ISBN 978-0-276-44280-3

www.readersdigest.co.uk

The Reader's Digest Association Limited, 11 Westferry Circus, Canary Wharf, London E14 4HE

# of love & life

Three novels selected and condensed
by Reader's Digest

The Reader's Digest Association Limited, London

# CONTENTS

# JULIA GREGSON

# EAST OF THE SUN

As the *Kaiser-i-Hind* leaves Tilbury Docks en route to Bombay, three young women stand at the railings, wondering what the future holds for them. Viva Holloway is seeking answers to her troubled past; Rose Wetherby, a naive bride-to-be is marrying a man she hardly knows; and Tor Sowerby, bridesmaid to Rose, is just desperate to find a husband for herself. Will they find all they are looking for in the twilight days of the British Raj?

# Chapter 1

London, September 1928

*Responsible young woman, twenty-eight years old, fond of children, with knowledge of India, will act as chaperone on Tilbury to Bombay run in return for half fare.*

It seemed like a form of magic to Viva Holloway when, having paid three and six for her advertisement to appear in the latest issue of *The Lady*, she found herself five days later in the restaurant at Derry & Toms in London, waiting for her first client, a Mrs Jonti Sowerby.

For the purposes of this interview, Viva wore not her usual mix of borrowed silks and jumble sale finds, but the grey tweed suit she loathed but had worn for work as a typist. Her hair—thick and dark and inclined towards wildness—had been clenched back in a bun.

She stepped into the genteel murmurings of the tearoom, where a pianist was playing a desultory tune. A small, bird-thin woman wearing an extraordinary blue hat stood up to greet her. By her side was a plump and silent girl whom Mrs Sowerby introduced as her daughter Victoria.

Both of them were surrounded by a sea of packages. A cup of coffee was suggested, but disappointingly, no cake. Viva hadn't eaten since breakfast and there was a delicious-looking walnut cake on the counter.

'She looks awfully young,' Mrs Sowerby immediately complained to her daughter, as if Viva wasn't there.

'Mummy,' protested Victoria in a strangled voice.

'Well, I'm sorry, darling, but she does.' Mrs Sowerby pursed her lips.

In a tight voice she, at last, addressed Viva, explaining that Victoria was shortly to go to India to be a bridesmaid for her best friend Rose, who was about to be married to a Captain Jack Chandler of the Third Cavalry, at St Thomas's Cathedral in Bombay.

Viva composed her features in what she felt to be a responsible look.

'I know Bombay quite well,' she said, which was true up to a point: she'd passed through that city in her mother's arms at the age of eighteen months, and then again aged five, and for the last time at the age of ten, never to return again. 'Victoria will be in good hands.'

The girl turned to Viva with a hopeful look. 'You can call me Tor if you like,' she said. 'All my friends do.' Viva noticed that Tor had wonderful eyes: huge and an unusual dark blue colour, almost like cornflowers.

When the waiter appeared again, Mrs Sowerby began to make a fuss about having a tisane rather than a 'normal English tea'.

'I'm half-French, you see,' she explained to Viva as if this excused everything. Then she asked, 'Do you know anything about cabin trunks?'

And by a miracle Viva did: the week before she'd been scouring the front pages of the *Pioneer* for possible jobs, and one Tailor Ram had placed a huge advertisement for trunks.

'The Viceroy is excellent,' Viva said. 'It has a steel underpinning under its canvas drawers. You can get them at the Army and Navy Store.'

An attractive older woman wearing tweeds arrived at their table.

'It's Mrs Wetherby.' Tor stood up and hugged the older woman.

'Do sit down.' Tor patted the chair beside her.

Mrs Sowerby turned to Viva. 'Mrs Wetherby is the mother of Rose, who is going to be married in India. She's an exceptionally beautiful girl.'

'I can't wait for you to meet her,' Tor said. 'She is so much fun, and so perfect, everybody falls in love with her—I've known her since she was a baby, we went to school together, we rode ponies—'

'Victoria,' her mother reproved. 'I'm not sure we need to tell Miss Holloway all this yet. We haven't decided. Where is Rose, by the way?'

'At the doctor's.' Mrs Wetherby looked embarrassed. 'You know . . .' She sipped her coffee and gave Mrs Sowerby a significant look. 'I'm meeting Rose again in an hour at Beauchamp Place—she's being fitted for her trousseau. Now, who is this charming young person?'

Viva was introduced to Mrs Wetherby as a 'professional chaperone'. Mrs Wetherby put her hand in hers and said it was lovely to meet her.

'I've done the interview,' Mrs Sowerby said to Mrs Wetherby. 'She knows India like the back of her hand, and she's cleared up the trunk business—she says the Viceroy is the only one.'

'The girls are very sensible,' said Mrs Wetherby anxiously. 'It's just quite comforting to have someone to keep an eye on things.'

'But I'm afraid we can only offer you fifty pounds for both girls,' said Mrs Sowerby, 'and not a penny more.'

Viva did some quick sums in her head. The single fare from London to Bombay was eighty pounds. She had one hundred and twenty pounds saved and would need some spending money when she arrived.

'That sounds very reasonable,' she said smoothly.

'Thank God!' Tor said. 'Oh, what bliss!'

Viva shook hands all round and left the restaurant with a new spring in her step; this was going to be a piece of cake.

Next stop was the Army and Navy Hotel to talk to a woman called Mrs Bannister about another prospective client: a schoolboy whose parents lived in Assam. The boy's name was Guy Glover.

And now she was sitting with Mrs Bannister, who turned out to be an irritable, nervy-looking person with buckteeth. She ordered them both a cup of tea with no biscuits or cake.

Mrs Bannister said that her brother, a tea planter in Assam, and his wife, Gwen, were 'slightly on the horns of a dilemma'. Their son Guy, an only child, had been asked to leave his school rather suddenly. He was sixteen years old.

'He's been at St Christopher's for ten years now without going back to India. If you can take him, his parents are quite prepared to pay your full fare,' his aunt assured her.

Viva felt her face flush with jubilation. If her whole fare was paid, and she had the fifty pounds coming from Mrs Sowerby, she could buy herself a little breathing space in India. It didn't even cross her mind to enquire why a boy of that age couldn't travel by himself.

'I'll send you a map of Guy's school and your first payment,' said Mrs Bannister. 'And thank you so much for doing this.'

How shockingly easy it was to tell people lies, Viva thought, particularly when it was what they wanted to hear. For she was not twenty-eight, she was only twenty-five, and as for knowing India, she'd only played there as a child, before what had happened. She knew it about as well as she knew the far side of the moon.

After coffee, Mrs Wetherby flew off to pick Rose up at the doctor's.

Tor's mother had her notebook out with the clothes list inside.

'Now jods. Jodhpurs. You'll probably go hunting in India. Ci Ci says it's too stupid to buy them all in London; she knows a man in Bombay who'll run them up for pennies.'

Ci Ci Mallinson was a distant cousin of her mother's and would soon be Tor's hostess when she arrived in Bombay. She had also heroically agreed to organise Rose's wedding without ever having met her. Her letters spoke of constant parties, gymkhanas, days at the races, with the occasional grand ball at the governor's.

'Quinine,' her mother was ticking away furiously, 'face cream, evening dresses, a campstool—oh, for goodness' sake! I think that's too Dr Livingstone—I'm going to strike that.'

'Mummy,' Tor leant across the table, 'please don't cross out the campstool. It sounds so exciting.'

'Oh, how pretty you look when you smile.' Her mother's face suddenly collapsed. 'If only you'd smiled more.'

In the silence that followed, Tor sensed a series of complicated and painful thoughts taking place under her mother's hat; some of them she was all too familiar with: had Tor smiled more, or looked more like Rose, all the expense of sending her to India might have been saved. Her mother seemed always to be adding her up like this and coming to the conclusion that she was a huge disappointment.

**W**hen they arrived at the riding department at Swan & Edgar, her mother asked for the services of a Madame Duval, a widow, she explained to Tor, whom she remembered from the old days.

Tor mentally rolled her eyes as Madame Duval complimented Mrs Sowerby on how slim she still looked. She watched her mother dimple and pass on her famous, much-repeated advice about lemon juice and tiny portions. Tor had been forced to follow this starvation diet herself, all through the season. Sometimes she thought her mother wanted to slim her out of existence altogether: their fiercest row was when her mother had found her one night, after another disastrous party where nobody had asked her to dance, wolfing down half a loaf of white bread and jam in the summerhouse.

That was the night when her mother, who could be mean in several languages, had introduced her to the German word *Kummerspeck* for the kind of fat that settles on people who use food to buck themselves up. 'It means sad fat,' she'd said, 'and it describes you now.'

'Right, now, I've got the larger size.' Madame Duval had returned with a flapping pair of jods. 'These might fit. Are we off to some gymkhanas this summer?'

'No,' Tor's mother answered. 'She's off to India, aren't you, Victoria?'

'How lovely, India!' Madame Duval beamed at her mother. 'Lucky girl!'

Her mother had decided to be fun. 'Yes, it's *très amusant*,' she told her. 'When these girls go out they call them the Fishing Club because there are so many handsome young men out there.'

'No, Mother,' corrected Tor, 'they call us the Fishing Fleet.'

'And the ones who can't find men there,' her mother gave Tor a naughty look with a hint of challenge in it, 'are called returned empties.'

'Oh, that's not very nice,' said Madame Duval, and then not too convincingly, 'but that won't happen to your Victoria.'

'Um . . .' Tor's mother said. 'Let's hope not.'

*I hate you, Mother.* For one terrible moment Tor imagined herself sticking a pin so hard into her mother that she made her scream out loud. *I absolutely loathe you*, she thought. *And I'm never coming home again.*

There was one last arrangement for Viva to make and the thought of it made her feel almost light-headed with nervous tension. An appointment at seven o'clock at the Oxford and Cambridge University Club in Pall Mall with William, her guardian and executor of her parents' will.

It was William who had, two months ago, set off the whole chain of events that now led her to India by forwarding a letter telling her about a trunk her parents had left in India. The writer, a Mrs Mabel Waghorn from Simla, said the trunk, which contained clothes and personal effects, was being kept in a shed near her house. The rains had been heavy that year and she was afraid the trunk would disintegrate should she leave it there much longer. She said that the keys of the trunk had been left with a Mr William Philpott, at the Inner Temple Inn in London.

William had attached his own letter to this. 'I don't think you need do anything about this,' he wrote. 'I would send the old lady some money and get the trunk disposed of. I have the keys should you want them.'

Viva had at first been convinced he was right. Going back to India would be like throwing a bomb into the centre of her life. No, it was ridiculous. For, finally, after six months and two dreary typist's jobs in London, she'd fallen into a position she adored as assistant to Nancy Driver, a kind, eccentric woman who churned out romantic novels at an impressive rate. Her new job paid thirty shillings a week, enough for her to move from the YWCA into her own bedsit in Earl's Court. Best of all, she had started to write herself, and had found—or was it stumbled into?— what she knew she wanted to do with her life.

She dreaded seeing William again—their relationship had become so soiled and complicated. She wrote to him asking if he could post the keys, but he'd refused.

So why, given all these new and wonderful opportunities in life, had another part of her leapt at the thought of seeing her parents' things?

In certain moods she could barely remember what her family even looked like. Time had blurred those agonising memories, time and the relative anonymity of boarding school and, later, London—where, at first, she had known nobody. Indeed, one of the things she most liked about the city was that so few people ever asked you personal questions. Only two ever had: first, the form-filler at the YWCA, querying the blank she'd left after 'Family's place of residence', and then Fran, the friendly typist in the next bed in her dorm. She'd told them both they had died in a car accident years ago in India; it always seemed easier to dispose of them both at once. She didn't tell them about Josie at all. *You don't have to say* was something she'd learned the hard way with William.

**H**e was waiting for her outside the club when she ran up the steps at around a quarter to seven. A fastidious man, he was wearing the pin-striped suit she had last seen folded over the arm of his chair in his flat in Westminster. She remembered how he'd lined up his sock suspenders on top of his underpants, a starched collar, his silk tie.

'You're looking well, Viva.' He had a sharp, slightly barking voice, used to great effect in the Inner Temple where he now worked as a barrister. 'Well done.'

'Thank you, William.' She was determined to stay calm.

'I've booked us a table.' He was steering her towards the dining room.

'There was no need to do that,' she said, moving away from him. 'I could take the keys and leave.'

'You could,' he said.

A waiter led them towards a table set for two in the corner of the grand dining room. William had been here earlier. A bulky envelope—she presumed it held the keys—lay propped against a pepper pot.

He settled his pinstriped knees carefully under the table, smiled at her blandly and told her he had taken the liberty of ordering a bottle of Château Smith Haut Lafitte.

The waiter took their orders: brown soup and lamb cutlets for him; grilled sole for her, the simplest and quickest thing on the menu.

A few stiff pleasantries, then William lowered his voice.

'Are you sure you want these?' He closed his hand over the envelope.

'Yes,' she said. 'Thank you.'

He waited for her to say more, then asked, 'Are you going back?'

'Yes.' She bit the inside of her lip.

'Can I remind you, you have no money—or very little.'

She forced herself to say nothing. *You don't have to say.*

He looked at her with his cold, grey eyes. He was still handsome in a bloodless sort of way. The waiter brought his soup.

'Well, for what it's worth,' he took a careful sip, 'I think it's an absolutely dreadful idea. Completely irresponsible. There'll be nothing in India for you,' he said, 'and I'm worried it will upset you.'

She gave him a quizzical look. 'It's a bit late for that, William,' she said. 'Don't you think?'

She picked up the envelope and put the keys into her handbag. 'I've made up my mind,' she said. 'One of the advantages of being an orphan is that I'm free to do what I like.'

'How will you support yourself?'

'I have already found two people willing to pay my fare—I am to be a chaperone and then I have some addresses in India.'

'A chaperone! Do you have any idea how irresponsible you are?'

'And I'm also going to be a writer.'

'How can you possibly know that?' She could see bright spots of colour on his cheeks. He simply couldn't bear not being in control, she could see that now. He preferred the wounded bird.

She ignored what he'd said. Now that the keys were inside her bag and she had said what she meant to say, she felt a surge of power, like oxygen in the bloodstream. She suddenly felt really hungry.

She raised her glass of Château Smith Haut Lafitte towards him.

'Wish me luck, William,' she said. 'I booked my passage on the *Kaiser* today. I'm going.'

## Middle Wallop, Hampshire, October 1928

On the night before she left England, Rose Wetherby had such an attack of cold feet that she seriously thought about going to her parents and saying, 'Look, scrap the whole thing; I don't want to go,' but of course it was too late.

Mrs Pludd, the family cook, had made her favourite supper: shepherd's pie and gooseberry fool. When it came, Rose wished she hadn't asked for it, because the nursery food made her feel even more desperate and clinging, and everyone was making a huge effort to pretend nothing special was happening. Her father tried to tell them a joke he'd obviously saved up for the occasion: a terrible joke, and when she and her mother fluffed their parts and laughed too quickly and in the wrong place, he'd given her such an unhappy smile that she could have wept.

*I shall miss you so much, Daddy; Jack will never replace you.* The violence of this emotion surprised her.

After dinner she'd gone into the garden. The last puffs of smoke from a bonfire of leaves rose and drifted above the tall branches of the cedar tree. It had been a cold but perfect day, with the sky clear as polished glass. The garden had never looked more beautiful.

She walked past the orchard to the stables and looked back at the house. She thought of all the life that had gone on there: the laughter and the rows, and shouts of 'Bedtime, darlings', the blissful sound of the supper gong when she and Tor and her big brother, Simon, whom they'd idolised, had been racing around in the garden playing cricket, or building dens or playing pirates in the stream.

Her pony, Copper, had his head over the stable gate. She gave him his bedtime apple, then let herself into his stable and collapsed over him weeping. Nothing in her life had ever made her feel this bad before, and at a time when she was supposed to feel so happy.

Copper pushed her gently with his head, and let her tears fall into his mane. She knew she wouldn't see him again, or the dogs, Rollo and Mops, who were getting on. Maybe not even her parents. Her father's wretched bout of pneumonia only last winter had left him with what he called a dicky motor and the doctor called a serious heart condition. He had not recovered. They talked about her wedding as if he was bound to be there, although both of them knew he wouldn't.

She was aware, too, of all the painful thoughts tonight would bring to all of them about Simon. Darling Simon had had all her father's goodness and gallantry as well as his steelier qualities. He was killed in France in the last month of the war. It was ten days before his twenty-first birthday. Her parents rarely spoke of it; but it was always lurking there, like an iceberg under the sunny surface of things.

She stayed for a while, desperately trying to calm herself. *Soldiers' daughters don't cry.*

Going up the backstairs to her room, she heard her mother call out from her own bedroom, 'Are you all right, darling?'

'Yes, Mummy,' she said. 'Good night.'

Inside her room, all her new clothes had been hung outside her wardrobe like ghosts waiting for their new life to begin. They'd had such a lovely day up in London with Tor and her mother, Jonti.

Her mother had taken her to a powder-puffy little salon in

Beauchamp Place that Tor's mother had recommended. They'd bought her trousseau there: thirteen pairs of cotton drawers; a corset that laced at the back; bloomers; two silk petticoats; and then the long peach silk negligee with a lace trim that made her feel like a glamorous stranger.

Rose had looked at her reflection in the mirror. The next time she wore this, she'd be in Jack Chandler's bed. Mummy must have been thinking along these lines too. She'd given a funny little grimace and shut her eyes. This was all so new for both of them.

That might have been the best time to have asked her about the bedroom side of things, but she'd been too shy. All that had happened in that department was a hot-making visit to Dr Llewellyn, an old family friend who hunted with her father, and who had offices in Harley Street. Blushing furiously and avoiding her eyes, he'd fished around inside her, hurting her horribly, and then handed her a small sponge. He'd explained how to use it. 'You put it in like this.' The back of his tweed suit had strained as he'd creaked into a squatting position and poked it between his legs. He'd given her a little cloth bag, into which it must return washed and powdered when it wasn't in use.

She longed to ask her mother for more information, but her mother, who'd left her at the gate of the doctor's surgery almost scarlet with embarrassment herself, had said nothing.

She'd met Jack at her friend Flavia's twenty-first, at the Savile Club in London; he had seemed so much older and more experienced than the other silly boys. He was handsome too, with his fine tall physique and blond hair. He wasn't at all a good dancer, and at first they'd both been hopelessly flustered and tongue-tied bouncing around the floor together to the New Orleans Rhythm Kings.

He'd asked her to come downstairs so they didn't have to shout, and then she had asked him about India. And been impressed rather than bedazzled. He seemed to her a proper grown-up man, and to have done so much: pig-sticking and chasing tigers and helping Indian people learn so much about themselves. He was very modest, saying he was simply doing his bit, but she could tell he'd been brave. He'd proposed four weeks after that first meeting and gone back to India a week later.

**A** soft knock on the door: her father. She hoped he couldn't see how red her eyes were from the big blub in the stables.

'Do you think you'll be all right, Froggie?' he asked.

'Yes, Daddy, I will.'

He sat on the bed beside her. His fingers, papery and old-looking in the lamplight, were plucking at the bedspread. 'My darling girl.'

When he turned, she was shocked to hear him swallowing, the breathless rasp of his lungs. The first time she ever saw him cry. She put her arms round him. How thin he was now! She inhaled him, pipes and soap and dogs, and fixed him somewhere deep inside of her.

'Good night, Daddy. Sleep well.'

'Good night, my darling, darling girl.'

'Would you mind turning off my light?'

'Will do.' The door clicked and the room went dark. She knew, and he did too: it was their last night together under the same roof.

**A** maid showed Viva into the sparsely furnished visitors' room at St Christopher's School in the village of Colerne, near Bath.

'I've come to pick up Guy Glover,' she told the maid. 'I'm his chaperone. I'm taking him back to India.'

'Mr Glover's in the parlour,' the maid said, 'but Mr Partington, his housemaster, would like a quick word with you first.'

Mr Partington, an exhausted-looking man with nicotine-stained white hair, entered the room softly. 'Miss Viva Holloway, if I'm not mistaken.' He shook her hand limply. 'Well, well, well, off to India then.'

'Yes,' she said, 'tomorrow from Tilbury. We're going down tonight.'

She waited for him to say the usual things masters say when boys are leaving, 'We'll miss him' or some such, but nothing came.

'Do you know Guy?' he said after an awkward pause. 'I mean, are you a friend of the family?'

'No, his parents contacted me via an advertisement in *The Lady*.'

'I've got something for you to take with him.' Mr Partington slid a letter from under the blotter and across the desk towards her. 'It seems, hah! that nobody has told you.'

'Told me what?'

'Guy's been expelled. Two boys in his dorm reported money missing; another boy lost a clock. He owned up right away. It wasn't a great deal of money, and there are some mitigating circumstances. His parents keep him very short of funds. But the point is, it's led to problems with the other boys,' he blinked at her, 'an understandable lack of trust. We sent a letter saying all this to his parents a few months ago, but they didn't reply except to send a telegram last week to say you were coming.'

Partington plucked another letter from underneath the blotter. 'Would you mind awfully giving this to them too? His report and his exam results. A disaster, I'm afraid—all this blew up before them.

Shame. Hah! On the right day and given a fair wind, he's perfectly capable of passing them—depending on his mood, of course.'

'On his mood?' Viva took the letters and put them in her bag, trying to sound calmer than she felt.

'He's not a strong boy mentally at the best of times. But his parents reassured me you were responsible and experienced and I—'

The maid appeared. 'Mr Bell wants to speak to you in the lab,' she said to Mr Partington.

'Oh God,' sighed Partington.

'Well, I won't keep you,' Viva said.

Mr Partington took her hand in his. 'The boy's waiting for you just across the hall. We've said our goodbyes.' He pointed towards the door opposite, then scurried off in the opposite direction down the corridor. He seemed in a hurry to get away.

**A** tall pale-faced boy stood up without smiling when Viva entered the room. He was wearing a long black overcoat; pimples stood out on his chin through the beginnings of a beard.

'Hello, my name is Viva Holloway. Are you Guy Glover?' she said.

'That's the name,' he said.

'Well, I'm very pleased to meet you.'

He shook her hand reluctantly. 'Charmed,' he said. 'I'm sure.'

When at last he smiled, she noticed he had the same buckteeth as his aunt. Also that his eyes couldn't quite meet hers.

'Well, shall we collect your things?' she said.

As she followed his long thin legs upstairs, she tried to neutralise the sense of panic she'd felt at Mr Partington's words. The entire trip was organised, she couldn't afford to exaggerate his crimes and, after all, she rationalised, lots of children did a bit of amateur thieving.

'So, how long have you been here?' she asked.

'Ten years.'

'Gosh, long time. It must feel rather strange leaving.'

'Not really.' His voice was completely without expression. She felt she must stop asking him questions. For all his assumed nonchalance, he might be upset at the thought of leaving this place under a cloud.

The door at the top of the stairs had a wadge of felt underneath it to keep draughts out. When he'd pushed the door open with his foot, she saw a row of ten white beds with green counterpanes folded neatly at the base of them. At the end of the room, a large window looked out onto a sky ready to dump more rain onto sodden fields.

He led her to a bed with two suitcases beside it.

'My trunk's gone on ahead,' he told her.

She was struck by the silence, the cold in the dormitory, and then relieved to see a note pinned to his pillow with his name written on it in an untidy schoolboyish scrawl, assuming it was someone wishing to say goodbye. Without reading the letter, he tore it up and dropped the pieces of paper into a wastepaper basket underneath the bed.

'There,' he said. 'All done now.'

The note had brought a flush of colour to his otherwise chalk-pale cheeks. His young man's Adam's apple bulged in his neck. She pretended not to notice. *He is more upset than I realise*, she told herself.

'So,' she said with an attempt at brightness, 'shall we be off? I've already spoken to Mr Partington.'

'Yes.' He was moving round his bed like a large stunned animal, looking about the room for the last time.

She carried one of his cases downstairs; he took the other. They crossed the polished hall together. She closed the door behind him and it was only when she was sitting in the taxi and they were halfway to the station that she realised that nobody: no boy, no maid, no servant, no master, had come to the door to say goodbye to him.

And her thought was, *The sensible thing now would be to ask the taxi driver to turn round and drive him straight back to school*. She would say, 'I'm very sorry, but I don't think this will work.' But that would mean no ticket and no India, so she ignored her feelings and told the driver to take them to the railway station in Bath.

# Chapter 2

Tilbury Docks, October 17, 1928

The *Kaiser-i-Hind* was a swarming hive of activity by the time Tor and Rose arrived. Red-turbaned lascars flew around with luggage; crates of fruit and boxes of food were being hauled up the gangplank and, on the quay, a band was wheezing its way through 'Will Ye No' Come Back Again?'. And all that Tor could do was smile and try not to stare too openly at all the men walking up the gangplanks: sunburnt men in naval uniforms, old colonels bundled up against the cold, young civil servants and one heavenly-looking man, who looked half-Indian, in the most beautiful cashmere coat.

Close to the gangplank, Tor and Rose's parents stood conversing with Miss Viva Holloway, who had been joined by a tall pale boy in a long dark coat, her other charge.

All of them had flown round for most of the morning exploring the ship, which was astoundingly spacious and opulent. Its gleaming wooden floors smelt of fresh polish; it had deep armchairs in the smoking rooms, lushly painted murals in the dining room, Persian carpets, fresh flowers, and when they walked in to look at the dining salon, a buffet was already being laid out with huge turkeys and hams and a sweet trolley, quivering with blancmanges, as well as neiges au crème, fruit salads and—Tor's favourite—lemon meringue pie.

Her mother had gasped with admiration, then spoilt it by stage-whispering, '*Somebody* will be in their element.' And then, 'Darling, please do try not to overdo it, there is *no more money* for any frocks.'

And for once, Tor's father had taken her side. 'Leave her alone, Jonti,' he'd said, his voice throbbing with emotion. 'Don't go on at her today.'

At the clang of a loud bell, the pulse of the ship had quickened; orders were shouted, the music on the quayside swelled to a sobbing pitch, and her parents had been sent ashore.

Tor's last view of her mother had been of her standing on the quay, a few feet away from her father. When Tor looked down, her mother looked up, lifted her bosom and gave her a significant look. '*Posture*,' her mother mouthed and Tor had immediately straightened up. *Her performing seal*, she'd thought bitterly, *right up until the end*.

Then the band had played a rousing farewell and suddenly she'd felt this lurch like a giant heartbeat and they were off. And while other passengers had wept and waved and strained their eyes towards the shore until their people were dots, Tor's heart had floated upwards and outwards in an ecstasy of flight. She was free.

**A**n hour later, Rose and Tor stood in a thumping wind on A deck clinging to each other. Rose's new coat suddenly ballooned above her head, making them both laugh a little too wildly.

'Are you all right?' Tor said. Rose looked as if she'd been crying.

'Yes, Tor, I'm fine—excited—*really*. But I do think I'll go down to the cabin now and unpack. Would you help me find it again? I'm afraid they all look the same to me.'

She was trying hard to smile and keep the wobble out of her voice, but poor Rose was in quite a state, Tor could see that. At school, Rose had always been the calmly efficient one; now Tor was the one holding Rose's hand as they wove their way down the deck. As the wind drew them in a sucking motion towards the steps, she saw the strange boy who'd been with Miss Holloway earlier, sitting on his own on a deck chair, staring out to sea.

'Oh, hello,' said Rose, 'have you seen Miss Holloway?'

'No,' he said. 'Sorry.' He looked intently at the sea again.

'Gosh, how *rude*,' Rose said as they walked down the stairs towards the cabins. 'I jolly well hope we don't have to eat with him.'

'We don't,' Tor said firmly. 'Because I won't. I'll talk to Miss Viva Holloway about it. I'll make some excuse.'

**A**lone in their cabin, Rose and Tor sat on opposite bunks and grinned at each other. The tiny room was already chaotic: they'd been down earlier and left heaps of clothes on the floor, too excited to unpack properly.

They were chattering when there was a knock on the door, and their steward walked in. He smiled at them radiantly. 'My name is Suday Ram,' he said. 'Babies want bat?'

'Sorry?' Rose said politely. 'I didn't quite catch that.'

Tor knew she mustn't look at Rose; they were in a mood to giggle.

'Do babies want *bat*?' he repeated more firmly.

He took them into the miniature bathroom, which had thick white towels and new soaps. He showed them how to get the rust-coloured seawater out of the taps and how to flush the water closet, which was most embarrassing. When he left, they exploded with laughter and said, 'Baby want bat,' several times until they'd perfected their Indian accents and Tor was so happy to see Rose laughing.

'Rose,' she said in her Indian voice when the man was gone. 'Go back into the bathroom and make a vish. I have big surprise.'

When she heard the bolt slide, Tor took the most magical thing she possessed out of her trunk and held it reverently in her arms. Its red leather box, with the little dog Nipper and a horn inscribed on its lid, still made her tremble with happiness.

'Don't come out yet,' she said. A few seconds later, the cabin exploded with the squeaks and bangs of J. B. White's 'Shoo Fox'.

'Oh, Tor.' Rose Charlestoned out of the bathroom in her stocking feet. 'Thank God, *thank God* you're here.'

They danced together for a while, then collapsed on the bed. Tor poured them both a crème de menthe and they lay on the bunk together, with their eyes shut, feeling the ship speeding them onwards.

Then Tor read the letter from the captain that had been left on their beds. 'We're invited to a cocktail party tonight, in the Taj Room. The voyage out will take three weeks. We'll stop at Gibraltar, Marseilles, Malta, Port Said and Bombay. Dancing each night in the Persian Room.

'No second-class passengers even to think of showing their common little mugs in first class,' Tor continued, 'and there will be fancy-dress parties, deck quoits and bridge evenings, a talk on snakebites and sunstroke in the Simla Bar given by Lieutenant-Colonel Gorman when we get to Port Said. Dinner jackets and long dresses to be worn each night.'

Rose took a sip from her glass, then put it down. 'What's that?' she said. There was a great creaking noise coming from the direction of the porthole, followed by the thud of an engine.

'Only the wind, my lovely.' Tor glanced towards the porthole, towards the waves, grey and tumbling.

'I shan't have any more crème de menthe,' said Rose, who was looking a bit green.

'Well, I will,' said Tor, 'otherwise I might just die of excitement.'

## Bay of Biscay

'NO CLICHÉS,' Viva Holloway wrote in capital letters in her new leather-bound journal. 'GET ON WITH SOME PROPER WORK.'

This habit of writing bossy notes to herself often resurfaced at times of strain. When she was a child, at her convent boarding school in Wales, she'd imagined them being dictated by her father, Alexander Holloway, railway engineer, late of Simla, who was in heaven but looking down on her, monitoring her progress.

'You must NOT go to Simla,' she wrote, 'until you have earned enough money to do so. VERY BAD IDEA!'

Money was something she worried about constantly. Guy Glover's aunt had promised to send her one hundred and sixty pounds in a banking order before the ship left, but the posts had come and gone, and the fare plus the money for their train tickets had come from her own dwindling savings.

At the last moment her old employer, Nancy Driver, had slipped a ten-guinea bonus into the leather journal that had been her farewell present. She'd been given twenty-five pounds by Rose's mother and twenty-five pounds by Tor's, but now survival depended on her being able to supplement her income by writing articles.

She turned another page and took a deep breath. She was sitting in the far corner of the ship's writing room where, at other lamplit desks, a handful of other passengers were dutifully scratching away.

'The Fishing Fleet by Viva Holloway,' she wrote in bold letters at the top of the page.

'There are, roughly speaking, three kinds of women on board the *Kaiser-i-Hind*,' she began.

She stared out to sea for a while, trying to decide whether she would post this, or try to send it by telegram, which would be expensive. Its final destination would be a shabby bedsit in Bloomsbury, where *The Voice*, a feminist magazine begun by two suffragette sisters, Violet and Fiona Thyme, had its headquarters. Mrs Driver had introduced her.

If they liked the story, the sisters had promised to pay her ten pounds for one thousand words. 'Lift the lid on what really happens to all those women going to India, and what they think they'll do when the whole thing collapses,' Violet had told her.

'First,' wrote Viva, 'there are the memsahibs—the name in Hindi means "the master's women", all of whom are travelling on this ship first class. Next, we have the skittishly nervous young girls who are collectively and unkindly called the Fishing Fleet. They are going to India to look for husbands, and they've been going there with their hooks baited ever since the early nineteeth century.'

She put down her pen for a while and thought of Rose, who was— Mrs Sowerby was right—ravishingly pretty. On their first night at sea, she'd gone to the girls' cabin to see if they were all right. Their cabin was next to hers. The door was unlocked, and when she'd put her head round the door, she'd found Rose lying face down on the bed quietly weeping. The girl had leapt up and mumbled something about her father—that poor man had looked devastated as she'd left—and apologised for being such a wet. *She's petrified*, Viva thought. *And why not?*

'And next,' she wrote, 'there are women like myself: single women with no sahib and no wish for one, who love India and like to work. You see, nobody ever really writes about them—the governesses, the schoolteachers, the chaperones—but we have our tales to tell.'

All of a sudden, her mouth filled with liquid and she put her pen down as the floor rose and fell along with her stomach. The walls creaked as she stood up. How hot-making! Not thirty-six hours out from Tilbury and she was going to be sick.

'Excuse me, madam.' A waiter appeared with a grey and pink box and a glass of water.

Oh no! Was it that obvious? She sat back with her eyes closed, trying not to feel the suck and swell of the waves. *Breathe! Breathe!*

'Missy.' The waiter stood at the door. He smiled kindly at her as she stumbled out onto the deck and into the deafening boom of the waves.

'Thank you. I'm fine, thank you.'

She rested her forehead on the railings and stayed there until she felt slightly better. What if she wasn't strong enough for this? she thought. What would that mean?

She saw Guy Glover sitting on a deck chair behind a glass screen that sheltered him from the worst of the wind. He was wearing his black overcoat and smoking a cigarette. When he saw her looking at him, he held her gaze for a moment and raised his cigarette to his mouth. The look in his eye said, *Try and stop me*. He inhaled deeply and exhaled, then ground the cigarette under his heel and sauntered over to her. Pathetic, she thought, in his too-large coat.

*He's just a child*, she tried to reassure herself, for the sight of him had made her anxious, *a foolish self-conscious child. Nothing to be frightened of.*

She'd shared a similar background, and her current thinking about him went as follows: like many boys of his class and background, he'd been turfed from the nest too young. Without parents on hand or, in his case, siblings to chivvy him along, he'd become a permanent defensive guest, unsure of his welcome, uneasy in his skin. Underneath the studied indifference, the coldness, there was, she was almost certain of it, a boy hungry for love, angry about having to ask for it. She should at least try to understand him even if she couldn't like him.

'I meant to tell you,' he shouted over the waves, 'there's some people on board my parents want me to say hello to. The Ramsbottoms from Lucknow. They've asked us for a drink in the music room tomorrow night. I'd like you to come too.'

Well, well, well, he'd made one unsolicited remark to her.

'Of course,' she said. 'Perhaps you and I and the girls can have dinner together at the early sitting first. We can all get to know each other.'

'I'd rather not do that,' he said. 'I don't want to eat with other people.'

'Why not?'

'My parents said we'd be eating alone,' he mumbled.

'Shall we talk about this later?' She felt too sick to think about food now and the girls were hardly going to mind.

'Of course.' He beamed his blank and insulting smile and shouted something else about parents that was swept away by the wind. He was going to be a handful; there was no doubt about it.

After this exchange, Viva went down to the cabin she was sharing with a Miss Snow, a schoolteacher who was going back to teach in a school near Cochin. The two had come to this arrangement in order to save money, but hadn't yet exchanged more than a handful of words.

Miss Snow was asleep under a mound of bedclothes with a green pail underneath her bed. Viva lay down on her bunk and thought about Guy again. The scary thing was, she thought, that he was her responsibility now. A wave of anxiety swept over her. Why in God's name had she taken all this on, particularly at a time when she had, at last, achieved a kind of independence?

It couldn't surely just be for the chance to open that wretched trunk—Mrs Waghorn couldn't have been more frank about the chances of her finding anything in it—but she had flung her life onto this slender thread. Why?

She thought back almost longingly to her basement flat in Nevern Square, not an abode of bliss, to be sure, with its gas ring and narrow bed, but a home nevertheless. She'd sallied forth each morning to work, leaving in the same foggy darkness in which she came home.

An older person might have seen nothing but drudgery in this existence, but for her, young and determined to survive her tragedies, independence had been a kind of drug. No more school dorms, no more spare rooms where relatives had to move things round to fit her in. This room was hers. On a lumpy single bed near the boarded-up fire, she'd put her only real heirloom, an exquisite patchwork quilt, made up of sari fabrics in jewel-like colours, with a border embroidered with fishes and birds. It had once been on her parents' bed in Simla, and in their other houses in Nepal and Kashmir.

She had a brass lamp, a few kitchen utensils stowed under the bed, boxes and boxes of books and typing paper and a Remington typewriter. What she wanted more than anything in the world was to be a writer. After work each night, she changed into some warm clothes, lit up one of the three Abdullah cigarettes she allowed herself each day and set to work. Around midnight, stiff and yawning, she undressed for bed and as soon as her head hit the pillow, fell dead asleep.

It was via the agency for whom she did temporary typing that she was sent to work for Mrs Nancy Driver, who was a prolific writer of romances, two of them set in India, where her husband, now dead, had been a major in the Indian cavalry. Mrs Driver, who spent much of her day furiously typing in a camel-haired dressing gown, might have seemed at first, with her Eton crop and fierce pouncing style of conversation, like an unlikely fairy godmother, but that was what she'd been.

She and Viva had settled into a routine together. At eleven thirty, when Mrs Driver had bathed and eaten her breakfast, she wrote furiously in longhand for an hour or so while Viva dealt inexpertly with her correspondence. After lunch, while her employer relaxed, Viva would type up the morning's work and, if a large red cross was in the margin, she was allowed to add what were called 'the spoony bits'. Mrs Driver was convinced, quite wrongly, that Viva, being young and good-looking, was having lots of exciting romances.

When Viva, shaking with nerves, told Mrs Driver over sherry one morning that she had dreams herself of writing some stories, Mrs Driver had been kind but pragmatic. She told her that if she was serious and needed to earn money immediately, she should try to sell to women's magazines, the kind of gentle romances they published on a regular basis. 'It will get you started and give you some confidence,' she had said. In the past six months, Viva had penned thirteen stories in which a variety of granite-jawed heroes seized women of the blonde, helpless and dim variety. Three had been published.

And oh, the impossible elation of that first moment of hearing that her first story had been accepted. She'd got the letter after work on a wet November evening, and run around Nevern Square on her own in the dark. She'd been so sure then—ridiculously sure in retrospect—that this was a turning point and that from now on she would be able to survive by her pen. So why, with everything at last moving in the right direction, had she decided to change all her plans and go to India?

## Poona

'Master,' Jack Chandler's bearer called softly through the bathroom door. 'Wake up, please, time is marching. *Jaldi!*'

'I'm not asleep, Dinesh,' Jack Chandler called back, 'I'm thinking.'

He'd been lying in the bath for almost an hour. His eyes were closed as he brooded about marriage and why men told lies, and Sunita, to whom he must soon say goodbye.

Normally, this was a favourite time of the day, when he peeled off clothes that smelt satisfactorily of horse sweat and stepped into warm water, with a whisky mixed just the way he liked it, before he went to the club. But tonight he was a bundle of nerves. That afternoon, he'd been to the church to talk to the vicar about arrangements for his marriage in four weeks' time. The vicar had informed him that you didn't need banns to get married in India; so many people, he had implied without actually saying it, did it on the spur of the moment here. And this exchange had further rattled Jack who was, generally speaking, a man with a logical brain who thought things through. So why had he jumped in, eyes closed, in the matter of finding a new wife?

He'd set himself the task of writing to Rose earlier that night and posting it to her in Port Said, where her ship would arrive in twelve days' time by his calculations.

'My dearest Rose,' he'd written. 'Today, I went to the church where we are to be married and—' He had crumpled up the letter, irritated with the banality of his thoughts and for not having the right words at a time when, surely, they should be tumbling out. But more and more, he found communications with her stilted. The excitement of their earlier letters had petered out into a dull exchange of plans.

He stood up in the bath: a tall man with a fine, sensitive face, wary eyes, strong sloping shoulders and the long muscular legs of a horse-man. He was far better looking now at twenty-eight than he had been when he first came out to India six years ago. Then, he was a tall boy just one year out of Sandhurst, skinny in spite of all the punishing exer-cise, the yard drills, the riding, the expeditions in mock deserts with thirty-pound weights on his back, all things designed to take the soft-ness out of young men.

'Sir, please.' Dinesh stood smiling at the door, a towel in his hand. He'd come to Poona three years ago, a refugee from a flooded farm in Bengal. Jack had first met him quite by chance in the house of a friend in Delhi, and had been struck, as everybody was, by the open radiance of his smile. Dinesh counted this job as his one blinding stroke of good fortune in a life full of tragedies.

Dinesh and Jack were a team now. The fact that Jack was a young officer with an Indian, rather than a British cavalry regiment and could—after quite a slog, for he was not a natural linguist—converse with Dinesh in almost fluent Hindustani was a point of pride with Dinesh. He'd served with a reverence and a passion that both humbled and worried Jack, for the wheel was turning again. All of Jack's servants—Dinesh and his wash man, his cook and her young daugh-ter—were acutely aware of their various positions in the house; they watched each other like hawks for any changes in the pecking order. The arrival of Rose, no question about it, would ruffle their feathers, and Jack hadn't found the words to explain that to her yet.

He walked into his bedroom. In the plain, low-ceilinged room an ancient fan ground away over his single bed with a mosquito net above it. On the bamboo chair in the corner of the room Dinesh had laid out a pair of linen trousers and a white shirt, all beautifully pressed.

Dinesh brought him a simple kedgeree for supper and he ate it on his own in the dining room. Normally, it was one of his favourite meals; tonight he pushed it around his plate—too nervous to eat much.

He drained a glass of beer. Six months ago, when he'd first met Rose, he'd felt an emptiness at the centre of this life, a hunger for someone to talk to about something other than politics or polo or parties, the staple diet at the officers' mess and the club. But now, a goblin in his head was whispering to him about the bliss of bachelorhood: not having to tell anybody when you're coming home from the club, being able to work until midnight when the heat was on.

He buried his head in his hands and heaved a shuddering sigh. Why not be honest, at least to himself? It was Sunita who filled his thoughts tonight. Sunita, darling Sunita, who knew nothing about the changes ahead and had done nothing to deserve them. But tonight, he had a cheque to give her after his speech, a donation he could ill afford, towards her future. His heart sank. For the first time in her life she might feel like a prostitute. He felt like a brute; but he had to do it.

They'd been together for three years. She'd been introduced to him by a fellow officer who'd been going home to England. She was refined, beautiful, well educated, well connected, even: her father, a liberal cultivated man, was a lawyer in Bombay, but she was not wife material. It wasn't as easily explained as snobbery, although snobbery did come into it. The problem was this: he loved his regiment and his fellow officers with a passion that bordered on the obsessional. No woman, Indian or English, would ever really understand what they meant to him, and as a group they strongly disapproved of fellows who took on native women and went what they called 'jungli'.

Part of him knew he would never have married her. In the end they were just too different. *With my body I thee worship.* No problem with that. *With my soul I thee wed.* That was the rub. If he had a soul (which he sometimes seriously doubted) it had been, in a hundred thousand ways, forged so differently from hers. In the end, it would be so much easier to marry a girl like Rose.

Lots of men carried on with their women after they were married, but he didn't want to. In old-fashioned language that strangely appealed to him, he had plighted his troth. He wanted to make Rose happy, to earn her trust and keep it.

So much of his life he already saw through her eyes now. Would she take to India in the way he had? He'd tried to be honest with her about the bone-shrivelling heat of summers here, the poverty of the people, the constant moves, the hard life of the army wife.

But he'd been desperate to woo her at the same time. Desperate in the way a man is who has fallen for a girl like a ton of bricks but who knows he only has a week's home leave left. A certain hard-headed practicality had crept into his warnings.

### Gibraltar, October 21, 1928

*Darling Daddy and Mummy,*

*We arrive in Gibraltar in about an hour's time, so will try to post this then.*

*I've been lying in my bunk reading my Spanish phrase book, and have just read this: Gracias a la vida que me ha dado tanto. (Thanks be to life, which has given me so much.) Isn't that lovely? It made me think about all the wonderful times we have had together.*

*There are so many nice people in first class, and also, don't worry about Miss Holloway being so young. She is very kind and keeps a good eye on us. Every night there are parties or entertainments planned, and we have found it easy to join in. One of our new best friends is Nigel, who has a junior post in the civil service; he is fairly quiet, but very clever and has a good sense of humour. Unlike most people on the Kaiser he is sick at heart at having to go back to India because he's done four years there in a remote province and wants to stay home. The other bods on board are tea planters, army officers and so on, also quite a few children and their ayahs.*

*Frank, the ship's junior doctor, is a good egg. He's working his passage to India so he can do some research out there on some sort of malaria. He's great fun and very good-looking. I think Tor has her eye on him!*

*Later: Sorry, didn't finish! Will post in Malta.*

*A party of eight of us went ashore, so there were lots of people to keep an eye on us. Frank knew a respectable restaurant overlooking the harbour. For lunch we had some sort of fish, caught that morning, and prawns, then the fat señorita who ran the place laid out three puddings of such deliciousness I thought I was dreaming. (Much more of this and I shall simply waddle down the aisle. Food is an obsession on board.)*

*Write soon. Give Copper a kiss for me and a handful of carrots.*

*With bestest love,*

*Rose*

# Chapter 3

*Kaiser-i-Hind,* 150 miles from Port Said

The sun woke Tor early in the morning and she basked in it like a cat on a windowsill and thought, as she had almost every morning since she'd been at sea, *How wonderful. I'm free.*

Today would start with tea in bed and a good gossip with Rose about the night before, then a wonderful breakfast, maybe kippers, or eggs and bacon, and delicious coffee, which she had only just started to drink. All kinds of games in the morning, and perhaps a turn around the deck with Frank, the ship's junior doctor, who was so good-looking and who, yesterday, had appeared on deck just as she and Rose were looking out to sea. And then, at six o'clock, Viva would appear in the cabin, for what they now called a bishi, the Marathi word, Viva had told them, for a female party.

Last night, during their bishi, the conversation had turned to the topic of what qualities they should look for in a man, and Tor had told Viva about Paul, the man who had broken her heart last summer.

'Perfect at first,' she said. 'We met at his parents' house at Tangley, not far from where we live. He was very dark and sophisticated, sort of tortured-looking. He'd been away working in Rome as an art historian for three years. My mother thought he was the perfect catch because his parents have money and we've become quite poor since the war.'

She was trying to make them laugh at her stupidity, but it hurt even now to remember how fated that first meeting had seemed.

'He was three years older than me,' she said, 'and more interesting by a mile than the other men I'd met. He took me to concerts where he read the scores, lent me books. He even told me what colours I should wear. I didn't even know I had olive skin until he told me.'

'He does sound interesting,' Viva had said—she seemed to love listening to their stories even though she never told them a thing about herself. 'What happened next?'

'He disappeared.' Tor suddenly hadn't felt like finishing the story. For reasons she still didn't understand, it had all gone so wrong.

He had asked her mother whether he might take Tor on a picnic to

Magdalen, his old college in Oxford. Her mother, sensing a proposal in the air, was ecstatic; she saw no reason why they needed a chaperone.

After lunch, under a willow tree near some historic bridge, he'd rolled up a towel and tucked it under her head. And suddenly—it had happened almost without her thinking—she'd turned to him, taken his face in her hands and kissed him.

And then, horrible, he'd leapt to his feet almost shouting at her. 'Please never do that again.' He'd brushed the grass from his trousers.

'Why not, silly?' She'd tried for a flippant tone that would not come.

He'd stood glaring and looking down at her.

'I can't do this,' he had said. 'It's ridiculous.'

'I don't understand,' she said, and even now it made her wince to think of it. 'I thought we . . . I thought you said you loved me.'

'You do have an awful lot of growing up to do,' he'd said as if it was all her fault.

She'd cried all the way home, hating her tears and at one point begging him to reconsider. But he hadn't. The next week he'd appeared, charming and kind again, to tell her a job had come up in Rome and he simply had to go. If he had, at any point, given her the impression of an engagement, he was terribly sorry.

Her mother had stopped speaking to her for two whole days. It was Rose who had held her in her arms, who had told her he was an absolute cad and a swine. Rose's kind words had helped, and being on the *Kaiser* was a tonic, but part of her was still bruised and bewildered.

The sun was rising in the sky, the sea a sapphire blue. Suday was walking into their cabin with a tray in his hands.

'Chai, my ladies. Chai and fruitycakebiscuit, hot roll, *irrawaddy*.'

Neither of them had the slightest clue what *irrawaddy* meant, but every morning their laughter made him laugh delightedly.

He poured tea for them with a flourish from a silver pot, then took hot rolls from a napkin and put them on their plates. He smiled when they told him what an absolute brick he was and shut the door behind himself still beaming.

'I love Suday,' said Tor sentimentally when he had gone. 'Now, get into bed with me, Rose. I need a gup.'

A gup, their new word for a gossip, was gleaned from the series of lectures they'd been going to called 'Kitchen Hindi for Memsahibs', given by Lieutenant-Colonel Gorman twice a week. Rose had listened avidly; Tor had gone along to keep her company.

Rose climbed in at the opposite end to Tor. 'First item on the agenda,' she said. 'Who were all those people you were dancing with last night? I got buttonholed by Mrs Llewellyn-Pearse, who told me all about the forty-seven varieties of rhododendron she saw in Simla last year.'

'Oh goodness, absolutely everyone. Philip, he is such a show-off. Colonel Green, who breathed garlic down my neck.'

'And Frank?' Rose widened her eyes. 'Were we dancing with Frank, Frank, Frank, Frankeee?'

'Oh, Frank.' Tor kept her voice carefully neutral. For the first time since the Paul fiasco, her heart had leapt when she'd seen him walk across the dance floor to ask her to dance. He was so endearing in his white dinner jacket and untidy hair. And a doctor was exciting, even though Mummy would think that was beneath them. *But danger!* her heart had said. *Red alert! Don't talk about him to anyone!*

'He's a sweet boy,' she said offhandedly. 'Oh, and I meant to say, he asked if you and I had any plans when we get to Port Said. He knows a splendid restaurant there—everyone's going.'

'Oh, darling, you know we can't,' said Rose. 'We promised your mother we wouldn't go ashore after Gibraltar, you know that.'

'She's obsessed with the white slave trade,' said Tor. 'It's ridiculous, and Frank is a grown-up: he's been on board lots of ships, well, at least two, and he's medically trained if anything happens to us.'

'Well, let's think about it,' said Rose in her sensible voice.

'Well, you can think about it, Rose. I'm going. And if you're going to get married soon, I suggest you learn to think for yourself.'

A shadow crossed Rose's face and Tor wished she hadn't said it.

'I'm not saying it to be bossy,' Rose said. 'It's just that you don't know him and . . .'

Tor knew exactly what she was thinking: *I don't want to see you hurt like that again.* But, a few moments later, when Tor was sitting in the bath, she thought, *I don't care. I'm ready again. For everything this time.*

**V**iva was sitting on her bunk, her typewriter balanced on a pillow; she was trying not to cry with frustration. Miss Snow had just walked in full of apologies—'Sorry, sorry, sorry!'—and was now organising what she called 'her kit': her underthings, her dresses and her books.

'You look awfully uncomfortable there,' Miss Snow said rather pointedly. 'Don't you find the writing room a more suitable place for work?'

She had tried. It was impossible. Four of the senior memsahibs on board had taken it over for a regular bridge four and the silence was punctuated by cries of 'Four in spades' or 'I say, what a wily bird you are' or 'Well done you!'

So far, apart from the evening bishis with Rose and Tor, she'd spoken to no one, apart from Miss Snow. The other young female passengers were perfectly polite to her, but she was a chaperone after all, so they, for the most part, excluded her from further intimacies. She felt angry with herself at times. Why mind being rejected by people she didn't want to be friends with anyway? It was absurd, illogical.

She shook herself out of these gloomy thoughts. She liked Rose and Tor more and more. Their evening bishis were fun. Last night Tor had wound up the gramophone and handed out the crème de menthe and taught her the Charleston.

The first-class dining room was humming with conversation when Viva entered it later that night. Such an elegant room with its richly painted murals, sumptuous chandeliers and mirrored walls. For a girl who'd been living on tinned sardines and baked beans heated up on a Primus hidden under the bed, it was like a dream to sit here and see the uniformed waiters buzzing around with silver platters, the sideboards heaped with exotic fruits and fine wines, the occasional glimpses of the scurrying, steaming world of the kitchen behind the swing doors.

Guy Glover was waiting for her in the corner of the room, looking pale and put-upon. He looked up as she approached and gave her a wan wave. She'd imagined when she'd taken on the job that once on the ship, the Great Sulky, as she now unkindly thought of him, would pal up with people of his own age, leaving her time to write. But not a bit of it: all he seemed to want to do was to gloom around the decks on his own, smoke cigarettes and sit and eat with her. If he'd made even the most minimal effort with her, she might have forgiven him, but he was almost impossible to talk to.

Now that the weather was so much warmer the other passengers had changed into summer clothes: lighter dresses for the women, dinner jackets for the men. But Guy, still wearing his long black coat, stuck out like a pallbearer at a wedding party.

Three waiters leapt into life as she sat down at their table.

One handed her a menu. She heard a burst of laughter coming from a nearby table. 'The Young', as the older people on board called any-body under thirty, had begun to eat at each other's tables. Rose and Tor were sitting with two other women, whose names she didn't know, and a young civil servant called Nigel.

'I'm sorry I'm late,' Viva said. 'Have you ordered?'

'Not yet.'

She picked up her menu with a heavy sense of duty.

'So, what would you like? Sole Véronique is the dish of the day. I think it's very good.' She hadn't a clue really, it was something to say. 'Oh good,' she said, 'pommes dauphinoise is on too.'

'I can actually read by myself.' Sarcasm had been added to his own limited menu lately.

'Sorry,' she said.

At first she really had tried with him: admittedly auntyish stuff about whether he was looking forward to going home. 'Not really.' And what kind of sports he'd played at school. 'None.' You had to start somewhere but now she had just about reached the end of her patience.

'Water?'

'Yes, please, and,' he gave her a look of barely concealed truculence, 'a bottle of Pouilly-Fuissé. Waiter!'

She'd offended him on the first night by asking him whether his parents allowed him to drink and he had not forgiven her. 'You do realise, don't you, that I am eighteen years old?' he'd said. Mrs Bannister had said he was sixteen but she let this pass. 'Not eight. I can't imagine why my parents thought I needed a chaperone.'

'So what about food?' she said. 'Are you ready to order?'

'Not yet.' He disappeared behind his menu.

'Well, I'm going to have a tournedos Rossini,' she said.

When it came, she listened to their knives and forks on the plates; watched the waiter take their plates away; looked at the old married couple at the table beside them who had also eaten in silence.

'It's Saturday night,' she told him. 'They've got a band up in the ballroom. They're supposed to be rather good. Do you feel like going?'

'No, I don't think so.' He sighed heavily.

'So, is there anything else you'd like to do then?' Oh, she honestly felt like striking him sometimes. 'Just say the word.'

The pudding trolley arrived bearing lemon meringue pies and fruit jellies, an apple soufflé, ice creams and the Indian julebis.

'More wine, sir?' The wine waiter's smile was a beam. 'We have some very nice Beaumes de Venise to go with the crème anglaise. Madam?'

'Just the lemon meringue for me, thank you.'

'I'll have a bottle of Beaumes de Venise,' Guy told the waiter.

'Who is going to pay for this?' she asked him in an angry whisper after the wine waiter had scuttled off.

'My parents,' he said prissily. 'Do stop fussing.'

As she watched the Young, chattering and laughing and starting to move upstairs, she felt what a luxury it would be to box him soundly round the ears. The room was half-empty now and he was scowling at her again with that look of barely concealed contempt.

'Will both your parents be in Bombay when we get there?'

'I don't know.'

She felt a sudden desire to make him feel something, anything—hurt, embarrassment, a sense that she existed too.

'My parents won't be there,' she said.

'Why not?' It was the first question he'd ever asked her.

'My parents and my sister died in India when I was ten. That's why I came back to England. One of the reasons I'm going back now is to pick up their things. They left a trunk there.'

He gazed at her, so blankly at first that she thought he hadn't heard. When he stood up his chair fell on the floor.

'Were they assassinated?' The expression on his face was one of genuine, even exaggerated horror. 'Did the Indians kill them?'

She felt a spurt of shame move from her stomach to her chest. She simply couldn't believe she'd blurted it out to him of all people.

'No.' She held her hands up as if to tamp him down.

'So why?'

'They just died,' she whispered. She felt a wave of heat go over her. 'I don't really want to talk about it. It was a car crash. I don't know where.' She hated it when people asked for details.

'I don't know what to say. Tell me what I should say.' His voice had risen and she wished she'd kept her mouth shut—she seemed to have unhinged him and wanted the silent boy back. He rushed off.

**W**hen she went on deck to look for him, the air felt thick and warm and the moon lay in a basket of cloud.

'Guy,' she called out, but the rush of bow-water and faint echoes of music from the ballroom muffled her voice.

'Guy?' She was near the lifeboats now. 'Guy, where are you?'

Half of her was inclined to let him stew in his own juices, but she was starting to feel worried about him. His almost hysterical reaction to her story, the wearing of that dreadful overcoat, even now with the glass regularly hitting 100 degrees—what if he was barking mad rather than simply churlish and self-engrossed?

After a fruitless search down empty corridors and on the landing of

A deck, she found him at last, hiding in a lifeboat, stretched out in his long dark coat. He was smoking a cigarette.

'Look,' she said. 'Lots of people have parents who died in India, so don't worry about it too much.'

The moon had gone behind a cloud, but she could still see the desperate intensity of his eyes. He was drunk, she was sure, and in pain.

'Why is life so awful?' he said.

'It's not all awful,' she said. 'Things change, improve. I really shouldn't have said it. I don't know why I did.'

He sat up and stared at her.

'Look, forget about me for a moment,' she said, realising that this might be her only chance. 'I want to ask you about yourself. I remember what it's like to be torn out of one place and put in another, that it's—' Her voice was stumbling but it was the best she could do.

'No, that's not it,' he interrupted. 'Not at all. Look, sorry . . . I'm going to bed.' He hauled himself out of the lifeboat and she watched him walk away with his stiff, high-shouldered gait.

'I'm so sorry,' a voice said from behind a pile of deck chairs. 'I feel I'm eavesdropping but I'm not.' A shadow stood up: it was Rose.

'I came out here to think,' she said. 'The others were so noisy.'

'Did you hear all that?' said Viva.

Rose looked embarrassed. 'Not all of it. I used to argue with my brother all the time—isn't it absolutely de rigueur?'

'I don't know if I can stand him,' Viva said. 'He's so contemptuous.'

A waiter had followed Rose in case she wanted anything.

'Coffee, madam? A nice liqueur? A cocktail? Emmeline Pitout will be singing her songs in the music room soon.'

'I tell you what.' Rose was smiling at her. 'Let's go mad and have a brandy. I think the worst thing about him not being your brother is you can't give him a fourpenny one. It would be so satisfying.' Rose had a wonderful laugh, warm and throaty. Its hint of wildness was what stopped her seeming too good to be true.

'It must be so strange for him going back to India.' Rose sipped her brandy. 'After all those years on his own.'

'Ten years,' said Viva, trying to calm down. 'And it is hell leaving India as a child—one moment, sun and freedom and blue skies, and lots of people running round after you who adore you. The next, well, you're breaking the ice on a washbasin in some freezing school.'

'Like being kicked out of paradise,' Rose said.

'Yes, but India isn't paradise. It has other ways of being awful.'

'Examples, please, but nothing too horrid.'

'Well, the heat for one thing; you have never, ever felt anything like it in England. The flies, appalling poverty, but if you love it, as I do, it gets to you, it bores its way into your soul. You'll see.'

'It's so odd to think I'm going to be married there soon,' said Rose. 'There is quite a lot to think about.'

Rose had confessed to her the day before, as if it were a splendid joke, that she'd met her fiancé a grand total of only five times. And Viva had wondered, *How could you give yourself away so carelessly?* Why had her parents allowed it? It wasn't even like an arranged marriage in India where the families would have known each other for generations.

'Yes, I can imagine,' said Viva.

'It's been such fun on the dear old *Kaiser*.' Rose was twisting the sapphire ring on her wedding finger, her voice dreamy and far away. 'All our new best friends, the sense that you're always on the way to somewhere else. In fact . . .' she looked at her watch '. . . we should be able to see Port Said soon, or so our waiter told us.'

She walked towards the ship's railings. 'Look. Oh, do look!' She pointed towards the horizon. 'You can see the lights already.'

Viva didn't want to move. She shouldn't have said all that to Guy.

'Do come! Do look! It is so thrilling. Is it Port Said? It must be.'

Together they looked out at a faint necklace of lights across a dark and crinkling sea.

'Tor's desperate to go ashore,' Rose said, sounding anxious. 'Frank's asked us all. What do you think of him, by the way?'

'Not sure,' said Viva. 'Except that he seems rather sure of himself and of his effect on women. I hope he doesn't hurt her.'

'I do too,' said Rose. 'She had such a rotten time during the season. I don't know why men aren't nicer to her.'

*She tries too hard*, Viva thought. *She doesn't mean to but she does, because she thinks she's not pretty enough.*

'Colonel Patterson told me yesterday that Frank had an older brother who was killed at Ypres,' Rose said. 'That's why he became a doctor. Colonel Patterson thinks Frank puts on a jolly front because he's still getting over it. He said it only came up because the colonel's son was killed there too.'

'Are you sure?' It took Viva a few seconds to absorb this information and feel the jolt of shame that came with it. *I do this all the time with people. I write them off before I know them, or I think that friendliness, a certain kind of openness, is a form of weakness.*

'That's what the colonel said.' Rose's beautiful blue eyes suddenly gleamed with tears. 'My older brother died in France—the one I used to row with, because I was so much younger than him and wanted to do all the things he did. Oh, let's not talk about it now. It's too awful. I can't bear it sometimes. The thing is,' she said in a firmer voice, 'Frank knows the most wonderful restaurant there, and a trip we can do to the pyramids. Tor's simply longing to go, but I did promise my pees I wouldn't go without a proper chaperone, so would you come?'

'I'd love to.' Viva tried not to sound too eager.

'But what about the boy?' Rose's expression was warily polite. 'I mean, he can come if he likes, but we probably seem like a crowd of ancients to him.'

'He wasn't keen when we talked about it earlier,' said Viva. What he'd said was, 'So, camel stools, perfume factories. How splendid,' his voice breaking on the splendid.

'He might actually like a day on his own.' Rose sounded hopeful. 'But do bring him if you have to.'

*No, no, no*, thought Viva. *I don't have to. He has made it perfectly clear he wants a day on his own.*

She had made up her mind already, and one day she would pay for it.

## Port Said, 1,300 miles to Bombay

Tor got up early, woken by the shouts of the boatmen in Port Said Harbour and a sense of queasy excitement about the day ahead. Picking up a bundle of clothes she crept round Rose and headed for the bathroom. She locked the door and put on a white toile dress first. She stood on the stool and lined up her reflection in the mirror. She took the dress off again. Too sugared-almondy and twee.

Ten minutes later, sweating and agitated, she stood in the middle of a clothes mountain in a pale green cotton frock and a pair of jade earrings, trying to imagine what Frank would think of her in this.

She had the most hideous crush on him. When he'd asked her, in the most casual way possible, if Rose and she had any plans for Port Said, she'd been sitting in the bar chatting to Jitu Singh. Jitu was the urbane young maharajah, down from Oxford and rumoured to have at least twelve servants with him, organising his immaculate suits and special food. Beside him, Frank, who had just worked a five-hour shift, looked adorably rumpled and creased.

Frank had said he'd be off-duty at twelve the next day and maybe they could all meet for lunch. When he'd smiled, she'd felt her hand go clammy round her glass and her heart skip. She'd started to look forward to him arriving every day. Only yesterday, he'd walked around the deck with her and, in between saying polite good mornings to the Groans (anybody over thirty), muttered scandalous accounts of their lives under his breath. *Murdered wife's best friend in a moment of sordid passion*, he'd said as they passed Major Skinner, quietly settling down to a few deck quoits with his family. *Senior member of opium gang*, towards Miss Warner, who had been sitting on her deck chair reading her Bible.

'It's certainly a thought,' she'd said, when he'd told her about the quick trip to Cairo they could do from Port Said. 'It sounds rather fun.'

She was proud of herself for sounding as if they had a million other possibilities there.

'I'll be up near the purser's office at ten tomorrow morning collecting my post,' he said. 'No need to let me know before then.'

'Honey pie,' Rose's voice came through the keyhole, 'any chance of using the bathroom before we get to Bombay?'

**F**ifty minutes later, Tor saw Frank standing near the purser's office.

'Oh, hello, Frank. Did you sleep well?' *Oh, how wonderfully original.*

'Hardly at all,' he said. 'I was on call and we were quite busy.'

'Any good scandals?'

'Lots,' he said. 'But I'm not allowed to tell you, or at least not until I've had at least three grenadines in the Windsor Bar.'

'Beast,' she said. 'Well, you may get one because we're coming.'

'I can't come until lunchtime,' he said, 'but I've got you a safe driver to drive you around Port Said. He'll take you to the station at twelve fifteen when the train leaves and we'll get to Cairo about four hours later. We can have lunch on the train. You'll have time to shop this morning if you want to.'

She felt a warm glow as she watched his tanned hand scribbling. He was so much manlier than the pale and artistic Paul Tattershall.

**S**even hours later, Tor, Viva, Rose, Nigel and Frank were in the Windsor Bar, in Shepheard's Hotel in Cairo. They were sunk deep into chairs made of old barrels, with piles of shopping bags full of what Frank called 'ill-considered trifles' all around them.

'I would adore a lime and soda,' Rose told Frank, who was ordering.

Tor thought Frank looked wonderful out of uniform. He was wearing a crumpled linen suit.

'A pink lady for me,' said Tor. 'Do try one,' she said to Rose. 'They've got grenadine at the bottom and brandy on top and they taste like pear drops—you'll love them. I say, it's not every day you have breakfast in Port Said and supper in Cairo.'

Tor's hair felt gritty from the train, her legs ached from the camel ride that had made them all shriek earlier—one had spat at Nigel straight in the eye—but she felt happy in a keyed-up sort of way. There was Frank, smiling his sleepy smile; her friends, Viva and Rose and Nigel, all drinking grenadines now. Nigel, the young civil servant, was one of their new best friends. He had lank sandy hair and a languid body. His pale fine-featured face quivered with intelligence.

'See all this.' Nigel waved his glass towards the Windsor's antique carpets and polished floor, the stuffed animal heads on the wall. 'It was once a very smart English officers' club; it'll soon be a piece of history.'

'Nigel, don't start all that hell in a handcart stuff,' Tor pleaded. 'We're having a jolly day out.'

'But it's true, though, isn't it?' Nigel turned to Viva.

When Viva looked at him and smiled sadly without saying anything, Tor thought how beautiful she was today in her scarlet dress, her loose hair looking artistic and dishevelled. She was an original, Tor decided, and admired the way she never looked as if she tried too hard. Frank was looking at her too, both men waiting eagerly for her to talk.

'Another grenadine, please,' Tor told Frank. 'Too delicious for words.'

The waiter arrived, plump and smiling with a napkin over his arm. They ordered far more than they needed: dishes of fat olives and plump little tomatoes, chickpeas, hummous and mouth-watering mounds of chicken and tabbouleh, all washed down with some local wine.

When Frank turned to talk to Viva, Tor watched them from the corner of her eye. He must have made a joke for she suddenly seemed to glow, and then she leant forward, saying something to him that Tor couldn't catch but which made him laugh.

'Have one of these.' Viva offered Tor a dish of olives, deliberately involving her again. 'And tell me if Frank is lying to me. He tells me some archaeologists have just dug up a pharaoh's tomb at Moukel al Tes and found inside it mountains of old hairnets, tweezers and pots of face oil.'

'He's probably lying.' Tor didn't mean to sound so sour.

'I'm not.' When Frank turned round to look at Tor, she was happy again. 'Why wouldn't good looks be as important to them as to us?'

'I feel a quote coming on,' said Viva. 'Hang on.' She thought for a moment. '"I am convinced that nothing in a man's life has as much importance as the conviction that he is attractive or unattractive." Tolstoy.'

'Perfect,' said Frank. 'My case rests.'

Tor, who had never read Tolstoy, gave a knowing smile.

Frank turned away from Tor again. 'Where are you going to live when you get to India?' he asked Viva.

She hesitated. 'I'm not sure yet. I have a few introductions. I'll be living on my wits for a while.'

Everybody waited for her to say more, but she didn't.

*That was the secret*, Tor thought, *be more mysterious*. She blabbed to everyone.

'So,' Nigel turned to Tor, 'what are *your* plans post-Bombay?'

'Well—' Tor was about to be elusive too when Rose interrupted.

'She's my chief bridesmaid,' she said loyally, 'and bestest friend in the whole world.'

'And is this a full-time job?' Frank teased.

'Yes,' Rose said, 'I'm hideously demanding.'

Tor had never heard her role in India sound so mundane, so childish.

'As soon as Rose is hitched,' she blew out some cigarette smoke, 'I'll be off like a shot, travelling, having adventures and so forth.'

'Oh!' Rose stood up. She looked as if she'd been slapped. 'Do excuse me,' she said. She pushed back her chair and walked off in the direction of the ladies' room.

'Is she all right?' Viva mouthed to Tor.

'I'm sure she is.' Tor was puzzled. Rose had never in her life walked off in a huff. 'I'll go and see her. Maybe she's not feeling very well.'

Rose was standing by an ornately tiled washbasin crying when Tor walked into the ladies' room.

'What on earth's the matter, Rose?' she said.

'You.'

'*Me?* Why?' Tor had never seen her so angry.

'I'm sorry, Tor,' Rose said. 'But I thought you were a little bit excited about being a bridesmaid and that when we got to India we would spend some time together enjoying things. But now, you seem completely bored by the whole thing.'

And suddenly Tor was shouting at Rose, because the whole day was turning out to be such a disappointment and she was absolutely fed up with being on the edge of everybody's dreams.

'Oh, so is my sole function in life to be your wet nurse?'

'No! No! No! But all you talk about now is going away and having adventures.' Rose gave a great whoop of despair and tears ran down her face. 'Can't you see, can't you see at all how strange this will be for me?'

For a few seconds, they both glared at each other, breathing heavily.

'Oh, Rose.' Tor put her arms round her. 'I'm so sorry. I really and truly am. I was showing off to Frank, and it's just that sometimes other people seem to have such interesting lives and I want one too.'

'You'll have one, Tor, I know you will.'

'Yes.' Tor straightened Rose's hair. 'I'll have one.' Her voice seemed to bounce in a hollow way off the tiled walls.

'Friends again?'

'Yes.' Tor hugged her. 'Friends. In fact, if you're not careful, I'll be on that honeymoon with you. Shall we go back and join the others?'

'Yes,' said Rose. 'Sorry if I was a bit of an idiot, but it is so strange.'

They walked back to their table. Nigel was sitting on his own reading a book of Arabic poetry. Frank and Viva had disappeared.

'Where is everyone?' asked Tor.

'Gone,' he said. 'While you were away, a chap came from the *Kaiser* and told Viva to get back to the ship as soon as possible. Something about an incident on board. Frank went with her.'

'What about us?' said Tor.

'He's ordered a car to take us to the ship.'

'How thoughtful.' Tor felt her heart turn to stone again. 'He's thought of everything.'

# Chapter 4

Port Said, eleven days from Bombay

When Viva got back to the ship, Mr Ramsbottom, the acquaintance of Guy's parents, stood at the bottom of the gangplank. Beads of sweat stood out on his forehead, and he was so angry he could not look at her.

Viva felt her mouth go dry. 'What's happened? Where's Guy?'

'You'd better come down and talk to him,' he said. 'I'll tell you what I think of your behaviour later.'

She followed his squared shoulders up the gangplank and then down three flights of narrowing stairs, down into the bowels of the ship.

'You had no right to fob him off onto us today,' he flung over his shoulder. 'We know his parents a little, but we don't know *him* at all.'

'Look,' she said. 'Tell me quickly, is he all right?'

'Well, you'll see him in a minute—he's being held in the ship's lock-up, brig or whatever damn thing they call it.' He was still spitting mad.

A uniformed officer took them into a small, airless suite of rooms that smelt faintly of urine and Dettol.

'Ah! Miss Holloway, the chaperone, good of you to drop in.' The duty officer was waiting for them. 'My name is Benson.' The two men exchanged looks full of male understanding about the unreliability of women. 'Mr Glover's been rather a busy boy during your absence.'

**W**hen she walked in, Guy was lying on a narrow bunk with his face to the wall. It was hot in the room, 105 degrees or so, but he was huddled in a grey blanket. His overcoat was hanging up on a hook on the wall. She could smell him from the door: alcohol and sweat.

'Guy,' she said, 'what happened?'

When he turned over, his face looked as if someone had stamped on it: one eye purple and swollen, his lips twice their normal size. A cut at the corner of his mouth was leaking watery blood.

'Why aren't you in the hospital?' she said.

He raised his voice and looked beyond her, to the officer who was keeping a protective eye on both of them.

'I want her away from me,' he said in a slurred voice. 'It's not her fault. Silly old sod Ramsbottom keeps blaming her.'

'Guy, Guy, shush, please.' As she sat down at the end of the bunk, she was conscious of the door closing softly.

'Look, he's gone,' she whispered, 'so tell me quickly what happened.'

'Nothing. That's all you need to know.' He crumpled up his face like a child about to cry, then closed his eyes and seemed to sleep.

'Miss Holloway,' Benson appeared at the door, 'he's been given a sedative, so I don't think you'll get much more out of him tonight. If you wouldn't mind,' he added, 'we'd like to ask you one or two questions.'

'Of course. Are you sure there's nothing I can do for you, Guy?'

'You can bring me a bottle of bleach,' he said, 'and I can drink the lot.' He turned to look at the wall again. 'A joke,' he mumbled.

'**H**e has to see a doctor,' she told the duty officer.

They were sitting in his cubbyhole of an office. Sweat was dripping from Benson's face onto the blotting paper. He switched the fan on.

'What happened to him?' she said. 'His eyes are so swollen. He must see a doctor.'

'Absolutely.' Benson scratched his forehead. 'I'll organise one right away, but what we'd most like to do is move him back to his cabin.'

'Wouldn't it be better if he was in the sanatorium?'

'Well, it's a bit complicated,' Benson said. 'While you were out sightseeing, Mr Glover attacked one of our passengers. An Indian passenger, name of Azim. They're a prominent Muslim family from the north. Mr Azim apprehended Glover in his cabin with a pair of cuff links and a small silver ornamental sword in his coat pocket. A scuffle ensued, nothing too serious at first, but then, according to Azim, Mr Glover punched Mr Azim hard in the face, then in the ear. Azim was in the san for five hours; they've discharged him now. At the moment, he says he does not want to press charges. That may change.'

'Who beat Guy up?' she said.

'Well, that's the point, we don't think anybody did. Your boy was seen approximately half an hour later by two members of staff, banging his own head against the stern railings.'

'Oh good Lord!' She stared at Benson in disbelief. 'Why?'

'We don't know, but now we have to sort out the best way of dealing with him. He said he did it for you. Something about being in love with you and voices telling him to do it.' Benson's face looked carefully blank.

'This is madness,' she said.

'Well, it may be,' said Benson, 'but, assuming that Azim doesn't press charges, here are our options: do we get the police involved, which could mean you disembarking and hanging around in Suez for an indefinite period; do we keep him locked up here and cause a scandal; or do we take the chance that it won't happen again? What do you think? You know him best. And technically, he is yours, although I'm surprised that his parents gave so much responsibility to someone of your age.'

She looked at him for a moment, trying to think.

'Do you know Frank Steadman?' she said at last. 'He's one of the medical officers on board. I'd like to talk to him before I make up my mind; he could check Mr Glover over at the same time.'

'That sounds like a very good idea.' The duty officer looked so relieved he actually smiled. 'Worse things happen at sea and all that. What if we arrange for Mr Glover to be taken back to his cabin tonight? I could arrange for Dr Steadman to meet you there.'

'Thank you,' she said.

'Just one more thing,' he said. 'I wouldn't tell anybody about this incident if I were you. Ships are funny places: rumours, fears spread like wildfire. I've said the same thing to Mr Ramsbottom and he agrees.'

'I won't say anything,' she said.

'It wouldn't look very good for you either,' he added slyly. 'It wasn't perhaps the wisest thing to leave him alone like that. It could have been very much more serious.'

It took two sailors to bundle Guy, still groggy from the sedative, back to bed in his own cabin. When they left, Viva bolted the door behind them and collapsed in a chair. Guy fell asleep almost instantly.

As she watched him sleep she felt a cold contempt for herself. She didn't like him, but it was dreadful of her to have left him behind.

A soft knock on the door made her spring to her feet.

'Can I come in? It's Dr Steadman. Frank.'

Relief flooded through her like new blood.

'Come in and lock the door behind you,' she whispered.

He was back in his uniform. He sat down on the chair beside Guy's bunk, a small leather bag at his feet.

'Don't wake him for a second,' he said. 'Tell me what happened.'

When she opened her mouth to speak, the boy's swollen eye flickered. 'Ah, Doctor,' he said. 'Good of you to drop in.' When he tried to sit up, she caught the smell of his stale air, his sweat and vomit.

'Stay where you are for a second.' Frank moved closer to him and gently touched the corner of the boy's eye. 'I want to have a look at this.'

Frank scrutinised the boy's face.

'You were lucky that whatever hit you missed your eye,' said Frank. 'What was it, by the way?'

'A thunderbolt.'

'I can't help you if you're going to play silly buggers with me,' Frank said. 'It looks like someone gave you an almighty punch. Was that it?'

'My business, not yours.' The boy turned his face to the wall.

'Look,' Frank said evenly, as if the boy hadn't spoken at all, 'before you go to sleep, I'd like to clean up your lip and put something on your eye to take the swelling down and then, maybe,' he looked at Viva for permission, 'I could talk to Guy on his own. Man to man.'

'Of course,' said Viva.

'Come back in about half an hour,' said Frank, 'then you could come to the surgery with me to get something to help Guy sleep.'

Viva walked down the corridor. A heavily made-up man wearing a frock suddenly appeared from one of the cabin doors. More people appeared from behind him, giggling and self-conscious, dressed in feather boas and clown suits, and she remembered it was the Eccentrics party that night. She had said she might go with Tor and Rose.

When she reached the purser's office, the clock outside said eight thirty-five; the lights were on inside. To fill in time and to hide from the partygoers she went in to ask whether there was a letter for her.

The clerk handed her a buff-coloured envelope with a telegram in it.

It was from the *Pioneer Mail and Indian Weekly*. 'Sorry,' it read. 'Insufficient funds to take on another correspondent in our Bombay office this month, but do come and see us if you are passing by.' It was signed Harold Warner. He was an old friend of Mrs Driver who'd been sure he'd be able to find 'some little job' for her.

She glanced at her watch. She'd been gone for ten minutes and would go back in ten. The worst thing about being on a ship was there was nowhere to hide when things went wrong. If she went to her cabin, Miss Snow would be there. If she went into supper, she'd have to face the Ramsbottoms. The only person she felt safe with was Frank.

He was still sitting in a chair by Guy's bed when she walked in.

'How is he?' she said.

'Fast asleep. Do you know anything about his parents?' he asked.

'I met an aunt once at my interview. She said something about his father being in the tea business in Assam.'

'They should never have put you in this situation,' he said.

'What situation?'

'Would you mind if we went into the bathroom?' he said. 'I don't want him to overhear.'

They crept into the bathroom together where they sat awkwardly at either end of the bath.

'To start with, how do you get on with Guy?' Frank asked.

'Honestly?'

'Yes,' he glanced at her quickly and smiled, 'always.'

'I can't bear him.'

'Well, that's pretty unequivocal,' he said.

'Look, I know boys of his age struggle with conversation,' she said, 'but he's barely uttered a word for the past two weeks, and when he does, I get the feeling he hates me.'

'He doesn't hate you,' Frank said at last. 'He hates himself.'

'But why?'

'That, I'm not sure of. Have you seen him in his own setting, at school for instance?'

'Well, I drove down there to pick him up, but when he left all the other boys seemed to be out. His dormitory was deserted.'

'That's pretty unusual. He told me he was leaving school for good.'

'He was.'

'Do you know why?'

'Yes, I do. Look, this is all my fault. I should have said something earlier. He'd taken things from other boys. I didn't take it seriously enough.'

'What did he take?'

'Not very much, the normal pilfering.'

'Don't blame yourself too much,' said Frank. 'The thieving might be part of a bigger problem. When you were out of the room he told me he hears voices sometimes. He said they come through his wireless.'

'But that sounds absolutely—'

'I know. He also said something about you being his chosen mother. He said he hates his real one.'

Viva felt her skin prickle. 'I shouldn't have left him. Do you think he's dangerous? Will it happen again?'

'I don't really know. His reaction did seem quite extreme. Obviously I'll have to talk to my senior, Dr Mackenzie, about it, but my instinct is to keep an eye on him for a couple of days. I'll attempt to persuade him to come into the san; we'll try to keep the lid on things. It's only ten days to Bombay and the weather will be too hot for anyone to do much in the Indian Ocean.'

'What's the alternative?'

'To put him off the ship at Suez, but then he'd have to wait for his parents to come and that won't do anything for his state of mind.'

'What if he won't go to the san?'

'Well, the other alternative is to keep him under some form of house arrest in his cabin. They'd fit his door with an extra lock, but how would you feel about that?'

She shuddered and shook her head. 'I honestly don't know. Did you know that his cabin is right next door to Tor and Rose's?'

'No,' he said. 'I didn't.'

'Shall I tell them?'

'Not for the time being. No point in frightening them.'

'What would you do if you were me?' she asked.

'I'd review the situation first thing tomorrow. I'll talk to Dr Mackenzie; you won't be left alone with this.' He looked at her again. 'Are you all right?'

'Yes. Why do you ask?'

'You look very pale.'

'I'm fine, thank you.' She took a step back from him. It was so instinctive not to ask for help, a habit she couldn't break. She shook his hand formally. 'But thank you,' she said. 'You've been most helpful.'

He smiled at her. 'Part of the P&O service, madam.' He was back to his bantering self again.

He turned off one of the lights in the cabin and straightened the blankets over Guy. She collected her wrap and her bag.

'Don't worry too much,' he said. 'I'm sure he'll be all right.' He brushed against her arm as he locked the cabin door. She stepped backwards into a figure in the corridor. It was Tor. She was dressed for the Eccentrics party in a black hooded cloak, with a rope tied round her neck like a noose. Attached to the noose was a bottle with the label 'The last drop' written on it. When she saw them both she stopped smiling.

## The Strait of Bab-el-Mandeb

Tor had looked forward to the next event, the Arabian Nights party, ever since she'd arrived on board. Held on full-moon nights, on the day before the ship slipped into the Red Sea, experienced travellers on board said it was one of the highlights. Exotic costumes were expected and the dress she'd planned to wear—long, slinky and made of fine gold silk— begged for a cigarette holder, red lips and a weary expression. It was a vamp's dress and any other mother but hers would have forbidden it.

She was to be an Egyptian goddess in it and she'd decided to wear it with a gold mask, a long rope of pearls and lipstick. Every time she'd thought of the party, she ran a little film in her head in which Frank took off her mask of gold, and looked deeply into her eyes. Sometimes he told her she had wonderful eyes, sometimes he simply led her down to his cabin where he made a woman of her. And, once again, her mind had raced ahead to babies and houses and photograph albums.

On the morning before the ball she woke early, furious with herself all over again. How long, she wondered, would it take her to get it into her fat head that men didn't like her?

She thumped her pillow and turned over. Jealousy was such a horrible emotion, she decided. The sight of Viva and Frank leaving Guy's room that night, looking so conspiratorial, had made her accept that Frank was not the slightest bit interested in her. Why she'd ever imagined he was, was a complete mystery to her now. But this time, she told herself, she would behave like a grown-up. *Stop caring so much*, had been her stern message to herself over the past few days.

The Arabian Nights party was in full swing when Tor went up on deck later that night. The sky flamed with the colours of coral and claret and all the faces of the partygoers were bathed in its light. The crew had scurried around all day, wrapping tables in pink cloths and piling fruits—figs, mangoes, pawpaws and sweetmeats—and Turkish delights on the tables. There were coloured lights hung around the deck rails, and the sports deck had been magically transformed into a sultan's tent.

There was a fire-eater inside the tent and a throng of shouting people in masks and Turkish sandals, saris and flowing robes.

Tor took a deep breath. *Shoulders back. Head up. Smile. Walk.* Her destination was the other side of the crimson deck where she could see her group drinking and laughing.

'Heavens,' said Nigel, bowing. He was wearing a sharkskin dinner jacket and a fez. 'It's Nefertiti, and how, um, how ravishing she looks.'

'Thank you, Nigel.' Tor kissed him on the cheek.

'Who are you?' she asked Jane Ormsby Booth, the strapping young woman by Nigel's side, who was not a natural candidate for the sari.

'Unsure,' came the good-natured reply. 'Someone foreign.'

'Thank you, darling.' Tor took a glass of champagne from Nigel and arranged herself casually against the deck railings. 'Isn't this divine?'

She was interrupted by a group of people saying, 'Ooooohh!' Rose had appeared in brilliant pink silk, and as the band struck up 'Ain't She Sweet?' she did a little jig in the direction of the colonels and the mems who were sitting at their own table. She was followed by Jitu Singh, who swaggered across the deck in a blue silk jacket and baggy trousers, a silk turban with a large diamond on his head.

'Jitu,' they called, 'come over here and tell us who you are.'

He walked over and salaamed deeply, touching eyes, mouth and chest. 'My name,' he announced, 'is Nazim Ali Khan. I am a Mogul emperor. I bring gold and perfume and diamonds.'

As he nuzzled Tor's hand with his lips, she hoped Frank was watching.

After the sun set in a final blaze of glory, the stars came out and the partygoers danced, then ate sitting on silken cushions arranged inside the tent. Afterwards, they played a parlour game called Who Am I?, in which you had a strip of paper stuck on your forehead with the name of somebody famous on it. You had to ask the others questions to guess who you were. It caused great mirth and when it ended most of the elderly passengers went to bed.

Tor watched it all from a table littered with snapped streamers and lipsticked cigarettes. Nigel had just left and she was summoning up the energy to go to bed when Frank suddenly arrived at her side. He looked pale and out of sorts.

'Have you had a good evening, Tor?' he said with unusual formality.

'Marvellous,' she said. 'How was yours?'

'I'm tired. I need a drink.' He poured some wine. 'You?'

'No, thank you.'

'Tor,' he said, looking at her very intently, and for one heart-stopping moment she thought she'd got it wrong and that he might kiss her after all, but instead, he removed a piece of paper from her forehead.

'"Virginia Woolf,"' he read. 'No, I don't think that's you at all.'

'Who do you think I am?' she asked. She'd hoped the question would sound light-hearted. 'Theda Bara? Mary, Queen of Scots?'

He shook his head, refusing to play her game.

'I don't know,' he said at last. 'I don't think you do either.'

She felt her face grow hot with dismay. And then she stood up and called, 'Jitu, don't sit on your own, come and have a drink with us.' Not because she wanted him to but for something to do.

'None of us knows.' Frank was staring glumly into his glass. 'We—'

But Jitu had arrived. 'I've been summoned by a goddess,' he said, sitting next to her. 'Might a mortal even dance with her?'

Frank's reply had really hurt her, and the whole evening put her in a strange, unhappy, slightly unhinged mood.

She smiled at Jitu. 'She *will* dance with you. Thank you for asking her.'

The day after the party, Viva, pale-faced from lack of sleep and air, went to visit Guy in his cabin. When she walked in, he was lying in bed playing with a crystal wireless set, unshaven and miserable-looking.

The cabin was now littered with papers and old sweet wrappers and some nuts and bolts that he'd removed from his wireless. He'd forbidden the cabin steward to enter his room for the past two days and became irritable when Viva tried to tidy up.

'Are you feeling any better this morning, Guy?' she asked.

'No,' he replied. 'I'd like you to get off my airwaves for a start.'

Her heart sank. She hated this wireless talk.

'I'm not quite sure what you mean when you say that,' she said.

'You do know,' he said. He gave her a bright I-wasn't-born-yesterday sort of look. 'You know you know.'

'Guy,' she tried again, 'Dr Mackenzie is coming to see you today. He needs to decide the best thing to do with you. We'll be in Bombay in five days' time. Your parents will be there.' He closed his eyes when she said that but she ploughed on. 'The thing is that Dr Mackenzie says there are quite a few people in the ship's sanatorium with upset stomachs but he can easily make room, if that's the best place for you.'

'I'm not ill. Why do you keep telling people I am?'

She ignored this. 'I think Frank will be looking in on you too.'

Every night now since Port Said, Frank had come down to sit with her in Guy's cabin. When Guy had fallen asleep, she and Frank had sat together in the half-light, talking about a range of things—books, music, travel—nothing too personal except for one night when he'd told her about his brother, Charles.

'He didn't die at Ypres,' he said in a low and scarcely audible voice. 'It's just easier to say that to most people. He was invalided home. He had injuries to his throat and trachea, and he wrote down on a piece of paper that he would like me to stay with him until the end. He asked me to talk, so we held hands, and I wittered on.'

'About what?' Viva stiffened—too much emotion in the room.

'Oh, I don't know, daft things: family cricket matches at Salcombe where we went for summer holidays, camping trips in the New Forest, eating Eccles cakes in Lyons Corner House, family meals, the usual sort of stuff. It was difficult for him though—he would whisper something to me, then I'd tell him what I remembered.'

Frank said it had been the strangest five nights of his life and the saddest, and that afterwards he had felt so relieved it was over and that his brother wouldn't have to live with his dreadful injuries.

Viva fell silent after this outburst—what was she supposed to say?

'Do you think that's why you became a doctor?' she said at last.

'Possibly,' he'd said, standing up. 'It's a fairly impressionable age, eighteen—Charles was ten years older than me.'

He'd turned towards Guy. 'I'm worried about this chap,' he said in a brisk new voice, 'and the amount of time you have to spend with him. It's not healthy, and it's not much fun for you.'

She'd gazed at him, conscious of having failed as a confidante.

'No, it's not,' she said. 'But what can one do?'

'I think it's time to explain the situation to Rose and Tor, for their safety if nothing else. They must be wondering where you are.'

'I sort of explained my absence by saying he had an upset stomach.'

She didn't tell him that when she'd told Tor she'd reacted very strangely: 'Oh, don't bother to make up a story,' she'd said with an icy look. 'I knew it from the start.' And then she'd walked off in the other direction.

**D**r Mackenzie was due in half an hour. Viva sat down to wait for him.

Reading was impossible in Guy's cabin, because he liked to sleep with the curtains closed, and writing seemed temporarily beyond her; all she felt capable of at the moment was a kind of dull worrying about him and about her. Everything was starting to feel precarious.

But then came a small break in the clouds. She'd just crept to the sink in his bathroom to wash her face when she heard him singing softly behind the thin partition wall. It was a song she remembered her own ayah singing, '*humpti-tumpti gir giya phat.*'

She put her head round the door. '*Talli, talli, badja baba,*' she sang to him and his pleased snort felt like the first bit of good news she'd heard all morning.

'Did they all sing the same songs?' He opened one bloodshot eye.

'Probably,' she said. 'Mine told me lots of stories that began "*Ecco burra bili da*"—there was a large cat,' she said.

'You can tell me a story if you like.' His voice sounded softer.

Her mind raced furiously, then went blank.

'Tell me about your school. Were they horrible?' he asked.

'They were very strict; we were hit on the hands with rulers and made to do penances, but that wasn't the worst thing. Homesickness was, missing India. In India we'd step over beaches as soft as silk, we swam in water as warm as milk. At school we had to crunch over huge, sharp pebbles into grey waves that smacked you bracingly round the face. The nuns had all sorts of strange punishments—one of them, Sister Philomena, she wore a leg brace, used to make us stand in a bath if we were naughty, then she'd turn the hose on us.'

He gave a short bark.

'Looking back,' she resumed quickly, 'I just wish somebody had told me that schooldays are often a pretty dreadful time of your life, but that they go so fast, they really do, and other things like being independent, making your own money, your own decisions, are so much more fun later.'

'I don't think I'm going to have fun later,' he said. He sat up and looked her in the eye. 'You see, I've more or less decided to kill myself.'

'Guy, please. Don't even say that as a joke.'

'It's not a joke,' he said. 'I wish it were. You'd better tell Dr Mackenzie that when you see him. He should know that too.'

She looked down at him. The skin round his eyes was still yellowish and marbled, but she could see it healing day by day. It was his eyes and their strange scattered expression that troubled her. This was the moment she decided to get help.

The ship's surgery was on B deck and ran from nine thirty until noon, when it closed for lunch. Viva arrived at five past twelve.

She ran downstairs again and in desperation knocked on Tor and Rose's door, not expecting to find anybody in.

Tor opened it, her expression frozen.

'Look, I wonder if you could help me?' said Viva. 'I'm in a bit of a pickle. Can I come in?'

Tor's shrug wasn't enthusiastic but she stepped back from the door.

Viva spent the next ten minutes trying to explain about Guy and his increasingly odd behaviour.

'I didn't tell you before because I didn't want to worry you,' she said. 'Frank's been wonderful, he's given him sedatives and me moral support, but neither of us feels it's right to keep you in the dark any more. Guy was expelled from his school. He stole things from the other boys. It's only fair to warn you.'

It was a surprise to feel Tor's hand on her shoulder, then to feel her quick hug.

'I'm sorry,' she said. 'Poor you—you look absolutely done in,' and then she shook her head and hugged her again. 'I've been so cheesed off with you, but don't let's talk about that now, this is important.'

Tor opened up a miniature of Drambuie, split the contents between two glasses, and said, 'Are you sure he's as bad as you say? I mean, I was fairly doolally myself at his age. I was always threatening to kill myself.'

'No, Tor, I'd like to think that, but this is different: much worse.'

'And my own father is quite odd at times too,' continued Tor, 'but that was mustard gas during the war. The thing is to give him plenty of treats, something to look forward to each day. I could take my gramophone in and play him some tunes.'

'Oh, Tor, you are kind.'

'I'm not very kind, actually,' said Tor, 'but we'll be in Bombay in a blink of an eye, so surely between us all we can keep him amused, then it's his parents' hard cheese.'

Rose appeared, pink from a game of deck quoits.

'What's going on here?' she said. 'A drinking den? Can anyone join?'

Tor sat her down and put her in the picture, ending up with, 'So I'm sure he doesn't need flinging in the brig or whatever they call it.'

'Don't feel you have to say yes,' said Viva, noting Rose's slight hesitation. 'I would understand.'

'Well, I would like to talk to Frank first,' Rose said.

'Oh, of course.' Tor smiled. 'We've all got to talk to Dr Frank.'

## The Indian Ocean, 500 miles from Bombay

Although Rose had decided to avoid the boy next door as much as possible, she had started to feel a strange and unhappy kinship with him. Viva had told her that he hadn't seen his parents for ten years, that his terror was growing as they drew closer to India.

She understood. Yesterday when she'd used the term 'fiancé' to describe Jack to one of the mems, the word had stuck in her mouth. In two days' time they'd be there, and one door would close for her on her childhood and a sort of freedom, and another would open on a world as foreign to her as the moon.

This thought brought a gnats' swarm of other fears into her brain. Would Jack even recognise her after their six months apart? And assuming he did recognise her, would he be disappointed? Or would she look at him and know in an instant, *I got it wrong—he's not the one?*

Even Tor, she thought, had never been rash enough to give her life away to a man she hardly knew, and anyway, she seemed to be palling up with Viva and helping the boy next door.

That morning, for instance, Tor had taken off with her portable gramophone and a stack of 78s, and right now Rose could hear the muffled sounds of 'Blue Skies' and three voices singing, 'Nothin' but blue skies from now on . . .'

The boy's mood, according to Tor and Viva, was still very up and down, but Tor had discovered he had a passion for jazz and for cinema and during his good moments she nattered away to him like an old friend. Rose thought that they should have handed him over to Dr Mackenzie right away, and had said so quite firmly when the matter had been discussed with Frank. But Tor, who had previously been so mean about him, had annoyed Rose by turning out to be the sympathetic one. She'd said they could all form a safety circle round him until he was handed over to his parents in a few days' time.

Rose closed her eyes and put her head against the cabin wall. She was cross with herself for having such dreary thoughts about love and its dangers. Mummy had warned her that most brides got cold feet before their weddings; maybe this was nothing more than that. What she needed to do was to start packing and stop thinking.

## Poona

Many things had frightened Jack during the six years he'd been a cavalry officer. Four months after his basic training in Poona he'd been sent to a remote hill station, near Peshawar, on the northwest frontier, to help patrol one of the most dangerous and unstable borders in the world. After nights spent on horseback on mountainous roads where you waited for every shadow to kill you, the muscles on your neck stood out like organ stops. But this was a new kind of fear. It clung to him like black netting. The thought that Rose was hours away now; the idea that in ten days' time he'd be married. *I don't know you.* He'd sat up in bed this morning with the words booming in his head.

He checked his watch. Twenty-one hours to go. To calm himself he went down to the stables and walked into the stable of his favourite horse, Bula Bula. The name was Urdu for nightingale.

'Bullsy, old chum.' He placed his hand on his horse's mane, kneading it between his fingers.

'Morning, sahib.' His groom popped out from underneath the horse, saluted and went back to his grooming. There was a clatter of hoofs. His friends, Maxo—Lieutenant Maxwell Barnes—and Tiny Barnsworth, had ridden into the yard and were calling for him. He watched them for a moment from the stable, against the dazzling sky. Tough young men in their prime. His best friends.

He saw them smile at him the way people smile at funerals. Everybody knew in the tight world of the regiment that when you married things changed.

Five minutes later they were coated in red dust, shouting, galloping like savages up the long side of the polo pitch, where they played a boys' game of polo pretending to clock balls to each other, then they took the long red path that led up to the racecourse where the horses leapt forward again, their hoofs pounding the red dirt, their sides sopping with sweat. And it was here that he found himself shouting and crying at the same time, grateful that nobody could see him. It felt like the last day of his life.

Three hours later Jack was sitting in Colonel Atkinson's office. He was shaved, bathed, uniformed, subdued.

'We had some rotten news last night from Bannu,' Atkinson said. 'Three of our men up there were ambushed and have disappeared. I'm going to make an announcement this morning. Reynolds, who's the senior man up there, is almost certain more attacks are planned.'

'I'm sorry to hear that, sir.'

'We all are, but the point is, it's not going to stop and it's almost certain we're going to have to take some more of you up there, and we'd like you to command a company. The timing, I know, is wretched.'

'When, sir?'

'Couple of weeks, maybe sooner. I'm sorry if this throws your wedding plans but my hands are tied.'

'Not your fault, sir. It's an honour.'

'Will your wife cope?'

'I'm sure she will, sir.'

'Good luck.'

'Thank you, sir.'

## Bombay, November 7, 1928

Tor and Rose's trunks had been packed and placed outside their cabin, when Nigel knocked on their door.

'Message from the captain,' he announced. 'Last service at sea will be at four thirty in the grand salon. Message from me, I have a large bottle of champagne that needs attention in my cabin at one o'clock.'

'Oh, Nigel.' Tor put her arms round him and hugged him. 'Do you honestly think you can live without us?'

He hugged her back, pink with embarrassment.

'Not sure,' he said. 'I'll write and tell you.'

Tomorrow, she knew, he'd take his train back to Cherrapunji, en route to the remote hill station he'd told them was one of the wettest places on earth. He'd mentioned in his offhand, jokey way that three of his predecessors had committed suicide there, driven mad by isolation.

'I must fly, I must pack,' he said, 'but don't forget the champagne and tell Viva to come too.'

Viva, looking pale and jumpy, turned up later for the drinks party. She, Tor, Rose, Frank, and Jane Ormsby Booth squeezed into Nigel's cabin.

'Oh delicious.' Tor closed her eyes and held out her champagne flute. 'What a good idea this is.'

'Not so fast, my child.' Nigel put down the bottle and picked up a book. 'I'm going to read you all a very short poem first. Oh hush! Wretched philistines,' he silenced their groans. 'It will take two minutes of your time and you won't regret it. The poem is called "Ithaka", but it might just as well be called "India".'

He sat down close to Viva and started to read.

> 'As you set out for Ithaka,
> Hope your road is a long one,
> Full of adventure, full of discovery.'

'Sorry,' interrupted Jane, 'I don't do poetry. What's he on about?'

But Viva and Frank shushed her and Nigel continued. There was a silence after he'd finished. He popped the champagne cork and filled their glasses. 'To all our Ithakas,' he said, his eyes bright with tears.

'Bravo, Nigel,' said Viva. She put her hand on his arm. 'Who wrote it?'

'Cavafy.' He looked at her. 'I knew you'd like it.'

'I do,' she said.

'So here's to Bombay,' Frank said.

'And to all of you for making this journey so ripping,' said Tor with such fervour that they all laughed, except Rose, who was looking pensively towards the horizon.

**A** little over an hour later, they sat in the upstairs salon, which had been made into a temporary church for the last service at sea. A Union Jack had been draped on a temporary altar, and from the windows they could see the faint blurred outlines of the coast of India.

A large, sweating woman plunged her fingers into the harmonium, then one hundred or so voices floated out into the clear blue yonder. Tor glanced at them: the long rows of memsahibs, all dressed up today, the colonels, Jitu Singh, the missionaries, the little children with their mothers and whose ayahs you could see outside the door in their brightly coloured saris.

The hymn ended and they all knelt down. Rose, who was sitting beside Tor, was praying so hard her knuckles shone.

Viva walked in late with Guy. He was looking mole-like and dazed.

Frank came late too. He stood on the other side of the aisle from them, looking handsome in his full uniform.

Last night, Tor had had a conversation with him that had hurt her very much, although he would never have known it.

They'd taken a turn together round the deck, and it had seemed so romantic that she'd thought, *If he's ever going to kiss me properly, it will be now.* But instead he'd looked out in the blackness and given a heartfelt sigh. Tor, trying to cheer things up, had said, 'I can't believe we'll be in Bombay tomorrow morning—it really is too thrilling.'

'How sweet you are,' he'd said sadly. 'So eager for everything.'

'Well, aren't you? Come on, Frank, you must be.'

'Not really,' he replied. He'd lit a cigarette and exhaled moodily.

And then in the next five minutes she learned that she was a brick, a lovely girl, etc., and under normal circumstances just the sort of girl he should be spoony on, but that he was in love with someone else.

Tor had forced herself to nod and smile.

'Anyone I know?'

He'd turned away. 'No. I don't think anyone does.' Then he turned to her and said with real desperation in his eyes, 'I've tried so hard with her, too hard probably, but she's frozen, all locked up, and now I won't be able to get her out of my head. Oh, Tor, why am I telling you all this? It's too sweet of you to listen.'

'Not at all. What are friends for?' She'd even added a little joke. 'It's what my mother calls doorknob secrets. The things you blurt out suddenly just as you leave a room. And this is the last night on board after all.'

He'd kissed her lightly on the tip of her nose. An uncley sort of kiss.

'And what do you want, you sweet girl? Romance? Babies? Parties?'

'No.' She'd been stung by this. 'More than that.'

'Don't be offended,' he said. He was staring at her. 'So what is it?'

'I don't know. Something solid. Something that can't be taken away.'

'Gosh, are you a suffragette,' he'd said bitterly, 'or has Viva been getting at you too?'

# Chapter 5

## Bombay

Viva spent the morning sorting out the rancid-smelling clothes Guy had refused to send to the wash and generally keeping a wary eye on him. It was partly a way of avoiding herself, for they'd almost arrived. Earlier in the day, standing on the deck and watching Bombay's skyline take shape, she remembered holding Josie's hand on another sunlit day like this. Her father walking out of the crowd to claim them; her mother, flustered and happy, talking nineteen to the dozen to disguise the shyness they always felt at first until they became a family again.

Later, there had always been a celebration lunch in the restaurant on top of the Taj Hotel. She and Josie with the pees again.

Opening her eyes and seeing the skyline shimmer, she felt for a moment almost nauseous with pain. They were gone, *they were gone*. She'd had fifteen years to get used to it, but this morning the wounds were open and bleeding.

'**M**iss Holloway?' The purser's assistant was at her side with a handful of bar chits for her to sign, for herself and the boy. Her stomach knotted again. They were thirty pounds over the twenty-five-pound allowance his parents had sent her. She'd be meeting them in less than an hour.

She could smell India from the ship—spices, dung, dust, decay: elusive, unforgettable. From the harbour came the sounds of cracked trumpets and drums and shouts from the chana wallahs flogging peanuts and gram.

'Viva! Viva!' Tor bounded towards her. 'Isn't this thrilling?'

'Is Rose all right?' Viva asked quickly.

'No, of course she's not, she's downstairs having kittens. She's decided against meeting him on the pier as all the mems will stare. Nigel's gone ahead to find him and to take him down to our cabin. Oh, Viva. Please promise not to ditch me the moment we arrive. You can show me round and I'll ask you to parties.'

Viva smiled but said nothing. How could she possibly explain her financial terrors to someone like Tor to whom a monthly allowance, however small, was as natural as blood pumping into veins? She had a grand total of one hundred and forty pounds left in the world, wired ahead of her to Grindlays Bank in Bombay, some for emergencies and accommodation, the rest to get herself to Simla to collect her parents' trunk. If she didn't find work almost as soon as she arrived, she had, she estimated, about a month's worth of funds to live on.

'Don't you dare bolt once the ship's landed,' Tor said again.

'I won't.' Shyly, Viva returned Tor's squeeze. She wasn't good at this kind of moment. 'I'd better go down and get Guy up,' she said, looking at her watch.

'Is he all right?'

'Not really. I'll be glad when today's over,' she said.

**G**uy came to the door, yawning and bad-smelling and affecting a nonchalance she knew he didn't feel. He was still in his pyjamas.

'Please, Guy,' she said, 'it's nearly twelve fifteen. Wash your face, do your hair, get cracking.' Impatience flared up in her again.

The night before, they'd been packing when he'd said in a casually offhand voice, 'When my parents arrive tomorrow, will you stay with me? They'll probably ask a lot of very boring questions.'

'Yes, Guy, I'll stay,' she'd said, 'but give it time. You'll soon feel like a family again.'

'They're complete strangers,' he'd said. 'But thank you for the advice.'

And now, they had definitely arrived: she felt the final bump and shudder of the *Kaiser* landing and then a loud roar from the pier.

Rose had arranged herself in a casual pose on a wicker chair between the bunks. Feet were pacing above her head, the squeak of shoes running along the corridor. She waited for what felt like an age, then at the knock on the door she sprang to her feet.

'Rose,' said a deep voice. And there he was, standing in the doorway, topi in one hand, flowers in the other. He was taller than she remembered and not as handsome, or maybe that was because his face seemed somewhat contorted.

'Well, hello!' he said. She hadn't remembered him being so hearty either. He handed her the lilies. 'These are for you.'

She thought he might kiss her but instead he said, 'May I?' and sat down. He cleared his throat.

'They're lovely, Jack. Thank you.'

'Nice of that fellow Nigel to come and find me,' he said. 'He seems a decent chap.'

'Yes, he's a civil servant, he's off to—gosh, I can't even remember, how silly. These are really *so* pretty.'

Smiling at the flowers again, she felt a disagreeable blankness where her heart was supposed to be.

'Tor and I had such a jolly trip,' she said after a while. 'Real life is going to be absolute hell!' The smile died on his lips.

*Oh no! What a perfectly idiotic thing to say*, she thought. *Now he'll be quite sure I regret the whole thing.*

'Well, you're going to be rushed off your feet here . . .' he started, then stopped.

The fan had gone off; her hand, which was now resting in his, felt embarrassingly sticky.

'Look, there's a slight change of plan about the wedding that I wanted to tell you about before anybody else did.'

When he said this she felt an immediate lightening of her spirits: the whole thing was off, this was a dream.

'Yes, there's been a spot of bother up on the northwest border recently; I can explain it all in more detail soon.' He was sweating, she noticed, and had a dimple in his chin. 'My CO has asked me to join a company up there but I don't know when yet. If there is any change to the date, Ci Ci Mallinson says you can move in with her for a while.

The season starts in November, so there'll be masses of parties.'

She laughed a little wildly for a moment. 'Darling.' It felt so strange to be using the word. 'Whatever you think is right.'

Relief flashed across his face like sunlight.

'I appreciate you not making a fuss,' he said. 'I'm afraid the one thing you can rely on in India is that no arrangement ever quite works out.'

**T**en minutes later, as they walked down the gangplank together, a thin woman wearing lots of lipstick and a cloche hat stepped out of the crowd to greet them.

'Darlings,' she said. 'Romeo meets Julietta at long last. I'm Cecilia Mallinson, call me Ci Ci.' When she kissed Rose lightly on both cheeks, she smelt strongly of cigarettes and perfume.

'Everything all right?' said Tor as they headed towards Ci Ci's car.

'Fine, thank you,' breathed Rose without moving her mouth. 'Simply lovely.' But then she stopped suddenly. 'Oh, how awful, I forgot to say goodbye to Viva. I can't believe it!'

'Don't worry,' Tor said, 'she knew you were in a state and so was she—the boy's parents had arrived. I gave her our address.'

They drove home in Mrs Mallinson's snazzy little car—a bottle-green Model T Ford. Tor sat in front, exclaiming and laughing at everything; Rose was behind with Jack, absurdly aware of where his square brown knees ended and her pink silk ones began.

Ci Ci turned to look at them. 'So, tour guide speaking,' she sang out. She seemed determined to be fun, which made Rose feel even shyer. 'Big pukka palacey-looking place on your left with the dome on top is the Taj Mahal Hotel, where we'll be having a party on New Year's Eve. Coming up on your left, Bombay Yacht Club, where we sail, another favourite watering hole, and beyond that—Oops!'

A sudden stop jammed Jack's leg against hers. A man carrying bananas stepped in front of them and crossed the road.

Rose saw Ci Ci's eyes gleam at them naughtily in her car mirror. She blushed and felt her heart racing. Jack was holding her hand again.

**November 9, 1928. YWCA, Bombay. Extract from Viva Holloway's diary.**

*I mst. write down what happened before it fades. Guy Glover is a rat, he laid a trap for me; he begged me to stay with him to meet his parents. Frank had agreed to stay behind to give his professional medical opinion on Guy, in case things got sticky for me, but at the last* minute was needed urgently in san. So I was left to deal with things on my own.

Eventually they came. She, Gwen Glover, drab, tearful little partridge of a woman; Mr G., a red-faced blusterer who immediately shook Guy's hand and clapped him on the shoulder.

'Well done, old boy, you got here in the end,' etc., etc. and 'Have you both had fun?' Fun! wld <u>not</u> be my word for it.

For the first five or ten minutes, Guy played the part of the prodigal son quite well, but when we started to collect his things, he suddenly left the room, slamming the door behind him.

While Guy was out of the room I handed over the two letters the school had given me for them. Mr Glover stuffed them in his pocket. He said he didn't have time to read them now, which made me wonder whether he didn't know already about the thieving, the exam results, etc.

I tried to explain the nervous strain Guy appeared to have been under on the voyage out, and how he'd been under doctor's orders, and then—it only seemed fair to tell them—about how he'd been seen banging his own head against the ship's railings.

'But this is preposterous,' Mr Glover said, turning redder. 'Are you suggesting my son is not mentally sound?'

'Yes, I think I am,' I said.

Mrs Glover started to cry and said, 'I knew something like this would happen,' and, 'It was only a matter of time.'

Mr Glover said, 'Shut up, Gwen,' and then, to me, 'How dare you.' He then marched outside and got Guy.

'Sit down on that bed, Guy,' he said. 'Miss Holloway claims you got involved in some fisticuffs on board.

Guy looked at me very coldly and shook his head. 'She's a liar,' he said. 'And she drinks; she said to put it all on your bill.'

At that precise moment, Guy's steward came in with another armful of chits, still unpaid from our bar bill. Mr G. spread them out on the bed. He got out a pad and a silver pencil. The bill was nearly ten pounds—the little rat had been drinking on the sly.

I was accused of being a drunken, irresponsible liar. If I hadn't been drinking so much I would have been more sensitive to the finer feelings of a boy who hadn't, due to circumstances beyond their control, seen his parents for ten years and was understandably nervous. In conclusion, he had no intention of paying me my money, I was jolly lucky not to be handed over to the police.

Perhaps there was some fear behind his bluster: when I invited him to talk to the ship's doctor to verify my story, he didn't reply, but instead

*offered magnanimously to pay off the bar chits, provided I signed a note
saying I would pay him off in instalments.*

*They left on the night train to Assam. Guy walked off between his
parents, and then ran back and tried to hug me, whispering, 'Don't let
the bastards get you down.' How dare he!*

*And then I was on my own in the middle of the Apollo Bunder, with
dozens of porters swarming round me. I asked a tonga driver to take
me to the YWCA, which Miss Snow had told me was a cheap, clean,
respectable and safe place to stay.*

*I'm paying two rupees a night here for a single room. My room,
though small, overlooks a huge and beautiful tree. It has an iron bed, a
table and a cupboard in the hall where I can hang clothes.*

*The clientele, as far as I can make out, consists of a mixture of
working Englishwomen and Indian women, most working in Bombay
as missionaries, students or teachers. The management seem friendly
tho' authoritarian. LOTS OF RULES.*

*I can just about afford the per diem, but even this small amount
frightens me. I HAVE NO MONEY, or practically none, if the cheque
for my first article does not come through. Must try and start any kind
of paid work right away.*

## Bombay, five weeks later

A week before Rose got married, Tor sat on the verandah of Ci Ci's
house in Malabar Hill with her feet up. She was writing a long-overdue
letter to her mother, who wrote lengthy letters full of unanswered questions every week. How was Tor, having a wonderful time? Lots of
parties and so forth? How did Rose feel about the wedding being put
off for two weeks? Jolly cross, she imagined.

Tor didn't quite know how or where to start, for, far from being cross
that the wedding had been delayed, Rose had seemed relieved. 'It's given
me breathing space,' Rose had explained in that rather careful way that
Tor found worrying. And from a perfectly selfish point of view, Tor had
felt thrilled to have two extra weeks with Rose in this fairy-tale house.

Tambourine House. Well, how to tell her mother, without sending her
completely mad with jealousy, quite how perfect the place was and how
well her cousin had done for herself, for Geoffrey Mallinson—whom Ci
said had done clever things in cotton—seemed to be stinking rich even
by the standards of Malabar Hill.

From where Tor sat she could see a curved sloping lawn that led down
to the Arabian Sea; a terrace bursting with bougainvillea and jasmine

blossom; a dazzling blue sky; and everywhere houseboys, maids, gardeners, sweeping and tidying, raking, washing, picking up and generally making things perfect. At this precise moment, six servants were putting up the spectacular maharajah's tent that Ci had planned as the centrepiece at the wedding reception next week.

Tor unscrewed the top of her pen and sighed. The simple answer to her mother's main question—'Are you meeting lots of nice young men out there?'—could easily have been, 'Mother, it's looking promising.' Already at the club and the Taj, where she'd been to cocktail parties and dances, she'd met young naval officers, cavalry officers, businessmen and some high-caste Indian men. And although it was true that no one had exactly seized her yet, there'd been plenty of flirting. After the many small humiliations of her London season, Tor could hardly believe that now she had some choice in the matter.

Ci Ci suddenly appeared wearing a lilac-coloured kimono and ballet slippers. During Tor's first days at Tambourine, almost everything about Ci—the bright red lips, the slouchy walk, the chic clothes—had made Tor feel huge and slow-witted and obvious. But now awkwardness had grown into a kind of hero worship. Careful examination of Ci, Tor felt, could teach her how to be sophisticated and fun and not care so much about what other people thought about her.

'So how's our little orphan this morning?'

This orphan tag was a new joke between them, for Ci actually had two children of her own—a boy and a girl at boarding schools in England—ghostly figures in silver frames on the mantelpiece. She rarely spoke of them, except in jokes, 'my rug rats,' she'd say, or 'the ghastly creatures'.

'Oh, marvellous!' Ci Ci was opening a large scarlet envelope. 'Oh, what fun.' She was reading the letter inside. 'Goofers will love this. Cooch Behar has asked us to go shooting with him in three weeks' time. He's got the most wonderful place. "Sadly places are numbered,"' Ci read on. 'We'll have to find a baby sitter for our little orphan, won't we, darling. I'm assuming you'll still be here?'

As she swept her eyes upwards, Tor experienced a moment of panic. Where else would she be? At the moment she had no other plans.

'I'd love to stay on for a bit more, if you'll have me,' she said humbly.

'We'll see how you behave,' said Ci. 'Oh damn.' She had opened another letter and was looking cross. 'The Sampsons can't come to Rose's wedding, what a bore, which reminds me, I meant to ask you this earlier. Your advice. Last week I had a slightly tense discussion with old frosty knickers, Captain Chandler, about the reception. I thought it was a bit of a cheek actually, because he seemed to be saying he only wanted about five people he knew really well to come to the party afterwards, but our lawn looks completely wrong like that—naked and sort of golf coursey—and I am the hostess, so I've invited a few amusing chums of our own to swell the ranks. I don't think Rose will give a damn either way, do you?'

Tor, flattered that Ci Ci should ask her advice, said without thinking, 'No, of course she won't mind, why should she?'

On the morning of the wedding Rose was awake early and had bathed and was dressed in pale stockings and her new silk underwear by the time Tor went to her room.

The first thing she said was, 'D'you know, I really *am* glad in the end Daddy didn't make the trip; I'm sure it would have been much too much for him,' as if this was what she'd wanted all along. But the pale skin above her petticoat was covered in the rash Rose got when she was frightened. She'd dabbed a few spots of calamine lotion on it.

After a breakfast that neither of them could eat, they went upstairs again together.

'Are you ready?' said Tor, determined to be motherly and protective even though she felt completely overwhelmed.

'Yes.'

Tor took the wedding dress off the hanger and let it slide over Rose in luscious waves. Rose stood stock-still and stared at herself in the mirror.

'Gosh,' she said. 'Caramba.'

'Now the veil.' Tor pinned it gently round Rose's face, thinking how innocent she looked, how young and hopeful.

'There. Let's have a look at you. You'll do for most known purposes,' she said to make Rose smile, for her eyes were full of terror.

At ten thirty, Pandit, in a red silk turban, drove the Daimler round to the front of the house. Geoffrey, gleaming with sweat in his morning coat, sat beside him in the front. Ci, wearing a purple cloche with a large scarlet feather in it, seemed distant and snappy, and when Geoffrey started a monologue about some company headquarters they were passing, and how it was going through lean times, she said, 'Shut up, Geoffrey—she doesn't want to hear all that on her wedding day.'

But Rose didn't seem to be listening to anyone anyway; she was looking towards the dusty streets.

When they arrived at St Thomas's everything speeded up. The garrison vicar almost bundled them out of the car and into the vestry, the 'Wedding March' played and Rose and Tor walked up the aisle between a crowd of hats. When the hats turned round to sneak a look at the bride, Tor didn't recognise anyone except Ci Ci and Geoffrey.

When Jack, stern and handsome in his blue and gold uniform, suddenly appeared and stood beside Rose at the altar, Tor longed for him to turn and gasp at the sight of Rose, but he stared stiffly ahead. The garrison vicar galloped through the ceremony. Rose's 'I do' was almost inaudible even to Tor who was standing right behind her.

When the service was done and they walked out into the harsh sunlight, a dozen or so men from Jack's regiment appeared, making an archway of crossed swords down the path. Rose blinked at them for a moment, then at Ci's friends pouring from the church. And then, in a moment that wrung Tor's heart, Rose scampered like a startled rabbit underneath the crossed swords and out the other side again.

'Don't abandon me at the reception,' Rose muttered to Tor before she disappeared with Jack in the Daimler.

When Tor saw Rose again at Tambourine House, she stood looking pale and much too young to be married, on the edge of a roaring mass of partygoers: Ci's friends had turned up in force. She searched for Viva, who had promised to come, but couldn't see her.

Tor gulped a glass of champagne down, then another. The whole morning had been such a strain and she was glad it was over.

After more drinks and delicious things to eat, Ci stood on a chair shouting, 'People! People!' through a megaphone. She announced that Geoffrey was going to make a speech in the pond garden.

The guests carried their glasses underneath the arch of wisteria blossom that led into the shady part of the garden where two stone nymphs gambolled under cascades of water.

When everyone was assembled Geoffrey stood up with a glass in his hand. 'Today,' he said, 'I'm here in lieu of Rose Wetherby's father, who I have not had the honour of meeting but who sounds like a very fine man. And what an awfully proud man he would be today to see this beautiful young girl who stands before us like a freshly plucked flower.'

Tor was so pleased to see Rose smile at him and then shyly at the crowd of strangers. Tor finally spotted Viva in the crowd, and thought that it was beginning to feel more like a proper wedding, but then Geoffrey spoilt it all by booming, 'To Rosemary.'

Nobody ever called her Rosemary. It wasn't even her name.

**B**y four o'clock that afternoon the sun reached its zenith in a perfect blue sky and some of the guests had collapsed in the heat.

When Rose appeared from the house again in her going-away outfit, Tor stepped up to say goodbye. She wanted to say something that would fill in the blanks of that strange and unreal day. To thank Rose for being the best friend a person could ever have, to wish her kisses and babies, but at the last minute her mind went blank with misery, and all she did was peck her on the cheek like a maiden aunt.

After Rose and Jack's car disappeared in a cloud of dust down the drive, she went up to Rose's bedroom. She took off her bridesmaid's dress and lay down on the bed in her underwear. She closed her eyes, which were suddenly full of tears, and slept fitfully for about half an hour, dimly aware of Ci's guests in the distance. When she woke up, she heard Ci shouting at her from the bottom of the stairs.

'Tor, come and play with me. I'm having a drink on the verandah.'

'Coming,' Tor shouted back reluctantly. She didn't dare say no, but she still felt shy on her own with Ci Ci.

She got dressed and went downstairs. Ci was lying in the half-dark in a kimono on a wicker lounger.

'I'm a rag,' she said. 'How are you?'

She must have noticed Tor had been crying for she pushed a glass of brandy towards her. They sat drinking together while the servants cleared away the wreckage of the day. Then Ci Ci said out of the blue, 'Most Bombay weddings are damp squibs, darling. But she'll be happy by now.' She smiled at her slyly. 'He's a wonderful-looking man.'

Tor looked at her. 'I don't like him,' she said. 'I think he's—'

'Think he's what?' Ci sounded impatient.

'Cold,' said Tor bravely. 'I kept wanting him to look happier.'

'What a silly thing to say,' Ci protested. 'None of us even know him.'

An awkward pause followed; they both took sips of their drinks, then Ci took Tor's hand in hers. She said, 'Might a chap say something?'

'Of course.'

'Don't be too fussy, darling; I'd hate to have to send you home a returned empty.'

Tor winced. Ci laughed as if she was joking, but Tor knew she wasn't.

Ci gave her a long appraising look. 'Darling,' she said after a longish pause, 'would you mind if I was incredibly frank with you? Because I think I could help you if you'd let me.'

'Of course.' Tor steeled herself for the worst.

'You're a big girl, aren't you, but you don't have to be if you don't want to be. All it would take would be no cake for two weeks, lemon and water in the morning, and I rather think we need a hair conversation with Madame Fontaine. With half an inch off this, you'll be fighting them off with a stick. Do you want to fight them off with a stick?'

'Yes,' said Tor, and even though at this precise moment she felt she could have died of shame, she made herself smile. 'I rather think I do.'

Then, the following night, something amazing happened. Ci Ci walked into Tor's room with Pandit behind her, his arms piled high with silk dresses, beaded shifts, shawls of shivery softness, necklaces, even earrings. Ci took the clothes from his arms and flung them on the bed.

'Darling, do me a favour and keep these,' she said. 'I need an excuse to buy some new clothes.'

'I couldn't!' Tor, still smarting from the conversation the night before, felt both thrilled and shamed.

'Why not?' Ci Ci said.

For the next two hours Ci, smoking and squinting, watched Tor try on the clothes. Apart from the few hems that needed taking down and waists out, some of the dresses fitted perfectly and Tor couldn't wait to wear them.

The following morning Ci drove her to the Taj Mahal Hotel, where Madame Fontaine danced around her, snipping, regarding, adjusting, while the pile of hair on the floor grew and Tor, watching herself in the mirror, saw a different kind of girl. Madame showed her how to apply kohl to emphasise what she said was her best feature. Her 'wonderful eyes'.

An hour or so later, Tor sat with Ci in the bar of the Bombay Yacht Club awed by her transformation. Her short hair felt so different, so suave and silky and modern.

Across the bar, two young naval officers drinking together had actually stopped talking as she'd walked in. One of them was still sneaking looks at her now.

'I'm going to buy my little Cinderella champagne.' Ci looked at her with real approval. 'Lots of glass slippers from now on, I think.'

'It feels like magic.' Tor couldn't stop herself grinning.

'It is magic,' said Ci. 'And it's all done with mirrors—you'll see.'

Viva's original plan had been to go straight to Simla to collect the trunk so she could tick this painful task off her list, then get on with the rest of her life. But the plan had gone out of shape, because she had no money or almost none now.

A job. That was the first thing she needed. She consulted her note-book. Before she'd left, Mrs Driver had scribbled down the names of a few people in Bombay who might help her. Top of the list was a Miss Daisy Barker who had come out to India to teach at Bombay University Settlement. Underneath, Mrs Driver had written, 'Mr Woodmansee, retired correspondent, *Pioneer Mail*.'

After breakfast she telephoned Miss Barker before she lost her nerve. 'Hello?'

The cut-glass voice at the other end of the line was brisk but friendly. Viva asked if she could see her today. Miss Barker said she was teaching a class at the university that morning, but they could meet after lunch at her new flat in Byculla. Did she happen to know the area? No, well, it was somewhat off the beaten track, but she would give precise directions for getting there. 'Bus or rickshaw?' she added, which Viva found a relief; taxis for the time being were out of the question.

**V**iva stepped down from the bus in Byculla and looked at her map before walking down a narrow street that led into a series of sinister-looking alleyways. Daisy had said her house was near the Umbrella Hospital, but all she could see were ramshackle shops built like dark cages in the wall. She poked her head inside one of the shops where an old man sat on his haunches ironing a pile of shirts.

'Where is the . . .?' she asked in Hindi, then she put an imaginary umbrella up above her head.

'It's over there.' He pointed towards the next corner where there was a crumbling block of flats with wrought-iron balconies on the front, most of them broken. She walked across the street and was about to ring the bell when a shutter opened above her head.

'Hello, hello,' a voice floated down. 'I'm assuming you're Miss Holloway.' A small round woman wearing a sunhat squinted down at her from the balcony. 'Hang on, I'll come down and get you.'

Shoes clattered down the stairs and then the door burst open on a woman whom Viva guessed to be at least thirty-five. She wore rimless glasses and a simple cotton frock and had a lively intelligent face.

'Forgive the shambles,' Daisy said. 'I only moved last week.'

The corridor smelt of old curries, and fly spray, but when they stepped into Daisy's flat, Viva liked it immediately. It had high ceilings and whitewashed walls and was airy and somehow purposeful-looking with its neat piles of books and bright cushions. On a desk in the sitting room, there was a typewriter and stacks of papers.

'Come and look at my new view.' Daisy led her through the sitting room and out onto a large balcony with a white mosaic floor and a view of roofs and a mosque. 'It's going to be a perfect party place,' she said. 'Now, tea? Sandwiches? Are you absolutely famished?'

Over tea, Viva decided she liked Daisy. Behind the kindly eyes she sensed a practical energetic mind that knew how to get things done. Daisy told her how she was part of a movement called the Settlement, formed by Oxbridge women graduates who had decided to come to India and teach the women at the university in Bombay.

Much later Viva learned that Daisy, with her dowdy dresses and cut-glass accent, had a titled father who owned estates in Norfolk; but that wasn't how she wanted to live her life. She had an urge to do things for other people, and was much-derided for it among the smart set.

'Indian women, at university?' Viva was amazed. 'Forgive me, but I thought most were illiterate?'

'Well, a lot of village people are, it's true.' Daisy looked pensive. 'But Bombay is very advanced in certain respects and we have female lawyers here, poets, doctors, artists, engineers. And they're a splendid bunch: bright, questioning, full of beans.

'And you?' Daisy continued. 'Have you lived in India before?'

'Until I was ten. Both my parents were killed in a car crash up north.' The lie slipped out so easily now it almost felt real. 'And I went back to England; I've come back partly to pick up their things. They've left a trunk for me in Simla.'

'Poor you, that will be sad for you.'

'Well . . .' Viva never knew what to say.

'Any work planned?'

'I want to be a writer.' When things weren't going well she felt so fraudulent saying this. 'I've had one or two things published in England.'

'Gosh, how exciting.'

'Not very, I'm afraid, at the moment. I wish it were. In fact, I'm looking now for any kind of work that can support me.'

Daisy said that she knew Lloyd Woodmansee. 'He used to be features editor at the *Times of India*, as well as working for the *Pioneer*. He's worth a try. ' She wrote down his name and address.

'What sort of money might one expect if I were lucky enough to get a story to write?' Viva's heart thumped.

'Oh, practically nothing, I'm afraid.'

'Ah.'

'Oh dear . . .' she said. 'Are you very short of money?'

Viva nodded. 'I have about twenty-five pounds left. My passage out was supposed to have been paid for, but my employer had other ideas.'

'That's not fair.'

'No,' said Viva, 'it was not.'

'I have another idea that may tide you over,' said Daisy.

In the next half-hour she told Viva that the Settlement supported two children's homes in Bombay: one in Byculla called the Tamarind, which served a midday meal to street children and gave them rudimentary lessons in reading and writing. They had a few children living there as temporary boarders and were missing one assistant at the moment. The pay was poor—one rupee a day—but the hours were flexible and might suit a writer. The job came with a small room, nothing grand, in a house nearby that was owned by a Parsee, Mr Jamshed, whose own daughters were at the university.

Viva thought for a bit. She put down her cup. 'I'll take it,' she said.

'Splendid.' Daisy shook her hand.


## Poona, January 1929

On the day that Viva started her first job in Bombay, Rose sat silently in the window seat of the *Deccan Express*. She and Jack had been married for three weeks and were on their way to Poona, where they were about to move into their first married quarters. Three weeks was long enough for her to know that he was a man who did not wish to be spoken to while he was reading the papers and that his plans, from now on, would generally be considered more important than hers.

This point had been made, patiently but firmly, in the bedroom of the old-fashioned guesthouse in Mahabaleshwar, where they had spent the four days of their honeymoon.

'What fun,' she'd said, clapping her hands with delight when he'd explained that they'd stop for a day or two in Bombay on their way back to Poona. 'I can go and see Tor, and maybe Viva.'

She was longing to catch up with them and hear their news. He'd frowned and she'd seen that pulse flicker in his cheek that she was beginning to register as a slight warning.

He'd explained that he had to go and look at a horse, then they'd need to do some shopping for the new house.

'There will be plenty of time once we're settled,' he'd softened immediately and put his arm round her, 'but we do need to get mobile.'

The honeymoon had not gone well. On their wedding night, she and Jack had eaten a quiet supper together in the guesthouse, with another couple at the next table, who didn't say one word to each other throughout the meal, which made Rose's attempts at conversation sound even more stilted. She'd talked a bit about Middle Wallop and her ponies. She'd asked him to tell her about the history of the Third Cavalry, which he had at some length. His face had glowed; she'd never seen him so animated as when he'd talked about his regiment.

After she'd finished her glass of wine Jack gave her a funny look and then whispered, 'You are beautiful, do you know that, Rose?'

And she'd looked at her plate. Then he'd said in the same low voice, 'Would you like to go upstairs ahead of me and get ready for bed?'

She saw the man and woman exchange a secret smile because they'd seen the confetti on her coat as she arrived.

In the bathroom, she felt her fingers tremble as she tried to get the sponge thing in place. Twice it had pinged out of her fingers, once landing under the bath. She'd had to crawl underneath it, terrified she'd find a snake or a scorpion there. While she was washing it again, she had heard the door to the bedroom open and close.

'Are you all right in there?' Jack called.

'Fine . . . thank you,' she'd replied.

'Come on, darling,' he'd called five minutes later.

She had her foot on the bathroom stool and was still desperately trying to get the thing in. Trying not to cry, she finally felt it pop into place. The peach silk negligee seemed absurdly too much in this spartan room, and she almost tore it when she put her foot in the hem.

When she'd stepped into the room, he didn't say anything. He was lying underneath the mosquito net in a paisley silk dressing gown, pretending to read the paper. A fan whirred overhead.

When he drew back the covers, she saw that he had put towels all over the sheets. He looked at her without smiling. 'We don't have to do this if you don't want to,' he said.

'I do want to,' she'd said without looking at him.

Tor had told her that if you did lots of riding it didn't hurt, but it did. Both of them were sweating with embarrassment when it was over and unable to look each other in the eye. No, it had not been a good start, and in the two nights that followed, it hadn't got much better.

The train was passing through some parched-looking scrubland. The chai wallah had stopped at their seats to offer them first brick-coloured tea, then fruit-cake and a pile of hectically coloured sweets.

'I wouldn't eat any of this, darling.' Jack had set aside his paper. 'I bet

Durgabai is cooking enough for an entire regiment this morning.'

Durgabai was the name of one of the four new servants she had yet to meet. Oh Lord, she was nervous.

Six hours later they arrived. A taxi picked them up at Poona Station and whisked them down through tree-lined streets, past the club, past the polo ground. And now they'd arrived at a nondescript little bungalow, and Rose had her eyes closed and was beaming. As Jack lifted her over the threshold, the thin part of her calf caught quite painfully on the lock, but she appreciated the romantic gesture and kept on smiling.

'How lovely to be here,' she said, opening her eyes.

She hoped he couldn't see how disappointed she was. She'd pictured, what? Well, something more like one of the many beautiful and spacious-looking bungalows they'd passed on their way here, with their wide verandahs and majestic trees. Not quite such a small dead-looking garden or this dark poky corridor smelling a bit of damp. But he had warned her that theirs was a junior officer's house.

'So, this is it,' he said brightly. 'Is it all right?'

'Darling, I love it, honestly,' she said.

He took her into the sitting room, which was small and unfurnished, apart from a bamboo sofa facing a single-bar electric heater.

'Look, we can get more furniture,' Jack told her hurriedly—his mouth went very small when he was cross—'and bits and pieces from the bazaar.'

'I adore arranging houses,' she said. But in fact, apart from lining up dolls on her bed at home, she'd never really done it.

'We will have to watch the pennies for a bit.' Jack turned his back to her. 'But lots of people hire furniture, particularly now.'

'Hire? Gosh, I've never heard of that before.'

'Well, things change very quickly here. People move all the time.'

They walked back into the hall together where a collection of calling cards sat on a small brass table.

'These came for you,' he said. 'The ladies at the club can't wait to meet you. One or two are battle-axes, but most are very nice. And two letters.' He read from one of the envelopes, '"To Mrs Jack Chandler."'

'One's from Tor.' She smiled properly for the first time that day. 'And it looks like Viva's writing on the other envelope.'

Jack told her to read them later. He only had half an hour for lunch and wanted to show her the kitchen first. 'Of course, darling,' she said. She put them in her pocket, but part of her did mind.

The kitchen was a dark room at the back of the house. Rose saw a pot of rice bubbling on its own on the stove.

'Where are the servants?' she said suddenly.

'Are you up to meeting them yet?' he said gently. 'I told them to go to their huts until you'd had a chance to look around.'

'Of course!' she said, although she felt like hiding. 'But can I see the rest of the house first?' She managed to make this sound like a treat.

'Well, there isn't all that much left.' He smiled at her, a bashful smile that wrung her heart. This was such a big change for both of them.

It would be so much easier next week, she consoled herself, when Jack was back with his regiment again and she could get on with something. And after that he'd hinted he might be away for two weeks doing something secret in a place she'd forgotten. He'd already told her that she must go and stay with Tor while he was away. Was it a bad sign, she'd wondered, that she was already looking forward to this so much?

They'd finished looking at the kitchen and now he put his arm round her and led her down another corridor, whispering, 'Our room.'

'I've never slept in a downstairs bedroom before,' she told him gaily, making this sound like a treat too. He opened the door on a small room crisscrossed with bars of sunlight falling through the blinds. In the middle of the room was a double bed with a white candlewick bedspread on which somebody had placed twigs to form the word GREATINGS.

'Durga and Shukla must have done that,' he said. 'How sweet they are.'

She bobbed her head and blushed. The bed side of things still made her feel rigid with embarrassment and strangely giggly.

One by one, the servants came forward to be introduced to her. First came Durgabai, the maid and cook, a fine-looking Maharashtrian woman with jutting cheekbones and large brown eyes; then Shukla, her seven-year-old daughter, hiding behind her skirts.

Next came Dinesh, stick-thin and immaculate, who bowed without smiling. Jack said Dinesh had been his bearer for the past three years. Then came Ashish, the wash man, the dhobi wallah, who had a withered leg and milky eye and was as shy as the little girl. Durgabai was sweet to her, smiling and wobbling her head and saying, 'Greetings, memsahib,' as if to make up for the awkwardness of the others.

After a lunch of pea and ham soup and a dry lamb chop, Jack took her out to show her what he called 'the grounds'—a stretch of concrete with a tiny lawn in it and some clay pots with roses inside that looked as if they could do with a water.

'Do you normally have lunch at home?' she'd asked him politely.

'No, at the mess, or on the trot usually,' he said, flooding her with relief. 'But it's lovely to come home and see you here.'

'Thank you.' She shot him a swift glance. 'Heavens,' she squinted up at a cloudless blue sky, 'can this really be winter? It's so beautifully hot.'

'Yes it is, isn't it?' he said. 'But nothing like as hot as summer.'

'I love hot weather.'

'Good.'

She stood on her toes and had decided to kiss him when she heard leaves rustling behind the trellis.

'Darling,' Jack pushed her aside, 'don't do that in public any more. It doesn't do in front of the servants. It offends their modesty.'

'I'm sorry, Jack.'

'Oh, Rose, don't look like that, there *is* so much to learn.'

What was she supposed to look like? Oh drat, she wanted to run into the house now and cry. 'Sorry,' she said again in a breathless voice.

When he went inside to collect his things, she stayed in her new garden, wondering if she'd made the worst mistake of her life.


# Chapter 6


Bombay, February 1929

It was starting to get hot in Bombay, a soupy, steamy kind of heat that weighed down on you and made you long for a cleansing burst of rain.

Tor, who had prickly heat, was sitting in the bath when she heard the phone ring.

A few moments later Ci, who was getting increasingly snappy about phone calls, shouted through the door, 'Someone called Frank, wanting someone called Viva. Don't know what in the hell he's talking about.'

Tor still felt her heart flutter.

'Hello, stranger in a strange land,' she said when she telephoned him back twenty minutes later. 'So, what brings you here?'

Frank said they must meet up but in the meantime, did she have any idea where Viva was. He had some urgent news for her.

'Well, that sounds rather exciting,' Tor had drawled. 'Might a chap know what it is?'

Maybe he would have explained and maybe not, but Ci Ci had appeared at that moment smoking furiously and pointing at her watch so there was only time to give him Viva's address and get off the phone.

Tor had honestly felt only a brief twinge after she'd hung up. In her heart of hearts, she'd always known he was keener on Viva than he was on her. And besides, she had more than enough on her plate now. She was in the throes of what Ci Ci called an '*amour fou*', a mad passion.

The affair had begun on December 21, 1928, at about ten thirty at night, when she'd lost her virginity to Oliver Sandsdown in a hut on Juhu Beach. The only casualty of the evening was Ci's silk Chinese jacket, which got tar on its sleeve.

Ollie had turned up at the Christmas party Ci had given at the Bombay Yacht Club. He was a twenty-eight-year-old merchant banker who loved sailing. He was short and dark, and Tor thought him fearsomely attractive because he was so confident. When they'd first met, he'd danced with her and said with a very social smile plastered on his face, 'I'd really like to go to bed with you,' which she found both funny and naughty. On the way out to the beach they'd sung 'Oh, I Do Like to Be Beside the Seaside' in the car, which he'd driven at a reckless speed. When they'd got to the beach he'd kissed her—a man's kiss that seemed to claim and demand. Her knees had literally buckled.

The hut itself had a low string bed in the middle of it where he'd taken her efficiently but without any particular ceremony. Afterwards, he'd made her stand still in front of him while he arranged her pearls against her nakedness and then he'd chased her into the sea. What her mother would have said about pearls in sea water wouldn't bear repeating, but she hadn't given it a thought. Swimming in sea as warm as milk, she'd felt savagely happy. A feeling she'd never had before. He'd held her again in the water and she had felt absolutely exhilarated and released. It was done! Wonderful! Perfect. She didn't have to worry about it any more and she was sure that in time she'd get to like it very much indeed.

After they'd swum, he dried her with an old towel, kissed her quickly and buttoned her up into the silk jacket, getting all the buttons wrong. Then he said some pals of his were in town and he wanted to have a nightcap with them in the Harbour Bar. They'd ended up in the water splash at the Taj Mahal Hotel.

Since the night at Juhu Beach, she and Oliver had had several afternoon assignations in his flat at Colaba Beach. For several days she'd had to powder over the faint bruises he'd left on her neck and right shoulder.

Ci had noticed. 'Don't let him mark you like that.' She'd raised one plucked eyebrow at Tor's shoulder. 'It's common.'

Which was when Tor, who had gone beetroot red, had tried to change the subject by asking Ci for a huge, *huge* favour. Would it be an awful bore if Rose came for one or two days the following week and had a what-the-hell day?

Ci Ci had introduced Tor to the whole idea of what-the-hell days when she'd first arrived in Bombay. These were days of pure hedonism when you weren't allowed to be a grown-up and only drank cocktails and saw amusing people and did exactly what you wanted to do for once. She said there was far too much seriousness in the world.

Ci had smiled and replied, 'Darling, what a good idea.' She'd even offered to lend Tor the car.

'Are you sure about the car? Why are you so nice to me?'

Ci Ci had popped a kiss into the air. 'Because you're fun and because your days are numbered. I got a letter from your mother this morning asking me to book your ticket home after the season ends in February.'

It had taken Tor a couple of hours to absorb the full impact of this bombshell, and even then she refused to believe it was true. Surely someone would propose to her, or something would turn up. At any rate, it now seemed absolutely and crucially important for her to see Rose as soon as possible.

Jack had answered the phone.

'Please can Rose come out and play with me?' she'd said in her whiny-child voice. 'I'll scream till I'm sick if you don't let her.'

And, oh, what a stuffed shirt he was, he'd replied as though she'd been completely serious.

'I'll have to check diaries, but I think that will be fine,' he said. Then there was a brief whoompf down the line and a thump.

'Tor, oh, darling Torrie,' Rose sang. 'I'm so happy to hear you.'

'Rose, this is an emergency,' she said. 'You have to come and see me. You can take the *Deccan Express* and we'll have a good gup. I'm bursting, I have so many things to tell you.'

'Hang on a tick.' Subdued murmurings in the background.

'That's absolutely fine, darling.' Rose was back. 'Jack says the ladies' carriage is perfectly safe.'

Tor didn't need Jack to tell her that.

But then Jack had surprised Tor by ringing back an hour later and whispering, 'I want to give Rose a surprise. Will you buy her a bottle of champagne when you go out to lunch? Tell her it's from me.'

Tor parked the car outside the majestic Victoria Terminus Station and ran through the crowd just in time to see the Poona train pull in and Rose, looking almost bizarrely pink and gold in the middle of so many brown faces, step out of first class. Porters were fighting to carry her case.

'Oh, Rose.' Tor flung her arms round her. 'I've missed you so.'

As they drove back into the city, Tor couldn't resist showing off. 'Cigarette, please, young Rose,' she said. 'They're in the glove box on the left. Oops!' She had to swerve to avoid a man selling peanuts. 'Sorry!' she sang out gaily.

'So,' said Tor when they stopped at the traffic lights, 'here's the plan: first stop, Madame Fontaine's to get the hair done. Then, lunch and a good gup at the club, then I'm going to drive you home to the Mallinsons' for a chota peg, then some friends may call, and we might go out dancing.'

Rose clapped her hands. 'Oh, Tor,' she said, lying her head lightly on Tor's shoulder. 'I can't believe you're allowed to do all this.'

'Well, I am,' said Tor, breathing out smoke in a film-starry way, 'but for God's sake, don't tell my mother. The silly woman already wants me home.' She said this so lightly that Rose said nothing and Tor was glad—the last thing she wanted Rose to feel was sorry for her.

Tor and Rose were in a room full of steam at Madame Fontaine's salon, their necks stretched over basins. They could smell sandalwood and pine, and coffee brewing.

'Now, Rose,' said Tor. 'To return to the big question of the day. They charge eight rupees here for the first-time shingling, and this is the place for it. But don't let me talk you into it and stop saying it won't suit you—you'd look good with a cow pat on your head.'

And they were giggling again, seven-year-old stuff, really, but such a relief.

'You have wonderful bone structure, and it's going to get jolly hot soon. Just a thought,' Tor added innocently. 'Your life, your hair.'

Rose looped her hair under and turned her head experimentally in the mirror. 'We've already got water restrictions up at the cantonment.'

'Will Jack mind?'

Rose hesitated and thought about this. 'He's never actually said he likes all this.' Rose lifted up her hands under her hair and let it fall like spun silk to her shoulders. 'So I honestly don't know.'

Tor was glad to hear Rose sound even faintly rebellious about him. If it was possible to be too good-natured Rose, was, and it worried Tor.

The Bombay Yacht Club was full at one fifteen when they arrived for lunch. As Rose, shorn and a little shy, made her way with Tor across the room, the conversation dipped for a moment and one old man screwed his monocle in and openly stared at her.

'Rose,' muttered Tor, 'the hair is a success.'

Their waiter led them to a table in the corner of the room that over-looked the harbour.

'Very lovely menu for today.' The handsome Italian maître d' flicked large linen napkins onto their laps. 'Fresh lobster from the harbour, sole Véronique, guinea fowl and pheasant à la mode. Champagne is on ice, madam,' he murmured near Tor's ear.

'Tor,' Rose whispered, 'I don't want to be a killjoy, but I can't aff—'

Tor held her hand up. 'Hush, child. The champagne was ordered by your husband, Captain Jack Chandler.'

'Jack!' Rose looked amazed. 'Are you sure it was him?'

'Quite sure.' Their eyes locked for a moment.

The waiter poured champagne; the bubbles made Rose's nose wrinkle.

'Rose.' Tor put down her glass. 'I don't want to go home. I can't—'

'Please don't,' said Rose. 'I can't bear it either. I—'

'Let's not talk about it yet,' said Tor. 'It's too serious for champagne.'

'Quite right,' said Rose. 'Anyway, I'm sure half of Bombay is already madly in love with you. Is there anyone special?'

'Well. There's a boy called Oliver, he's a banker and we're having quite a jolly time of it.'

'Tor, I believe you're blushing. Is he husband material?'

'I don't know.' Tor pulled her bread roll to bits. 'Probably not—how can you tell? He's good fun and very manly, but—'

'Tor, please can I say one absolutely serious thing?' Rose said. 'Don't, whatever you do, rush into it. It's such a huge change in your life, and Middle Wallop isn't so very awful. And you've got to know at the very least that you can, or I mean, that you do love the person.'

They exchanged another quick look. And Tor got a stabbing feeling seeing how quickly Rose's face had flushed with emotion. She wanted to ask, 'Is everything all right, Rose? Does he make you happy?' but you didn't ask Rose things like that. She was a soldier's daughter.

After two hours of talk, the waiter brought them coffee and sweetmeats. Tor leant back in her chair and appraised the room in a genial way.

'Oh God!' She suddenly froze. 'Am I going completely mad or can you see what I see?'

A group of around eight people, Indians and Europeans, were gathering up their things and preparing to leave. Guy Glover had already seen them. He had a camera over his shoulder and when he saw Tor he got up and swaggered over to see them.

'Good Lord,' he drawled, 'what a surprise.'

'What are you doing here, Guy?' Tor did not return his smile. 'Viva said you were ill and had to leave rather suddenly.'

'I was ill. But I'm much better now. In fact,' he said, eyes darting, 'I've got a job. I'm a photographer now.'

'A photographer?' Tor was amazed. 'Who for?'

'For a film company here,' he said. 'They're bringing talkies to Bombay, and some English actresses and they need—look, this is awfully boring of me but I've got to go. Everyone is waiting for me outside.'

'So you're better now.' Tor's tone was unusually icy. 'Viva will be relieved to know that.'

'Yes, much better, thank you.'

'Damn,' he said, patting his pockets, 'I've left all my cards at home. But if you see Viva tell her I haven't forgotten her, she's due a little windfall. And by the way,' he stepped back and gave Rose a prissy little smile, '*love* the hair. It makes you look like a beautiful boy.'

*Love the hair*. When Guy left, Rose and Tor made each other laugh by imitating him, but now Rose felt less sure about her dashing new look.

Last night, as she'd stared at herself in the Mallinsons' bathroom mirror and tried to see it through Jack's eyes, she'd felt that seeds of terror had been planted in her. Twisting and turning in the half-light she could see how fashionable she looked with it, but so different too, like another kind of person. She had no idea whether Jack would like it or not; there was still so much about him she couldn't predict.

As the train approached Poona Station she could see Jack standing in his riding clothes on the platform, his head moving rhythmically from side to side as he looked for her. *My husband*, she thought, *my spouse*.

The train was slowing to a halt. She stuck her head through the window and mouthed, 'Jack!' She showed him her hair. 'Do you like it?'

His expression froze, then he shook his head. Jack didn't tell lies. She knew that already—he'd pointed it out to her as a matter of pride. But wasn't it better sometimes to be kind rather than to be absolutely truthful?

The train stopped. Porters in bright red jackets came rushing towards them, but he waved them away. He pecked her cheek and put his hand into the small of her back and pushed her through the crowd.

She'd had such a wonderful time with Tor in Bombay—swimming and riding, good laughs and long easy talks—but as he drove her home she felt all her happiness draining away.

She tried talking for a bit: she said she'd bought him a shirt at the Army and Navy; he said that was good of her. He told her about some dinner party they'd have to go to next week, a polo match he'd be playing in on Friday, but his voice was so flat she knew he was livid.

When they were home again, Dinesh helped carry her suitcases in, and he seemed to greet her stiffly too. She thought, *He resents me for being home again; he'd rather be with Jack on his own.*

Durgabai padded in and handed Rose a cup of tea. A horrible cup with the usual bright globules of fat swimming on it, but she felt absurdly grateful for it and could have kissed Durgabai when she pointed towards her new hair and said, 'Nice, memsahib.'

Jack said he'd like a wash before he went back to work. In the same constricted voice he said he had a meeting with the polo club committee after work. Rose didn't believe him.

'Big baby,' she muttered to herself. 'It's not that bad.'

Shortly after that Jack walked out of the house. He slammed the door hard, and left without patting her arm or smiling or anything. How mean of Jack to react like this. How utterly childish.

Crying, she discovered that night, this sort of comfortless, adult crying, made your eyes swell and gave you a ravenous thirst.

But just before dawn, when she'd all but convinced herself the marriage was a disaster, he'd come to her from the spare room where he'd been sleeping. He got into their bed, put his arms round her and muttered, 'Oh, my poor Rose, please don't.'

Which had made it worse. She'd said with a spluttering laugh, 'You must think you've married a madwoman.' She'd put her hot cheek against his chest, and hugged him blindly.

'But this *is* different. It's hard. I do forget that.'

She wanted him to keep holding her like this. It was all she wanted. But then she felt him lift her nightdress and stroke the inside of her thighs and do all the other things that made her feel so embarrassed.

'Don't fight me, Rose,' he said. 'Let me . . .'

And for the first time, she felt a definite something, not the overwhelming thing she'd dreamt of but a glimpse of some animal comforts being given and received, something better than words.

And they'd slept for the first time in each other's arms.

When Frank phoned Viva to say that he was back in Bombay and wanted to come and see her, Viva didn't answer at first.

'Frank from the ship,' he prompted her. 'Do you remember me?'

'Of course I remember you,' she said, smiling. She felt a flush of heat.

'I'd like to come and see you and talk to you about Guy Glover.' Frank sounded guarded. 'Something's cropped up.'

'Oh no, not Guy,' she said. 'What's he done now?'

'I'll tell you when I see you. Not for discussion over the phone.' Frank's voice had lowered almost to a whisper. 'Can I come and see you? What time do you get back from work?'

She worked out how long it would take her after work to wash, to dress, to do her hair and look presentable and then was annoyed with herself. What on earth did it matter what she looked like?

'I'm busy tonight,' she said. 'How about tomorrow?'

He said tomorrow was fine.

She gave him her address and he rang off.

After she'd spoken to him she stood and looked at her room, trying to see it through his eyes. When she'd first arrived, less than a month ago, she'd thought the tiny room horrible, a true sign that she had come down in the world and would probably go down further.

The room was free, as Daisy had promised, and its location, above Mr Jamshed's shop on Jasmine Street, was central, but with its badly painted walls, its one naked light bulb, the thin rush matting and the curtain with the gas cooker behind, it had reminded her of the meanest kind of London bedsit, only sticky and hot. On her first night here, she'd sat out on her tiny balcony smoking a cigarette and looking down on the street, wondering what madness had brought her here.

The next day, she'd scrubbed her room until it was spotless. She'd burned a stick of sandalwood incense to take the smell of old food away. She'd put her parents' quilt on the bed; its squares of red, green and purple silk lit up like stained glass when the sun rose.

The following weekend, she and Daisy had gone to the Chor Bazaar—the Thieves' Market—and bought cutlery and a kettle and a fine-looking chair that she'd re-covered in an old Kashmiri shawl. She'd found an old blue and green enamelled mirror, which she'd put above the sink. At last, the room felt like hers.

On her first night, Mr Jamshed, who was large and jolly and noisy, had beckoned her over the threshold of the household. He'd made her sit in a chair near his window and brought her chai to drink. He'd introduced her to his daughters, Dolly and Kaniz, beautiful confident girls who bobbed their hair and wore lipstick and evidently ran rings round their father. 'They are very much for teasing me,' he'd told Viva, his eyes shining with pride and delight.

Mrs Jamshed, plump and shy at first, had insisted she stay for dinner and they'd sat around a long table in the courtyard and piled her plate with a stuffed fish covered in a leaf, and rice and vegetables, and then, later, a sweet custard pudding, until she felt she would burst.

**H**er job at the Tamarind Home in Byculla began two days later. She'd taken the job with the quite cynical intention of earning enough money to write, perhaps get some good stories and then go up to Simla. It hadn't worked out like that.

She'd been shown round the dark corridors and spartan dormitories of Tamarind House by Joan, a cheerful Scottish midwife who said she was going upcountry soon to do a survey on village midwives.

Joan told her they had room for fifteen to twenty girls here, and that they were mostly orphans, some abandoned at their gates and some found by a team of volunteers who went out three times a week in search of children who might need a temporary roof over their heads. A few boys were allowed in, but they preferred to keep the sexes apart.

The home was open to Muslim and Hindu alike, and the aim was to return children eventually to their families or to provide suitable homes.

While they were walking across the courtyard, a fluttering, cooing troop of small girls in brilliant saris suddenly landed beside them, touching Joan, and smiling and laughing at Viva. 'They want to sing you a song,' Joan explained. When they'd burst into song, Viva thought, *You never see Europeans with their eyes this bright, their smiles so wide.* Poor they might be, but they burst with life.

At lunch, eaten at tables in the courtyard with the children, she was introduced to Clara, an Irish nurse who was large and pale and freckled and struck her as being a bit of a sourpuss.

Clara took her to see the row of children waiting to be assessed by the visiting doctor. The children stood behind locked gates, barefoot and ragged. They'd salaamed her, made small chewing gestures with their mouths, tried to touch her through the railings. Every one of them seemed to be saying, 'Help me.'

One of the girls broke into a wild torrent of words to Clara. 'Her mother died a few months ago,' Clara explained to Viva. 'She's walked here from a village seventy-five miles away. Her father is dead too, and her relatives don't want her.'

And Viva had felt a shaming, a husking of the soul—the task of helping seemed so overwhelming and she was trained for nothing.

They gave her easy things to do at first. Joan told her to sit at a table in the courtyard and when the children arrived she, with the help of a Maharashtrian woman who worked as an interpreter, recorded their names in a large leather ledger. On her first day at this job, halfway through the morning, the wonderfully reassuring Daisy Barker had bounced through the gates, followed by a line of chirping little girls who fought to bring her a glass of water. She sat down beside Viva.

'Surviving?' she'd asked.

'I'm fine,' Viva had said, but she'd felt shaken to the core.

'You know, one day,' Daisy said before she left, 'you might write more than their names in a book. You could write their stories.'

On the Monday of her second week there, things changed again. Joan, breathless from running across the courtyard, came with news that 'all hell had broken loose' in a nearby slum behind the cotton factory.

A water pipe had burst, and twenty had already been drowned. Half an hour later a stream of slum-dwellers arrived, plastered in a foul-looking mud; many crying and pleading for help. The adults were sent to a local hospital where there was a temporary shelter; children who appeared to have no adults were to stay. Tin baths began to appear in the courtyard and some kerosene stoves were lit to warm up food.

A girl called Talika was plucked from the crowd of children cowering near the school's iron gates. About seven years old, she was pitifully thin with huge brown eyes and matted hair. She had a label round her neck that read, 'Hari kiti'—help me. When Talika prostrated herself before Viva, her small rag doll fell in the dirt beside her.

A line of temporary cloth cubicles was swiftly erected in the courtyard. Daisy and Clara ran round putting tin baths in each and distributing bars of soap and towels.

Viva had led Talika behind one cubicle. She'd never done anything like this before; both of them were embarrassed.

'Take this off.' She'd pointed towards the child's muddy dress and the child had looked at her with huge appalled eyes, put her doll down on the cork matting and stepped out of her clothes. She shuddered as she stepped into the cold water, but soaped herself obediently all over, her little fingers working busily but her eyes downcast. Viva had poured water over the small head and rubbed in the special carbolic soap Daisy had given them for head lice. Talika had stood there, numb with shock.

When she was dry, Joan came and gave the child a new dress and a new doll—the old one was taken away to be fumigated. She was taken to the dormitory on the first floor she'd share with ten other girls.

At the end of that day, Viva had been standing near the gates when she'd seen Talika again. She'd been given a brush and, as she swept up leaves from the tamarind tree in the courtyard, her expression was grave. She had a job to do; she would do it well. And the thought that passed through Viva's mind was, *Well, if she can hold her life together, so can I.*

**O**n the evening when Frank was due to visit, Viva had been exhausted and she'd fallen asleep as soon as she'd come home. Now, she sat up in bed when she heard the knock on the door. Behind the frosted glass she saw a dark silhouette bobbing. She put on a silk kimono and tried to put the lights on.

'Wait a second. I fell asleep.' She fumbled with a candle. 'Power cut.' They were always having them.

'Viva.' His voice was muffled behind the glass.

'Frank, wait.'

When she opened the door, he was standing in the yellow light of an oil lamp. He was thinner than she remembered, less boyish, but with the same shock of butterscotch-coloured hair, the same smile.

'I'm late,' he said. 'There was an emergency at the hospital and no one could cover for me.'

He was staring at her as if he couldn't quite believe she was there.

'Can I come in?' he said.

'Give me a moment.'

She closed the door on him and flew around in the shadows, putting on her red dress. She lit two more candles.

'Right,' she said, opening the door again, 'you can come in now.'

He stood at the door as if reluctant to come in. She could feel his eyes taking stock of everything: the charpoy, the typewriter, the picture Talika had made her that hung on the wall above her worktable.

The flickering lights made the atmosphere between them seem hectic, unstable, and when they went out again entirely, it was a relief. 'I can't think in the dark,' he said. 'Let me take you out to dinner.'

**I**t was a warm night in Jasmine Street; squares of yellow light fell from the higgledy-piggledy houses on either side of them, and the streets were full of people walking slowly home as the bazaars closed for the night. A few street girls hung around on the corner.

'If you don't mind walking,' she said, 'there's a place called Moustafa's a few streets away. He makes the best *pani puri* in Bombay.'

'Sounds good to me,' he said. He smiled at her almost bashfully; much of the cocky self-assurance of the ship seemed to have gone.

On the next corner, a group of men sat in a café playing draughts in a fug of smoke. When one of them turned to look at her, she felt Frank's grip tighten on her arm.

'Do you walk alone here?' he asked her.

'Yes,' she said, 'I'm not frightened.'

'Maybe you should be.'

'What's the point of being frightened about things you can't control?' she said. *When the worst has already happened*, she thought to herself. 'And anyway, I can't believe how kind most people are here,' she said out loud. 'They put us to shame.'

'You're on your own,' he said, 'don't take too much for granted.'

This remark annoyed her. He had no right to talk to her like that, she thought.

'Look,' he said, 'I am worried and you will understand when I tell you why. Has Guy Glover tried to contact you?'

'No.' She stopped under a lamppost. 'But Rose wrote to tell me that she and Tor had bumped into him at the Bombay Yacht Club. I think he said something about paying back the money he owed me.'

'Don't take it,' he warned her. 'Promise me you won't. If you need money, I'll lend it to you or you can ask your parents.'

'I don't have parents,' she said. 'They died years ago.'

'I'm sorry.'

'It's not your fault,' she said, her usual glib response.

'I know it's not,' he said, but she'd made him look sad. He was about to say something else, but she stopped him. 'We're here,' she said.

She'd grown to like Moustafa's café with its scuffed tables and old chairs. Its owner was an unshaven Greek, a warm, humorous man, dressed this night in a long Kashmiri tunic. He beamed at them, brought them a bottle of wine and olives and nuts and meze.

'Tell me about Guy,' she said.

'Guy's parents threw him out last month—I think they were starting to get frightened of him. His mother wrote to me, a pathetic letter, and a sort of apology in a way. She said they'd had no idea about the state he was in. After he left, she started tidying his room and found all sorts of odd things: diagrams, diaries. She said there was quite a bit about you in them—something about a dark avenging angel.'

'Oh God! What does that mean? Is he mad?'

'I'm not sure. I've been reading up on some literature on mental states since I met Guy because he interested me. The voices he heard and so forth. There is this new thing called schizophrenia, a chap called Freud has been writing about it. It means 'split mind'. Before, the treatment for people like this assumed they were either depraved or wicked, but they're starting to think it might be a proper sort of disease of the mind. The point is, well, I don't want to scare you, but I think he could be dangerous. The man he beat up on the ship was not a pretty sight. Nothing may come of it. I'm simply passing on the facts.'

'All right,' she said, 'but I still don't quite see what I can do about this.'

'Lock your doors for a start, be careful about who you ask back to your room. One of the diagrams his mother found was of the house in Jasmine Street. She has a hunch he may have got himself a room nearby. There's a distinct possibility he has a sort of fixation on you.'

'Oh God.' Viva shook her head. 'What a mess. But I don't ask people into my room,' she said, looking at him.

He looked straight back at her. 'Good,' he said.

'Is that all?' she said.

'No, not quite. There's one more thing. The police came to see me. I have no idea how they found me, but they asked if I knew anything about the All-India Muslim League. They're a political party actively campaigning for a separate Muslim India.'

'Why would Guy be involved in that? He never talked about politics.'

'No? Well, he may not be but there are a number of young Englishmen out here actively working for them. Some of his new chums on the fringes of the film industry are not what they seem: they're revolutionaries, political hotheads, and it suits their purpose to infiltrate a world where many Europeans and Indians mix more freely. Some of them are violently against Gandhi's policies of non-violence, if that makes any sense to you.'

'Not much.'

'Well, what it means is that when the time comes to boot the British out, some of them think we should leave with a bloody nose.'

'I still don't see what I've got to do with all this,' said Viva.

Frank looked worried. 'I don't know yet either, and I might be wrong about all of this, but he's an obsessive and you are on his list. My fear is that if he starts coming round to see you, the police will think you're involved too.'

While they'd been talking, she could see Moustafa out of the corner of her eye, hovering with menus, and now he broke into their conversation, chiding them for looking so serious, and insisting they ate tonight's best dish, which was spicy meatballs and naan bread.

'He's right.' Frank smiled. 'Let's eat and forget the ghastly child.'

So they ate and afterwards they took their coffee out on the street where the air felt warm and heavy.

'I'm starting to love it here,' she told him. 'It's really got under my skin again.'

'Me too,' he said. 'And I don't know why.'

Some of the shyness had gone between them. Over their liqueurs, when he talked to her about Chekhov, whose short stories he had just discovered, his face lit up with pleasure and it had occurred to her again that she may have misjudged him. He was intelligent and passionate about life. The sight of the loose button on his linen suit made her feel she would like to sew it back on again, a feeling of tenderness she tried to squash. So many girls had had crushes on him on the ship—including Tor—that not being bowled over by him had given Viva a different feeling, almost, you could say, a thrill.

She wanted to hold on to it.

'Have you been up to Simla yet?' he asked.

With a shock, she remembered she must have told him at some point about the trunk without telling him about her parents. It was hard sometimes keeping all her evasions clear, even in her own mind.

'No,' she said. 'Not yet.'

'Ah,' he said. 'That was where your parents lived.' It was more of a statement than a question, and she could feel him thinking again behind that intelligent gaze, trying to put it all together.

'Yes,' she said. 'Years and years ago.'

'Ah.' When he held her gaze for a moment, she felt cornered and a little panicked, so she told him about the children she had met at Tamarind.

'Will you write about them?' he asked. He'd remembered that too and she could do nothing about the quiet spurt of happiness that followed.

'If I could do that, well,' she said, 'that would be something.'

'You'll do it,' he said. 'I can feel you will.'

That was all. And when he didn't even try to kiss her on the way home, she was not disappointed.

*He's right*, she thought, *I will do it.*

Lying in her bed an hour later, she was surer than ever that it was a job she needed, not a man.

# Chapter 7

Bombay, April 1929

April came in like a fire-breathing dragon and Viva and Rose both got a telephone call from Tor. The Mallinsons, finding the heat unbearable, had taken themselves off to a hotel in the hill station of Mahabaleshwar for three weeks. Tor had the house to herself. She needed them to come and stay with her. Simple as that. She was tempted to add, 'It's an emergency,' but hoped that if she had enough baths and drank enough gin, she could keep one mortifying secret to herself.

Rose—the reliable—had phoned immediately, saying of course she would love to come, for a week if that was convenient. Jack was all for it (*Oh, hooray for Jack*, thought Tor sarcastically) because the weather in Poona had been very hot and he knew she'd be more comfortable in Ci Ci's house.

'If we swim,' Rose warned, 'you're not to laugh at my cossie—I look like a baby whale in it.' She was four months pregnant.

Viva, to her considerable surprise, had also responded quickly. She said she was working at some children's home, and could stay only one night or two at the most. She'd write during the day but they could spend the evenings together. Tor could hardly wait to see them.

On the day before they came, Tor woke, as she had on every one of the mornings since her monthly period had failed to arrive, sweating with fear and pleading with God to put her out of her misery. For the rest of the day she made the *bhisti*, the water man, run up and down the stairs, bringing hot water in relays to her bathroom. She'd already taken five miniatures of Gordon's gin from Ci Ci's drinks cabinet and hidden them underneath her bed in the guest room. She'd almost fainted after her second bath but nothing had happened.

Thank God Rose and Viva were coming, she thought. She was definitely going mad.

**R**ose was here. Plumper but still pale and beautiful—even with her bob half grown out. She was wearing a blue maternity dress and when she flung her arms round Tor and said, 'Oh golly, I've missed you,' Tor felt the hard bump of Rose's tummy against hers and had to bite the inside of her lip to stop herself crying. Why did Rose always do things so well, and she always got things so wrong?

Her friend looked so happy to see her, and Tor, not wanting to spoil things immediately, took her out to the verandah for tea and cakes.

Rose sank into a deep chair. 'Oh, thank the Lord,' she said, crossing her still-perfect legs. 'What bliss to feel halfway cool again.'

They gossiped for a while about this and that and, after tea, Rose fell asleep in her chair.

Tor put a cushion behind her head and crept upstairs again. There was just time, she estimated, for one more bath before supper. Pandit, who had to go off to find the water man, who was probably in his hut having supper, stomped off downstairs and made no secret of his irritation this time. He was bound to tell Ci when she came back.

A quarter of an hour later, Tor sat in her bath, weeping. *Please, God, please, God, please, God. Please don't make me have this baby.* She drank another tumbler of gin from her toothbrush glass, crying. After a few more minutes, feeling dizzy and sick, she got out of the bath and dried herself slowly, still waiting for the miracle to happen. Nothing.

'Tor, are you all right?' Rose said, as she walked into the living room dressed in her favourite, midnight-blue, dress. 'You look puce. Are you sickening for something?'

At that moment, Pandit arrived to ask them what time they would like to dine. He'd brought soda fountains and glasses with whisky in them, and small bowls of olives and cheese canapés.

'Come on, out with it,' Rose said when he'd gone. 'Something's up.'

Tor took a deep breath and was about to answer when the doorbell rang. Viva had arrived, on the back of a motorbike driven by one of her friends from the children's home. She burst through the door, her hair wild and dusty, and carrying her clothes in an old satchel.

'Sorry I'm late,' she said. 'There was a huge demonstration opposite the VT Station. They were burning Union Jacks; there were fire engines, policemen. I didn't actually think I'd get here at all. Would it be a nuisance if I had a quick bath before dinner?'

Pandit stomped up the stairs again with the water man.

**D**inner was served early in a long candlelit room, kept bearably cool by fans whirling slowly overhead. The French windows were open; the air was saturated with the scents of mimosa and frangipani. Beyond the garden, a vast yellow moon was sinking into the sea.

When they asked Rose about the new baby, she said, yes, it was a lovely surprise, wasn't it? Jack was delighted, and so was she. The only fly in the custard was that Jack's entire regiment might be moved soon to Bannu on the northwest frontier, which was very dangerous, but they'd cross that bridge when they came to it, she said serenely.

Tor put down her soup spoon. 'Hang on, Rose, what does this mean for you? Will you have to go too?'

'I've no idea yet—it hasn't been decided if wives are wanted.'

'But don't you have *any* say in this at all?' said Viva fiercely. 'I mean, you're having a baby.'

'No, I don't,' said Rose. 'I'm an army wife now, and it's not Jack's fault.'

Tor could suddenly feel her own heart pounding. *How precarious all our lives are*, she thought.

'Viva. What about you? What about this job of yours? You're always such a woman of mystery.'

'Am I?' Viva said. 'I don't mean to be.'

'You are,' Tor agreed. 'Are you still going to be a writer?'

'Well, I am, or at least I hope to be. I've just sold my first proper story, a small piece about the children's home, to *Blackwood's Magazine*.' Threads of excitement ran like electric currents through Viva's voice as she said this, even though her expression was carefully impassive.

'That's amazing,' said Rose. 'Why didn't you say immediately?'

'Because I can't quite believe it myself,' said Viva. 'My first few weeks here were so dreadful. I could hardly afford to pay my bill at the YWCA, but then I got work at the children's home. I've been writing at night. I'm going to try and get the children at the home where I work to tell their own stories in their own words.'

'Gosh.' Rose folded up her napkin and put it carefully into the silver ring. 'I do admire you. I don't think I could do it.'

'Yes, you could,' said Viva bluntly. 'My life is probably a lot easier than yours. It's a question of choice.'

They had coffee on the verandah and some crème de menthe for old times' sake.

'Tor, you're so lucky to live here,' said Rose. 'I think it's the most wonderful house I've ever been in.'

Tor burst into tears. She felt in the pocket of her dress and handed a piece of paper over.

'"*Empress of India*,"' Rose read out. '"Miss Victoria Sowerby, May 25. Single." Oh, damn it, Tor,' she said quietly. 'I can't bear it. And you've been so brave all evening.'

They sat on either side of Tor, holding her hands as she cried—great heaving, gulping sobs. 'I'm sorry,' she said eventually. 'I'm being the most awful wet, and I knew I had to go home eventually, but I'd so hoped my mother had forgotten about me—I was supposed to go back in March.' She gave a strangled gulp and wiped her eyes.

Rose said they should go upstairs to Tor's bedroom, for the night servant had stirred in the shadows and this was private.

It was too hot to sit in Tor's bedroom, so they went out onto the balcony and sat down on three rattan chairs. They took their stockings off, and the sea breeze on their bare legs felt good.

'So what happened to Ollie?' Rose asked. 'I know for a fact,' she told Viva, 'he was absolutely mad about her.'

Tor felt so grateful to Rose for saying this.

'You see,' Tor explained to Viva, 'I was almost engaged to a man called Oliver Sandsdown. We met at a party at the Taj and fell madly in love.'

The madly in love bit was a bit of an exaggeration, but there was only so much pain you could let out all at once.

'We had a wonderful few weeks—picnics, parties, moonlit swims. He was so much fun,' Tor wailed.

'So what happened then?' asked Rose.

'Well, we went to this marvellous party at the Taj Mahal. He told me I was the most beautiful girl there and that he loved me.' Tor looked at them defiantly: this was her story and she could tell it any way she wanted, and besides, there was plenty of humiliation to come.

'Ci left me there. She said Ollie could take me home. Anyway, Ollie and I got into this tonga. It was so romantic. We went along the seafront and we could see all the lights from the ships. When we got to the esplanade he turned to me and he asked me to marry him.'

What he'd actually said was that she was the sort of girl he should marry if he had any sense.

'I don't suppose you'll be too shocked to hear that I went back to his flat that night. I only meant to stay for a cup of coffee,' Tor continued, 'but he begged me to stay, and then . . . well, I'm not ashamed to say that I have been to bed with him several times, because he did say he loved me.'

'And then what?' Rose and Viva were agog.

'Oh. Well.' She gave a deep sigh. 'One morning, when I got up and went to the bathroom, I found some face creams in his medicine chest. I shouldn't have looked but I had a headache. When I asked him if he had another woman, he flew into a terrible rage.'

In fact, it had been worse than that: he'd said, 'God, you're boring, Tor. What did you expect?' As if it had been her fault all along.

'Oh, what a complete *rat*,' said Rose. 'So then what happened?'

'Nothing.' Tor had no energy left for embellishment. No tearful apologies, no late-night phone calls professing undying love. Nothing.

Three days later, using a fake Scottish accent, she'd phoned his office and asked to speak to him. 'Is that Mrs Sandsdown?' the voice at the other end had said. 'No,' she'd said, 'it's Victoria Sowerby.'

'Oh heavens! Sorry!' the voice had said. As she hung up she heard people laughing.

'Married!' Rose was appalled.

'Yes,' said Tor. 'Wife in England. I suppose everybody knew but me. Not only married but with lots of other girls too. Trust me to pick him.'

'But lots of other people can't have known,' said Rose, 'else Ci would have warned you off him.'

'Well, it doesn't matter now. Back to Middle Wallop and my mother. Spoilt goods,' she said bitterly.

'Oh, Tor, please don't call yourself that, it's horrible,' said Rose.

'That's what the old biddies at the club call girls like me,' Tor told them. 'Ci Ci will, of course, dine out on it after I've gone. And there's more to come. Much worse. I'm three weeks late with the curse. I'm having a baby.'


## Poona, May 1929

Jack was out on the Poona Cantonment number-two practice ground lining up polo balls and smashing them as if to smash the universe into smithereens. Bula Bula, his favourite polo pony, was panting and foaming with sweat and Jack's entire body blazed with heat, but some demon was driving him today.

Jack cantered towards a line of balls about fifty yards from the goalmouth. *Thwack.* He leant down and made a fluid shot that sent the ball like a bullet through the scuffed posts. He galloped the length of the polo field again, lifting himself in his stirrups and slashing left and right with his mallet, until his horse's sides were heaving.

*Calm down*, he told himself as he went back to the stables. *None of this is Bula's fault.*

Or Rose's. When he looked up, he saw her watching him. She was sitting on a bench about seventy-five yards away, an innocent speck of blue against a wide horizon, and the sight of her brought shame and, for one blessed moment, a feeling of tenderness.

It wasn't her fault that Sunita had written to him last week to tell him she was married now. She was very, very happy, she said, and much more settled. '*I hope you are happy too*,' she'd added innocently. He'd cried when he read that.

He cantered over to where Rose was sitting. When he came to a halt, Bula put his head about an inch from the ground, his sides still heaving.

'Poor Bula.' She patted the horse's neck. 'It's much too hot, isn't it?'

She shot Jack an unhappy smile.

'I've brought you some lemonade, darling,' she said.

'Kind girl,' he said as he leapt from his horse.

'So how was Tor?' he asked.

She looked surprised—it was rare for him to ask her about Tor.

'You haven't told me anything yet.'

'I didn't think you'd be interested,' she said. And then he was embarrassed to see her chin wobbling. *It must be her condition*, he decided. She'd turned the taps on a bit in the first three months of their marriage, but she hardly ever cried now.

'Of course I'm interested,' he said.

She told him that Tor would be leaving on May 25.

'You'll miss her.'

'Yes.'

He touched her hand but found he didn't want to hold it. The threat of tears had put him off. He wished he could have liked Tor better but he didn't. There had always been some sort of rivalrous edge to their conversations that he didn't understand.

'Anyway, I'm determined to go to Bombay and say goodbye to her when her ship leaves. I've got to.'

'It sounds to me as if you've made up your mind,' he said.

'I have,' she said.

He was trying not to lose his temper—it wasn't up to her to tell him where she was going and when. And then he felt relieved. Earlier in the day he'd decided against all his better judgment to see Sunita one more time. *I hope you are happy too.* Such banal words; they'd hurt so much. If Rose insisted on doing what she wanted to, well, he could too.

Later that night, unable to sleep, he got up and walked into the kitchen for a glass of water. It was a quarter past three, the air felt soupy and thick, the walls of the little house seemed to be closing in on him, and he could hardly breathe. He went into the living room and was sitting in an armchair reading the letter again when Rose walked in.

Half-groggy with sleep, she sat down on the armchair facing him.

'I can't sleep,' she said. 'It's too hot.'

As he lifted his eyes to hers, he saw coloured lizards dart across the wall behind her head and felt his whole life crash before his eyes.

'Jack,' she said, 'why are you crying?'

'Am I?' he said. He hadn't realised.

'Yes, you are.'

He didn't want her to walk over to him or to sit on the arm of his chair and stroke the side of his face. If she hadn't done that he might have held it all inside, but he'd felt his guts about to explode with sorrow at the mess he had made of things, and this sweet girl trying to work it all out. He sat there frozen while she tried to hug him.

'It's me, isn't it?' she said in a low voice. 'I'm doing this to you; I'm making you so unhappy. I can feel it.'

He tried to tell her no. He buried his head in his hands so she wouldn't see how much he hated his cowardice.

'It's not you,' he managed to say.

'Is it the baby then? You didn't seem very excited when I told you.' Her voice was gentle, there was no reproach.

Excited! No, that would not be the word. If he'd said what was in his heart that night, he would have said, *I'm angry at you for taking over my life in this way, for making me feel so out of control. I don't want my wings clipped in this way, I can't afford it, I don't know enough about you. I'm not even sure I love you yet.*

In the event he had forced out some stiff words of congratulations and gone out for a drink in the mess.

'What's this?' Rose swooped forward and picked up the letter that fell from his dressing-gown pocket as he reached out for a cigarette.

'Don't read it,' he'd almost shouted. 'It's mine.'

'What is it?' He saw fear growing like a fire in her eyes. 'Jack, tell me. *Tell me*. What is it?'

He looked at her and thought, *I can't do this to her. She doesn't deserve it.*

'Read it then.' He sat there like a cowering dog while she sat down again and read the letter.

'Who is this?' Rose said in a trembling voice. 'I don't understand.'

'Her name is Sunita. She lives in Bombay now. She was my lover.'

'Your lover?' Her voice was raised; her eyes looked wild. 'Was, or is?'

'I don't know, I don't know.'

'Is she Indian?'

'Yes, but educated. Her father is a barrister.'

'Do you love her?'

'I don't know.'

'You must love her. If you didn't love her you'd just say no.'

She got up. The look in her eye was so strange that he thought for one muddled moment that she might thwack him one round the face. Instead she gave him a look of such pain and confusion that he wanted to howl like a dog. What a worthless shit he was.

'I hate you for doing this,' Rose said. 'For having this secret, and not telling me, for letting me think I was getting everything wrong. Why in God's name did you let me come?'

'I'm sorry, Rose.'

She brushed the apology aside. 'Will you see her again?'

'No—anyway, the regiment's still on alert for Bannu.'

'Is that the only reason?'

He'd never seen her more furious and he shrank back from it. 'No.'

'It had better bloody well not be.'

The small part of him that wasn't frozen in shock admired the graceful way she held herself as she left the room. There was dignity in that straight young back, a refusal to sag and collapse.

It was only later, through the thin walls of the spare room, that he heard her being sick, and then the stifled moans of pain. He'd never hated himself more.

**I**t was late morning at the children's home and Viva was sitting underneath the tamarind tree in the middle of the courtyard, cutting up bits of tissue paper for the kites they were making. From where she sat, Viva could hear the hubble-bubble of children's voices, talking in a bewildering variety of languages: Hindi, Marathi, English, for some, with snatches of Tamil and Gujarati thrown in. And through all this cut the fluting tones of Daisy, who was talking to them while they worked.

Viva glanced at Talika. She sat at the end of the bench, completely absorbed, small hands busily working the scissors, dark eyelashes cast down. No one would have recognised the pathetic scrap Viva had bathed a few months ago, but she was still much too thin.

'Watch me, watch *me*, Wiwaji,' said Talu, a tall, thin boy with a pronounced limp. None of them could say her name properly. They either called her Madam Sahib, the Bombay version of memsahib, or Miss Wiwa, or sometimes as a term of endearment Wiwaji.

'I'm cutting out a peacock's tail for my kite,' said Talu.

Talika got up from the table with her half-finished kite. 'Mine is a bird,' she said, releasing its string. 'Watch me.'

She kicked off her sandals and started to dance, stamping her feet in precise little patterns on the ground, her kite a swirl of colour above her head. Twirling, prancing, she closed her eyes and began to sing. Viva hardly noticed that Daisy had sat down beside her.

'Well, somebody looks as if she's feeling better,' Daisy said.

'Wasn't that wonderful?' said Viva.

'Actually, Viva, I meant you,' said Daisy. 'You look much happier than when you first came here.'

'I do like it here, Daisy,' she said.

'Can I give you a piece of advice,' Daisy put a gentle hand on her arm, 'don't overdo it. Last year, half our staff went down like flies; this year we're insisting on time off. Didn't you say when you first came that you planned to go north and see your parents' old house?'

'Did I?' Viva felt herself stiffening. 'I don't remember saying that.'

'Oh sorry.' Daisy's eyes blinked behind her glasses. 'I thought you did.' They exchanged a strange look. 'Well, here's another suggestion. If you feel like a week off, my friends run a delightful boarding house in Ootcamund—it's a perfect quiet place to write and it's not expensive.'

'How kind you are,' said Viva, 'but it's funny, I almost feel I can't leave at the moment.'

'It gets you like that at first,' Daisy said. 'For the first time in your life, you're not thinking about yourself. That's such a relief, don't you find?'

'Daisy, do you think I'm any more self-absorbed than anyone else?'

'Self-absorbed, on second thoughts,' Daisy said, 'is unfair. Self-protective might be a better word. You're very reserved about yourself, or maybe you keep that for your writing.'

'Maybe I do.' Viva didn't want to feel hurt, but she was. Sometimes she just got so tired of being accused of keeping secrets she didn't understand herself.

Over lunch she brooded about why she was still so neurotically private about her past and her parents. There was no disgrace about their passing. If the details had been scarce—Father killed in a raid on the railway line by bandits, Mother dying a year later (of a broken heart, she'd been told by the nuns)—it was probably for no other reason than that nobody in England knew her parents that well. Her parents had been exiles for years, grown out of touch with family and friends.

When at the age of eighteen she'd been old enough to take an interest in them, she'd felt a sudden desperation to find somebody, anybody who could talk to her about them without seeming shifty or impatient. Which, of course, was where William had fitted in. What a gift he'd seemed at first, not only the executor of her parents' will, but so handsome, so articulate and compassionate; he'd taken plenty of time with her. Dinners, long walks, evenings over a bottle of wine at his flat.

He'd known them very well, he'd told her on their first meeting. Same quad as her father at Cambridge, stayed with them once in Kashmir before she was born. He remembered Josie, so red, so funny-looking as a baby—they'd called her 'the Nawab' because of the imperious way she'd reclined on her charpoy drinking her bottle. The night he told her about Josie was the night he'd dried her tears, gently, gently, and had given her a little sip of wine and taken her to bed.

And then, much later, she'd made the big mistake of asking him about Mother. She and William had been going up in the lift to his flat, when she'd said out of the blue, 'Did Mummy have a weak heart when you knew her?' This was the story she'd been told by one of the nuns.

He'd turned and said coldly, 'I was her executor, not her physician.' And then, later, he said, 'What's it really got to do with you in the end?' as though she was being nosy about some chance acquaintance.

It made her cringe, even now, to think of how meekly she'd accepted this rebuke. He had a nasty tongue and he knew how to use it, and by the end it seemed to her that she'd become so wary of him, so watchful that she'd handed over part of her own tongue as well as half her brain to him.

Darkness fell with its usual suddenness as she walked home that evening, and fragile strings of fairy lights appeared around the street stalls that sold fruits and cheap clothes, palm juice and papier-mâché gods. When all the rows of lights suddenly went out, she could hear soft laughter from one of the stallholders—having electricity in Byculla was still the big surprise, not when it failed.

Opening the door of her flat, she saw that Mr Jamshed had lit an oil lamp and put it in the stairwell. As she looked up the four steps that led to her rooms, a shadow passed behind the frosted glass in her door.

'Mr Jamshed,' she called, 'is that you?'

She opened the door and saw the outlines of a body lying on her bed in the shadows in the corner of the room. The shadow stood up. It was Guy Glover. He was wearing his black coat. He was waiting for her.

'Shush, shush, shush, shush,' he said in a gentle scolding voice when she called out in alarm. 'It's only me.'

'What on earth are you doing here, Guy?' she said. 'Who let you in?'

Her eyes had adjusted to the light; she could see that he was wearing no shirt under his coat, and that his white bony chest was sweating.

'No one. I told your landlady you were my big sister.'

When he smiled, she remembered everything she disliked about him: the thin adolescent voice that could never decide between being a baby and a bully, his weak smile. Even the smell of him, sweet and stale.

She lit a candle and looked quickly around the room to see if he'd moved anything.

'Look, Guy, I don't know why you're here, but we've nothing to say to each other any more, so I want you to go away right now, before I call the police.'

'Calm down, Viva,' he said, sounding hurt. 'I've brought your money back, that's all.'

When the lights came on again, they seemed brighter than usual.

Her patience suddenly snapped, 'I don't know how you had the nerve to come here like this. You told a pack of lies to your parents about me. I—'

'I've got a job now,' he interrupted. 'I'm—'

'I don't care. I had no money at all when I came here, thanks to you.'

'You're lucky to have lost your parents,' he interrupted her. 'I have nothing in common with mine.'

'Look, I talked a lot of rot on the ship.' She felt a wave of revulsion at herself. Why hadn't she kept her mouth shut? 'And I'm tired. Just go.'

'Don't you even want to know where I'm staying?'

'No, Guy, I don't. I couldn't care less—my responsibility for you ended when the ship got to Bombay.'

'That's not what the police think,' he said softly. 'They're bastards, but you could be in a lot of trouble if you don't pay up.'

'For goodness' sake, Guy, stop play-acting,' she cried.

'I'm not,' he said. 'I'm frightened. There's a man after me.' He sat down on her bed, put his head in his hands and then looked at her through his fingers. 'He says I hurt his brother on the ship, but he hurt me too.'

'What does he say you did to his brother?'

'He says I hurt his ear and now he can't hear, but he did hit me first. That's why I think you need this. Take it.' He handed over a stained bundle of rupees in an elastic band. 'You may need it when they come.'

'When who comes?'

'The police—you see, in law, I'm your baby.'

She turned the notes over in the palm of her hand, her mind working furiously. Was this what Frank had tried to warn her of: the dreadful, unthinkable possibility that, in the eyes of the law, he belonged to her? She snapped the elastic band. She could feel without counting 100, maybe 200 rupees there: enough at least to offer something to the police if they came round for bribes, but she suspected it wouldn't cover the amount she had lost chaperoning Guy to India.

'I think you should apologise to me for being so rude,' he said prissily. 'I suppose you can see now that I was only trying to help you.'

'Guy,' she said, 'I don't think I need to apologise for what is mine.'

He gave a sudden radiant smile. 'So, I am yours after all?'

'No, no, no . . . I didn't mean that. I mean this,' she held up the notes, 'the money was owed to me.'

She saw the light die in his eyes, but didn't care at all.

'Who told you I lived here?' she asked.

'It took me ages to find you. So I rang Tor and she told me.'

'I see. Didn't I hear you have a job? Where are you working now?'

'Nowhere,' he mumbled. 'Actually, I've lost my job. I was taking film photographs. The men who were running the company were clots.'

'So you're going home now?' Even the thought brought some relief.

'No.' He shook his head. 'I live here now: on Main Street behind the fruit market.' He looked at her. 'Oh, and there's one more thing. Stop telling everyone I'm sixteen when I'm actually nineteen.'

'I'm not going to fight about that, Guy. What difference does it make when you take no responsibility for yourself?' She glared at him, still furious at this invasion of her privacy, and the loss of her evening, 'and you tell lies to get yourself out of trouble.'

He stepped back. 'That's a really beastly thing to say,' he said. 'I was always going to pay you back. I've been waiting for the right time.'

'Oh really?' She didn't even pretend to believe him. 'Well, next time, do it in the right way: ring the doorbell and wait for me to let you in.'

As she showed him towards the door, she could feel a blister on her heel break and the sticky liquid run down into her shoe.

'Don't come back again, Guy,' she said as she let him out.

'It's all right, it's all right,' he said as if she'd asked for some kind of reassurance. 'I've promised to pay you back and I'm going to.'

The following morning, Viva phoned Tor in a fury.

'Tor, how could you? He's going to haunt me now.'

'Hang on.' Tor sounded sleepy as if she'd just woken up. 'Who are we talking about?'

'Guy, you bloody idiot. You gave him my address.'

'He said he had your money. I thought you'd be pleased.'

'Pleased! He frightened the life out of me. He was lying in the dark waiting for me in my room, and now he says the police are after him.'

She heard Tor gasp at the other end of the phone. 'Oh, Viva, I'm so sorry,' she said. 'But he said he had a job and money, and I thought you—'

'Tor, you weren't thinking at all.'

Tor blew her nose and decided, unwisely, to change tactics.

'Are you sure you're not blowing this out of all proportion, Viva?' she said. 'I always got on with him rather well.'

'Oh, for heaven's sake,' Viva exploded. 'He's completely doolally—even your darling Frank said so.'

'That's mean,' Tor said. 'He was never my darling Frank. If he was anybody's he was yours.'

Viva thumped the phone down and instantly picked it up and dialled again.

'I'm sorry, that was mean of me,' she said.

'I know.' Tor was crying. 'It's just that I get everything so wrong now and I'm still so worried about you-know-what. Can we meet somewhere for a drink? The Taj or Wyndham's or your place?'

Viva hesitated. 'I'm not sure you'll be able to find me here, Tor,' she said. 'It's slightly off the beaten track.'

''Course I could.' Tor sounded relieved. 'I'd love to see your place, and I could bring my gramophone. Look, thanks for forgiving me about Guy,' she added as an airy afterthought, 'but at least you've got some money now—I'm completely Harry broke.'

There were times when Viva wanted to crown her.

**W**hen Viva hung up she looked at her watch. Eight fifty. She dialled the number at the hospital Frank had given her.

She got through to reception. 'Gokuldas Tejpal Hospital,' said a sing-song voice at the end of the line. 'May I help you?'

'I need to speak to Dr Frank Steadman,' she said.

'I don't know where he is,' said the voice. 'Will you wait?'

She waited. Five minutes later, Frank picked up the phone.

'Frank, it's me. Viva. I can't talk for long, I'll be late for work. I wonder if I could ask for your professional advice on one of the children at the home who isn't doing very well?'

'It'll have to be after lunchtime.' The crackling line made his voice sound impersonal. 'Shall I come to the home?'

'Yes.'

'Good. Two thirty all right?'

'Two thirty will be fine,' she said. 'I'll see you then.'

At two o'clock that afternoon, Viva was sitting in the courtyard underneath the tamarind tree supervising a group of six children when Frank walked in carrying his doctor's bag. It worried Viva how happy she felt to see him again.

'Now, children,' she said in Marathi, 'settle down and be quiet for a while. We have a visitor.'

'My God,' he said. He'd taken the chair beside her. 'I wish my ear for languages was that good.'

'Daisy Barker's been teaching me,' she said, 'and it's not as good as it sounds. I can only say "pipe down" or "eat up" or "go to bed". Do you know Daisy? She runs this place.'

She looked at her watch. 'Girls and boys,' she said, 'we can break for half an hour's play now. Say goodbye to Dr Frank. But, Talika, please stay for a moment.'

'Goodbye, Daktar Frank,' they chorused, and raced off to play.

'Talika's the girl I wanted you to see,' she told Frank. Viva squeezed the child's hand. 'She's not doing too badly; in fact, we're very proud of her, aren't we, Talika? But, as you can see, she's very thin.'

'Can I listen to her chest?'

She went to get one of the cotton screens they used for consultations.

'Don't be frightened, Talika,' she said, as she placed the screen around them. 'The doctor won't hurt you.'

Frank got out his stethoscope. As he put it in his ears and listened gravely to the child, her large terrified eyes did not leave Viva's.

'Your heart is strong, your chest is clear.' He tried to smile at the child but she wouldn't have it. 'I'm sure the clinic doctor has ruled out the usual,' he added, 'TB, worms—she doesn't look rickety.'

When he released the child, she shot back across the courtyard like a frightened fawn desperate to join her herd.

'Poor thing,' he said when she was gone. 'She looks haunted.'

He looked up and held Viva's gaze for a moment. 'And what about you?'

'I'm all right.' She stood up quickly.

'That's good,' he said gently, packing his stethoscope away in his bag.

'Except,' she could feel him about to leave, 'I may have done something rather stupid last night. Guy Glover turned up in my room. It was a shock. He said he'd come to give me my money back.'

'Did you take it?' He looked at her anxiously.

'Yes.'

'I wish you hadn't done that.'

'I do too now, but I was . . .' She stopped herself saying the word flustered. 'I was persuaded by him that the police might want to see me and that I'd need it for bribes. There is a certain logic to that.'

His expression was grim. 'What he wants is to go on pestering you. He's an obsessive and you're on his list. Why on earth did you let him in?'

'I didn't—he was in my room when I came home.'

Frank groaned. He thought for a while and said, 'Look, Viva, I don't want to worry you but this could turn into a nasty situation. Is there anyone here at the home you can really trust?'

'I trust Daisy Barker,' she said. 'Absolutely.'

'Well, tell her right away,' he said. 'That way, when the police come round she'll be warned.'

'Do you really think they'll come here?'

'They might. They've probably already got their eyes on you anyway, a group of European ladies running a place like this at a time like this, when everything is so uncertain.'

'Oh God.'

'Now I've frightened you,' he said more gently. 'The police have plenty of other things to do at the moment, so don't worry too much, but just be more careful, please.'

They found Daisy sitting in what was grandly called 'the back office'— a dark, humid room in the depths of the building with a large overhead fan. The room had a desk, a chair, an old filing cabinet and on the wall a calendar, on which a woman in a sari floated down the Ganges in a boat extolling the joys of drinking Ovaltine.

'Daisy,' said Viva as they walked in, 'this is Frank. He's a locum at the Gokuldas Tejpal. We met on the ship.'

'Oh, greetings.' Daisy jumped up and pumped his hand. 'Well, we're never ones here to look a gift doctor in the mouth—if you ever have any spare time.' She took her glasses off and smiled winningly.

Viva took a deep breath. 'Daisy, do you remember me telling you about the boy on the ship? The little monster it was my misfortune to chaperone? Well, there's a new episode. He punched one of the passengers on the ship, the son of a prominent Indian businessman. No charges were pressed at the time, but it seems that the victim's family are now after some kind of revenge and I could be implicated.'

'Why you?' Daisy's clever eyes blinked behind her specs.

'Because technically, we were in foreign waters and he belonged to me.'

'That sounds absolute codswallop to me. Are you absolutely sure?'

'No, I'm not,' said Viva. 'The boy loves dramas, he says all kinds of strange things to draw attention to himself, and this could easily be another, but the point is, he came round to see me the other night. He claims the police might be interested, and if he or they come round, I— well, Frank thought I should let you know what's going on.'

Daisy seemed to take all this in her stride. 'I think you should leave town for a few days to put this young man off. Go and stay in Ootcamund. I've been trying to persuade her to do this anyway,' she said to Frank. 'I think she looks tired.'

He glanced at her impersonally, and she felt she had become, in that moment, another one of his patients.

'I'm not tired,' she said.

'It's going to get even hotter than this soon, Viva,' said Daisy. 'It's imperative to take breaks. Don't you agree, Frank?'

'I do,' he said. 'I think they're essential.' He looked at his watch. 'But, ladies, you'll have to excuse me. I'm on duty at four. Leave a message for me at the hospital if you want any more help.'

'Gosh,' Daisy said after he left, 'what a good-looking man,' adding more professionally, 'and how useful that he works at the Gokuldas.'

'Yes,' said Viva. The suddenness of his exit had registered as a slight shock to her, a feeling that there were other things she'd meant to say.

It was Tor's private opinion that Viva had been *un peu* hard on Guy, even on the ship. Of course he could be silly and affected, and maybe he did occasionally make things up, but what sixteen-year-old didn't?

But even so, she was tremendously relieved when Viva phoned on Tuesday morning to apologise once more for her outburst. When Viva had suggested a short holiday in Ooty, she said she'd love to come.

'The timing could not be more perfect,' she'd added significantly. 'You see,' she lowered her voice to a mutter, 'it came.'

'What came?'

'You know, *it*. The thing I was worried about. *My friends.*'

'What friends?' Viva sounded baffled.

'*The curse.*' Honestly, Viva, for an intelligent woman, could sometimes be very obtuse. 'I had so many hot baths I practically dissolved, but oh, the relief. It was the worst four weeks of my life, Viva.'

'Well, thank God for that. What a relief.'

'It was and I'm sure that's what made me so switched off about the Guy thing. I couldn't sleep, I couldn't even eat, can you imagine? Also Ci and I have had the most appalling row. I'll tell you when I see you. I've started to hate her,' she whispered. 'I can feel her marking off the days till my ship leaves. I honestly think she's gone mad in the heat.'

**A**lthough Tor had tried to joke with Viva about her awful row with Ci, it had hurt so much. She thought about it when she put the phone down: about which parts she could bear to tell and which parts must stay hidden inside her huge humiliations file and buried for ever.

Even Ci must have known she'd overstepped the mark. She'd tried to blame it later on the heat and the fact that Geoffrey's cotton factory was losing money.

The tension had begun building when Ci came back from her hols in Mussoree, looking more drawn than when she'd gone away. She'd started to stare at the phone in a funny way and to smoke more than usual. Tor was almost convinced now that Ci had had a lover. But, whoever it was that had been sending Ci flowers was no longer sending them and now she no longer cooed, 'Dahhlling,' into the phone like a dove.

The row began quite late one night when Tor was sitting at her dressing table, half-undressed for bed, and Ci had walked into the room.

'Darling,' she said, 'you know all those clothes I lent you when you first came out? I'd like them back, please.'

Tor wanted to cry at the meanness of this, for Ci had said she could keep them. 'Do you want them now, Ci?' she'd asked warily. The Chinese silk jacket still had tar on its elbow. She'd stuffed it to the back of the wardrobe thinking she'd sort it out later.

'No time like the present.' Ci's smile was a grimace.

Tor, feeling bulky in her sleeveless nightgown, had been forced under Ci's eagle eye to lay all the clothes out on the bed.

'Darling, I feel I must say something to you,' Ci had said. 'You see, nothing happens to you in life without self-discipline. I mean how much, for instance, do you weigh now?'

Her eyes had swept Tor's expanding girth. *I hate you*, Tor had thought. *I hate the way you talk, I hate the jokes you make about me to your friends*.

'Ten and a half stone,' Tor had said. A lie.

Ci was holding her green Chinese silk jacket up in front of her. 'What have you done to this?' she was shouting. 'This jacket was embroidered in Paris. It's absolutely and completely ruined.'

'I wore it on the beach.' Tor had wondered for a second who this woman was who was roaring at the top of her voice, and then realised with a queer thrill that it was her. 'I got tar on the sleeve,' she'd shrieked. 'Clap me in leg irons, why don't you?'

'Oh yes, that's right,' Ci had roared right back, her eyes bulging. 'Oh, very grateful! I mean, all I've done for you in the past six months is to clothe and entertain you, you *great fat fool*.'

After Ci said the 'great fat fool' bit, her mouth had clamped shut. Even she knew she'd gone too far.

And only later could Tor appreciate the wonderful irony of what happened next. As she and Ci faced each other—red in the face, breathing heavily—Tor had suddenly felt the pop of air between her legs, the unmistakable stickiness of blood. Shouting had done what gin and hot baths had failed to do. She'd suddenly beamed at Ci, who must have thought she'd gone mad. 'I'm fine!' she said. 'I'm absolutely fine.'

**A**fter speaking with Viva, Tor phoned Rose to see if by some miracle she could come to Ooty too.

'Do try and come. Tell Jack I'm leaving India in the blink of an eye, that I desperately need you and you'll probably never see me again.'

'No need for any of that,' Rose said crisply. 'I've already told Jack what I'm going to do.'

*Well, bully for you*, thought Tor. Rose sounded so much more in control, almost steely when she spoke about Jack.

The plan was that Tor and Viva would take the train to Ooty the following morning. Rose would meet them up there.

# Chapter 8

Ootcamund

It rained heavily the night before they arrived, and as the tonga carrying Tor and Viva clip-clopped up the steep hill that led to the Woodbriar Hotel, the ground was strewn with dashed rose petals, and the air smelt of roses and wet grass. They breathed in deeply. After twenty-four hours on the train, their limbs ached and it was bliss, they agreed, to feel almost cold again.

At the end of a pine avenue, they climbed towards a house on stilts that seemed to float in mist on the edge of a hill. A hazy figure stood up on the verandah and began to wave frantically.

'Rose!' shouted Tor. She leapt from the tonga and, narrowly avoiding the horse, ran up the drive, up the stairs, then flung her arms round her friend.

'Darling Rose.' She beamed, hugging her. 'Look at you! You're vast!'

A slight exaggeration this, as Rose's mound was small and neat and hardly showed under her blue smock.

'Oh, Tor.' Rose squeezed her eyes shut and hugged her again. 'I've missed you so much. Come inside and have some tea,' she said, giving Viva a hug. 'You're going to love this place.'

They did. The hotel's owners, Mrs Jane Stephenson and her friend, Bunty Jackson, were the merry widows of army officers. Lean and vigorous, they bred Welsh mountain ponies, adored their garden and served up the kind of food—shepherd's pies and rhubarb fools—that made their mainly British clientele misty-eyed with nostalgia.

In the sitting room there were comfortably dilapidated chintz sofas set beside roaring fires, mildewed copies of *Country Life* resting on antique tables and, on the walls, Stubbs prints and photographs of favourite dogs.

Over coffee with Jane on the verandah, Rose told them she had got a lift up to Ooty from a friend of Jack's, a Colonel Carstairs and his wife.

Viva thought that Rose looked peaky. There were dark circles under those formerly cloudless blue eyes. She also looked older in some way that Viva found hard to define, more wary.

'Did Jack mind you coming?' she asked. It was not exactly normal for a man to allow a wife in this condition to travel alone in India.

'I don't think he minded.' Rose fiddled with her biscuit. 'The heat in Poona has been frightful, and he's been so busy, and this really is my last . . . and, well, it's just so lovely to be here.'

There was a silence until Bunty strode in wearing a tweed hacking jacket, stood with her legs apart like a young subaltern and asked if they'd mind ordering their supper in advance—they were doing *She Stoops to Conquer* at the club and there was a seven o'clock rehearsal. Dinner would be set up for them in a private room where they could talk in peace. Would mulligatawny soup, local trout, a dish of pommes dauphinoise and apple amber for pudding fit the bill?

'That sounds delicious,' Rose said. 'But where are the other guests?'

'Oh, only four this week, and all either fishing or riding,' said Jane. 'We're very small here, and you'll hardly be aware of them.'

After supper, it was arranged that Viva should take the bothy—a small guest room separate from the house—and that Tor and Rose would share a room on the first floor of the house.

After Viva went to bed, Tor and Rose went upstairs to their room. When they'd washed and put on their nightdresses, Rose went to the window and opened the shutters.

'Look,' she said.

The rain had ceased and a pale moon had stopped between their muslin curtains; it hung there in a skein of mist.

Rose's bed was near the window and had been made up with beautiful crisp linen sheets. They both got into it, and opened the shutters wide so they could see the outlines of the hills in the distance.

Rose closed her eyes and pulled her eiderdown up over her stomach.

'Close your eyes, Tor,' she murmured, 'and tell me we're at home. Mrs Pludd will be up any minute now with cocoa.'

Tor shut her eyes obligingly, but she didn't like the game.

'Perfect, Rose,' she said. 'All those lovely walks up to your waist in mud, ice on your washstand water in the morning, chilblains.'

But then she felt mean. Rose was entitled to feel homesick with a baby on the way and other things, for she'd confided over supper that her mother had written to tell her that her father had had a chest infection and was 'not feeling one hundred per cent', which, in Wetherby speak, meant he was practically at death's door.

'Do you miss it very much, Rose?'

'Sometimes. But I suppose there are days when everybody hates it here: the heat, the stinks, the club.' This from Rose who never complained.

'Please tell me what's wrong, Rose.'

'I can't.'

'Why not?'

'Because I'm married now and you can't just blab—it's not fair.' Rose's voice had risen. 'It's not fair to the person you're married to.'

Tor flopped back on her pillow. This was exhausting. When she put her arm round her, Rose clasped her hand hard.

'Sorry if I seem nosy,' Tor said.

'Not nosy,' said Rose in a muffled voice. 'You're the best friend ever.'

Tor waited again, but nothing, and then Rose fell asleep.

The following morning, Jane Stephenson strolled in after breakfast, with a dog under her arm, suggesting they might have a picnic that day at Pykeva Lake. They were very welcome to take her tonga.

When Viva, Tor and Rose stepped into the morning sun after breakfast, it was dazzling: every leaf and flower seemed to have been rinsed clean by the rains the night before and the air was full of birdsong.

Their tonga arrived pulled by a smart Welsh mountain pony, and their driver, a handsome fellow in crimson turban and white puttees, salaamed them into their little carriage. A touch of the whip on the pony's fat little bottom and they flew down a winding road overlooking blue hills and lakes, and a vast expanse of blue sky beyond.

Their driver found them a fine picnic spot under a group of banyan trees overlooking the hills. They unpacked freshly made rolls packed in blue-and-white-checked napkins, thin slices of roast beef, curried eggs, fresh mangoes, a large Victoria sponge and homemade lemonade carefully wrapped in pages from the *Ootcamund Times* so it didn't drip.

'This is the best picnic I've ever had,' Tor said between mouthfuls of her sandwich. 'By the way, why did our driver show you that terrifying dagger in his belt, Viva?'

'To protect us from the *badmash*, the villains, on these roads. But we're safe, or so he says. This is Snooty Ooty after all and the locals like English people.'

'Just what they thought at Amritsar,' joked Tor, 'before they sliced off their heads.'

Viva said, 'They didn't slice off their heads, they—'

'Don't talk about it,' Rose said suddenly. 'I'm sick of that sort of talk. It goes on all the time now in Poona.'

'You're right, Rose,' Tor poured the lemonade, 'no gloomy talk, so don't mention ships or home or my mother. Let's drink to us.'

After they'd eaten, Viva took out her journal and started to scribble.

'Oh, for heaven's sake, Viva,' Tor teased, 'put that thing down and behave like a normal person for once.' Tor snatched away her pencil. 'Have some of this.' She put a piece of cake in her hand.

Viva put a piece in her mouth.

'That's perfection, isn't it?' Tor was watching her eat and smiling.

'Delicious.' Viva smiled at her. One of the many things she had come to like about Tor was her enthusiasm for small things—cakes and Jelly Roll Morton, dogs, sunsets.

Viva stretched out on the rug and closed her eyes. How lovely this was after the busyness and heat of Bombay, to doze on a rug and feel your friends nearby, to hear wind shushing through pines. As she drifted off to sleep, she could still taste lemon in her mouth and before she could stop it, felt the soft brush of Frank's lips on hers.

'Oh God!'

She sat up quickly, bumping into Tor, who was lying beside her.

'What happened?' said Tor sleepily. 'Were you stung by a bee?'

'I'm all right,' said Viva. 'I'm all right. I nearly fell asleep.' But she lay there with her heart racing as if she'd escaped some crash or fall.

It was starting to rain again. Their driver was approaching them. He was pointing towards the other side of the valley, where thick grey clouds were massing.

'Blast!' said Tor. 'We're going to get soaked.'

The grey pony cantered all the way home, but they were still drenched by the time they got back to the hotel.

They were running towards the verandah when Rose stopped so suddenly that Viva banged her nose on the back of her head.

Frank was standing near the door smiling at them. He was wearing a crumpled linen suit, carrying his hat in his hand.

Viva felt her heart cartwheel when she saw him, and in the next moment, she almost hated him. What a cheek to imagine he could just turn up in the middle of their holiday as if that was all they wanted.

'Frank.' Viva coolly took his hand. 'What brings you here?'

'There's been a spot of bother in Bombay. I thought I should come and escort you all home. Daisy told me where you were staying. I've ordered tea,' he said, 'in the parlour where we can talk.'

They ran upstairs and changed quickly out of wet clothes, then they walked into the parlour together where the red curtains were still open on what were now sheets of rain. Frank sat down on the fender with his back to the fire and with his legs sprawled in front of him.

When Bunty appeared with a tray of tea and scones, she'd changed into a floral dress—the first dress they'd seen her in.

She gave Frank the first cup of tea, and made a fuss about scones and jam for him. Viva heard the ticking of the grandfather clock near the window, then became aware of him looking at her over his teacup. Flustered, she turned away and made a point of telling Bunty what a perfect day they'd had.

Bunty was clearly eager to get back to talking to Frank about his doctoring, as she rather archly called it. 'I mean, you honestly work in a *Bombay* hospital,' she said, as if he'd descended to the last circle of hell. 'How awfully brave! Are you what the natives would call a *niswarthi*?'

'What does that mean?' Tor asked bluntly.

'It's a Hindi word for a selfless man.' Bunty beamed at him.

'Oh Lord, no, not that.' Frank stretched his legs out and smiled the smile. 'I'm only doing it for the beer and cigarettes.'

And there he was again, Viva decided, a fine young male animal surrounded by a pride of admiring females. The same Frank she'd mistrusted on the ship. Well, it was a relief at least to have got that straight.

**B**unty retired after tea to supervise the clearing of the gutters and to check that all the animals' shelters were rainproof.

'So, Frank,' teased Rose, 'tell us about this spot of bother in Bombay, or was that all a ploy to come on holiday with us?'

'Unfortunately not.' Frank's playful manner had gone. 'The Muslims and the Hindus have been rioting in the streets for two days now. Some of it has been fierce: I saw them set light to a man in the street. They poured petrol over him. He went up like a guy on Bonfire Night.'

'Oh my God.' Viva was thinking of the home, of Talika and Daisy and Mr Jamshed.

'Don't worry yet,' he said. 'It's all fairly localised in the hutments around Mandvi. Byculla's quiet, and so's Malabar Hill. But I didn't like the idea of you travelling home alone and I had two days off.'

He looked directly at Viva as if explaining himself to her.

'We thought you should get back before Tuesday—there's a big Congress meeting then, and there could be riots around the VT Station. They're certainly laying on extra beds at the hospital. Your husband phoned Mrs Mallinson,' Frank told Rose. 'He was going to take the train down to Bombay to meet you, but he can't—all leave is cancelled.'

Rose's expression did not change. 'How kind of you both to think of it, but I'm sure there's nothing to worry about.' With that she stood up, saying she was very tired and thought she would go to bed.

'Who's worried?' said Tor, standing up to follow Rose. 'Anything that stops me going home is fine with me.' They all laughed as if she was joking but she wasn't.

'I'm going to bed too.' Viva stood up.

'Stay for a moment, Viva,' he said. 'There's something else I need to tell you. Sit down first.'

He reached over and held her hand.

'I'm afraid there is no easy way of saying this, so I'll say it quickly. There's a rumour that Guy's been murdered. I'm so sorry.'

'What?' She stared at him stupidly. 'What are you talking about?'

'It's a rumour,' he said. 'It may all be wrong, but the police say he's not in his lodgings, and when his parents were contacted, they said they hadn't seen him for weeks. A burnt overcoat with his name in it was found in a street near your house. He moved there a month ago.'

Viva felt her stomach tighten. 'Oh no! Are you saying they torched him?' She thought she was going to be sick.

'I don't know,' he said.

She rubbed her eyes and shook her head. 'Tell me what happened.'

'Nobody really knows yet, but the policeman told me that the brother of the man Guy beat up on the ship is called Anwar Azim. He's very powerful, very political, and he is part of the All-India Muslim League, with which Guy, for reasons still unclear, has got himself involved. Azim made his own enquiries about the incident on the ship, then took matters into his own hands.'

'But surely our police will do something about this?'

'Not necessarily. Quite frankly, it's all too messy. It couldn't have come at a worse time.'

'Is it that bad?' Her voice had started to judder.

He put his arm round her, but she drew away.

'Nobody really knows.' He was trying to soothe her.

'Who told you all this, about Guy I mean?' Her mind seemed to be going backwards and forwards.

'The police. They gave me this.' He handed her a thin wallet and a packet of photographs. 'They said they were his. They asked me to give them back to his parents.'

'Perhaps we should look at them first.'

'I already have. Some are of you. Look.' He pointed towards a close-up of Viva walking in the street near the children's home. She was wearing a summer dress and smiling at Parthiban, the man who sold her mangoes on her way to work. Underneath it, he'd written in black ink, in a childlike scrawl, '*Mataji*'—my mother.

'He's been following me,' she said.

'If it hadn't been you, it would have been somebody else,' said Frank. 'He's desperate for someone to love, or blame.'

'How horrible.' She was starting to shake. 'I didn't love him at all, I almost hated him. I should never have taken him on.'

'This is not your fault,' he said gently. 'He was sent back to England, alone, at the age of six. He was warped from that moment on—even he knew that. I'm also convinced he has serious mental problems.'

'I don't think we should tell Rose and Tor until it's confirmed,' she said. 'What's the point of frightening them until we're sure it's true?'

Frank screwed up his face. 'I thought about that all the way up,' he said. 'But it's a lot for you to have to carry on your own.'

She got up with the vague idea of going to bed; she was dizzy and felt his arm again.

'Let me help you,' he said gently.

'I'm in the cottage across the lawn,' she said.

As they walked across the sodden grass, a gust of wind flung her coat around her and a faint wash of light lit up the hills across the valley.

'There's a big storm coming,' he told her.

'Horrible, horrible, horrible.' She was crying now, thinking of Guy's hair burning, his clothes on fire. 'He didn't deserve it.'

She felt Frank's arm round her shoulder.

'We don't know yet,' he said. 'Hold on to that.'

There was a boom in the distance, another flash of light, the rain unleashed itself in one sudden sheet of water and they were drenched.

Her hands were trembling so violently it took her ages to find her key in her handbag. When she handed it to him, she saw his wet shirt showing every rib and the hollows of his shoulders, the curve of his waist.

'You're wet to the skin, Viva,' he said. When he touched her, she cried out and then he touched her very gently again, her shoulders, her belly, her arms, and she closed her eyes and put her head on his shoulder.

There was one small light burning beside the bed in Viva's room. He took a towel from the stand beside the bed and rubbed her face dry. She had no words for the tears that poured down her face, or for the shivering that had started in her body. Tenderly, he rubbed her hair; he took off her soaking coat, then her cardigan and dropped it on the floor. He wrapped a dry towel round her.

'Stay with me for a while,' she said, feeling him about to leave. Her teeth were chattering.

When he lay down, she hugged him like a child with her eyes squeezed shut. Somewhere dimly in the background she could hear the sharp pebble-like sound of the rain falling on a tin roof and everything became simple as she pulled him on top of her: her hunger and his young man's body on top of hers, blocking out death.

When it was over, he looked at her. He shook his head and both of them looked at each other in fear and wonder. Then he gathered her up, all of her, and groaned and shook his head again.

'Don't say you love me,' she said.

For their own safety, Frank insisted they travel first class on their way home, but even so Tor felt like crying—everybody seemed so out of sorts. Frank and Viva sat across the aisle from her, as far away from each other as possible. Rose was silent and bunched up near the window, and Tor, realising nobody wanted to talk, felt all her high spirits draining away.

She found herself brooding about India. In two weeks' time all of this—the huge blue sky, the mud huts flashing by, that donkey, that woman in a pink sari waving at the train—would be gone, and would soon become faded in her mind like pictures in an album. How bloody unfair that was when, in spite of everything that had gone wrong, she had been so marvellously happy here.

Her sigh left a circle of condensation on the window pane.

'Are you all right?' Rose asked.

'I don't want to go home,' Tor blurted out, then regretted it. There had been an unspoken agreement between them both on this holiday not to discuss the unthinkable: in two days' time, Rose was going to take the train to Poona, and then what? Jack was supposed to get home leave every three or four years. But who knew if he'd take it, or where they'd go. They might never see each other again.

'I'm sorry too,' said Rose carefully. 'It is going to be funny being back in Poona again after having such fun with you chaps.' To Tor's horror, she'd turned red and her voice had cracked.

'Rose,' Tor said, 'I'm trying hard not to pry, but is everything all right?'

'No,' Rose said when she could speak, 'I mean, yes—it's just that Jack really might be sent to Bannu soon. They've been threatening this for months and, you know, my life's not my own any more.'

'I know, Rose.' Oh, poor Rose, she looked so upset and embarrassed. To change the subject as quickly as possible, Tor looked across the aisle to where Frank and Viva were sitting.

'What on earth is going on there?' she whispered. 'They look so mis, like stone statues.'

'Very odd,' Rose whispered. 'I saw him leaving her room early this morning. I couldn't sleep and was watching the sun come up. But now look at them; they haven't spoken one word to each other for almost the entire trip. Did something happen?'

Tor shrugged. 'I don't know,' she mouthed. 'Do we dare ask her?'

While Rose mouthed, 'No!' Viva half opened her eyes, looked in their direction and closed her eyes again. She wasn't very good at pretending to be asleep.

'Darling sweets.' Ci pounced the moment they entered the hall at Tambourine House. Geoffrey Mallinson had picked them up from the station and persuaded them all to come back for lunch. He'd explained in a hearty bellow that he'd driven himself in the Daimler because walls had ears and he didn't entirely trust his servants at the moment.

Ci was wearing an orange silk dress, more suited to an evening party than lunch. 'Lovely, lovely, *lovely* to see you all,' she said. 'And who does this divinely good-looking young man belong to?' Visibly brightening, she put a hand on Frank's arm. 'Pandit,' she shouted, 'I think we all need rather a large gin—in the drawing room, if you please.' She snapped her fingers.

Tor said, 'How very kind of you to stay in for us, Ci Ci.'

'*Stay in for you.*' Ci turned to look at her. There was something frantic about her eyes. 'I haven't stepped foot out of this house *for days.*'

'Well, it's even more kind of you to ask us for lunch,' Rose rescued Tor. 'Were the riots horribly frightening?'

'Not a bit,' said Ci Ci grandly, 'they're two-hatted oafs.'

'Cecilia refers to the fact that Hindus often carry Muslim hats in their pockets, so they can change if they wander into the wrong area,' Geoffrey said helpfully—always happy to translate.

'And vice versa,' Ci added indignantly, 'and it's all rot, so let's all have a very large gin and forget about the lot of them. Pandit! Where are you?'

'Well, actually,' said Frank, 'I'm afraid I can't.' He looked at his watch and frowned. 'I'm on duty at six.' He was speaking to Viva as if she was the only person in the room, but Viva shook her head and turned away.

'Oh, don't go. One little drinkie won't hurt.' Ci was almost pleading. 'I've done the whole thing for you really, to thank you for rescuing the girls. And everything's on the table. Our chauffeur will drive you both back—you won't have a hope of a taxi from here, not at the moment.'

Frank and Viva looked at each other again, and there was another awkward pause.

'How very kind,' Frank said. 'But I must be gone by four at the latest.'

He looked most peculiar, thought Tor, and again she saw that when he glanced at Viva, she turned away.

Ci Ci sat down unsteadily at the end of the table. 'Now,' she said, when everyone had taken their first sip. 'I've been sitting here, *God help me*, with Geoffrey for the last few days, so what I need is a good gup. Tell me something I don't know. Astonish me.'

Tor, Rose and Viva shot desperate looks at each other.

'Well, they say they had a very jolly time in Ooty, dear,' Geoffrey prompted helpfully.

'Oh, did you?' Ci said. 'Any amusing people there at this time of year?'

Rose gamely stepped in. 'Well, it was quite quiet, but it was such fun being together again, Ci Ci,' she said. 'The Woodbriar is every bit as nice as we'd been told it would be, and Jane spoilt us and packed us splendid picnics and it was so nice to feel cool again.'

She sipped some water and came to a sudden halt—Ci's eyes over the rim of her glass had gone perfectly blank.

'And what about our Tor?' At last Ci had swivelled round to talk to her. 'Any decent men there, or was it all picnics with the girls?'

'No men at all.' Tor was not in a mood to placate her. 'But lots and lots of lovely lemon cake.'

'Oh, I remember that *wonderful* cake.' Poor Geoffrey was all over the place like a man who'd invited a semi-wild tiger into his sitting room to entertain the guests.

'So Tor's been eating again, *what* a surprise,' said Ci Ci.

'Darling!' Geoffrey jumped up so quickly he dropped a crystal finger bowl on the floor, and shards of glass and water spread over the Persian carpet. Ci looked at it perfectly expressionlessly for a few seconds.

'God, you're a clot, Geoffrey,' she said at last. 'A clumsy clot.'

'Ha, ha, ha, ha,' Geoffrey laughed as if this was a splendid joke; he clapped his hands. 'D'you know, she's right for once? Vivash will clear it up,' he said.

'Not for long, Geoffrey,' Ci reminded him softly.

**B**efore Ci went upstairs for her afternoon siesta, she remembered that a man had called for Tor and she'd meant to give her the message.

'Oh heavens, who?' Tor tried to sound unconcerned. *Oh, Ollie, please, please, God, let it be Ollie.*

'Now, who in the hell was it?' Ci thought for a moment. 'Oh, I know, I know. What was his name? Toby Williamson. He said we'd all met at the Huntingtons'; I had no memory of it. He wanted to know you were safe in the riots. He left a telephone number.'

Tor's heart sank instantly. 'How kind of him,' she said.

She'd met Toby at some do at Government House. A sweet man, she remembered, who did something to do with teaching boys at a school somewhere. He'd talked to her about birds, and she, totally in the grips of Ollie obsession, had hardly heard a word.

When Ci had left the room, Rose said, 'Will you phone him back?'

'Not sure,' said Tor. 'He was a bit of an egghead.'

'Nothing to lose,' said Rose lightly. 'Except your ticket home.'

'No,' agreed Tor.

**W**hen Viva and Frank got in the back of the Mallinsons' car after lunch, she pulled the seat rest down between them.

'I can't stand that woman,' she exploded as soon as they were in motion. 'She's pure poison. How dare she speak to Tor like that?'

'Careful.' Frank looked at the chauffeur.

She felt his hand touch hers.

'Viva,' he said, 'I'm worried about you going back to Byculla on your own. Let me stay with you for a while.'

'No,' she said. 'No. You can't come back.'

'Talk to me, please,' he said. 'There's hardly any time left now.'

'I am talking to you,' she said childishly, pulling her hand away.

'We can't just pretend nothing happened.'

*Yes we can*, she thought. She'd done it before and she could do it again.

The most disturbing thing of all was that she felt so intensely alive sitting next to him like this, so aware of his hand resting casually on the seat rest. Her body was blazing with sensation in a new way, and all of this felt wrong and muddled up because Guy could be dead, and surely nicer or better people would be in mourning, not in lust.

'I want to see you again,' he said. 'I must. What happened has nothing to do with the riots or with Guy. You know that's true.'

She said nothing because that felt safer.

She was trying to hold on to the idea that the night before had been a moment of temporary madness, a lapse in discipline. Nothing hurt as much as love, that was what she had to remember.

'Not yet,' she said. 'It's all been too soon, and so . . .'

When the words were out, she felt vaguely nauseous. What she most wanted was to wash, to sleep, to stop thinking for a few hours.

'How far is it to the hospital?' She was longing suddenly for his confusing presence to be gone.

'Two streets from here.'

She could hear him trying for a more conversational tone to give himself more time. 'I've been offered a job in Lahore,' he said. 'That research job I told you about.'

'Will you take it?' She looked straight ahead of her.

'I haven't decided yet.'

One side of her mind now watched the street sellers setting up their stalls; the other wondered if she would regret it for the rest of her life if she let him slip through her fingers like this.

He looked exhausted, she noticed, and pale. His eyes searched her face for clues. 'Don't say anything you don't mean,' he said, 'but promise me that you won't feel ashamed.'

'I'm not ashamed,' she said. 'I feel as if I've been through an earthquake.'

He gave her a steady look. 'Ah, now that I understand,' he said.

He was about to say something else, but she put her hand over his mouth. 'No,' she said. 'Don't. Please. Not yet.'

She let herself into the house—everything was the same: bicycles in the hall; the smell of Mrs Jamshed's curries in the air.

Mr Jamshed was in his front room in the middle of his afternoon prayers. She stood at the door waiting.

When the door squeaked, he opened his eyes. 'Miss Viva.'

'Forgive me for interrupting you, but is everybody all right?' she said.

'We are tolerably well,' he told her. He looked at her, polite, distant. 'No riots in the streets, thanks be to God. But other things have been going on here that I am not happy with. Come. It's better I show you myself.' He put on his battered sandals and padlocked the front door behind him, something she'd never seen him do before.

'You see,' he explained as they were walking upstairs, 'while you were away, an unruly element broke into our house. They made a mischief in your room and did other things.'

When he opened the door to her room, she cried out with shock. The curtains were closed, but even in half-darkness she saw her typewriter slung on the floor; her dresses, knickers, blouses, pictures lay in random heaps.

'Oh no!' She ran to the little pine cupboard beside her bed where she'd kept the first draft of her book. It was still there.

Mr Jamshed drew the curtains with a scraping sound.

'That's not all,' he said. 'Look.' He pointed to the wall. She saw a photograph of herself leaving one of Daisy's parties, looking drunkenly dazed and happy. 'Whore' was written in large untidy letters across the corner of it. In another picture, she and Frank were leaving Moustafa's. On the bed, was an out-of-focus photograph Tor had taken of her and Guy side-by-side on deck chairs.

'I know who did this,' she told Mr Jamshed. 'But he may be dead. I don't know yet.'

As soon as the words were out, she realised how peculiar they sounded. 'You must think I'm mad,' she said.

'Madam,' Mr Jamshed spoke very formally, 'I don't think you're mad, but I cannot allow you to bring danger and other things to our house.'

'What do you mean?'

'You know what I mean. How can your father or your brothers let you live like this?'

'I don't have a father or a brother,' she said.

'Who is he?' He pointed to Guy.

'He's just a boy. I brought him over on the ship. I was paid to do it. I didn't even know him before.'

'*You didn't know him,*' said Mr Jamshed. 'And you, a young girl, were paid to bring him? No, I don't believe. Even in England, they wouldn't let this happen.'

His eyes were large pools of suffering. His forehead deeply furrowed.

'Madam, I am a Parsee, we are broad-minded people, but I found alcohol bottles in your room too, and now this. And I'm very worried for my family. I already get stick from some local people for letting my girls go to the university—more shame for me.'

'Mr Jamshed,' she said, 'I understand how this looks, but I must ask you something as a matter of urgency. Did anyone see this boy in the building?' She pointed towards the picture of Guy.

'This boy?' Mr Jamshed examined the photo closely. 'My neighbour, Mr Bizwaz, described a fellow like this. He said he looked like an Englishman. He went out into the street; he took off his coat and shoes and set light to them. He shouted after him but he ran away.'

'Oh God,' she cried. 'But this might be good news. We thought he might be dead.'

'You thought he was dead?' Mr Jamshed scratched his head. 'Mrs Daisy Barker told me you were a very respectable young English lady, and now this too. Crisis for me, Miss Viva,' he said. 'I can't let you stay here. Tomorrow you must leave. You can't stay here.'

'May I say goodbye to Mrs Jamshed, and to Dolly and Kaniz? You've all been so kind to me.'

'No,' he said. 'I'm sorry. Daughters are home but I don't want them to see you again.'

Viva had heard of the phenomenon by which certain people—the feeble-minded, she'd always assumed—had only to be accused of a crime to feel themselves guilty of it. The next day, as she walked through the gates of the children's home, she understood it: she felt as if she were carrying a bomb with her.

After Mr Jamshed left, she'd spent over two hours pulling down the creepy photographs and putting them in the rubbish bin, and then packing up her room.

After that, she'd hardly slept at all, her mind whirling with thoughts of Guy and Frank and where she would go next.

She found Daisy in her office. She was sitting, a small solitary figure, behind a pile of letters. When she saw Viva, she stood up beaming.

'Oh, greetings! How nice to see you. Did you have the most wonderful time?' She'd stuck a pencil absent-mindedly through her bun.

'I did, Daisy. But I'm afraid I have rotten news to tell you.'

Daisy listened carefully while Viva poured out her story, only punctuating the silence with a mild 'Oh golly' and 'Oh goodness me'.

'What a terrible shame if he stops Dolly and Kaniz coming to the university,' was her first reaction. 'They're brilliant students and they love their work. But what about this business with Guy? Do you think he's been spreading rumours about us? That could be very serious.'

'Oh, Daisy. I am so, so sorry,' said Viva. 'None of this would have happened if I hadn't come here.'

'No, that I can't accept. That's nonsense,' said Daisy briskly. 'There are spies everywhere and none of the locals really know what to make of us: why should they? They've never seen women like us before. And when people like Guy start spreading rumours it doesn't help matters.'

'So what can we do about him?' said Viva.

'Good question. You can't arrest someone for setting their coat on fire.'

'But he broke into my room.'

'So what do you think?'

'I think the police should be told.'

'Maybe.' Daisy hesitated. 'But if we do that, we open another can of worms. The police have already been under pressure from hotheads in the new Congress to try and close us down. So far we've resisted.'

'What about our people, what do they think?'

Daisy fiddled with her papers. 'The last time a government official came here, he admitted we were doing fine work but thought we should close down; he said that they could no longer guarantee us protection. That was before you came. Perhaps I should have told you.'

The two women looked at each other.

'When I told the staff and children, they all wept and begged us not to go. These children, Viva, have nothing. I'm not saying they all want to be here, they don't, but if we leave them, they'll die or end up on the streets. Someone has to understand this.' There was a long silence.

'I'm so sorry,' Viva said at last. 'You've worked so terribly hard here.'

'I need the children as much as they need me,' Daisy said quietly. 'That's the truth. But onwards. Let's get back to the horns of this particular dilemma. Do you think that this Guy Glover person will strike again, or was this a silly prank?'

'I don't know,' said Viva. 'But I don't want to go to the police. There's too much to lose.'

'Are you sure? I don't want you to be in any danger.'

'Quite sure,' she said. 'I think he's made his showy gesture, and now he'll go home.'

'Positive?'

'Positive.' Then they smiled at each other as if they'd understood that some lies were worth telling.

**E**ight days after this conversation, Viva moved into a new room on the first floor of the children's home. It was bare as a nun's cell when she arrived: an iron bed, a scuffed wardrobe and a temporary desk—a wide plank placed on two packing cases—the sum total of its furniture. She liked it this way. It looked like a place for work, even for penance, and she was drawing in on herself again. After Viva's conversation with Daisy, both of them had agreed a new timetable for her. Four hours' teaching in the morning, followed by lunch, and in the afternoon she was to write the children's stories.

When she opened the battered shutters, she could see the feathery foliage of the tamarind tree. Daisy had told her that in northern India the shade of this tree was thought to be sacred to Krishna, the god who personified idealised love. That Krishna had sat underneath a tamarind tree when separated from his loved one, Radha, and experienced the fierce delight of her spirit entering him.

But Talika had told her a much bleaker tale. She said the tree was haunted. She'd shown her how the leaves folded in on themselves at night and said that many ghosts lived there. Everybody knew that.

**O**ne afternoon, Viva was sitting at her desk typing, when there was a soft knock on the door.

'Lady has come to see you, madam.' A shy little orphan called Seema put her head round the door. 'Name is Victoria.'

Tor burst into her room and flung her arms round her.

'Viva,' she said, 'I need to talk to you immediately. I'm in such a state I think I'm going mad!'

'Good Lord!' Viva looked up from her work. 'What on earth's going on?'

Tor flung off her hat, sat down on a chair and let out a burst of air. 'Do you have a drink?' she said. 'I don't know where to begin.'

Viva poured her a glass of water. 'Begin at the beginning,' she said.

'Well,' started Tor, 'do you remember that awful lunch at the Mallinsons' when Ci told me a man called Toby Williamson had phoned to ask if I was all right. Well, I phoned him at the Willoughby Club. I felt I had nothing to lose and I needed a lift. I knew I had to get Mummy a present.

'He came straight over. His car was so scruffy—jammed with clothes and books—and Ci, who was hoping someone fun had arrived, looked him over as if he was something the cat had sicked up.

'He wanted to take me first to a place called Bangangla. It sounded jolly boring to me. I put my foot down and said I really had to go shopping. I explained that I would have to buy Mummy a present.

'Well, to nutshell it—he drove me to the Army and Navy Store. "Tell me what she's like," he said when we were in the hat department. "I'm good at presents." "You won't believe this," I told him, "but she's tiny, like a bird."

'And then he reached out and put one of those dreadful ostrich-feather sola topis on his head and squawked like a bird, and we both looked at each other and had complete hysterics. It's never happened to me with someone I don't know before but it was bliss.'

'So what happened then?' Viva was starting to enjoy this.

'We ended up buying her a teak elephant. After the shopping, he drove me to Bangangla. It's such a funny place, a sort of secret lake, right in the middle of Bombay, with steps all around it. It was so peaceful.

'We ate lunch at a little restaurant near there, and afterwards we sat on the steps and talked and talked and talked, first about his work— he's a biologist or something like that, but he's working in a boys' boarding school up north to make money—and then about absolutely everything: our childhoods, our parents, all the kind of ordinary things.

'Here is the best bit,' she said. 'All the time we were talking I noticed what a nice mouth he had and that if he had a decent haircut, he'd be almost handsome. And then he started to say some poetry to me and I said, "Look here! I must warn you—I'm very dim and I only know one poem and it's called 'Ithaka' and I think it's codswallop."'

Viva laughed. 'What did he say?'

'He said, "Why?" and I said, "Because it's a lie. It's all about finding diamonds and pearls on your travels and coming back a richer person, but if anything, being in India is going to make me feel much poorer, because if I hadn't come, I wouldn't know how wonderful life can be."

'He didn't say anything for a while. A funeral party had come down to the lake and we watched this man strip down to his dhoti, wash himself and scatter his father's ashes on the surface of the lake. That was quite sad and Toby explained how the man was saying goodbye.

'In the car going home he said that he didn't agree with me about "Ithaka" being just about the joys of setting out into the unknown; he thought it was about finding yourself, something like that anyway.

'Then he stopped the car near Chowpatty Beach. The sun was setting and he kissed me—oh, Viva, have I finally gone mad?' Tor's beautiful big blue eyes lit up.

'Go on! Go on!' Viva was the one on the edge of her seat now.

'He said, "I have a preposterous idea to put to you. You don't want to go home and I want to get married, so let's get married. It'll be an adventure, and I already know you make me laugh."'

'Oh no, no, no!' Viva put her hands over her ears. 'This can't be true.'

'It's true.' Tor folded her hands in her lap and looked down at them.

'Tor, you went out with this man for one afternoon. You can't do it, you simply can't.'

'But it's not like that. That's the funny thing. You know how sometimes you just know.'

'No, I don't,' said Viva. 'Not like this.'

'Toby says it's more like an Indian marriage except that we've arranged it ourselves.'

'But it's nothing like that, Tor,' Viva protested. 'You know nothing about him or his parents and they know nothing about you.'

'I know that his mother lives in Hampstead with his father, who is an architect, and that she writes poetry and that she goes swimming in a pond in Hampstead Heath every morning with a kettle in her hand.'

'Oh well,' Viva said, 'everything's understood now.'

'It's to make the water warmer,' Tor added helpfully.

'Wonderful.'

'Oh, Viva.' Tor clasped her hands together. 'Try to understand. I don't have to go home to Middle Wallop this way. I shall have a house of my own. He said our life together would be a journey of exploration.'

'How old is he, Tor?' Viva asked more gently.

'Twenty-seven, and he earns one and a half thousand pounds a year teaching at a school in Amritsar. We'll have our own house there.'

'And has he actually proposed to you yet?'

Tor looked secretive. 'Well . . . I am already betrothed.' Tor rolled back the cuff of her dress and showed Viva a silver bracelet round her wrist. 'He gave me this—in the Hindu religion it means "beloved".'

'But you're not a Hindu, Tor.'

'I know, and I couldn't give a fig. We went to the Bombay Registry Office yesterday and I have this too.' She showed Viva a gold band, which she'd hung on a chain inside her dress. 'We're eloping tonight. I shall leave a note for Ci Ci and I've already sent a telegram to my mother, and the best thing of all about this, Viva,' her eyes blazed with excitement, 'is that it's too late for anyone to do anything about it.'

# Chapter 9

WHEN TOR HAD LEFT with the same speed at which she'd arrived, Viva sat down on her bed, poleaxed by her news. The madcap speed with which Tor had donated herself to this Toby person seemed to her to border on insanity. The only thing she was grateful for was that Tor had been so bound up in her own news she hadn't asked about Frank.

Viva didn't want to talk about him. It was over.

She'd sent a letter to Frank a week ago informing him that Guy was still alive, and it seemed that his 'death' had been some sort of prank that had fooled them both, but as a result of it, she had had to move from Mr Jamshed's.

'I think it would be better for us not to see each other again,' she'd written. 'I want to finish my book now, and when it is done, I shall go to Simla and pick up my parents' trunk,' she'd said. 'Good luck to you in your future endeavours. With kind regards, Viva.'

Later in bed, and unable to sleep, she thought of how it had been in that little guesthouse in Ooty in the pouring rain, and pain turned to anger at herself. She deserved everything she'd got, and now the thought of her tears, her moans, the way she'd clung to him dismayed, repulsed her, and she wished with all her heart she'd kept her distance.

This keeping of distance was no mere figure of speech for her. After Josie and her parents died, she'd learned—and partially succeeded, right up until the William fiasco—not to trust, not to hope and, above all, not to reveal. Life was easier that way.

Frank wrote back two days later.

*Dear Viva,*

*Thank you for letting me know about Guy. It is a great relief to hear he is not dead. You will now, no doubt, deal with the situation as you think fit and need no further warnings from me. I have definitely decided to take the job in Lahore. I leave next week. I doubt you will, but don't try to contact me before I go.*

*Yours sincerely,*
*Frank*

She was sitting on her bed in her new room as she read the letter. Afterwards, she'd crumpled his words in her hand and thrown them in the bin, and then, in a mood of feverish energy, picked up a broom and swept the floor. Then she scrubbed out the large wardrobe with carbolic soap, relined it with paper, and arranged her few clothes inside. She'd lined up her writing paper, pens and typewriter on her desk, put her pile of notebooks in order of date on her one shelf, and finally pinned a timetable on the wall near her desk. Good, her life was back in some sort of order again. Let work begin.

Later that night, exhausted and numb, she'd lain down in her iron bed near the window. Drifting towards sleep, with her own arms wrapped tightly round her, the last thing she heard was the cry of a baby owl who was nesting with its mother in the tamarind tree. Talika had told her once it was an omen for disaster. She was glad she did not believe in such things.

**A**fter months of speculation, Jack and twenty other members of the Third Cavalry Regiment had been sent to Bannu to plug some gaps on the northwest frontier after a raid that had killed five members of an infantry column. His job now was to take two- or three-day treks into the hills in order to decide which areas were suitable for future operations. After the first morning's ride, the hills became so steep that the only communication possible with Bannu was by carrier pigeon.

Jack had begged Rose not to come. Everybody knew that this area, with its steep mountains and treacherous ravines and fierce, trigger-happy gangs, was one of the most dangerous places on earth. But Rose had insisted on coming. They'd expected to live in Peshawar Cantonment, where there was a reasonable military hospital, but a flash flood two weeks before they arrived had made the fifty or so houses there uninhabitable. The only other alternative, so the duty officer had said, was that Jack move into the officers' mess and for Rose to return to Poona.

'She'll stay,' Jack had said woodenly. 'If you can find us another house.' He knew it was pointless to argue with her any more.

On a baking-hot day in late August, they'd been given the keys to a deserted-looking bungalow surrounded by red dust and scrub. Rose had felt the hammer blows of heat strike her as she got out of the car.

In shock, she'd walked round the house with Jack, almost unable to focus her eyes, feeling the heat radiate off the walls. In the room where they were to sleep, their iron bed had bird droppings on its straw mattress; the walls in the dusty sitting room were covered in a green moss left from the last monsoon and the broken commode in the bathroom was full of dark brown urine. Outside her kitchen window was a woodwormy verandah, and beyond that the red dirt track leading to Bannu.

She should never have come, it was her fault, not Jack's, and he'd tried to warn her over and over again.

When he'd first seen the house Jack had shouted, 'Oh for Christ's sake, what a bloody shambles.' It was the first time she'd ever heard him swear, although they had had several shouting matches after he'd told her about Sunita.

Ten minutes later there had been a knock on the door and a tall Pathan woman arrived. She wore a dark blue shalwar kameez and had a gold ring through her nose. Addressing Jack in Pashto, she said her name was Laila and she was from the next village. She would help them in the house. Standing behind her was her husband, Hasan, as handsome as she was. He said he would be their driver and gardener.

It had taken Rose and Laila four days of scrubbing with carbolic soap to get the place even half habitable. When it was clean, Baz and Imad, Laila's two sons, who worked in Bannu in a carpenter's shop, came and put up shelves, and mended the bed and the hinge of the wooden box bought for the baby's new clothes.

On the morning her mother's letter arrived, along with one from Tor's mother, by mail lorry with the weekly newspapers, Rose had been on her own for a week. Jack was on patrol near the village of Mamash, an area where tribesmen had killed one of the soldiers. He hoped to be back in the next few days.

She made herself a jam sandwich and took the battered envelope that held her mother's longed-for letter back to bed with her. She read it greedily, so many questions, mainly about Tor, she didn't know how to answer. She'd hardly heard a word from Tor herself except to say she was madly in love and was never going to go home again.

Since Jack had told her about Sunita, she'd told nothing but lies to her parents and she was just so sick of this new person she'd become: outwardly huge and lumbering, inwardly thin-skinned, unreliable, unsure of everything. Jack had sworn he would not see Sunita again. But the atmosphere was so strained between them now that when Jack left the house, Rose experienced a physical feeling of relief. On the nights he was home, their conversation was so stilted she sometimes had this image of them all out to sea on a dark night in two small and separate boats drifting further and further apart.

They'd had such rows about her coming here; they'd raged for weeks in the privacy of their bedroom before he'd finally relented.

'Why are you so determined to come?' he'd shouted on the night of their worst row.

'You know why,' she'd shouted back. 'Because I'm having our baby and because if I lose you now I'm never going to find you again.'

She felt she was hanging on to him by only the slenderest of threads. That if she let that snap it would be over.

That night, he'd told her there was a hospital in Peshawar where she could have the baby. The muscle in Jack's jaw that twitched when he was angry had twitched during this announcement; she'd ignored it but was sad because she felt in that moment that she hated him.

As she finished reading Mrs Sowerby's letter, the distinct outline of her baby's foot appeared through the side of her smock. She doubled up with pain, then felt a whole new swarm of anxieties. She was so ill-prepared, but with two weeks to go before the baby came she didn't want to make a fool of herself by admitting herself into the very basic military hospital in Peshawar too early.

When the kicking stopped, Rose took a deep breath and sat quietly. Through the thin walls of the house, she could hear the gentle padding of Laila.

'Memsahib.' Laila had brought a glass of lemonade for her.

'Thank you, Laila. I think we should unwrap the tea service today.' She pointed towards a packing case in the corner of the verandah. 'I'll help you.'

Laila, who didn't understand a word of this, smiled attentively. A few moments later, Rose was on her hands and knees taking china from bits of newspaper when she felt the odd sensation of a cork being popped between her legs. Now water was streaming down her legs and splashing her shoes. How humiliating! She'd spent a penny on the floor in front of Laila. Her next thought, as she scrambled round trying to mop it up, was relief—thank God Jack hadn't seen that.

But Laila seemed to know what to do. She held up her hand and smiled widely. 'Baby comes,' she said in faltering English. 'Is all right.' She'd patted her softly on the back.

Rose, gasping from the shock of her first proper contraction, said, 'Laila, get the doctor, please. *Daktar, daktar.*' She wasn't sure that Laila understood her and was cross with herself for not making more effort with learning her language.

A few minutes later she saw Hasan whipping up his skinny horse and galloping towards town.

'Memsahib, sit.' Laila had made up a nest of cushions for Rose on the cane recliner in the corner of the verandah near the packing cases.

*The important thing is to stay calm*, she told herself. The corkscrewing pains she was feeling inside her womb she pictured as waves, which could easily be jumped, and when they went away they left her on a smooth flat beach.

Laila was standing at her elbow and leading her so respectfully around the verandah. When she suddenly doubled up with pain, Laila rubbed the small of her back. The sun had dipped behind the mountains. Rose lay down again.

'Oooh! Oooh!' she heard herself groaning like an animal. 'Sorry, sorry,' she said when Laila leapt to her side and started to shush her softly. 'OOOhhhh. Help!'

She looked at her watch. Seven o'clock and dark now. She'd never felt more alone in her life. 'Where is Hasan? *Daktar*? Captain Chandler?' She was trying not to shout, but Laila just shrugged.

'Help me,' said Rose, who was trying to sound calm. 'I think it's coming.'

Laila took her into her bedroom and helped her sit down in a chair Laila removed the sheet and put a clean tarpaulin on the bed.

'Don't worry about that.' Rose watched her impatiently from the chair. She wasn't hurting; all she wanted was to lie down. 'Doctor here soon.'

'Memsahib, sorry, sorry,' Laila said.

Rose fought her off at first, she was unbuttoning her skirt, she was pushing her down on the bed. She heard herself screaming. Nobody, nobody had told her it hurt this much.

'It's fine, Laila,' she said politely, when the pain went again. 'Thank you so much.' How awful to be seen like this.

And then the pain again: a bucking bronco kicking her to death from inside. When her screams stopped, Laila parted her legs and started to mutter words she didn't understand. Laila put both of her hands together to indicate a circle the size of a grapefruit.

But then nothing. The baby wasn't coming. Rose muffled her screams in her pillow at first, but then she called out, 'Mummy, Mummy, help me, Mummy.' Only pain now; she was on the side of a mountain waiting to fall. She didn't care if the baby died, she didn't care if she died, she wanted it to stop.

Laila's hand was holding hers: a hard-working hand, tough, strong, skin like sandpaper. She squeezed it; Laila was her world now, the rope that stopped her falling.

An hour before dawn, when she felt she would die soon of the pain, the baby shot out and another woman, perhaps the village midwife—she never did know who—burst into the room and cut the cord.

In the chaos that followed she felt Laila put the child in her arms. She heard herself shout, 'My baby! My boy!' in a choked voice. Her first miracle. The pain was there but in the blink of an eye it meant nothing. A feeling of vast exhilaration swept over her. She wanted tea, she wanted food, she wanted to kiss everybody and everything in the world.

Laila brought the boy back washed and in a muslin nightdress.

'Give him to me, Laila.' Rose couldn't stop smiling. Her eyes brimmed with happy tears, and the two women beamed at each other in delight.

Then Laila put the baby on her breast. How funny it was, but she had never felt so tired or so necessary.

'Sleep, memsahib,' Laila said softly when the baby fell asleep on her breast. She turned down the lights and straightened Rose's blanket.

'Thank you, Laila,' Rose said. 'I can never thank you enough.'

Laila put the palms of her hands together. She bowed her head. She smiled at her, a smile of sweetness and understanding that seemed to convey an equal joy, a delight that she'd been there too.

At ten o'clock that night Jack went into the bedroom where Rose and the baby were asleep. He lifted up the oil lamp he was carrying and saw that his son had a garland of marigolds round his neck. Rose looked pale lying beside him, and there were dark circles under her eyes.

'Darling.' Jack put out his hand. 'Darling.' He touched the baby's hair softly, then Rose's hair, still damp with sweat.

When she woke up, he was standing in his sweaty jodhpurs, crying so hard he couldn't speak. She used the corner of her nightdress to dry his eyes, then he kissed her.

'He's beautiful,' he said at last.

She put her hands over his lips, and smiled at him radiantly.

'Yes,' she whispered. 'The most beautiful thing.'

Jack got into bed in his underwear and lay down beside them.

'The doctor will come soon,' he whispered. 'He's on his way now. There was a small landslide on the road, it's cleared now. I can't believe how brave you've been.'

They lay in the dark holding hands. The baby lay on top of them, a sleeping Buddha.

'I have a son,' he said out of the dark. 'I don't deserve him.'

He could feel his son's head against his arm. The soft silk of his hair. Rose squeezed his fingers. 'You do,' she said.

Viva was playing tennis with her best friend Eleanor when the nun came to tell her that her mother had died. Sister Patricia had beckoned her off the court; they'd walked back down the path towards the school, and all Viva could remember now was how hard she'd had to concentrate not to put her feet on the cracks in the crazy paving. And how blank she'd felt inside—a muffling feeling like snow.

It was months before she had properly cried. The school had taken a group of girls to a production of *Snow White* in Chester. Viva, sitting in the darkened theatre with a bag of Liquorice Allsorts, had been enjoying herself, until the prince sang to Snow White 'A Pretty Girl Is Like a Melody'. Her father's favourite song. Viva had to leave the theatre with a cross, postulant nun who'd been enjoying this rare treat. The nun had loaned her a used handkerchief and watched her, standing under the Christmas lights outside Debenhams, heaving and sobbing, until she'd collected herself sufficiently to join her own group again.

Everyone had thought it kinder to ignore this outburst, and on the way back to school in the bus, she felt so ashamed that she'd told herself that this must never happen again. That the world would set traps and that she must from now on avoid them, and that the best way to avoid them was to hang on to the frozen feeling that had, up until now, kept her safe. It was songs and soppiness she should beware of.

This by now ingrained training persuaded her to feel glad after Frank left, relieved he'd gone, glad that he had not tried to contact her again before he had gone to work in Lahore.

Work was what mattered now. Now at night, long after the children had gone to bed, she would sit at her desk near the window. And then she would write, often until the early hours of the morning, these children's stories. Children who were often described as plucky and resilient—as she herself had been once—but who mostly had learned not to step on the cracks.

The book was harder to write than she thought it would be. But bit by bit, day by day, the sheets were piling up on her desk. Daisy had already shown some of the stories to a friend of hers at Macmillan, the publishers, who'd said if she could produce more chapters of this quality, they might be interested.

At the beginning of November, all the children started to get excited because the full moon would soon be in Kartika and that meant their biggest festival of all had come: the Festival of Diwali, the Hindu Festival of Lights. Held on the darkest night of the year, it marked the arrival of winter, the return of the Hindu divinities, Sita and Ram, a time for celebrating light over the forces of darkness.

For weeks now, lessons had been interrupted by local tradesmen calling in to ask for donations to help build *pandals*, the huge floats that would soon be transporting gods down the streets of Byculla. The dormitory above Viva's head had vibrated with the feet of children scrubbing their rooms from top to bottom, whitewashing walls and then making their own statue of Durga—a towering edifice of tinsel, paper and lights—which Viva had been called upstairs several times to admire and advise on.

The children insisted that Viva dress up for Diwali. At five o'clock that afternoon, as she put on her red silk dress, she could already hear drums beginning to beat in the streets outside, the cracked sounds of horns, and shouting and laughter.

A few moments later, there was a knock on her door. Talika stood there dressed up in her new finery: a beautiful peach-coloured sari, her skinny arms covered in glass bracelets, kohl round her eyes, her small ears weighted down with gold hooped earrings.

Behind Talika was little Suday, a boy who had come to the home with a badly burnt leg. He was wearing a brand-new khurta and had a gold crown on his head.

'How do I look?' Suday asked her.

'You look wonderful,' she said. 'Like Lord Ram himself.'

He squeezed his eyes shut, and shuffled his little wasted leg. This was almost more excitement than he could bear.

**A**n hour later, when Viva stepped out into the streets with her little charges, they were watching her face and when she gasped, they laughed and clapped their hands. The dingy shopfronts and collapsed verandahs of the street had been transformed into an explosion of lights. Every inch that could be lit was ablaze; windows were filled with clusters of candles, skinny trees were garlanded and glowed like Christmas trees against the sky, and crowds of people, dressed up to the nines and dripping with jewels, greeted each other in the street.

She wandered with the children for a while between stalls sagging under the weight of sticky sweets, carrot halvah and almond cakes. She heard drums, a discordant trumpet and then above the swaying heads of the crowd came a lopsided *pandal* with a gorgeously decorated goddess inside it, garlanded with magnolia flowers.

Talika was tugging at her sleeves. 'Mamji, Mamji,' she said. She often called her mother when she was excited. 'Lakshmi comes tonight.'

Lakshmi was the goddess of wealth. Viva knew already that tonight every single door in Byculla would be open so she would come and spread her munificence around. And then the fireworks: catherine wheels spitting like fat in the orange night air, as well as banging rockets, which stained the faces of her charges with blue and yellow and pink light and made the huge crowd gasp with delight.

Tonight, on the darkest night of the year, in one of the poorest countries on earth, hope was being celebrated. And she was part of it, standing there, gaping, humbled by their undefeated joy, their faith that things would get better.

'Isn't this fun?' Daisy had appeared at her side, a piece of tinsel hanging from her hat. 'I hope you're planning to come to my party later?'

'Try and stop me, Daisy,' she'd said, grinning. After weeks of hard work she suddenly felt lit up and ready to enjoy herself.

**I**t was midnight by the time the street celebrations started to die down and she'd got the children to bed and stepped out into the street again. Small crowds were drifting home through the haze of multicoloured smoke from the spent fireworks.

Stepping from the kerb, she heard the ping of a bell, then the whirl of wheels, the soft touch of a hand on her arm.

'Madam sahib.' A wiry little man with one eye cloudy pointed inside his rickshaw. 'Miss Barker sent for you. Get in, please.'

Once she was seated he set off, and she, tired from the evening, settled back against the shabby seat and dozed for a while. When she woke, she pulled back the canvas flap that separated her from the road and saw that they were bumping down a narrow dirty street.

'This isn't it,' she said. 'Miss Barker lives near the Umbrella Hospital. Could you stop, please?'

But the wheels kept on whirling and he didn't turn.

'Stop now!' she called, but he didn't reply. The next thing she felt was a jarring bump and her heart thumping as she looked around her and saw nothing that she recognised. 'Excuse me! Excuse me!' It felt important to be polite to him. 'This is not where I want to go. Wrong street!'

They were jolting down another narrow cobbled street. To the right of her she could see the slum dwellings the locals called *chawls*, a grim collection of buildings where itinerant workers could stay.

She felt the rickshaw stop. A cloudy eye appeared round the curtain. She felt the tip of a knife underneath her ear.

'Get out,' he said.

Her black notebook had flopped to her feet in the gutter. It had all the notes in it she'd planned to type up the following day.

'I want that,' she said. 'Can I please pick it up?'

'Don't move,' he said and kicked the book into a heap of rubbish.

'Please,' she said. 'Take my money, but give me my notebook back.'

The knife jumped against her throat this time.

She heard him sigh. His right leg hooked the book towards her.

Briefly, as he picked it up and handed it to her, the knife went away. 'Thank you,' she said, but he shook his head.

He punched her roughly in the back. 'Walk,' he said.

He led her down a passageway so narrow that she had to walk ahead of him. He prodded her painfully from time to time, muttering, '*Gora*' —foreigner—and obscenities she recognised from the street boys.

At the end of the street, the rickshaw man stopped. They'd reached a high narrow house with a solid-looking studded door.

'We're here,' he said.

The door opened. She felt arms pulling her down a narrow corridor lit by an oil lamp. There was a soft patter of feet. Someone held her hair back, and before she had time to scream, a petrol-smelling rag was forced between her lips.

A door opened; she was pushed so hard into the clammy darkness that she hit her head on a solid wooden object, a chair or a windowsill. She heard a man shout, the scrape of a chair as she fell down. The last thing she felt were ropes being tied round her wrists and neck, then a blow and a darkness that tasted of metal.

**W**hen Viva woke, a man, middle-aged and wearing an embroidered cap, was staring at her.

'She is awake.' He spoke in Hindi to someone she couldn't see.

She was cold. There were red swellings on her wrists, and marks where they had been tied tightly with rope.

'My name,' the man in the cap said, 'is Anwar Azim.'

He was a small but powerfully built man, with a large nose set slightly off-centre, and a sprinkling of gold teeth set in a fleshy mouth with a ridge on the lower lip where it looked as if he'd been cut and had stitches. He had the deep phlegmy voice of a heavy smoker, but he spoke good English. 'I've been wanting to meet you for some time.'

Her head ached so badly it was hard to focus on him or the room she was held in, but she saw it was small, about ten foot by twelve, with stained walls and a torn carpet.

She must have lost consciousness then, because when she woke up again, a young man with a wispy beard and a pleasant face was looking at her. He was lying on a charpoy placed in front of a locked door. A bolt of pain shot through her head as she turned to look at him.

'I'm thirsty,' she said. 'Can I have a drink?'

To her surprise, he leapt up immediately.

'Of course,' he said. He picked up a carafe of rust-coloured water and poured her a glass.

He held the glass to her lips and she heard her noisy gobbles.

'I'm sorry,' he said in a posh, precise voice, 'this place is a bit of a fleapit. I have no idea what sanitary arrangements will be here.'

She felt herself gaping at him. 'Why am I here? What have I done?'

'I can't tell you,' the young man said. 'It's not my part of the ship. Mr Azim will return later. In the meantime, do you want something to eat?'

'I want to go home,' she said. 'I've done nothing wrong.'

Her head was hurting so badly it made her feel sick, and although one part of her knew she was in danger, a huge lassitude was creeping over her like a fog and what she most wanted was to lie down, to go to sleep and let what would happen happen.

**W**hen she woke again, she looked towards the window where a closed wooden shutter filtered bars of light across the room. The rope round her wrists had been untied and her hands lay uselessly in her lap.

A fat woman in a dirty sari stood in front of her with a tray holding two chapattis and a small pot of dhal. Viva wasn't hungry but forced herself to eat. She looked at her watch—eight thirty-five in the morning. Surely they'd be looking for her at the home by now?

When she had finished her meal, the woman came back with a rank-smelling bucket. The woman tied her up again after she'd used it. The look she gave her was curiously blank but at the sound of heavy male footsteps, both of them stiffened, and the woman's movements became jerky and rushed as though she was scared too.

Anwar Azim opened the door.

This morning, his clothes were a perfect mixture of East and West. Over his shalwar kameez he wore a beautiful butter-coloured camel-hair coat. The conker-coloured brogues he wore under soft linen trousers were expensive and polished to a high shine.

He drew up a chair and sat opposite her, close enough for her to smell his cigarettes, the mustard oil on his hair.

'Good morning, Miss Viva,' he said softly. 'How was your night?' he asked in his plummy accent.

'Unpleasant,' she said. 'I don't know why I'm here.'

He yawned elaborately, showing gums and teeth. 'Don't worry,' he said. 'You have a few easy questions to answer then you can go home.'

He took out a mother-of-pearl case, put a cigarette between his plump scarred lips and lit it with an expensive-looking silver lighter.

'So,' he said when his head was enveloped in a blue haze. 'I won't beat about the bush with you. Mr Glover has been keeping an eye on you, or he was until we lost him. Anyway,' he continued mildly, 'tell me what you do on Friday nights at your children's home.'

The request surprised her. 'Well, nothing much,' she said. 'We all have supper with the children, then we read stories to them, then they go to bed.'

'What kind of stories?'

'All kinds: adventure stories, legends, Bible stories, Ramayana stories.'

'So there is no truth in the rumours circulating that you make the boys bathe with the girls at your home? Or that you wash provocatively in front of the children?' His voice had become cold as steel.

She felt fear fly through her body. 'Did Guy Glover tell you that?'

Mr Azim just looked at her.

'If he did, he's lying,' she said. 'We respect the children and they respect us. If you came to look around you would see.'

'We have had people looking around,' he said. 'And we have seen and heard many bad things. Why do you question our children all the time and write their names down in a book?'

He pulled open his coat and from its lining produced her notebook.

'That's mine.' She moved towards him.

'Sit down.' He was shouting at her like a dog. 'Answer my questions.'

With huge self-control she said, 'I'm writing the children's stories.'

'Why?'

'Because they're interesting.'

'They're nothing; they're street children, life dust. What other books have you written?' he said. 'Can I buy them?'

'No,' she said. 'It's my first.'

'Your English is very good,' she said after a long silence. She had decided to soft-soap him, or at least to try. 'Where did you learn it?'

'I was at Oxford University, like my brother,' he said coldly. 'Before that St Crispin's.'

She'd heard of it, it was one of a number of Indian public schools that claimed to be 'the Eton of India'. They delivered Western-style education and values to the sons of maharajahs, and anyone who could afford it and who felt it beneficial to have a veneer of Englishness.

When he left the room quickly, she assumed it was for his noon prayers. While she waited, the young bearded man stood guard at the door, pointing the barrel of a gun in her direction.

Half an hour later, Azim came into the room again.

'Did you go to pray?' she asked.

'No,' he said. 'I am not a religious man. Not all of us are.'

He moved closer to her. 'I am going to make it clear to you why we are holding you here,' he said. 'What goes on at the children's home is a side issue; our main aim is to find your friend, Guy Glover.'

'He's no friend of mine.'

'No? You shared a cabin with him on the *Kaiser-i-Hind*.'

'I didn't share his cabin,' she said. 'I was his chaperone. I was paid to take care of him.'

'Don't start by telling me lies, Miss Viva,' he warned her. 'I don't want to have to hurt you.'

A sour feeling like nausea began at the pit of her stomach and travelled up through her spinal cord into her mouth.

'He was a schoolboy,' she stammered. 'I needed a job. I was there to look after him.'

'Well, you didn't do your job very well,' he said softly.

The photograph he took out of his coat pocket was of a smartly dressed young man with oiled black hair crimped into waves. He was sitting in a dinner shirt on a chair in a resplendent ship's cabin. His lip was swollen, his eye half-closed and shiny.

'This is my younger brother,' said Azim. 'Your friend Guy did that.'

'I knew about it,' she was forced to admit. 'But I had no part in it.'

'Did you know Guy Glover was a thief?'

'I did. And so did your brother. Why didn't he press charges?'

He looked at her for a while.

'Because,' he said, 'we were able to persuade Mr Glover to work for us instead, and now we are very angry with him for giving us the slip. We hear he may be going back to England. He may even be on his way now. As soon as you can help us find him, we will let you go.'

Before he left he said, 'My brother is a peaceful man. He didn't want me to do this. He doesn't believe in your eye for an eye, tooth for a tooth business. But your friend left him deaf in one ear. You can still see the marks on him. I should have killed Mr Glover then, but I thought he might be useful to us. He has not been useful to us. He has betrayed us. Now, it is my duty to avenge my brother.'

**O**n the fourth day, after a breakfast of dhal and chapattis, the woman arrived and allowed Viva to wash in a trickle of rusty water, then to use the bucket while she averted her eyes. Viva hated this bit. When this was done she was tied up again and heard the descending tinkle of the woman's bangles as she walked downstairs. She'd begun to associate this sound with a pounding in her heart, a dryness in her mouth—after it, Azim would appear.

The pattern of his interrogations was unpredictable but again and again he returned to a familiar obsession of his.

'What do you do on Friday nights at the children's home?'

'Nothing very special,' Viva replied. 'We have a meal with the children who are boarders, and we sometimes have readings afterwards.'

'What kind of readings?' Mr Azim asked suspiciously.

'I've told you, poetry, Bible readings, sometimes the children will tell us a story from the Mahabharata, or some local fairy stories—it's a way of understanding each other's cultures.'

He gave her a look of deep disgust. 'So how do you explain this to the children?' He shoved a book near her face. 'Do you understand what this is?' He was trembling with barely suppressed emotion.

'I do. It's a holy book—the Koran.'

'And this. This is a great insult to a Muslim.' He grabbed her hair and shoved her face towards the book. There were torn pages in the middle.

'I know.' Her lips were so dry she could hardly speak.

'We found it in your room.'

'We didn't do that, Mr Azim,' she said. 'We're non-sectarian.'

'Don't try to pull the wool over my eyes, Miss Viva.' He stood up. 'Tonight is the last night of the Diwali Festival. It's time for us to decide what to do with you.'

Viva tried to sleep to blot out the fear but woke half an hour later frozen and with a crick in her neck.

She wondered if she would leave here alive. If Guy had been blackmailed to spy on them all at the home, God knows what he might have told Mr Azim about her.

She thought about Frank. He had tried to get close. He had opened his heart to her, made no secret of his feelings. How brave that seemed.

In the darkness she thought about the night at the guesthouse at Ooty. 'Promise me that you won't feel ashamed,' he'd told her afterwards.

What a fool she was. What had the poor man done wrong in the end, except step across some line she'd drawn too many years ago to make any sense now? Frank had liked what she was and had made love to her straightforwardly, like a man. Why had she said no in the morning?

'Frank,' she whispered into the dark. All she wanted was to hold him. She'd missed her chance.

When Mr Azim arrived in the morning, she'd decided what to do.

'I've been thinking,' she said. 'There is one house in Byculla where I think Guy could be hiding.'

He looked at her suspiciously. 'Why are you telling me this now?'

'I was thinking about your brother last night,' she said. 'How much you must have looked forward to seeing him again and the shock of seeing his face like that. It must have been horrible.'

'It was,' he said. 'He didn't deserve it.'

She leant her head towards him and made herself look into his eyes.

'But the real truth is, I'm tired,' she said. 'I'm hoping after I've led you to him you'll let me go.'

'This is not in your dispensation,' he said. 'It's mine.'

'Of course,' she said. She forced herself to smile. 'I just thought if I could help it would be silly not to.'

He stood up and sighed. 'Where is he living in Byculla?'

'In a flat near the fruit market,' she said. 'I can't remember the exact address, but if you take me there I will be able to find the way.'

His eyes brooded over her, hooded and suspicious.

'I'll come back at half past five,' he said.

**H**e came back again on the dot of five thirty, this time with a tunic and a Kashmiri shawl, which he flung on her lap.

'Time is running out.' He sat on the chair in front of her, legs akimbo.

'Where are we going?' She hated hearing her voice tremble like that.

'Out in the streets to see if your memory is jogged.'

'I think that's a good idea,' she said. 'I'll try my hardest.'

'Tell me again where he lives in Byculla,' he said.

She closed her eyes, pretended to think.

'It was near the fruit market or a small flat near the Jain Temple on Love Lane,' she said at last. 'You'll have to be patient with me— everything looks so different during Diwali.'

His eyes swept over her coldly. 'Not that different,' he warned. 'And Byculla is not a big place. If you try to give me the slip, I am going to kill you. For me,' he said, 'it would not be a sin but an honour. I don't like women like you. You bring shame to us and our children.'

She tried not to flinch when he brought a vicious-looking knife towards her. The sliced rope left three deep red marks on her wrists.

'Don't move,' he said when she tried to rub them. He put the knife back in a leather holster he wore on his belt.

When he left the room, she got dressed, supervised by the older woman. She was given a chapatti to eat, a drink of brackish water, and then, suddenly, she was led downstairs and out into daylight again.

**W**hen they got out in the streets she was bundled into a rickshaw. She sat thigh to thigh with Mr Azim, which terrified her. Before they had left, he'd shown her a gun. He said, 'If you make things difficult for us, you will be sacrificed.'

It was six o'clock now, not cold but dull and damp with all light bleached from the sky.

Azim rattled off some orders to the rickshaw driver, who looked cowed and terrified himself, then he turned to her.

'So where does he live?'

'I think it's near the Jain Temple.' She was determined not to stammer. 'Please be patient with me. I've only been there twice.'

He glanced at her sharply and she heard him sigh. He took out his gun, laid it on his lap, and then covered it with the flap of his kameez.

The grim street they were passing through was empty, apart from a mother kneeling on the steps, with two little girls who were drawing what looked like Diwali patterns on their doorstep.

They crossed into Main Street where the evening sky was mottled and bruised-looking. To their right, in the middle of a row of dilapidated houses, she saw a small temple lit up like a fabulous jewellery box with hundreds of small candles around the shrine.

'Where is he?' he said to her suddenly.

'I'm not sure yet,' she said. 'Could you tell me where we are?'

'Fruit market is there,' he said. He pointed towards the vast sprawling building, almost unrecognisable tonight under its weight of lights and tinsel. A small crowd forcing a lurid-looking papier-mâché goddess above their heads was slowing them down and making Azim angry.

'I need to find Glover tonight,' he said. 'I've been told he might leave India tomorrow on a ship.'

'Here's what I remember,' she said. 'The two times I went to his flat I took a short cut across the market and then—I'm sorry.' She shook her head. 'I'm going to have to see it again.' She saw him freeze momentarily while he thought, then he shrugged.

'I shall be walking right behind you,' he said. 'If you try to run away, I will shoot you, not now but later and nobody will ever know what happened to you. Do you understand?'

'I understand.'

He barked at the rickshaw driver. The little carriage stopped.

'Get out,' he said.

He prodded her in the back and they walked through the doors and into the market where she was deafened by the sound of bleating sheep and goats and the screech of caged birds. She was starting to panic. The taste of metal in her mouth was fear. She scanned what felt like a solid wall of sounds and faces with no plan yet apart from escape.

Two young girls were walking very slowly ahead of her. They were dressed up to the nines in their saris and jewellery and nattering happily to each other. Azim couldn't see them; he was prodding her in the spine with his gun. '*Jaldi, jaldi*,' he said.

'I can't go any faster,' she said.

Now she could see the vast door at the end of the market open underneath rafters where pigeons sat. Beside the door were the caged birds: each cage was lit tonight with Diwali lights.

Outside the door, she saw another crowd, moving swiftly in the direction of another teetering *pandal* surrounded by musicians. In the crush of the fruit market, she felt the strong tug of the crowd, like an undertow, then the hardness of his gun in her back warning her not to run, but she had no choice now and nor did he. She heard someone laugh and then a scream. The smell of smoke in the air, someone else shouting, '*Jaldi!*' and then she fell, and a scuffed shoe kicked her hard in the teeth. A jarring pain in the side of her head, thousands and thousands of feet thundered through her brain, then nothing.

She woke up with the taste of old fruit in her mouth and then thought all her teeth must have been kicked in because of the pulpy feeling round her lips. She was lying on a lumpy mattress. When she touched her head it was bandaged and she had the most excruciating pain in the roots of her teeth as though they'd all been pulled. Her eyes flickered open, but the light hurt too much. A young Indian woman with a calm, gentle face was bathing her forehead.

'*Mi kuthe ahe?*' Where am I? she asked. When her eyes flickered open again she saw a slatted roof, a dirty window. She was in a slum or *chawl*.

'*Kai zala?*' What happened? she said.

'You were knocked and kicked,' the woman demonstrated. 'Don't worry,' she added in Marathi, 'you're all right now, they are coming to take you home.'

*Coming to take you home. Home soon, home soon. Daisy will come.*

She opened her eyes again. When she touched the side of her head, she felt the stickiness of old blood through the bandage. The pain in the nerve endings of her teeth was still excruciating, but when she checked gingerly with her tongue, her teeth were still there.

From behind her bandage, she heard a door open, voices, the creak of wooden floorboards.

'Daisy?' she said.

Nobody answered. When she tried to sit up, she felt a hand close round her wrist.

'It's Guy,' he said.

'Guy,' she whispered, 'why are you here?'

'I don't know. Some stupid person in the market found you knocked out. They said an English girl was hurt. I wanted to help, but now I don't—you're frightening me like that.'

'Calm down.' Her mouth felt as if it was packed with cotton wool. 'All you need to do is to go to the home and get Daisy Barker; she'll help me.'

'I can't, they'll catch me. I'm in too much trouble myself.'

'Guy, please, that's all you have to do.'

'I'm leaving tomorrow. Ask someone else to do it.'

He was drumming the pads of his fingers on a tabletop and humming in the way he had on the ship when he felt most agitated.

'Guy, why did all this happen to me? What did you do?'

'I wanted to get you out of the home,' he whispered at last. 'It was bad for you there.'

'There were other things too,' she said.

'I can't remember them, they've all got muddled. Mr Azim was trying to hurt me—he was frightening me.'

She felt his mouth draw close to her. 'Listen,' he whispered. She felt his hand brush her temples. 'You're *my* mother. I chose you.'

'No! Guy, no! I'm not her!'

'Yes.' She heard the slow exhalation of his breath. 'You saw that school. They hung me out of a window there on sheets. My other mother chose that school; she wanted me to stay there. I want to kill her,' he said calmly. 'She jams up my wireless.'

'Guy, *listen* to me. This isn't right.'

'I loved you.' He was panting and she was frightened.

'Listen to me,' she said. 'I know exactly what you've got to do.'

'Um.' He'd turned his back on her; his shoulders were slumped. He clicked an invisible switch behind his ear. 'What?'

'I know you've been worrying about a lot of things for a very long time,' she said. 'And you need to stop for a bit, to rest.'

'I can't,' he said. 'They're after me, and you. That's why I have to go back to England again.'

'All you have to do is go back to the home; tell them where we are.'

'I can't,' he said in a muffled voice. 'They'll find me and hurt me.'

'Well, find someone to take a message there,' she said with her last ounce of strength. 'Tell them to come and get Viva, Guy, then, if you like, you can come back with us and we'll find people who can look after you until you're better again too.'

He got up and walked around the room hugging himself. 'There are too many people on my airwaves,' he said. 'My father's looking for me too. He's angry as well. He gave me a thrashing after I got off the ship; he said I was rude to him.'

'Here.' She leant forward and turned off his invisible switch. 'Turn them off if you don't want them. Nobody else can control you. They can say things, they can ask you to do things, but you can say yes or no. All I'm asking is for you to let me help you. I won't let you down.'

'Everyone lets me down. No one likes me.'

'I know you think that, but it's not true and there comes a point in your life when you can't go on getting so angry with other people.' He was listening to her intently, but he looked perfectly blank.

'People will love you if you let them,' she continued.

'You can't,' he said. 'I've asked you.'

There was a silence. 'I think we could be friends,' she said at last.

'And walk into the sunset,' he sneered. 'Holding hands.'

'No, don't be silly. What I mean is, I'll listen to you. I think you're tired of running and you need some rest.'

She prayed to God she had hit some sort of target, but the effort of talking had worn her out. Her head slipped down the pillow and she was fast asleep again before she heard his reply.

## St Bartholomew's, Amritsar, December 1929

Sometime before Christmas, Daisy wrote to Tor out of the blue saying that Viva had been hurt in an 'unfortunate accident' during the Diwali celebrations but was well enough to travel and was there the slightest chance that Viva could come and stay during the Christmas holidays? She needed a change of scene, she said. All would be explained when Viva saw her.

Tor was upset to hear that Viva had been hurt, but excited at the thought of seeing her again. An idea gradually snowballed in her mind: if Viva was coming for Christmas, why not Rose and Jack too? She nervously broached the idea to Toby.

'Why are you sounding so Tiny Tim about it?' he'd said, surprised. 'There's tons of extra rooms in the school if our house gets too small.'

'Our house', how she loved to hear him say the words. It still made her heart swoop with pity and love to remember that when she'd first seen the bungalow, Toby's bedroom was the only properly lived-in room. She'd looked at its iron bed, the thin, green chenille bedspread, mosquito net and framed insects on the wall, and thought it looked like the room of a boy left behind for the holidays in a deserted school.

Tor, in an enormous rush of energy, had set about redecorating the three-bedroomed bungalow with the help of two new servants: Jai and Benarsi, bright good-looking boys from the local town who adored Toby because he spoke fluent Hindi and made them laugh.

Then to her astonishment, her mother had sent a cheque for fifty pounds, stipulating that it must be spent on furnishings. The money came in handy—Toby was only teaching part-time at the school this term while he finished his book, *The Birds and Wildlife of Gujarat*. In a fever of excitement they'd gone out and bought their first double bed, then a bedspread from the local bazaar embroidered with birds and flowers. A new sisal rug went on the floor. Next, Tor had supervised whitewashing, carpentry and floor scrubbing.

The garden had been cleared and replanted. Their little sitting room had fresh coir matting, an old sofa and two cane chairs. She had a proper table at last for her gramophone, and Toby had spent five nights designing and putting up shelves for his books and her records.

'So, I really can ask them?'

'Last Christmas,' he said melodramatically, 'was so awful I almost went home and drank arsenic.' He'd spent it in the club in Rawalpindi, drinking port in a paper hat with a drunken tea planter and a missionary. 'I can't believe how my life has changed,' he added quietly. That was one of the best things about being with Toby: so silly and playful one moment, and in the next, so able to say what mattered most.

Anyway, Rose had written back almost immediately to say she'd love to come and that Jack—whose regiment was off doing something frightening in the mountains—would try to come, at least for a day or two. But would it be too stinking fish of her to stay for longer? She was dying for Tor to get to know Freddie.

**I**n early December, Tor told Toby to stop being a boring swot and have a what-the-hell day with her. For the past three weeks, he'd been working feverishly on his book trying to get it finished before Christmas.

The following morning, they moved Toby's telescopes and bird books, his sitar and his piles of wildlife photographs from the guest room into the main school. Toby went into the woods to look for a Christmas tree. He came back with a baby monkey puzzle tree, which he planted in a pot. He put on some Beethoven and they painted the tree's tips with gold, then they turned off the lights and danced together through the moonbeams that fell through the windows of their sitting room.

Tor so hoped that when Viva and Rose came to stay they would see Toby like this: silly and full of life, and incredibly clever too—he'd read all kinds of books. Naturally they were suspicious of him. He'd proposed so quickly they probably imagined that he was either desperate or criminal or unappealingly overconfident. He was none of these things. He could be terribly shy and awkward with people he didn't know. He had been with her at first.

The day after their registry office wedding in Bombay, her mood of reckless euphoria had sunk like a blancmange. They'd driven north in his battered Talbot, and he'd talked for what seemed like hours in a monotonous drone about shops and clothes. He told her later his mother had once said the way to a woman's heart was to take an interest in her, so he had at least tried. But on that day, Tor had sat in growing panic. The man was a crashing bore! She'd made the worst mistake of her life. On and on the car had chugged, farther and farther away from Bombay, through miles of desert and dun-coloured plains, until it got too hot to talk, and she drifted off to sleep.

When she woke up and saw the gold band on her finger, she thought she should at least ask him to explain in some detail what he did. He'd perked up immediately. He had already told her that he taught history and science at St Bart's but then he said that he was also writing his life's work, a book on the thousands of extraordinary birds there were in India, many of them sacred. He'd then glanced sideways at her across the car and asked if she'd mind if he told her a secret.

'Not a bit,' she'd said, glad things were loosening up between them.

Then he told her how one morning he'd been walking across the school playing grounds when he'd found a small bantam's egg lying on its own in the grass. It had lost its mother, so for the next six weeks he'd held the egg under his arm until it had hatched. He'd felt the shell crack, the fluffy little head emerge. 'So now I know what it feels like to have a baby,' he'd said softly and she'd glanced at him in the darkening car.

'Gosh,' she'd said, 'how sweet of you.' But really she was thinking, *What if he turns out to be barking as well?* 'What a marvellous story,' she'd added, thinking she sounded exactly like her mother.

On that night, she'd tried to tell herself that she must think of this marriage as a more or less practical arrangement: if you didn't expect too much, how badly wrong could it go?

Now it pained her to remember she had ever thought of him in such a cold and practical way. The bantam story, so typical of his kindness, melted her heart. She also loved the way his hair felt silky when she ran her hands through it in the mornings. The way he went to sleep with his arms round her. His jokes, the cups of tea he brought her in the morning with some special treat to eat. The way he pursued his work with energy and passion, the way he read to her at nights: Conrad, Dickens, T. S. Eliot—all the books she'd once thought she was far too dim for.

It was her love for Toby that she was really celebrating this Christmas, for he was the greatest gift of her life so far. She so hoped the girls would like him too.

Mind you, she still hoped he wouldn't tell the bird-under-the-arm story too early on in his acquaintance with Viva and Rose. It did take time to get to know a person.

# Chapter 10

AFTER HER PARENTS' DEATH, Viva had often spent Christmas in the houses of people she barely knew: cousins, and once, when nobody else could be found, with her school's head gardener, whose childless wife had made it clear, during a sullen Christmas lunch, that she expected to be paid for the privilege of serving her turkey.

So when Tor's invitation came—in the form of a lurid cardboard elephant on which she had written, 'Christmas at Amritsar—do come!'—her immediate response was to say no. She loathed Christmas with a passion, and even without Christmas, she was feeling awful.

Her escape from Mr Azim had left her with a cut eye that needed five stitches, a cracked rib, headaches and insomnia. It had shaken her confidence profoundly. She'd been interviewed at length by Sergeant Barker, an irritable Scot who'd implied that if she, a single woman, chose to live in one of the less salubrious suburbs of Bombay, she'd had it coming to her and was lucky not to have been killed.

But at least she and Daisy had managed to find Guy a room at a Bombay rest home. Dr Ratcliffe, the gentle, gaunt-looking man who ran the home, had once been a victim of mustard gas and was both sympathetic and successful with patients with nervous disorders. He too was of the opinion that Guy appeared to be suffering from a kind of schizophrenia.

Guy was put in a tranquil sunlit room on the edge of a courtyard. They'd put him on a regime of nourishing foods and exercise. His room overlooked a small garden in which Guy enjoyed working.

When she was well enough, she went to see him. They sat together in the courtyard drinking lemonade, and the last time she'd visited, he'd actually said, 'I'm sorry I hurt you. I didn't mean to.' It was the calmest she'd ever seen him, the most happy and in control.

But four days after that, Guy's father had arrived from Assam. He came to the home especially to tell Daisy and Viva that he didn't hold with trick cyclists. He said he'd brought a one-way ticket for Guy to get back to England again. An old pal of his was in the army there and they felt sure he would find a place for him in his regiment. In spite of everything that had happened, when Guy, looking pale and shaken, had come to see her for the last time, she'd felt the old tug of guilt and responsibility and a kind of quiet anguish that he was being thrown to the wolves again.

Guy had asked Dr Ratcliffe to drive him over to the children's home especially so he could say goodbye. They'd been sitting on a bench outside Daisy's office when he'd suddenly put his arms round her and buried his head in the side of her neck like a child.

'I don't want to go,' he'd said. 'Can't you do something?'

'No,' she'd said, and realised, finally, that this was true. She wasn't his mother or his guardian. Guy was outside of her control. There was nothing she could do to mend his life.

He'd hugged her again. 'You're beautiful,' were his last words to her. 'I'd like to marry you one day.'

The incongruity of this had made her head reel.

**W**hen the train arrived in Amritsar two weeks before Christmas, Viva was relieved to see Tor was on her own. She didn't feel up to meeting anybody new.

'Viva!' Tor hugged her hard then looked under her hat.

'Good heavens!' she said. 'Your eye! What happened?'

'Oh, nothing, *nothing* really.' Viva had dreaded this. Her eye still felt like a badge of shame and, although she still lived in fear of Azim, she tried her best to gloss over the incident. 'I had a little adventure, then a fall. It looks far worse than it is. I'll tell you all about it over supper.'

**T**or drove them back to the school. Half an hour later, she stopped near a gate with a huge coat of arms above it.

'This is it,' she said. 'Home sweet home.'

They drove up a short drive, towards the flamboyant main school building, all flourishing carvings and mini-turrets, and a properly green front lawn. Behind them was a sign saying, 'St Bartholomew's College for the Sons of Gentlemen and Maharajahs, aged seven to fourteen.'

'Not our house, so don't get too excited,' Tor said gaily.

The car bumped along a gravel path beside a cricket pitch.

'Now,' Tor glanced at her as they headed towards a circle of trees beyond the cricket pitch, 'close your eyes, we're getting warm.'

It still hurt Viva to close her eyes. The doctor said she'd been lucky not to have lost her sight.

'Now!' Tor took her hand and squeezed it hard. 'Open.'

Viva heard herself laugh out loud for the first time in a long time.

She'd stepped into a child's fairy tale. There was a fat Father Christmas sitting on the chimney; every window twinkled with candles; icicles made of string hung from the bougainvillea pots. Above the door, in silver letters a foot high, a sign said, 'Happy Christmas.'

'We've put them up miles too early,' Tor said, 'but we couldn't wait.'

'It's wonderful, Tor,' Viva laughed. 'What genius lives here?'

'Well, genii actually—if that's the plural.' Toby had appeared carrying glasses, champagne and cheese straws.

'Hello, friend of Tor's,' he said awkwardly.

Viva thought how young he looked—tousled hair, slightly inky fingers, a shirt tail that hadn't quite been tucked in—and innocent: she'd imagined he'd be smoother and far more devious-looking.

'Darling.' Tor put her arm round his waist. 'Darling, this is my friend Viva. She's going to tell us about her eye later, so don't ask now.'

'Greetings, Viva.' He shook her hand warmly. 'How about a glass of champagne?'

'I'd love one,' she said.

'Oh drat!' When he poured the bubbles straight over the glass, Viva thought, *He's as nervous as I am.*

When they'd given her a new glass, she took a deep breath, then a sip. *See!* she addressed the part of her that was always frightened. See—there were already three things to celebrate: that she'd travelled here on her own; that Toby didn't look like an obvious drunk or wife beater; that nobody had yet mentioned Frank, whom she didn't want to talk about. So, even though the whole thing was kicking off earlier than she would have chosen, let Christmas cheer commence. No whining, no brooding, no dreading, no looking backwards or forwards.

She raised her glass towards Tor. 'Happy Christmas,' she said.

**W**hen Rose turned up the following day with four-month-old Freddie in her arms, Toby teased the girls for going gaga. But he was such a beautiful baby, with Rose's silver-blond hair, a perfect little chiselled dimple in his chin and intelligent blue eyes.

Even when he was only chuckling in his bath, or lolling around having his nappy changed, Freddie seemed to increase the emotional temperature of the house, as if he was a little fire burning away.

'Oh Lord,' Toby complained to the girls when he was at last allowed to hold him. 'The memsahib is going to want to be in foal right away now,' and then, just as Tor had feared, he launched into his story about keeping the egg under his arm and what that had meant to him.

'So what happened to your bird?' Viva enquired gently.

'Two months after it had hatched, I trod on it. I was running to get the post. Sorry, darling,' he said to Tor, 'didn't tell you that bit. I've only just been able to talk about it.' He was not joking.

'That's dreadful,' said Viva softly. 'You must have loved that bird.'

'You're right,' he said. 'I did love that bird.'

The sun was shedding a lavish apricot-coloured glow over the playing fields and the woods beyond where, from time to time, a flock of dark birds rose and wheeled around in the sky, settling in the tops of trees. A few seconds later, it was dark and a scattering of stars had appeared on the horizon. Toby came out onto the verandah and sat down beside Viva who had been watching the sunset.

'Are you all right there?' he said gently. 'I mean, is this a private think, or can anybody join in?'

'Not private at all,' she lied. 'It's so lovely to have the luxury of not racing around like a mad thing. Tor seems so . . . Well, I just wanted to say I've never seen Tor so happy.'

'Oh, I do hope so! I still can't quite believe it. I understand you had some doubts?' His grin in the dusk was mischievous.

Viva laughed, embarrassed. 'Well, I do admit—even by Indian standards it was pretty speedy.'

'I know,' he said. 'We took the most gigantic risk, but they're always the best, don't you think?'

'I don't know. I'm not very brave like that.'

'Oh, come on, Tor's been telling me about your work, your book. You sound very brave to me.'

A peal of laughter coming from the baby's room made them both look up. A few seconds later, Freddie appeared in Tor's arms flushed from his bath and smelling of soap and talcum powder. 'Say good night to Uncle Toby and Auntie Viva,' she said.

Viva kissed the baby's forehead. His skin smelt like new grass.

'Good night, Freddie darling,' she said. 'Sleep well.'

After Tor left the room, Viva felt cross with herself for starting to feel low again. If she was going to be the ghost at the wedding, she should at least have had the decency to stay in Bombay.

'You know, it's awfully good of you to have us all,' she said to Toby.

'The more the merrier as far as I'm concerned,' said Toby. 'Shame, though, that your doctor friend couldn't make it. Lahore's really no distance at all from here, and I would have liked to talk to him about blackwater fever. We lost a couple of boys to it here last year.'

'What doctor friend?' She stared at him. 'I didn't know he'd been invited.' She put down her drink. 'Who invited him?'

'Oh Lord,' he said. 'I've put my foot in it? What an idiot.'

'No, no, no, not at all,' she said with a lightness she did not feel. 'He was everybody's friend on the ship. I hardly think of him but . . .' She looked at her watch. 'I'm going to go to my room and freshen up—it's nearly supper time. I enjoyed our chat, thank you for it.'

**U**pstairs, she locked herself inside her room, and sat doubled up at the foot of her bed. So this was the end of it: he'd been asked; he didn't want to come. How much more clearly did she need to be told? And then she felt pain blooming inside her and there was nothing she could do about it. A winding kind of pain as if she'd been dealt a blow in the solar plexus. *This is the end of it*, she told herself again. *He'd been asked, he'd said no. Get this into your fat head*, she raged at herself, *and don't you dare cast a cloud over Christmas because of it.*

**O**ver supper, Toby, who said he was learning to carve and usually did it like an axe murderer, managed a decent job on a joint of roast beef. Jai came in and lit a flare path of oil lamps round the verandah, then they opened a special bottle of wine Rose had brought with her and they toasted each other.

The talk was jolly and open, and Viva did her best to join in.

Over pudding—a very good treacle tart—they had a conversation about the difference between a friend and the kind of chap you'd choose to go into the jungle with.

'I'd never choose you for the jungle,' Tor teased Toby. 'You'd be crawling around looking for the greater spotted titmouse or some such and we'd never get out. No, I'd take Viva with me.'

'Why me?' she wanted to know.

'You're brave and you don't go on about things. I mean, take this mysterious thing that happened to you in Bombay. If I'd had stitches in my eye, or been knocked out, I'd dine out on it for months.'

'Oh, these.' Viva touched the side of her eye. *Trapped.* 'Well . . . it was nothing really; well, it was *something* but not as bad as it will sound.'

She had rehearsed this moment on the train on her way here, but even her light-hearted version of her kidnapping, starring her as terrified maiden in red dress, Azim as pantomime villain, drew gasps of horror from them.

'But you could easily have been killed!' said Tor.

'Why didn't the police come?' said Rose.

'Well, they did. But you know how these things get swept under the carpet here,' she said.

'Not usually when they concern English people,' Toby said drily.

'Don't forget,' she reminded him, 'that the governor has warned us twice to think about closing the home, but no one can bring themselves to. It's a complicated situation.'

'But, Viva,' Tor suddenly turned to her, 'finish your story. What happened to that little rat, Guy?'

So she told him about Dr Ratcliffe and his home. How well he was doing there until he was whisked away.

'He's gone back to England now. It's the saddest thing. His father got him a commission in the army. Can you imagine anything he'll be less suited for? What do they see when they look at him?'

'We do not see things as they are, but as we are,' Toby said quietly. 'That's from the Talmud.'

'I've been guilty of that,' she told him.

'And, Viva,' Tor could be remarkably persistent when the mood took her, 'where will you move to if the home does have to close?'

'I don't know,' she said. 'I hadn't really thought about it. I—'

'Have one of these.' Toby pushed a box of chocolates in her direction. He seemed to be trying to come to her rescue. 'By the way, I've been meaning to ask you, whereabouts in India did your parents live? Wasn't there something about a trunk you're supposed to pick up?'

Thinking that she wouldn't notice, Tor put down her pudding spoon and mouthed 'No' to Toby. After a brief moment of panic he went on smoothly, 'When I was a boy we moved all the time too—my father was a scientist, but he worked for the Forestry Department in India for years, so I never really knew where I lived either. Quite fun in a way, but the only problem is'—Viva saw him glance at Tor as if to say, *How am I doing?*—'one's inner globe is always slightly spinning.'

'Mine isn't,' said Tor. She stood up and put her arms round him. 'I absolutely love it here.'

Viva watched them with hunger. How at Tor's touch he squeezed his eyes shut and laid his head against hers. She felt a wave of desolation sweep over her. She shouldn't have come; she wasn't ready yet.

'Viva,' Rose said, 'how would you feel if we asked Frank again, just for Christmas lunch? He was this very good-looking ship's doctor,' she explained to Toby. 'We were all very spoony on him.'

Viva felt a spurt of anger—how trivial she made it sound.

They looked at each other, and Viva swallowed.

'I'd rather you didn't,' she said. 'He's said no once.'

The following morning, Tor said that Viva and Rose should go for a ride on their own together.

Toby drew a map for them. The school, he said, had twenty acres of riding tracks, one of which led to a lake that was a lovely spot for a picnic. And an hour or so later, Viva and Rose were trotting between an avenue of poplar trees that led into a wood. Viva's pony, a grey Arab wearing a scarlet bridle, was delicate and frisky and made bug eyes at everything that moved: parrots, leaves, spots of sunlight on the path.

Ahead of them Viva saw a winding track that led up a short incline between misty trees. Rose said it was the perfect place for a gallop.

'Ready?'

'Ready.'

Rose disappeared in a cloud of dust.

When Viva let go of the reins, her pony took off like a rocket, fighting for its head. On and on they sped, the scrub whizzing by and then through a muddy track past cinnamon-scented trees; and then, when they halted at the top of the track, the ponies were slick with sweat, and they were laughing and far more relaxed with each other.

'Oh, what bliss!' Rose, cheeks flushed and with her blonde hair flowing loose, suddenly looked about twelve. 'What absolute and utter bliss.'

They could hear the burblings of the stream that followed the track. When they got to the stream, they let the horses drop their heads to suck up a few greedy mouthfuls.

'You look so much better, Viva,' Rose said.

'Do I?' Viva picked up her reins. 'I am fine,' she said. 'What about you?'

Rose gave her a strange look. 'Truth or flannel?'

'Truth.'

Rose said, 'I don't know where to start. So much has changed in this year. Coming here. India. Everything. I came without giving it a second's thought.'

'D'you think anything really prepares you for India?' Viva said. 'It's like a vast onion: every layer you unpeel shows you something else you didn't know about it, or yourself.'

'I'm not just talking about India,' Rose went on doggedly. 'I'm talking about getting married to Jack. It was so awful at first.'

Viva was so shocked her scalp prickled. She'd always assumed Rose was silent about Jack because she didn't want to gloat about her handsome husband in front of Tor.

'Absolutely ghastly,' Rose insisted. 'I felt so shy, so homesick, so completely out of my depth with him and everything.'

'Gosh,' said Viva after a while, hating this. 'How is it now?'

'Well,' Rose fiddled with her reins, 'some of it got better—at least the bedroom side of things—at first it seemed so *rude*.'

They burst out laughing and a partridge flung itself croaking out of the undergrowth.

'But it's better now?' Viva asked cautiously. 'You know, the other things.'

'No—well, only partly . . .' Rose was faltering. 'You see, it got worse.'

'How?'

Rose gave a deep sigh. 'Something happened. A horrid thing.' There was a long silence before Rose found her voice again. 'One night I went into the sitting room and Jack was sitting there reading a letter. He was weeping. When I asked him why, well, you know Jack, well, you don't really, but he's sometimes *hideously* honest.' Rose heaved a big sigh. 'He confessed straight away.'

'About what?'

'About his other woman.'

'Oh no.' Viva put her hand on Rose's arm. 'How horrible.'

'He didn't have to tell me; in some ways, I still think it might have been better if he hadn't. Even though it finished when he married me, all the time when we were on the ship he was seeing her. He said he'd found it hard to say goodbye. I was so shocked at first. I felt so far from home and so awful.'

'Was it somebody you knew?'

'No.' Rose took a deep shuddering breath. 'Her name is Sunita. She's Indian. She's a beautiful, educated Bombay girl. When I asked him if he loved her, he said he felt immensely grateful to her, that she'd taught him so much, and that she was a fine person. In other words, he loved her.'

'Oh, Rose, what a thing.'

'It was the worst thing ever and I was too proud to tell anyone.'

'So what did you do?'

'Well, I've really never felt so mis. I felt I loathed him for a while. One of the most infuriating things was the way he apologised to me; it was so stiff.' Rose did his voice. '"Look, sorry, Rose, but men are men and these things happen." And then he went all sulky as if somehow this was my fault. Oh, I was livid. It wasn't that I wanted him to grovel, but I was so hurt and the worst thing was that I had actually started to really love him. Not like in books, or in plays, but small things: like having his arm round me in bed and caring about what he ate.'

When they reached the lake, three herons flew away with a light flapping of wings.

'I hope you don't mind me telling you all this.' Rose looked pale as they sat down together on the rug.

'I think you've been very brave,' Viva said. She could never talk about herself out loud like that.

'There was nothing a bit brave about staying.' Rose took off her helmet and shook out her hair. 'What were my alternatives? To go back to Hampshire, divorced and expecting a baby? It would have broken their hearts, and besides, I'd been telling them in letters what a whale of a time we were having here. So much has gone wrong for my mother since the war, my brother dying and then Daddy being so ill, I feel she needs things to go well for me.' Rose closed her eyes in pain. 'Jack didn't mean to be cruel.'

'Does he talk about her?'

'No, well, yes, but only once when I insisted on it. He could think of nothing bad to say about her. I rather admired him for it. I only needed to look at his face to know he still loved her, maybe still does.'

Viva looked at her in astonishment. Rose was so fair.

'I felt horribly jealous—if it hadn't been for Freddie, I can't say what would have happened. The birth was awful. It happened at home by mistake and we were miles away from hospital. Jack came back that night, and when he saw me from the door with Fred in my arms, he broke down and cried. He said he was sorry and that he would protect us until his last. It was such a funny old-fashioned thing to say but it meant so much—but by then, I didn't need it. Everything had changed again. He got into bed and put his arms round me, and Fred lay on top of us, and when I looked outside and saw, I don't know, how huge the world was—the moon, stars—I knew I'd never felt more in my life. I can't even properly put it into words. I also knew that if I left him, I would leave half of me behind.'

After lunch, Rose fell asleep on the rug; her confession seemed to have exhausted her. Viva went to check on the horses, who were tethered and munching grass, then she went back and lay beside Rose, thinking about how Rose had told her own story simply and from the heart. How Rose had assumed Viva must know about this catastrophe if they were to be properly close. *And the truth shall make you whole.* But could you know another person only to the extent that they were prepared to show their true selves to you? That thought gathered at the edge of Viva's mind like a cloud.

She could easily, at that moment, have told Rose about what had happened at Ooty, about Frank, and Guy. Rose, who'd proved rather unshockable, would have understood, and maybe have some sensible advice for her. But her door seemed jammed—opening it was too frightening—there might be a howling wasteland beyond.

A more painful thought followed: that all the energy Rose had spent on trying and, by all accounts, succeeding in loving a flawed man, Viva spent in not caring, on a kind of willed heartlessness. She did it—at least this was her excuse—so she could work and survive. Who was right? She was trying to think of it in purely abstract terms when Frank's smile—his dimples, the sudden sweetness of it—made her squeeze her eyes tightly shut. She mustn't think of him again like that. Her chance had gone. It was over.

**W**hen Rose woke up, Viva was lying next to her with her eyes open.

'What are you thinking, Viva?' she said.

'That we should ride home soon.'

Rose suddenly felt furious with her. Both she and Tor had been shocked at how ill Viva looked. It wasn't just the bruised eyes, both of them had agreed; all her fire seemed to have gone.

'Say something to her while you're riding,' Tor had said. 'I would but I'll only put my foot in it, and you know how prickly she can be.'

So Rose had tried, and because Viva was a good listener, she'd said far more than she'd meant to. Now she felt angry and stupid, because Viva had just stood up and was smiling at her in a superior, chaperone-ish way, as if she felt sorry for her.

She took a couple of deep breaths. 'So aren't you going to say anything?' The words were out before she thought of them.

'About what?'

'About yourself?'

'But I thought we were talking about you, Rose. I'm so sorry.'

'You don't understand, do you?'

'I don't know what you're talking about, Rose.'

'About saying things. You know, friendship. I tell you something that's important to me, then you say something about you that's important to you. It's called letting your guard down.' Rose was shocked to hear herself practically shouting.

'Rose!' Viva moved away from her so quickly she knocked over the hip flask. 'I do tell you things. Sometimes.'

'Oh, rubbish,' shouted Rose. 'Absolute rubbish.'

'This is not a game of tennis,' Viva roared. 'Why do I have to confide in you just because you have in me?'

'Well, drop it then, Viva,' Rose bellowed back. She couldn't stop herself now. 'Just drop it. I'll overlook the fact that you've lost about a stone in weight; that you look absolutely done in; that someone tried to murder you and you don't want to talk about it; and that Frank, who is clearly mad about you, has been sent away with no reason. Let's just talk about ponies and Christmas pudding. I'll pretend not to notice any of that—it's just silly little Rose who has all the problems and makes all the mistakes, and Viva, the magnificent, is still divinely in control.'

'How dare you say that.' Viva's fists were balled. 'What do you want me to say?'

'Well, you could start with Frank. Most friends would at least tell each other what happened.'

'Nothing happened,' said Viva. 'We had a brief whatever it was, but I needed to work, to finish my book, to try and earn my own living. I don't have a mummy and daddy in the background to help me along.'

'No, you don't,' Rose admitted. 'But that doesn't mean you can tell lies about yourself.'

'What lies?' Viva's voice was cold.

'About how you feel.'

'Don't you dare judge me.' Viva's eyes had gone as black as coals.

'I'm not trying to judge you, I'm trying to be your friend. Viva, please,' she touched her gently, 'sit down.'

Viva sat down at the far end of the rug and glared towards the lake.

'Look,' Rose tried again after a long silence, 'it's absolutely none of our beeswax, but we do care. We were with you in Ooty—we saw you with Frank, you seemed mad about each other.'

'All right, if it makes you feel any better, I made a bloody great mess of the whole thing. Now do you feel better?'

'No, of course I don't,' Rose said quietly. 'That's mean.'

Viva stood up suddenly. 'I'm sorry. But I'm hopeless at this sort of thing. Thank you for trying, really, but I think we should go home now.'

'Say something, Viva,' Rose pleaded.

'I can't. There's nothing really to tell; it's all such a muddle in my mind.' Viva's sigh sounded like a dry sob from deep inside her. There was another long silence.

'All right.' Viva had turned her back to her and her voice was muffled. 'Do you remember the night Frank came to Ooty? After you went
to bed, he came to my room. He stayed the night. Are you shocked?'

'Of course not. Things happen in India that are different from home,
and besides, it was so blindingly obvious!'

'Was it?' Viva looked up reluctantly.

'Yes, it was. You both looked so different, sort of spellbound.
I remember feeling jealous, thinking that's the way I hoped I'd feel on
my honeymoon.'

'I didn't feel spellbound, I felt, well, it was so confusing.'

'But,' Rose was perplexed, 'forgive me, but did something go wrong?'

'No.' Viva's voice was almost inaudible. 'That part was wonderful.'
She gave a soft squeak of pain.

'So you sent him away because it was wonderful.'

'I felt so guilty—because he'd come to warn me that Guy might have
been killed in the riots. I was sure he was dead.'

'It wasn't your fault that Guy did what he did.'

'Look, Rose.' Viva's face was white. 'I said I didn't want to talk about
it and I don't, so can I stop?' She stomped towards the horses. 'I really
do want to go home now,' she said.

Tor was standing in the kitchen when Viva walked into the house. She
shut the door so hard that a wreath fell onto the verandah. She heard
her shoes click up the corridor, then the door to her bedroom close.

Rose was hanging up her riding hat in the corridor and looking
towards the closed door.

'Rose, what happened?' said Tor. Her heart sank.

'Disaster,' whispered Rose. 'She's absolutely livid. She really does hate
talking about things.'

'Shall I go?' Tor mouthed. 'I could take her a cup of tea.'

'I'd leave her for a bit,' said Rose. 'I really do think she wants to be on
her own. Is it all right if I give Freddie a bath?' she said loud enough for
Viva to overhear.

Tor felt her spirits plummet. While the girls had been out riding, Jack
had telephoned to say he was back temporarily in Peshawar, but it was
looking unlikely that he would make it for Christmas. He'd started to
explain but the line had sounded like a forest fire. Rose would be upset.
Viva was hardly the life and soul, and with eight days to go before
Christmas, Tor envisaged quiet meals with herself overdoing it as usual.

These gloomy thoughts were interrupted by bird-like chirrupings coming from the bathroom, where Freddie was in the old zinc bath.

'Freddo, darling, who's a pretty baby boy,' Rose crooned lapping water up his fat, creased little legs. The baby gave a reckless, gummy smile, then kicked his legs out.

Tor joined Rose in the bathroom. 'Do you think Viva's going to be all right?' she asked Rose. How nice it was, she reflected, rolling up her sleeves and kneeling on the other side of the bath, to have at least one jolly person in the house.

'I hope so,' whispered Rose. 'But she is infuriating sometimes. I mean, we did talk about Frank a bit, but it really was like pulling teeth, and then she got—well, you saw her stamp in.'

'So what to do?' Tor hissed back. 'It'll be so awful if nobody speaks over Christmas.'

'That's unlikely,' said Rose. 'If you put that towel on your knee, I'll pass him to you. Careful, he's slippery . . . Wheeee!'

The dripping baby was held up in the air and passed from friend to friend, landing up on Tor's knee.

'You are a *burra* baby,' Tor told him, kissing his toes, 'and a fine horseman.' She clicked her tongue and bounced him up and down on her lap. 'This is the way the ladies ride, clip-clop, clip-clop, clip-clop.' When she bent down to kiss him again, he shot a jet of urine into her eye.

And suddenly they were in hysterics, doubled up and shrieking breathlessly. While they were laughing, Viva walked into the room and sat down on the cork-covered stool beside the bath.

'This sounds fun,' she said.

'It is,' Tor choked. She put a towel on Viva's lap and passed the baby to her. 'That child has a lethal aim. He just pee-peed into my eye.'

Viva smiled and played with his fingers for a while. She looked as if she wanted to laugh but was too worn out.

'Tor,' she said at last, 'how far is Frank's hospital from here?'

Tor beamed, she couldn't help herself. 'Oh, it's nothing, absolutely nothing—half an hour, maybe three-quarters at the most.'

'Well . . . Toby's been telling me about his last Christmas at the club; it sounded horrible—of course Frank may have other plans by now, but I don't think it would do any harm to go over and wish him a happy Christmas—even if he can't come. What do you think?' She looked at Rose and then at Tor. She was trembling.

Tor walked over to Viva and kissed her gently on the head. 'I think it's a wonderful idea,' she said.

# Chapter 11

THEY LEFT FOR LAHORE the following day, Tor at the wheel of Toby's Talbot, Rose with the map on her knee beside her, Viva in the back seat.

The car was too noisy for Viva to join in the hum of conversation, a relief since the idea of arriving unannounced at Frank's suddenly seemed completely preposterous.

'Viva,' Tor flung over her shoulder, 'when we get to Lahore, do you want us to stay with you or shove off? Moral support and all that.'

'No,' said Viva quickly. 'Don't stay.' She couldn't bear the thought of anyone watching this debacle. 'Come and fetch me at four o'clock; that should be plenty of time. I'll just walk round if he isn't there,' she added. 'It'll be fun. And of course, it's quite likely he's had a lot of invitations for Christmas by now,' she said. 'But at least we'll have asked him.'

She saw Tor glance at Rose, then shake her head very slightly.

They'd reached the outskirts of Lahore, a flat city dominated by one high hill. It took half an hour and lots of frantic hootings on Tor's behalf to force their way through the narrow teeming streets, then all of a sudden they were clear of the bazaar area and lurching up the drive towards a grandly dilapidated mongrel of a building.

'This is it.' Tor's foot pressed the brake. 'We're here: St Patrick's Hospital, home of Frank.'

Inside the hospital, a uniformed man with an enormous waxed moustache was sitting at a desk cordoned off by a length of rope. Viva's shoes clicked down the marble floor towards him. When she stood in front of his desk, he stopped writing in his appointment book and looked at her.

'How may I assist, madam? I am supervisor here.'

'I'm looking for a Dr Frank Steadman,' she told him.

His face was a sudden ballet of smiles and dimples. 'Please sign here, memsahib,' he said.

He produced a form, thudded it with stamps, shot out an order to a boy, who had appeared at her side. 'Take Madam Memsahib to Dr Steadman's room,' he said. 'Quick sticks.'

'**F**rank.' She knocked gently. 'Frank, it's me. Can I please come in?'

The door opened; he stood there half-asleep, butterscotch-coloured hair sticking up like a child's. He blinked a few times. He was wearing blue striped pyjamas; his feet were bare.

'Viva?' He was scowling at her. 'You'd better come in,' he said coldly.

When he'd closed the door behind them, he looked at her and said, 'So why are you here?'

She forced herself to stand tall. 'I was hoping we could talk for a bit.'

'I'd like to get dressed first.'

He put a pair of trousers over his pyjamas; she looked away.

His room was anonymous, an exile's room. The wardrobe behind his head had two large suitcases on top of it covered in P&O labels.

He lit a lamp, pushed a chair towards her.

'Why are you here?' he said in the same flat voice.

She took a deep breath. Now he was sitting opposite her and she could see his face properly: his skin, his hair, his full mouth. She felt such a wave of emotion she was almost in tears before she began.

'Would a glass of water be out of the question?' she said at last.

'Of course,' he said in a polite voice. 'Some brandy in it?'

'Yes, please.'

He produced two glasses, swearing softly when he spilt some on his desk.

'What's wrong with your eye?' he said when he sat down.

'I had a fall,' she said. 'In Bombay, in the market, I hit my head on the kerb. I'm much better now.'

He leant towards her. He ran his finger along the length of her eyebrow, and looked at her.

'Daisy told me you were abducted,' he said.

'She did?' She could feel herself burning with shame.

'She was petrified,' he said. 'She thought you were dead and that's why she contacted me.' When he looked up, his face was full of a quiet, confused pain. 'You could easily have died. I sent two letters to the home, and I didn't hear from you or from Daisy for that matter. After that, I didn't want to know. Look,' he said angrily, 'I've stopped thinking like that. I don't want to any more. I don't even know why you're here.'

She heard herself babbling. 'I didn't get the letters, I swear. They were all intercepted; everything's such a mess there now. The home is in a shambles—Daisy's been told to close the whole thing down,' and suddenly to her disgust her cheeks were wet with tears.

He said nothing for a while, then, 'Did you finish the book?'

'No,' she said. 'Most of the typed pages were destroyed. Oh, I've got the notebooks, but I don't think I could do it again. So there we are. I'm sorry if I gave you a shock.'

It was the first time she'd told anyone about the book; most of the manuscript pages had been either torn or defaced while she was at Azim's. They'd been waiting for her in her cupboard when she returned. A terrible silence fell between them.

'I'm staying at Tor's house near Amritsar,' she said at last. 'I don't know how much of this you know, but Tor got married, to a man called Toby. Rose is there with her new baby. They asked me to persuade you to come for Christmas.'

'I know,' he said. 'Tor was the one who told me you were all right.' The muscle in his cheek had started to work again. 'She's already asked me; I've said no.'

She felt a crushing sadness all over again. *I've lost him*, she thought, *and it's all my fault*.

'I don't blame you,' she said.

'I couldn't bear the thought of it. So!' He tried to smile, then looked at his watch as though he couldn't wait for her to leave.

There was so much pain in the room, such a weight of things that could not be said, that she stood up and wrapped her arms round herself.

'Is there anything I could say that might help you change your mind?' she said. 'There's still time.'

'No,' he said. 'I don't think there is. You see, I don't like people who pretend.'

Viva felt fear under her ribs. 'I wasn't pretending.'

'Ah, well, all better now,' he said drily.

'All right. Look,' she was almost shouting, 'I'm sorry. Does that make you feel any better?'

'No,' he said, so sadly she knew he wasn't trying to be unkind. 'Funnily enough, it doesn't.'

She took his hand. 'Look, I *was* dishonest about Ooty. It frightened me. Can't you understand?'

'No.' He shook his head.

When she looked up, she noticed he'd grown thinner in the past few months. There were the beginnings of lines around his mouth. *I've done this to him*, she thought. *I've made him look older and more wary*. She knew that if she didn't make a stand now, it would soon be too late.

'Please come for Christmas, Frank,' she said. 'I can't say everything to you all at once.'

He got up and rested his head on the bars of the windows.

'No,' he said. 'I can't change everything on a whim again.'

She'd passed on her hurt to him. She saw it in the way he held himself, by the look in his eyes. She'd never seen it quite so clearly before.

'Frank,' she took a deep breath and decided to jump, 'I'm not using any of this as an excuse, I couldn't, that would be disgusting of me, but do you remember on the ship when I told you my family had died in a car crash? That's not true. They all died separately.' She gripped the arms of the chair to stop herself shaking.

'My sister died of a burst appendix. If we'd been closer to a hospital she would have been all right. She was thirteen months older than me.'

'Viva,' there was an edge of anger in his voice again, 'you should have told me. I would have understood.'

'I couldn't.'

'I don't think you can have any idea how closed off you can be. It's like a moat appears around you. But go on, your father.' He was listening intently. 'Tell me now.'

She took another deep breath. 'My father was killed shortly after; he was found with his throat slit on a railway track near Cawnpore with seven of the men he was working with. They think bandits killed him.'

'Oh God. What an awful thing.'

'It was. The worst thing possible. I loved him so much. He was a brilliant man and he tried so hard to be a good father to me.' She looked at him wildly. 'The awful thing is, I can't properly remember now what he sounded like, or what he looked like. If Josie hadn't died we could have reminded each other, but the memories are all fading. I hate that.'

'But what about your mother?'

'No, no, she died a year later.' She squeezed her eyes shut. 'Someone said of a broken heart—is that really a medical possibility?' She tried to smile but he didn't smile back. 'And anyway, we were never really close,' she continued. 'And I can't really remember why. Shortly after my father's death, she took me down to the railway station in Simla and put me on a train back to my boarding school in England. I don't know why she didn't want me with her. I never saw her again.'

'You should have said this before.'

'I couldn't.'

'Why not?'

She felt exhausted. 'I don't know—partly it's because I can't bear people feeling sorry for me.'

'Did you think I made love to you because I felt sorry for you?'

'No.' She could hardly speak. When she looked up at him he had turned away again.

'Please come for Christmas,' she said. 'We all want you to come.'

'No,' he said. 'I'm glad you felt you could tell me, but I can't.'

They sat in silence for a while.

'Look,' he said at last, 'when you left, I had to rethink everything.'

'I—' She started to speak but he put his hand over her mouth then took it away again as if she was on fire.

'Don't say anything,' he said. 'Let me finish. What happened that night at Ooty didn't surprise me. I knew it would happen and I thought you knew it, but afterwards you made me feel, you made me feel . . .' his voice broke, '. . . like a rapist when I was already so in love with you.'

'No, no, no, no,' she said. 'It wasn't like that.'

He pulled her towards him, then pushed her away.

'You've had months to get in touch with me, even if you didn't get my letters. At first I waited, then I thought, I'm going to be slowly murdered by her if I go on like this.'

She took his face in her hands then stopped. Outside the window, she could see Tor and Rose being led into the quadrangle.

'This is hopeless,' she said. 'Listen,' she said quickly, hearing the crunch of their feet on the gravel, 'I've just decided. Before Christmas, I'm going up north to Simla. It's where my parents are buried. I've got a letter from an old girl there. A trunk I was supposed to collect years ago. Once I've faced that, maybe . . .'

He was about to answer when the door flew open.

'Frank!' Tor flung her arms round him. Rose stood behind her with two parcels in her hand. 'Gosh, are you all right, Viva?' Tor said with her usual tact. 'You look as white as a sheet.'

Frank offered them a drink but seemed relieved when they said no. Rose, who'd read the atmosphere correctly, walked to the door and said that she could already see one or two stars had come out. It would be safer for them to drive home before dark.

So this was it. When Viva explained to Rose and Tor the following morning that she was going to take the train up to Simla to pick up her parents' trunk, she tried to keep her voice as calm and as even as possible, so that they didn't realise how frightened she was. When they offered to come too, she said no, she'd be back in time for Christmas and it was better they stayed put.

Now she was sitting in the window seat of the *Himalayan Queen*, the train that her father had helped to build and maintain on its circuitous route up through the Himalayan foothills. As the train worked its way through tunnel after tunnel, in and out of bright sunshine and shadowy rocks, she tried to stay calm and at one remove.

*Daddy, Mummy, Josie*—such a long time since she'd dared to say all their names together. She was eight, maybe nine, when she'd sat on this train with them for the last time. How strange to have got this old without them. On their last ever journey together, Josie sat next to her mother and Viva sat opposite them in a patch of sunlight next to her father. She felt again the sun on her hair, her joy at being beside him.

She thought of Josie. After her appendix burst, and they'd taken her to the graveyard, Viva had been obsessed for months and months with the thought of her turning into a skeleton there. She'd seen freshly dug earth round all the other little gravestones; she'd pestered her mother for details of how the other children had died. There was a small boy, she recalled, who had toddled over to a snake and tried to shake hands with it; a baby who died of typhoid the day after Josie.

Did she ask too many questions? She must have. Or maybe her mother couldn't bear her for looking like Josie but not being her, or because she'd refused stubbornly for a while to accept that Josie had gone. She had said so many prayers. She'd put Josie's pyjamas on the bed at night, put a biscuit under the sheets so when she came back she wouldn't be hungry, gone to the temple and put rice and flowers out before the gods, before she'd given up believing all together.

Shortly after, she'd been sent home to the convent. Her memory was that she'd gone alone—but surely not? She was ten years old. There must have been a companion. Why had her mother not come? Did she kiss her goodbye? These were the details that silted up your mind and made you feel like a liar to yourself and to other people.

Twenty miles or so away from the station she found herself weeping uncontrollably. She shouldn't have come, she knew it, *she knew it.* It took her a while to get back in control, to mop up the tears, to stifle the sobs by pretending she was having a coughing fit. Then she fell asleep, and when she woke, the woman opposite was tapping her on the arm. The train had reached the end of the line. She was back in Simla.

She stood for a moment in the spot where she'd stepped down from the train. She looked at the trees dusted with snow, at the thin horses covered in burlap sacks, waiting for passengers.

In front of her, in the station forecourt, was a tonga driver.

'Are you waiting for your sahib?' he asked her.

'No,' she said, 'I'm by myself. I'd like to go here,' she handed him the piece of paper.

Frowning, he looked at Mabel Waghorn's map.

'This no good.' He handed the map back to her. 'Lower Bazaar—no English pipples live there.'

'I don't care,' she said. She lifted her own case into the carriage before he changed his mind. 'That's where I'm going. It's in the street behind the Chinese shoe shop,' she added, but he had already picked up the reins and was touching the horse's rump with his whip.

They passed through a busy street, where she saw mostly English people walking in front of charming, half-timbered houses. In the gaps between the houses, she saw snow, mountains, forests, rocks.

They stopped at the next crossroads. A black cow with a brass bell round its neck was airily depositing dung on the street corner. Viva leant out of the carriage so she could see the shop signs: Empire Stores, Tailor Ram's, Military, Army, Civilian Uniforms, Himalaya Stores.

'Stop!' She'd seen the shoe shop with 'Ta-Tung and Co. Chinese shoe makers', written on it. She got out her map again.

'You can put me down here,' she told the driver as she held out her money. 'My friend lives in the street behind this shop.'

He muttered and shook his head as if she would shortly see the error of her ways.

She stood for a while in the street, trying to get her bearings. To the right of her was the smart European street, well swept, and with gay little tubs of flowers; below this and down a long flight of steep and winding stairs was the native quarter, a rabbit warren of small streets and tiny lamplit shops. She walked down the first flight of stairs.

*I've made a mistake,* she thought. Mabel Waghorn had been a schoolteacher, perhaps even a headmistress. The map must be wrong. The street was too shabby. Flustered, she sat down on the step, then she saw a house behind a row of ramshackle tin roofs that might just be it.

Walking closer, she stopped in front of a two-storeyed tenement clinging to the side of the hill and stared at it. Surely not. She drew closer, still not believing, but there it was: 'Number 12', drawn in flaked green paint on a front door with a rusty grille. To the right of the grille was a brass bell with a rope pull, underneath it a sign written in Mabel Waghorn's quavery writing: *'I am on the first floor.'* When she rang it, there was no answer.

On the second ring of the bell, an old woman stepped out onto the verandah above. They looked at each other, Viva unwilling for a few seconds to believe that this frail-looking person was Mabel Waghorn.

'Good Lord!' The old woman stared at her intently. 'No!' she said.

'No! No! No!' She had to shout to avoid the catastrophe. 'My name is Viva—I'm her daughter.'

'I'm frightfully sorry,' the woman said, 'but have I asked you to come?'

'I should have written,' Viva apologised. 'You asked me ages ago. Do you mind if I come up? It won't take long; I'm sorry if I frightened you.'

'Come up then,' she said after a long pause. 'I'll send Hari down.'

A few seconds later, Hari, a handsome smiling boy in a Kashmiri tunic, creaked open the front door and beckoned her inside. He took her suitcase and led her down a corridor that reeked of old cats.

'Follow me, please,' he said. 'Mrs Waghorn is upstairs in her study.'

When they reached the first landing she heard the yapping of a small dog, the scrape of a stick.

'Hari?' called a voice from behind the door. 'Is that her? I'm in here.'

'Go inside,' he said. 'She is waiting for you.'

The room seemed so dark when she first walked in that she thought Mrs Waghorn was a pile of clothes left on a chair. When her eyes adjusted, she saw the old lady sitting in front of a paraffin heater. At the end of her knee perched a tiny bat-like dog with tragic eyes.

'Come in,' she said. 'And sit down where I can see you.'

She pointed towards a sagging sofa piled high with papers at one end. The voice, though breathless, was authoritative.

They looked at each other for a few seconds.

'I'm Alexander and Felicity Holloway's daughter. Do you remember me? You were kind enough to write to me ages ago about a trunk they left with you. I'm sorry I've taken so long to pick it up.' Viva gazed into her watery eyes. 'I must have been about eight or nine when we first met. I remember you—I was a little bit scared of you because you were a headmistress.'

'Yes, indeed. You're absolutely right. I was head for ages there.' Mention of the school seemed to perk the old lady up. 'My husband, Arthur, and I ran the whole show: forty boarders, thirty day pupils, Indians and English. It was called Wildhern School. That's where I met Hari—' She broke off suddenly and looked at her long and hard.

'I do remember Felicity. A lovely woman.' She gazed at Viva intently. 'Now I look at you,' she said at last, 'you don't look as much like Felicity as I thought you did, more like your father.'

She began to cough, a painful rattling sound. 'Sorry, darling.' Mrs Waghorn stopped spluttering.

Viva said, 'I don't have long in Simla, and I'd very much like to see my parents' trunk. That's why I'm here.'

'Oh my goodness, of course, of course. Heavens! Let me think.' She put her finger to her temple. 'It's in the box-room,' she said, after a silence. 'It's filthy, I'm afraid.'

'That's all right,' Viva said.

'The box-room floods in the monsoon. I haven't been down there for years.' The old lady was breathing jerkily. 'If you don't mind,' she said, 'I shan't come down with you. Hari will take you.'

As they stepped outside the house, Hari was explaining to her that the box-room was awkward to get to. They really should have one inside. He led her towards a broken path that went round the house.

A few seconds later Hari stopped and pointed towards a ramshackle shed that seemed to be loosely attached to the verandah at the back of the house.

Hari took a key from a chain he wore round his waist and unlocked the door. The black gloom inside smelt like the bottom of a pond.

'One moment, please,' said Hari before he closed the door behind them. He put a match to an oil lamp he carried in his other hand. 'It's very dark in here, and there are plenty of rats.'

She sneezed several times. When he lifted his lamp she saw in its yellow blur several collapsed bales of straw, held together with rotten string. Weak shafts of light shone through a hole in the roof.

'Follow me, please.' Hari's lamp was moving past the hay bales and towards the back of the shed, where the ground felt slimy and unreliable underneath her feet. Now she saw some white shapes in the dark, furniture perhaps, and on top of them a jumble of old suitcases.

It took a while for her eyes to adjust again, but when she saw it, she heard herself gasp. The large battered trunk in front of her looked for that moment like a freshly dug-up coffin. It sat on a low deal table, covered in dirt and green mould.

When Hari put his lamp down on top of it, she saw its wooden lid sweating and mossy, almost like a live thing.

Hari stood by her, polite, impassive. She took a deep breath.

'Well, here it is then,' she told him. 'It won't take me long to go through it.'

*Oh, Mummy! Oh, Josie—I left it too long.*

She took the keys out of her pocket. Some twigs protruded from the lock and when she tried the key, it jammed immediately. She pushed again but felt it catch on the rust and grit.

'I'll need your help, Hari,' she said. 'The lock's stuck.'

'Please, memsahib, hold the light and I will have a go.'

He tried the key left and right and then again more forcibly.

'Step back, memsahib, please,' he said at last. He took a knife out of a leather sheath attached to his pocket and inserted it under the lid. With one foot braced on the wall he leant into the trunk. Both of them yelled as the lid flew open.

'I'm quite sure there's nothing here,' she told Hari breezily as she looked down on the bundle of old clothes. 'I'll have a quick look through, then I'll be off.'

She heard her own jagged breath as her fingers reached out and touched something damp. A slimy sweater, then slacks, a torn pair of cricket trousers, a paisley eiderdown with a scattering of mouse droppings in the seams.

*Oh dear, oh dear, still trying hard not to think or mind. Too late! Too late!*

'Could you leave me on my own for a while?' she said to Hari.

'Of course,' he said. He looked relieved. 'I shall leave the light with you. When should I come back?'

'Half an hour will be fine, thank you, Hari,' she said. She felt an urge to say something more: to thank him for his grace, his reticence, the gentle concern she saw in his eyes, but the door had shut behind him and she could already hear the soft slap of his shoes going upstairs again.

Alone again in the dark, she fought against a choking feeling of panic. She'd taken so long she couldn't funk it now, but the sour decaying smells, the pointless emptiness of their clothes running through her hands was horrible. Her fingers closed round something soft and pliable wrapped up in a tea towel. A softness she recognised even before she'd unwound the cloth and seen Susie, Josie's favourite doll. Josie had loved this scruffy thing with its sausagey legs and gingham frock.

Now there were rat-like bite marks on its arms; most of the kapok had been removed up to its knees. When she squeezed it, it fell apart in a foul puff of air. *Horrible.* She felt saliva come into her mouth. Susie was lying in Josie's arms on the night she died; she remembered the screams coming from her bedroom, wave upon wave of them. The sounds of vomiting, shouts of 'Do something, Mummy! Help me.' All night, feet running up and downstairs, as it dawned on everybody this wasn't just another bout of gippy tummy. Viva's own ayah had tried to stop her hearing by putting her hands over her ears, but Viva had fought free and crouched in the cupboard by Josie's door. And some time after midnight, she'd heard the screams go weak, then tiny rabbit-like squeaks and then nothing. *For Christ's sake, somebody do something!* Her mother's shriek had torn through the dark like a wild animal, a raw and bloody sound. And then the door slammed shut.

*Darling, darling Josie.* The doll collapsed underneath her fingers leaving a trail of grey dust down her blouse. *My sister. My only sister.*

She put the doll aside. There must be something here she wanted, could keep and make sense of. She dug down a little deeper, finding a few old letters, mostly bills, and a small household account book. In a tin was a pink bridge with two false teeth set in it. Her father's. She crammed them into her pocket.

This was it. An insult, a joke, a great big bloody waste of time. She closed the lid again, folded her arms and leant her head on the top of the trunk. Nothing had happened. And what on earth had she expected after all this time? Some great transfiguring moment? Parcels filled with damp but usable banknotes? Parental letters from beyond the grave full of stirring advice about how to live life from now on? So much energy squandered on a heap of rotten clothes—it was almost funny when you thought about it.

A pair of her mother's snakeskin shoes had fallen beside the trunk. One of her father's trains had lodged in its toe. A wooden train with the words '*Himalayan Queen*' painted carefully in his hand along its side. She crammed the train inside her pocket alongside his teeth.

'Viva? Miss Holloway.' She almost jumped out of her skin. 'Are you there?' Mrs Waghorn was standing at the door with a hurricane lamp in her hand, a wraith-like figure in the gloom. 'Are you all right?'

'Yes, thank you,' she said coldly. She hated being seen like this. They stood looking at each other.

'Please don't cry.' She felt the old lady's papery hand. 'It's my fault and I've found something I'd like to show you. Come upstairs and have a drink with me. I think you've done enough.'

'I don't know how much to tell you,' Mrs Waghorn said when they were back in her chaotic sitting room again. Mrs Waghorn had her back to the window; Viva was sitting on the chair opposite her. Hari had put glasses of brandy in their hands.

'How did my father die?' Viva said. 'Tell me everything you know.'

Mrs Waghorn looked surprised. 'Surely you know.'

'No. Not really. It's all got so confused.'

'He died of overwork,' said Mrs Waghorn simply. 'He had been racing around the country working on the trains, and they found him one morning at the club in Quetta. He was dead.'

'Are you sure? I was told he was set on by bandits, his throat was cut.'

'Who told you these things?' Mrs Waghorn's face sagged with disbelief. 'It's absolute tosh. He died putting on his shoes. It was very quick.'

'I don't know who told me,' said Viva. 'I was at school . . . I can't remember now, somebody must have told me.'

'Not necessarily. Sometimes adults fudge even the simplest facts of life when they talk to children.'

'Please,' Viva said, 'tell me everything. It's all slipping away, and I can't bear it any more. I need to know what's real and what I've made up.'

'I didn't know them all that well,' Mrs Waghorn began cautiously. 'But we did like each other.' She was tapping her fingers against her palm in an agitated way. 'I'm not very good at talking about them either.'

'Please.' Viva took her jittery hand in hers and held it there. 'Don't be frightened. The worst thing for me is feeling so cut off.'

'Well.' Mrs Waghorn fiddled with her cigarettes, then lit one. 'I've thought about this quite a lot; I'm talking about your mother now. At first your mind goes round and round and you look for reasons.

'Here's what I've come up with. Your mother was a good-looking woman; you've seen the photographs. She was great fun to be with, an asset to your father, but I always thought of her as a Saturday's child, or she should have been. You know, the one that works hard for its living, but it was frightfully difficult with your father moving so much.

'His work came first, of course. But your mother had gifts of her own. She painted very well and, as you probably know, did these wonderful things. Have you seen them?'

She put a small, hard object into the palm of Viva's hand. She took it to be a navy-blue button at first: a toggle-shaped button of some elaborate design. Looking closer, she saw a woman, wrapped in a shroud or a shawl and carved out of a dark blue marble-like stone. The tiny figure, no bigger than her thumb, seemed to radiate life. It felt important.

'I think I remember my mother doing pottery classes,' she said at last. The memory was so vague it was almost forgotten. 'But never when we were around. But are you quite sure she did this? It's like something you'd see in a museum.'

'When she gave it to me . . .' Mrs Waghorn had taken the figure back. 'she wouldn't let me thank her for it. She said, "It's a gift from the fire."'

You see, one day, I'd walked into her studio unannounced. Well, it wasn't a real studio, a hut shall we say, in the grounds of our school. She was on her knees, in tears in front of her kiln. The heat was too high, and hours of work had ended in what looked like a row of burnt cakes. We had a cup of tea, and I said to her—I can't remember my exact words, but the effect was—"This doesn't look much fun, why bother?"

'And it was then she explained with more passion than I ever heard her express that sometimes when you opened the kiln there was something there that was so magical, a pot, a figure, so much more beautiful than the one you'd thought of that you tingled for hours afterwards.

'Tingled!' Mrs Waghorn laughed delightedly. 'She told me potters call these offerings—these divine mistakes—the gift of the fire. A damn shame she stopped, wasn't it?'

'I don't know.' Viva had a hollow feeling inside her heart, a feeling that she'd been cheated of something she'd never had. 'But why did she stop? Was it when Daddy died? When Josie died?'

'I can't remember, I really can't, but why does anyone stop? Husbands, children, moving too much. All I can tell you was that she left things of value, and that she worked very hard for them.'

'I don't remember her like that at all,' Viva said, 'but then I was a bit of a daddy's girl. I only really remember her as, well, you know, somebody who did things for you: organised meals, name tapes, journeys.'

The sketching. Out of the blue she remembered it. How the pencil and the book had often appeared with the picnic things and how cross it had made her—it was time taken away from her.

'She was consumed with her work—the pottery, the paintings, the tiny sculptures—and felt guilty about it,' Mrs Waghorn went on, 'so she tried to hide it. It was considered not the thing to work. Still is, but it was much worse then. For women that is, the men never stopped.

'So she was a misfit. She was tremendously good fun as well as everything else. A marvellous mimic. One of the very best things about her was that she didn't take herself too seriously. But it was also her downfall, if you see what I mean.'

No, Viva was trying not to look too astonished; five minutes into the conversation and they were talking about a complete stranger.

She remembered her mother in two ways—rustling of a taffeta dress, waft of scent on her way out to some do at the club or in the mornings, permanently rushed, often tired and always in her father's shadow.

'I'd like another glass of brandy,' Mrs Waghorn said. 'Help yourself too. Now, are you the sort of person who likes the truth?'

'Yes,' said Viva, 'I am.'

She felt Mrs Waghorn's hand close round hers. 'Dear girl, please don't cry. None of this is your fault.'

'It is.' Viva could no longer stop the tears running down her face. 'I should have come earlier.'

'You are *not* to feel guilty,' Mrs Waghorn said with some force. 'Do you hear? It was nothing you did. They wanted you away because nobody wanted you to know.'

'To know what?' Viva felt her whole body freeze.

Mrs Waghorn started to mutter in some agitation to herself; she was talking herself into or out of something.

'Tell me.' Viva dried her eyes, and made a huge effort to look in control. Mrs Waghorn must not stop talking.

'Your mother took her own life,' she said. 'I thought you knew.'

Viva heard herself groaning. 'No,' she said. 'No.'

'Yes.' Mrs Waghorn's eyes were bright with tears. 'But I must tell you this: she was the last person on earth who I thought would ever do such a thing. Oh, she had her ups and downs, but she was so full of beans and she loved you so much, but such a lot went wrong. This is no consolation, but it happens to so many people out here. They get lost.'

'Oh God.' When Viva put her head in her hands she felt herself floating hazily above her own body.

'Are you sure?'

'Quite sure,' said Mrs Waghorn. 'I was the one that found her.'

# Chapter 12

VIVA BOOKED IN at the Cecil Hotel and went straight to her room and lay on the bed, rigid with shock. Then as the shock wore off she wept uncontrollably. She'd been so angry with her mother for so long without ever thinking about her as a separate person with her own complicated life. She felt ashamed, revolted by her own stupidity. How could she have got it so wrong—dramatising her father's death, burying her mother under a heap of carefully nursed old grudges?

When she got up, exhausted and red-eyed, the day was over and there were stars outside her bedroom window. It was nearly ten o'clock.

She went into the bathroom and turned on the taps. Her body felt stiff as if she had been pummelled, and on her hands she could still smell the damp and camphor from the trunk.

She stared at the dirt that was flowing from her; she had been buried alive. She scrubbed her neck, her legs, her breasts, her arms; she washed her hair, then she lay in the water until it got cold, thinking about her mother again.

She felt already that sometime soon she might be released from the darkness. An easing—something like space or lightness.

At least she knew now. Before, she'd blamed her, even hated her for so many things: for not keeping Daddy alive, for not wanting her more, for not keeping her with her in India, when the truth was she'd been cut off from the two things that might have kept her going for a little while longer—her work and her child.

Viva got out of the water and reached for a towel. She saw her face blurry and indistinct in the steamy bathroom mirror. Maybe she'd been a ghost for years without really knowing it. That line of poetry lodged in her brain years ago at school, something about being 'half in love with easeful death'. The other half floating out from herself, longing to slip away into the darkness like a boat in the water, to where Josie and her parents waited for her.

She climbed into bed, putting the little blue woman her mother had made on the bedside table. Before they'd parted, Mrs Waghorn had pressed it into her hand.

'Keep it.' She'd closed Viva's fingers around it. 'It's yours. I want it to be the first thing you see when you wake up tomorrow morning.'

She was calmer now and saw it more clearly: the careful arrangement of the woman's shawl, the quizzical intelligence of her eyes as if she were in on some private joke. Its perfection hurt and thrilled her—how could something so small be so full of life?

She turned out the lamp and lay in the dark thinking about her last conversation with Mrs Waghorn.

'My mother and I had the most terrible row the last time we were together,' Viva had confessed over tea. 'I can't for the life of me remember what it was about now, or why I was so angry. I think I might have told her I hated her. *I can't wait to go back to school.* I wanted to hurt her as she had hurt me. It was the last time I ever saw her.'

'You were ten years old. All children of that age are foul sometimes,' said Mrs Waghorn. 'Particularly when they're about to be sent away. She understood.'

'You don't know that.'

'I do. She was heartbroken.'

'No—don't say it, you don't have to.'

'I do. After she'd said goodbye to you she walked up to the school and had a drink with me. She was desperately upset; she knew she'd acted strangely with you, that she was losing her grip. I remember it so well because she said to me, "I couldn't even kiss her goodbye," and she'd longed to—it was so horribly sad. Too much for everyone; but why should you take the blame for that?'

Mrs Waghorn had become emotional herself at this point. She'd squeezed her hands together and swallowed several times. Viva sat there frozen and immobile as though parts of her had jammed, watching tears flow down the deep lines in Mrs Waghorn's face.

When she had composed herself again, Mrs Waghorn had shuffled over to a locked cabinet and shown her several more pieces of her mother's pottery. A celadon green teapot, a plate, a bowl. Beautiful things.

Viva had pored over them, desperate for clues.

'Why did she leave them with you?' she'd asked.

'They were precious to her, and she'd lost so much in transit—she wanted me to take care of them.'

*Why the pots and not me?* she'd wanted to ask but hadn't. The question sounded so nakedly self-pitying.

'I still don't understand why she sent me home?' she asked instead. 'Did I do something?'

'No, no, no, nothing like that.' Mrs Waghorn had bowed her head. After a long silence she'd looked up. 'It was my fault, I'm afraid. I said, "Send her back to England." I probably talked about the need for fresh air, the company of other children. All the things I used to say to anxious parents, and it was a ghastly mistake. And of course I did think at the time that she would eventually join you. I had no idea how desperate she was. I'm so sorry,' she said almost inaudibly.

Viva had made the usual gestures of forgiveness, squeezing Mrs Waghorn's hand, saying it wasn't her fault, she was only following the rules and so on, but another part of her cried out in agony.

She thought back to the day after the row, when she and her mother had parted: the stiff hugs, the brittle jokes they'd made, her muffled howls of pain later, doubled up in the ladies' lavatory in some railway station on her way back to school. They should never have let go. That was the truth, terrible and simple. In the end they'd died to each other, not all at once, but bit by bit, by making themselves less vulnerable. A shocking, ridiculous, waste of love.

**W**hite muslin curtains, more stars, a silvery-green crescent moon hanging low in the sky. From downstairs she could hear puffs of music coming from a dance band, distant laughter. Her parents would have come to parties here. 'Your mother loved dancing,' Mrs Waghorn had said.

Now she pictured her laughing and glamorous in her green silk dress and snakeskin shoes and felt another shift inside her. She knew something now, and must never forget it. It was money in the bank.

However sad her mother's ending had been, she had known deep pleasures: a husband she adored, work that she was good at, children. Mrs Waghorn's laughter had rung out like a girl when she'd remembered the fun they'd had together. These things were real.

A thought had come to her, clear and strong. She must tell Frank about everything that had happened that day. If she didn't tell him quickly, she'd find other ways of hiding it and the truth would be smudged or rearranged like footprints in the sand and they'd go on not telling the secrets that were at the heart of them. That was dangerous.

She dressed hurriedly, tugging on her stockings, dashing a brush through her hair. What had to be done must be done now while the pain was real—if she left it too long she could lose her nerve.

She glanced at her watch. Ten forty. The hotel's front desk might be closed, the hall porter off duty. She ran out of her bedroom into the corridor and across the hall, almost throwing herself on the lift button. Her blood was racing as the brass doors closed behind her with a thunk.

The lift took a long time to wheeze its way down to the ground floor. When the doors were open she sprinted across an expanse of highly polished cedar floor towards the turbaned man on the desk.

'I want to send a telegram,' she told him, almost grabbing the pencil out of his hand. 'To Lahore, tonight.'

He handed her a form.

'It's over,' she wrote. 'Stop. It's done. Stop.' She felt her heart jump in her chest like a large fish. 'Please come for Christmas.'

**B**ecause Tor was atrociously bad at keeping secrets, she'd been forbidden by Rose and Toby to pick up Viva at the station. In the end, they'd relented—after all, the whole thing had been her idea and it seemed mean to exclude her from the excitement.

'What happened?' she said, when she first saw Viva almost running down the platform. 'You look different.'

'I feel different.'

'So, tell all.' Tor ignored Rose's quelling look. 'Was the trunk stuffed with buried treasures? Did you see anyone you knew?'

Viva tried to smile, said something about being too ravenous to talk yet and, as they were walking across the car park, said casually, 'Oh, by the way, did anyone leave a message for me?'

'No,' they both said together.

'I didn't think they would,' Viva replied, and then, 'I honestly can't believe it's Christmas in two days' time,' as if that was what they'd been talking about all along.

'Sorry.' Tor didn't like to see her look suddenly so tired and upset.

Tor glanced at Rose. 'But we do have a small surprise for you. An early Christmas present you could say.'

'Honestly, Tor.' Rose shook her head. 'I could throttle you sometimes.'

'Why?' said Tor. 'What did I say wrong?'

Nobody mentioned the surprise again until after Viva had had a bath and washed her hair and they were taking tea on the verandah. They were draining their cups, when Tor said she thought they should stroll down to the stables and watch the horses being fed. She said it was one of her favourite things to do at this time of the day.

Viva, who was still looking pale and rather strained, said that it would be good to be out in the fresh air. She hadn't yet said a word about Simla, but they'd grown used to her being reserved about things like that by now and didn't press her.

By the time they'd organised Freddie and his ayah and told Toby they were going out, it was dusk and the whole sky had turned into a gaudy fanfare of shocking pinks and oranges. As the girls walked arm in arm down the path together, their faces absorbed the light and they were laughing because Rose's blonde hair had gone pink.

At the end of the red dirt track, they turned to the right down an avenue of poplar trees that led to the polo ground. They sat for a moment watching a couple of men playing. Their distant yelps, the rolling thunder of hoofs, made Rose sigh suddenly quite heavily.

Viva said, 'Do you miss Jack?'—the kind of intimate question she usually went out of her way to avoid.

Rose didn't seem to mind. She said yes, she did miss him—and then she said, in a wifely exasperated way, that Jack had managed to telegram them only yesterday to tell them that there was no chance that he'd make it home for Christmas. Something about a huge fall of snow north of Peshawar. Jack would be stuck in some miserable hut in the middle of nowhere with only two of his friends from the regiment for company. It was a shame for him to miss Freddie's first Christmas.

At the end of the polo ground, they stood for a while watching in silence the birds floating and turning against the crimson sky. The men cantered side by side down the long side of the pitch.

Rose was smiling.

'Isn't India the most magical place on earth sometimes?' she said as they walked into the stable yard.

'I mean, honestly, would you have missed it for anything, Viva? Even the bad bits. Do you feel that?'

'No. I mean, yes.' Viva had hardly heard a word. 'I don't know.' Her heart had started to thump uncomfortably. What was this surprise the girls had concocted?

They'd reached the stable yard. Two tiny Shetland ponies were stretching over their stable doors to look at them and whickering.

Tor stopped and put her hands over Viva's eyes '. . . here's your surprise.' She pushed her towards the stable door. '*Look*,' she whispered softly into her ear. 'He came after all.'

Viva's heart leapt in her chest and there was a shrill sound in her ears, but when she saw it, she had only a second to adjust her expression.

It was a foal. Nothing but a foal—still wet from its birth, lying on a heap of bloodstained straw. Above it an exhausted-looking mare stood with a damp tail and sweaty sides.

And all the way here, lit up inside, excited by the sunset, she'd imagined—oh, it didn't matter what she'd imagined—that he would be here after all, and that she'd be able to talk to him, and tell him about Simla and all the new things she'd learned there. *Stupid, stupid, stupid. There is life as it is and life as we are* and she was always confusing the two.

The foal got to its feet, tottered over to them to sniff their hands; they stroked its wrinkled little nose and said it felt like velvet.

'The mare lost her last foal, so she's in heaven,' Tor whispered.

Viva made herself concentrate. If she started to cry now she might never stop and her humiliation would be complete.

'Was the birth frightening?' Viva felt punched. *Stupid, stupid, stupid.* She must stop thinking like this.

'No, we weren't frightened at all.' Tor was looking at her strangely. 'We were lucky to have a professional here.' And it was then that Viva felt Rose's nails dig into the palm of her hand. When she turned round, Frank was there.

And then, she'd done something so unlike herself that the girls had teased her about it for months afterwards. 'You,' she'd almost shouted. She'd put her arms round him and hugged him fiercely; she'd burst into tears. It was just that the sight of him in that marvellous light was so overwhelming, so absolutely the most beautiful thing she'd ever seen that she couldn't stop herself. *Sometimes you know so quickly it frightens you. Your mind lumbers behind trying to make sense of it.*

He was wearing his battered linen suit; he was smiling at her and shaking his head as if he couldn't believe it either.

*Thank you, God*, she thought when her head was buried in his chest. *Thank you, thank you, thank you.* When he hugged her back, she cried some more.

'I got your telegram,' he said. 'I was going to go to Simla, but thought you might have left already. I decided to meet you here instead.'

'He drove like the clappers.' Tor had tears in her eyes too.

'Do you promise you didn't guess?' Rose was beaming. 'I thought Miss Tor was about as subtle as a blow over the head.'

'I didn't guess. No.' Viva could hardly speak—it was all too much.

Tor checked her watch. 'I have an idea,' she said. 'There's two hours, at least, before dinner. Why don't you two go for a walk . . .? You could actually go for quite a long walk if you wanted to,' she added innocently. 'Supper will be late as usual.'

When they were alone again, they laughed, because they'd heard Tor boom, 'See, I *can* be tactful,' to Rose as they'd walked off.

Then Frank touched her lightly on the arm. 'There's a summerhouse near the river—we could talk there. Is that what you want?'

'Yes,' she said. 'That's what I want.'

He borrowed a lamp from the grooms at the stable. She followed him back down the path towards the water.

Their footsteps had quickened and when they came to a small slatted bridge, he took her hand and helped her over it. On the other side was a grass clearing and a white wooden summerhouse.

'Quick.' He pulled her inside and when she shut the door behind them, she felt her blood leap.

The hut was simple and bare. There was a desk in the middle of the room with a pad of paper on it and some pencils, a charpoy with some faded cushions and a set of cricket stumps propped up against the wall.

'It belongs to one of the masters,' Frank explained. 'He's on holiday.'

When he lit the oil lamp, turning the wick down low, she saw his long brown fingers, the blondish-brown hairs on his strong forearms, and shivered again. She'd never felt so out of control, so alive.

'Sit down,' he said. 'Here, with me.' He pulled her down beside him on the charpoy under the window.

'I've been so worried about you,' he said. 'It nearly killed me. I . . .'

He put his hands under her hair and kissed her—a long slow kiss that felt like a claiming. When she came up for air, her shoe had fallen off and every cell in her body felt alive and singing. It was terrifying.

'Talk to me first. What happened in Simla?'

She took a deep breath and began by telling him about the trunk—trying to make a story of it at first.

'I mean, really, it was almost a joke—a few sodden bits of clothes, my father's false teeth. And when I think how long I'd put off claiming it.'

She told him about seeing their old family house again—Hari had taken her on their way to the railway station. How irrelevant it had looked standing in the mist, all neglected and forlorn with the woods round it. And that was it. No ancient retainers had rushed out to tell her stories from her past, no neighbours who remembered them, no further clues, just the dense forest closing in on a borrowed house.

She told him how, on her last day, Mrs Waghorn had taken her to the Sanjauli cemetery where they were buried, and she'd seen all three of them for the first time, laid out in a row. It was peaceful there. She'd weeded the graves and put the flowers into a vase she'd brought with her and filled with water from the stream that ran nearby.

He listened to this intently, his green eyes trained on her.

'So,' he said, 'maybe in the end it was a good thing; maybe it helped to set your mind at rest—somewhat,' he'd added uncertainly.

He looked so anxiously protective when he said that, she knew this was a turning point. One part of her brain was telling her, *People keep things hidden from each other all the time: the soothing lie could be told, no one need ever be the wiser*, but another part of her recognised that if she fudged this, some door would be slammed inside her for ever.

She looked at him. 'My mother took her own life.'

Mrs Waghorn had added more details before they'd parted, and now, it was a great comfort to tell him as simply and fully as she could. 'She got malaria. She recovered, but apparently got very homesick and low in spirits. When I think of it now, she must have been reeling from Josie's death, then my father's. I'd never really thought of it like that before.

'She rode a horse up to a hut on the ridge, half a mile north of Wildflower Hall—a beautiful place where you can see the Himalayas. She used to go up there sketching. She'd left a note saying how much she'd loved us all, but that her life was no longer bearable. "Sustainable" was the word she'd used. She must have stayed on the side of the mountain until she'd frozen to death. She'd left a couple of hay nets for the horse, so it would have something to eat until somebody found her.'

He put his arms round her. He stroked her hair.

'I had no idea,' she told him, wild-eyed. 'I'd been so angry with her for so long. I'd blamed her for everything, and almost everything I said about her was a complete lie.'

'Don't you think most people make their parents up?' he said. 'When you're a child, you're not really ever interested in them, and later, if you talk to them at all, you have all the wrong conversations. Oh, my love.'

He leant over and wiped away the tears that were starting to pour down her face.

'You don't have to say it all tonight if it's going to hurt you,' he said. 'Let it come out bit by bit.'

And she had a spacious sense that this was right. There would be time to talk, and, at last, she could tell the truth. She thought of something else along these lines: that if you were lucky, very lucky indeed, there were one or two people in your life to whom you could tell the unvarnished truth. People like Frank, and Rose and Tor. And that these people held the essence of you inside them, just as Mrs Waghorn had held the essence of her mother inside her. The rest would be conversations with people that ended when night fell, or the dinner party ended.

'Come here,' he said. He put his arms round her and rocked her.

'But the point is,' she told him fiercely, 'no one can ever really say why she did it. We want a simple explanation and what if there isn't one? What if all you can say is sometimes awful things happen to the best people? I think it's better to throw up your hands than try to square everything up.'

'Do you want me to tell Tor and Rose for you?' he asked. 'They were so worried about you, they had a sense something like this might happen.'

'How did they know?' She was genuinely amazed.

'I don't know,' he said. 'Friends are another mystery.'

'Not yet,' she said, all this emotion had made her feel momentarily giddy and off-centre. 'I want to show you something first. Look.'

She tipped the blue woman into the palm of his hand where it lay between his lifeline and his thumb.

'Something else I didn't know about her—she was a sculptor. She made this.'

And later, she realised this was another kind of turning point between them, that if he'd flipped the little figure over and said something polite and automatic, she wouldn't have been able to stand there feeling such pride, such a strong sense that she could hold her head up high.

He turned it over, his brown-blond hair forming for a moment a screen between her and the blue woman. And she could tell by the way he was looking at it that he understood, and that as far as anyone is really safe in this world, she would be safe in his hands.

She and Frank had walked back together through the darkness, the lamplight glancing off the poplar trees. Holding hands all the way, they'd taken the red dirt road back to Tor's house for supper. He'd stopped near the wooden bridge and pulled her behind a jasmine bush for a long, slow kiss that, even when she thought of it now, made her go weak at the knees.

She knew that for the rest of her life when she smelt jasmine, she would think of him: his arms round her, the smell of his hair, the way the kisses had changed tempo—gentle at first, then so passionate they'd had to stop, breathless and laughing and amazed.

He said he had never felt anything remotely like this before. She said she felt the same, then felt tears run down the sides of her face.

When they reached the house it was blazing with Christmas lights. With the lights and the music wafting out, it looked like a mad little pleasure craft against the dense darkness of the trees all around them.

They ate dinner in the small dining room where Tor and Rose had lit candles and set the table with flowers. With her friends all around her, a glass of champagne in her hand and Frank beside her in the candle-light, she'd felt so full of life she could have died.

Dinner—roast chicken, rice, champagne and afterwards a dish of lemon fluff—had gone on for hours. There was so much to celebrate and, eventually, they wound up the gramophone and danced the var-sity rag on the verandah. Then Tor cracked open a bottle of crème de menthe, and tried to teach Toby to tango. Their noise woke up baby Fred. He was carried into the dining room by his ayah. They put a Christmas hat on him and even though he was still half-asleep, they'd made him chuckle, which was never hard to do. And when Viva had looked at Frank she'd known with certainty that sooner or later they would have children.

Three weeks later, Viva moved in with Frank into a three-roomed flat in Colaba. It had a wide half-glassed balcony on the front of it from where you could see, if you stood up and leant to the right, the sea, the boats and the misty outlines of Elephanta Island.

This was the island where the caves were full of what Tor called 'socking great' sixth-century carvings of the Hindu gods Shiva and Parvati. Colossal, magnificent, they showed the gods making love and playing dice, quarrelling and laughing. They had been there twice already, taking a picnic lunch, which they ate on the island.

During the hot days, as she sat on her own verandah, shaded by a bamboo blind, Viva often glanced across the sparkling water and towards the island. Typing and looking, typing and looking, at the island, the harbour, the boats coming and going.

Finishing the book had almost been a condition of her marriage. She'd come back from Amritsar certain most of her notes had been destroyed. He said she must try again.

A few days later, when she'd gone back to work at the home, she found a pile of torn and crumpled notes in her washstand drawer, and it turned out that Daisy had kept another chunk of the torn and defaced pages in an envelope just in case she could ever face them again.

When the children heard their stories had been revived, they got excited about the book all over again and began drawing pictures for it and writing poems. They'd helped her stick the notes together, and filled in any gaps. Once they'd started, the job had not been huge.

And it was in the flat, on April 12, 1930, that she typed the full stop that ended her book. *Tales from the Tamarind: Ten Bombay Children Tell Their Stories.*

Frank, who was back working shifts at the Gokuldas Tejpal Hospital until his new research project began, was in their bedroom when she typed the last full stop. She took the pages in her arms and hugged them to herself for a moment, then she walked into their room, put the book on the bedside table and got into bed with him.

'It's done,' she said. 'I've finished.'

'Good,' he said. He took her in his arms and held her tight. 'Good,' he said again.

There were tears in his eyes and in hers. He'd known all along how important this would be.

And lying there in the crook of his arm, she felt how much lighter she'd become in the last few months. It was incredible. Like a great big stone lifted off her chest. So much had changed.

Frank was on the early shift the next morning. She got up with him at five thirty in the morning and made him scrambled eggs on toast. After he'd eaten, they sat together on the balcony drinking coffee and watched the fishing boats coming in with their night's catch. And beyond them, just breasting the line of the horizon, they could see another P&O liner on its way to India. They came only twice a month now. Watching the scattered lights come into focus, she remembered standing with her group: Tor and Rose, Frank and Guy. Poor Nigel had gone—he'd taken his life during the rainy season just as he'd predicted he might. She remembered their uncertain hymns, the childlike paleness of Rose's face, and poor old Guy—hard to imagine him square-bashing in England now.

'I've got some strong paper in my desk,' said Frank. They'd been talking about the safest way to send her book back to London. 'I'll help you wrap it and if you like, we can drop it off at Thomas Cook later.'

'Yes,' she said. She felt a drunken feeling of relief at having finished the book. He'd seen what she needed; she hadn't. When you're used to looking after yourself, you don't always get it right.

Three weeks after that, they were married in the Bombay Registry Office. They'd decided to hold the reception at the children's home at Tamarind Street, which was still, by a miracle, open, although the authorities were threatening to close it in June of that year.

On the morning of the wedding, half-dreaming, half-awake, she experienced the old familiar pain: it was her wedding day, Josie and her parents should have been there, but the moment came and went more calmly now. What she'd come to understand, what India had helped her see, was that mourning was no crime. It wasn't her feeling all boohoo sorry for herself, or being disgustingly self-engrossed, it was what you had to do to go on.

And she knew that for the whole of the rest of her life, there would be moments—today, for instance, or when her children were born, or when something trivial came up that she longed to tell them about—when she would have to love them and leave them over and over again.

Three people came to the registry office: Daisy, and Tor and Toby, who'd taken the train down from Amritsar. Tor was the first person Viva saw as they stepped out of the tonga. When Tor hugged her, she whispered in her ear that she and Toby were having a baby in October.

Rose couldn't come. In her reply to Viva's wedding invitation, she said she'd be on a ship on her way home then. Her father had died before Christmas. Her beloved father dead for six weeks before she'd even heard about it. Six weeks! She was mortified to think of her mother suffering on her own.

'I'm staying for a few months to help her pack up the house,' she wrote, 'and to introduce her to Freddie.' Jack, she added, would be staying on in India. She said he would try and come to the wedding.

'He won't come,' Viva had said to Frank.

'You never know,' Frank had said. 'He'll be lonely without them.' Viva wasn't sure about that.

But when Viva and Frank arrived for the reception at Tamarind Street, Jack was there. Thinner and older-looking, he stood apart from the cheering children and Tor and Toby. When she waved at him, he touched his hat and raised his hand shyly, and she was glad to see him.

There was no time to talk. Talika, Suday and a chattering, laughing group of children dragged her back up to her old room overlooking the tamarind tree. The girls dressed her in pale green, explaining that green was an auspicious colour for a Maharashtrian girl to be married in. They put green glass bangles round her wrists, took her Western shoes off, helped her bathe her feet and put a fine silver ring round her big toe.

Down in the courtyard, the drums had started up, and a flute. A fire had been lit in a brazier and placed in the middle of the paving stones.

Talika ran to the window. 'They're ready for you,' she said.

Talika's eyes glowed as she held the corner of her sari. On their way downstairs she had to talk fast to tell her all her news. She told her how she'd performed the Shiva *puja* so Viva could find a good husband, how she'd drawn a picture for her and hoped it might go in the book. And Viva, looking into those eager, forward-looking eyes, saw in a jolting moment how much she owed this child, how much she'd taught her.

There was another surprise in the courtyard: Mr Jamshed, plumper than ever and wearing an embroidered tunic, stepped forward and handed her flowers and a box of Turkish delight. Behind him was Mrs Jamshed and Dolly and Kaniz, looking as though they'd stepped from the pages of *Vogue* magazine in their silk dresses and smartly buttoned shoes. They were grinning their heads off.

For reasons she would probably never fully understand, they'd forgiven her. More than forgiven her. Daisy explained that Mrs Jamshed had got up early to help supervise the cooking of a special feast for them: a fish curry served on glistening banana leaves, all kinds of *pakwans*, desserts, *modak* and dumplings with coconut, all laid out on long tables in the courtyard.

The feast took two hours, and after it, much giggling and jangling behind a thin rattan curtain, and then Talika had appeared resplendent in a tangerine sari.

She cleared her throat. 'Miss Wiwa, this is our special dance for you,' she'd announced, and with a stern glance towards the troop of little girls, they'd appeared. Each girl had worn a red, an amber or an orange sari. The hundred little bells worn round their ankles had made a thrilling shivery sound you felt in your spine as they'd walked round the perimeter of the tamarind tree, the boys sweeping the path before them. Musicians appeared: Suday, playing tabla, a trumpeter from Byculla. And then the music and dance had exploded, the girls stamping and twirling, their arms graceful as saplings in the wind.

Frank held her hand tightly and, barefoot, they'd walked round the sacred fire four times, praying for long life, harmony, peace, love.

After the ceremony, Viva made a point of going over to speak to Jack, who was sitting on his own looking amused and watchful. But when she sat down beside him, she saw that what she'd taken to be English reserve was in fact an attempt to control some violent emotion. He was swallowing hard and clearing his throat.

'Well done,' he said in a constricted voice. 'First class.'

'I wish Rose could have been here,' she said. 'I don't think I'd be here without her.'

'Ah, well.' He glanced at her quickly. 'Have you heard from her?'

'Not much,' she said. 'A quick letter, last week. She didn't say much.'

'No.' Jack seemed to be focusing on a spot above her head. 'Tricky time. I think her mother needs her for a bit, and the regiment's all over the shop, so I'm hardly ever home. So—' He made himself look at her again. 'What about you? Where are you chaps going to live?'

She told him about going back to Lahore—that Frank's work on blackwater fever would resume this summer. She was, she said, determined to go too—she could work almost anywhere.

'Yes, go,' he said, with surprising ferocity. 'It doesn't work staying apart. You've got to be one thing or the other. I haven't been. I've been—' He said something else but she missed it. A sound drew their attention away. Suday was blasting away at his tabla again; a group of children were blowing on recorders, others through combs onto Bronco paper. Frank moved towards her. He was laughing; he put his arm round her and she felt the extra glow of life beginning in her again.

Daisy, the sun bouncing off her spectacles, stood up on top of a box that had been decorated with crepe paper. She beamed at them. She hit a glass with her teaspoon. Tor, standing beside her, winked at Viva.

'People, people! If I might.' Daisy, head cocked, waited for silence. 'This is a good news day,' she said at last. 'Daktar Frank and Miss Viva are married, the sun is shining, we are at the feast of life. Hard times will come.' When she closed her eyes, everyone knew she was thinking about the home again. 'But we must not get ahead of ourselves.'

'Hear hear!' said Toby stoutly.

'We owe each other so much,' said Daisy in a faint voice. 'We owe you so much,' she told the children.

Then Talika stood up on the crepe-covered box Daisy had vacated.

'Sanskrit poem,' she said. She took a deep breath.

*'Look well to this day*,' she read out in her piping voice.
*'For it is life.*
*In its brief course lies all the realities of existence.*
*For yesterday is but a memory and tomorrow only a vision.'*

But then a gust of wind tore her poem away. It stirred the leaves in the tamarind tree and when a donkey honked thunderously in the street outside the children burst out laughing.

'Look well to this day.' Talika made a last-ditch effort to be heard and inject some solemnity into the proceedings.

Everyone cheered; she hopped down and bobbed her head shyly.

Viva glanced at Tor, who was smiling. She thought of water rushing by, of a huge sky above them all, of being so lost she thought she'd never be found again, then Talika tugged at her fingers. They were ready to dance again.

## Julia Gregson

**Before becoming a journalist, you had a variety of jobs in the Australian outback. What took you to Australia?**

My family moved to Australia because my father was stationed there with the Air Force. I attended school and then worked as a jillaroo—a female ranch hand. I helped look after the horses and exercise them every morning. I was only sixteen and was in heaven. I also worked as a groom and a shearer's cook, and as a nanny for a very uptight lady who kept an immaculate house in a dusty outback town in New South Wales. Ironing in 100 degrees—no fun.

**You then ended up modelling for Hardy Amies in London. How did that happen?**

I think my mother felt I needed civilising after being in the outback, so she sent me to the Lucy Clayton Modelling School in London. Hardy Amies were looking for a house model and I turned up one day. The job was mainly sitting around in a silk dressing-gown, or drifting up and down in front of clients in all the beautiful clothes. I earned eight pounds a week and lived in a grotty flat.

**What then led you to become a journalist?**

I married young and my then husband (now deceased) was doing a Ph.D in English Literature. He encouraged me to do a mature student degree in the same subject. That re-awoke an ambition to write. Then one day, when I was riding horses on the film set of *Ned Kelly*, back in Australia, I was asked to ride out with a young baby-faced rocker called Mick Jagger. I wrote a story about it, and it was published on the front page of the *Sydney Morning Herald*. Getting that story printed was a turning point. I'd found what I wanted to do. I instantly gave up my day job which was stupid. I didn't sell another story for a year.

**Did you travel to India to research *East of the Sun*?**

I had been to Bangladesh as a foreign correspondent after the war there in 1973, to do a series of stories on orphanages, and to interview women who had been raped during the war. My descriptions of the orphanage at Tamarind House in *East of the Sun* drew on this experience. During the writing of the book I went back to India twice: once to Rajasthan and Shimla, with my husband and daughter, and once, on my own, to Bombay.

**How did you research the fishing fleet?**

My husband Richard's mother, Violet, went out to India as a member of the fishing fleet, and he told me some wonderful stories about her. I also interviewed a number of memsahibs, and listened to tapes of a childhood heroine of mine, a Mrs Smith Pearse, who was also part of the fishing fleet.

**Would you like to have lived in the Twenties?**

No. I think that underneath the bursts of gaiety it must have been an incredibly sad time with a whole generation of young men lost in the war. I set my book in this period because it was such an interesting time of transition in India.

**Of your three heroines, which one did you empathise with most?**

I empathised with Viva's longing to write, and her sense of always being an outsider, but, like Tor, I've never been very good at being mysterious and slightly envy people who are.

**What is your favourite Indian food?**

Almost any recipe from Madhur Jaffrey's cookbooks.

**What would your perfect 'what-the-hell' day be?**

That's hard. Pink champagne would come into it, and a long-distance ride on a horse. But then I'd want to dress up and have a jolly evening with my husband and friends, maybe in Paris or London. Am I having too much fun?!

**And do you have any unusual hobbies? Although with two Welsh cobs, a Shetland pony, two dogs and a writing career, I guess you don't have too much spare time!**

Long-distance riding is a passion of mine. I find riding frees the mind and takes me out of my everyday self. Perfect recreation for a writer.

*Jane Eastgate*

# The Sugar Queen
## Sarah Addison Allen

Josey is desperately unhappy.
She spends her days running around after
her demanding, widowed mother and her
nights alone in her room, reading
romance novels and eating junk food.
But Josey dreams of a different
life and a handsome prince to rescue
her—all she needs is a fairy godmother
to wave a magic wand . . .

# 1
## Everlasting Gobstoppers

WHEN JOSEY WOKE UP and saw the feathery frost on her windowpane, she smiled. Finally it was cold enough to wear long coats and tights. It was cold enough for scarves and shirts worn in layers, like camouflage. It was cold enough for her lucky red cardigan, which she swore had a power of its own. She loved this time of year. Summer was tedious, with the light dresses she pretended to be comfortable in while secretly sure she looked like a loaf of white bread wearing a belt. The cold was such a *relief*.

She went to the window. A fine sheen of sugary frost covered everything in sight, and white smoke rose from chimneys in the valley below the resort town. Excited, she opened the window, but the sash stuck midway, and she had to pound it the rest of the way with the palm of her hand. It finally opened to a rush of sharp early November air that would have the town in a flurry of activity, anticipating the tourists the colder weather always brought to the high mountains of North Carolina.

She stuck her head out and took a deep breath. If she could eat the cold air, she would. She thought cold snaps were like cookies, like gingersnaps. In her mind they were made with white chocolate chunks and had a cool, brittle vanilla frosting. They melted like snow in her mouth, turning creamy and warm.

Just before she ducked her head back inside, she looked down and noticed something strange. There was a ladder propped against the house, directly underneath her window.

She leaned back in quickly and closed her window. She paused; then she locked it.

She turned and walked to her closet, distracted now. The tree trimmers from yesterday must have left the ladder. Yes. That had to be it. They'd probably propped it against the house and then completely forgotten about it. She opened her closet door and reached up to pull the string that turned on the light.

Then she screamed and backed away, stopping only when she hit her desk and her lamp crashed to the floor.

'Oh, for God's sake,' the woman sitting on the floor of her closet said, 'don't have a cow.'

'Josey?' She heard her mother's voice in the hall, then the thud of her cane as she came closer.

'Please don't tell her I'm here,' the woman in the closet said. Despite the cold outside, she was wearing a cropped white shirt and tight dark blue jeans that sat low, revealing a tattoo of a broken heart on her hip. Her hair was bleached white-blonde with about an inch of silver-sprinkled dark roots showing. Her mascara had run, and there were black streaks on her cheeks. She looked drip-dried, as if she'd been walking in the rain, though there hadn't been rain for days. She smelt like cigarette smoke and river water.

Josey turned her head as her bedroom door began to open. Then, in a small act that changed everything, she reached over and pushed the closet door closed as her mother entered the room.

'Josey? What was that noise?' Margaret asked. She'd been a beautiful woman in her day, delicate and trim, blue-eyed and fair-haired. There was a certain power beautiful mothers held over their less beautiful daughters. Even at seventy-four, with a limp from a hip replacement, Margaret could still enter a room and fill it like perfume. Josey could never do that.

'My lamp,' Josey said. 'It attacked me out of nowhere.'

'Oh, well,' Margaret said distantly, 'leave it for the maid to clean. Hurry up and get dressed. My doctor's appointment is at nine.'

'Yes, Mother.'

Margaret closed the bedroom door. Josey waited until the clump of her cane faded away before she rushed to the closet door and opened it again.

Most locals knew who Della Lee was. She waitressed at a greasy spoon called Eat and Run, outside the town limits. She haunted bars at night. She was probably in her late thirties, maybe ten years older than

Josey, and she was rough and flashy and did whatever she wanted.

'Della Lee Baker, what are you doing in my closet?'

'You shouldn't leave your window unlocked. Who knows who could get in?' Della Lee said, single-handedly debunking the long-held belief that if you dotted your windowsills and door thresholds with peppermint oil no unwanted visitors would ever appear. For years Josey's mother had instructed every maid in their employ to anoint the house's casings with peppermint to keep the undesirables away. Their house smelt like the winter holidays all year round.

Josey took a step back and pointed. 'Get out.'

'I can't. I need a place to hide.'

'I see. And of course this was the first place you thought of.'

'Who would look for me here?'

Rough women had rough ways. Was Della Lee trying to tell her that she was in danger? 'OK, I'll bite. Who's looking for you, Della Lee?'

'Maybe no one. Maybe they haven't discovered I'm missing yet.' Then, to Josey's surprise, Della Lee reached over to the false wall at the back of the narrow closet and slid it open. 'And speaking of discoveries, look what I found.'

Revealed now was the large secret space behind the closet. There were stacks of paperback romances and magazines on the floor, but most of the secret closet was occupied by shelves piled with food—packaged snacks, rows of sweets, towers of colas.

Josey's entire body suddenly burned with panic. She'd never be the beauty her mother was, or have the personality of her late father. She was pale and plain and just this side of plump, and she accepted that. But food was a comfort. It filled in the hollow spaces. And it felt good to hide it, because then she could enjoy it alone without worrying about what others thought, or about letting her mother down.

'I need to figure some things out first,' Della Lee said, sliding the door back in place, her point made. She was letting Josey know that she knew her secret. *Don't reveal mine and I won't reveal yours.* 'Then I'll be moving up north.'

'You're leaving Bald Slope?'

'Like you don't dream of leaving this stupid town,' Della Lee said, leaning back on her hands.

'Don't be ridiculous. I'm a Cirrini.'

'Correct me if I'm wrong, but aren't those travel magazines in your secret closet?'

Josey bristled. She pointed again. 'Get *out*.'

'It looks like I got here just in time. This is not the closet of a happy woman, Josey.'

'That's it. I'm calling the police.'

Della Lee laughed. 'And what will you say? There's a woman in your closet, come get her out? They might find your stash.'

'So you stay, you don't tell anyone—is that it?'

'Sure,' Della Lee said easily.

'That's blackmail.'

'Add it to my list of sins.'

'I don't think there's room left on that list,' Josey said as she took a dress from its hanger. Then she closed the closet door on Della Lee.

She went to the bathroom down the hall to dress and to pull her very curly liquorice-black hair into a low ponytail. When she walked back to her bedroom, she stared at her closet door for a moment. Maybe she'd imagined the whole thing.

She opened the door.

'You should wear make-up,' Della Lee said.

Josey reached up and grabbed her lucky red cardigan off the high shelf, then closed the door. She put the sweater on and closed her eyes. *Go away, go away, go away.*

She opened the door again.

'No, really. Mascara. Lip gloss. Something.'

Josey sighed. The sweater was probably just rusty. Good things happened when she wore this sweater. She'd had the best haircut she'd ever had while wearing it. When she'd slept in it once, it snowed for three days straight.

And she'd been wearing it the day she first met Adam.

'Eyeliner?' Della Lee said.

Josey closed the door and walked away.

The Cirrinis' new maid spoke very little English.

Helena was hired to help Margaret after her hip replacement. Basically, her duties were light housekeeping, preparing meals and learning English by gossiping with Margaret.

When Josey and Margaret arrived home from Margaret's doctor's appointment, Josey heard the vacuum cleaner humming upstairs. She helped her mother into her favourite chair in the sitting room, then she went upstairs, where Helena was vacuuming the runner in the hallway.

Josey approached Helena and tapped her on the shoulder to get her attention. She got her attention, all right. Helena screamed.

'It's me,' Josey said. 'I didn't mean to scare you. Are you OK?'

Helena put her hand to her heart, breathing heavily. She nodded.

'Helena, did you, um, clean up the broken lamp in my bedroom?'

'I clean.' She crossed herself; then she kissed the crucifix on her necklace. 'Oldsey's room strange today.'

'Strange? Did you see anything . . . unusual?'

'See, no. *Feel.* Cold in Oldsey's room,' she said.

Josey sighed in relief. 'Oh, I opened my window earlier, that's all.' She smiled. 'Don't worry about vacuuming up here. Mother is downstairs in the sitting room.'

'Oldgret downstairs?'

'Yes. Margaret is downstairs.'

That would keep them both occupied and away from Josey's room for a while. Margaret liked to watch Helena clean. And Helena, as far as she was able, liked to spread the latest gossip.

Josey went to her bedroom. Her stomach growled as she stared at her closet. Her food was there. All her lovely food.

The secret closet was the closet in the adjoining room. That bedroom had a huge armoire in it, a heavy old Cirrini heirloom. It took up most of one wall and hid that closet. She'd found the door between the two closets by accident, when she would sit in her closet and eat candy she hid in her pockets when she was young. Now she stocked the secret space with magazines, paperback romances and sweets. Lots and lots of sweets. MoonPies and pecan rolls, Chick-O-Sticks and Cow Tales, Caramel Creams and Squirrel Nut Zippers, Red Hots and Bit-O-Honey, boxes of Little Debbie snack cakes.

Josey took off her coat and put it and her bag on the blue tufted chaise longue, then went to the closet and opened the door.

'Did I just hear your maid call you and your mother Oldsey and Oldgret?' Della Lee asked, laughing.

Of course Della Lee found that funny. Some people liked to call Josey and her mother the Cirrini Sisters. Josey was only twenty-seven, so they were essentially calling her an old woman, but they were comparing her to Margaret, who was once the belle of Bald Slope, the woman married to the late, great Marco Cirrini. Josey looked like a thick dark blob next to her. *Sisters?* Margaret would say. *We look nothing alike.*

Josey's shoulders dropped. 'It's a wonder she didn't see you. You're going to get caught.'

'It's just for a little while.'

'Define "a little while".'

'However long it takes, I guess. Days? Weeks?'

'Excuse me,' Josey said as she leaned in and slid back the false wall.

Della Lee scooted to a corner. Josey grabbed a red tin of Moravian cookies and went to her desk and sat. She opened the tin of cookies and started eating slowly, savouring each thin spice-and-molasses bite.

Della Lee turned and sprawled out on the floor of the closet, staring up at Josey's clothes. 'So this is the life of Josey Cirrini.'

Josey focused on her cookie. 'If you don't like it, you can leave.'

'I didn't know your life was like this. I used to envy you when you were a kid. I thought you had everything.'

Josey didn't know what to say. She couldn't imagine someone as beautiful as Della Lee envying her. Josey only had money.

Suddenly her head tilted to one side. Like magic, she felt him getting nearer, felt it in the pit of her stomach. Like the best kind of expectation. Ice cream expectation. Chocolate expectation.

'What's the matter?' Della Lee asked as Josey pushed back her chair and went to her window.

He was coming up the sidewalk. He was early today.

The Cirrini house was located in one of the oldest neighbourhoods in town. When Marco Cirrini made his fortune with the Bald Slope Ski Resort, he bought a house in the neighbourhood he'd always dreamed about living in, then promptly tore the house down. He built a large bright blue Victorian lady in its place. He said he wanted a house that would stand out even among the standouts.

Adam would be at the door in no time.

Josey hurried out of the room.

Helena and Margaret were talking in the sitting room when Josey came down the stairs, slowing her pace to a walk. 'The mail is here,' she called to them.

Margaret and Helena didn't stop their conversation.

Josey opened the front door; then she pushed open the screen, her eyes on the front porch steps. The screen door abruptly stuck, hitting something soft. She realised, to her horror, that she'd hit Adam Boswell with the door as he was putting the mail in the black-flapped mailbox hanging to the right.

'Whoa,' Adam said, smiling. 'What's your hurry, Josey?'

He was dressed in his cooler-weather uniform, the trousers covering the scars on his right leg, the leg he favoured. He was a good-looking, athletic man. His round face was always tanned—golden, in fact, like something warm and bright was glowing inside him. He had curly dark blond hair he sometimes pushed back with a bandanna tied round his head. He was in his thirties, and he had a secret. She didn't know what it was, but she could tell.

Adam wasn't from here, Josey knew that much. Three years ago he'd shown up on her doorstep, mail in hand, and her dreams had never been the same. Adventurous types flocked to Bald Slope and its famous steep ski runs. Though her mother had sold the resort shortly after had Marco died, it made Josey feel happy to think that she had something, however tenuous, to do with Adam being here.

When she just stood there and stared at him, he said, 'Josey, are you OK?'

She felt herself blush. He was the only person in the world she was tongue-tied around, and yet the only person she really wanted to talk to. 'I'm sorry,' she said. 'I didn't know you were already here. You're early today.'

'The mail was light. This is all I have for you,' he said, handing her the catalogue he'd been about to put in the mailbox.

'Thank you.'

'Beautiful day, isn't it?' he said, taking a deep breath. The cool noon air was flavoured with the mulchy scent of fallen leaves. 'I love fall.'

Josey froze, completely enchanted by him. 'Me *too*.'

'It makes you want to do something, doesn't it?' he said, grinning. 'Like get out and . . . play in trees.'

That made Josey laugh. Adam watched her as she laughed, and she didn't know why. It was like she'd surprised him.

Adam finally said, 'Well, I'll see you later.'

'Right,' she said. 'Bye, Adam.'

He walked down the steps and crossed the street. As soon as he reached the other side, she went back into the house.

She walked into the sitting room, where Helena had set up the ironing board to press some of Margaret's dresses.

'Only a catalogue in the mail,' Josey said. 'I'm going to take it to my room, OK?'

'Wait,' Margaret said, squinty-eyed as she looked Josey over. 'Were you wearing that sweater at the doctor's office?'

Oh no. She meant to take it off when she came in. 'Yes,' she said, then added quickly, 'but I had my coat on over it.'

'Josey, I asked you to get rid of that sweater last year. It's been washed so many times that it's far too small for you. And red isn't a good colour on you. Try white. Or black.'

'Yes, Mother.'

Josey walked back out of the sitting room. She went up the stairs to her room, where she sat at her desk and stared at the wall.

'So who is he?' Della Lee asked from the closet.

'Excuse me?'

'The man you ran out of here to see.'

Josey sat up straighter. 'I don't know what you mean.'

Della Lee was silent for a while as Josey pretended to look at the catalogue. 'It feels like he's taken your heart, doesn't it?' Della Lee finally said. 'Like he's reached in and pulled it from you. And I bet he smiles like he doesn't know, like he doesn't know he's holding your heart in his hand and you're *dying* from him.'

It was the truest, purest, saddest thing she had ever heard spoken. Josey turned to look at Della Lee.

'You're wondering how I know. Girls like us, when we love, it takes everything we have. Who is he?'

'Like I would tell you.'

'I can help you, you know.' Della Lee leaned back.

'You're in no shape to help anyone. What happened to you, Della Lee? You still look like you're wet.'

Della Lee looked down at her clothes, then she touched her hair, which was heavy and flat. 'Oh, I forgot,' she said. 'I took a little dip in the river.'

'You swam in the river at this time of year?' Josey asked.

'Seemed like a good idea at the time. The last stupid thing I did before I went up north.' Della Lee shrugged. 'Like redemption, you know?'

'Redemption for what?'

'More than you could ever imagine. Listen, I want you to go to a sandwich shop on the ground-floor rotunda of the courthouse. A woman named Chloe Finley owns the place, and you'll love her. She makes a grilled-tomato-and-three-cheese sandwich that will make your head spin it's so good. Get me one, will you?'

Josey, stuck on the image of Della Lee in the cold Green Cove River, dunking herself in her own version of a baptism, was caught off guard by the sudden change of subject.

'You want me to get you a sandwich right now?'

'Why not?'

'Because I have to eat lunch with my mother at twelve thirty. Then I have to sit with her when our financial adviser comes by this afternoon.'

Unfazed, Della Lee said, 'Tomorrow, then.'

'I take my mother for her manicure and pedicure tomorrow.'

'No wonder you have so many travel magazines. If you ever manage to get off this gerbil wheel, I bet you'll take off.'

'I *will not*,' Josey said, indignant, because respectable daughters stayed. Never mind that she dreamed of leaving every single day.

Della Lee snorted.

Josey put the lid back on the cookie tin and stood. She returned it to the closet. 'You can eat anything you want in here. I'm not getting you a sandwich.'

'No, thanks. I'll wait.'

'You're going to be waiting a long time.'

Della Lee laughed. 'Honey, I've got nothing but time.'

## 2
## Swee Tarts

FOR NEARLY A CENTURY the town of Bald Slope barely sustained itself as a High Country summer getaway for the hot, wilted wealthy from North Carolina's Piedmont. The town slept like a winter beast during the cold months, its summer houses and most of its downtown shops boarded up, the locals getting by on money they'd earned in the summer.

Marco Cirrini had been skiing on Bald Slope Mountain since he was a boy, using the old skis his father had brought with him from Italy. Marco led groups of local boys up the mountain, showing them how to make their own skis and how to use them. When he was nineteen, he decided he could make great things happen in the winter in Bald Slope. Cocky, not afraid of hard work, and handsome in that mysterious Mediterranean way that excluded him from mountain society, he gathered investors to buy the land and construct the lodge. It took fifteen years, but the Bald Slope Ski Resort was finally completed and was an immediate success.

Stores didn't shut down for the winter any more. Bed and breakfasts and sports shops and restaurants sprouted up. Instead of closing up their houses for the winter, summer residents began to rent them out to skiers. Some summer residents even decided to move to Bald Slope permanently. Marco himself was welcomed into this year-round society. Finally it didn't matter where he came from. He'd saved Bald Slope by giving it a winter economy, and he could do no wrong. This town was finally his.

Josey stopped in front of a small yellow bungalow and compared the number on the mailbox to the address she'd copied out of the phone book that morning. This was it. Della Lee obviously hadn't tended to her yard since summer. Garden gnomes and plastic flowers still lined the walkway to the porch, and there was a long plastic chair for sunbathing still in the yard, now covered with small red-black leaves that had fallen from the dogwood by the house.

Josey put the large gold Cadillac—her mother's idea—in park and cut the engine.

This blue-collar neighbourhood was one Josey was faintly familiar with because her father would pass through it on their Sunday drives when she was a child. Josey lived for those drives. It was the only time in her entire childhood she ever felt calm. The rest of the time she was locked in a constant power struggle with her mother. She had no idea why she'd been so mean as a child. She had no idea why she'd pitched such fits. But during those drives, Josey would relax while Marco talked. He knew everything about Bald Slope. He was in his late sixties when Josey was born, an established figure in town, rich, silver-haired and swaggering.

Marco died when Josey was nine, and all she had left was her mother. That's when she decided, if it took for ever, that she was going to make it up to her mother for every horrible thing she'd done. The day her father died was the first day Josey bit her tongue, the first day she took criticism and didn't fight back, and the day she began to realise how hard it was going to be to change the way people saw her as a child. Almost twenty years later, she was still trying.

Taking a deep breath, Josey got out of the car.

She'd caught a lucky break that day after taking her mother to the salon. Josey usually sat and waited for her, chatting with the older ladies. But her mother reminded her that she had to pick up the peppermint oil specially made for her by Nova Berry, the woman whose family ran the organic market.

Josey went to pick up the oil, but Nova didn't have it ready yet. She said to come back in a few days. After leaving the market, Josey only meant to drive by Della Lee's house. Della Lee had been in Josey's closet for two days now, and Josey was still no closer to figuring out why she was there or how exactly to get her out. Maybe Della Lee's house would give Josey something to bargain with.

Nothing like a little breaking and entering to liven up a day.

When Josey reached the porch she was surprised to find the door open. She knocked on the screen door. No answer.

'Hello?' she called.

Still no answer. She opened the screen door and entered.

The place was a mess. There were beer cans everywhere. There was a broken coffee mug on the floor and a chair was overturned.

She had only taken a few steps in when she stopped short, her heart jumping against her rib cage like a startled cat.

*There was a man sleeping on the couch.*

She stood there for a few moments, paralysed, afraid that she might have made enough noise to wake him. He was, very clearly, not the kind of man you wanted to wake.

He didn't have a shirt on and his muscles indicated he spent a lot of time in a gym. His cheekbones were high and his hair was long, straight and dark. He smelt of alcohol and of something else, like if you took a match to a rosebush. It smelt good, but dark and smoky, and it made Josey feel heady, like she was losing herself in it somehow.

All at once she understood. This was the reason Della Lee left.

She felt a connection to Della Lee at that moment, one she couldn't explain. She *felt* her here, felt her genuine, profound unhappiness like it was her own.

She turned her head slightly, and she could see down a short hallway. She took a few slow steps backwards, keeping her eyes on the man's face, watching for movement. She then turned and walked down the hallway, bypassing small piles of his dirty clothes.

Della Lee's bedroom walls were painted purple, and there were sheer lavender curtains on the single window. There was a white mirrored dresser that had make-up tubes and bottles littered across the surface. Some tote bags were stashed in the corner near the dresser.

Josey grabbed a few bags and slowly slid open the drawers until she found socks and panties and bras. She stuffed one bag full, then she put the make-up in another bag.

Her heart beating thickly, she went to the closet and took clothes off the hangers as quietly as possible. She knelt to get a few pairs of shoes. She was just about to stand when she noticed the cardboard box in the corner of the closet. It had sweaters stacked on top of it and PRIVATE written on the side in green marker.

She crawled to the box. Inside were dozens of old spiral notebooks, bundles of letters and photographs. There was a yearbook from Bald Slope High, with Della Lee's name embossed on it.

She suddenly heard some movement coming from the living room. She turned her head, brushing a coat that was hanging above her, and it swayed precariously. She heard the man sigh and then the squeak of the springs on the old couch.

He was coming down the hall.

She strained to hear what he was doing. It took a moment to realise that he was using the bathroom, which shared a wall with the closet. The commode flushed and he shuffled out into the hall. His steps were slow, sleepy.

The squeak of the couch springs again.

Silence.

Josey waited until her muscles were quivering with tension from keeping the same awkward position for so long, then she scooted out of the closet with the box. She grabbed the tote bags, went to the bedroom doorway and peered out before slowly walking down the hallway. She stopped just before the turn into the living room.

She could hear him breathing. But was his breath shallow enough to indicate he was asleep again? She screwed up her courage and took that final step into the living room.

Then she almost dropped everything she was carrying.

*He was sitting up on the couch.*

But then she saw that his head was resting back against the cushions. He'd fallen asleep sitting up. On the coffee table in front of him was a scuffed leather pocketbook with a shiny purple wallet sticking out of it with the initial *D* on it in white.

Della Lee would need her ID.

Josey was trembling as she took those few steps to the pocketbook. She had to lean down, box and tote bags and all, to get the wallet and slide it out.

Josey then backed quietly to the door, pushing open the screen with her butt, her eyes not leaving him until the last possible moment, when she had to turn.

She tried to catch the screen door with her elbow so it wouldn't slap shut, but she was too late. It hit the casing with a bang.

She took off down the steps. She fished her keys out of her coat pocket and opened the trunk at exactly the same time the screen door to the bungalow slapped shut again and the beautiful long-haired man walked out onto the porch.

'Hello? What are you doing?' the man called out to her. His voice was melodic and the air carried it to her like a present.

She actually stopped for a moment and turned to him. Seduction was his sixth sense and he knew he'd caught her.

'You,' the man said, smiling with an edge as he walked down the steps towards her. 'Were you just in my house?'

She heard the caw of a crow nearby, a portent of danger, and she gave a start. Snapping out of his spell, she quickly threw the things into the trunk, then slammed the lid closed.

Josey hurried to the driver's side and got in. As she drove away in the largest Cadillac in the entire Southeast, the man stood on the sidewalk and watched, his stare as dark as a Gypsy curse.

After getting her mother settled in bed that night, her sleeping pill and water beside her on the nightstand, Josey crept down the stairs and outside to the car. She took the things up to her room, then opened her closet door and set the box and bags in front of Della Lee.

'What is this?' Della Lee asked, surprised. She had washed her face since Josey had last seen her earlier that day, so the mascara streaks were gone. How she'd managed to do that without anyone noticing was a mystery.

Josey smiled. 'A surprise! I went to your house today.'

'You did *what*?'

Josey went to her knees and opened one of the bags. 'Look. I picked up some of your things. Here are some clothes and make-up, and here's your wallet. And this box. It looked like the kind of thing you wouldn't want to leave behind.'

Della Lee was shaking her head, slowly at first, then more and more quickly. 'Was Julian still there?'

'The man with long hair? He was asleep on the couch.'

'But you saw him,' Della Lee said.

'I saw him.'

'Then you understand.'

Josey swallowed. 'Yes.'

'You have to promise me not to do anything else like this, Josey. Don't go back there to him. *Promise!*'

'OK, OK. I promise.'

'I can't believe you would do this for me.' Della Lee scooted the box towards her. It made a loud scraping noise against the hardwood floor.

'Josey!' Margaret called from down the hall.

'No one's ever done anything like this for me.' Della Lee suddenly grabbed the bags and brought them towards her, hugging them. 'Could I have a little privacy here?'

Josey hesitated at first, then got to her feet.

'Close the door, will you? And don't forget to go see Chloe at the courthouse and get my sandwich,' Della Lee said as she brought a shirt out of one of the bags.

Josey shook her head, thinking, If Della Lee were a candy, she would be a SweeTart, the chewy kind you had to work on and mull over, your eyes watering and lips turning up into a smile you didn't want to give.

'Josey!' Margaret called again.

Josey turned quickly and went to check on her mother.

Margaret liked to look at one particular photo after she took her sleeping pill, because sometimes it made her dream of him. She was thirty-one in the photo, but she looked much younger.

Long ago, when she was a young woman, younger even than in the photo, she thought she would be happier here in Bald Slope than she was in Asheville. She would be away from her family and their demands of her. She was only twenty-three when she married Marco. He was almost twenty-two years her senior, but he was rich and charismatic. Still, it didn't take long to understand that Marco only wanted a beautiful wife and the cachet of her old Southern family name. He didn't want *her.* But when she was thirty-one, for one brief, wonderful year, she wasn't lonely. She was happy, for the first and only time she could ever remember.

The photo had been taken at a picnic social, and he wasn't supposed to be in the picture. He was caught by accident so close to her. She'd cut the photo in half years ago, when she thought cutting him out of her life was the right thing to do. But she could still see his hand in the photo, a young man's hand, just barely touching hers. The hand wasn't her husband's.

Josey tapped on Margaret's bedroom door and entered. 'Is something wrong, Mother? Do you need something?'

'What are you doing in your room? I heard a scraping sound.'

'I was sitting at my desk,' Josey said. 'I pulled back the chair. I'll go to bed now. I won't make any more noise.'

'All right,' Margaret said. Josey started to turn. 'Josey?'

'Yes, Mother?'

'Did you get rid of that sweater like I asked?'

'Yes, Mother.'

'I wasn't trying to be mean the other day. It just doesn't look good on you.'

'Yes, Mother,' Josey said.

The truth was, that sweater, that colour, looked good on her daughter. And every time she wore it, it hinted at something that scared Margaret. Josey was growing into her beauty.

Margaret watched Josey leave.

She used to be a beautiful woman, the most beautiful woman around. She brought out the photo again.

But that was for ever ago.

# 3
# Rock Candy

ACROSS TOWN, early the next morning, Chloe Finley stared at the door of her apartment. Her boyfriend, Jake, was on the other side of the door, outside in the hall.

She couldn't believe this was happening. She'd just kicked Jake out after he'd admitted he'd cheated on her. Dazed, she turned round . . . and tripped over a book on the floor.

She looked down at it and sighed. She'd half expected this. Whether she liked it or not, books always appeared when she needed them. Since she'd moved in with Jake five years ago, books had come to her less frequently. When they did show up, she ignored them. After all, how did you explain such a thing? Books appearing all of a sudden?

She could remember clearly the first time it happened to her. Being an only child raised by her great-grandparents on a farm miles from town, she was bored a lot. When she ran out of books to read, it only got worse. She was walking by the creek along the wood line one day when she was twelve, feeling mopish and frustrated, when she saw a book propped up against a willow tree.

She walked over and picked it up. It was a book on card tricks.

She sat under the tree by the creek and read as much as she could before it got dark. She wanted to take it with her when her great-grandmother called her home, but she knew she couldn't. The owner of the book would surely want it back. So she reluctantly left it by the tree and ran home.

After dinner Chloe took a deck of cards out of the kitchen drawer and went to her bedroom to try some of the tricks. She couldn't get them right without following the pictures in the book. She sighed, and that's when she saw the book, the same book she'd left by the creek, on her nightstand.

For a while after that, she thought her great-grandparents were surprising her with books. She'd find them on her bed, in her closet, in her favourite hide-outs around the property. But when her great-grandparents confronted her about all the books she had and where she got the money to buy them, she realised they weren't the ones doing it. The next day, under her pillow, she found a book on clever storage solutions. It was exactly what she needed, something to show her how to hide her books.

She accepted it from then on. Books liked her.

She slowly picked the book up from the apartment floor. It was titled *Finding Forgiveness*. She stared at it a long time, anger bubbling inside her. What the hell did books know about forgiveness?

She went to the kitchen, put the book in the refrigerator and shut the door. She slid her back down the door and sat on the floor. Jake had woken her up that morning by kissing his way down her stomach. She could feel her abdominal muscles clench at the memory, even though she was furious with him now, *livid*. But she could never seem to help her physical reaction when it came to Jake. She'd never loved anyone as much or felt such passion. To this day she could make tap water boil just by kissing him. As he had moved over her that morning, she'd said, 'I would die before I could ever be with anyone else.'

Jake had suddenly closed his eyes, and that's when he told her.

He made a mistake. He hadn't meant for it to happen. It was just one time, he'd said. Three months ago. The law office had been celebrating after winning the Beasley murder case. Everyone had committed so much time to it, and there had been all this stress, all these emotions, and before he knew it he'd done it.

He loved Chloe, not the other woman.

He begged her forgiveness, telling her he'd do anything to make this right. Anything, it seemed, but tell her the name of the woman he'd slept with.

Chloe sat on the floor in front of the refrigerator and stared into space until the phone rang. The voice that came over the machine belonged to one of the security guards at the courthouse. He was wondering where she was.

She got up, got dressed and went to the door. The book was sitting on the console by the door. She frowned at it as she left.

It was on the passenger seat of her car when she got in.

It was lying on the counter by the cash register when she lifted the security gate to the shop.

**D**owntown was busy that afternoon. Josey had forgotten that preparations had begun for the three-day Bald Is Beautiful festival, which was held every year to kick off the ski season. It took Josey longer than she thought it would to find a place to park. When she entered the courthouse, she walked across the cavernous pink marble rotunda and went to the small shop Della Lee had told her about. It looked like a newsstand from a distance, with shelves of magazines and newspapers and paperback books, but as she got closer, she noticed a sandwich counter and two small café tables.

There wasn't anyone there when she approached.

Suddenly she heard from the back room behind the counter, 'Would you please go away? I don't need you!'

'Excuse me?' Josey said, surprised.

A young woman with the most beautiful hair Josey had ever seen popped her head out of the doorway. 'Oh, I'm sorry,' she said as she walked all the way out of the room. 'I didn't know anyone was out here. Can I help you?'

Her brown eyes were shining. Her gorgeous red hair was a thick mass of curls that fell down her back. She looked like a painting, fragile, caught in a moment she couldn't get out of.

'Are you all right?' Josey automatically asked.

The woman's smile didn't quite meet her eyes. 'I'm fine, thanks. What can I get for you?'

'A grilled-tomato-and-cheese sandwich to go, please.'

'Coming up,' the woman said, and turned round to the grill.

Josey sat at one of the small café tables anxiously checking her watch. She had sneaked out of her mother's ladies' club meeting. She had about twenty minutes to get back before the meeting ended. Josey

wasn't a member of the group, and she always stood off to the side with
the nurses and paid companions of some of the older ladies. Not even
they paid any attention when she slipped out. The only person who
seemed to notice was Rawley Pelham, the older man who owned the
local cab company. Some mysterious part of the Pelhams' family tree
forbade them from breaking promises. Once a Pelham gave you his
word, he had to keep it. If Rawley promised he'd pick you up at ten
o'clock, he was always there at ten o'clock. Annabelle Drake hired him
to take her to these meetings, and he always waited outside. He smiled
at Josey as he leaned against his cab, his collar up against the cold wind.

Josey suddenly felt a pull in the centre of her body. She heard the
courthouse metal detector go off and turned.

It was Adam. He was emptying his pockets before walking through
the metal detector again. He had on a well-worn blue fleece hoodie,
and a bandanna was pushing his hair back.

He didn't look at her as he went straight to the counter. 'Chloe?'

The woman turned from the grill, saw who it was, then turned back
round without a word.

'Come on, Clo. Talk to me. I just got home from work and found
him on my front step.'

'I don't care,' Chloe said.

Adam stared at Chloe's back. 'He never meant to hurt you.'

That made her turn again, spatula in hand. *You knew about it?*

Adam hesitated. Whatever it was, he knew.

Chloe turned back round. 'Just go.'

'Listen, he asked me to go over to your place and get some of his
things. I'll call you tonight before I come by. Jake will be staying with
me for a while.' He waited for her to say something, but when she
didn't, he finally turned and walked away. He glanced at Josey as he
passed her and took a few steps before he stopped. 'Josey,' he said.
'What a surprise.'

'Hi, Adam,' she said breathlessly.

'What are you doing here?'

'I'm waiting on a sandwich.' She quickly added, 'It's not for me.'

'Oh, right.' He studied her for a moment. 'Are you OK?'

'You ask me that a lot.'

'Do I? I'm sorry. You just seem a little sad.'

She shook her head. 'I'm fine,' she lied.

'Well, I'll see you later.'

She watched him go. 'Bye.'

'Here's your sandwich,' Chloe said, putting a white paper bag on the counter.

Josey stood and approached the counter as Chloe punched some buttons on the cash register. 'So, you know Adam?' Josey asked as casually as possible.

'He's my boyfriend—my *ex*-boyfriend's—best friend,' she said. 'It's four dollars even.'

'Oh.' Josey dug around in her bag a little too long, working up enough courage to ask, 'You mean you and Adam aren't a couple?'

'No,' Chloe said, surprised. 'How do you know him?'

Josey finally handed her the money. 'He delivers my mail.'

Chloe took the money. 'Do I know you from somewhere?'

'I don't think so.'

Chloe suddenly smiled. 'Oh, I know! You're Josey Cirrini. There's a portrait of you and your father in the lobby of the ski lodge. I see it every time I go there.'

Josey hadn't thought about that portrait in a long time. 'I'd almost forgotten about that. I didn't know it still hung there.'

'Adam never said he knew you.'

Embarrassed, Josey picked up the warm white bag. 'He doesn't,' she said, and turned to leave. She knocked a book she didn't know was there off the counter. She picked it up and looked at the cover. *Finding Forgiveness*. 'I'm sorry. Is this your book?'

'Unfortunately.' Chloe took the book. As Josey walked away, Chloe went to the back room, saying, 'I said, *go away*.'

'**A**nd then Adam walked in! I couldn't believe it! Apparently, Chloe's boyfriend is his best friend, and he's staying with him now. I think she kicked her boyfriend out.'

Josey was sitting on the floor in front of the closet, talking with animation. The bag with the sandwich in it was sitting on her lap.

While Josey was out, Della Lee had obviously occupied herself by playing with the things Josey had brought from her house. She was wearing a child-sized tiara and some old necklaces from the box, and she had put a rhinestone-studded denim shirt over her T-shirt.

'Who is Adam?' Della Lee asked.

'He's my mailman.'

'Aha!' Della Lee said with a triumphant smile. '*He* was the reason you ran out of here so quickly the other day.'

Josey felt like she'd been caught with a mouth full of jellybeans.

'I always worried about Chloe being so wrapped up in Jake,' Della Lee said, flopping onto her back on the sleeping-bag and pillow Josey had given her.

'You know these people?' Josey asked.

'Not personally.' Della Lee stared up at Josey's clothes. 'But I know Chloe is a good kid. She's . . . twenty-five, I think. I remember I was ten when you were born and twelve when she was born.'

Josey looked at her oddly. 'You remember when I was born?'

'Of course. You were Marco Cirrini's *beloved only child.*'

'Oh.' Della Lee hadn't made a move for the bag, so Josey proudly put it on the floor in front of her. 'Here's your sandwich!'

Della Lee turned her head to look at the bag. 'I ate some things from your closet while you were out. *You* eat the sandwich. You know you want to. Get me another one tomorrow.'

Josey eyed the bag. 'Are you sure?'

'Positive,' Della Lee said. 'Go on, eat. And tell me about seeing *Adam*. The more I know, the better I can help you.'

Josey sighed and opened the bag.

**W**hen Chloe heard the knock that evening, she muted the television with the remote and took the book that had appeared beside her and stuffed it under the couch cushions. 'Behave,' she told it.

She walked across the open living-room/dining-room area and took a deep breath before she opened the door. She knew who it was. Adam had called earlier and said he was coming by. She waved him in. 'His suitcases are under the bed.'

Adam entered the apartment. 'How are you doing, Clo?' he asked as he unzipped his jacket.

'I'm great. Let's go to the bedroom and get this over with.'

'I can't tell you how many women have said that to me.'

Chloe had to smile. Everything about Adam made him seem care-free—his sense of humour, his tanned skin, his curly blond hair. He looked part surfer, part ski bum. And it was true—if there was an extreme outdoor sport, Adam had done it at least once. Up until three years ago, that is. After his accident, he said it was time to settle down. No more risks for him. But Chloe always sensed he wasn't really happy here. She followed him and watched from the bedroom doorway while he took the suitcases out and began to put Jake's clothes in them.

'Josey Cirrini asked about you after you left the shop today,' Chloe said, because that was neutral territory for her. 'She thought you and

I were a couple. She seemed relieved that we weren't.'

Adam stopped packing, giving Chloe the strangest look.

'I take it this is a surprise to you?'

'She's a nice woman and I deliver her mail, that's all.'

'She is nice,' Chloe said. 'Come on, I know you've noticed more than her mail.'

'She smells like peppermint,' he said, giving it some thought.

'You *have* noticed.'

But he didn't say anything else. He disappeared into the attached bathroom, and she crossed her arms over her chest and looked down at her feet.

'I'm going to lose you, aren't I?' she said when he came out of the bathroom with Jake's toiletries.

She liked Adam, but he was friends with Jake first. Everything had been Jake's first. The apartment was Jake's, a stylish red-brick place in the historic renovated firehouse downtown. It had been a gift from his parents when he graduated from law school. She had some furniture left from her great-grandparents' house, along with hundreds of boxes of books that had appeared over the years, in a small storage rental. She'd never asked to put her things here. She didn't know why. She guessed she didn't think they would fit.

Adam walked over to her and put his hands on her arms. 'You're not losing anyone, least of all me. It was a one-time thing, three months ago. He was stupid. People do stupid things.' He dropped his hands from her arms. 'I guess I should be going.' He went back to the bed and zipped up the suitcases, then he noticed a book on the nightstand. 'Is this your book?' he asked as he picked it up.

She looked over at it, expecting it to be that damn book that had been following her all day. But no. This was a new book. *Old Love, New Direction.*

'This is good, Clo.' He held the book in the palm of his hand like a scale, as if the words had weight. 'It's good that you have this.'

Confused, Chloe leaned out of the room and looked over to *Finding Forgiveness*, back on top of the couch cushions in the living room. Good Lord, it had called in reinforcements.

'I should go,' Adam said, putting the book down. He slid the suitcases off the bed and she followed him to the front door. 'Do you want me to tell Jake anything?'

She opened the door. 'No, I don't want you to tell him anything. Good night, Adam,' she said, and closed the door behind him.

She whirled round. *Old Love, New Direction* had joined *Finding Forgiveness* on the couch, like they were waiting to have a talk with her. Great. She was being stalked by self-help books.

The next day at work, *Finding Forgiveness* kept appearing by Chloe on the counter, nudging her, reminding her. At least *Old Love, New Direction* had decided to stay at home. She had just knocked the book off the counter again when she saw a woman crossing the rotunda towards her.

'It's you!' Chloe said, unreasonably glad to see her again. 'Another grilled-tomato-and-cheese to go?'

Josey walked up to the counter. 'You remembered.'

'I remember what everyone orders. I get that from my great-granddad.' Chloe turned and started to assemble the sandwich. 'He used to run this shop. He left it to me. I don't get too many orders for grilled-tomato-and-cheese. There was this one woman who always ordered it, but I haven't seen her in a while.'

'Oh?' she heard Josey say, as if that interested her.

Chloe shrugged and said, 'A pretty woman, older, a little rough. Blonde hair and lots of make-up. Every time I saw her, she was coming from court. Domestic disturbance. Every time.'

As soon as the bread turned golden and the cheddar and Colby and Jack cheese began to melt and sizzle onto the grill, Chloe scooped the sandwich up with a spatula and wrapped it in wax paper. When she turned, Josey had the money ready.

She was dressed that day in a long grey coat, its cloth-covered buttons secured all the way to the top, where a red cardigan peeked out from under the collar. It was easy to overlook, but she was really very pretty. She had beautiful pale skin, which was a stark contrast to her dark eyes and hair, like black marble and snow. She smelt sweet, like candy. No, that wasn't it, Chloe thought. She smelt like *Christmas.* 'Adam's right,' Chloe said as she set the bag on the counter in front of Josey. 'You smell like peppermint.'

'Adam said I smelt like peppermint?' Josey said, her voice pitching slightly.

'Uh-huh. Last night when I talked to him,' Chloe said. She rang up the purchase just as the elevator furthest from them opened and a wave of suits poured out. Court had recessed.

Chloe looked up and found him right away.

Jake looked embarrassed. He didn't know how to handle this any better than she did. He began to walk towards her shop. He had dark hair, and his eyes were light green, a striking shade she could make out even from across the rotunda. He was so intense. A single hard impulse hit her and she wanted to go to him. He'd hug her and they would kiss and the water in the coffeemaker would start to boil and everything would go back to the way it was.

But she stopped herself. That wouldn't make it right. You didn't forgive because it was the only choice you thought you had. That didn't make it forgiveness, that made it desperation. She'd always been too desperate about Jake. *Always.*

'Excuse me,' she said to Josey, starting to turn, to hide in the small storeroom.

'Are you OK?'

He was getting closer. 'I'm just trying to avoid someone.'

Josey turned to see who it was. 'Jake Yardley?'

'You know him?'

'Sort of,' Josey said, turning back round. Chloe wasn't surprised. As prosecutor, Jake had been on the television news almost every night for the duration of the Beasley murder trial.

'He cheated on me,' she said.

'Oh,' Josey said.

Chloe hurried into the storeroom. 'Clo, please come out here,' she heard him call.

'I don't think she wants to.' Chloe cocked her head. That was Josey's voice.

'Chloe, if you don't come here, I'm coming back there.' He was ignoring Josey.

Chloe steeled herself for his presence. He could make her forget that it was desperation. He could make her forget everything.

'You're not going back there,' Josey said.

'Who *are* you?' Jake demanded in his lawyer voice.

To Chloe's surprise, she heard Josey say with some exasperation, 'I'm Josey Cirrini, Jake. I stole your piece of chocolate cake at your grandmother's Christmas party when I was six and made you cry.'

'Josey!' Jake said, as if his memory had suddenly kicked in. 'Where is your mother? What are you doing here?'

'I'm helping out a friend.'

'I know all of Clo's friends.'

'Maybe you only thought you did,' Josey said. A few moments of silence passed before Chloe heard, 'He's gone.'

She walked out sheepishly. 'Thank you,' she said.

'I hope I didn't . . .' Josey waved an arm in the direction Jake had obviously left. The movement revealed the watch on her wrist. When she looked at it, she said, 'Oh no. I have to go.'

'I'll walk you out,' Chloe said, falling into step with Josey as she grabbed the sandwich bag and hurried into the rotunda. They reached the doors and walked out into the cool afternoon. The park in front of the courthouse was a flurry of last-minute activity before the kickoff to the Bald Is Beautiful festival that night. Leaves skittered across the grass on the breeze created as the canopies went up. The clouds were low in the sky, bright grey and full of sparkles. 'Wait,' Chloe said as they reached the courthouse steps. 'Are you going to the festival tonight?'

Josey looked out over the park warily. 'No. Are you?'

'I usually do. I mean, I always went with Jake. I'll go if you go.' She met Josey's eyes. They were about the same height, and their eyes were the same shade of dark brown.

Josey shook her head. 'I haven't been since I was little,' she said. She looked down, confusion coming to her face. She picked up a book that was lying on the steps. 'Isn't this your book?'

Chloe sighed. 'Yes. I think I will go tonight. I didn't do anything without him. That's going to change. I'm going to do this.'

Josey's eyes went from the book to Chloe's face. 'Do you think you'll forgive him?'

'I don't know what I'm going to do yet.' She took a few steps over to a large green trash receptacle and threw *Finding Forgiveness* away. 'Listen, I'll be at the stage around eight o'clock if you change your mind and want to come tonight.'

'Here, eat this, quick,' Josey said as she opened her closet door. She put the sandwich bag in front of Della Lee, who was sitting on the floor on the sleeping-bag.

Josey took off her long grey coat, then slipped out of her lucky red sweater. Was today really lucky? She didn't know how to feel exactly. Things were changing, in tiny ways, but enough to throw her off her normal course.

'Why eat it quick?' Della Lee asked.

Josey walked over to the chaise longue and set her bag, sweater and coat on it. 'I wanted you to eat it warm, so I put it in my bag when I brought in the groceries. But I think my mother smelt it on me.'

'So what?' Della Lee said.

'So, I don't want her to find it here. If she thinks I'm sneaking food in here . . . well, it would embarrass her. And I think I've embarrassed her enough as it is.' The truth was, she sneaked food in all the time—there was just never anyone else involved.

'What have you done to embarrass her? It seems to me that you've given up all semblance of a normal life just for her.'

Josey shook her head. 'I was a terrible child.'

'So what?' Della Lee said again.

'So, I owe her this. And she's my family, my only family.'

Della Lee laughed. 'That you know of.'

'What is that supposed to mean?'

'Joke. It was a joke.' She shook her head. 'Thank you for the sandwich, but I already ate. Here.' Della Lee set the bag outside the closet. 'You eat it.'

Josey sighed and walked over to Della Lee. She sat on the floor in front of the closet and opened the bag. 'I talked with Chloe today. She remembered you, that you ordered this.' She unwrapped the sandwich. 'She said you were always coming from court.'

Della Lee smiled. 'Chloe remembered me? That's nice. I wasn't sure she would.'

'She asked me to go to the Bald Is Beautiful festival tonight.'

'That's great! I knew the two of you would hit it off.'

Josey shook her head and took a bite of the sandwich. 'I can't go.'

'Why not? Wear that sweater you like so much, the one you just took off. It looks good on you. Go, then come tell me everything. I'm forming a plan for you.'

'Della Lee, you're living in my closet. You need to form a plan for yourself.'

Della Lee shook her head. 'I gave up on me a long time ago. There's still some hope for you, though.'

Josey approached the stage, where a band was now setting up. There were lots of college-aged kids milling around in groups, laughing, waiting for the music. She spotted Chloe by her hair, a blaze of red shining in the stage lights. like spun cinnamon sugar.

Josey made a beeline for her. She knew people weren't really looking at her. It only felt that way because Della Lee had insisted she wear her hair down, and she was wearing some of Della Lee's make-up.

Make-up. She couldn't believe it.

She'd never worn make-up in public before. Her mother always said that, with Josey's colouring, it would only make her look cheap. That's why Josey had decided not to tell her mother she was going out tonight. It's why she'd waited until her mother had taken her pill and was fast asleep.

Chloe looked relieved to see her. 'Josey! I was about to give up on you.' She stepped back. 'You look great. Wow.'

With her gloved hand, Josey touched her cheek self-consciously. 'I don't usually wear make-up.'

'You should. The hair, the make-up. It looks like you.'

Josey hesitated, then pushed her curly hair behind her ears, feeling better. 'So, what do we do?' she asked.

Chloe said, 'Want to get something to eat?'

That wasn't something Josey normally admitted in public, but Chloe was already heading to the food booths, so Josey followed. The area smelt like sweet vanilla cake batter you licked off a spoon. Chloe and Josey ate caramel apples and pecan cookies made by tiny old women from madly competitive church groups. Snow flurries began to fall and swirled around people's legs like house cats. It was magical, this snow-globe world.

They were at the end of the craft booths, ready to go towards the stage, when they suddenly turned at the sound of someone calling Chloe's name. Jake Yardley was standing under the colourful lights strung above the walkway formed by the booths. He was a mesmerising man, intense and smart, with those strange green eyes all Yardley men had. People used to say that Yardley eyes could see right through you.

'Clo, *please*,' he called, his voice desperate, a little slurred.

'Crap. I didn't think he'd be here. And I think he's been drinking,' Chloe said tightly as she led Josey away, looking over her shoulder as they walked. 'Oh, good, at least Adam is with him.'

Like a hypnotist's command, that made Josey stop and turn, as if not of her own will. Adam was trying to talk to Jake, standing in front of him and pushing him back. Jake gestured in Chloe's direction and Adam turned his head. He froze, his mouth open as if in mid-sentence. His eyes had fallen on Josey. Did he recognise her? What was that look? Men didn't look at her that way. *He'd* never looked at her that way. Long looks from head to toe were for women like Della Lee and Chloe, not for Josey.

Adam turned away and pulled Jake with him.

'How long?' Chloe asked.

Josey turned to find Chloe looking at her thoughtfully. 'Excuse me?'

'How long have you been in love with Adam?' Chloe smiled.

'Since the moment I saw him,' Josey said quietly.

'I don't think he knows, Josey.'

'Oh, I know he doesn't.'

Chloe looked again to where Adam and Jake had disappeared, then she locked her arm in Josey's. 'Come on.'

It was crowded in front of the stage as Josey followed Chloe into the frantic hive of people. It was like nothing she'd ever experienced before, the movement and cohesion. It was like being enveloped by a warm wave of humanity. Josey felt anxious at first, as if she was going to lose Chloe, or suffocate. But then she let herself move with the flow, like water.

And she *loved* it.

The band's heavy bass boomed so loud she could feel it vibrate from the ground through her boots. For years Josey would lie in bed and hear the music from the festival, but she never dreamed she'd actually be here like this.

About an hour later, Josey suddenly stopped moving with the crowd. She knew he was there before he spoke.

'Chloe?'

Chloe turned her head slightly. 'Adam,' she said.

'I took him home.' Adam leaned forward, talking loudly in order to be heard. 'He was a little sauced. He's trying to give you space, he really is. He feels horrible about what happened.'

'Good.'

Adam's eyes fell on Josey, curious. 'Well, hello, Josey.'

'Hi, Adam.'

He straightened and she turned back to the stage, but she was acutely aware of his presence. He was now standing directly behind her. She closed her eyes. She could feel him move a little closer. Was it her imagination, or was he leaning down, his nose close to her hair?

She opened her eyes. He was *smelling* her.

Oh God, she thought. Was this really real? Or was she making it up? The fear was so real that she turned round quickly, just to make sure. And she bumped right into Adam's chest.

His hands went out to steady her, and she looked up at him. His blue eyes had seen too much sun. Papery snow flurries were sticking to his curly blond hair.

She immediately turned back round and his hands slid off her arms.

'I should be going,' she leaned over and said to Chloe.

Chloe looked from Josey to Adam, then back again. 'Are you OK?'

'Yes, I'm fine. I just have to go.'

'OK. Adam, will you walk Josey to her car?'

'No!' Josey said frantically. Then she tried to smile. 'No, I'm fine. Really. To walk. To my car. Thank you. I'll see you soon.'

*Stupid, stupid, stupid*, she said to herself as she walked away.

Adam and Chloe watched Josey disappear into the crowd.

'You know she's in love with you, don't you?' Chloe said.

He hesitated. 'Excuse me?'

'Josey Cirrini is in love with you,' she said in a louder voice.

'That's ridiculous.'

'She told me. She said she's been in love with you since the first day she saw you. Open your eyes for once, Adam. That mountain didn't kill your libido. Don't mess this up. Why do men have to mess things up?' Chloe turned and left him there.

He watched her go, stunned.

He'd always liked the way Josey smelt. He thought about how she was wearing her curly black hair down that night, how she was in that tight sweater he'd seen her in so many times, the red so striking against her pale skin. And damn if she wasn't wearing make-up.

Was it for him? He suddenly felt uneasy, the way he felt about anything that involved chance.

Oh, hell. His leg was hurting. It was time to go home.

The next morning Adam got up and went to the kitchen of his small home. It had taken him months of searching to find just the right place, with just the right view. He wanted a place that would let him see Bald Slope Mountain, as if he had to keep an eye on it.

This morning his leg burned like a red-hot poker. He'd grown up in the California Sierras. He'd been a competitive skier in high school. He loved the snow, but he was paying now for standing out in it last night. Enjoying snow was yet another thing the mountain had taken from him. Every day, he woke up humbled by that mountain, his aching leg a constant reminder of what you got when you teased fate to the point of payback. That was it for him. No more taking chances. He'd settled down in the place that had broken him. He was safe here.

He knew he couldn't go back to practising law. His older brother, Brett, had an established law firm, so the job had been waiting for Adam when he graduated. But he'd hated it.

He turned, startled, when he heard Jake stumble down the hall. It was hard to get used to having someone else in the house. When Jake appeared in the doorway, Adam said, 'You look like hell.'

'That's a relief. It's not all in my head. Give it to me straight. How big of an ass did I make of myself last night?'

'You don't remember the motorcycle gang? Doing the striptease in front of them at the bar? The iguana? Good God, man. Tell me you remember the iguana!'

'You're a funny guy. I remember seeing her. Who was she with?'

Adam turned to get a bottle of Tylenol from the cabinet. 'A woman named Josey Cirrini.'

'Oh, yeah. She never said she knew her. So I didn't talk to Chloe? I didn't say anything stupid to her?'

'No.' Adam downed three pills and turned back round. 'I have a question for you, Jake.'

'Don't make it a hard one.' Jake went to the coffeemaker and poured a cup. 'My head might explode.'

'Why in the hell did you tell her? She never even suspected.'

'You sound like my father.' Jake took a gulp of the coffee and set the cup down. 'I told her *because* she never suspected,' he finally said. 'She trusted me, and I let her down. And I was just walking around like it didn't happen. Like I got away with it.'

Adam crossed his arms over his chest. 'Let me get this straight: you told her to punish yourself? Like there was no other way to do that except by hurting her?'

'I'm not saying it was the smart thing to do. I love Chloe. I can't believe I did this to her. I wish to God I could take it back. I wish I could take everything back.'

Adam shook his head. Sometimes you weren't supposed to share pain. Sometimes it was best just to deal with it alone. 'Stupid, man. Stupid.'

'I know.'

The mail was heavy on Monday. It meant Adam was later getting to the Cirrinis' neighbourhood. Until now, he'd never paid much attention to the fact that he saw Josey almost every day, that she always seemed to know when he was coming up her walk.

The front door of the immaculate Victorian house opened as he walked up the steps, and she appeared like a spirit in a black dress. The scent of peppermint reached out to him as he got nearer. Damn, she smelt good. He made it to the top step and stopped.

'Hi, Adam,' she said as she walked up to him.

'Josey,' he said cautiously, handing her the mail.

'Thank you.'

'You're welcome.' His smile faded. Then he didn't know what else to do but turn and walk away.

She looked confused as he left. She watched him cross the street before going back into her house.

He walked into the Fergusons' yard, feeling like a jerk. Hell, he didn't want to hurt her. But he didn't want what she wanted . . . whatever that was. What *did* she want?

Mrs Ferguson, a stout woman of about sixty, was hand-trimming the grass bordering her driveway. She was bundled in a fuzzy wool cardigan, and she wore a pair of pink gloves with the fingers cut out.

'Hello, Mrs Ferguson,' Adam said as he opened her box and put the mail in.

'Nice to see you, Adam,' she said. 'That happens every day, you know.'

He stopped. 'I'm sorry, what?' he asked absently.

'Josey. She watches you walk across the street every day.'

Adam looked up.

'She's a nice girl.' Mrs Ferguson lifted herself to her feet with a grunt. 'It's too bad no one sees it.'

'What do you mean?'

'You aren't from here. You don't know the reputation Josey earned when she was a child.'

'What sort of reputation?'

'That girl was the meanest, rudest, most unhappy child I've ever known. She could pitch the loudest fits when she didn't get what she wanted. I think she broke just about everything her mother ever owned. And she threw tantrums in public just as often. Margaret had to hire tutors to teach her at home.'

'*Josey?*' Adam said incredulously.

'I know. She grew up to be so pleasant. But she looks sad, don't you think? She reminds me of Rapunzel. You know, like in the fairy tale. The only time she leaves that house is to take her mother to her few social activities or to run errands for her.'

No, Adam thought. That's not the only time she leaves. He turned to look at her house, more curious than he wanted to be.

Rapunzel had been sneaking out of the castle.

# 4
# Lemon Drops

ALL WEEKEND, alone in the apartment, Chloe would catch herself almost calling for Jake when something funny was on the television, or when she was doing a crossword puzzle and had a question. It finally occurred to her on Sunday evening that this was probably what Jake intended. *He knows you want your space*, Adam had said. Space enough for her to see how much she needed him.

Chloe knew some people from Jake's office went for after-work drinks at Jiggery's, the pub on the square across from the courthouse. Jake wouldn't be there on Monday because it was his dinner night at his parents' house, so she made plans to be at the pub that night. She wanted Jake's coworkers to see her. She wanted it to get back to Jake that she was happily out on her own, thank you very much. And maybe, just maybe, she could get some information from his co-workers. She desperately wanted to know about the woman who had caused all this trouble.

After work on Monday, she went home and changed clothes and carefully applied her make-up. She wanted to look good, but she didn't want to look like she was trying too hard. It took a while to find the balance. A few hours later she walked into Jiggery's, feeling excited. She stood just inside the door and looked around . . . and slowly realised she didn't see anyone she knew. She'd spent so much time getting ready that she'd got there too late. Her shoulders dropped as she went to the bar and ordered a lemon drop.

She was aware of his stare before she was aware of him. It was like feeling rain in the air before it falls. She found him on the other side of the bar, staring at her. He was beautiful, and she was a little startled, when he moved, to see that he was real. He picked up his drink and walked towards her.

'I don't want to bother you,' he said when he reached her, his voice the melody to all her favourite songs, 'and I swear I'm not trying to pick you up, but would you mind if I sit here? I'm meeting some friends and I can see the door better from this side.'

She was finally able to take a deep breath. What was the matter with her? Why was she panicking? It wasn't like she'd never been hit on before. 'Be my guest.'

He took the stool beside her. 'Are you OK?'

'I'm fine,' she said, because she didn't want to say that she felt like she'd lost her left arm. 'Why do you ask?'

'The look on your face, for one. This book, for another.' He gestured towards the bar without taking his eyes off her.

She finally looked away from him and found, next to her drink, a book titled *A Girl's Guide to Keeping Her Guy*. On the cover was a young woman circa the 1950s, wearing a crinoline, high heels and a creaseless half-apron. 'Oh, that,' she said. She quickly turned the book over, hiding its cover.

'Are you worried about keeping your guy?' he asked gently.

'It's just . . .' *Crap*. Books had gone crazy. That was all there was to it. She wouldn't be admitting this to a stranger if it weren't for them. 'I found out last week that my boyfriend cheated on me.'

'Damn,' he said. He looked away and lifted his beer mug to his lips. 'Looks like we're in the same boat. Last week my girlfriend took off without a word.'

'Damn.'

He smiled at that. 'Hearts break. There's nothing you can do except wait for them to heal. Alcohol helps. So does talking to someone about it.'

That was all the prompting she needed. 'I want to know who it was,' she confided, moving in closer to him. 'I can't stop thinking about it. All I know is that she was at an office party three months ago and that's when it happened. Some people from his workplace come here. I was going to ask around, but I got here too late.'

He was nodding as she spoke, encouraging her. 'The courthouse crowd?'

'The DA's office.'

'How about this: I'll keep my ear to the bar for you. See what I can find out.'

His offer startled her, but at the same time she accepted it without question. 'I've never seen you here before.'

'And I've never seen you. I'm here most weekend nights. I just happened to be here tonight to meet some friends.' His eyes drifted over her shoulder. He grabbed his beer and slid off the stool. 'And they just walked in. If you ever want to talk again, you know where to find me.'

She turned as he moved past her. His hair was pulled back in a long and beautiful tail. 'Wait—what's your name?'

He smiled at her over his shoulder. 'Julian.'

Jake's cellphone rang just as his mother served cocktails in the living room. It had been a long time since he'd had to have dinner at his parents' house alone. Sitting there without Chloe, he felt like an exposed wound his mother wanted to bandage but his father kept poking.

'Jake, you know I don't like you to answer calls while you're here. We don't get to see you enough as it is,' Faith Yardley said in a mock scold.

He set his drink down and took his cell out of his pocket. 'It might be work.' He took the phone out to the porch. The night was blue-black and brittle, a perfect late-fall evening.

He flipped open his phone and said, 'Hello?'

'Jake, it's Brandon.'

It *was* work. Brandon was a fellow ADA. 'What's up, Bran?'

'I'll get straight to the point,' Brandon said. 'I went to Jiggery's after work, and then came home and realised I'd left my wallet there. Long story short, I went back and Chloe was there.'

Jake, pacing the porch to keep warm, suddenly stopped. 'Chloe was at Jiggery's? Alone?'

'No. That's just it. She was talking with someone. His name is Julian something. I've seen him in court a few times. Petty stuff, but he's a hitter. I know you and Chloe are having some problems, but I thought you needed to know this.'

Jake's body felt coiled, ready to spring. He was not going to let Chloe get hurt again, by anyone. 'Thanks, Bran. I'll go now.'

Jake closed his phone and put it back in his jacket pocket. He turned to go inside, to get his coat and make his excuses, only to find his father at the front door, leaning in the doorway with his drink in his hand. 'Trouble?' Kyle Yardley asked.

'I have to go, Dad. I'm sorry. It's work—'

'No, you don't. I heard the whole thing. It's Chloe. I told you this when she kicked you out, son. Give her some space. You're not doing yourself any favours by having people keep tabs on her. You shouldn't have told her in the first place.'

Though everyone in the DA's office that night had agreed not to say anything because it would jeopardise all the work that had gone into winning the Beasley murder case, word had somehow leaked out about Jake-the-Wonderboy's indiscretion with an unnamed woman. It had eventually reached his father, who just happened to be the mayor of Bald Slope.

'I'm not trying to keep tabs on her,' Jake said.

'Let her realise she needs you. If you push too hard, she's going to walk. Chloe is good for you. You messed up once. Don't do it again, because if you do it again, you'll lose her for good. Do you want that?'

'Of course not.'

Kyle pushed himself away from the doorway. 'Then come inside and assure your mother that everything is going to be all right.'

'I don't suppose you ever did anything like this,' Jake said as he watched his father disappear inside.

'If I did, you can be damn sure I never told your mother about it,' Kyle called out into the darkness.

On Tuesday afternoon, after a long day of pushing *Finding Forgiveness* off the counter eighty-two times, Chloe was about to clean the grill and reluctantly go home. But then she saw Josey walking across the rotunda towards her, and her day suddenly got a little brighter.

'Josey!' she said. 'I'm so glad you came by. You rushed away so quickly at the festival. I didn't have any way to contact you to find out if you were all right.'

'I know. I came by to tell you I'm sorry,' Josey said as she approached the counter. 'I have a cellphone. I'll start checking messages if you want to call me. Do you have something to write on? I'll give you the number.'

Chloe took one of her business cards from the little stand by the register and handed it and a pen to Josey. Josey turned the business card over and wrote a number on the blank side, capping the pen and putting it beside the card after she'd finished writing.

'Go ahead and take a business card,' Chloe said. 'You can call me here if you want. The bottom number is my cell.'

'I didn't know this place was called Red's,' Josey said, reading the card.

Chloe smiled when she thought of her great-grandfather. 'A family tradition. My great-grandfather had red hair. So did my mother. Why don't you stick around for a minute while I clean up? We can leave together.'

Josey leaned against the counter as Chloe turned round to scrape the grill. 'I see you fished the book out of the trash,' Josey said.

Chloe looked over her shoulder. *Finding Forgiveness* was back on the counter. Josey was stroking the cover. 'Um, yeah.'

'Where do you get your books? The library? The bookstore?'

Chloe hesitated. She'd always wanted to reveal her relationship with books, about how they came to her. She wanted to be told it was all right, that strange things happened to other people too. But she could never bring herself to do it. 'I collect them,' she finally said, going to the sink. 'I have hundreds of boxes of them in storage.'

'Wow.'

'Do you read a lot?' Chloe shut the water off after washing a few things.

'I have favourites I read over and over.'

'You can borrow any of mine,' Chloe said, wiping her hands. 'In fact, let's go to the storage rental now!'

Josey looked surprised. 'Now?'

'I just need to cash out, then I'm finished here. Do you mind?'

'No,' Josey said. 'But you don't have to do this just for me.'

'It's for me too. I haven't been to the storage rental in a while. I have some of my great-grandparents' things there. Maybe it's time I decorate the apartment with some of my stuff.' Chloe cashed out and put the money bag in the safe in the back room. After she locked the security gate, they walked outside. 'I walked to work today. My apartment is about two blocks away, if you want to take my car.'

'That's OK. I'm parked right there.' Josey pointed to a metallic gold Cadillac across the park. She laughed as they walked down the steps. 'It's on loan from Elvis.'

When they got in, Chloe told her the name of the storage rental. Josey knew where it was and headed towards the highway. For the first few minutes, Chloe surreptitiously looked around the car. Everything inside was very neat. There was nothing personal, or even the slightest bit messy, about it. It wasn't Josey at all.

When she finally looked up from her perusal and saw where they were, she suddenly said, 'Oh, wait! Stop right here!'

Josey stopped abruptly. 'What? What's wrong?'

They were on a street called Summertime Road. Small, boxy houses lined the street, looking like old wooden children's blocks left outside, light pink and yellow and green.

'Right here,' Chloe said. 'This house. What do you think of it?'

Josey stared at the buttercup-yellow house with white trim. There was a realtor's sign in the neat front yard. 'Same owners for over thirty years. A neighbourhood that's being revitalised, lots of young families moving in.' Josey shook her head. 'But they're asking too much for it. It's been on the market for over a year and they haven't budged on the price. They're too emotionally attached.'

Chloe laughed. 'How do you know all that?'

'It was brought to us as an investment opportunity.'

'Oh.' Chloe turned back to the house. At that moment she envied Josey's wealth. 'They've had a couple of open houses over the past year. It has the most wonderful library, to the right, just off the entrance. That window there. See? When I first walked in and saw it, I remember thinking, *This is it.*' Chloe sighed. 'I love this house. I pass by it all the time. Jake thinks it's funny.'

'He doesn't like it?'

'He likes it. He likes it because I like it. But at the price they're asking, we'd never be able to afford it without asking Jake's parents for money. Jake has big issues with that.' The car was quiet for a moment. 'That's it. I just wanted to show it to you.'

'It's a beautiful house,' Josey said as they drove away.

'Yes, it is.'

The sun had almost set by the time they reached the storage rental place—a large, sprawling maze of low-slung buildings on an inky-black tarmac. When Chloe lifted the bay door to her unit and turned on the overhead fluorescent lights, Josey walked in and said, 'Wow, look at all this stuff.'

Chloe followed her. She had forgotten how much this place smelt like the farmhouse. She felt calmer all of a sudden. Why hadn't she come here sooner? She walked to a long bank of boxes stacked chest high. 'So, what do you like to read? I have mysteries. I have romance. I have history. Self-help. Classics.'

'Romance,' Josey said.

'I have the most of those, ironically,' Chloe said, walking over to the boxes on the far end. Josey followed. 'I read these just before I met Jake. Tons of them. As soon as I finished one, there was another.'

'How magical,' Josey said.

Chloe shifted uncomfortably. 'Books aren't always right. But maybe they weren't meant for me. Maybe they were meant for you. For you and Adam.' She lifted the lid of one box and said, 'Help yourself.'

Josey paused. 'Um, about Adam. Would you mind not saying anything about me to him? He seems distracted lately, anyway.'

'Uh-oh,' Chloe said. 'I sort of already told him that you've been interested in him for a while.' She laughed at Josey's expression, then reached out and took her hands. 'It's a good thing, Josey! Adam isn't seeing anyone. He needs to get out more. You could ask him out. There's nothing wrong with that. Are you all right?'

Instantly, Josey smiled and nodded. 'Oh, yes. Yes, I'm fine.'

'Are you sure?'

'Of course! What could be wrong? I have my choice of romance novels. I'm in heaven.'

Josey began to go through the books, so Chloe walked around, touching things, smiling. There was the headboard of her old childhood bed. The pie safe. The jelly cabinet. These things weren't meant to just take up space. They'd been waiting all this time for her to *use* them. Furniture was a lot more patient than books.

About a half-hour later, Josey had a respectable pile of books on the floor. 'I'll get these back to you as soon as possible,' she called.

Chloe wove her way around ladder-back chairs and braided rugs. 'Take all the time you need. They'll make their way back to me eventually,' she said. She found an empty box, and together they loaded the books into it. 'What are you doing this weekend?'

Josey shrugged. 'Taking my mother to tea on Saturday. That's about it.'

'Do you want to go out?'

'Maybe,' Josey said doubtfully. She put the lid on the box and picked it up. 'So, what did you decide to take with you?'

Chloe turned and looked around the storage bay. 'Nothing.' She took a deep breath, and the decision was there before she was even fully aware of it. 'I think I need to move out of Jake's apartment.'

On Saturday afternoon Margaret changed her shoes three times and her handbag twice and snapped at Josey for no other reason than that she was standing there, waiting patiently to take Margaret to tea.

Margaret *hated* having tea with Livia Lynley-White. She knew she should be past the point of feeling intimidated by this woman. Livia was ninety-one years old now. No one that old should still have so much power.

But she did have power. She was the only person in town, besides Marco, who knew about Margaret's affair. It had happened over forty years ago, but Livia would not let it go. Every month, like a queen, Livia commanded Margaret to join her for tea, and every month Margaret had no choice but to go. They met in a private, sectioned-off area of the tearoom in what used to be Livia's old family home, the oldest home in Bald Slope. Thirty years ago Livia had donated the house to the preservation society, and it was turned into a museum with a tearoom. Though it had been three decades since she'd actually lived in the historic home, Livia still thought it her right to come and go as she pleased.

Josey finally drove Margaret to the Lynley-White Historical Home, though Margaret still wasn't happy with her choice of shoes. Once there, Josey walked with Margaret into the private room.

Livia was already seated. When they reached the table, Livia said, 'Josey, wait outside.'

'Yes, Mrs Lynley-White,' Josey said, then left.

'Margaret, what are you waiting for? Sit down.'

'Yes, Livia.' Margaret pulled out the chair and sat down.

'Your daughter looks different,' Livia said, her long knobby fingers toying with the pearls at her neck. 'What's different?'

Margaret put her napkin in her lap. 'I don't think anything is different.'

'She was never a pretty child, was she?'

'No, Livia.'

'We're ready!' Livia yelled, and the curator rolled in the trolley with the tea service. She set small bowls of sugar cubes and lemon wedges on the table, then a three-tiered server laden with cucumber finger sandwiches, flaky raspberry jam puffs and thin slices of rum-and-butter cake. She left without a word. Lucky woman.

Livia stirred two sugars into her tea. 'So, tell me about your month. I heard you went to the ladies' club meeting.'

'Yes. It was very nice.'

'Rawley Pelham still takes Annabelle Drake to the meeting in his cab, doesn't he?'

'I believe he does, yes,' Margaret said.

'He might be sweet on her, I heard.'

Margaret reached for the sugar tongs. 'Oh?'

'Interested, Margaret?' Livia said slyly.

Margaret wondered at the power of her own heart. All these years and her damn old heart still hurt for him. Three sugars later, Margaret managed to say, 'No, Livia.'

'Bald Slope is a different place from your Asheville. We have different rules here. Rules that can't be forgotten. Everyone said you knew the rules. Pretty little Margaret from Asheville. *She doesn't do anything wrong.* But I knew you weren't good enough for Marco.'

Livia had been in love with Marco. Margaret knew it from the moment she met her. And Livia had watched and watched for some misstep, anything that would dishonour Margaret, make her not worthy of the great Marco Cirrini. And Livia found it, all right. She had to have known about all of Marco's affairs, but that was acceptable in Livia's eyes. Perhaps she'd even hoped that one day he would have an affair with *her*.

But for Margaret to have a little happiness?

That would never do.

**W**hile Margaret was suffering through tea, Chloe was across town going over apartment rental listings in the newspaper. Jake was doing it again this weekend, not contacting her. He was just waiting. Waiting for her to come to her senses.

She angrily circled another listing in the paper. She didn't have to depend on Jake for her social life, for the roof over her head, for her sense of security. She was going to take steps to forget all about him. Soon she would manage to forget about his voice, how good it felt to have him around.

She set her pen down on the newspaper. Julian had been in the back of her mind all week, lingering, not pushing. He said he was at Jiggery's most weekends. She could go there tonight and maybe talk to him some more about their shared misery.

She spent a lot of time with her hair and make-up again. She wore her heeled boots and her short wool plaid skirt and her favourite soft cabled sweater. When she looked at herself in the mirror, she liked what she saw.

When she got to Jiggery's, she spotted Julian right away. He was seated at the bar, surrounded by women, women who existed only at night, thin sheets of steel, all sharp edges and shine, undulating and unsteady. He was something different to each of them, and that made them swoon and think the other women were no competition at all, because each thought she had the true Julian.

When Julian saw her, he immediately left them to come and see her, which felt nice. 'Hello there,' he said. 'I didn't get your name last time.'

'It's Chloe.'

'Would you like a drink, Chloe? Let's sit.' He led her to the end of the bar, past the shiny, undulating women, who would simply wait there for him to come back to them. He and Chloe sat, and he ordered their drinks, remembering that she'd been drinking a lemon drop last time. 'How are you?'

She nodded. 'Fine. Better.'

'I'm glad you came. I've been wanting to talk to you. Your boyfriend, would his name happen to be Jake Yardley?'

She felt a slight pinch of apprehension. 'How did you know?'

'I've been asking around, and I might have some leads. There's only been one soap opera in the DA's office in the last three months, and I was told it had to do with a golden boy named Jake Yardley. No one has wanted to give up the details yet.'

'I can't believe you'd do something like that for me. You don't even know me.' She put her hand to her chest. His eyes followed the movement to her breasts.

'I know hurt when I see it. I guess my next question is, Do you want to know her name? There's no going back once you know.'

'I want to know,' Chloe said without hesitation.

'Then I'll find out for you. I have some connections at the courthouse. I've had plenty of legal matters settled there.'

Their drinks arrived, and Chloe took a sip of hers, trying not to stare at him. 'So, um, have you heard from your girlfriend?'

'No.'

'This must be so hard for you. Did she leave you a note, anything?'

'No.' He put both his hands round his beer mug and stared down into it. 'We've been fighting a lot lately. After our last fight, she got in her car and left. Someone came and took her clothes and her wallet, so I know she's still around. She just doesn't want to see me.'

'So, is it over between the two of you?'

'Probably.' He met her eyes. 'What about you and Jake?'

'I don't know.'

He smiled slightly. 'You still love him.'

She looked away. 'I can't seem to help it.'

'Your Jake, is he tall with blond curly hair?'

She turned back to him curiously. 'No.'

'Then is he medium height with dark hair and light, eerie eyes?'

'I wouldn't say they were eerie, but yes. Why?'

'Because a big blond and a shorter guy with those eyes just walked in and zeroed in on us. And they look none too pleased.'

She looked over to the door and locked eyes with Jake. The force of it nearly knocked her over. As much as Julian could do, as much as he wanted to do, he could not affect her the way Jake could. It was the difference between a tickle and a punch.

Jake walked towards her, Adam on his heels. They got caught in the group of shiny women on their way. Walking through that group was like walking into a sudden dust devil. They emerged on the other side looking rumpled and wind-blown.

By the time they reached her, Julian had disappeared.

'Clo, what are you doing?' Jake said. His eyes were all over her, drinking her in like sweet tea with lemonade. He *missed* her.

She got off her stool. 'It's none of your business.'

'You don't know that guy. He's bad news.'

'Oh, really?' she snapped. 'Let me tell you something, Jake. You lost the right to have any say in my life the moment you slept with another woman.'

'I didn't sleep with her. I had sex with her. That was all it was. It didn't mean anything. Everyone was tired, everyone was high on winning, and there were all these emotions looking for release. I didn't make a conscious decision—'

'Get out of my way.' She tried to push him, but he didn't budge.

He took her by the arms. 'Chloe, please, just promise me you'll stay away from him. I don't trust him. He has a record.'

She sucked in air so quickly she almost choked. 'How do you know that? Have you been spying on me? You don't think I can handle myself. I'll show you, Jake.' She barrelled past him this time. 'I'll show you.'


Chloe woke up feeling parched and headachy.

'Jake,' she said automatically, reaching for the other side of the bed. He always made her feel better when she was ill. But when her hand touched his flat, empty side of the bed, she remembered. He wasn't here and she was. In bed. In her clothes. She sat up slowly, squinting through the pain in her head.

She moved her legs to the side of the bed and sat on the edge, putting her head in her hands. She'd spent hours crying when she got home, crying in a ball on the floor, crying so hard her chest felt as if it was going to cave in.

She began to shiver, so she grabbed her jacket from the bottom of the bed. She slowly got up and headed to the kitchen for some water. As she walked, she stuffed her hands into the pockets of the jacket. She felt something in the left pocket and pulled it out.

She stopped and stared at it. It was a cocktail napkin, and on it was written a phone number and a name.

*Julian.*

# 5
## Sugar Daddy

ON MONDAY AFTERNOON, on her way to the organic grocery store to pick up the peppermint oil that was finally ready for her mother, Josey stopped by the courthouse to see Chloe. The moment she caught sight of her, she knew something was wrong. Chloe was sitting at one of the tables by the counter, a cup of coffee in front of her, staring into space.

'Chloe?'

She immediately looked up. When she saw who it was, she smiled. 'Oh, hi, Josey.' She didn't have on any make-up, and her red hair was pulled up into a tangled ponytail. There was sadness under her skin, giving her a fragile, matte pallor.

'What's wrong?'

Chloe shrugged, her movements uncomfortable. 'I guess I was in shock for a while—Jake telling me he'd slept with another woman, then kicking him out. This weekend I think it finally hit me. Bam!'

Josey tried to think of something comforting to say, like when all else fails, it helps to eat chocolate.

But then Chloe shook her head. 'I'm sorry. I didn't mean to put that on you. Would you like a sandwich?'

'I have to go to the organic grocery for peppermint oil. I just wanted to stop by to say hello and to thank you for the books again.'

'Peppermint oil? Is that why you always smell like Christmas?'

Josey laughed at that. 'My mother insists that peppermint oil be used on the casings of our house. It's supposed to keep unexpected guests from arriving on the doorstep. I'm pretty sure the old herbalist at the organic grocery propagates these superstitions for profit. She claims that she can whip up love potions, elixirs for pleasant dreams, charms that will give you more hours in a day. Nova Berry, she's quite a character.'

'I've never heard of her.'

'Not many people have. She works with referrals only.'

Chloe said thoughtfully, 'Do you think you could refer me?'

'Well, sure. What do you need?'

'I don't know,' Chloe said. 'Maybe she can tell me.'

Nova Berry looked like a hickory switch—tall, thin and knobby. These days people treated what she did as a novelty, but there had been a time when the Berry women had been known far and wide for their natural remedies. Slippery elm for digestive problems. Red clover for skin conditions. Pot marigold for certain monthly female ailments. Nova made it known that her cure for heartburn also mended a broken heart, and her cure for cramps also made you more fertile—or less, if that's what you wanted.

Nova's children ran the market, and Nova had her workroom in the back. Josey led Chloe there, pushing back the curtain that separated it from the rest of the store. Nova was sitting at her workbench, crushing lavender with a mortar and pestle.

She looked up when they entered. 'Josey! I have your mother's peppermint oil right here. Please tell her I'm sorry it took so long.' She got to her feet and gave Josey a small glass vial, then gestured to the explosion of knitted scarves and dried herbs in the corner. 'Now, can I interest you in a scarf? Red is your magic colour, Josey. Try red.'

'No, thank you.'

Josey gestured for Chloe, who was standing by the curtained door, to come forward. She did, but leerily. Josey took her hand and pulled her the rest of the way. 'Nova, this is Chloe Finley.'

Nova looked her up and down. 'What can Nova do for you?'

Chloe cleared her throat. 'I want to forgive someone,' she said, 'or I want to move on. Do you have anything that would help?'

Nova thought about it a moment. 'You need a tisane of stinging nettle.' She went to her workbench and opened one of the dozens of clear glass jars. 'You use this like tea leaves, to drink.' Nova scooped some of the dried plant into a small paper envelope.

'Stinging nettle,' Chloe said, trying to laugh, but she sounded nervous. 'That sounds painful.'

'Love sometimes hurts. This is painless, though. It tells your heart what to do. Your heart, child, remember. When you have a decision to make, listen to your heart.'

Josey dropped Chloe off at the courthouse, then went home. As soon as she walked through the door with the peppermint oil, Margaret admonished her for taking too long, then grabbed the oil and went in search of Helena. The oil had to be put on the casings immediately, she said, because Thanksgiving and Christmas were almost upon them and people didn't think twice about dropping in during the holidays.

Margaret wanted to nip that in the bud.

Josey unbuttoned her coat as she walked into her room. She went straight to her closet. When she opened the door, Della Lee was sitting where she always sat, on the sleeping-bag. She was holding the small tiara in her lap, looking at it wistfully.

'Della Lee?'

She looked up and smiled. 'I won this in the Little Miss Bald Slope pageant when I was six years old.'

Josey went to her knees. 'You must have been a pretty child.'

'I was.' Della Lee put the tiara on the floor. 'Josey, there's something important I have to tell you,' she said seriously. 'I've been debating whether or not it really has anything to do with me being here, but I think it does, so I think you should know.'

'Let me guess: you're a serial closet squatter and I'm not your first victim.'

'No.' Della Lee reached into a corner of the closet and brought out the box Josey had taken from her house. She set it in front of her, then she pushed it halfway between her and Josey. 'Look inside.'

Josey lifted the lid.

'See those notebooks?' Della Lee said. 'Those were my mother's. Go ahead. You can look in them.'

Josey lifted the first one out. It was a regular spiral notebook, the kind kids carried to school in backpacks. 'Are these diaries?'

'More like logbooks. My mother liked to follow Marco Cirrini and write down what he did. She did it for almost twenty years. When I was a child she would drag me around town in our car, driving wherever he drove. She was obsessed with knowing what he was doing and who he was with.'

Josey looked over a few pages, feeling uncomfortable. Most of it was written like this entry, dated March 30, twenty-three years ago:

> Marco drove down Highland Street.
> Marco parked in the seventh parking space from the corner.
> Marco was wearing his grey suit with a red tie.
> They stood on the sidewalk and talked.
> Marco laughed three times.
> She touched his sleeve.

Josey closed the notebook, shutting out the frantic energy emanating from the pages. 'I don't understand. Why would your mother do this?'

Della Lee ran her tongue over her front teeth, thinking about her answer. 'My mother was a troubled person,' she finally said. 'And she was too beautiful for her state of mind. She left home when she was sixteen. She dropped out of high school and got a job as a check-out girl at the Winn-Dixie. When she met my father, she thought he was going to be her saviour. She loved to tell me the story of how she was sitting on a bench downtown one Saturday when he walked up to her and said, "You are the most beautiful creature I've ever seen. Can I buy you dinner?" It was like something out of a movie. I came along nine months later. She was eighteen.'

Josey vaguely remembered Della Lee's mother, small and pretty and rough like Della Lee, but with big green doll eyes. 'Your mother was Greenie Baker, right? I remember seeing her around.'

'I'm not surprised. Following you and your father on your Sunday drives was one of her favourite things to do.'

'Were you with her?'

'Sometimes. But as soon as I was old enough to stay home alone, I did. I hated following you. Hated it. But then I would always hear about it when she got home, where he took you, how you used to laugh when you were with him. I didn't want to hear about him acting like a good father with you.'

'What happened to *your* father?'

'He died when I was nineteen. I didn't even know who he was until I was nine. He paid off my mother when I was born. Bought her the house. Bought her a car. Bought her silence.'

'Why would he do that?' Josey asked, absolutely transfixed.

'Probably so his wife wouldn't know. But my mother, God bless her, went to his wife when I was nine. "This is your husband's daughter," I remember her saying. "Look at her. His own flesh and blood, and he won't even see her."'

'That must have been horrible for you.'

'Actually, that was the day everything made sense,' Della Lee said. 'That was the day I realised why my mother was following Marco Cirrini around town.'

'Why?'

Della Lee's eyes went past Josey's shoulder. She looked around the bedroom. 'I've been in your house once before. That day when I was nine years old. I stood in your living room. I couldn't believe how beautiful this place was. It *smelt* rich.'

Josey started coming back to herself, pulling away from the story. No, no. She didn't want to hear the ending.

'Your mother gave my mother more money. Bought her silence again. That Margaret is one smart cookie,' Della Lee said, shaking her head. 'It was well known that Margaret and Marco didn't want children, but a year after Margaret found out about me, suddenly there was Josey, their late-in-life baby! The baby that would bind Margaret to Marco's fortune, no matter what.'

Josey stood and backed away from the closet. From across the room she stared at Della Lee in horror.

'Hi, sis,' Della Lee said.

It seemed like hours passed.

They just stared at each other. Della Lee was sitting crosslegged with her hands placidly on her knees. Josey was breathing heavily with anger and indignation.

'That's it!' Josey said. 'I've had enough!'

'Finally,' Della Lee said.

'I mean I've had enough of you! I will not tolerate anyone saying such things about my father. Everyone knows he was a great man.'

Della Lee rolled her eyes. 'Oh, grow up, Josey.'

'*This* is the real reason you decided to come to my closet. It had nothing to do with running from Julian. If you needed money, why didn't you just say so? You didn't have to go through this whole production of pretending you wanted to help me.'

'I don't want your money,' Della Lee said, moving her box back into the closet. 'And I do want to help you. That's why I'm here.'

Josey snorted. 'Nothing you say is true.'

'You love your mailman. Is that not true? You feel stuck here. Is that not true? You're trying to make up to your mother for something you did as a child, something she's never going to let you live down. Is that not true? You want to leave this place. You want to wear red. You want to take your candy out of your closet and eat it in front of everyone!'

'My father did not have a child with another woman.'

'You don't believe me? Ask your mother,' Della Lee said.

'No!' Her mother would have a fit if she got wind of Della Lee's allegations. 'And don't you dare say anything about this to her.'

'OK, ask Samuel Lamar.'

'My father's old lawyer?'

'Yes. Who do you think set up the money, house and car transfers? The confidentiality agreement?'

Josey stared at her, not saying anything. She couldn't believe this was happening. She should have kicked Della Lee out that first day. 'Fine,' she finally said. 'I'll write to him right now.' She went to her desk and pulled out a sheet of paper. 'But I want you to agree to leave when I get his answer. When he writes and says my father never had any other children, you will leave this house and never bother me again. Understood?'

'Sure,' Della Lee said. 'But calling would be faster.'

'I'm writing to him.'

'If you really wanted to know the truth, you'd call. Be sure to ask him about all of Marco's affairs. Ask him about the other woman, besides my mother, he paid off.'

Josey had got as far as 'Dear Mr Lamar'. She stopped and turned to Della Lee. 'You're really starting to get on my nerves.' She turned back to the letter.

'Sibling rivalry,' Della Lee said. 'It happens to the best of us.'

Chloe couldn't bear the thought of waiting hours to try the stinging-nettle tea. What if this was the thing that was going to make everything all right? She started getting excited about feeling better. At four o'clock she closed the shop early.

She dumped her bag and coat on the floor when she got home and went directly to the kitchen. She ferreted out her tea infuser, then boiled water in a cup in the microwave. When she finally took that first sip, she was surprised to find it bitter. She had imagined it sweeter. She gulped the rest of it.

She put the cup down and started to pace. Half an hour later, several things were definitely more clear. She decided to take a long bath later that evening. She decided to have pesto pizza for dinner. She also decided to wait to vacuum until next week.

But nothing was any more clear when it came to Jake. It wasn't working. The tea wasn't going to tell her what to do.

She sat at the dining-room table and put her head down, resting her cheek against the smooth, cool surface. She felt tears come to her eyes. Why had she thought it would be so easy? She squeezed her eyes shut. When she opened them again, she saw that she was eye-level with the salt and pepper shakers. There, tucked in between them, was the cocktail napkin with Julian's number on it.

She reached for it, then sat up and stared at it.

Everything came back to this. She needed to know who had caused Jake to stray before she could decide if she could forgive him.

She went to the phone and dialled.

'Hello?' Julian answered. His voice was strangely calming.

'Julian, this is Chloe.'

'Chloe, sweetheart, I've been waiting to hear from you.'

'I'm sorry about Saturday night.'

'Don't be. I know how a man gets when he thinks he's lost the love of his life.'

'I know you do,' she said with sympathy. 'Still no word from your girlfriend?'

'No.'

'Have you, um, learned anything more about who Jake might have slept with?'

'As a matter of fact, I have. Let's get together tonight. I'll tell you then.'

'Why won't you tell me now?'

'Because I'd like to think I can also be a friend to you, not just a source of information about your cheating boyfriend.'

That made sense. At least she thought it did. 'We can't go to Jiggery's. Jake might be there.'

'My favourite weekday haunt is Nite Lite. Meet me there around nine.'

Julian hung up before she could say no.

Chloe chewed on her lip for a minute, then she went to her bag. She dug out the card with Josey's number written on it and dialled.

She heard the phone pick up on the other end. 'Hello?'

'Josey?'

'Yes?'

'It's Chloe. I was wondering if you would do me a favour.'

'Of course I will. What is it?'

She liked that Josey said yes without even knowing what the favour was. 'I know this is a lot to ask, but would you go to a bar with me tonight?'

'A bar,' Josey repeated. 'I've never actually been to a bar.'

'Then now's the perfect time to experience one! I wouldn't ask if it wasn't important. Someone there has some information for me that could really help me with my situation with Jake.'

'What kind of information?'

Chloe pinched the bridge of her nose. She didn't want to tell Josey. It made her feel trite and desperate. But she finally said, 'He knows who Jake slept with.'

'Chloe,' Josey said gently, 'is this something you really want to know?'

'It's something I *have* to know. Please come with me.'

Josey took a deep breath. 'OK. I'll go.'

**N**ite Lite was located on the winding road leading up to the ski resort. The sign by the road read HAMBURGERS! KARAOKE! COLD BEER! Josey figured it had probably been designed to attract the college kids who were on their way up the mountain to ski, but from the looks of things when Josey and Chloe entered, it ended up being a hangout for bearded men in flannel shirts.

They stopped at the door, letting their eyes adjust to the dimness. 'I don't see him here yet. Let's get something to drink,' Chloe said, going to the bar.

Josey followed, feeling conspicuous. She had picked Chloe up after Margaret had gone to bed. When Chloe had opened her apartment door, she had taken one look at Josey in the same black dress and coat she'd worn earlier that day and grabbed a bold yellow-and-red rugby-striped scarf off the coat stand. She'd looped it round Josey's neck and said, 'Now, you have colour. Perfect!'

Once at the bar, Chloe ordered a lemon drop, so Josey did too. When the drinks arrived, Josey pretended to sip hers. She tried to make conversation, but Chloe was distracted, constantly looking around and saying every ten minutes, 'He said he'd be here.'

Two hours later Chloe was flat drunk and Josey was trying to figure out a way to get her to leave. Chloe had refused every attempt. Josey couldn't even stop her from calling Jake and leaving him a slurred message, telling him she was at Nite Lite and having loads of fun without him. But it was far from the truth. Chloe was more miserable than Josey had ever seen her. Josey squeezed her eyes shut.

What would Della Lee do?

Della Lee would take charge. She wouldn't care about being nice.

Josey said, 'We're leaving.'

'No, Josey, we have to stay,' Chloe said. 'Just a few more minutes. Pleeease?'

'I'm going to the rest room. When I get back, we're leaving.'

Josey slid off the bar stool and went to the ladies' room. Ha! Easy as pie. Strawberry rhubarb pie with fresh vanilla ice cream.

She walked back out into the dim neon-lit bar a few minutes later, but she only took a few steps before she stopped short.

Julian was sitting with Chloe. What the hell was he doing here? They were leaning in towards each other, smiling, laughing. Chloe was entranced by him. She couldn't get out alone.

Josey rubbed her aching forehead. What would Della Lee do?

When it came to Julian, Della Lee would run. OK, Josey could do that. She just had to get Chloe first.

The bar was dark enough that there was a chance Julian wouldn't recognise her as the woman who'd been in his house. She walked over to them sideways, like she was doing a line-dancing step to the music from the jukebox. Keeping her back to Julian, she angled her way between them. She grabbed Chloe's bag and coat from the bar. 'Come on, Chloe. We're leaving.'

'No, we don't have to go now,' Chloe said jubilantly. 'Look, Julian finally made it! Julian, this is Josey.'

Josey gaped at Chloe. She'd come here to meet *Julian*?

'It's nice to meet you,' Julian said, leaning to the right, trying to see Josey's face. 'You look familiar.' He touched her arm and she stepped away quickly, facing him now.

'She's Josey Cirrini. *Cirrini*. Shh, she's rich,' Chloe said.

Josey tried to coax Chloe off the stool. 'Come on. Let's go.'

Chloe held on to the bar rail with both hands, refusing to budge. 'I can't go. I haven't found out her name yet.'

'Come on, stand up.' Josey kept tugging at Chloe, but Chloe had suctioned herself to the bar, and the harder Josey pulled, the harder Chloe hung on.

Suddenly, from behind them, Josey heard, 'Chloe? Josey? Are you two all right?'

Josey let go of Chloe. They both turned.

'Adam!' Chloe said. 'What are you doing here?'

Adam's brows lowered. He did not look pleased. Still, Josey didn't think she'd ever been so happy to see someone. Adam was wearing a soft brown leather jacket over a turtleneck and a blue scarf the exact colour of his eyes. He looked *wonderful*. 'You called me, Clo. You left a message on my answering machine. Obviously you intended the message for Jake.'

'Oops!'

'Let's go, Clo,' Adam said, trying to get her off the stool.

'Hold on,' Julian suddenly said. When Josey looked at him, he was looking right back at her. 'You,' he said, pointing a finger at her. 'I know who you are. You broke into my house! You took my wallet!'

'Come on, Josey,' Adam said. 'Help me with Chloe.'

'You owe me money, you fat bitch!'

It happened so fast, it was almost a blur. Julian was in the process of standing when Adam turned and punched him across the jaw with absolutely no warning. Julian fell backwards, and people around them stopped talking and turned to stare.

'Up, Chloe.' Adam literally lifted her off the stool and tore her away from the bar. 'Josey—with me, now.'

Josey forced her feet to move. She ran to the door and held it open as Adam hauled Chloe out.

Chloe was calling, 'Julian! Julian! I'm so sorry! Let go of me!'

The night outside was a shocking contrast to being inside Nite Lite. It was cold and quiet, and Josey immediately felt like she had cotton in her ears. 'Who drove?' Adam demanded as Chloe struggled in his arms.

'I . . . I did,' Josey said.

'Where is your car?'

'Over there.'

Adam crunched across the gravel lot towards the car, saying, 'Unlock it.' She hurried after him and electronically unlocked the doors. He opened the back door, and together they got the squirming mass of red hair into the back seat. 'Sit back there with her and give me the keys.'

She hesitated, and he started to say something. 'OK, OK,' she said, handing him the keys and sliding in beside Chloe.

He slammed the door, then trotted round the car and got behind the wheel.

Josey put her arm round Chloe, and soon Chloe's head fell on her shoulder. Adam didn't say anything the entire drive to Chloe's place. He didn't even speak as they carried Chloe up the long interior steps that cut the old firehouse into four apartments. Josey got the keys out of Chloe's bag and opened the door.

She followed his lead to the bedroom. As soon as they had Chloe on the bed, Adam rounded on Josey. 'How could you let her get so hammered?' he demanded. 'Are you drunk?'

'I didn't have anything to drink,' she said. 'And I kept trying to get her to leave. I had no idea she was going there to meet Julian.'

'You know that guy? You didn't really break into his house and steal his wallet, did you?'

She hesitated, 'It wasn't his house, and it wasn't his wallet.'

'You stole someone else's wallet?' he asked incredulously.

'I didn't steal anything. I got a friend's wallet back.'

Adam's jaw worked back and forth. 'What's got into you lately? Does your mother know you're doing this?'

That did it. 'I'm twenty-seven years old! What does my mother have to do with this? But that's how everyone sees me, isn't it? Poor Josey. Fat, unsocial, under her mother's thumb. I'm so tired of worrying about what people think of me.'

He took a step back, like she'd scared him. 'Look,' he said, 'all I'm saying is that Chloe's vulnerable right now. You should be nudging her back in Jake's direction instead of going with her to dives.'

'I'm not going to *nudge* her in any direction. This is her call. Whether or not she and Jake get back together has nothing to do with me—or you, for that matter.'

He waved his hand dismissively. 'You don't know anything about this.'

'I know enough to stay out of it. Like I know you've got a secret. But have I ever asked you about it? No.'

She'd surprised him. A couple of seconds ticked by before he said, 'What?'

'You're hiding something. You're hiding *from* something. I've known it since the moment I first saw you.'

He met her eyes, his head tilting slightly. 'You've known a lot since the moment you first saw me.'

The room suddenly fell quiet. He had just said he knew. He knew she loved him. Embarrassment felt a lot like eating chilli peppers. It burned in the back of your throat, and there was nothing you could do to make it go away. You just had to suffer until it eased off.

When he spoke again, his tone was softer. 'I'll let you get her undressed.'

As soon as he left the room, Josey sighed and reached down to take off Chloe's boots. She managed to get Chloe out of her coat and sweater, leaving her in the T-shirt she wore underneath. She then took off her watch and earrings. She tucked the blankets round her. Then she walked to the bedroom door, took a deep breath and opened it. Adam was sitting on the couch, waiting for her.

'Give me my keys,' she said, walking up to him. 'I'll drive you back to the bar to get your car.'

'I'm not letting you go back there.' He jiggled her keys in his hand absently as he looked up at her. 'I'll get Jake to take me in the morning.'

'Then give me my keys and I'll take you home.'

He suddenly stood and brushed by her. 'I'll drive,' he said, walking to the door. He opened it and waited for her.

This night was never going to end. She walked to the door and out into the hallway. She headed for the staircase, hearing him close the apartment door, then the fall of his footsteps as he followed her. Josey got in the passenger side of the car and stared straight ahead as he took his time getting behind the wheel.

'This is a nice car,' he said as he pulled out of the lot. 'Did your mother pick it out?'

'Yes, she picked it out.' She could have sworn she saw him smile. 'Stop looking so smug.'

'Smug?'

'Yes, like everything you thought of me has fallen back into that nice safe place you had it in before.'

He seemed to ponder that for the rest of the drive. Soon, he pulled to the kerb and stopped behind another parked car.

She knew this neighbourhood, unique because the houses on one side were high above the street, each with steep concrete steps from the sidewalk all the way up to the front. Adam's house was a single-storey clapboard with a large front window.

Adam cut the engine. Josey got out and began to walk round to the driver's side. But by the time she reached the front of the car, Adam had met her halfway. He looked down at her, and she had to fight the urge to step back. His eyes dropped to her neck. 'That scarf looks familiar.'

She shrugged. 'I got it from Chloe. She wanted me to wear it.'

'Why would she want you to wear it?' he asked.

'She said for colour.' Adam Boswell, fashion critic? Oh yes, finding out that she had feelings for him *of course* gave him leave to find all the things wrong with her.

'This is Jake's scarf,' he said, reaching out to touch it. Her body gave a start, and he hesitated. He wrapped his fingers round the scarf and pulled slowly, causing a warm friction against her skin. As soon as he had it pulled off of her, cold air darted into the collar of her coat and she shivered.

Adam unwrapped his own light blue scarf and looped it round her, their hands touching briefly. She could only stare at him. He stared back at her for several impossibly long seconds, his hands holding the ends of the scarf as if holding her to him. Finally he dropped his hands and brushed past her. Up the concrete steps he went, then he disappeared inside.

**W**hen Josey got home, she stood on the porch in the dark, holding Adam's scarf. She reluctantly hung it on the mailbox. It was a pity scarf, she decided, and she wanted nothing to do with it.

No, that was a big fat lie. She wanted *everything* to do with it. She wanted to sleep with it, dance with it, snuggle it like a pet. But that's exactly what Adam thought she'd do, and she wasn't going to give him that satisfaction. She decided she wasn't going to run to the door every day just to see him any more.

She silently unlocked the front door, crept into the dark house and clicked the door closed.

'**S**o, did you have fun with Chloe?' Della Lee said to Josey when she opened the closet door.

'*No,*' Josey said vehemently.

'What happened?'

'Do you know who she went to the bar to meet?' Josey said. 'Julian.'

Della Lee blinked a few times. 'My Julian?'

'Yes.'

'Holy crap! Keep her away from him, Josey. She's no match for him, especially not in her state. That man could ruin her life.'

'Like he ruined yours?'

'He was just one more destructive tendency.' Della Lee shook her head, like she was looking back on something she'd done a long, long time ago. 'That's why women are drawn to him, don't you see? He'll ruin her by giving her exactly what she thinks she wants.'

# 6
# Snow Candy

JOSEY HAD TO TAKE her mother to the annual Baptist Women's charity luncheon the next day, Tuesday. But before they were to leave, Josey decided to call Chloe to see how she was doing. In the closet, Della Lee was trying on all of Josey's shoes.

'Hello,' Chloe finally answered after several rings. She sounded sick.

Josey sat on the edge of her bed. 'Chloe, it's Josey. How are you feeling?'

'I'm so sorry about last night, Josey,' Chloe said, and her voice started to tremble. 'I never thought I would be the kind of woman to act like this, to fall to pieces, but I . . . I can't seem to help it. It hurts so much. I feel like I'm going crazy.'

Josey hesitated. Della Lee watched her curiously. 'I'll be right over,' she finally said.

As soon as she hung up, Della Lee said, 'You're going to see her?'

Josey picked up her grey coat from the chaise. 'Yes.'

'Instead of taking your mother to her luncheon?'

'Yes.'

'Oh, my baby is growing up.'

'You're psychotic,' Josey said, leaving the room while dialling another number on her cellphone.

**A**dam didn't see the scarf draped over the mailbox until he was halfway up the steps. He pulled the buds from his iPod out of his ears.

It had been strange seeing Josey in Jake's scarf last night. *Chloe* should wear Jake's scarf. But when he took it, Josey then didn't have a scarf. So he gave her his. It was cold. She needed one.

He took the scarf off the mailbox and put the Cirrinis' mail in. He hesitated and looked at the door. Josey usually came out before now. He looked over to the driveway. Her car was there.

Where was she?

He shook his head. He wasn't going to let her do this. He went to the door and raised his hand to knock, not sure what he was going to say. All of a sudden, the door opened and there was Josey.

She looked tired. But her hair was so curly it could never get limp. And the paler her skin, the more striking her dark eyes seemed. She looked . . .

OK, he could admit it. She looked beautiful.

When she saw him, she seemed momentarily nonplussed. She reluctantly stepped outside and closed the door behind her. 'Hi, Adam,' she said, looking down to button her long grey coat.

He held out the scarf. 'You could have kept this.'

Her eyes darted up briefly, embarrassed. 'I know.'

'Have you talked to Chloe today?'

'I'm going to see her now.' She went to the steps and started walking down.

He turned quickly to join her. 'Listen, I'm sorry I was so rough on you last night. I was just . . .'

'Angry,' she said.

'No, not angry.' He stopped her when she reached the bottom step, putting his hand on her arm. 'I could never be angry at you, Josey.'

She considered him for a moment, as if to gauge his honesty. She stared at him so long he dropped his hand.

'I've, uh, been thinking about what you said last night,' he said. 'Why do you think I have a secret?'

'I don't know. Maybe you don't. Maybe I was just projecting.'

'You have a secret?'

She gave a small laugh and shook her head. 'Well, not any more,' she said, and walked to the driveway and the enormous gold Cadillac parked there.

Why hadn't he seen it before? *Three years.* Why hadn't he known she was in love with him?

He felt a strange stirring, something he hadn't felt in a very long time. It felt a little like when a limb falls asleep but then slowly, surely, there's a tingling, an almost uncomfortable sensation . . . of waking up.

After stopping by the store for noodle soup and 7-Up and Milky Way ice cream, Josey knocked on Chloe's door.

When Chloe opened it, she looked miserable. She was wearing a thick terry-cloth robe and her hair was all over the place.

Josey held up the bags and said, 'In all my life, I've only ever been sure of one thing. Food makes everything better, at least until it's gone.'

Chloe smiled.

And then she cried.

Josey walked in and closed the door behind her. She made a nice pot of stinging-nettle tea, which made the decision to eat the ice cream first much easier for them.

Margaret sat in the sitting room, confused. Here she was, all ready to go, and Josey just came down the stairs and said she had something else to do! A friend, Josey said. She had to help out a friend.

That was clearly a lie. Josey didn't have friends.

Not ten minutes after Josey left, there was a knock at the door. Helena appeared in the sitting-room doorway. 'A man at the door for you. He say he drive you.'

'Drive me?'

'Yes, Oldgret.'

Margaret got up and followed her maid. When Helena opened the front door, Margaret felt slightly woozy, strange memories coming to her, memories of the last time he'd stood on her porch like this. 'Rawley Pelham,' she said, giving a nervous pull to the hem of her yellow suit jacket, 'what on earth are you doing here?'

Rawley turned to Helena. 'Please tell Mrs Cirrini that her daughter called me a few minutes ago and I promised I would take Mrs Cirrini to her luncheon.'

'Josey called you?' Margaret asked. 'She made you *promise*?' Pelhams didn't make promises easily, because they knew they couldn't break them. It was astounding that Rawley had not only promised something, but promised to do something for *her*. He hated her.

'Please tell Mrs Cirrini yes,' he said to Helena.

Well, there wasn't really any choice now. If Rawley promised, he had to do it. He would take Margaret to this luncheon whether she liked it or not, or die trying. 'Helena, get my coat and cane.'

Rawley walked with her to his cab in the windy noon air. She felt herself leaning towards him, as if he had a gravitational force. He opened the cab door for her, his face without expression. She awkwardly sat, and he closed the door.

When he got behind the wheel and pulled out, she stared at the back of his head. She'd always been attracted to Rawley, from the moment she saw him. Ladies in their circle never drove themselves anywhere. They had chauffeurs, or they called a cab. The first time she saw him— she was in her late twenties at the time—he was helping one of her friends out of his cab at a social function. She'd asked, 'Who is *that*?'

All the ladies who were natives of Bald Slope knew Rawley, and they were more than glad to tell her. He was beneath them, but so pretty to look at with his healthy good looks, blue eyes and russet hair. After high school he'd gone into the service. He'd just come back to Bald Slope to work for his father at Pelham Cabs.

He met her eyes that day, and it was the start of three years of long looks, three years of her dismissing the chauffeur for the day, then suddenly realising she had to go somewhere, so of course she had to call a cab. And it was always Rawley who came. She never had to ask for him by name.

It was so innocent at first. He talked with her, laughed with her. She'd lived for those rides. She was lonely, and he was kind.

Then it happened.

Rawley had driven Margaret home on the evening of Christmas Eve, after the church programme. All the servants were gone for the holiday, and the house was dark. Not even Marco was home. By that time she'd known about his other women.

She'd looked up at the house that night and felt empty. She hadn't talked to her family in Asheville since she'd left almost ten years ago. Her father was a hard man who'd clung to his old Southern name. His family lost all their money in the market crash, but they never lost their pride. Margaret was the oldest of his seven daughters, and she had taken care of her loud, needy sisters after her mother died. She cleaned the house from day to night. Even working as hard as she did, her father expected her to keep her appearance impeccable, because he said her beauty was his only thing of value. She thought he meant he valued *her*. Later, when he brought Marco to dinner, when he forced Margaret to sit next to Marco at the table, she understood. All she was to him was an investment. After that, she couldn't wait to get away.

Rawley had opened the door for her and she'd stepped out.

'Good night, Mrs Cirrini,' he'd said. 'Have a joyous Christmas.'

'Good night,' was all she'd managed before her voice broke. She tried to hurry away, but Rawley caught her hand.

'What's wrong?'

'Nothing. I must be tired, that's all.' Then, before she knew it, she was crying. Bawling. She couldn't control it.

Rawley had taken her into his arms. Oh, it had felt so good, just to be held. She'd wept for a long time, until at last there were no more tears.

'Better?' he'd asked, and she heard his words in his chest, her ear to his heart.

She looked up at him and nodded. They'd stared at each other for a long time.

He slowly lowered his head, slowly enough for her to pull away if she'd wanted to. She should have. But she didn't move.

His lips finally touched hers, and she suddenly felt alive, melting slowly. If it weren't for Rawley, she never would have felt her own heart. He'd shown her she actually had one.

And in return, she'd broken his.

She felt a cold gush of air and snapped out of it to see that they'd stopped in front of the newly renovated Downtown Inn, where the luncheon was being held. Rawley was holding the cab door open for her. She looked up at him, the wind blowing his hair.

Rawley slowly extended his hand to help her out.

And with a deep breath, she touched him for the first time in more than forty years.

The next afternoon, mail in hand, Adam walked up the steps to the Cirrinis' porch. It was finally snowing. He'd felt it coming for days. He always could.

He put the mail in the Cirrinis' box and waited for Josey to appear. When she didn't, he frowned. This was ridiculous. So he knew she loved him. He still wanted to see her. He didn't want things to change. Without another thought, he knocked on the door.

A small, pretty woman with caramel-coloured skin opened the door. She looked at him curiously.

'Mail?' she asked.

'Oh. Right.' He reached over to the mailbox and took out the mail, then he held it up to show her. He felt like an idiot. 'Is Josey here?'

'Oldsey?'

'No, Josey.'

'It's OK, Helena. I'll take care of this,' Josey said, suddenly appearing behind her.

Helena skittered away, leaving Josey there in the doorway, staring at him guardedly. But then her eyes slid past him, and she smiled.

'It's finally snowing!' she said, opening the screen door. 'I've been waiting for this for days.'

She went to the porch railing and stuck her hand out, the rainy snow pooling on her palm. She loved snow. He knew she loved snow. He knew that from three years of coming to her door.

'It's so beautiful.'

'It's going to be deep. Great for snowmen,' he said as he came to stand beside her.

She laughed, as if the thought had never occurred to her. 'I've never made a snowman.'

'No?'

She shook her head. 'It's a neighbourhood rule.'

He was staring at her now, her skin so fair it looked like cold fresh cream. 'You don't have to avoid me, Josey,' he said. 'We're OK. I like what we have.'

'Yes, I'm sure you do.'

'What's that supposed to mean?'

'It means, Adam, that *you* get to be the object of someone's affection. I don't.' She suddenly waved her hands as if to erase what she'd said from the air. 'Oh God,' she said, turning to him. 'Forget I said that, please.'

He couldn't help but smile.

'Listen, while you're here, I want to talk to you about Chloe,' she said, changing the subject in a flash.

He nodded, encouraging her to talk, to interact. 'OK.'

'The reason Chloe keeps seeing this Julian person is because he's telling her he knows who Jake slept with.'

'Damn,' Adam said, surprised. 'I'll let Jake know.'

'No, please don't tell him,' she said. 'Just see if you can find out who it is, OK? I'm trying to keep her from seeing Julian again.'

She'd never asked him for anything. How could he say no? He handed her the mail. 'I'll see what I can do.'

'Thanks.'

He watched her walk to her door. *You get to be the object of someone's affection. I don't.* 'Josey?' he suddenly said.

She turned.

He hesitated. Don't change things. 'Have a nice Thanksgiving.'

'You too, Adam.'

**A**t first the snow was light and mixed with rain. It was not enough, Margaret decided, to keep her from her hair appointment that afternoon. Thanksgiving was a day away, and this was the last opportunity to get her hair done before the start of the Christmas social season.

'I want you to go to the grocery store while I have my hair done,' Margaret said as Josey drove her to the salon.

'Maybe I should stay with you,' Josey said, her eyes on the road. 'The snow is going to get heavier, and I might not be able to get back to you.'

'Don't be silly. Go to the store. I made a list.' Margaret snapped open her handbag and put the list on the dashboard.

Josey sighed as if she was trying to see her breath in the cold. 'It's the day before Thanksgiving, and it's snowing. The grocery store will be a madhouse.'

Margaret stared at Josey's profile. Something was changing with Josey, and Margaret didn't like it at all.

**W**hen Margaret entered the salon, she was relieved to see that Annabelle Drake was there. That meant Rawley had already dropped her off and left.

The salon was busy. It took longer than it usually did for her hairdresser to finish with her hair. Afterwards she went to the reception area, expecting to see Josey waiting for her.

But Josey wasn't there.

Margaret had just walked up to the receptionist's desk to ask if her daughter had called or been by, when the bell over the door rang. Relieved that Josey was now there, she turned, but it wasn't Josey she saw. It was Rawley Pelham.

His jacket and moleskin driving cap were covered in snow, and he took a moment to brush them off before he walked further in.

'Mrs Drake will be finished in a few minutes,' the receptionist told Rawley. 'Would you like a cup of coffee?'

He took a seat on one of the couches. 'That would be nice. Thank you.'

The receptionist went to get his coffee, leaving Rawley and Margaret to stare at each other. He was in his mid-sixties now, his hair silver.

*Talk to me*, she thought. *Say something.*

When the receptionist came back and handed Rawley a cup of coffee, Margaret finally turned away and headed to the ladies' room, where she intended to hide until Rawley left.

The phone rang as she was walking away. The receptionist called, 'Wait, Mrs Cirrini. Your daughter is on the phone.'

Margaret hastily walked back and took the receiver. 'Josey? Why aren't you here?'

'I'm just leaving the grocery store,' Josey said, sounding tense. 'It's going to take a while to get there.'

'Why?'

'Because the roads are terrible and there's a ton of traffic.'

Rawley stood and walked to the desk. 'Will you ask Mrs Cirrini if I could speak to her daughter?' he said to the receptionist, though he was looking at Margaret.

'Mrs Cirrini . . .' the receptionist started to say.

'Why do you want to speak to my daughter?' Margaret asked.

He took a few steps to her and gently took the phone away from her. 'Josey, it's Rawley Pelham. Where are you?' he said into the receiver, watching Margaret the entire time. 'I see. You'll never make it here, not in that car. Go home and be careful. I'm here to pick up Annabelle Drake and it would be no problem at all to drop your mother off at your house. I have chains on my tyres.' Pause. 'You're very welcome. Remember, be careful.'

'I can't believe you just did that,' Margaret said as he handed the receiver back to the receptionist. 'Did you ever think to ask me if that was what I wanted?'

Rawley turned to Annabelle, who had just appeared at Margaret's side. 'Annabelle, will you help Mrs Cirrini outside when I pull the cab up to the front door? Josey can't make it here in this snow.'

'I don't want you to take me home,' Margaret said desperately.

'Come with us, Margaret,' Annabelle said, patting her on the arm. 'You'll be our chaperone. There's a rumour going around about me and Rawley, you know, because we spend so much time together in his cab.'

Margaret watched him walk outside.

It had ended at a summer party Marco had thrown. Marco threw the best parties. Everyone clamoured for an invitation. This particular party was island-themed, complete with a tiki bar in the back yard, paper lanterns hung in the trees, and waiters who wore white trousers and Hawaiian shirts. Each guest was even given a lei.

Livia Lynley-White wore a godawful muumuu, and she watched Margaret at the party. She always watched her, and that's how she eventually found out. Margaret had been seeing Rawley secretly for over a year now, and she was getting careless.

It was dusk, and Mrs Langdon Merryweather was ready to leave, so Margaret went inside to call for a cab.

Margaret knew it was Rawley coming to pick up Mrs Merryweather, so she made an excuse to stay in the house, near the front windows, to watch for him. She wanted him to see her in her outfit, in her sarong and sandals and her tight sleeveless button-down tied at her waist so that a strip of skin at her stomach showed.

She saw him drive by the house. There wasn't anyplace to park in front of the house because of the party, so he had to park down the block. She left and met him halfway, on the sidewalk by the boxwoods in the Franklins' front yard.

His eyes scraped her body and he smiled as she walked towards him.

'Hello, Rawley,' she said.

'Hello, Mrs Cirrini.'

'Hot evening, isn't it?'

'It is indeed.' She stopped in front of him on the sidewalk. 'You look incredible,' he whispered.

She looked over her shoulder. No one knew he was here yet. They had a few moments, so she pulled him into the Franklins' yard, behind the boxwoods. No one would see.

They kissed, his big hands going all over her. She loved this about him, how eager he always was. She thought about him all the time. Sometimes this was all they had time for, a fast, passionate encounter. Sometimes, though, she would hire him to take her to Asheville to shop, but they'd stop halfway there and have a picnic on the Parkway, and they'd talk all day. He was a good man, earnest and smart. He could have stayed in the army, or gone to college, but he came back to help his family with their business. He was their only son. Their joy and pride surrounded him like a halo. When she thought back, she always lingered on that. She'd never known another man like him. His family loved him, and he gave his love so effortlessly. She wanted that.

He'd had her shirt unbuttoned, his mouth trailing down her neck, when they suddenly heard, 'Well, well, well.'

They pulled apart and Margaret's hands went to her blouse, fumbling with her buttons.

'I knew it,' Livia said. 'I knew if I just waited long enough, I would find out who you really are. Adulterer. *Slut.*'

Margaret had known she was doing the wrong thing. But she had not then, and still would not, apologise for it. 'Leave, Rawley,' she said flatly.

'I'm not leaving you.'

She whipped her head round and said, 'Rawley, for the love of God, just go.'

When Rawley left, Margaret very calmly made a deal with Livia. Margaret didn't ask her not to tell Marco. She just asked that Livia not say it was Rawley. He was young. He deserved to get on with his life. Livia had agreed, because she got the best of both worlds: she got to tell Marco *and* hold something over Margaret.

Marco had been livid, of course. He'd yelled at Margaret, even pushed her against a wall in their bedroom. He wanted to know who it was. Livia had been vague. She said she'd seen Margaret with someone, but she couldn't make out who. But Marco couldn't break Margaret, no matter how angry he got. He would never trust her again, he said. And he *would* find out who she had been with.

Then he would ruin him.

Rawley came to the door late that night, banging on it. He was going to take on the great Marco Cirrini. Thank God, Marco was already passed out upstairs. She could remember fragments of what came next. She remembered telling Rawley that she didn't love him, that she didn't know how to love. She told him she was older. She was married. He needed to move on.

She remembered him begging. She remembered trying not to cry, desperate for him to just go away.

She'd found how to give love from somewhere deep inside her, a place she never knew existed. She'd been mad at Rawley for making her capable of feeling this way. If he hadn't shown her, she wouldn't be hurting so much.

And finally, she remembered watching him walk away. The words 'Please don't leave' stuck in her throat.

And to this day, Rawley had never said another word directly to her.

# 7
## Mellowereme Pumpkins

SHE WANTED TO DO THIS, Chloe told herself. She made another cup of stinging-nettle tea that afternoon, hoping to feel like the decision was the right one. But the only decisions the tea made easier were whether or not to cook a turkey this year (she decided against) and whether or not she should wear a hat if she went out (she decided for). Whether or not she should actually go out with Julian that night was still as murky as the Green Cove River. What to cook and what to wear were not what she needed help with. Maybe Nova hadn't given her a high enough dose of the stuff.

Chloe poured the rest of the tea into the sink and watched it swirl down the drain. She was depressed about tomorrow being Thanksgiving. This was going to be Chloe's first Thanksgiving alone. Friends and acquaintances had been calling and leaving messages all day, wishing her a happy holiday. She didn't want to talk to them. In fact, the only person she wanted to talk to was Josey, who had called earlier to check up on her. She'd tried calling Josey back, but got her voicemail. That's when Chloe got it in her head to call Julian. She hadn't contacted him since the incident at Nite Lite. She should at least apologise, wish him a happy Thanksgiving.

And, of course, maybe he would finally give her the name of the woman Jake had slept with. If she just found out who it was, then everything would get better.

Julian had answered right away, as if he'd been expecting her.

'Hi, Julian, this is Chloe. I'm so sorry about Monday.'

'All is forgiven, sweetheart,' he said. 'Why don't you come over to my place this afternoon? I'll tell you all about this other woman. I'll even show you where she lives.'

Once again, he wouldn't tell Chloe her name over the phone.

Later, when Chloe walked outside, the snow was coming down heavier than it had a few hours ago. She was surprised to see how much of it was on the sidewalk and street. It was a wet, heavy snow, and it already reached her ankles. When she got to her VW Beetle in the parking lot beside the building, she noticed something strange. There, at her back tyre, under the snow, was a book. She brushed the snow away and picked it up.

*Madame Bovary.*

She rolled her eyes and threw the book into a snowbank. Books thought she was going to cheat on Jake. That was rich.

Traffic was mad, the heaviest snow falling just as people were getting off from work early for the holiday. The secondary roads were quieter, so Chloe cut through Summertime Road. She had to take the highway to get to the address Julian had given her, but traffic got backed up on the ramp. That's when her little car got stuck. Some people behind her helped her push her VW Beetle to the shoulder.

The tea hadn't made her decision easier, and the snow had taken away the choice altogether. She felt strangely relieved. Now all she wanted to do was go home.

It took Chloe nearly an hour and a half to walk back to Summertime Road. The snow on the ground was so high now, she was forced to adopt a high step that made her thigh muscles burn. She finally let herself stop for a breather when she reached the yellow house that had captured her imagination since the day it had gone on the market. She stood there and stared at it so long that her footprints were covered with snow and it looked like she'd grown there, right out of the sidewalk.

She was startled when the door to the house suddenly flew open and a bald man ran outside to the tiny porch. He was wearing oven mitts and carrying a turkey pan, the turkey inside charred and smoky. He threw the turkey, pan and all, into the snow.

A short woman in her sixties, wearing overalls and bright purple high-tops, stood at the door, shaking her head. 'I told you I smelt something burning,' she said to the man.

'I followed the directions!' he insisted.

'You put it on broil! I told you we shouldn't have cooked.'

Almost simultaneously they turned, both becoming aware of the person watching them from the sidewalk.

'Hello!' the man called, waving an oven mitt at Chloe. 'Are you all right?'

She snapped out of it. 'Oh, yes. I'm sorry. I didn't mean to stare.'

'You look like you've been out here a while,' the man said. 'I thought you were a snowman.'

'My car got stuck on the highway. I was walking back home.'

'You've walked all the way from the highway?' the woman said. 'George, help her in here.'

George immediately walked down the front steps and into the snow. 'No, I'm fine.' Chloe waved to get him to go back. 'It's just another couple of blocks.'

'You'll get frostbite,' the woman called.

Chloe was too tired and cold to argue, so she let George lead her inside.

'I'm Zelda Cramdon and this is my husband, George,' Zelda said when she closed the door behind them and they all stood in the small hallway.

'I know,' Chloe said. 'I've met you at your open houses.'

'You know, you do look familiar, now that I see you up close,' Zelda said, helping Chloe out of her coat. 'I remember your red hair. What's your name?'

'C-Chloe Finley,' she said, trying to get her boots off herself, but Zelda had to help her.

'Come with me, Chloe, and I'll get you some dry clothes,' Zelda said, leading her down the hallway.

'Am I interrupting your Thanksgiving preparations?' Chloe asked.

'No, no. Our daughter, her husband and the grandkids were coming in, but they got as far as Asheville and the snow stopped them,' Zelda said, showing Chloe into one of the bedrooms that had obviously been made up for her incoming family. There was a water pitcher on the nightstand and a stack of folded towels on the bureau. Zelda took one of the towels and handed it to Chloe. 'That's when George decided to cook his first Thanksgiving dinner ever—hence the black bird in the yard.' Zelda went through the drawers and brought out a pair of socks, pink sweatpants and a Yale sweatshirt. This, Chloe guessed, had been their daughter's room.

'I'm sorry your family can't be here,' Chloe said.

Zelda focused on Chloe with her sharp bird eyes. 'Can I share something with you?'

'Of course,' Chloe said, rubbing the towel vigorously over her hair.

'Our daughter bought us a house last year, near her home in Orlando. She said, "When you're ready, come down and live close to your grandkids." So we put this house on the market, but we priced it so high that we knew no one would be interested. We weren't really ready to leave, you see. Now a year has gone by and we've missed the birth of another grandchild, and now Thanksgiving. We need to be closer to them. George and I decided just this afternoon that we have to move. We're lowering the price on the house.'

Chloe stopped drying her hair at that startling news. 'That must have been a hard decision to make.'

'It was. But we made it, then we said we would wait for a sign that it was the right decision. That's when the smoke alarm went off. Then we opened the door, and there you were.' Zelda turned to the door. 'I'll leave you to change. Just drape your wet clothes over the radiator.'

When Zelda left, Chloe peeled off her clothes. They were lowering the price on this house. Her house.

After she'd put on the dry clothes, she left the room. She found George and Zelda speaking in serious tones in the kitchen. Flour coated the floor. Pots and pans were everywhere.

They stopped talking when she entered. 'I'm going to try to salvage what's left in here,' Zelda said. 'George, show her around.'

George led Chloe out of the kitchen. 'You said you've been to our open houses. Do you go to a lot of others?'

'No, just this one. Just this house.'

'Do you have a favourite room?'

'Yes.'

'So quickly she answers. Which one?'

'The library,' she said softly.

George smiled. 'My wife's favourite too. Lead the way.'

There was a fire in the fireplace, and it made the dark wood of the ceiling-high built-in bookcases glow. There wasn't an inch of wall space that didn't have a shelf occupied by books.

George sat in the window seat by the bay window and crossed his legs, resting one ankle on the opposite knee. 'What would you do with this room, if it was yours?'

'Nothing,' Chloe said as she walked around. 'It's perfect as it is. I have books. Hundreds of boxes of them. They would all go here.' She stopped. 'I have a . . . special relationship with books.'

'Books can be possessive, can't they? You're walking around in a bookstore and a certain one will jump out at you, like it had moved there on its own, just to get your attention. Sometimes what's inside will change your life, but sometimes you don't even have to read it. Sometimes it's a comfort just to have a book around.'

Zelda came out of the kitchen. She handed Chloe a cup of coffee.

'We've got ourselves a reader, Zelda.'

'Really,' Zelda said, looking at Chloe thoughtfully. 'Well, dinner will be ready in a little while. We can talk books, Chloe. How would you like that?'

'I'd like that very much.'

'When I first heard your name, I knew it sounded familiar,' Zelda said. 'I finally remember why. I remember there being a Finley farm off the highway.'

'Yes! That's where I grew up.'

'Whatever happened to it?'

'My great-grandparents raised me. When they got sick, I had to sell it to pay their medical bills.'

'That must have been hard for you.'

'Giving up a house you love is always hard.'

'That,' Zelda said, 'was the perfect answer.'

Josey had turned off all the lamps in her bedroom so she could stand at her window and watch the snow fall in the darkness, but Della Lee wanted the light on in the closet so she could see to cut photos from Josey's travel magazines. She was going to make a collage. Josey had given up trying to make sense of Della Lee, but she figured it really didn't matter now. As soon as Mr Lamar's letter came, she would be leaving anyway.

It wasn't as comforting a thought as she wanted it to be, mostly because when Della Lee left, Josey wouldn't even have Adam any more. He said he didn't want things to change, but they already had. She could feel it.

With no more distractions, Josey would be able to focus solely on her mother again, and that would make Margaret happy. Margaret had come in after Rawley had walked her to the door and had gone directly to her bedroom. She hadn't said a word to Josey.

'You have a message on your cellphone from Chloe,' Della Lee said from the closet.

Josey turned to her. 'How do you know that?'

Della Lee shrugged as she carefully cut out a photo of the Eiffel Tower with the scissors she'd filched from Josey's desk drawer.

Josey sighed. 'I'd be mad about you using my cell, except I never get messages and I never would have checked.' Josey went to her bag and got her phone. She retrieved the message and listened as Chloe told her that she was fine and that she'd call Josey on Thanksgiving. She didn't sound as bad as yesterday, and Josey was glad. Maybe Chloe was over the rough part now.

Josey put her phone back in her bag. Now, to take care of *her* rough part. 'Della Lee,' she said, turning to her, 'I think we need to talk about what you're going to do when Mr Lamar's letter arrives. You don't have much time, so you need to start planning.'

'It's all planned,' Della Lee said.

This was news to Josey. 'It is? Then where are you going?'

'I told you, north.'

'But where north?'

Della Lee just smiled.

**F**or three years now, Adam had been going to Jake's parents' house for Thanksgiving, which they always celebrated on Wednesday night instead of the traditional Thursday. This was the first year, however, that he'd gone as Jake's date.

'This feels strange without Chloe,' Adam said as they walked up the steps to the door.

'Everything feels strange without Chloe.'

They brushed snow off their coats, then stomped off what little was on their shoes.

'I'm dreading this,' Jake said, pushing the doorbell.

A maid opened the door and they were shown inside. Faith Yardley had outdone herself with the decorations for this year's Thanksgiving party. There were crystals that looked like snowflakes hanging on strings falling from the ceiling. The cornucopias and the leaf arrangements on the mantels and tabletops had been lightly sprayed with artificial snow.

They walked into the grand living room with the large fireplace. Despite the snow, the Yardleys' dinner party still had a good turnout. There were about thirty people there this year, a large enough number to get lost in.

Faith was the first to greet them. She was beautiful in a red off-the-shoulder dress. 'My baby,' she said, hugging Jake. 'I'm so sorry Chloe couldn't be here.'

'I am too, Mom.' He gave her the box of candy he brought her every

Thanksgiving. She took the box like it was the best gift she'd ever received.

'And Adam, I'm glad to see you again.' Adam handed her the bouquet of flowers he always brought for the hostess, and she gave him a hug.

'I like your mom,' Adam said as they watched her walk away.

'She's a saint.'

'Jake,' his father called.

Kyle Yardley approached them, smiling and saying hello to guests he passed along the way, kissing women on the cheek, clapping men on the back. 'Jake, I just got a very interesting call from Howard Zim,' Kyle said when he stopped in front of them. He held out his hand to Adam. 'Good to see you, Adam.'

Adam shook his hand. 'Kyle.'

'Who is Howard Zim?' Jake asked.

'He's a realtor. I play racquetball with him. I told him about your troubles with Chloe.'

Jake was instantly riled. 'Why in the hell did you—'

'Just listen to me. He knows about your troubles with Chloe, which is why he thought I might like to know that the Cramdons on Summertime Road called him not an hour ago to say that they were ready to lower their price on the house and they wanted to give first dibs to a charming young woman named Chloe Finley.'

The shock of this obviously had Jake reeling. He couldn't seem to say anything.

'You should have listened to me in the first place. But now you have to focus on stopping her from making this terrible mistake. You should consider buying the house out from under her.'

Jake's face was tight, growing red. Before he totally lost it, he turned and left the room.

Adam caught up with Jake in the hallway, getting his coat from the maid. 'Jake, you're not really going to buy it, are you? Chloe's always loved that house.'

Jake jerked his coat on and walked out.

Adam nodded to the maid and she handed him his coat too.

When Adam got outside, Jake was on the porch, staring into the snow-covered yard. 'He told me to give her space, to let her realise how much she needs me. What a load of crap! He doesn't know Chloe. I know Chloe. She quit college to care for her great-grandparents. She had to sell the house that had been in her family for generations. She moved into the storeroom of her shop and didn't complain because her great-grandparents were being taken care of and that's what mattered most to her. She's as strong as hell, Adam. But she was devastated when her great-grandparents died. They left her alone. I knew she hated to be left alone. And I left her alone.' Jake slapped one of the porch pillars. 'I've lost her, haven't I?'

'No, you haven't. Don't go there.' Adam thought of what Josey had told him earlier that day. For her, he asked, 'Who was she, Jake? Who was the woman you slept with?'

Jake shook his head. 'No one.'

'Chloe wants to know. Why not tell her? It might help.'

'I can't.'

'Why not? Don't you think Chloe is more important than keeping this a secret? What's the point?' Adam said, stuffing his hands into his coat pockets.

'For the love of God, Adam, you know Chloe is the most important thing in my life. But it's not my life I'm worried about.' Jake suddenly barged down the front steps. 'I'm an idiot,' he said.

When they got to Adam's house, they ate in front of the television. Jake went to bed early after trying to call Chloe several times and not getting an answer. Adam stayed up. He turned off the lights and opened the blinds in the living room. Off in the distance he could see Bald Slope Mountain.

He'd been thinking about Josey all day. It was easy to resent people who forced you to see things in a different way. And that's exactly what Josey was doing, by telling Chloe that she loved him, by stepping outside of the confines of what people expected of her. He supposed he did resent it at first, because her changing meant everyone around her had to change. It meant *he* had to change. But when he finally gave in to it that evening, staring out at Bald Slope Mountain, he found it was surprisingly easy. He wanted things to stay the same between them, but he knew now they couldn't, and he was almost . . . excited about it.

He grabbed his coat and went to the door.

Josey suddenly opened her eyes. The sound of something hitting the side of the house had drawn her out of her sleep. 'Della Lee?' she whispered.

'Yes?' Della Lee called from the closet.

'Did you hear that?'

'It sounded like it came from your window.'

Josey sat up. Her stomach felt jumpy, but she wasn't hungry. She was startled again by the sound, like a wet slap against the side of the house. 'What is that?' She went to her window, opened it and stuck her head out. It had stopped snowing. The world outside looked as if it was coated in a thick layer of white cake frosting.

'Josey,' someone called in the quiet night.

She looked down to see a figure standing in the yard. His head was tilted back as he looked up at her. He was grinning, his entire face illuminated by the moonlight. 'Adam?'

'Your mailman?' Della Lee asked from the closet, sounding equally surprised.

'Come down,' he called, like in a fairy tale. 'Let's make a snowman.'

Josey couldn't believe it. 'What are you doing here?'

'I told you. Let's make a snowman.'

'Are you insane?'

He knelt and scooped up a handful of snow, then he packed it between his hands. 'Come down, or I'll throw a snowball at you.'

'You wouldn't dare.'

His grin turned cunning. 'Are you sure about that?'

'OK. I'll be right down.' Josey quickly ducked back inside and closed the window. She just stood there for a moment.

'Well, this is interesting,' Della Lee said. 'What does he want?'

'To make a snowman.' Josey was wearing pyjamas; she fumbled around in the darkness until she found her snow boots and a sweater. Then she put on her long black coat and grabbed a wool cap and gloves on her way out.

'Have fun. Use condoms!' Della Lee called after her.

Josey went downstairs to the front door, then stepped outside onto the porch. Adam was waiting there for her. Waiting for *her*. This made no sense. She closed the door behind her and crossed her arms over her chest. 'Are you drunk?'

'No.'

'And you couldn't make a snowman in your neighbourhood because?'

'Because you weren't there.'

Words left her.

'You told me today you've never made a snowman. I want to teach you.'

'Oh.' He was feeling sorry for her again. 'Well, I'm sorry you had to come all this way, but we can't do this here,' she said, taking a step back towards the door. 'It's against neighbourhood rules.'

'Who's going to know it was us?' He turned. 'Come on.'

'What about your leg?' she asked. He was struggling a little with it as he walked down the steps.

'To hell with my leg.' He got to the bottom step and looked up at her. She'd loved this man for three years, but she knew so little about him. She'd been too afraid to ask him about his injury, to ask him anything personal, because then he might suspect how she felt. But now that he knew how she felt about him, what was the harm in asking?

'How did you hurt it?'

'Come make a snowman with me and I'll tell you.' He held his hand out to her.

So what if this made her pitiful? This was Adam holding his hand out to her. Of course she was going to take it. Just for tonight. Because when would it ever happen again?

Snowman 101 included instructions on the art of packing a firm snowball, putting it in the snow, and then rolling it around the yard in a wide circle, letting it pick up snow and grow. Adam made it look easy. She kept trying, but her snowballs all fell apart when she tried to roll them.

'You're pressing too hard,' Adam said.

'I am not. I just want a small snowman.'

When he laughed at her, she picked up her pitiful snowman ball and threw it at him.

He straightened slowly. 'The young apprentice has provoked the master.'

Josey started to run, but his snowball hit her in the back. She made an indignant sound and stopped. This was war.

He had better aim than her, but that didn't matter once she got close enough to pelt him. She hit her target several times, once even in the face. Unfortunately, she was close enough now for him to grab her by the arm, then drop a handful of snow down the front of her sweater. She shrieked, slipped, then suddenly fell back into the snow, taking him with her. He was halfway on top of her, his hands in the snow on either side of her shoulders.

She threw her head back and laughed so hard her eyes filled with tears. When had she had a better time? Letting go felt so good. When she was finally able to catch her breath, she saw that Adam was staring down at her with the most serious look on his face. His eyes went to her lips and lingered there a moment.

Then he suddenly rolled off her and got to his feet.

'I hurt my leg skiing on Bald Slope Mountain,' he said, extending a hand to her.

She sat up, dazed. *What just happened here?* She looked up at him, then took his hand. He pulled her to her feet. 'It must have been a bad fall.'

'It was. No more skiing for me. No more skiing, no more sailing, no more cliff diving, no more mountain climbing. No more travel.'

It all sounded so exotic. 'You used to do all those things?'

'Yes.' He turned and walked to his snowman-in-progress.

'Did you like travelling?'

'I loved it. Here, help me lift this middle ball onto the bottom one.'

She walked over to him, and together they lifted the big snowball. 'So you haven't left Bald Slope at all since your accident.'

'Maybe sometime in the future I'll go see my brother in Chicago. See some old friends there. I'm not ready yet.' He started making the last ball.

'I didn't know you lived in Chicago.'

He smiled as he rolled the ball around, making it bigger. 'I was a lawyer in Chicago. Before the accident.'

Her brows rose. Adam was a lawyer? This was like *candy*. 'Did the accident make you give up the law?'

'No. I gave it up because I hated it.' When he got the head of the snowman the right size, he picked it up and walked back to the body. His limp was getting worse the longer he was out there.

'Why didn't you give it up before the accident?'

'I don't know,' he said, setting the head on top with a plop. 'I guess almost dying makes you re-evaluate things.'

She couldn't speak for a moment. 'You almost died?'

'It was the first time I was ever hurt. Broken femur. Broken back. Internal injuries. Lost my spleen.' He said it mechanically, hiding the emotion.

She looked at him carefully in the moonlight. 'You're afraid to leave, aren't you?' she said. 'It happened, and you're afraid it's going to happen again if you do . . . anything. That's your secret.'

'I'm staying still. There's nothing wrong with that,' he said.

Josey felt strange, like there was a shifting in the universe somewhere. She followed the light shining on him through the snow-laden trees, across the sky and to the moon. She stared at it as if seeing it for the first time.

It took her breath away.

Chloe rolled over onto her side on the bed in the Cramdons' guest room and looked through the window at the same moon at the same time, and felt exactly the same shift.

She stuck her arm under the pillow to snuggle it to her. But then she paused. There was something under there.

She sat up and brought out a book.

*The Complete Homeowner's Guide.*

She put her head back on the pillow, staring at the book. Finally, a book that didn't have anything to do with her love life. It felt like a reward. She brought it to her, wrapping her arms around it, and looked back out into the cold, silent night.

Then she closed her eyes and went to sleep.

# 8
# Candy Hearts

MARGARET BARRELLED INTO Josey's bedroom on Thanksgiving morning. 'There's a snowman in our front yard!' she said, as if locusts weren't far behind. She walked to Josey's window. 'Look!'

Josey got out of bed and joined her mother at the window. The neighbourhood was pristine, the snow evenly coating everything . . . except their front yard. It was a mess. The snow was pockmarked by footprints, and then there was the snowman, which looked like it had been sprayed from a can of Reddi-wip.

With Adam's blue scarf wrapped round its neck.

Josey pinched her lips together to keep from smiling.

'Who would do such a thing to us? Call our lawn man,' Margaret said as she walked away. 'Tell him to come over and smooth our snow.'

She stopped in the doorway suddenly when a chirping sound came from somewhere inside the room. Josey felt a jab of dread and slid her eyes to her bag.

'What is that?' Margaret asked, looking around.

Josey went to her bag. 'It's, um, the cellphone ringing.'

'You gave out the number? To whom?'

'Her name is Chloe Finley,' Josey said, bringing out the phone.

Margaret's face grew tight. '*Finley? That's* who you've been seeing? Who told you about her?'

'What are you talking about? Told me what?'

'Nothing.' Margaret turned with her cane and left quickly.

Josey answered the phone, watching her mother leave. 'Hello?'

'Happy Thanksgiving!' Chloe said, sounding better than she had in all the time Josey had known her. 'Josey, you're never going to believe this. I'm going to buy the house on Summertime Road!'

Josey rubbed her eyes with one hand. 'What? Really? How?'

'I met the owners yesterday. Long story. Anyway, they had just decided to lower the price. And they agreed to sell it to me!'

Josey laughed. 'Oh, Chloe, that's fabulous!'

'I have so much to do. My mind is spinning.'

'If you need any help, I'm here for you.'

'Thank you. But I can do this on my own. I've been putting money into savings for a long time.'

'Good for you, Chloe. Good for you.'

'I'll talk to you soon.'

'Congratulations,' Josey said as Chloe hung up.

'What was that all about?' Della Lee called.

Josey went to the closet and opened the door. 'Chloe is buying a house.'

Della Lee was wearing the sweater and snow boots Josey had worn outside last night. 'It's nice that you offered to help her. You two stick together, OK?'

'Why? What do you mean?'

Della Lee shrugged. 'Nothing.'

Josey sighed and turned away. Again with the *nothing*.

**T**wo days later, on Saturday, Chloe called again and wanted to give Josey a tour of the house on Summertime Road. Josey agreed to meet her there that afternoon, glad to get out of the house. Margaret was emitting a constant level of vexation, making the air around her hum and crackle. And Josey had avoided Adam both Friday and Saturday when he'd been by with the mail, which seemed to make the days even longer. She didn't feel like finding out which Adam was there—the one who liked things the way they were or the one who came to her window to make a snowman.

Snowploughs had cleared the roads and there was a lot of traffic as Josey headed out to see Chloe's new house. The Christmas season was officially under way, transforming Bald Slope into a snowy picture-postcard paradise.

The Cramdons were happy to let Chloe show Josey around. They were very fond of Chloe. And, judging by the amount of books they owned, it was clear Chloe had found her lost tribe. Chloe loved everything about each room. She told Josey about what pieces of her great-grandparents' furniture would go where, sometimes stopping herself when she mentioned something she remembered belonged to Jake.

The last stop was the kitchen, where George and Zelda were having coffee. Zelda poured cups for Josey and Chloe.

'I can tell why you're friends,' Zelda said. She had sharp, intelligent eyes, like she knew more than she would say. 'The two of you even look alike.'

Josey and Chloe looked at each other, surprised. Chloe laughed and said, 'Oh my gosh, it's true! We even have the same colour eyes. And all this wild curly hair.'

Something suddenly occurred to Josey. No, it couldn't be.

*Damn it, Della Lee*, she thought.

Chloe was chatting with the Cramdons and they said something about the back yard.

'Oh, the back yard!' Chloe said. 'Josey, I want to show you the back yard.'

Cups of coffee in hand, they went outside to the screened-in porch. The back yard was large, large enough for a swimming pool, Chloe said, if she wanted one. But the Cramdons had gardened for years and the soil was good, so she might try her hand at that first.

'Did you know your father?' Josey suddenly blurted out.

Chloe raised her eyebrows at the sudden change of subject. 'No, actually. I have no idea who he is. My mom got pregnant with me when she was eighteen. Three days after I was born, she left town. I was raised by my great-grandparents.'

'Have you ever tried to find out who he is?'

'No,' Chloe said. 'When I was young, I lived on fantasies of who he was—royalty, a rock star. But I realised long ago that if I really knew who he was, I'd only be disappointed. Why do you ask?'

'I was just thinking of my dad.'

'He was a great man.'

Josey nodded absently.

'Girls,' George said, sticking his head out of the back door, 'who's up for pie?'

'You wanted me to ask Mr Lamar about the other woman my father paid off. You think it's Chloe's mother, don't you?' Josey demanded when she finally got home late that afternoon and went straight upstairs to Della Lee in the closet. 'You kept sending me to her for sandwiches you never ate.'

'Well, that took you long enough. What are you, blind?' Della Lee said, looking up from her collage. 'It's all in my mother's notebooks. She documented their entire affair.'

Della Lee's complete confidence in something so wholly improbable was getting under Josey's skin. 'Della Lee, don't take this the wrong way, but I think you might need professional help. I can help you. I can pay.'

Della Lee snorted. 'Oh, don't give me that. You're saying you haven't even considered the *possibility* that your father *might* have had other children?'

Josey hesitated before saying, 'You think my mother paid off your mother, that my mother knew about you. Do you think she knew about Chloe too?'

'I'm sure Margaret knew about all of Marco's affairs.'

Could that be why her mother had such a reaction to Chloe's name? No, Josey thought. She wasn't going to go there. Mr Lamar's letter was going to settle everything anyway.

'So you don't want to go?' Adam asked Jake, waving the invitation as if that might make it more enticing.

Jake was sitting on the couch in Adam's living room, flipping through the television channels with the remote. 'While going to the retirement party for your postal supervisor sounds like loads of fun, a bunch of us at work will be staying late Monday night.'

'You're a lousy date anyway.' Adam tossed the invitation on the coffee table and sat beside Jake. It wasn't like anyone expected him to bring someone to these functions. So why was he staring at the invitation instead of watching the television?

Because of Josey.

She was still avoiding him. He knew he had told her he liked the way things were, but that was before Wednesday night. She had somehow reached into him and seen exactly what he was trying to hide. He missed his old life. He missed it so much that sometimes his body would shudder, as if fighting with his mind to put him in motion again.

'I think I'll ask Josey Cirrini to the party,' he suddenly said to Jake, who muted the television and turned to him. 'I like her.'

Jake just stared at him, uncomprehending. '*What?*'

'She's nice.'

'Well, yes, I guess she is. She sent me a card my first week at the DA's office, saying congratulations on my new job. And she was the first person to send my mother flowers in the hospital when she had her hysterectomy. But you know what my mother said? "I can't believe *she* sent me flowers." Yes, my nice little mother said that. Apparently, when Josey was a little girl, she kicked my mother in the shin in the grocery store. She left a scar.'

'She apparently did something to everyone in this town. What did she do to you? Out with it.'

'She stole my piece of chocolate cake,' Jake mumbled.

Adam laughed. 'So naturally you're scarred for life.'

'Well, I love chocolate cake.'

Adam couldn't imagine what it was like for Josey to be constantly reminded of, and judged by, something she did when she was so young. He suddenly grabbed the phone book and left, Jake watching him curiously. When he got to his room, he sat on the edge of his bed and looked up her number. He couldn't believe how nervous he was. It felt like being at the starting gate at a downhill competition.

He dialled and their maid answered. 'Cirrini house.'

He cleared his throat. 'Could I speak with Josey, please?'

'Oldsey?'

'No, Josey.'

'I get. Who speak?'

'This is Adam Boswell.'

'Ahhhh, the mail,' she said, sounding pleased. 'Hold. I get.'

He stared at the floor, taking deep breaths, his heart pumping heavily. A few minutes later Josey came on the line. 'Hello?'

His head jerked up. 'Hi, Josey. It's Adam.'

Pause. 'Hi, Adam.'

'I haven't seen you in a couple of days. Are you OK?'

'Oh, yes. I'm fine,' she said awkwardly. 'Thanks for calling.'

'Listen,' he said. 'I'm thirty-four and I haven't done this in a long time, so forgive me my teenage-boyness.'

'What are you talking about?' she asked.

'I'm asking you out on a date.'

Silence.

'It's a retirement party on Monday night. Feel free to say no.'

'Of course I'll go out on a date with you,' she said simply.

*Of course.* Like how could he have thought otherwise?

'OK then. I'll pick you up on Monday at seven o'clock.'

'Oh, no. Don't pick me up here. I can meet you somewhere.'

'I want to pick you up.'

'I can't let you do that. Seriously, I can meet you somewhere.'

'Seriously, I want to pick you up,' he insisted.

'For a date,' she said, as if to verify that she didn't have it wrong.

'Yep.'

He was smiling when he went back to the living room. God, he felt good. He'd made it to the bottom of the hill. A hell of a ride.

On Monday night Josey looked in the mirror over her dresser and tugged at her lucky red cardigan. She wore it with a grey wool skirt she rarely went out in because her mother didn't like it. She didn't have a turtleneck that matched, so she was actually wearing one of Della Lee's, a Lycra one that was too small, but if she kept her cardigan buttoned, hopefully Adam wouldn't be able to tell.

Her hair was down, her curls tamed. And she was wearing make-up, thanks to Della Lee's tutelage. Josey finally turned away from the mirror and picked up her coat.

She walked to her window for the fortieth time. She felt a catch of panic that made her lose her breath. There was an SUV there that wasn't there before. 'Oh God. He's here.'

Della Lee looked up. She was still working on her collage, using a glue stick to paste all the images she'd cut from the travel magazines onto the flat surface of the lid from her private box. 'I don't understand you, Josey. Shouldn't you be a little happier? I thought this was what you wanted.'

Josey turned to her. Della Lee had, inexplicably, several pencils in her hair today. 'This is what I want,' Josey said. 'I just wish I knew what *he* wanted.'

'Because asking you on a date is so unclear?'

'That's just it. Why did he ask me? Is this just a friend thing? Maybe he only needed a date for this specific function, and any woman would do. Maybe it's just a pity date.' She suddenly wanted Mallomars and Jelly Nougats and creme-filled cookies. Her eyes went to the wall at the back of the closet.

'Oh, no. No, no, no,' Della Lee said when she saw the look on Josey's face. 'Nothing is real in here. Your life is outside. It's waiting for you.'

Josey closed her eyes. There was only one thing she wanted more than Mallomars and Jelly Nougats and creme-filled cookies.

Adam.

She picked up her bag, then hesitated at the door. 'You'll be here when I get back, won't you?'

'I'm not going anywhere yet,' Della Lee said. 'For God's sake, smile. This isn't an execution.'

Josey walked downstairs and into the sitting room. Helena was sewing, and Margaret was reading a magazine.

Margaret lifted her head and stared. 'What is this?'

Josey straightened her shoulders. 'Mother, I know this is going to come as a surprise, but someone is about to come to the door. I have a date tonight.'

'You're wearing that sweater again,' Margaret said, as if she hadn't heard a word Josey said. 'You told me you threw it away.'

'Mother, did you miss the part about me saying I had a date?' There was a knock at the door and Josey felt light-headed. 'There he is. I warned him, but he wants to meet you anyway. Please be nice.'

'You warned who? What did you say about me?'

Josey walked to the front door and opened it. Adam looked wonderful in a cream-coloured sweater and leather jacket. He was smiling. But for how long? She took him by the arm before he could say anything. 'I apologise in advance,' she said as she pulled him in.

She led him to the sitting room. She started to take her hand off his arm, but he put his hand over hers and kept it there. She could have cried. 'Adam, this is Helena. And this is my mother, Margaret Cirrini.'

'We've met a few times before,' Adam said affably. 'But it's nice to be formally introduced to you both.'

Margaret's brows rose. 'You're the mailman.'

'Yes.'

'I can't believe it,' she said, laughing. 'Oh, Josey, Josey, Josey.'

Adam looked at Josey curiously. Josey just shook her head and took comfort in his hand on hers. *Hold on*, she wanted to say. *Don't let go.*

'I apologise for my daughter,' Margaret said to Adam, her laughter fading to a chuckle. 'She's not very schooled in these matters. I've always known she liked the mail, but it never occurred to me it was the *mailman* she liked. Josey honey, he doesn't come to the door every day just for you. It's his job. He does it for everyone. This is certainly awkward. If you'd like to leave now, young man, you may. There is no obligation.'

'Actually, for years now I *have* come to the door just for her. Good evening, Mrs Cirrini.' Still holding Josey's hand on his arm, Adam turned and led her out to his SUV, then he helped her in.

Minutes of awkward silence passed while he drove. Finally he cleared his throat and said, 'So, tell me about your mother.'

Josey shifted uncomfortably. 'What do you want to know?'

'Is she always like that?'

'I tried to warn you.'

He gave a low whistle. 'Did I mention you look beautiful tonight? I've always liked that sweater on you.'

She turned to him. 'You recognise this sweater?'

He nodded. 'You were wearing it the first day I met you.'

Well, if she'd had any doubt before, it quickly disappeared. This sweater really *was* magic. 'Just don't ask me to take it off.'

'Excuse me?'

'Oh no, wait, I didn't mean it like that,' she said quickly. 'I just meant that the turtleneck under this sweater is too tight. It's a little obscene.'

He cut his eyes at her and smiled. 'Now I'm intrigued.'

'You look very nice tonight too,' she said, trying to change the subject.

'I'll take off my sweater if you want me to,' Adam offered. 'It's not obscene, but I have some really interesting scars.'

'Well, I think this is going well so far, don't you?' Josey sighed.

But Adam laughed and said, 'In case I forget to tell you at the end of the night, I had a great time.'

The retirement party was held in the VFW hall. There were paper streamers and garlands and tables piled high with fried food and desserts with frosting. Mostly, though, there was laughter. The hall echoed with it.

Adam and Josey drew a lot of interest when they walked in. He figured that would happen. What he didn't count on, however, was the fact that they had no sooner made it to the punchbowl than Josey was descended upon and taken away by some women at the party. Josey gave him a questioning look over her shoulder. He smiled and was about to go after her when one of the women said something to her and Josey suddenly laughed.

It stopped him short.

He didn't think he'd ever heard Josey laugh, not like that, unrestrained, unselfconscious. It was as clear and pure as water. He spent the rest of the evening watching her from across the hall. She surprised him by socialising with his coworkers better than he did. She was having a wonderful time. Without him.

Sure, he hadn't dated in a while, but he was pretty sure the purpose was to spend time *together*. So what was he doing all the way over here?

As things were winding down, Adam finally walked across the hall to where she was sitting with a few other women. 'Are you ready to go, Josey?'

One of the women nudged her, like they'd been talking about him.

They walked outside after they'd said their goodbyes. The stars were out, pinholes in dark fabric. They lingered at his SUV.

'Want to get some coffee, maybe walk through the park?' Adam asked. He held his breath, waiting for her to answer, waiting to hear she actually wanted to spend time alone with him.

'I'd love to,' she said.

'Good.' He opened the passenger-side door for her. She got in, brushing him with the scent of peppermint.

They got coffee at Dang! That's Good, the bookstore-café downtown. The bookstore, the newly renovated Downtown Inn and a curving line of other shops surrounded the courthouse and the large open park. All the shops were decorated for Christmas, with twinkling white lights and foil and tinsel. Even the bare trees in the park had lights in them. The library, one street over, rose up behind the buildings, its dramatic arches almost white in the moonlight.

'Look at that,' he said, pointing to the library as they walked slowly through the park, cups in hand.

'Beautiful, isn't it?' she said. 'It's been for ever since I've been in there. I had a tutor named Holly who convinced my mother to let us go to the library to study several days a week. We would spend all day on the Internet there, just goofing around. I loved that.' She turned to him with a smile. 'I was home-schooled.'

'I know. Your neighbour Mrs Ferguson told me.'

'I get the feeling you've heard a lot about me.'

He leaned in closer to her, nudging her playfully. 'That's because you're the daughter of the late, great Marco Cirrini.'

'But who are you, Adam Boswell? Even your coworkers don't know much about you. I think they wanted me to give them some sort of inside information. But I didn't have anything to tell.'

'I'll tell you anything you want to know, Josey,' he said. 'Just ask.'

She hesitated. 'Listen, if tonight was just about needing a date for a function, I understand. This doesn't have to be serious.'

'So *that's* what this is all about,' he said, and he could have laughed at how relieved he was. 'Josey, I didn't just need a date for a function. I wanted a date with you. *You.* Just ask.'

She hesitated again. 'I think I've lost my train of thought.'

'OK, so I'll tell you.' He told her about growing up in California and about his competitive skiing days, about how he ended up here after hearing about Bald Slope's steep runs. He told her about his brother, that Brett called every week telling him to come back to Chicago.

'But you don't have any plans to leave,' Josey said.

'You've brought that up before. Why? Do you want to leave?'

'I want to leave so badly I can't stand it sometimes,' she said vehemently. 'Too many people see me the way I was as a child.'

Adam stopped under the light of an old-fashioned streetlamp and threw away their coffee cups.

'What would you do if you left?' he said, something almost like panic in his chest.

'I'd go everywhere, see everything I could.'

'What about your mother?'

'Sometimes it seems like I'm just waiting for her to say she's finally forgiven me for all the things I did, waiting for her to say, "You can go now. Go live your life."'

'You don't need anyone's permission, Josey. You could do it. You have the rest of your life in front of you, wide open. I can't even explain how that makes me feel. I want to take some of what you have and eat it. I want to feel that way again.'

'Do you?' she asked. 'Do you really?'

The moon spun a spiderweb of light around her hair. He took a step towards her. 'Yes, I do.' He bent slowly, stopping several times along the way to gauge her reaction.

'Adam?' she whispered when he was close enough to feel her breath. 'Don't do this unless you mean it. Don't do it because I want it, or because you feel sorry for me, or anything like that.'

'Oh, I mean it, Josey.'

'Right. OK then,' she said seriously.

He slowly, slowly touched his lips to hers. He wasn't prepared for what he felt. His panic and tension suddenly dissipated and he was filled with her—open, expressive, hopeful Josey.

His kiss went deeper. He raised her hands and put them round his neck, then he wound his own arms around her, inside her coat, and pulled her to him. To this place. The right place. Right here. She made a sound somewhere deep in her throat, a moan, an acquiescence, trembling with need and uncertainty.

Suddenly he stopped and stepped back. He took an impossibly deep breath, then whooshed it out.

'I . . . I should take you home.' He ran a hand through his hair.

'Promise me you're going to mean this again,' she said softly.

He laughed. 'I'm going to mean this every chance I get from now on.' He put an arm round her waist, his fingers tight, like he was hanging from a cliff by them, as if he might fall.

Together they started walking again.

**T**ell me again,' Della Lee said into the darkness late that evening, just as Josey was falling asleep.

'He kissed me,' Josey said into her pillow.

'No. Say it like you said it before.'

Josey smiled. 'It was the best first kiss in the history of first kisses. It was as sweet as sugar. And it was warm, as warm as pie. The whole world opened up and I fell inside. I didn't know where I was, but I didn't care. I didn't care because the only person who mattered was there with me.'

Della Lee said, 'I think heaven will be like a first kiss.'

'I hope so,' Josey murmured.

'Me too.'

**T**he December meeting of the ladies' club was the following Thursday afternoon, and Margaret half expected Josey not to take her. She'd even worked up a fair amount of indignation, ready to be left at home, forgotten. But exactly on time, Josey walked into the sitting room and asked if Margaret was ready to go.

When Josey parked in front of Mrs Herzog's home, where the meeting was held every month, Rawley was already there, helping Annabelle Drake out of his cab. When Annabelle saw Margaret, she waited for her, and they walked up to the front door together. Josey followed.

'I knew it had got too much for him, all those rumours about us,' Annabelle said. 'Rawley said to me in the cab today, out of the blue, "It was nice having Margaret ride with us, wasn't it?" I think it would make him feel better if someone rode with me all the time. Why don't we ride together more often, Margaret?'

Margaret looked over her shoulder at Rawley. He was watching them walk away.

The meeting was late to begin because everyone was talking about the latest news: a body had been discovered in the Green Cove River that morning. Margaret had heard all about it from Helena at breakfast. The Beasley murder case was still fresh in everyone's mind, and the ladies at the meeting were saying, 'Was it murder?' 'Again?' 'Are we not safe in our own homes?' But Margaret tuned out the gossip. She went to the window and looked out. Rawley was standing there at his cab. She couldn't believe he would say something like that to Annabelle. He had to have known it would get back to Margaret. She turned and walked to the door.

No matter the weather, Rawley always leaned against his cab and watched the house. He straightened as she approached.

'Annabelle told me what you said. You will have to find someone else to ride with you so no one thinks you're having an affair,' she said bitterly when she reached him. 'It won't be me. I will have nothing to do with this. Nothing at all, do you hear me?'

Rawley's brows lowered, but he didn't speak.

'Marco would have ruined you,' she said, even though she knew the explanation was too late. 'As long as he didn't know who you were, the identity of the man I was with that night, you were safe. You could move on and have a good life. But when Marco died, and you still hadn't married, I thought things might change between the two of us. I was wrong, obviously. I understand why you still hate me. But that doesn't mean you can put me in the middle of your affair with Annabelle. I may deserve it, but I don't think my heart could take it.' She turned and walked back into the house, clinging to the last of her dignity.

When the meeting was over, Rawley was still there, waiting for Annabelle, but his eyes zeroed in on Margaret and followed her intently, almost angrily, as she and Josey walked to their car.

When they arrived home, Josey hurried to her room. Margaret just sighed, asked Helena to bring her a pain-relief pill and walked to the sitting room. She stiffly sat in her favourite chair.

There was a knock at the door, and Margaret almost groaned. She was in no mood for company. Shortly, Helena walked into the sitting room without the pain-relief pill.

'Who was—' Margaret started to say, but stopped when Rawley Pelham walked into the room behind Helena.

'If you'll excuse us,' he said to Helena, 'Mrs Cirrini and I need to talk in private.'

Rawley shut the sitting-room door behind her and turned to Margaret with an ominous look.

'Now,' he said, speaking to her directly for the first time in forty years, 'it's time to get a few things sorted.'

Margaret sat up straighter. *He was speaking to her.*

'First, I'm not having an affair with Annabelle Drake. Second, I had no idea that you protected my identity from your husband. All these years I thought he knew. Third, you know very well that the reason I don't speak to you is because you made me promise never to speak to you again in public.'

Margaret jerked as surprise entered her body. It travelled through her nervous system, setting every hair on end. 'Excuse me?'

'You don't remember?' he asked incredulously. 'We stood there on that porch. I was ready to fight your husband. But all you wanted was for me to go away. You were so miserable that night. I would have done anything to make you feel better. You made me promise to never speak to you in public.'

She shook her head in sharp, jerky movements. 'That's not possible. I can't believe I would make you do such a thing,' she said. 'I was always careful about promises around you.'

'Not careful enough.'

Everyone knew Pelhams didn't make promises easily, because they were incapable of breaking that promise, once made. It simply was not possible for a Pelham to go back on his word. And it wasn't good old-fashioned taught honesty, either. It was in their genes, like their blue eyes and their russet hair.

'And of course the only time I saw you after that was in public, so how could I say to you how much I missed you, how much I wanted you? How could I say, when your husband died, that I had never stopped dreaming of you? Do you remember, under the tree in the woods behind the old theatre?'

Her hand went to her heart. 'Of course I remember that place.'

'We were making love one day, and you looked up at me with those beautiful blue eyes. I said, "I love you, Margaret. I will love you for ever." And you said, "Promise?"'

'Oh God,' she whispered. How could she have done such a thing?

His gaze was steady. 'Every day since then, my life has been about wanting. Wanting you, Margaret. It's been my choice, and I've revelled in the beauty of it. *My choice.* Promising to love you has been the easiest promise I've ever made.'

She had to look away. This was too much. When she heard the scrape of the doorknob turning, her head shot up.

'Wait, Rawley,' she said.

He paused in the doorway, his back to her.

She took a deep breath and said what she should have said forty years ago. 'Please don't leave.'

## 9
## *Life Savers*

CHLOE HAD JUST got in from work late that afternoon when there was a knock at the apartment door. She put down her coat and answered it. Julian was leaning against the wall directly opposite her door. He didn't move, just smiled at her. His long hair was down and seemed to float around him. She could feel his pull from here.

'Julian,' she said, 'what are you doing here?'

'I haven't heard from you in a while. I wanted to see if you were all right.' His words surrounded her like perfume.

'I'm sorry. I've been busy.'

'Back with your boyfriend?' he asked, but he already knew the answer. 'No.'

'Are you ready to find out who Jake slept with?' he said gently.

She felt a ping of excitement. 'Is that why you're here?'

'Of course, sweetheart. I've been sitting on all this information. It's not doing me any good. Come on.' Julian pushed himself away from the wall and walked down the stairs.

'Where are you going?' she called after him.

'To your car. Don't you want to see where she lives?'

She stood there for a moment. Which would be worse, spending the rest of her life knowing who it was or spending the rest of her life not knowing? 'I'm coming,' she said, grabbing her coat and bag.

When they got in her Beetle, Julian said, 'All right. Go left at the end of the street. Head east towards the Catholic church on All Saints Boulevard.' Once she reached that, he said, 'Turn on Saint Joseph's Lane. It's number twelve.'

She pulled over and parked opposite the house. It was a beautiful colonial-style home behind an iron security gate.

'This place looks familiar,' she said.

'This is where Eve Beasley lives.'

She jerked her head round to face him. '*Beasley?*'

'You have no idea what I had to do to find this out. I feel so dirty,' he said, grinning.

'Jake slept with *Eve Beasley?*' Chloe said, completely bowled over.

'You know her?'

'You don't?'

He shrugged. 'I've never heard of her.'

The Beasleys were fairly new residents in Bald Slope. They'd bought a vacation home and spent about four months out of the year there. Wade was a fifty-five-year-old retired stockbroker, and Eve was his beautiful forty-five-year-old wife. Wade Beasley had murdered their housekeeper and dumped her body off a trail near the state park.

There was only circumstantial evidence tying Wade to the murder, and halfway through the trial Jake was prosecuting, it had looked like the jury was going to acquit. But then Eve Beasley, who had stood by her husband from the beginning, suddenly filed for divorce and agreed to testify against him. She was the only one who knew her husband had sexually harassed their housekeeper. She'd seen it. She was the only one who had experienced his violence first-hand. She'd been away visiting her sister when the murder occurred. When she came back and found the housekeeper gone, she'd asked her husband what happened. Wade had said, 'She couldn't take it. She wasn't as tough as you.'

That turned the jury around quickly.

Jake had worked closely with her. He used to talk about her, how he felt sorry for her and how sweet she was. Everyone blamed her for not speaking up sooner. But Wade Beasley had abused her for years. She was terrified of him. Chloe knew that Jake made her feel safe. Jake was the one who had ultimately convinced her to testify.

Then, when the case was over, when everyone was celebrating, *they'd slept together.*

Chloe knew now. She understood why he couldn't tell her. If this got out, there was the possibility of a mistrial. Wade Beasley might go free because of this.

'Ah, look,' Julian said. 'I'd hoped we would be here for this. She leaves for church every day about this time.'

Chloe ducked as the gate opened and Eve Beasley pulled out, driving an Audi. Chloe peered out of the window as she passed. Eve was an elegant-looking woman, her hair prematurely silver, but her face was unlined and her skin was absolutely luminescent.

'Jake and an older woman,' Julian said as he watched her car disappear. 'Not much of a scandal, but people make do, I suppose.'

It was obvious Julian hadn't followed the trial. It was obvious he didn't know what was at stake. 'Jake is called the Wonderboy at work. I'm sure everyone had a good Mrs Robinson laugh,' Chloe said, to keep Julian on the wrong track. She still wanted to be angry with Jake, but she found the hurt was fading.

'Now you know,' Julian said, watching her carefully. 'Here, sweetheart. Let me drive.' He got out and walked round the car to the driver's side. Chloe obediently scooted to the passenger seat. She wasn't sure she could drive anyway.

Instead of driving back to the apartment, Julian took her to his house. She was just going to drop him off and go home. She wanted to call Josey. 'I need some time to take this all in,' she said.

'Sweetheart, the last thing you need to do is think.' He got out, taking her keys with him. 'Come inside.'

She followed him to the door of the yellow bungalow. When they stepped inside, Julian immediately picked up some piles of clothing from the living-room floor and threw them into a bedroom.

'I guess you still haven't heard from your girlfriend,' Chloe said.

'No. And I'm not much of a housekeeper. Sorry.'

Chloe looked around. There were feminine touches everywhere—baskets on the wall with artificial roses in them, a white wicker rocking chair with pink pillows. 'This still looks like her place.'

'It is, actually. She owns the house.'

'It's like living in Jake's apartment.'

'Exactly. I know what you're going through.' He took her by the hand and sat her on the couch. 'Let's get drunk.'

Margaret and Rawley took dinner together in the sitting room, behind closed doors, while Josey ate in the kitchen with Helena. It was well into the evening when Margaret finally walked him out, speaking to him softly. Josey and Helena came out of the kitchen to watch her. Margaret smiled slightly but didn't offer any explanation. She simply walked up to her room.

'What do you think that was all about?' Josey asked Helena.

'Oldgret like cab.'

'Hmm,' Josey said thoughtfully as she walked to the staircase. She retreated to her room. She went to her closet and opened the door, then she took a startled step back. Della Lee was standing there. She'd never seen Della Lee stand in her closet before. The first thought that struck her was, *Something's wrong.*

'What took you so long to get up here?' Della Lee demanded. She was nervous. Scared, almost. Tension was undulating from the closet like heat. 'Check your messages.'

'What?'

'Check your cellphone messages!'

Josey went to her bag on the chaise. She pulled out the cellphone. There was one message.

'Hi, Josey. It's Chloe.' Pause. 'I really wish I could talk to you. Um, I'm at Julian's house right now. Out of the blue, he came to see me today. He took me to see the woman Jake slept with. I'm not sure why I thought it would make me feel better. It made me feel worse, because I know now why he wouldn't tell me and it really was for a good reason. I miss him, Josey.' Another pause. 'Anyway, I'm here with Julian. He's in the next room, pouring drinks. He's not all bad, you know. I . . . kind of like him. Not in the way I like Jake, but he doesn't have to be Jake. I'll talk to you tomorrow.'

Josey slowly lowered the phone.

'Go,' Della Lee said frantically. '*Go!*'

Josey turned and ran out of the room.

She got in her car and raced down the street. She made it to Della Lee's house in under fifteen minutes. Chloe's car was there and Josey pulled to a stop behind the Beetle at the kerb. The lights were on in the living room, and music was pounding from the house. It was a wonder the neighbours hadn't called the cops. Josey got out and ran up the walkway, then up the steps. The door was locked, so she knocked. When that didn't get a response, she began pounding on the door and calling out Chloe's name until her fist hurt and her voice turned raspy. If Della Lee and all her rough ways couldn't handle Julian, Chloe didn't have a chance.

The only thing besides her keys that Josey had taken with her was the cellphone she still had clutched in her hand when she ran out. She went back to her car and got in. She fished the phone out from under the seat where it had fallen and called 911.

'This is Marcie Jackson and my neighbour won't turn down his music,' she said, exaggerating her accent. 'It's so loud that it's shaking my windows and it woke up the baby. The whole neighbourhood is complaining. He's a nuisance.'

She gave the address and they promised to send someone out. Josey hung up and stared at the house. She suddenly caught some movement coming from inside. A shadow moved by the curtains.

She got out of the car again. She was at the bottom of the porch steps when she heard the tumble of the deadbolt, and then the door flung open. Chloe appeared, her shirt half off and her lipstick smeared. She was carrying her coat and bag, and she was saying something muted by the music.

Josey started up the steps as Julian came up behind Chloe and put his arms round her in an embrace, causing her to drop her coat and bag. 'Come on, baby,' he said, talking loudly over the music. He sounded drunk. 'Don't make me do it like this. It'll be good. I can make everything OK. I'm magic that way. You'll see.'

'Let me go, please,' Chloe said weakly. Julian pushed her into the living room. He tried to close the door, but Chloe's bag and coat prevented him from doing so. He knelt to move them out of the way, and when he looked up, Josey was there.

'I'll be a monkey's uncle,' he said, slowly straightening. 'The thief returns.' He was wearing boots and unbuttoned jeans, but nothing else. His bare chest almost crackled with electricity.

Josey called into the house, 'Chloe? Chloe, come on.'

'Josey? Is that you?' Chloe came running up to the door. Julian blocked her way, his hands gripping the door casing. He tried to close the door in Josey's face, but Chloe's coat and bag were still there.

Josey caught the door and pushed against it as hard as she could. He pushed back for a few seconds, then he quickly stepped away, sending her flying into the house.

Julian kicked Chloe's things out of the doorway and started to close the door. Josey took Chloe's hand and was about to run to the bedroom at the end of the hall. She prayed the door had a lock and that they could get to it before Julian got to them. The police would surely be here soon.

But then Julian's long hair suddenly flew behind him, off his shoulders, like a sharp wind had blown through the door. He staggered back towards the kitchen at the other end of the living room.

'What the hell?' he said, when the wind blew at him again, sending him falling through the swinging kitchen door.

Josey saw the clear path and darted for the front door with Chloe.

She had no idea what was going on until she heard Julian say, 'Della Lee, is that you?' Josey grabbed Chloe's coat and bag and ran out just as they heard one crash, then another, like dishes being thrown, broken. 'Get away from me!' Julian yelled.

How on earth did Della Lee get here? She must have come in through the back door.

Josey rushed Chloe to the Cadillac and got her into the passenger seat. She saw the police cruiser at the four-way stop down the street. Thank God. She ran to the other side of the car and got in, pulling away from the kerb as the cruiser turned down the street. In her rearview mirror she saw the cruiser come to a stop in front of Della Lee's house. Two patrolmen got out. She parked at the end of the road and watched as they walked up the steps and banged on the screen door.

Julian shot out of the door. One of the patrolmen caught him by the arm and Julian struggled against him, swinging his fist and catching the patrolman across the jaw. The other patrolman tackled Julian on the porch and together they cuffed him.

Julian was yelling, 'Get her out of my house! She's crazy!'

One of the patrolmen entered the house, and a few seconds later the music stopped. The patrolman came back out shaking his head.

'She's in there, I swear to God! She threw plates at me!'

Chloe was leaning her head against the passenger-side window. 'I'm going to take you home now, OK?' Josey said.

Chloe nodded.

Chloe stared out of the car window. Her stomach was churning. If she didn't move, maybe she wouldn't get sick. She bolted out of the car right after Josey parked and raced ahead. She knew Josey was following her, so she left the apartment door open and ran to the bathroom. She went to her knees in front of the commode and started to retch.

She stayed there on the cool tile floor for about ten minutes, her eyes closed, images of the evening swimming through her head. Desperation. She'd been desperate with Jake. She was desperate without him. When would it ever stop?

Suddenly she knew she wasn't alone any more. She'd left the bathroom door open, so she assumed it was Josey. She shakily made her way to her feet and turned, but no one was there. Her eyes went to the floor and there, in the doorway, was a stack of books. The book on the bottom was *Finding Forgiveness*, the old warhorse.

'You're going to get wet,' she said as she walked to the sink. She turned on the faucet and splashed her face, then washed her mouth out. She dried her face and pulled her hair back into a ponytail. When she turned to leave, the books were still there.

She picked them up—*Finding Forgiveness*; *Old Love, New Direction*; *A Girl's Guide to Keeping Her Guy*; *Madame Bovary*; and *The Complete Homeowner's Guide*. She carried them into the bedroom and set them on the nightstand. She stared at the stack, the syllabus of her life for the past month, a map of what she'd been through. Then she couldn't look any more and turned away.

After changing into sweats, she walked back into the living room. Josey was pacing, but stopped when Chloe appeared. 'Are you OK?'

She was grateful for Josey, for her friendship. It had come at the most unexpected time in her life. 'I don't know. I don't know anything any more. How did you know where Julian lived?'

Josey hesitated. 'It's a long story. Did he hurt you?'

'No.' Chloe went to the couch and sat, tucking her legs under her. 'I thought I could do it. It wouldn't have been cheating. Jake and I aren't together. But I couldn't. I love Jake too much. Why didn't Jake love me enough not to do it?'

'It wasn't because I didn't love you enough, Clo,' Jake said from the doorway. Josey and Chloe both turned, startled. Jake was standing there, his hair dishevelled, his coat buttoned wrong. Adam was behind him in the hallway. 'I love you more than my own life.'

Chloe looked at Josey.

'I called Adam while you were in the bathroom,' Josey said. 'I'm sorry. I didn't know what else to do.'

Jake entered the room and Adam followed, reaching round Jake to take Josey's hand. 'Come on,' Adam said. 'Let's go.'

'No,' Josey said, trying to shake him off.

'It's OK, Josey. Really,' Chloe said. This needed to be done.

Chloe watched Adam lead Josey towards the door. As soon as the door closed, Jake knelt in front of the couch where she was sitting and said, 'Chloe, look at me.'

She met his eyes. Those magnetic light green eyes.

'It was Eve Beasley,' he said.

'I know.'

Jake looked poleaxed. 'You do? Who told you?'

'It doesn't matter.'

'I didn't mean for it to happen. Neither did she. We instantly regretted it, and we haven't seen each other since. I am to blame. I know I am. If I could take it back, I would. I'm so sorry.'

There was a thud, and a book that was sitting on the arm of the couch fell to the floor beside them. *Finding Forgiveness.* Chloe pinched her lips together, tears coming to her eyes as she stared at the book.

'Let's start over, Clo,' Jake said, and she lifted her eyes to meet his. 'Let me call you up and ask you on a date. I'll knock on the door to your house. I'll have flowers. I'll be nervous. I'll wait until the third date to kiss you, though I'll think about it every second until I do.'

The first time, they didn't have a conventional courtship. It had been very hot very fast. Could they really start over, and then do it the traditional way?

'Never do this to me again, Jake.' Her voice shook.

'I won't.'

She lifted her chin. 'I have books. A lot of books. And they're going to be around from now on. You have to accept that.'

'I've never had a problem with your books, Clo. They're who you are.'

Jake slowly leaned in. He wrapped his arms round her. She found herself nuzzling him, hiding her face in his neck. She would always be desperate about him. But she wasn't as disorientated as she used to be. She felt a strange sort of grounding, as if she knew she wasn't going to lose her way any more.

She turned her head on Jake's shoulder to look at *Finding Forgiveness* again.

But it was gone.

Josey kept looking back at the door as Adam led her down the stairs. 'She'll be fine. You know they need to do this or you wouldn't have called,' he said. 'Bringing them together tonight is good for them. They're going to be fine. I promise.'

Out on the sidewalk she could see that he'd parked on the street. Her car was looming large round the corner in the parking lot.

'Do you want to go somewhere?' he said. 'Get something to eat, maybe?' He stared at her. 'Or we could go to my house,' he said with a significance she couldn't ignore.

She felt her chest catch, setting off a wild array of racing shivers. This past week they'd upped the notch of intimacy every time they met. Short, desperate surges in the dark of her porch or his SUV after she'd sneaked out. No one could see. No one would know. It was a secret, like almost everything else in her life. It was easier that way, easier to work round her fear rather than face it, easier not to tell her mother. Now he was asking her to put it out in the open, and despite everything, she hesitated. 'I don't know.'

'You're scared.'

'If I stay with you tonight, it will be all over town by tomorrow.'

He looked genuinely confused. 'So?'

'You really don't understand, do you? I still hide. I still sneak out of my mother's house because I don't want her disapproval. I still worry about what people here think of me.'

'Then let's leave,' he said quietly.

She gaped at him. 'You're not serious.'

'I'm completely serious. Neither of us want to be here. Let's go.'

'You would leave?' she asked incredulously. 'Really?'

'I would leave.' He took a deep breath. 'But only with you.'

She couldn't believe what she did next.

She left, all right.

And ran home.

Helena met Josey at the door. 'Oldsey, Oldgret want to see you.' She pointed towards the light coming from the sitting room. 'She wait up.'

Oh, hell. Josey tried to smile. 'Thanks, Helena.' Then she did the death march to the sitting room.

Margaret was in her nightgown, sitting in her favourite chair. She looked up and set aside her magazine. 'Where have you been?' she demanded. 'I won't have you acting this way, do you hear me? Imagine my surprise when I got up to tell you something, only to find you gone. For days now I've suspected you've been sneaking out after I've taken my sleeping pill. Well, I didn't take one tonight. You're not a silly teenager, Josey. I won't have you acting like this.'

'I'm sorry, Mother.'

That was what Margaret wanted, Josey thought. She wanted Josey cowed. Margaret stood up and said, less harshly, 'I wanted to tell you to pick up pork tenderloins at the grocery store tomorrow. Rawley Pelham will be dining with me tomorrow, and I remember he likes them. Also, I won't be needing you to drive me to my eye appointment tomorrow. I'll be taking a cab for the foreseeable future.'

Josey watched her mother walk towards the door with her cane. She couldn't believe what she'd just heard. 'What am I supposed to do, then?'

'You're supposed to behave. Don't see that Finley girl or the mailman. And don't sneak out again. What would the neighbours think if they saw you? And what if I had needed you tonight?'

'You just said you *didn't* need me, Mother!' Josey laughed, but with an edge, very close to crying. She'd just run away from the man she loved because she couldn't let go of the faraway hope that, if she stayed long enough, one day Margaret would love her, accept her, *forgive her.* 'When is it ever going to be enough? When are you ever going to forgive me? Why did you even have me? Was it really just to keep his money?'

Margaret set her jaw and walked past Josey. 'I'm going to bed now.'

Josey followed her and stood at the base of the steps as her mother walked up. 'Was he really that bad?'

Margaret didn't answer until she reached the top of the steps. Then she stopped, her back to Josey. 'Yes, he was,' she said as she disappeared down the hallway. 'And you look just like him.'

Josey stared at the place her mother had been. It had taken her twenty-seven years to finally figure this out. Margaret wasn't going to be happy as long as Josey was there, but she would never tell her to leave. And Josey wasn't going to be happy until she left, but she wanted her mother to tell her to go.

This wasn't about forgiveness. It never had been. This was about two women punishing themselves for no good reason.

And it was time for it to end.

**T**wenty minutes later, Josey said, 'Can I come in?'

Adam hesitated in his doorway, then stood back. 'Of course.'

She walked into the living room of his house. It was sparse, temporary. Secondhand furniture for the most part, blue couch with purple cushions, a 1970s-era orange reading chair. The large leather recliner and flat-screen TV above the fireplace stood out. Those were deliberate purchases for comfort.

'I think I'm scared of your furniture,' she said, trying to smile.

'I was living day by day here at first, not sure what I should do. I bought a bed, the recliner and the television. Then, every once in a while, someone at work would say they were getting rid of something, and I asked if I could have it.'

She turned her back on him to look around some more. The television was on and she pretended to watch it. He came up behind her and took off her jacket. She jumped a little and turned to face him. They stared at each other for a moment.

'Why are you here, Josey?'

She took a deep breath. 'You go, I go.'

He dropped the jacket, and in one step he was in front of her, his hands on her face, kissing her. There was no lead-up. It was all at once frantic, hands everywhere. Still kissing her, he backed her to the couch, then pushed her down to the cushions, angling his body over hers. His kiss was deeper this way, hungry, like she was candy. He *feasted* on her. His hands went to the sides of her sweater and slowly brought it up. He looked down at her, breathing heavily.

'I was afraid I'd pushed you away for good tonight. It was all about speed with me. I've always gone too fast.'

'But that's exactly what I need, Adam.'

'You go, I go,' he whispered as he kissed her again.

She was distantly aware that the eleven o'clock news had just come on, and the lead story was the body that had been found in the Green Cove River that morning. Not breaking their kiss, Adam stretched one hand above her and reached for the remote control on the end table.

The news anchor started the broadcast by saying, 'We are now able to confirm identification of the body as that of thirty-seven-year-old Della Lee Baker of Bald Slope.'

Josey suddenly sat up. 'Wait. Stop,' she said, putting her hand on his and lowering it so he couldn't use the remote.

'Baker's abandoned car was found in a grassy area this afternoon near the Green Cove Bridge, where officials also discovered what appears to be a suicide note. Baker had a long criminal record that included assault, convictions for driving while intoxicated and shoplifting.' They showed an arrest photo of Della Lee. 'In breaking news, we've also learned that her live-in boyfriend, Julian Wallace, also of Bald Slope, was arrested tonight on unrelated charges—assaulting an officer who was responding to a disturbing-the-peace call at the home the couple shared. Wallace confirmed to police that Baker has been missing for weeks, which supports the coroner's initial findings that the body appears to have been in the water for an extended period.'

'Josey, what's wrong?' Adam said, trying to get her to look at him. But her eyes were fixed on the screen. 'You look like you've seen a ghost.'

That made her turn to him. Suddenly her chest hurt. She couldn't breathe. She quickly stood, disengaging herself from him in a tangle of arms and legs, pinches and pulls. She grabbed her sweater from the floor. 'I've got to go home.'

'What?' he said, clearly thrown by her abrupt change in mood. 'Wait, Josey . . .'

But she was already out of the door.

Josey shot into her house and ran up the stairs in the dark. When she got to her bedroom, she threw open the closet door.

'Thank God,' she said, going to her knees in front of Della Lee, who was in her familiar sitting position on the sleeping-bag. 'You'll never believe what they're saying about you on the news!'

Della Lee just stared at her. She didn't seem curious at all.

'There was a body found in the Green Cove River. Your car was found near the bridge, so they think it's you!'

She still didn't say anything.

Josey's heart was pounding. 'You know what's funny? There was a moment there—you're going to love this—when I thought, what if it's Della Lee's ghost in my closet?'

Della Lee remained quiet. She didn't even blink.

Cold prickles rose on Josey's skin. 'Isn't that funny?'

'It's time for me to leave, Josey,' Della Lee said.

Josey laughed, a tad hysterically. 'What are you talking about? Mr Lamar's letter hasn't even come.'

'Josey . . .'

'And we both know what it will say, right? You'll wait until the letter comes and we'll laugh over how you tried to convince me—'

'Josey!' Della Lee said loudly.

Josey finally stopped.

'You made the right decision tonight. I could feel it. You don't need me any longer.'

'Della Lee,' Josey said, her voice thick. 'I don't understand.'

'I didn't know how to change,' Della Lee said, and as she spoke, smudges of mascara slowly appeared under her eyes like bruises, trails of it snaking down her cheeks again, just like that first day Josey found her in the closet. 'I didn't know how to be around decent people, or how to live without stealing or lying. I didn't think genuine happiness was possible. So I gave up. I was standing on the bridge and my last clear thought was of you. Then suddenly I was here, in your closet, and it became clear to me what I had to do. Maybe by helping you, I might mean something. *That* makes me genuinely happy.' She smiled. 'You're going to be OK now, Josey.'

And Della Lee was gone.

'Della Lee?' Josey stuck her head in the closet and searched the dark corners. Della Lee's bags and the box were still there, but not Della Lee. Josey pushed back her clothes, then slid back the secret door. She wasn't in the candy closet, hiding behind the bags of marshmallows or between the towers of cola. 'Della Lee!' Josey turned round, her eyes searching the room. She went to her knees and looked under the bed.

Josey sat down on the floor, bringing her knees to her chest. She looked back into the closet and saw Della Lee's collage sitting there on the sleeping-bag. She crawled over to it. Della Lee had cut out every photo from Josey's favourite marked pages. Next to the BON VOYAGE at the top, Della Lee had cut out five more letters and put JOSEY.

She suddenly heard heavy footsteps in the hallway. 'Josey?' Adam called. 'Josey, where are you?'

She craned her head over the side of the bed. He stopped in her bedroom doorway. He looked worried, tense. When he spotted her, he walked round the bed.

'Josey, what's wrong?' He knelt in front of her, putting his warm hands on her knees. 'Why did you run away? Why are you crying? Talk to me.'

She looked up at him. 'The woman on the news tonight, the woman in the river, I knew her.'

He lowered himself to the floor beside her, his stiff leg not giving way easily. 'Oh, honey,' he said, putting his arm round her. 'I'm so sorry.'

'Adam?'

'Yes?'

'She was my sister.'

# 10
# Now and Later

Dear Josey,

I loved the postcard from Sweden. But you have to stop asking me to join you. How many times do I have to tell you, I am not travelling with you on your honeymoon?

Everything is fine here. You can stop pretending that your visit next month is just the whim of you two world travellers. I found the ring. Jake thought he could hide it behind my books in the library. The minute I walked into the room, I knew which book it was behind. Oh, Josey, it's so beautiful. I stood there and bawled like a baby when I found it.

Then I heard Jake coming and put the ring back and ran to the kitchen, where I started chopping an onion to explain my tears.

I saw your mother yesterday. What is up with her and this cab driver? I see them all the time. Yesterday she was in the back of his cab, which had stopped at a red light downtown. She was talking nonstop. And the cab driver was smiling and nodding, but not saying a word. He was watching her in the rearview mirror. The light turned green and he didn't even know, he was so busy watching her.

Last week I went to the cemetery, like you asked, and put flowers on Della Lee Baker's grave. It's been a year and people are still talking about it. One day you're going to have to tell me why you paid for her funeral.

I had a weird dream about her the other night. I dreamed you and Della Lee and I were walking down a busy street somewhere, but the road was gold, like in *The Wizard of Oz*. Our arms were linked and we were laughing. Why am I dreaming about a dead woman I didn't even know? Is that creepy?

I guess I'll go now. No, not yet.

I've been thinking about this for a while . . . and I want to tell you something, something I've never told anyone.

OK, you know about me and books, that I have so many, that they're always around. The thing is, books just appear to me. Out of nowhere. I haven't bought a book since I was twelve. I'll walk into a room and there's a book that wants me to read it. They follow me sometimes too. I'm always worried people are going to find out and think I'm crazy. But I thought, I don't know, that you'd understand.

I'm going to send this now and regret it. Just remember, if you sic the men in white jackets on me, you don't get to be my matron of honour.

Love,

C.

Adam came up behind Josey and kissed her neck. Josey closed Chloe's email.

'Chloe knows about the surprise engagement party,' she said, staring out at the sea as Adam moved her hair away for better access.

'Jake was never good at keeping secrets,' he said into her skin, and it made her shiver.

Josey closed her eyes. The things this man could do to her. She was still amazed. Her eyes flew back open when her laptop almost fell off her knees to the balcony floor.

'If you keep this up,' she said, 'we're not going to leave the room. Again. I want to see the ship in the daytime at least once.'

He laughed and straightened. He looped one of her curls round his finger and gave her hair an affectionate tug. 'Tell Chloe I said hello,' he said, then walked back into the stateroom.

Something caught Josey's eye, and she turned. Della Lee had suddenly appeared by the railing at the corner of the balcony. She was gazing out at the water.

Della Lee turned her head and looked at Josey. She nodded in the direction Adam had gone and winked.

Josey smiled and quickly moved her laptop aside. She got up and went to the railing beside Della Lee. She missed having her around. She missed talking to her. Della Lee rarely spoke these days. In fact, the last time Josey remembered her saying anything was in Las Vegas. Chloe and Jake had flown in with Adam's brother to attend Adam and Josey's wedding ceremony. Chloe had just walked down the short aisle ahead of Josey. Josey was about to follow when suddenly she saw Della Lee, standing there to her left.

'Congratulations, kid,' she'd said.

Sometimes months would go by without Josey seeing her. But just when Josey would start to worry that she'd gone away for good, Della Lee would always return.

They stood like that for a while, both staring out at the sea. Josey didn't know how much time had passed before Della Lee turned to her, her brows raised, as if she knew what Josey was thinking.

It was time.

'Stay here,' Josey said. 'Don't go yet, OK?'

Della Lee nodded.

Josey went into the stateroom. She could hear the shower water running and Adam singing. She went to her luggage and dug out her passport wallet. Tucked into a pocket inside was a folded envelope. It was the letter from Samuel Lamar. She took it with her wherever she went, convinced there would be a right time to open it and learn the truth.

She walked back out to the balcony and stood by Della Lee at the railing again. She stared at the plain white envelope. Della Lee watched her curiously.

Taking a deep breath, Josey tore the envelope in half, then in fourths, then eighths. She tossed the pieces into the wind, where they turned into paper birds that floated through the air, finally landing peacefully on the water.

Della Lee laughed, but no sound came out.

Josey smiled at her, then turned back to the water, satisfied that she'd made the right decision.

When she turned back again, Della Lee was gone.

She returned to her seat and picked up her laptop.

Dear Chloe,

We're slowly crossing the ocean towards you as I type. How do you know our coming back to Bald Slope for a visit isn't just a whim? (I have to say that, you know. I promised Jake. But I can't wait to see the ring!)

I don't understand what's going on between Mother and Rawley. When I call, Helena says she's happy. She says that Rawley actually spends the night there sometimes too, though no one is supposed to know. Maybe I'll finally talk to Mother this visit. Or maybe, like last time, she'll refuse to see me. I know this has less to do with me personally and more to do with memories she won't share, memories of my father. But there's nothing I can do about it.

Thank you for taking the flowers. Della Lee was a special person. I'll tell you about her someday. I promise. In fact, there's a lot I need to tell you.

And about the books, I don't think you're crazy. Not at all.

Josey looked up to the place Della Lee had stood.

In fact, I understand completely.

Love,

J.

Sarah Addison Allen

**Whereabouts in the United States were you born?**
I was born and raised in Asheville, North Carolina, a place *Rolling Stone*
magazine once called 'America's New Freak Capital'.

**When you were a child, what was your dream job?**
When I was a kid, I wanted to be a trash man. I would spend hours
daydreaming about riding on the back of a garbage truck, jumping off at every
house and dumping people's trash into it.

**What did you study?**
I have a BA in Literature from the University of North Carolina at Asheville, a
major I chose because I thought it was amazing that I could get a diploma just
for reading fiction. It was like being able to major in eating chocolate.

**Interesting fact about yourself?**
I can't turn away stray cats and I'm convinced they know this.

**Interesting fact about your father?**

My father was a copy editor, reporter and award-winning columnist for our local paper.

**Interesting fact about your mother?**

My mother has a nose ring, but we pretend it's not there.

**Any siblings?**

One sister, Sydney, who has been married four times, which I think is enough for both of us.

**When did you start writing?**

I graduated from college in 1994, and that's when I started writing seriously. I sold a few small things along the way, but *Garden Spells* didn't sell until 2006. That's twelve years writing as close to full-time as I could manage, folks. Twelve long years.

**Did your first novel, *Garden Spells*, start out as a magical novel?**

No. It was supposed to be a simple story about two sisters reconnecting after many years. But then the apple tree started throwing apples and the story took on a life of its own . . . and my life hasn't been the same since.

**Is *The Sugar Queen* a continuation of *Garden Spells*? If not, do you think there will ever be a sequel?**

I love that people ask this question. I had no idea people would care so much about these characters, enough to want to see their stories continued. *The Sugar Queen* isn't a continuation of *Garden Spells*, but there's a possibility of a *Garden Spells* sequel (or maybe a prequel) in the future. It might take a while. My next few books are either already written or already in the pipeline.

**Interesting snippet about writing *The Sugar Queen*?**

When I began writing what would become *The Sugar Queen*, Josey's name was Evelyn, and I called the project 'Evelyn's Closet'.

**I've never heard of some of the sweets mentioned in *The Sugar Queen*. How do readers find out more?**

Go to my website: www.sarahaddisonallen.com and click on the Candy page. There's an image of every sweet in the book. I tried every candy/cookie/sweet mentioned in *The Sugar Queen*. More than once. For the sake of research, of course. I gained eighteen pounds while writing the book!

**Do you have a lucky colour?**

Red.

**What is your next book about? When will it be released?**

The next book has romance and magic and, of course, another quintessential Southern setting. In North Carolina it's also used as a primer for barbecues, a religious experience around here. It will be released in 2009.

# CATHERINE LAW

# A Season of Leaves

*In 1943, when German attacks on Britain were at their peak, Rose Pepper went to work as a land girl on a farm in Cornwall to escape the bombs—and Will Bowman, to whom she was reluctantly engaged. It was there that she met and fell madly in love with a young Czech soldier, and where her story began . . .*

# Prologue

## *Cornwall, June 1992*

THE FLOORBOARD had been squeaking for months. Wincing as she knelt down, her arthritic joints creaking in protest, she coaxed the nails with the claw end of the hammer. Aged and rusty, they came out easily, like pulling a knife out of butter. The furrows in her brow relaxed. Irritation was replaced by satisfaction: one more tiresome chore—boringly regular in this old house—was dealt with. Lifting the small section of floorboard, she stopped. She caught a glimpse of what looked like paper in the gap between the joists. As she lowered her hand into the void, her fingers brushed the letters in their dusty grave.

Holding the envelopes in her hands, she was struck by a bright, soul-cleansing understanding. The letters were still sealed and were addressed to her. Many minutes passed as she stared at them: moments when she knew not the difference between happiness and grief; life and death. She knew he would speak to her again one day; she knew he'd let her know, somehow. In her hands were his letters to her: unread, unknown, unearthed forty-six years after she had last seen his face.

How could it possibly be any other way?

## *Cornwall, September 1992*

LEANING OUT OF HER bedroom window, Rose Pepper could see to the edge of her world. Beyond her garden wall lay the churchyard, where long grass between the graves was hazy in the Indian-summer light. Rising cheerfully above the headstones sat the granite church, squat and small. She squinted. On one side of her garden was the postwar cube of the new vicarage and the cluster of stone cottages that made up the hamlet of Trelewin. To her right were the stile and footpath that led to Pengared Farm. These days, the church was her boundary. What lay beyond was softened and blurred as if by tears, but really, she corrected herself, by geriatric myopia.

She rested her arms on the stone sill, feeling the residual warmth from the sun that had long moved round to the front of the house, which faced the sea, its golden light sparkling like diamonds on the water. Her home, the Old Vicarage, had stood there on the cliff for a hundred years: granite walls and a Gothic façade withstanding all that the Cornish weather threw at it. If she cared to observe, she would see a century's worth of scars: rainwater stains, a leaning chimney, a loose roof tile here and there. I have lived in this house for nearly half of its life, she reminded herself, rubbing at the smooth stone sill with her fingertip. And for three-quarters of my own.

Her daughters often wondered why she chose to use this room at the back for a bedroom. After all, the great bay window at the front commanded the sea. But Rose knew what constituted a good view. The garden lay before her, shimmering. Butterflies bounced among frothing purple lavender; roses melted into one another like scoops of ice cream. Her eyes rested on the corner by the far wall where, under the spreading boughs of a cherry tree, lay a patch of long, glossy grass. The tree had been planted in the year after the war, and she had watched it grow. Every autumn, leaves fell from the cherry and covered the grass around its trunk; she never raked them up. Nettles flourished in this corner, for the butterflies, she conceded, and she allowed ivy to grow wild, crawling from the stone wall between the garden and the churchyard to tangle itself around the tree. Every year, the creeping ivy fingers reached further still. I like this bedroom. I like this view, she told herself. I can keep watch from here.

She used to be able to see so much further from the window: beyond the stile that marked the edge of the glebe, even to where the footpath snaked over the rise of the headland on the far horizon. She could, however, still make out the old postbox that once belonged to Pengared Farm. It stood, rusting on a pole by the stile, guarded by brambles. During the war, the postman only went so far, and it was up to Betony or Ted Cumberpatch to come and fetch their own post, walking the two miles across the headland from Pengared Farm to Trelewin. A lifetime ago.

From the cooking aroma rising up the stairs, Rose calculated she had about fifteen minutes' peace before she'd be called by her daughters for dinner. Lara was cooking chicken fricassee downstairs in her kitchen. It was one of Betony Cumberpatch's recipes 'which *always* work': a special meal before the three of them left tomorrow on their trip to Prague. That was Lara's thing: cooking. Her elder daughter Nancy's thing was finding fault.

Rose sighed, squinting hard through the fading late afternoon light at the rusting postbox, remembering how, when she worked as the Cumberpatches' land-girl, she used to reach in past cobwebs and snails for their post. She wanted to go down there now and grasp that stupid pole, wrench it from the ground and sling the whole thing over the hedge. She did not want a celebratory meal. She did not want the fuss. But ever since she had found the letters under the floorboard in the spare room, her life had become one big fuss. They were such innocent things: three simple brown envelopes. Krystof had addressed them so diligently to her at Pengared Farm, and yet they never made it to her. They only got as far as that cursed postbox for Pengared.

When she unearthed them—was it really three months ago?—her tremendous shock, crumbling voice and darting fingers compelled her daughters to fill her head with their voices and their concern. The trip to Prague was their idea. They tried to make it all right, but all she wanted was the peace and space to remember.

She leaned a little further from her window, tasting the sweet, balmy air tinged with a tang of sea salt. In Krystof's language, September was *Zári: the month that glows with colour*. How right he was. She kept his words alive, kept his memory bright. In the dark every night before she drifted off to sleep, the thoughts and words spinning through her head were in Czech.

It had been another warm day, the day of the haymaking at Pengared during the war, when she and Krystof had laughed deeply into each other's faces, their clothes stuck with seed heads, their eyes full of the low golden sun. Krystof's scent and the vibration of his laughter sunk under her skin. And stayed there. That had been July. By the time September, *the month that glows with colour*, was over, he was gone.

'Mum? Are you OK?' Nancy walked in without knocking and eyed the almost empty suitcase on the floor.

Rose kept her face to the window, willing treacherous tears to disappear. 'I'm fine,' she lied easily, picking up some knickers and throwing them into her case. 'There! Nearly done.'

Her daughter sighed without humour. 'I know how you hate packing,

304 | Catherine Law

so I thought I'd better check up on you. Dinner will be ready soon. Lara's sauce is bubbling and the wine is breathing. Not sure if fricassee is right for such a warm evening, if you ask me.'

Nancy was a tall, handsome woman, who always knew better. She had strong, well-placed features and a habit of padding around the farmhouse at Pengared in one of her husband Mo's old shirts. Sensibly, once she'd hit forty, she cropped her thick dark hair into a choirboy style, although Rose thought it made her look like a beanpole.

Now Rose felt her daughter's dark, scrutinising stare.

'Look, Mum, are you sure about going to Prague? I'm beginning to think it's not such a good idea, going back after all these years. It seemed such a good thing to do, with the Wall coming down, and everything. But are you really ready to go back there?'

Rose was unable to answer. Trying to distance herself from the trip, the letters, she asked after Nancy's mother-in-law: 'How's Betony? I haven't seen her for a while. Still cooking her wondrous meals?'

Nancy was baffled. 'Of course she is. And a good job too. Mo hates my cooking. I let her get on with it. There must be some advantages to living with your husband's mother. That's one anyway. Ah, I see you've managed to pack *something*.' Nancy stooped to the case and picked up the bundle, wrapped carefully in her mother's silk scarf. Rose's hand rose in reflex, like a cat's paw, to grab it back. She stood rooted, seething, while Nancy sifted the flimsy envelopes in her hands.

'I see. You're waiting until you get to Prague before opening them. I don't know how you can bear it. Just think of what lies inside these letters. The truth, I suppose. I can't see why you won't just rip them open here and now.' There it was: that little piece of her father, Will, behind her eyes. *His* handsome eyes. The desire to control, and then the panic when that control starts to slip. 'Don't you think you should open them now? Get it over with?'

'Not at all.' Rose could not look her daughter in the eye as she reached for the letters. Cradling Krystof's letters, so fragile, so *light*, she noticed how they were disintegrating at the folds, a little torn. Like me, she thought. His looping hand was off-centre, the inked postmark, *Praha, June 9, 1946*, fading. She wrapped them tenderly back up in the scarf and stowed them in a corner of her suitcase.

Nancy would not take her eyes off them. 'I still can't believe my father stole them. You reckon he took them from the old postbox and hid them? I wonder what made him do it? I'm so sorry, Mum.' Nancy sat on the bed with a flump, a great sigh rushing forth. Her large hand, as red and calloused as any self-respecting farmer's wife's should be, swept back through her cropped hair. 'What a bastard.'

Rose was struck by how vulnerable her hard-faced Nancy was for a fleeting moment. She said, gently, 'You have no need to apologise for something that man did. For someone you never knew. Something so long ago . . .' She sat down at her dressing table, catching Nancy's eye in the mirror. It seemed easier than face to face. 'You're right. I have always hated packing,' she said lightly. 'Packing a suitcase always means an end of something. It means I have to *think*.'

'Look, I'll help you. I'll do it for you.' There it was, the controlling streak: Will Bowman manifesting again, and again.

Rose flinched. 'No, thank you, Nancy. I can manage. I am not feeble and decrepit yet. Even at *my* age.' She looked at her reflection. 'What is it they say? You know you're getting old the moment you look in the mirror and see your mother staring back at you.'

A sixty-seven-year-old woman was staring back at her. She saw a high forehead, softly lined. Her eyes—still as green as a cat's—had kept their pretty almond shape, even if they were a little hooded. Her hair was still glorious. Thick and glorious. Her land-girl friend Meg Wilson had once told her it was as red as a fox's tail. Now the grey still glowed warm from the odd auburn hair that stayed with her and refused to leave.

She glanced out of the window at the turning season's gilding of the countryside, blurred before her eyes. Now she was here, in the autumn of her life. Realisation hit her with a jolt of sadness: she had always thought that, by now, she'd be in Prague once again; living, laughing, loving. Walking beside Krystof across the Charles Bridge. She shook away the image, telling Nancy, 'But of course my mother never made it anywhere near this far. Poor dear Mother . . .'

Nancy was uncharacteristically quiet.

'Well, the years are certainly passing,' said Rose, rallying. 'Look at my scar. I hardly notice it now. I've carried that round with me since I was eighteen. And now, good heavens, it's all but faded away.'

Nancy peered over her mother's shoulder at her reflection.

Irritated, Rose said, 'There. That crescent-shaped mark on my cheek.'

Nancy shrugged. 'It's so small I've never really noticed it. It's always been part of your face. It's not important, Mum.'

Nancy didn't know how wrong she was.

Lara called up the stairs. 'Dinner's ready! Come on, you two.'

Nancy put her hand on her mother's arm. On reflex, Rose drew away and then, ashamed, tried to make amends by leaning closer.

'Before we go down,' said Nancy, oblivious to her discomfort, 'I just wanted to remind you that Cringle Cottage is always ready for you if you want it. If you want to leave this old place, put it all behind you, and start afresh. Don't worry, it hasn't been left to rack and ruin since Meg died. Mo's been painting it. Whitewash everywhere. He's fixed the roof and the chimney doesn't smoke any more; he's tested it.'

Rose glanced again out of her window, her eyes darting in protection of her thoughts, worried that Nancy would read them. 'I like this house.' There was the lie. 'It's been my home for so long . . .'

'But, Mum, this huge old place . . . the running costs. You're rattling around in here. Oh, I know it's lovely in the summer but . . .'

'There was a time'—Rose, turning and walking out of the bedroom, laughed suddenly—'when you couldn't wait to get your hands on it. Both of you, seduced by the pictures in glossy magazines. Lara sorting out my kitchen and bathroom; putting in the roll-top bath. You doing up the hallway, fixing those floor tiles . . .' They were now at the top of the landing looking down on the large, square hallway below. The floor was Victorian mosaic in black, terracotta and cream. 'And now you want me to leave it all behind,' Rose chided.

'We loved it as kids,' mused Nancy. 'This rambling old place with its dusty corners: a perfect playground. But things are different now.'

'But you never knew about—' Rose stopped and shook her head. 'Nothing,' she said, forcing another laugh. Her daughters had never been aware of the chilling, draining emptiness of the rooms once their playing was over and they were tucked up in bed; the loneliness that followed her solitary figure upstairs every night.

'It's just a thought, Mum,' Nancy was saying. 'We could put this place on the market; I'm sure you'd make a good profit. Live in Cringle Cottage. You'd be five minutes from me, Mo and Betony, not half an hour's walk over the headland. It could be a project.'

At my age, 'on the market' meant surveyors, buyers, people who would prod and poke. The longer she held out, the less likely she'd have to face it. The longer she could protect her daughters, and herself. With Ted, his brother Hugh and now Meg gone, her secret remained with just herself and Betony.

'Don't know why,' said Nancy, standing at the top of the stairs, 'but I always feel uneasy walking around this landing. Maybe I fell as a child.' She stopped and her eyes burrowed into Rose's. 'Did I fall down the stairs? There's something odd about it. Some strange memory.'

Rose's hand gripped the banister. She dared not answer.

'**D**id I hear Nancy mention the *project*?' cried Lara, her bright face greeting them as she peered over her shoulder while energetically draining the veg over the sink. 'Don't you think Cringle Cottage is perfect for you, Mum? Keep talking, while I finish this.'

Rose stopped at the kitchen threshold, her spirit draining clean away, her eyes filled suddenly with Krystof's face. His deep grey eyes now belonged to Lara, the joy for life that surrounded her like a halo was his. He was standing there: his face behind Lara's eyes. Even the way her fair fringe fell over her forehead.

'Nothing has been decided,' Rose said, her voice weary. 'One thing at a time, please, girls. My, that smells good, Lara. I can't wait.'

She felt them both back down; they knew not to press her.

'Go through to the dining room then,' Lara said cheerily.

'Come here first,' Rose said, holding her arms open. 'Both of you,' she added quickly.

Her daughters stepped forward and she hugged them together. Why was she always struck by how unalike they were? What did she expect? Their fathers had been as different as heaven and hell. She had tried to bring them up as equals; tried not to have a favourite. But with Nancy, Rose's guilt worked its mischief in so many ways. The secret about her father, Will, which she would take to her grave, had built an invisible wall between them. Even now, married to Mo, the son of Rose's old friends Betony and Ted, and living at the farm where Rose herself had once lived and worked, Nancy seemed as far away as ever.

In the kitchen, Nancy's embrace was stiff with pent-up frustration. Lara just fell into her arms, pressing her face into her mother's cheek.

'**S**o, which area did you live in, Mum?' asked Lara as Nancy poured the coffee. They had cleared the dessert plates away and continued to sit at the dining table. Lara was leafing through a book open before her on the cloth. Rose stared at it, feeling her lip curl with distaste.

'What on earth is that?'

'The guidebook I bought,' Nancy answered, affronted.

'I won't be needing a guidebook,' Rose said.

'But think how much has changed since the Wall came down,' Nancy pressed on. 'We're talking nearly fifty years. The Communists booted out. The Prague we lived in then has all but disappeared.'

'I hope to God some aspects of it have.'

'Well, of course, all the important things will still be there: the Charles Bridge, the Old Town Square, that amazing astronomical clock.' Nancy reeled off the tourist sites. 'But the atmosphere will be different, the *people* will be. You forget that I can't remember any of it. I will be discovering it for the first time for myself. I can't tell you how helpful it's been corresponding with those students at the university. They're very interested in our case. When I last wrote they agreed to meet up with us one afternoon—did I tell you?'

'Our case . . .?' Rose felt Nancy was racing ahead of her.

Lara, flicking through the book, raised her head. 'I'm glad we're going. This is just what I need.' She looked at her mother. 'Oh, I know the trip is for you, Mum, of course, but now my divorce has come through, I want to focus on myself and have a nice little holiday. It will help me forget a little, while hopefully it will help you remember.'

Rose was desperate to change the subject. 'So, Lara, have you heard from Greg recently?'

'No, which is a good thing,' retorted Lara. 'Anyway, I don't want to talk about him. This is about us. And our quest . . . our case, as you put it, Nancy. Now let's see, where is the university? Oh, I see, right by the river. I take it the students will help us find my father?'

Rose's stomach balled into a hard stone. She held her breath, trying to stop the eruption of a huge, uncontrollable sob. Prague surfaced in her memory: bells rang out over the fairy-tale spires and red-tiled roofs; the majestic castle presided from the hilltop; the insides of churches dripped with gold; birds circled the river in the light of the setting sun. And then the deep-freeze of winter when the river lay cold and stiff under the arches of the Charles Bridge and birds fell frozen from the sky.

She saw Lara's face, struggling to show empathy, looming towards her. 'What happened, Mum? Will we ever know? The letters will tell us, won't they?'

Nancy shook her head at her sister.

'No, no, Lara's right, Nancy.' Rose sounded very old and very tired. 'I'll tell you what I remember. The letters can wait.' She took a deep breath. 'Krystof's house was opposite a monastery in the *Stare Mesto*, the Old Town.' She waited as Lara eagerly turned pages, tracing columns of text with her finger. 'It was a tall house. Built of stone. Crumbling stucco. Truly beautiful, faded and grand. It had been in Krystof's family for a century at least.'

'How many floors?' asked Lara.

'Four. But we had to give them up to the Communists. They put us in the attic. Crammed in we were: Krystof, Babička, Nancy and me.'

'Oh, Babička! The old lady,' cried Nancy. 'How funny that I should suddenly remember her. She was Krystof's granny, wasn't she?'

'I wonder what else you will remember?' said Rose. 'We were there for less than a year, you know; you were very young. You had your second birthday there in June 1946, just before we left.'

Nancy swept her pensive eyes over the photographs in the guidebook. 'I keep having snippets . . .' she said. 'I remember there were a lot of stairs in the house in Prague. And in my mind, narrow streets. And Babička; she had rather large, wrinkly hands and long white hair. I also remember crying . . . the cold.'

Rose swallowed hard. 'Do you remember Krystof?'

Nancy wrinkled her nose. 'Hardly. Hardly at all.'

'He was a father to you.' *For less than a year. That's all we had.*

Nancy was blunt, defensive. 'I don't remember.'

Rose was incensed. Nancy was quick to apologise when she didn't have to, for her own father's cruelty and madness. For someone she never knew. But she would show no contrition for not remembering Krystof. To distract herself from her anger, Rose looked over at Lara.

'You've taken to wearing your hair in a ponytail. It's just how you wore it as a child. What traumas we had, trying to get a brush through it.' Her ponytail would swing behind Lara as she ran, Rose remembered. Every day, she had wanted Krystof to see his daughter run; her hair bouncing; her smile a mirror of his.

*Am I the only person, apart from Betony, left alive who remembers him?*

'The Communists were taking over,' Rose went on. 'It began to get dangerous, and, soon after your second birthday, Nancy, Krystof and I decided we had to leave. You know all this.'

'But you've never really told us. Not properly,' persisted Lara. 'Why didn't Krystof come with you?'

Rose rested her thumping forehead on the coolness of her hand, shielding her eyes, which were screwed up tight with pain. She whispered, 'He couldn't. He simply couldn't.'

**R**ose could not sleep. In the silence of her bedroom she listened to the small hours marked by the chimes of the church clock and Krystof's voice saying over and over, '*Ruzena*, I will follow.'

She replied, '*Následujte me* . . . follow me.'

Three years ago, in 1989, she had watched the Berlin Wall come down on the evening news. She saw the joyful people jumping on graffiti-splashed chunks of mortar; she saw their ecstasy and their open arms as, like a surging tide, Easterners piled through the gaps. She wondered and dared to hope. *Now he will contact me. He knows where I am. He must reach me here.* But she didn't know that his letters had already reached her and had been sleeping—crumbling—for forty-six years under her floorboards. He might phone, she had thought. Funny to think they had never spoken on the telephone. His voice. Oh, to hear his voice again. She could not remember it.

The bedroom window was open and the waves of Trelewin Cove below were breaking and receding on the sand. She found herself remembering how Krystof had marvelled at the sea's vastness, its freedom. How he had cried with joy that it existed.

She knew what she would do with his letters. Once they had got their taxi from the airport into Prague; once they had been dropped off at the hotel and had some light refreshment; once her daughters had consulted the guidebook and decided what to do, she would leave them. She would take a tram to the river. She'd find a spot where she could see the Charles Bridge downstream. Then she would take the bundle of letters and gently unwrap them. She'd take her life in her hands. Using her handbag-sized magnifying glass, she would carefully check each postmark, check each date. And one by one, in the order that Krystof sent the letters and in the order that Will Bowman concealed them, she would slit each envelope open and read . . . and read . . . and read.

At last, the truth . . . their truth.

A tap on the door, gentle at first. She thought she was dreaming. But then it grew urgent. Rap rap rap. The bedroom door opened.

'What? What is it?' She hoisted herself upright against her pillows. 'Is that you, Nancy?' Of course it wasn't Nancy; Nancy never knocked.

'No, it's me.' Lara's tall, slim figure in a white nightie slipped into the room, quickly shutting the door behind her. 'Oh, Mum, I can't bear it. Switch your light on. Switch it on!'

Rose fumbled in the dark. 'Lara, whatever is the matter?' She peered at her daughter as the sharp light from the bedside lamp hit her.

Lara was hiding something behind her back. She bit her lip as she carefully brought her hand round, clutching what looked like an old towel. It was wrapped round something heavy. She placed it on her mother's lap and it sank into the bedclothes.

'Tell me what it's doing here. I can't believe it was there, right there in the cupboard.'

'Why were you looking in your cupboard at this time of night?'

'I wasn't. It was earlier. Just before getting into bed. I wanted to find my old walking boots to take with me. Instead I found this disgusting thing. I haven't slept at all. Mum, what on earth is it doing here?'

The weight of the object sat between Rose's knees. Willing her tired eyes to focus, she pressed her fingertips into the towel and found cool metal. She ran them along the length of it until she touched the smooth wooden handle, her finger alighting on the trigger.

'It's Krystof's gun,' she breathed. 'Oh God, I'd forgotten . . . Oh, Lara. What a shock for you. I'm so sorry.'

'But what's it doing in the cupboard?' Lara shrieked.

'I doubt it's loaded,' Rose said, remembering, with a thrill of pleasure, the crack of the bullets as she fired them off one by one. She gazed down at the pistol as if it was an old friend: a Model 24, standard Czech armed forces issue. It was quite a dinky thing: it used to fit in the palm of Krystof's hand, and it slipped inside his coat pocket with ease.

'You've got to get rid of it!' hissed Lara.

A strange, sweeping lethargy filled Rose's limbs. 'You know, Lara,' she whispered, 'I am so sorry about this. Of course, it is horrid, but it means a lot to me. It was the last thing your father touched.'

'You mean, he really is dead? He died using it? Did someone shoot him? Was he shot dead?'

'No, no . . . what I meant to say was: he had been carrying the gun before we parted. I can't explain to you . . .' Her eyes slipped sideways to Krystof standing on Prague station as her train pulled away.

'But it's a gun. And you're just sitting there!'

Rose was weary. 'Lara, I can't get worked up over this. I can't let myself. I have been through so much, that the sight of this gun right now is really not having an effect on me. Not the horror that you expect me to feel. I'm sorry about that.'

She watched her daughter's open, incredulous face close down with fear. 'Well, you must be made of concrete then,' Lara snapped.

'Maybe I am.' Rose wrapped the pistol up again. 'Tomorrow, before we leave, I'm going to take this thing and throw it into the sea.'

'Good.'

'But for now, it is going in the bin.' She reached out and tossed Krystof's gun into her waste-paper basket.

Temporarily satisfied, Lara retreated to the door. 'You're so calm, Mum. I don't understand.'

'I don't either. Concrete, you see.' She managed a smile. Inside her chest her heart was turning itself inside out. She could barely manage to keep her voice smooth and motherly. 'But right now, Lara, you are going to sleep, and so am I. We have a long day tomorrow.'

Lara opened the door. 'You don't have to throw it into the sea, Mum. Not if it was the last thing my father touched.'

Rose switched off her light and lay in the darkness listening to her thoughts: '*Skutečný* . . . and *skutečný* . . .' and marvelling at how the words for truth and reality were the both the same in Czech.

A light aircraft droned across the sky. She was grateful to the unknown pilot for breaking in and stopping unpleasant thoughts from spiralling towards unimaginable horror; the horror, truth and reality that she was keeping from her daughters and from herself.

But then her concrete heart tripped over its beat and the sound of the plane's engine turned a fresh page in her memory.

Planes in the sky, a whole squadron, a bank of them seven miles wide, like a great storm approaching. Sharp-eyed navigators looking down on the English countryside, at the line of the coast and the treacherous breaking waves. Planes in the sky over Plymouth docks: battle-black, shiny-nosed Dormiers with a heavy cargo to offload.

And there she was, down in the street. Tiny Rose, trapped by the rain of bombs, trapped by the fire; trapped in the air raid with Will Bowman. She sank deeper into her bed, helpless to the memory, wretched with it all.

The night of the raid was the night that changed everything; changed the truth; changed the reality of what Rose Pepper was to become.

# PART ONE

## *Cornwall, January 1943*

## One

CIGARETTE SMOKE BURNT her eyes and seeped into the very weave of her clothes. Standing patiently in the Anchor pub, down at the Plymouth docks, Rose reluctantly breathed in the fug. She wanted to be home in her parents' back parlour listening to the Light Programme. Last orders had been rung out. Surely she could go home now? Her legs itched under her nylons, courtesy of Will and his nudge-nudge contact. No, it looked as though he was getting in one last round.

The crowd grew noisier. Able mariners on leave were clinging drunkenly to their mates. Girls with watery eyes waited for a last goodbye, or wore bright red lipstick as a banner of bravery. A group of privates was singing 'Tipperary'; in a corner, an officer was kissing a Women's Voluntary Service girl.

Everywhere Rose looked she saw a uniform: the Tommy khaki and forage cap, the voluminous fatigues of the mariners, the buttoned-up and commanding Air Force. She felt a patter of pride in her chest; very soon even she would have a uniform of her own. Will's Air Raid Patrol get-up was not quite as endearing as the forces' issue: baggy overalls and a black tin hat with a luminous white 'W' on the front. He was exempt from active service because of his chronic asthma but still did his bit. He was the hero of the air raids, so he told her—all rotas, buckets and stirrup pumps—and her parents thought he was wonderful. But she often had to stifle a laugh when he called in to see them on his rounds: the hat was far too small for him, perched there on top of his large, handsome, humourless face.

His fingers gripped hers now as he paid for his beer and a port and lemon for her. He leaned aggressively on the bar. When he was agitated or determined, his wheezing grew louder and she could hear it now as she waited. He did not ask what she wanted to drink. She did not want anything. All she wanted was to be at home.

Disappointment nagged at her as he pulled her behind him through the pub and sat her down at a corner table.

'What's that face for?' He pulled out a chair and perched beside her. 'Looks like you need a little trip. How about in the spring, Rosebud, I take you up to town? The raids on London have stopped now. How does tea at the Ritz take you? The building's steel-framed, you know. Safe from bombs. We could stay the night. Live it up a little.'

'Will! What are you suggesting?' She blushed. 'What would my parents have to say?'

He supped his beer. 'Sylvia and George like me.' His confidence in using her parents' first names irritated her.

'Have you forgotten?' She mustered a good-natured smile. 'I start my training next week and my duties at Pengared Farm in March. There's no time for a trip to London, Will, however much my parents like you.'

He put his large hand flat on the table and gave her an unnerving stare. 'You're not still serious about this Land Army lark, are you?' He was incredulous. 'I can't quite see it, if you ask me. All that muck and manure. Far too much like hard work for a nice girl like you.'

'I'm used to early mornings at the shop,' she said, hating the defensive note in her voice. 'I lift sacks of flour, tins of stuff.'

'What, with old Mrs Brown and her black-market butter under the counter and her firm hand on the ration books? You don't know you're born, Rosebud. You wait until you're up to your neck in muck, breaking your back. It's not all chirping birds and haystacks, you know.'

'I want to do my duty.'

'Ah, now, Rosebud.' His fingers grabbed hers and he began to play with her engagement ring. 'I'd say it was your duty to marry me.'

A year ago, she would have giggled. Handsome Will Bowman—senior clerk at the Western Bank, with his bachelor maisonette and sleek Ford car—was going to marry her. Now, in the Anchor pub down by the docks, feeling tired and wretched, she extracted her fingers from his.

'We've talked about this, Will,' she said patiently. 'We must wait for the war to be over. And then of course, you know . . .' She paused. 'When it's all over, I want to go to college. I want to be a journalist.'

'You mean learn typing and shorthand? I'll say it again, my Rosebud. If we are to be married, won't all of that rather get in the way?' She felt his finger press under her chin and he made her look at him. He gazed at her from under long lashes, his blue eyes melting momentarily. 'I remember when I first saw you, Rosebud,' he said, holding her hand, 'when I gave your dad a lift back from the bowling club. In your school uniform, you were, doing your homework.' His fingers tightened. 'And then your mother invited me in for tea on a run of Sundays. She knew what was going on, did Sylvia. She's not blind. She saw the looks you gave me. The looks I gave you.'

Yes, Rose remembered the pulse of pleasure at the attention from this man of twenty-eight, when she was a mere girl of sixteen. She squinted now through a curl of cigarette smoke blown their way from the next table. A trickle of worry made her mouth twitch.

'What's that look for, Rosebud?' Will's face hardened again and he shrugged, turning away from her to survey the room. 'What's the use of college? A land-girl first for a month or two, until Churchill and his cronies get their act together. And then of course, Mrs Bowman. So, what's the use of it all, when there'll be babies to look after?'

Her face stiffened in shock but Will did not notice. She watched as his eyes explored once more, resting on the slim back of a Wren near the bar. Something sank into her, then, a strange understanding. Was it the way his eyes darkened? Was it the way the Wren turned her head, her red-lipped smile making it all the way round to him?

'Is that her?' hissed Rose, leaning over the table. 'Is that her?' Her hands clenched into fists. She wanted to throw her drink over him.

'What are you talking about?' He turned reluctantly towards her. His face closed down, his eyes searching for a way out. He was caught.

'Will. Answer me.'

'Let's not do this here, old girl. Not in front of this ship-load.'

'Mrs Brown saw you. Kissing that *girl*,' she whispered, her voice thick with anger.

Will pushed his face close to hers. 'There's a war on. Things like that happen all the time. And Mrs B is a nosy old cow.'

'Two minutes ago, you wanted me to be your wife.'

'Look, poppet, she was probably drunk. I know I was. I took her for a walk over the Hoe. Probably missing her fiancé or something. I was probably missing you. It doesn't really matter, does it, Rosebud?'

She knew that he was right: it didn't really matter. The war changed everyone. You hardened to it. Took it on the chin.

'I give them no encouragement, you know. A lot of the girls, they get sexy, missing their men. They meet a nice fellow like me and with the blackout down, and everything, they get fruity. You can't blame them.'

*Them?* He said *them.*

'So, how many *have* there been?' she snapped. She began to twist at her finger. Her teeth were bared in anger as she pulled off the ring.

'Don't you dare.' Will's breath was sharp, his wheezing rattled. He grabbed for her hand. 'Forget all this rubbish. It means nothing. You and I are going to be together. You know it.'

'I know nothing of the sort, not now.' She held the ring out to him; her fingers trembled. 'This has just confirmed everything. I had my doubts and now I know. I don't love you, Will. So take your ring back, please. It's over.'

Will glared at her, and she felt the full force of his anger as he took the ring, brandishing it back at her. His face drained of colour.

'It's not true. You do love me. Silly little girl. Grow up, will you?'

His words failed, drowned by the sudden haunting wail of the air-raid siren. The whole pub reacted as one, tipping back chairs and jostling for the door. Rose stood up and was instantly carried along in a wave of shoulders and elbows. Will disappeared in the crush. They all knew the drill. The navy lads would run to their stations, air-raid wardens would clap on their tin hats; firemen would stand by their pumps; policemen would blow their whistles. The rest of them, if they had any sense, would head for shelter.

Rose was on the pavement. The blackout in the streets by the harbour was intense. There were no friendly lights, just white search arcs needling the sky over Plymouth. In the intermittent light she could make out the dark bulk of the surrounding hills, the quiet, cowering suburbs. She crunched up her shoulders as the crowd dispersed. A weird calm settled in the air. The sky was empty—and silent.

Will's hand closed round the top of her arm, tight like a tourniquet. She jumped. 'Come with me, Rosebud.' She heard his voice in the dark. 'Let's get to the shelter before the fireworks begin.'

'Leave me alone.' She tried to shake herself free. 'I'm going home.'

An ARP warden strode round the corner. 'Oi, you two fools,' he bellowed, 'get in the bloody shelter.'

'Don't worry, mate.' Will's voice was suddenly light and friendly. 'It's Bowman, St Budeaux Division. Just sorting this out.'

'Ah yes, Bowman. Shelter's down Tobacco Street. That way. Get there quick, I would.' The warden hurried on.

Rose twisted her arm. He held her fast.

'Now listen to me.' He shook her. She smelt his beer and his hair cream; sensed his familiar, menacing face close to hers.

'I will not. I'm going home.'

'You stupid girl!'

Rose shuddered. Faint at first, and then expanding by the second, came the awful rumbling of the bombers. A heavy, broken throb curved over the sky and put a hard lid on it, trapping her. Antiaircraft guns on the hills overlooking the Sound began their retort. *Ack-ack. Ack-ack.*

'What use are they!' she screamed, sickened by the noise.

And then, the inevitable. The invisible bank of planes let loose their bombs and they began to stream down, whistling like deadly rain.

She felt the first crump deep inside her body as the dockyard exploded and the hard cracking noise split her ears. Another cluster of mines, then another: so precise, so steady. The noise and the violence were all she knew: above her head and in the earth beneath her feet. She collapsed against the pile of sandbags by the pub wall. Three years into the war and she never got used to the terror.

Will leaned over Rose, making her stand up. Her legs would not straighten. Her knees were water. He pushed her against the sandbags. 'This isn't over between us,' he hissed into her ear. 'Raid or no raid.'

Another stick of bombs fell, this time right at the end of the street. She crumpled again into shock. A belch of pressure pressed down on her as the houses on the corner blew out their guts. Flames poured like water over windowsills and doorsteps. Her hearing was blasted away.

'Get away from me, get away!' she screamed into his face. He grasped her arms and hauled her upright. 'Take the ring back,' he yelled, gripping it in his fist. 'Take it back and tell me you love me!'

He hit her in the face. She screamed and cowered, her hand over her cheek where the ring had cut her. Her body folded in half. Her knees hit the pavement hard.

Half inside her body, half outside her body, Rose was alternately carried and then marched down steep steps into the confines of a tunnel, propelled by the strong arms that trapped her, held her up. Her ankles twisted painfully, her grazed knees buckling, stockings torn to shreds. Her shoes scuffed without mercy on the floor.

Slowly, with every breath of smoky, stale air, her senses returned to her. She was sitting on a slatted bench. Dark figures loomed in the shelter; some leaned forwards, blocking their ears, others held children, constantly soothing. The sound was muffled, as if under water. Somewhere, there was the hiss of a Primus stove. Someone was making a cup of tea.

The seat beneath her shifted and thumped; the earth was flinching from the *crump, crump* of the bombs. Her nausea returned as she was suddenly aware of Will jammed against her.

A woman sitting opposite her leaned forward. 'Did you hit your face, darling. Was it shrapnel? Bit of a war wound, I'm afraid. Damn those Nazi bleeders. Here, have a cup of tea.'

Rose held out her shaking hands for the steaming cup. Her arms ached, her head felt as if it had been cracked wide open.

Will's bulky body both shielded and trapped her. Along the tunnel someone was praying. Rose sat up. 'My parents!'

Will's arm tightened. 'They have their Anderson,' he said.

'But they don't know where I am.'

'They know you're with me. They know you're safe with me.'

Will's fingers tipped her chin up to face him. He avoided her eyes and looked, instead, at the cut on her cheek.

'Just a scratch,' he told the woman opposite, speaking over the top of Rose's head. 'She'll be all right in a day or two.'

'Might leave a scar though,' replied the woman. 'Never mind, lovey, something to remember this night by. And a bloody night it is too.'

After an age, there was a merciful, unbelievable silence from the streets above and then the all-clear rang out. Will whispered in her ear. 'Here, Rosebud, we mustn't lose this again.' His face softened into a smile. He slipped the ring back on her finger.

# Two

A CORNISH MORNING in spring: a sun-bright watery sky with the breath of sea on the breeze. Rose stood at the side of the lane, her shadow long and her suitcase set down next to her regulation Land Army shoes. Hawthorn hedges rambled vertically; two or three slate roofs peeked out above. Behind them was the square, granite church tower; between them a blue slice of the sea. She wriggled her toes, relishing the ability to stretch her legs after her two-hour bumpy ride on the bus from Plymouth. The driver was revving the engine, ready for the off. She called to the conductor, 'Is this Pengared? You said "Pengared next stop". Which way's the farm?'

The man glowered at her. 'This is Trelewin, miss. We don't go any further than this. Pengared's over that way, two miles across the head-land, is all. There's no lane to it that'll take a vehicle like this. I suppose you hoity-toity Devon town girls aren't used to a bit of walking. You're in the real country now. You're not at some college, learning how to milk off a pretend cow with a bag for udders.' He bared his teeth. 'Bloody ridiculous. How are you going to cope up at the farm?'

Rose opened her mouth to remind him about what she and the rest of Plymouth had had to cope with: air raids and burnt-out lives. But her voice was drowned out by the bus driver's insistent revving. The conductor hopped back on and, belching fumes, the bus roared off.

She pulled out her letter from Mrs Pike, district commissioner, South Cornwall Land Army Division.

*Your employers, Mr and Mrs Edward Cumberpatch, expect you to arrive on 15th March, 1943, at 09.00 hours sharp. I suggest you take the earliest bus from Devonport and disembark at Trelewin. To reach Pengared Farm, you must take the footpath by the Old Vicarage, past the church.*

Rose found the footpath beside an old empty house. Huge blank windows veiled by ivy were like mournful staring eyes; the chimney stacks a little wonky. Altogether it looked a rather sorry sight.

Brushing along the path through nettles and brambles, Rose was grateful for her thick Land Army socks and breeches. The graveyard between the old house and the church was quiet and sleeping. She spotted a tin letterbox on a post, with rusted lettering on its side, *Pengared Farm*, and felt her first duty was to check for Mr and Mrs Cumberpatch's post. The box was empty. Hurrying along, she was soon over the stile, climbing higher and higher across the open headland.

Her case grew heavier and her shoes began to pinch, even though Mrs Pike had assured them all they'd soon wear in. She stopped to rest, undoing the buttons of her greatcoat. Her shirt and tie made her feel proud and professional. On her head was clamped the cowboy-style hat. *Don't forget the hat, girls. Rather snazzy, isn't it?*

Halfway up the breezy headland, the footpath split and one path disappeared into ferny undergrowth down to the sand and grey wire of Trelewin Cove. 'We'll fight them on the beaches,' Mr Churchill had boomed. Rose shivered. The water looked so peaceful and innocent, but she knew full well that under the waves U-boats cruised. Thank God she didn't know of anyone out there at sea, or in North Africa or Singapore. Her father was too old, and had done his bit in what he called 'the last lot'. She had no brothers. And Will, of course, was exempt. Rose picked up her suitcase. She didn't want to think about Will.

'Don't worry about us, Rosie,' her father had told her as she boarded the bus at Devonport earlier. 'Your mother and I will be fine.'

'But the raids, Dad,' she'd said. 'I'll be so worried.'

'The skies have been quiet since January, since the raid on the docks.' Her father hoisted her suitcase after her. 'I think Hitler's got another agenda. We have Will to look after us. And we have our Anderson.'

Her mother, nervous and frail through lack of sleep, stood on tiptoe to kiss her cheek. 'Take care, Rosie,' she whispered.

Standing on that bright clifftop above the sea, Rose was seized by a new thought. It was spring, a new year: surely the war couldn't go on for much longer? Here, at Pengared Farm, among strangers, working in the fields that rolled to the sea, she would be free of that grinding fear that had enveloped her for years. She could escape the war. She could escape Will. And her parents had their Anderson.

She grasped her suitcase handle and headed for Pengared.

Nestled there in the valley was a little group of buildings: cowshed, stable and barn with its great door propped open. Hens strutted in the yard. Across the way was the old rambling farmhouse. Yellow clouds of lichen bloomed over the ancient slate roof; tiny casements were tucked under the eaves. Rose breathed in the scent of hay and the green whiff of cows as she unlatched the five-barred gate and entered the yard. In a flash she was surrounded by a terrific commotion as two sheepdogs bounded from nowhere and streaked past her legs.

And then, too late, she noticed the sign on the gate: *Do not open. Please climb over.* She called, 'Here boy, here boy,' but was ignored as the dogs ran this way and that out in the rutted track. She looked round in embarrassment to see a young woman with curlers in and a topknot scarf rushing towards her from the house.

'You let them out. Oh, now what? They never come to me. Mutt! Jeff! Heel! You see? It's no use.'

'I'm so sorry. I didn't see the sign. I'm Rose Pepper, from the Land Army. Not a good start, is it? I'm afraid I'm no good with dogs either.'

The woman barely looked at Rose. 'Not a good start, no. He's been waiting four weeks for the likes of you. That Pike woman promised us months ago. He's not pleased on the Land Army and he's not going to be pleased on this either. Mutt! Jeff! Blast you, wretched dogs!'

Rose set her suitcase down and quickly undid the latches.

'Don't unpack here. They'll savage it!'

'Biscuits. Mother packed me biscuits.' She rummaged under her clothes. 'Saved her coupons for me. This might just do it.'

Rose opened the tin and, in a flash, two wet noses prodded at her fingers, snapping up the biscuits.

'Oh, you wasted good biscuits. Now these dogs are spoilt as well as stupid.' The woman latched the gate behind them, aiming a kick at the one leaping up, resting his muddy paws on Rose's arm.

'I'm awfully sorry,' Rose said. 'Is Mr Cumberpatch or his wife at home?'

'I'm Mrs Cumberpatch.'

Rose looked the woman full in the face for the first time and extended her hand. Instantly, her eyes flicked to Rose's cheek. 'That looks nasty. How did you get that then?'

Rose touched the scar on her face with a nervous finger. 'During the blackout. Walked into a door. So clumsy.'

'Have you tried lanolin to fade it? Sheep's fat, you know. Old wives' remedy. Folks round here swear by it. I've got a jar in the cupboard.'

Mrs Cumberpatch was certainly *not* an old wife. She was stick-thin, a shade older than Rose, with huge blue eyes and a smooth open face like Olivia de Havilland. Even in her curlers she had a pure, still beauty.

'Come on.' She picked up Rose's suitcase and marched off across the yard with the two dogs snuffling after her. 'I'll show you in. Meg, the other land-girl, is with him out on the top field. Sowing barley. It's going to be a long day. Ah, here's Mo.'

Mrs Cumberpatch dropped Rose's case on the step and bent to pick up a grubby toddler who was making his escape from the kitchen. A toothless smile nearly split his face in two.

'What a beautiful babe.'

'He's our Maurice, but we call him Mo. Say hello to . . . em . . .'

'Rose. Rose Pepper.' She followed her employer into the kitchen, where the smell of fresh-baking bread made her sigh.

Mrs Cumberpatch jiggled the baby up and down on her hip. 'I see you're missing your home-baked bread.'

'We haven't had a good loaf in months.' Her mouth ached for it.

'I bake every other day. We had a store of wheat left over from last year. Home Office don't know about it, mind. This year he's doing only barley. Orders from on high. They want us to break up the meadow next year for sugar beet. First time in four hundred years, he reckons, it would have been ploughed. That's the war for you. I was conceived in that meadow. That's why my mother called me Betony. After the meadow flower. Have you got your ration book?'

Rose handed it over and Mrs Cumberpatch put it in the dresser drawer. 'We have our own butter. And eggs. I expect you're used to just one egg a week on the ration. Not healthy, I say.'

'My parents keep chickens, so we do all right.'

'I sell them down the village through Jack Thimble. Black market and all that but who's going to say anything?'

'Jack who?'

'You know, Jack Thimble. The grumpy bus conductor. He's cross because the Yanks commandeered his new bus. He was hopping mad. Hasn't cracked a smile since. Come upstairs. You'll share with Meg. Hope you don't mind, but I can't help you if you do.'

Betony Cumberpatch hooked Mo onto her hip and clomped up the dark stairway. Rose followed her along a dim landing. 'Bathroom's in there. One bath a week, of course. And the lavvy's outside. Ah, I see from the look on your face, you're not used to that sort of thing.'

They went up another narrow stairway into a stuffy bedroom under the eaves. One of the twin beds was made up with a neat counterpane and a patchwork quilt; the other was unmade, strewn with socks.

'We need you girls,' said Betony. 'His brother's in Malta, far as any of us know. He's sore about it. Worried sick, if you ask me. The sky caved in when Hugh said he'd enlisted. I say it was either that or wait for the call-up. He's been in a permanent bad mood since.'

'You mean Mr Cumberpatch?'

'Yes, my Ted. Call him Ted. And you must call me Betony. Like I said, my mother fell for me in Pengared meadow. Funny how I ended up marrying a Cumberpatch and came to live here. But then you should see Ted. Anyone would want to marry him.'

Betony bumped Mo onto the floor. 'Meg works like a carthorse,' she said. 'Can't fault her. You . . . you look a bit thin. Although you are tall. How strong are you?'

'I have my paperwork here.' Rose pulled out her official form signed by Mrs Pike. 'It tells you everything you need to know. Everything I've been trained in: ploughing, milking, hen work, pig farming . . .'

Betony wrinkled her nose. 'I don't . . . I can't. Show it to him if you like, but he'll not be interested. He'll want to *see* what you can do. You can have some soup and bread, and then you have to get started—oh! Look at that sparkler! What's his name?'

'Will. Will Bowman. He's back in Plymouth.'

'Navy?'

'Not in the forces, he's . . .'

'Reserve occupation?'

'No, he's in the bank.'

'Can't do without him, can they? Must be very important.'

'He's exempt. He has a chest condition. But he does his bit, he's a . . .'

'Ah.' Betony's face fell blank. She plucked Mo from the floor and left the room.

Rose began to unpack. She took off her engagement ring and hid it in the pocket of her dressing gown. She pulled her overalls over her breeches and jumper. 'If you're going to be a land-girl, Rose Pepper,' she said to the wall, 'you'd best get started.'

**I**n the kitchen, she hurried her soup and sank her teeth into the delicious bread, while Betony stood next to her on the threshold of the kitchen door, pointing the way. 'Go across the yard. Over that gate. Follow the path by the meadow. See that line of trees? That's the path that leads to the top field. You can't miss them. They'll be waiting.'

Rose scurried across the yard. Mutt and Jeff bounded after her, while the long face of a chestnut mare watched her from a half-open stable door. The horse's eye was rolling and white. She heard Betony call after her, 'That's Blossom. Ted's mare. You'll get used to her.'

'I don't want to try,' Rose muttered to herself, remembering the donkey that had kicked her in the stomach when she was eight.

Her stride had purpose but her ears rang with nerves. She felt like an impostor, a hoity-toity Devon town girl, as she skirted Betony's meadow on her way to her first job-of-work.

The air around her was full of the fresh breeze from the sea. Catkins shivered and blackbirds hopped in the dirt. Young wild daffs opened their yellow faces in the hollows of tree roots. Her ears pricked to the rumble of an engine and in automatic fear she tilted her head to the sky. But then she saw the green army truck with a rounded bonnet and a yellow star on the door trundling along the top road.

'The Americans!' she cried in relief. The Americans were their saviours, here to help. Rose felt them very welcome.

'Hey, Ginge!' came a woman's cry over the hedge. 'Stop gawping at the Yanks and get a move on! We're waiting! Oi, over here!'

There, beyond the gate of a freshly turned field, was a girl in overalls. With her was a man in a trilby and a youth lounging against the trailer.

'Yes, Ginge, I mean you!' The girl, her mouth bright with lipstick, was puffing on a cigarette. Her dark curls were encased in a topknot scarf, while Rose's hair was being whipped by the wind. In her haste to leave the farmhouse and not keep them waiting, she'd forgotten her scarf.

'Hello, I'm Rose Pepper,' she piped up and, not daring to undo the gate, began to climb over.

'Well, put up the flag. I'll tell Winston,' said the girl in a rolling St Ives accent. 'She's arrived.'

The man stepped forward. 'Now, Meg, simmer down, girl.' He looked at Rose. 'Good afternoon Land-Girl Pepper. Ted Cumberpatch.' He held out his thick-palmed hand. 'This here's Meg, you might have guessed, and Joel here helps out. We needed you a month ago.'

'Well, I'm here now, and eager to get on with the job.'

Meg gave her a slow handclap.

'Show some manners, Meg,' grumbled Ted. 'And you, come here.' Rose obeyed, stepping forward and watching nonplussed as Ted unknotted the scarf from round his neck. 'Here, lovely, use this on that wild-fire hair of yours. It's already driving me mad.'

Flushing, she took the scarf. 'Thank you.'

She put Ted at anywhere between thirty and fifty. Deep lines carved up his weathered, handsome face. His shock of russet hair was clamped tight by his trilby and his body was sheer weight of muscle. She had no doubt where little Mo got his looks from.

'Right, as you know, Ginge, we're here to sow barley. Here, Joel, you get the shovel. You, Meg, start filling this sack. I'll get Ginge started.'

Rose followed the others and grabbed a stomach-shaped canvas sack. Joel climbed up into the back of the trailer, stood on the huge pile of silvery seed and began to shovel it into the sack that Meg, cigarette in the corner of her mouth, held wide open for him.

'Well, well, Meg,' said Ted, scratching his chin to hide a smile. 'I was wondering if we'd got the timing right.'

Meg's face was a picture, her dark eyes flicking sideways to Rose. 'Yes, Ted. What *is* that old country lore you keep spouting? You can't sow barley until the soil is warm to your bare backside?'

Joel blurted a laugh, his neck red beneath his collar.

Ted said, 'Now, Meg, I'm glad it was you who said that, and not me.' He turned on Rose. 'Well, Ginge, I know it's your first day and all, but we need to test it for sure. How about it?'

Rose looked from Meg's sharp, mocking eyes to Ted's crinkled, half-serious face to the boy covering his mouth with a grubby hand. 'I am quite sure that is not the official method of assessing when the soil is ready for barley. What would Mrs Pike say, I wonder?' She paused and caught Ted's eye. She began to laugh, getting the joke. 'All right, Ted. I'll do it,' she said. 'But only if you show me first.'

**R**ose trudged up the vast top field with the heavy sack of barley seed across her shoulder, and then she trudged back down again. With every third step she dug her hand into the bag, pulled out a dusty handful and broadcasted it with a wide swing of her arm.

'Sweep it. Sweep it. Keep the rhythm!' Ted yelled at her.

Her arm was screaming, the muscles burning. She was breathless, the seed dust was getting into her lungs and her boots were caked with soil. She stopped to watch Joel and Ted proceed across their section.

'Too much for you, Ginge?' Meg called out.

'Just taking a breather,' she shouted back.

'Well, don't spend too long on it. We've got barley to sow.'

'Onward and upward,' Rose muttered, her heart not in it. How could she do this, day in, day out? She was utterly beaten. How could she have imagined she could ever be a land-girl? Will was right.

'Ugh!' she breathed. 'Damn him!'

'What was that?' Meg called.

'Just wondering if there was a chance of a hot bath tonight.'

'Not on your life. Saturday is bath night. There won't be any hot water. And remember, Ginge, whenever there is, I go in first.'

'How did I guess?'

Meg stopped and looked across at her. 'Hey, do you like the way this field has been turned? I did it. All by myself. Finest, straightest furrows Ted's ever seen. Can you plough?'

'I like to plough. I can drive an Allis.'

'Whoopee. I used Blossom to harrow and roll it. Hitched her up like in the old days. Saved on petrol. Bloody glorious it was.'

'Is she easy to handle?'

'Absolute nightmare!' Meg laughed. 'Oh, I see that's not good news for you, Ginge. Maybe you should ask Ted to keep you away from the horse, if you're that scared.'

'I'll do whatever is required. I'll do my bit.'

'Yes, yes . . .' Meg waved her away.

Rose returned to the trailer for more seed, her eyes streaming from the cold wind. Her nose was red and her lip wobbling. Ted met her there. 'Right, Ginge, that's enough. I think you're through. You're no good to me dead. Finish now. Go back to the house. Bet will have some tea on.' He peered at her. 'Well done, Ginge.'

'Thank you.' She bit her lip, determined not to cry. 'Ted, can I ask you something? Can I ask you not to call me Ginge?'

'Sorry, my lovely. But it's up here now.' He tapped the side of his head. 'Don't worry, you'll get used to it. Like you'll get used to all of us.'

The cool spring day drifted into a cold spring evening. Betony dished out mutton stew and potatoes at the table by the warmth of the black lead range. Rose was ravenous. She fell on her plate.

'Hold on, greedy,' hissed Meg at her side. She nodded towards Ted and Betony who were saying grace, eyes closed, mouthing a prayer.

'You'll learn, Ginge,' said Ted. 'Every evening we say a prayer for our Hugh. Last we heard he was in Malta.'

'Who will you pray for?' asked Betony, as she tucked into her meal.

Rose straightened her shoulders. 'No one in the forces, I'm afraid— as you know . . .'

Meg turned on her: 'Oh, don't be *afraid*. There's no need to be *afraid*. You should be grateful you have no one out there. I wish that was me.'

'Her fiancé is in the bank, in Plymouth,' said Betony.

Meg piled in. 'Is it war work? Can't do without him, can they?'

Rose said, 'He has an important job in the bank, yes. But he is also exempt on medical grounds. He has asthma.'

Meg tutted. 'Asthma? *Asthma?* My little brother Bertie lied about his age. Went over with the British Expeditionary Force. Got a bullet through his back in the fiasco that was Dunkirk. Didn't kill him, though. He drowned in two inches of sea water.' Meg was screwing her napkin up in her fists.

'I'm sorry,' said Rose.

'No, you're not, you're relieved. Your fiancé is safe. My Bertie is under the mud in some French field. Will they bring him back when all this is over? Who knows? Who cares? I know Whitehall doesn't.'

'Hush, Meg,' Betony whispered, glancing at Ted's stricken face.

Meg sank back in her chair. 'Sorry, Ted, I do go on.'

Ted looked up, beaming a false smile. 'Hugh writes when he can. That lad is certainly seeing the world. But he'll come home.'

Betony rested her hand on her husband's arm. 'That's more like it.'

Rose felt uncomfortable witnessing the mutual compassion in their eyes. She piped up, 'My fiancé, Will, is an air-raid patrol warden.' But no one seemed to notice. Aware of Meg prickling at her elbow, she tried again. 'Meg, I'm sorry for your loss.'

Meg turned her eyes on her, wet with unshed tears. And then she gave her a crooked smile, before putting a forkful of stew in her mouth. 'This war touches everyone, doesn't it. Just you wait until it's your turn.'

The attic bedroom was cold, damp and stuffy.

'Do you mind if I open the window?' Rose asked.

'Yes, we'll freeze,' said Meg, taking off her clothes and throwing them on the floor. The blackout blind was drawn and the small oil lamp gave off an insipid yellow light. Meg's face was a white oval against her black hair. 'Hey, Ginge, is that a war wound then?' She pointed at Rose's face.

Even though she was so bone-tired that she felt as if she had been run over by Jack Thimble's bus, Rose gave in to her constant need to be courteous. 'If you mean my scar . . . yes. It's nothing, really. I was caught in an air raid with Will. The last big one we had, back in January. Flying glass. I got caught by flying glass.' She sat down on her bed, amazed at how easily the lies tripped off her tongue. And how difficult it was proving to get her story straight.

Meg turned off the lamp. Rose fumbled with her clothes and felt her way into bed. She lay her head on the cold, unfamiliar pillow, imagining her own fresh linen and silky eiderdown back home. Hot tears began to soak into her hair.

'Hey, Ginge,' came the whispered voice in the darkness.

Rose's shoulders tensed in agony. *Oh, leave me alone.*

'Oi, Ginge! I just want to say . . . the war does terrible things. Losing Bertie has made me rotten. I'm a bit of a piece these days.'

Realising that this was a mild apology, Rose mustered some strength to ask, 'How do you mean?'

'The Yanks,' whispered Meg. 'I just can't have enough of them. It's my way of coping. You wait. Next village hop at Polperro and we'll go.'

'Really, Meg. I'm engaged.'

'Oh, I know that. Do you love him?'

'Well, really. I don't think I have to explain myself to you, do I?'

'Listen, Ginge. At dinner. You hardly defended him, did you? If someone said what I said to you about the man I love, I would have let them have it. I insulted him and his work. I don't know any different, do I? He could be an amazingly brave man. But you said nothing.'

The silence in the bedroom pressed down on Rose's ears.

'I don't think you do,' Meg said.

'What?'

'*Love* him.'

She opened her mouth to speak, but could not.

'We'll leave it now, shall we?' came Meg's satisfied voice. 'Can't wait to show you my Yanks. They're such gentlemen. All *Hi* this and *Ma'am* that. They dance like Fred Astaire. They give you ciggies and gum.'

Rose rallied. 'I don't smoke.'

'How did I guess? Then they take you for a walk, wrap you up in their coat and give you something else too!'

'Meg, really.' She tried disapproval.

'Shush! Listen a moment. There they go,' giggled Meg. 'Drives me mad listening to that when I haven't had any.'

In the dark, Rose rocked her head. 'Goodness!' she cried, horrified but fascinated at the same time. 'I thought they weren't at all suited.'

'Oh, they are. She's the backbone of them. Without her he'd crumble. She gives him heart. They are truly in love.'

Rose pulled the covers over her head to try to muffle the intimacies from the marriage bed downstairs. Were she and Will ever in love? Would she crumble without him? Her indignation began to recede, only to be replaced by a cold bite of emptiness.

**R**ose was shaken from sleep by the rattling alarm clock. She was warm and surprisingly comfortable. A few weeks on at Pengared and the lumpy mattress had begun to mould itself to her body. She lay for half a minute, wiggling her toes, enjoying the moment. Then she had to move.

Back went the covers and bare feet touched the rug over the chilly lino. On went shirt, breeches and jumper, her fingers feeling for buttons. She wrapped her hair up tightly while Meg moved with equal speed. No one spoke until hot tea was poured in the kitchen.

Downstairs by the warmth of the stove, they sat at the table holding their steaming mugs and taking slices of toast provided by Betony.

'How did Mo sleep?' Meg asked Betony once her tea had sunk in.

'Oh, very well. I didn't tell you, Mrs Thimble's evacuees have nits.'

'Ew, keep them away from me.'

Rose piped up, 'Is that Mrs Thimble, wife of Jack the bus conductor?'

She was ignored. She continued to nibble in silence on her slice of toast, sighing with relief when Ted came in. 'Cows, Meg,' he announced. 'I've just brought them in.'

'Who's to help me?'

'Joel is already there.'

Meg gave Rose a smug look. Ted never asked Rose to help with the milking, even though she had been given a merit by Mrs Pike. She longed to be inside that shed with the soft-faced sleepy cows, the humming of the cooling machine, the smell of silage and cud, Joel painstakingly sluicing the gutters.

'Yard, Ginge,' he said. 'Then see to the hens. You can muck out once the milking's done.'

'Yes, Ted. Then what?' She hoped for some tractor work, hauling bales of straw, perhaps. She loved being out in the fields.

'Later on? Hoe the sugar beets. Meg, the Allis needs an oil change.'

There was another look of triumph from Meg.

'Breakfast in two hours,' said Betony, stoking the fire in the grate. 'Oh, Ted, didn't you need Blossom for something?'

'Yes. Meg, when you've finished the milking will you harness her, please?'

Rose felt her shoulders sink with relief. At least she did not have to go anywhere near that horse.

She picked up the heavy yard broom and felt creeping discontent as she bent her back to the mess of straw and dung stuck to the cobbles. She swept and sweated, then bent to shovel the muck into her barrow.

Wheeling her third barrow-load to the muck heap she paused to rest, glancing at her red, chapped hands and her black nails. She watched Meg, over the way, languidly urging the herd back out to pasture.

Meg noticed her. 'Your engagement ring won't look so nice now, will it, on those hands. Anyway, stop preening, Ginge. You can get started in the cowshed now.'

Irritated, Rose called back, 'I always do the henhouse before breakfast, to get it out of the way.'

Meg shrugged and went on her way.

Rose opened the door to the henhouse to let the chickens out onto new straw that she had strewn for them in the yard. 'Go on.' Rose used the toe of her boot to nudge the reluctant ones. 'Mucky little devils.'

Then she stooped to the small door in the side of the hut to collect the eggs, still warm from the hens' bottoms. She carefully placed the precious brown eggs in Betony's wire basket, took them to the kitchen and put them on the dresser. Then she took a deep breath.

Hen dung was far worse than cows' could ever be. On her knees with her head and shoulders stuck right inside that musty little shed, the stink of it reached right down to her stomach, sending a queasy rush back up her throat. She took up the small trowel and began to scrape the splattered hen muck from the perches, some of it crusted, some of it still wet. Even though she held her breath, she could taste the smell.

At last, she shuffled back out. By the time Rose had put away her tools, she heard the metallic clop of Blossom's hoofs on the cobbles. Meg proceeded across the yard towards her, holding the leading rein like a natural horsewoman. Rose moved to one side.

'She's really quite harmless, Ginge,' Meg trilled. 'She's just an old lady.'

'She's a cantankerous old lady.'

'Why not be friendly? Stroke her nose. She can sense your fear.'

Suddenly the roar of an engine ripped across the sky. Rose ducked, glancing up to see blue and red circles on the underbelly of a Spitfire as it thundered towards the sea. Blossom—spooked by the plane—jerked her head, rolled her eyes and flattened her ears.

Meg clung to the rein, her arm stretching out as Blossom yanked in terror. She yelled, 'A dogfight! My first dogfight!'

'Is there another plane? Did you see a German?' Rose spluttered, her own fear escalating as the horse grew more and more agitated.

Suddenly, her eerie whinny rising in pitch, Blossom wrenched her head from Meg's grasp and reared up. Hoofs pummelled the air over Meg's head. The horse's body all but blocked out the sun.

'Steady girl, steady!' came Meg's cry. 'Oh my God, steady!'

Through the explosion of hoofs and the animal's awful noise, Rose saw its heavy chin crack down on Meg's face, sending her reeling to the ground, clutching her nose.

Without a moment to think, Rose stepped forward and reached towards the horse. The rein was flying around like a whip but a calm voice inside her head told her to grab it. She tugged it down in one deft movement, placing her hand flat on Blossom's nose.

The horse snorted and foam flew in Rose's face but she kept a firm grip. She spoke the same calm words out loud that she could hear inside her head. Finally, Blossom stood still, her sides heaving like bellows. Meg scrambled to her feet, her nose bloodied.

'There wasn't another plane, damn it!' Meg cried, craning her neck towards the sky. 'He must have been answering some scramble.'

Rose snapped with a surge of anger. 'Is that all you care about? Plane spotting? Trying to wave at the pilot? You could have been *killed*!'

'What do you mean, *killed*? It's only old Blossom.'

'I couldn't have controlled her for much longer.'

'But you did control her.' Meg reached forward to stroke the animal's nose and asked, 'Have you got a handkerchief for my nose?'

'Here, take this. Keep it.'

'Thank you. And sorry.' Meg bit her lip. Her voice had a humble ring.

In silence, as a team, they walked Blossom back to the stable.

'Best stay in there for a bit,' Meg said to the horse. 'Got to keep calm, old lady.' She looked across at Rose. 'You know, when I used to do the henhouse, I always put a dash of cologne on a scarf and tied it round my nose and mouth. Helps with the pong.'

'That's a good idea. It doesn't half smell.' Embarrassed by Meg's humility, Rose couldn't look at her. She gazed at Blossom instead. 'She still looks a bit loopy. She certainly had a fright.'

'So did I,' said Meg. 'But you saved it, Ginge.'

'I did, didn't I?'

They smiled at each other across Blossom's shoulders.

Even in the darkness of her sleep, Rose heard the planes. The gnawing drone came from the back of her dream, driving forwards until her eyelids opened to agonising reality. She sprang awake and crouched on her bed, frozen. Fear flashed like a beacon inside her head.

'They're not after us; they're flying too high.' Meg was beside her, lighting the lamp. 'Must be Birmingham, Bristol or Plymouth.' Meg peered at her in the gloom. 'God, sorry, Ginge, I didn't think . . .'

Ted was knocking on the door. 'Get going, girls. We never hear the blessed siren out here, when the wind's the wrong way.'

Meg grabbed Rose's dressing gown and wrapped it round her,

pulling her down the stairs. They found Betony crouched under the kitchen table with Mo. Ted pulled the ring on the trap door in the flagstones. 'Down in the cellar. Come on, all of you.'

They bent double to take the stairs down into the dank space. Rose's ears filled with the sound of her own fear as she remembered the shelter in Tobacco Street. In the raids, she thought, when we go underground, it's as if we are burying ourselves alive.

Ted lit the lamp to reveal the Cumberpatch shelter: a cosy den with two battered old armchairs. He got the little Primus going for tea, while Meg tucked a blanket around Betony and Mo in one of the chairs.

'Sit down, Ginge,' she said, pointing to the other chair.

'The animals, Ted?' blurted Rose. 'What about the cows? Blossom?'

'Didn't know you cared so much about the old girl,' came Meg's voice. Rose felt Meg's warm hand on her knee.

'I can't do anything for them, can I?' Ted replied. 'That's what's so frustrating. Being totally at those bastards' mercy.'

'Must bring it back for you, Ginge,' said Meg, turning on her side on the floor, making a pillow out of a blanket and curling up to doze.

'Ginge,' said Ted, peering at her in the gloom. 'Buck up. You can phone home in the morning.' He settled himself on a box of apples. 'We've been tough on you since you arrived, Ginge. All of us.'

'I'm getting there,' Rose said, mustering a little strength.

'You've been through a lot,' said Betony, lifting her head up to listen. 'You've had to live through all these raids. I'm sorry. I realise your parents might be in the thick of all this now, and your fiancé—'

'He'll be out doing his rounds,' she interjected.

'Ah, you see,' said Ted. 'Not a complete shirker then.'

'Oh!'

'He's playing with you, Ginge,' said Betony, lowering her voice. 'And Meg admits she has been particularly awful to you about him. But I think you know why she's like that. Her brother—she's still hurting.'

Rose glanced down at the sleeping Meg. She said, 'She tells me that's why she likes the Yanks, and they like her.'

Ted raised an eyebrow. 'We know what she's like. And you, Ginge, we're getting to know you. You two are chalk and cheese. You don't mind Ginge really, do you?'

'It makes me smile. So there. Makes me feel . . .'

Ted teased her. 'Singled out, picked on? *Special?*'

'Oh, yes, very special.' She laughed out loud. She rested her head on the back of the chair. She felt safe with the Cumberpatches.

In a mere moment, Rose was woken by a frantic ringing of the telephone and a trample of feet over her head. It was morning and she had been fast asleep in the cellar. Betony was calling her to the phone. She rushed up the steps and through the trap door. The receiver was lying on the stand in the hall. She lifted it and held it to her ear. Her knees gave way when she heard her mother's voice. 'Thought we'd better call, darling. Surprised the line's not down.'

'Oh, Mother, are you all right?'

'We're fine. It was a light raid. Will came round especially this morning to check on us. They were just dropping off after Bristol.'

'And Dad?'

'Yes, yes, we're all fine. Will not so. Says he hasn't had a letter from you in weeks. Says he wants to visit. See what's keeping you from him.'

Her mother's voice sounded rather accusing. Rose's stomach dropped. The thought of him here at Pengared was astonishing.

'How is it being a land-girl?' her mother went on.

'Fine; hard work, but fine.' Rose brightened now as she glanced through to the kitchen where Betony was slicing yesterday's bread for toast and Meg was pouring the tea.

'Come home and see us soon, darling,' said her mother and Rose opened her mouth to reply, but the operator interjected and their three minutes were up. She stood for a moment in the hallway and then, suddenly remembering, put her hand into her dressing-gown pocket. It wasn't there. Somewhere between the attic bedroom and the cellar floor, her engagement ring had been lost.

# Three

FROM THE ATTIC WINDOW in the early evening, Rose saw a shimmering haze of silver-green over the top field. As if overnight, the barley she had helped sow on her first day was springing out of the red soil. The weeks had spun quickly past, the season had changed and she was part of life at Pengared Farm. She missed her parents and sometimes longed for home, but she knew that as soon as she arrived at Stanley Crescent,

Will would be there. And she knew that he'd beg forgiveness for what happened on the night of the raid. He'd stare into her eyes, turn it all around and make her feel small and sorry.

'Stop dreaming,' said Meg, 'and help me with my buttons.' She turned her back so that Rose could do her up. Everything about her was circular, from the polka dots on her red dress to her dark eyes, black curls and large, round bosoms. Rose felt flat-chested, boyish and a frump by comparison.

'What's the matter with you?' Meg scolded. 'You can take that look off your face. We're going dancing, remember.'

'Oh; it's just this dress,' Rose said, smoothing her hand down her dark blue frock. 'I should have brought my best dress with me, but I didn't think I'd be going *dancing*. This one is so old-fashioned. You look so wonderful. So bright and pretty. I feel like a granny.'

'Enough of that; the blue suits you. Brings out your eyes.' Meg reached forward and undid one of the buttons at the neck. 'That's a start.' She spun Rose round to face the mirror and scrutinised her. 'What sort of colour is your hair, anyway?'

'My mother says it's Titian. After the great artist. This red was a colour he always used.'

'I bet the GIs will love it,' laughed Meg. 'That's it. You're smiling now. I don't know Titian but I know what a fox's tail looks like. And look at that face.' She carefully rolled up two locks of Rose's hair and pinned them around her forehead. 'There, now the Yanks will see more of you. They'll die for that skin and those freckles.'

'Do you think so? I hope not. I don't want to encourage anyone.'

'What are you saying, Ginge? That you don't want to meet anyone new? Even though you don't love the incredibly brave and dashing Mr Will Bowman?'

'Did I *actually* say that?' Rose felt swamped by the emptiness again.

'No, you didn't have to.'

She felt ready to confide. 'Did I tell you, he had an indiscretion with a Wren? Mrs Brown, the lady who runs the corner shop, told me, and he didn't deny it. I saw the Wren in the pub and it was so obvious.'

'Ugh, Wrens. They're the worst. You should have broken it off there and then. Why haven't you, for goodness' sake?'

'I tried to the night of the raid. He wouldn't have it.' The sudden truth of it made her relax. 'I'm thinking about ways of telling him. I'm going home next weekend. It's best I do it face to face. I'll do it then.' The thought of it made her blood run cold.

'I think you're too kind.' Meg was cross. 'All he needs is a *Dear John*. You've changed these last few weeks. You don't love him. Now come on, Titian beauty,' she said. 'I can hear Ted grumbling from here.'

In the evening half-light, squeezed into the front seat of Ted's old truck, they drove along the top road to Polperro, the fishing village. Ted peered through the mud-splattered windscreen. 'I must say, it's a fine evening for this abomination.'

'Whatever do you mean?' Meg pretended to be indignant.

'Those Americans and you girls at this shindig. It's so bloody obvious. It will be like a cattle market. Ginge, remember you're spoken for.'

Rose kept quiet and watched hawthorn blossom falling like gentle snowflakes on the bonnet of the truck.

'Hey, Ginge.' Meg dug her in the ribs. 'When this bloody mess is over, I'm going to drive the Allis tractor along here all the way to Polperro and get myself a drink. Are you going to come with me?'

'Of course I will. I can't wait for this awful war to be over.'

Ted grumbled, 'Something tells me we're all in for a long wait for that day.' He pulled up at the top of the village street. 'This is as far as I'm going,' he said. 'Polperro's far too steep for motors. You're on your own now. You girls be careful,' he called after them as Meg slammed the truck door shut. 'I'll be in the Sailors' Arms, ready to go at eleven. Sharp. Any trouble, you know where I am.'

'You won't leave without us,' Meg said.

'Be late and you'll see.'

'Good old Ted,' said Meg, linking her arm through Rose's. 'He had to dig up one of his petrol cans buried in the orchard for tonight. Betony persuaded him. At least he gets a night out at the boozer for his trouble. I like it when he goes all big-brother-ish on us.'

Laughing, they clipped down the cobbled hill past rows of white-washed fishermen's cottages. In Polperro harbour, fishing boats bobbed in the sheltered water. Rose sighed. 'How lovely it is here.'

'Never mind *lovely*,' Meg retorted. 'We're not here for the view.'

Meg pulled her up some steps into a tin-roofed church hall and through the door under a fluttering Union Jack. They paid their pennies and walked into a chattering crush of people.

'Oh, my goodness,' Rose said as they stepped into the throng, feeling the heat, breathing the cigarette smoke and absorbing the swing of music. 'A real band! I've never been to a dance like this before.'

'Oh, Ginge, welcome to the world!'

And what a wonderful world it is, Rose thought. The rhythmic brass and relentless drumming broke over her in a rocking wave; so different from what she listened to on the cosy wireless in her parents' parlour. Here the music was raw, insistent, live. She caught sight of a banner over the stage: *Polperro welcomes Hank Ancourt and his Band.*

'This lot are stationed round the headland. I saw you gawping at them the day you arrived. They've brought their own band with them, the lovely Yanks,' cried Meg, her face rosy with excitement.

The floor was bouncing with dancers. The American GIs, British sailors, Wrens, Auxiliaries and Polperro villagers all bobbed, twirled and jived to the muffled trumpets and infectious beat, their bright faces transfixed with pleasure. Rose was mesmerised. She clapped her hands with joy. 'Oh, I love it! I love it!'

'Hi, girls, care for a drink?' A close-cropped, red-necked GI elbowed his way to them.

Meg looked him up and down. 'Yes, please. Two beers, please.'

The GI brought the drinks over to their table. As he set them down, Meg gestured towards Rose. He took the hint and grabbed Rose by the hand. 'Care to dance, ma'am?'

'Go on,' said Meg. 'I'll guard your beer.'

She assented for she didn't know what else to do. He was tall and thickset and instantly her face was pressed close to his scratchy lapels. She cautiously lifted her chin to look at his face.

'Private Solwell, ma'am. From Ol' Kentucky.' He beamed down on her. 'You'all dance good, ma'am.'

'Pleased to meet you. I'm Rose Pepper, from Plymouth,' she said. 'Thank you, but it's you. I don't dance *good*. *You* dance well. You're leading. I don't know what to do.'

She tried to keep up with him, shuffling her feet as best she could, wishing she had learned how to dance. She glanced over her shoulder and saw that a pretty blonde girl was sitting in her seat, leaning close to Meg and chatting in her ear. The song finished and Kentucky bowed. 'Thank you, ma'am, you'all enjoy your beer.'

'Oh, he was so polite,' she told Meg, 'but I really can't dance.'

'This is Mabel Brown,' said Meg, and the blonde girl gave Rose a quick smile. 'She's over at Hunter's Farm. She's lonely, never gets out.'

'Got my eye on that big fella,' said Mabel, tucking a cigarette between her lips and smoothing her red dress over her skinny hips.

'That's my girl,' laughed Meg.

Mr Ancourt counted in the next tune: 'One, two, you know what to do.'

Another GI appeared by the table. 'You like Glenn Miller?' He moved in close, smelling of beer.

Rose smiled politely. 'Yes, I do. My parents like him, so I . . .'

'You a land-girl, huh?' He pulled her out into the melee of the dancers. 'Do you know any haystacks nearby?'

From their table, Meg and Mabel giggled, digging each other in the ribs and nodding fierce encouragement at her.

'I beg your pardon?' Rose had to shout over the music.

The GI moved her closer to his barrel chest and pressed his wet lips to her ear. 'I said, do you know of any haystacks where we could . . .' His hand slipped down to her bottom.

'How dare you! I'm not that sort of girl!' she cried.

She glanced over her shoulder and saw that Meg and Mabel had been cornered by two GIs. Meg was sitting on one man's lap, supping her beer and arching her back, showing the tops of her stockings, while Mabel was running her hand inside the collar of the other's shirt.

Rose tried to extract herself, but the GI's damp hands clamped tight to her hips. 'My, you're a tall girl. I love it that you are. Hey, I'm just about level with your titties. Just right for—'

'Leave me alone.' She wrenched herself away and walked off to sit down in a corner, away from the dance floor. It was spoilt now. Next to her, a couple were holding hands sedately across the table.

'Oh, don't look so affronted, love,' said the woman, glaring at her. 'No need to look down your nose at them. They're here to help us.'

'I know that,' she snapped. 'I just wish they wouldn't take advantage. They start off all polite, and then they . . . misbehave.'

'You bring it on yourself. After all you came with *her*.' She nodded to where Meg was sitting on a lieutenant's lap, her face being devoured by his moustache. 'They think you're the same as her. By association.'

'My friend is only being like that because she is in mourning.'

'We *all* are. But we don't *all* behave like that.'

Rose stood up and made for the door. She slipped out of the fuggy dance hall into the caress of the sweet night air. Relief swept over her as she began to walk down the dark street, drawn by the stillness of the sleeping harbour. The sun had long set but the sky was still light in the west and the harbour walls were lapped by inky water. It was a bright night, a bombers' night. In that peaceful, empty moment she suddenly sensed someone watching her. The man was reclining on a bench, feet propped up on the harbour wall, hands in pockets, uniform hat pulled right down over his nose.

The stranger spoke: 'Such a perfect English night.'

She glanced at him, wondering if the man was talking to himself, then demurely fixed her eyes on the line of fishing boats.

'And you the perfect English rose.'

In one swift motion, he sat up on the bench and removed his hat.

'I beg your pardon?' she asked, suddenly nervous.

'The perfect English rose, if you don't mind me saying.'

His accent was heavy, definitely European. She tilted her head to hear him better. She could not place it: he hissed his 's's, he emphasised the wrong syllables. Confused, her mind reeled to the constant warnings about Nazi parachuters.

'Oh my God,' she blurted, 'you're not a German, are you?'

He leapt to his feet, crying, *Jezis-Maria!* What an insult.'

She was horrified as he sprang forward, his face young, open and utterly shocked. She muttered a quick apology and turned to go.

He cried after her, 'Please. I did not mean to shout. Do not leave.'

'Tell me who you are then!' she blustered.

'Don't be frightened. Please. I am a Czech soldier. I am Czech.' He fumbled in his top pocket for his papers. 'Captain Novotny. 29th US Regiment. I am taking the air, just like you.' He took a step towards her. 'Far too hot in there. All those people. So *noisy*. I came down here to be near the sea,' he said, revolving his cap round and round in his hands. 'Back home we are landlocked, so, being here in England, I can't take my eyes off the water. And if I can't see it, I love to smell it. And if I can't smell it, I love to hear it. It gives me peace.'

He moved closer towards her, and on reflex she turned away.

'No, please.' His voice was soft. 'I said please not to go away. Please, English rose. I'm with the Americans, but I can see from your face that that is perhaps not a good thing. What I mean is, I am stationed with them, but I am not *like* them.'

Her shoulders relaxed. 'But I do have to go,' she insisted. 'It sounds like they're playing the last songs. The love songs.'

'Ah, you don't like that?'

Rose watched him, suddenly trusting him enough to tell him, 'I can't bear it. All the sentiment. All the "We'll meet agains". This bloody war.'

'It makes you sad. You have a love somewhere?'

'A love?' Her mind went blank. Of course, there was no *love*. 'No, nothing like that.' She stifled a laugh. 'Well, good night.'

'Please, don't go. Not yet!' he implored her.

Rose looked at his face more closely. He was fair-haired and his face had a creaminess, a freshness. His eyes were deep grey and issued a pure light; his smile was bright and open.

'Please? Dance with me?' he asked.

She laughed. 'Here?'

'Why not? We can do whatever we want.'

'But that's what they are doing in there. *Whatever they want*. And taking advantage, using the war as an excuse.'

'Ah, but they are doing it with their bodies, not with their souls.'

She waited as this expression sank into her consciousness, and then, feeling a sense of peace settle inside, she surprised herself and stepped forward into his arms. Gently, he took her hand in his own soft, cool palm. His fingertips were tender on the centre of her back. He barely touched her as he swayed her to the music drifting down the street. She felt her feet become light. She felt as if she could dance, *really* dance.

'Just one moment of bliss,' he mused, his strange voice a caress.

'Did you leave someone behind in Czechoslovakia?'

'I left everything behind.'

Suddenly understanding his immense sorrow, Rose held his hand tighter as they danced with light, sensitive steps on the cobbles. She turned her head and smiled into his eyes. 'You don't have to use the word "English" when you address me.'

He cocked his head, half amused, half puzzled.

'You called me an English rose. But my name is—merely—Rose.'

His eyes shone as he understood. 'I knew it. Such beauty, like the flower,' he whispered, and then corrected himself. 'I'm sorry, Miss Rose. I am being very forward for a Czechoslovakian officer and gentleman. What I meant to say was that you do look lovely tonight.'

'Thank you.' She accepted the compliment with grace. 'And you? We haven't been properly introduced.'

'My name is Krystof. And, as I was saying before, I am from Czechoslovakia where we have no sea and I can't take my eyes off . . .' he winked at her and let his gaze drift with mock reluctance over her shoulder, '. . . the sea.'

Laughing, she told him, 'I know a lovely cove near the farm where I work. If you squint past the wire and imagine children playing in the rock pools, it's heaven. And the sand is so soft between your toes.'

'I have never felt sand between my toes!'

'You should.'

'I will, with you at your cove.' He glanced towards the sound of voices outside the church hall. 'Looks like the dance is over.'

'Hey, Ginge,' came Meg's whooping cry, as she skipped down the steps. 'Time to go.' Mabel was hoofing up the street with a man in uniform, throwing back her head in laughter.

Krystof asked her, 'What is this "ginge"?'

'That's my friend Meg, and I won't introduce you, if you don't mind. I have to go. It was lovely to meet you.'

'You cannot go, Rose. You haven't told me where you are staying!'

Meg's urgent cry broke the spell. 'Come on, Ginge—let him go. Ted's taxi service to Pengared is waiting. Mustn't make him mad.'

'You live at Pengared? I think I know it. Is it close by the camp? These Cornish names. They are difficult for me. Do you mind if I . . .?'

She felt a gentle flipping under her heart. 'No.'

He bowed. 'Until next time, English Rose.'

In the morning, as Rose opened the bedroom window to let in the fresh air, Meg rolled over and begged for water.

'Never again?' Rose asked her.

'Never again,' Meg muttered, reaching for the glass. 'Tell Ted I'm poorly, will you? I can't do the cows. I'll make it up to you. Promise.'

'At last,' Rose teased her, 'a chance to milk the cows.'

After tea and toast with Betony, Rose got up from the table, pulled on her jacket and headed out into the bright sunshine.

'And where do you think you're going?' Ted called across the yard.

'To collect the eggs, as usual, and see to the hens. Why, do you want me to do the cows instead,' she asked eagerly, 'seeing as Meg is unwell?'

'That girl better haul herself out of her bed and quick!' he called up in the direction of the attic casement, knowing Meg would hear him. 'No, I'll see to the milking.'

'What, then?' Rose asked, downcast.

'Don't look like that, Ginge. I'm giving you the morning off.'

'Are you sure?'

'Stop procrastinating, Ginge.' Ted nodded towards the farmyard gate. 'You're keeping him waiting.'

'Oh goodness!' She had not seen Krystof there, leaning on the gate, his peaceful face soaking up the sunshine. Trying to compose herself, her heart racing, she hissed at Ted out of the side of her mouth, 'Are you really sure, about the morning off?'

'I want to know if *you* are sure, Ginge,' he said, gravely. 'I'd like to know what your fiancé might think of this.'

Rose lowered her head. 'We'll go for a walk. What's the harm in that?'

Ted growled, 'Go now, before I change my mind.'

She thought quickly. 'Ted, can I take the dogs?'

'If you must. If you feel that will break the ice, then yes.'

He strode away across the yard, laughing. Then she heard the casement rattle and a dishevelled Meg leaned out.

'Yoo-hoo, Ginge, I knew it!' Meg cried. 'When I saw you with him, dancing by the harbour, I knew it!'

Rose blushed and pressed her finger to her lips. 'I'm surprised you can remember anything about last night.'

With a schoolgirl giggle, Meg slammed the casement shut.

Rose waved at Krystof to wait and hurried back to the kitchen to grab the dogs' leads from their hook. She suddenly realised why Betony had been grinning at her across the table.

'Did you know he was there? All this time?'

Betony nodded in response, her eyes shining. 'He was there at first light. Asked Ted if he would allow you the time off; permission to take you for a walk. Said something about the cove.'

In the yard, she hooked the leads onto the dogs' collars. They were being surprisingly obedient: they sensed escape and they had never forgotten her biscuits and lived in futile expectation of more.

The dogs trotted beside her as she walked towards Krystof, both leads in one hand. She felt a strange stew of confidence and butterflies fluttering in her stomach. Had everything she had felt when they danced and held each other and looked into each other's faces been in her imagination? Had he felt it too?

He took off his cap, a deep smile curving his face, his head gently nodding. Suddenly, deep down, she realised she had been expecting him. She reached for the latch on the gate.

'No, wait,' he cried. 'Look, look at the sign. You should not open the gate. It says so. See, I am good at English. I can read the sign. Look!'

'It's all right,' she said. 'That only applies when these two are loose in the yard. But now they are on the lead, and under my control.'

The dogs trotted round the gate as she opened it.

'So many things are in your control.' He glanced at her.

'Hardly many things. I can count only the dogs at this precise moment.' She looked at him. 'I hope you are not suggesting that *you* are in my control. It's far too early to be saying that sort of thing.'

'Early? It's eight o'clock in the morning. In farming, that is not early.'

'I mean—' She stopped, yanking the dogs back. 'Ah, I see, you are teasing me.' She watched pleasure break over his face.

'You don't mind, do you?' He laughed.

She walked in one wheel rut and he walked in the other.

'Are you taking me to your *cove*?' he asked, saying the word carefully.

'That's where I'm going so . . .'

Sunlight dappled through trees and a lacy froth of blossom grew on spiky hawthorn hedges. 'English springtime,' said Krystof, watching the benign blue sky, 'is very beautiful.'

'You remembered where I lived, then?' she asked, feeling shy.

'I forgot at first,' he said. 'These Cornish names tie me in knots. But all I had to do was ask some of the platoon. They remembered you from the dance. The fiery redhead, someone said, the firecracker. But *Ginge*? That's what your friend called you. Not sure I like that name.'

'I'm not sure either.' She smiled. 'But part of me finds it endearing.'

They walked up the footpath that snaked over the headland. Gulls were swooping, their calls keening overhead.

'The sea cannot be far away,' he said. 'The birds always stay close. It's like they are keeping watch over us.'

She noticed their steps were in rhythm, their strides the same length.

'I hope it is acceptable for me to call on you.' He looked at her, just as she caught his eye. 'I have a morning pass from my commander. I hope you don't mind.'

'Mind?' She pondered on it, smiling at the formality of his words. 'When I woke up I was thinking how much I wanted to show you the cove; how strange that you have not seen the sea until you came here. I was also thinking that your English is very good.'

'I have been with the Americans for nearly four years, so I have picked it up, as you say.'

They had reached the brow of the hill and suddenly the sea broke before them: the rolling waves, the expanse of grey-blue that was not quite yet a picture-postcard colour. Rose let the dogs off their leads.

Krystof fell to his knees. 'Oh, the agony,' he cried out, laughing at himself. 'The agony. The beauty. Look at it. See how far it goes. It's enormous. Take me there. I want to touch it.'

She led him to the path that took them down to the cove. Soon enough, gravity began to propel them into a tunnel of shady hawthorns and they were enveloped by greenery and silence. The dogs crashed ahead. The sound of the sea was muffled by the undergrowth, but then she turned a corner and the cove was there before them, perfect.

Krystof cried out and ran over the smooth wet sand, dodging rock pools and the wave-licked boulders. He stopped abruptly at the twists of wire strung between wooden props following the shoreline like an ugly scar.

'I want to go in. I have to touch it.' He hopped on one leg to loosen a boot and then fell onto his backside as he struggled to pull off the other.

'Krystof! Are you mad? What about the wire?'

'You think I haven't breached tougher wire than this?' Krystof called. 'It might try its best to keep *them* out, but it won't keep me in.'

He took off his shirt and rolled up his trousers. Rose let out a short burst of laughter and then clapped her hand over her mouth. She had never before seen a man without his shirt on. Not her father, nor Will. She could not pull her eyes away from Krystof. His skin was creamy, smooth, not a mark on it. Downy golden hair covered his chest and rounded muscles defined his arms.

He stepped back a few paces, judged the distance and then pelted to the wire. She squeezed her eyes shut as he sprinted past her and heard him yell with joy as he breached it in one bound. He plunged into the water, kicking great plumes up with his legs.

'Be careful,' came her feeble voice, but she began to laugh.

He stood to attention, facing her, saluted and fell backwards flat into the water. The splash obliterated him and he came up floating, his feet like a rudder. He tipped his head backwards and drank a hard mouthful of sea water, which he spouted like a whale.

'Keep your mouth shut!' she called.

'I can't stop laughing!' he called back, and then shouted out in Czech.

'What did you say? What are you saying? Tell me.'

He sank under the waves and leapt up like a glistening dolphin. 'I said, "You don't know what this means to me." And, "I love the sea like I love my mother." And, "Why can't I live like this for all time?" And, "How is it that you aren't in here with me?"'

'Because I—because I can't jump as high as you.'

He stood up and waded back to shore, his trousers clinging to him like a second skin. Then he reached out and beckoned her towards him. She stepped forward. The wire was as high as her shoulders. She stared at it, at its twisted violence, dividing them. And then she looked beyond it to Krystof.

'*Polib me*, Rose,' he said. 'Kiss me. Say it, Rose.'

'I'm not going to say that! Who do you think you are? You be careful.' She tried to sound cross but it wasn't working. He reached his fingers over the wire and held them towards her. She copied him, tentatively. Their fingertips touched. His fingers felt warm. They felt *right*.

She realised she was holding her breath. 'Come back over, Krystof.'

He turned from her and walked back into the sea, dug his heels into the wet sand and then sprang forward. She clapped her hands over her eyes; she could not watch. He did not have enough space to run. He might not make it. She heard a lot of splashing and a yell and then Krystof was in a ball in the sand at her feet, clutching his bare foot.

She yelped in panic. 'Let me see.' She knelt down and took his foot in her lap. He lay back on the sand, groaning.

His foot was strong and wide, his skin was perfect. 'There's nothing! There's nothing here, you rascal!' She dropped his foot and stood up.

He stayed where he was, lolling on the sand. '"Rascal"?' he called. 'What is this strange word? I merely wanted you to touch my foot. We've touched hands, now we touch feet.'

Rose gazed at him, liking the way he found joy in every little thing; liking the way his eyes shone at her, laughing with pleasure; liking the rush of bliss surging through her body. She had to shake it off. She had to remind herself: she was engaged to be married.

Abruptly, she turned from him and walked towards a boulder to sit down. Krystof ran after her and sat next to her, squeezing out his trouser legs to make watery indents in the sand.

'What is it about the sea, Krystof?' Rose asked, eventually.

His eyes squinted, as if he was peering beyond the water, beyond the landmass of Europe, all the way to Czechoslovakia. 'Imagine growing up in a country where the sea is a fable, a fairy tale. We can only dream of it. Never see it or smell it.'

'It's lovely here. So peaceful.' She glanced shyly at him. 'It's lovely by the harbour at night.'

'Such a moment,' he said, equally shy. 'When I sat there last night, that was the first time I had been truly close. I see glimpses as we go about our ops, and on a ferry over from France. But to just sit still and watch it, listen to it in peace. The sound. That push and pull. It's like breathing.'

She loved to listen to his voice. She wanted to rest her head on his shoulder.

'Why are you quiet, Rose?' he asked. 'I am sorry I teased you. Sorry I asked you to kiss me. It wasn't correct of me, was it?'

Rose jolted, realising she hadn't minded at all. 'I'm just thinking . . . thinking about a lot of things.' She sighed. Her life had changed so much in the past few months. 'This is my first time away from home,' she said. 'Breaking my back on the farm, making friends with Meg the hard way. Overcoming my fear of horses.' She laughed. 'Oh, yes. I have come a long way. And here I am, my first morning off, after my first proper grown-up dance, larking about with a Czechoslovakian soldier I met only the night before. Who would have thought it?'

Krystof touched her face with his hand. '*I* would have thought it,' he said gently. 'It's your adventure, Rose. Your life. All these things are good things. Your new experiences. It's only just beginning.'

His touch surprised her; drew her to him. There was an unexpected warmth, a tugging in her belly and she found herself wanting to sink into the deep grey depths of his eyes. He enfolded her hands in his own—soft and strong—and leaned his face towards hers.

'Krystof!' she squealed, flinching back. 'I'm engaged to be married!'

He recoiled, looking at her in confusion, disappointment flickering through his eyes. 'I see. I did not know.' His voice was calm and serious. He looked down at her hand. 'But you're not wearing a ring. I assumed you were . . . not engaged. How silly of me.'

She twisted her fingers together on her lap. 'I'm sorry. So sorry. I lost the ring. I have been engaged a year,' she rattled on, desperate to explain. 'His name is Will. He is twelve years older than me. Friend of the family. But truth be told . . .' She felt peculiar, crushingly disloyal, but not to Will. She had deceived Krystof by coming here when she was promised to another man.

'Oh!' she cried with sudden bitterness. 'This bloody war! Three long years and it just keeps spreading. I just want it to end.'

'The war, Rose? The war?'

'Yes, of course the war. But also . . .' She looked at Krystof, knowing that he understood her. 'I left home because I wanted to do my bit. But really, I wanted to get away from *him*.' She looked at Krystof. 'You're right. I just want it to end.'

He turned his face away from her.

'Listen to me,' she muttered, ashamed, 'ranting on about my silly little worries.'

'We all have our own stories, our own troubles. It has been a long, hard journey for me to be sitting here, talking to you.'

Humbled, she asked, 'What happened to you, Krystof?'

He stared at the wire. And then he told her how angry he felt when the Germans invaded in March 1939 and Czechoslovakia fell, and Britain did not declare war but turned a blind eye.

'The Nazis took our uniforms and our dignity,' he said. 'They changed the map without asking anyone. I couldn't believe it when my commander surrendered, but it was orders from our government.'

'You were *ordered* to give up?' she asked.

'Yes, but a band of us from my regiment crossed the border to join the Polish army. When the Germans invaded in the September—and the war proper was declared—we headed off again while the borders were still open. We made it to Paris, crossed the Channel on a ferry, arrived in London. I went straight to the War Office to offer my services, and they stationed me with the US army.' He stopped to pick up a shell. 'Over the years, Rose, I have watched the Allied failures. The Sudetenland, Prague, Poland, Dunkirk, the fall of France. *That* was the worst day, wasn't it? But I was at victorious El-Alamein and now I see a change. We're getting stronger.'

'You've come through so much, Krystof. I feel ashamed at bombarding you with my so-called troubles.'

'I've come through so much, but now all I see is you.'

'What about *your* family? The people you left behind?'

'We live on a farm near a village, not far from Prague. We have a farmhouse there and a town house in the city. I can only guess that they are tolerating the Nazi regime. My country has been dismembered, but my family still has to run their farm. But I have no idea, really. I have no idea where, what . . . anything.'

'Nothing?'

'Only silence.'

Rose bit her lip. 'I'm sorry, Krystof.'

His voice brightened. 'I think that if I picture them there at the farm—my mother, father and brother, Tomas—then they *will* be there. They would love to know you, Rose. One day, perhaps, they will.'

She watched his face as he put his hand over hers and, again, felt the warmth of his body close to hers. She sighed and closed her eyes. She waited. This was their moment. Forget Will.

The moment passed and she opened her eyes. Of course, he didn't want to kiss her, not now he knew she was engaged.

But Krystof was peering over her shoulder, towards the top of the cliff behind them. 'There's someone there, watching us,' he said.

She stared towards the top of Trelewin cliff. The silhouette was unmistakable. 'Oh God, it's Will,' she cried. 'How did he know?'

'Will? Your fiancé Will?'

She felt inexplicable panic rising fast. 'We'd better go.'

'Why on earth, Rose? We have done nothing wrong.'

She looked at him. 'You wanted to kiss me, remember?'

'But I didn't.'

Rose wrung her hands. 'You stay here; I'll go up.'

Krystof looked at her. 'So I see. It was your day off. You were to meet him here anyway. You are playing with me. I am a fool.'

'No, not at all. I can't believe he's here. Oh, what shall I do?'

'All right, we go up the path together. We have nothing to hide. Why are you so agitated? Why are you so . . . frightened?'

'It's nothing. Nothing. Just the shock of seeing him here, and here I am enjoying myself with you—oh!' Her hands fluttered. 'The dogs?'

'Here, here they are.' Krystof's voice soothed through her panic. He bent to the animals and clipped on their leads. 'There, they are safe.'

She looked at him standing there, so generous, so calm. She knew that she loved him.

'Come on, Rose,' he said. 'I will escort you up the path.'

**W**ill's face was frozen. He did not say a word and yet his eyes spoke to her. They were hard, like Cornish granite. At his feet was set a hamper, which she recognised from home. It was her mother's.

'Will!' She tried to call gaily, but her mouth was dry. 'What a surprise! I had the morning off so I . . . I didn't know you were coming. How did you find the place? Did the bus conductor tell you?'

'I motored here and parked by the church.' Will's words were measured and even, his mouth a grim, set line. 'Used my precious petrol. Wanted to surprise you. Looks like I've had a bit of a surprise myself.'

Rose glanced at Krystof behind her, whose face was a picture of composure. 'Er, Will, this is . . .' she began.

Krystof interjected, 'Thank you for showing me the cove, Miss Rose.' He stood to attention and saluted. 'I bid you a very good morning.' He handed the dogs' leads to Rose, turned on his heel and marched off.

Will stared after him before picking up the hamper. He began to walk over the headland in the opposite direction to Krystof, towards Pengared. Rose, in confusion, felt obliged to step in beside him.

It was a long-drawn-out minute before Will spoke again. 'Showing Slovak conscripts the sights, are we?'

'He dropped by the farm. He's stationed nearby. He had never seen the sea.' She paused, feeling a sting of anger. 'And he is Czech, not Slovak.'

'Is he indeed?' Will stopped and looked down at her. 'Well, he can look at the sea all he wants. He doesn't need a female companion to join him. He does not need my fiancée to join him, does he?'

'He's a long way from home, he . . .'

'So he's lonely. A lot of people are these days. Just like my Wren was, out on the Hoe. But he's gone now, back to his barracks, no doubt. Just like my Wren. Long gone.'

He took her hand, and she bit her lip for his flesh felt cold compared to Krystof's. She mustn't think of him. She must concentrate on Will. This was her chance to face him and be strong.

'I have some news for you,' announced Will, suddenly bright and cheerful. 'That's why I came by today. I wanted to see for myself what draws you so strongly to this blessed, out-of-the-way corner of the country, and stops you coming home to visit your parents—and me. I wanted to see what prevents you from picking up a pen and writing to me. Once, it has been, Rose. Once in two whole months.'

'Will, I have been so busy. The farm . . .'

'Ha, I see that the Yanks are based nearby, with the other foreign soldiers, but I will skirt over that. And, yes'—he gave a perfunctory scan of the bay from their vantage point on the headland—'it is pretty enough here, but can't we do something about these blessed dogs?'

Mutt and Jeff were sniffing about the bottoms of Will's trousers.

'Here, give me the leads.' Will took the leads from Rose's hand and marched the dogs over to a fence where he promptly tied them up and left them there, straining and yelping in surprise. 'That's better,' said Will. 'Shall we sit?' He produced a blanket and shook it out over the grass. 'I thought we'd have a picnic, Rose. This is what folks do in the country, isn't it?' He unpacked a Thermos, some sandwiches wrapped in paper and two slices of cake. 'Your dear mother made this for us. And look here. Champagne!'

'Goodness,' said Rose. 'How did you get hold of that?' Then she caught his eye.

'Don't ask,' he said, knowingly. He popped the cork and splashed champagne into two tumblers.

'It's far too early in the morning for champagne,' she said.

'Not when you have something to celebrate,' he countered.

Confusion made her mute.

'Did you ever notice the old house over there?' Will persisted. 'Between those trees? Trelewin, is it?' He passed her a tumbler.

She found her voice. 'If you mean the house by the church, that's the Old Vicarage. It's derelict, I think.'

'Not so much of the derelict, if you please,' he said. 'I want us to celebrate, Rosebud. To put all our troubles behind us.' She saw him glance at the scar on her cheekbone and watched his eyes ineffectively shield his guilt. He said, 'I feel we are equal now, what with my little indiscretion and now yours . . . That old house?' He pointed back towards Trelewin. 'You'll never guess what. I've just bought it. For us. For you.'

Rose's head jerked forward. 'You what?'

'For you and me, my dear. Our marital home. Thank goodness for this war, I say, for I got it dirt cheap. Staff mortgages are such a good perk. The agent showed me round. One quick look was all I needed.' He got up, knelt by her. 'Your mother tells me you love this place, so I was thinking only of you.' His voice was like syrup. She thought she was going to be sick. 'We can get away from Plymouth, live a real country life. Visit your parents of a Sunday. Perfect.'

'Oh, Will no . . .' Her voice cracked with shock. She shook her head.

'And next weekend,' he blundered on, draining his glass of champagne, 'when you're home, we can tell your parents. Name the day. Make it official. Just look at you, Rosebud. Country air agrees with you. I can see a flush on your cheeks, a spark in your eyes.'

But her cheeks were crimson with embarrassment; the spark was unshed tears. She searched desperately for a way to tell him it was over, but how could she now? 'Will, I really don't think that—'

'Oh, do stop talking, Rose,' he said, 'and kiss me.'

'Will, I think you've drunk too much . . .'

'What rubbish. It's only a bit of champagne.' He leaned over her, his breath fired with alcohol. When she flinched away, he grabbed her hand to pull her back. He stopped. 'Where is it?' he asked, his voice cold again. 'Where's your ring?'

'Somewhere safe, in my bedroom,' she lied. 'You don't want me to lose it around the farm, do you?'

Irritated, he picked up the bottle and refilled his own tumbler.

'Have some more champagne, will you?' he snapped. 'You're cold as ice. Come and lie here!'

She flicked his hands away, stood up and brushed off her trousers. 'Really, Will.' She looked down at him. 'I think you're a little drunk. What would my parents say?'

'Oh, yes, mustn't upset the in-laws. I can't wait till next weekend,' he said. 'To see their faces when they know you'll be mine.'

Rose knelt by the hamper and put the picnic back in, tipping away the rest of the champagne. Panic made her fingers shake but inside she felt a hard core of reserve return. 'I'll show you the farm if you like,' she said.

'Oh, yes, Rosebud. The little farm.'

She felt proud as she opened the gate to the yard and shut it firmly behind them, letting the dogs off their leads. 'We have a small herd of Friesians. Over there, in the stable, is Blossom the mare.'

'Looks like that horse is ready for the knackers.'

She soldiered on. 'There's the apple orchard. The blossom was lovely. We have three pigs and a flock of smelly hens. And there, on that hill, is the crop of barley that I helped sow on my first day.'

He barely glanced at the field before fussing with his shoes, which were immersed in a muddy puddle. 'Bloody muck,' he mumbled.

Reluctantly, she said, 'Come into the kitchen and meet Betony. I'm sure we can have some tea.'

As she pushed open the kitchen door, she saw Betony slicing bread on the dresser, her back to the door. 'Well, Ginge,' Betony said, facing her shelf of white plates, 'and how was your walk with your young man? We were only just saying how nice and handsome he looked—'

Betony turned her head and her words failed. She peered beyond Rose's shoulder to the tall dark man behind her. 'Oh,' she said.

'Betony, I'd like you to meet my fiancé, Will Bowman.'

'Oh,' Betony said again.

Meg barged through the door from the stairs, calling, 'Ginge is back! She's back, she's back, with the man of her dreams!' The shocked silence that stilled the air inside the kitchen was broken eventually by Meg's giggling. 'And here *he* is! Pleased to meet you.' She held out her hand to shake Will's, her other hand keeping her dressing gown together. 'Please excuse me, I have been rather indisposed this morning. But it is lovely to meet you at last, Will Bowman. We've heard so much about you.' She flashed Rose a glare from her currant eyes. 'Give me a moment; I'll just fix myself up. Be right back.'

Will's confusion was modified by an unsightly leer as his eyes rolled over Meg's curves pushing at the folds of her dressing gown. 'No need to on my account,' he said.

'Tea anyone?' Betony squealed. 'Bread and butter?'

Will stared openly around the Cumberpatches' frugal kitchen. Rose watched him take in Betony's slender back as she bent to fetch some better crockery from the dresser, his eyes resting on her for far too long. Suddenly, he caught her looking at him and swiftly came to her side. 'We've been having a romantic time,' he gloated to Betony. 'A champagne picnic out on the headland. We're celebrating!'

Ted opened the back door and stomped his way in. Rose watched his face twitch in confusion as he walked forward automatically to shake Will's outstretched hand. 'Welcome to Pengared, Mr er . . .'

'It's Will,' insisted Betony. 'Will Bowman. It's Rose's fiancé.'

'Did I miss something? Did I hear you say you were celebrating?' asked Meg, coming back downstairs in her work clothes.

'Do you good people know the Old Vicarage at Trelewin? I've bought it. I and my lovely wife-to-be will soon be living there.'

'Jeepers, Ginge!' cried Meg, her voice loaded with meaning. 'I can't keep up with you!'

Rose stared at her, begging for some help.

'Well, our Ginge here is a dark horse,' said Ted gruffly.

'We'll be neighbours, my good man,' Will went on, 'and this little lady will no longer be a land-girl. No longer up to her elbows in all this muck. She'll be my wife. A banker's wife. How very grand.'

Rose's shoulders sank as the drowning sensation returned; the disappointment radiating from her three friends only added to her misery.

# Four

UPSTAIRS IN THE ATTIC, Rose dug her fingers into pockets and opened drawers. 'Oh, where is it? Where is it? Oh, Meg, I can't finish with him if I can't give him back the ring,' she wailed.

Meg rolled over on her bed. 'Yes, you can.' She peered at Rose through her dishevelled curls. 'You're not having second thoughts, Ginge?'

'It's just that he gets so *cross*. And I can't bear it.'

'You won't have to bear it for much longer if you tell him straight. He's not right for you. You're not in love with him.' Meg's gimlet eye bore right through her. 'I just want you to bear that thought in mind when you see him this weekend and tell him it's over once and for all. And that he can keep his stupid house. We all hated him, by the way.'

Rose ignored her. 'I'll just have to say I forgot it in my rush to get the bus.' She wrenched open yet another drawer.

'You've already looked in there,' said Meg. 'And off you go again, thinking of ways to explain yourself. Just tell him to get knotted.'

Rose snapped her suitcase shut. If only it was that easy.

'Are you ready now?' asked Meg. 'I'll walk over with you.'

Outside in the yard, as they lifted the suitcase over the gate they heard the clatter of a bicycle on the stony track. Skidding to a halt in front of them, the messenger, all of fifteen, hopped from the saddle. 'Telegram for Cumberpatch,' he announced.

'I'll take that,' said Meg. 'It's War Office. Official stamp, look.'

Rose followed her back over the gate. 'Heavens, Meg, you don't think it might be Hugh?'

'It most probably is.'

Crestfallen, they dragged their feet back into the kitchen. Betony's smile fell away as she saw their expressions.

'A telegram?' Betony choked on the word. 'God. No.'

She slit it open, her head shaking. 'I can see "Hugh" here . . .' She began to cry. 'But I can't read anything else. I can't . . . you know I can't.'

Rose stepped forward, her insides twisting. 'Here, give it to me.' Her hand juddered as she read the telegram in one breath. She sighed. 'He's fine, Betony. He's fine. It just says he's coming home. He has leave.'

'God damn it!' Betony cried. 'If only I didn't have to put myself through this every time.' She raced from the kitchen, calling, 'Ted!'

He must have heard from inside the barn for he came running. He gathered Betony tightly, pressing her to him, rubbing off her tears with his muddy hands.

Watching them, Rose felt jealous. Ted and Betony loved each other. She wanted what they had and she knew she'd never have it with Will. Her mind drifted to Krystof.

Meg dug her in the ribs. 'Come on, let's leave them to it.'

The bus rumbled across the bridge over the Tamar into Devon, leaving Cornwall and Pengared far behind. From her seat near the back Rose could see Plymouth spread out below her. Somewhere down there was the Anchor pub. The building had survived, that much she knew, but how much of her old life remained since that awful night?

Alighting at North Prospect, she walked along streets that no longer existed. Terraces of solid granite, built a hundred years ago, were as they should never be seen: with their guts hanging out, front doors dangling, possessions ragged and scattered. Rose felt sad that she was used to it. How *normal* the horror was these days. Rose's mother had told her that most people had been moved on, but she caught sight of a woman, hollow-eyed and stooping, washing her front step. Behind the doorway was a jumble of rubble and twisted joists, a dusty sofa and a battered bed; there was no house.

'Good afternoon.' The woman stopped her mopping. 'Post's still being delivered up and down here. I don't want to miss out on letters from my boy, do I? Postie's got to have somewhere nice to put them.'

Rose stared at the woman, who was nearly cross-eyed with fatigue. 'It does look nice,' she lied. 'You've done well to keep it so.'

What she wanted to say was that it looked pathetic and degrading. If this was the British bulldog spirit Mr Churchill was booming on about, then he could keep it.

'Can't be much longer, can it?' muttered the woman, bending to her filthy bucket. 'Then my boy will be home.'

'Let's hope so.' Rose walked on. 'Keep smiling through,' they all sang. Hope was so tenuous, she decided. But it was the only thing that kept them all going. She thought of Krystof and how far he had travelled to keep hope alive and suddenly a weight lifted from her shoulders.

She began her climb up the hill to St Budeaux and its leafy avenues of semidetached houses. And here she was: Stanley Crescent. Sight of the road sign lifted her with joy. Hope returned.

But first, there on the corner, was Brown's the grocer's shop.

She pushed the door and heard the familiar tinkling of the bell. All was quiet inside: Mr and Mrs Brown must be out back. The light was dim because they used oil lamps. Polished wood shelving reached to the ceiling, arranged with a meagre display of tinned food: National Household milk, oven-baked beans and custard powder. Mrs Brown liked to arrange her packets and tins in fancy patterns, so that Sunlight soap might sit alongside Woppa peas. Anything to brighten her, or her customers', mood these days, Mrs Brown would say. Potato Pete and Oxo advertisements on the wall advised Rose how to cheer up her vegetables, and subsequently, herself.

'Be with you in a moment,' Mrs Brown called from the back.

Rose breathed the warm smell of the shop and remembered her happy mornings here, checking ration books, weighing flour from the tub, slicing bacon and wrapping it in paper, carefully arranging packets of dried eggs in the window to emulate Mrs Brown's artistry.

'Rosie, my lovey.' Mrs Brown was an energetic woman with sparkling eyes behind horn-rimmed spectacles. She stepped forward to peck Rose's cheek, rubbing her hands down her white overall. 'Lovely to see you. Look at your flushed cheeks and your uniform. Ooh, you do look the part. Proper land-girl. Farm work doing you a power of good?'

'It is, Mrs Brown. I'm home just for the weekend. Thought I'd drop by on my way. How's Mr Brown?'

'Taken poorly. Nerves, poor devil.' Mrs Brown bit her lip. 'When North Prospect got the worst of it last time, I tell you, he'd had enough. He got blown to hell at Passchendaele, as you know, and now it's happening all over again. It's the noise he can't stand. He built the deepest Anderson in Plymouth in our back yard but he won't go in it. Reminds him of the trenches. Doesn't want to die like a rat in a hole.'

'Oh, Mrs Brown.'

'First time he's opened up in twenty years. It's brought it all home.' The shopkeeper paused. 'Listen to me go on. It's not as if we're the only ones, is it? And you, my Rosie, how have you been? Have you preferred being . . . away from it all?' Mrs Brown lowered her chin and stared at her over the top of her specs.

'In a way,' Rose said brightly, 'but I miss Mother and Dad. I—'

'What about being *away*?' Mrs Brown wanted her to understand.

'Yes, yes,' she said, understanding full well. 'Being away has helped.'

Mrs Brown's eyes shot to her left hand and they gleamed some more when they spotted the ringless finger.

Seeing her gaze, Rose lifted her voice. 'Now, what can I get Mother?'

Mrs Brown took her cue to bustle back behind the counter. 'There's not a lot here, lovey. But how about some carob?'

'Doesn't have quite the same ring to it as a nice box of Milk Tray, does it?' she laughed. 'Even so, I'll take it.'

'Two shillings, lovey, and I must say'—Mrs Brown pressed the change into her hand—'I'm so sorry for what I told you about Mr Bowman and the Wren on the Hoe. But I felt I had to—'

'Thank you, Mrs Brown.' Rose broke in to stop her. 'Everything is fine.'

As she strolled along Stanley Crescent, the pleasant scene of bay windows, tiled roofs and gables unfolded before her. She focused on the spot where her house would appear from within the curved street and averted her eyes from the reminders of war: white lines painted on lampposts, tape criss-crossing everyone's windows. At last, she saw her bedroom bay. She began to hurry and in one breathless moment she was standing at her own front door, with the small window above it depicting a ship in full sail, unaware of the tears streaming down her face. Home. She was home.

Suddenly she was gathered into the hallway by her father in his sleeveless sweater, and her mother in her apron, both crushing her tight.

'Where've you been, girl? Where've you been?' Mr Pepper growled. 'How are the yokels? How is that damn farm?'

'It's damn fine,' Rose laughed, brushing at her tears. 'They call me Ginge. I don't like it, really, but they *are* lovely.'

'*Ginge* indeed,' said Mrs Pepper, tapping her own red hair. 'I wouldn't have it if I were you. Your hair is new. Are you rolling it differently?'

'Meg taught me. Meg is the other land-girl.'

'Oh, yes, and what's she like?'

'Where do I start?' Rose laughed.

They walked through to the back parlour. 'Don't get too settled there at the farm,' said Mrs Pepper, trying to mask her trifling jealousy. 'This is home, remember.'

'How could I forget?' Rose's insides settled as she looked around the familiar room: the chairs by the tiled hearth, the standard lamp, the small curve-backed sofa. There was her mother's knitting basket and this week's copy of the *Radio Times* next to the radiogram.

'How long have you got?' asked her father, stepping towards the sideboard where he set out three tiny glasses. 'A toast, I think.'

'I've got today and tomorrow. I'd better get the last bus.'

'Well, we're going to make the absolute damn best of it,' said her father, bending over the cupboard to search for the sherry. 'And we've got a smashing dinner today, haven't we, Sylvia?'

'Oh, yes, Rose. Dad wrung Emily's neck specially.'

'Dad!'

He said, 'Well, she hadn't been laying well. And it is a special occasion, after all. Roast chicken, your favourite.'

Her mother said, 'And first-crop peas out of the garden. None of your tinned stuff. And Will is coming for tea.' Her eyes brightened. 'Then everything will be complete.'

An immense silence filled Rose's head. 'I'll just take my bag upstairs and get changed. I'll be back down for sherry.'

As she went upstairs and opened her bedroom door, her smile returned. How wonderful it was to be back there. Her bed was made up with fresh sheets and her pink satin eiderdown. Not a thing was out of place and she thought briefly of Meg and her mess. Meg was welcome to that attic room tonight. Setting her bag on the Lloyd Loom chair by the bed, she went to her wardrobe and took out her Sunday best dress with its pretty print and puffed sleeves. She took off her uniform and put her dress on. The silkiness of the fabric felt strange against her skin after the stiffness of her shirt and breeches. The bodice had tiny shell buttons all the way down and it fell in flattering pleats over her bust. She caught sight of herself in the mirror and decided to take the dress back to the farm with her. She wanted Krystof to see her wear it. Her heart began to tap delightedly at the thought of seeing him again.

'Rose,' called her mother up the stairs. 'Dad's found the sherry.'

'Hurry up, though,' he added. 'There's not much left.'

Sipping her thimbleful of sherry, Rose followed her father through the French windows and down the concrete steps.

'Look at my rose beds,' he said. 'Fine cabbage patch they make now. Cabbage roses, you could say—ha! And see the leeks and potatoes?'

She looked around the garden, which had once rambled with roses and hollyhocks and which, for three years now, had been turned over to vegetables, the chicken run and the great hump of the air-raid shelter right in the middle of the lawn. Mr Pepper had certainly dug it deep.

'I see you've managed to sow grass seed over the top of the Anderson, Dad,' she said. 'It'll make good camouflage.'

'Damn sure it will,' he said, glancing up at the sky. 'Sorry about Emily, Rose. But Jessica and Martha have lived to scratch another day.'

'Do you think they miss her?' Rose squatted down by the chicken coop to peer through the wire. 'Are they laying all right?'

'Not too well. Haven't had an egg in weeks.'

'I should have brought some from the farm,' said Rose. 'If only you'd told me the hens weren't laying.'

'I shouldn't complain,' her father went on, 'when so many people make such sacrifices, like those poor devils in the Atlantic.'

Mother emerged from the kitchen with a dab of flour on her face.

'Lunch won't be long.' She linked her arm through her daughter's. 'You do look well, Rose,' she said.

'It's all that good country air and good country cooking. Not that your cooking isn't—' Rose stopped herself as her mother's eyes filled with tears. 'Has it been tough here, these past few months?'

Her father cleared his throat. 'Yes, yes, it has. The raids just get you down. There's fewer of them now, though. Jerry's giving us a break.'

Rose was aware of her mother scrutinising her. 'Your scar hasn't faded, has it? What a dreadful night that was. I'll never forget it. We thought we'd lost you.'

Mr Pepper said, 'But thank goodness for Will.'

Her mother said, 'He'll always be my hero, the way he took care of you that night. He keeps me sane. He pops in here every other night on his ARP round, checking we're OK. Quick cup of tea and off he goes into the blackout. Like I said before, our hero. I can't wait for you two to be married. How happy I'll be.'

Rose saw the tiredness briefly lift from her mother's face and felt a thud of dread in her stomach.

It was a fine meal, Rose conceded: new potatoes roasted in chicken fat, peas from the garden and little pieces of Emily smothered in gravy.

'Here's the wish bone, Rose,' said her father.

Rose squeezed her eyes tight and tugged on the bone, thinking girlishly of Krystof, finding herself clutching the larger piece.

Her father said, 'Now your wish will come true.'

Her mother poured water into glasses. 'And I think we can guess what she wished for. We know how you feel about Will.'

Rose looked down at her plate. 'I'm sorry, Mother, Dad,' she said, her voice caught in her throat, 'but you don't know how I feel about Will. And neither does he.' She lifted her eyes fearfully. 'I don't love Will,' she said, louder, 'and I don't think I ever did.'

Abruptly the sound of eating stopped. Her father put down his knife and fork. 'What's this, Rose? What are you telling us?'

'I've met someone else,' she blurted, shocking herself with the utter joyful truth of it. 'He's a Czech soldier. He fought at El-Alamein. I met him at a dance. We've had just moments together, but he is—'

Her mother's cutlery crashed on to her plate. 'Oh, but Rose! *Someone else?* What about Will? How could you do this to him?'

'Now, Sylvia,' said her father, putting his hand on his wife's arm, 'let Rose speak. Let her tell us what's going on.'

Her mother roared, 'She doesn't know what's going on! Rose, you've just been taken in by the romance of it all. A brave soldier. Yes, I'm sure he's very nice. But Will? How could you? He's brave, too, and so dependable. After the war, what will happen to this Czech chap? He'll have to go back. He can't stay here. But Will will be here. You're a fool to let him go for some fly-by-night squaddy who'll be gone in a few weeks. Will is your future, your life. What are you *thinking?*'

Rose watched, aghast, as two angry spots of colour tinged her mother's pale cheeks. 'Mother, with respect,' she said, 'I have done nothing but think about this since I started at Pengared. It's not so much to do with the man I've just met. It's to do with Will and me—'

'I can't talk to you any more.' Her mother's voice lifted to a wail. 'Is this is how you want to be? A silly war bride? Don't you see . . .' She rounded on Rose. 'When there's a war on, you need something strong in your life? You can't do better than Will. He's even bought you that house over near your beloved Pengared! Think of all the poor girls who have no fiancé, no husband. Think yourself lucky!'

'Oh, Mother, I know I'm lucky.' Rose heard a shrieking edge to her own voice. 'I have a wonderful home here with you and Dad. But don't you see, you have both been plunging on pell-mell with the idea of Will and I getting married. You *love* the idea. It would make *your* wishes come true. But I don't love Will.'

'*Love!*' her mother spat the word into her hanky and stood up with a harsh scrape of chair legs over the parquet. '*Love!*' She left the room.

Rose felt as if all the air had been sucked out of the room. Did this mean her parents no longer loved each other?

Her father cleared his throat, then spoke wearily. 'Your mother is trying to protect you, Rose. She thinks the world of Will—'

'Doesn't she want *me* to be happy?'

'She wants you to be safe and content. Not chasing a dream which, let's face it, could be dashed and broken in an instant.'

'But how could she be so scathing about being in love? Is that it? Is that how it is with her?'

Her father's eyes narrowed. 'Oh, she loves—deeply. She tells me every time the sirens wail that she wishes she did not love us. The *both* of us. Because of the pain. The night you were caught in the raid on Devonport, she prayed for you. She believed you would be safe with Will, and she was right.'

Rose opened her mouth. She wanted her father to know the truth of what happened that night; she touched a shaking finger to the scar on her cheek. Then she looked at her father's earnest face and sank back.

His eyes were watery. He said, 'I think your mother's view is that if you don't love, then you won't get hurt.'

'Dad, I can't let this bloody war change my life . . . take over my life.'

'But it does. It did for me in the last lot. I came home broken. But when I met your mother, she transformed me.'

'Because she *loved* you.' A weary sigh escaped her. 'Oh, Dad, if only you met Krystof . . .'

Her father broke a smile. 'Ah, so he has a name.'

**R**ose tapped on her parents' bedroom door. 'Mother? Mother? Are you awake? I've brought you a cup of tea. Can I come in?'

Rose placed the cup and saucer and box of carob on the bedside table and sat gently down beside her mother, who was curled up on top of the candlewick bedspread. 'Did you sleep?'

'A little. What time is it?'

'Just after three.'

Her mother hauled herself up. 'What's this?'

'My gift to you, with my first wages.'

'That's lovely.' Her mother's voice was soft now. She took a sip of tea. 'What's he like then? Your brave Czech soldier?' There was a thin smile on her lips.

'I can't say he's *mine*, exactly,' Rose said shyly. 'As I told you, we've only had a short time together. But meeting him has made me realise that I don't want to be with Will.' She held her mother's stare. 'I'd love you and Dad to meet him. He is Captain Krystof Novotny, now stationed with the Americans near Polperro.' She felt her voice lift with pride. 'He was in the Czech army, but left when Germany invaded—'

'No, no. Not his potted history,' her mother interrupted. 'I'll hear that another time. I want you to tell me about *Krystof*.'

Rose faltered. How could she explain to her mother that when she looked into his eyes, she *recognised* him; that she saw herself there?

She wanted to tell her mother: he is a wonderful sportsman, someone I can trust, someone I can talk to, someone who makes me laugh. But she could not, for she did not know these things. But she *knew* him.

'Mother, I don't know him—I just *feel* . . . '

Her mother leaned back against her pillows. 'We were blind, I suppose. About Will. We wanted the best for you, our lovely Rose. I truly hope you will be happy. I truly hope your captain will make you happy.'

'Will you give me your blessing?'

'I will. But put Will out of his misery. He's expected at four. Your father and I will take a walk. To be honest with you, after all this upset, I don't think I can look him in the eye.'

**R**ose heard Will's knock at the door. There he stood, with his trilby shading his eyes, holding a bunch of roses as if he were a matinée idol. Her mouth went dry.

'Ah, Rosebud. Hello, my love.' He beamed. 'May I?' He planted a peck on her cheek, then stepped past her to tuck his hat onto a coat hook before marching off down the hall, calling, 'Hello, George. Hello, Sylvia.'

'My parents are not at home,' she said, reluctant to close the door now that he was standing in the hallway, filling it up.

'Oh? So I've got you all alone? Clever little Rosebud.' He moved back towards her, proffering the flowers. 'Roses for my Rosebud. I can't tell you what lengths I went to, but ask no questions . . .' He cocked his head, waiting for praise.

'They're lovely.' She uttered a perfunctory response. 'I'll get a vase.'

'Not just yet.' Will took the flowers back from her and tossed them onto the sofa. He caught her hands; his eyes danced over her face and down her body and she cringed under his gaze.

'Now, Rosebud,' he said gravely, 'I have a lot of apologies to make to you. Our little picnic last weekend was not a complete success.' He sighed dramatically. 'I was jealous of your Slovak because I love you—'

'Will, I—' She lifted her eyes to his face. A strange grin fixed his jaw. Fear coiled inside her chest. 'I'll just make some tea.'

His face dropped and he held up her left hand, peering at it in an exaggerated fashion. 'Still no ring?'

'Silly me. I took it off last night for my bath, put it somewhere safe. In my rush this morning, I must have forgotten it.'

'Silly Rosebud. Did you say something about tea?'

She found she could breathe again. 'Yes, yes. You sit down.'

'No, I'll help you. I'll put the flowers in water.'

Confused by this uncharacteristic offer to help, she found him a vase in the sideboard and went into the kitchen. Will was right behind her. She gave him the vase and turned to light a flame under the kettle.

'Forget the flowers,' he said, dumping them on the kitchen table this time, 'it's you I want.' He stood close behind her, his hands on her hips. She felt his hot breath all over her hair. 'I hope you're pleased with the house,' he whispered. 'We'll arrange for you to look round before long. As soon as you can stop that silly work at the farm, we can be married, make it our home.'

'It's rather a large house,' she muttered, flinching away from him. She could not face him. 'Will, I'm not sure. I want to tell you . . . I . . .'

'Such a pretty dress,' he said. 'I always liked you in it.' He ran his knuckle up her spine and rested it on the nape of her neck, then lifted her hair to plant a kiss behind her ear.

'Stop it! Please, Will. Not now.' She turned to face him.

'Come on, Rosebud, we've made up now. We can put all those things behind us.'

She gritted her teeth. 'I can't put the night of the raid behind us.'

He ignored her. 'Here we are, with the house to ourselves. Don't tell me you didn't plan this. Persuaded your parents to go out, so we could be alone. I knew you'd surprise me one day. Little minx.'

Anger flashed like searchlights from her eyes. 'How dare you say that! It was my parents' idea that they go out because they know I have something I wish to say to you.'

'Not the Wren again. I thought we'd got over that.' He pressed his thumb to her scar. 'I thought we were even, Rosebud.'

She gritted her teeth. 'Please don't call me that.'

'What does *he* call you then? Your little Slovak.'

'Nothing. He doesn't . . . He's not . . .' She trailed off, biting her lip.

'Those country folk,' he said. 'That Meg girl. They all knew, didn't they? They all knew about your fancy man. What a fool I am.' He rested the weight of his hands on her shoulders. 'You and me, Rosebud,' he said. 'There's nothing that can beat us. No silly Wren. No silly Slovak. They're both passing fancies. Let's put it all behind us.'

His body loomed over her. Will's strength was like a wall she could not climb. She felt rage, a need to defend herself. She wanted to be free. Why had she let it go this far? She reached up to her shoulders to push his hands away. He resisted and then she saw him look into her eyes.

'You are so cold, Rosebud,' he said. 'I've always thought it. Frigid.'

'Will,' she said, 'I have been trying to tell you for so long. I do not love you. I am breaking off our engagement. I want you to leave.'

His eyes narrowed to two pinpricks. 'We've been here before, haven't we?' he leered. 'You tried this in the pub back in January.'

'This time, Will, it's real.'

'Why the sudden change?' He suddenly sounded weaker.

She braced herself. 'No change. I have never loved you.'

There was silence. Then a sharp intake of breath. Without a word he picked up the flowers on the kitchen table and thrust them at her. As she lifted her arms to shield her face from the thorns and stems, he yelled in anger, slung the roses to the floor and crushed them under his heel. She crouched down as he loomed above her. He bent over and held her shoulders like a vice, his tortured breathing spluttering over her. 'How dare you,' he snarled. 'After everything I have done.'

A sudden shriek pierced the air, like a screaming, scalded cat. He released her and backed away. She slid to the kitchen floor and instinctively curled up, trembling with terror as the screaming persisted. 'A raid?' she whispered. 'Is it a raid?'

He leaned over her again. 'You silly, silly girl.'

She garnered dignity to hiss at him, 'Get out.'

He walked away, down the hall, slamming the front door behind him as he left.

After some moments, Rose pulled herself up, shaking, her head still full of the wailing. She gingerly lifted her eyes to glance towards the hob. There was no raid. The kettle was just about to blow its top.

She slept in her bedroom, curled up on her eiderdown. When she finally woke, she could hear the rattle of the grate. Her parents were home. It was teatime.

Later, she sat in the parlour next to the wireless. The French windows were wide open to the June evening and the dusk light was soft and pure. Her father flicked through the *Radio Times* and turned to the Light Programme.

'It's that lovely Glenn Miller,' sighed her mother, closing her eyes.

'What a beautiful evening,' Rose said. 'I wish it would never end.'

'It must, of course,' said her father, catching her eye. 'I'm glad to see you looking so happy. I hope all is well.'

'All is well, Dad.'

She didn't want to say any more. She didn't have to.

Later, Rose fell into bed and hugged her pillow, willing herself back to Pengared, and to Krystof.

# Five

WITHOUT HESITATING, Rose stooped to Blossom's grazing mouth and hooked the leading rein onto the harness. 'Not so much of a *night*-mare now, are you?' she told the horse. 'You old softy.' Shadows were melting from the corners of the pasture as the short summer night evaporated into dawn. 'Walk on, old girl.'

Voices reached her from Betony's meadow as she made her way down the bridleway. Long grass billowed over a good four acres, sprinkled with a mosaic of buttercups, daisies and the ubiquitous purple betony. Tiny waking butterflies fluttered and, under the hedge, blackbirds hopped for worms. Over in the corner, Joel was sharing a cigarette with Meg, while Ted, oiling his mowing machine, gave her a welcome salute.

She helped Meg harness the horse to Ted's cutter, speaking deeply into Blossom's velvety ears, which were pricking this way and that.

'Who's she seen, then?' Meg looked over her shoulder. 'I don't wish to make a bad joke, Ginge, but It's That Man Again.'

'What? Oh, goodness. Krystof.'

He was ambling across the meadow, knee-deep in wavering grasses.

Ted called out to him, 'Good of you to help out, Captain Novotny! We need all the hands we can get today, but don't you go distracting any of my workers here.'

Rose felt herself blushing furiously as she caught Krystof's eye. Suddenly, overwhelmingly, she was shy of him. It had been two weeks since their walk to the cove, and so much had changed. She felt her life was starting over. And now that he was unexpectedly here, in Betony's meadow, possibilities opened before her like a long, wide valley.

Krystof smiled, equally shyly, and said to Ted, 'Good morning, sir. I told my commander, haymaking is war work. He gave me a day pass.'

'Good morning.' Meg bounded over to Krystof, all smiles. 'Here, tie this string round your trousers. You too, Ginge.'

Krystof asked, 'What is this for?'

'Stops the mice climbing up your legs,' Meg trilled. 'They're driven mad by the cutter as it gets nearer and nearer them in the long grass. Then, whoop, up they go. A safe haven, so they think. Worse are the rats. Could give you a nasty nip or two.'

Catching one another's eye, Rose and Krystof duly bent in unison to tie the string just below their knees. She felt a giggle rise in her chest and glanced at him. His shoulders were shaking as he tried not to laugh, all thumbs as he fumbled with the string.

'Sounds like a Gestapo torture method to me,' she chuckled.

'It hardly bears thinking about.' She felt his fingertips on her arm. 'It's good to see you again, English Rose,' he said.

Ted called, 'Right, you lot! You, Joel, keep Blossom's head straight. Make sure she keeps a steady line. You three, start raking behind the mower. Meg, your extra task is to keep us all fed and watered.'

'And what will *you* be doing, Ted?' Meg teased.

'Well, I'll be in the driving seat, of course. Like I always am.' He sat himself on the little seat of the cutter perched above the blades between the two spindly wheels and took up the slack on the reins. 'Right, last time for Betony's meadow. Get up there!'

Blossom's harness jangled as she plodded forward and the clack-clacking of the mower began.

Meg handed Krystof and Rose a rake each.

'What did he mean by "last time"?' asked Krystof.

'Orders from the Min of Ag,' said Meg. 'The meadow is to be ploughed for sugar beet or turnip next spring. Need to feed people, more than animals.'

'But it hasn't been ploughed for four hundred years,' said Rose. 'What about the cows? They need to be fed.'

'Not if they're dead they won't. Next spring, slaughterhouse for the lot of them.'

On the hillside, Ted's gentle, black and white cows lowered their heads to pasture. So much was expendable, thought Rose. So much lost. Animals. People. Expendable.

Meg was watching. 'Don't go all misty on me, Ginge. Come on.'

Standing alongside Krystof, she began to swing the wide head of the rake over piles of grass that had fallen in the cutter's wake. She relaxed, breathing the green-scented balmy air. She absorbed the perfection of the day, caught in a capsule of time, watching Krystof surreptitiously out of the corner of her eye as he concentrated on raking and turning the cuttings. Piece by piece, Betony's meadow fell.

'How many days' work do you think, Captain?' called Ted.

'Two, I'd say.' Krystof stopped to rub his back and flex his fingers.

'You know your farming, sir, don't you?'

'I have a farm in Czechoslovakia!' he called back.

'Need to get a crack on!' cried Ted. 'Won't be many more days like this left.'

Something in Ted's tone made Rose stare after him. 'He doesn't just mean the fair weather, does he?' she said to Krystof. 'He means the end of a way of life. In so many ways.'

'But a new beginning also,' smiled Krystof. 'Change is good, remember.' He came near her and put his hand on her waist. 'Is everything all right, Rose?'

She gazed at his face, nodding slowly, aware of the firm warmth of his hand through her cotton shirt. 'Yes. Indeed it is,' she said.

She was solemn, hoping that he understood. She looked into his eyes, as the air once again filled with chaff and petals. The scent of the earth, the work of the day, filled her body with satisfying vibrations.

Sensing his sorrow, she said, 'Your farm will still be there.'

'You're right. The Germans still need hay and cattle, so it will be. And one day you will see it, Rose.'

'I'd love to,' she whispered.

His kiss was so light, like a feather on her lips.

Meg called out, 'Oi, you two. No slacking!'

Ted reined Blossom in on the stroke of twelve and they all rested by the hedge, knowing that Betony was on her way with the lunch pail and a flask of tea. Meg spotted her near the gate. 'Yoo-hoo! Over here! We're parched and starving.' Then she jumped up to attention, shielding her eyes. 'My, my. *Hello*, soldier!'

Rose squinted to see Betony strolling into the meadow cradling a milky-skinned Mo. With her was a man in khaki.

'Dear Christ! It's Hugh!' cried Ted. He greeted his brother in an enormous embrace.

'How wonderful,' Rose breathed.

'Indeed it is,' said Meg. 'How do I look, Ginge?'

'Fine, Meg,' she said, appraising the wild curls escaping her friend's topknotted scarf and her dungarees cinched tightly in at the waist and clinging to her rounded bottom. 'You're bound to be a hit.'

Meg laughed and licked the corner of her hanky to wipe her face.

Hugh Cumberpatch was a younger version of Ted, a little taller and a little leaner. His face had been tanned by the Tunisian sun, making his smile brighter than anyone else's, yet his eyes looked tired and dazed. He strolled over and saluted Krystof, instantly recognising rank.

'So you're with the Americans, then, sir?'

'For my sins, Sergeant,' said Krystof. 'They're a good bunch. A brave lot. Seems like there is a bottomless well of new recruits waiting to swell the ranks. It's good to know you've got that behind you.'

'That's enough war talk,' Betony snapped.

'Sorry, Bet. God, I've missed you.' Hugh hugged her.

Betony poured tea and began to hand round doorstep sandwiches.

Hugh was fumbling in his top pocket. 'Before I forget. Rose Pepper? I have a letter for you. I checked the postbox on my way.'

She took the letter. It was from her mother.

'I'm Meg Wilson, by the way,' chimed in Meg, leaning forward to shake Hugh's hand.

Rose slit open the letter. Her mother wrote:

*Dad and I are both well . . . Jessica and Martha are laying again . . . Mr Brown has been taken away in an ambulance . . . Will has visited; he's not himself, fairly distraught. But he's bravely trying to forget you . . . Will is a good man. I do hope you will be happy with your soldier. Please visit us once the harvest is done with.*

Rose folded the letter away.

Hugh said, 'Midday on the first day, Ted? We'll have to do better than this. I'm going to fetch out my old scythe from the barn. See if I can't help you out a bit.'

Meg squealed, 'I'll come with you,' and trotted after him.

Ted held back until they were both well out of earshot before saying, 'Well, he has been in North Africa for a year.'

Joel, lazing quietly over by the hedge, began to chuckle.

**A**t five o'clock, with the sun slanted long and golden across the meadow, Ted surveyed the work. 'Good job, everybody,' he said.

'I'll finish the last square by hand,' said Hugh, brandishing his scythe.

'We'll take Blossom back,' said Rose.

Krystof joined her to lead the weary horse up the hill to the pasture. Rose let Blossom canter off and watched her dip her long head and fall gracefully to her knees, rolling on her back to scratch away the ghost of the harness, grunting with pleasure.

She scooped her hand into Krystof's. 'Would you like to walk to the cove?'

They strolled down the bridleway, hand in hand. The pressing of his flesh against hers was right and good. Her excitement began to bubble.

'What's this place?' he asked, pointing to Cringle Cottage, nestled in the crook of the valley.

'That's the old gamekeeper's cottage,' she said. 'It's empty.'

'It would make a lovely place to live in peacetime when all this is over,' said Krystof. 'What do you think, Ruzena?'

'Ruzena?' she asked.

'Yes,' he said. 'Everyone else seems to call you anything but your real name so I thought I'd try. *Ruzena* is Czech for Rose.'

'I like it,' she said. 'Better than Ginge.'

As they passed by the house, she said, 'Do you mind awfully if I change? I want to stop being a land-girl for a few hours.'

Up in the attic room, she stripped off her work clothes. Pouring water into the bowl, she splashed her naked skin to wash away the toils of the day. Outside her window she saw Krystof holding his head under a torrent of water from the pump.

Clean and refreshed, she put on the dress with the pearl buttons.

Drowsy, but light-footed and a little frisky, she walked by Krystof's side over the headland and down the steep, shady path to Trelewin cove. They slipped off their shoes and ran barefoot across the baked sand to their rock. They rested in silence, enjoying the peace. Beyond the wire, the water shimmered like a million diamonds.

'You will love Praha—Prague,' said Krystof.

'Tell me all about it.'

She got down from the rock and stretched out on the dry sand. It gave way like a feather bed. He joined her and she rested her head against his crooked arm, looking up at the sky.

'Before all of this, before all of this *war*, our country was a beautiful republic. It was a golden era. Such prosperity. We Czechs love our land.' She listened to him drop his consonants, making his 's's sound like 'v's. He chuckled. 'We Czechs love our land-girls. They appear on posters advertising beer and on biscuit tins, with rosy cheeks, frothing tankards and wheat sheaves.' She felt him pause to think. 'But now, who knows what's become of them all? I can't bear to think of jackboots tramping through our countryside, tramping across the Old Town Square.'

She gripped his hand and pressed it to her lips.

He said, with bitterness, 'The enemy is too big, too vile for me to deal with on my own. So much sacrifice,' he went on, except there was no 'c'. 'So much *sacrif-y*. And what for, Rose?'

Suddenly, she was angry. 'For you and me, Krystof, and for our families. Don't give up. I need you to be strong, and then I can be.'

'Brave Rose,' he said, gazing at her.

His kiss found her mouth, and she folded her body against his, taken aback by the rushing in her head.

'Goodness,' she breathed.

Krystof gathered her hands together, planting kisses all over her face. She felt the delicious weight of his body on hers, the delightful brushing of his lips down her neck.

Presently he said, 'I can be brave if you are. I can go on, if you can.'

'We'll see it through,' she whispered.

'We, Ruzena?'

'Yes, we.'

'Are you truly'—he dipped his head shyly—'*free*?'

'I am,' she said, understanding him without him having to say another word. 'It's over. I told him.' She smiled at Krystof's happiness. 'And,' she went on, 'Mother wants me to visit after the harvest. Will you come too? I want you to meet them. I want them to meet you.'

He sat up and held her close. 'If I can get a pass, of course I will come. But everything is tightening up. We are to start training. Mock battles on Dartmoor. It's leading to something. Oh, I shouldn't be telling you this, but I have to share everything with you, Ruzena.'

She felt tears sting her eyes. 'Don't tell me, Krystof, I don't want to know.' She sat up and let him rest his head on her lap.

'Time I was back at base,' Krystof said, reluctance dragging his words.

They stopped at the gate to the farm, watching Mutt and Jeff bounding over to greet them.

With a catch in her voice, Rose asked, 'When will we see each other?'

'Soon. I'll tell my commander that there's a harvest to bring home.'

He wrapped his arms round her and she felt his heart beating. They held onto each other. There was no need to speak.

Eventually he glanced over her shoulder. 'I know you don't want to hear bad news, so do you want to hear something funny instead?'

She pulled back to study his face. He was grinning. 'Always,' she said. 'Look behind you.'

Across the yard, Hugh was gingerly opening the barn door. Glancing left and right, he gesticulated into the darkness behind him. Out came Meg, tugging at her belt buckle, tufts of straw clinging treacherously to her curls. They both trotted off in different directions.

'Oh, Meg Wilson,' tutted Rose.

Krystof laughed. 'Oh, Sergeant Cumberpatch.'

Rose was wrapping up the first crop of apples in newspaper when she heard—and felt—the rumbling. The ground beneath her feet vibrated and the misted pane of glass in the shed window rattled. Ducking outside into the yard, she spotted a convoy of heavy khaki trucks, their canvas roofs flapping, swaying along the top road.

'If I'm not wrong that's Fourth Division, Ginge,' called out Ted. 'On manoeuvres, as they say. Wonder where they're off to?'

She squinted to the brow of the hill, seeing the familiar US army star on the door of a truck. 'I wonder,' she said, shielding her eyes from the low September sun. She swallowed hard. What about Krystof's division? A coil of fear plummeted through her.

She and Krystof had barely seen each other since the day of the haymaking; just snatched, precious moments over a long, hard summer of toil. This bothered her and her mother's words echoed: 'Fly-by-night squaddie.' But Rose resolutely ignored them. Tomorrow they were going to spend the day at home with her parents; and then her mother would see how it really was.

Rose turned her puzzled face to Ted. 'I wonder what's going on?'

'Perhaps this man can tell us,' said Ted, looking behind her.

Silhouetted against the sunlight was a familiar figure.

'Krystof!' she cried, running over to him. She hugged him, pressing her face into his uniform. 'You're a day early. My day off is tomorrow. I doubt Ted will let me go today, there's too much work to do . . . What, Krystof? What is it?'

He would not look at her. 'I have eighteen hours.'

'Until what?' Her voice gurgled in her throat.

'Until I go. The leave I had authorised for tomorrow has now been brought forward to today. Today is my embarkation leave. This is it.'

She had no idea she was crying until she felt his fingertips gently wipe away her tears. She heard a footstep behind her.

'Ted?' she asked, turning to face her employer.

'Don't even ask me,' he said. 'Just go.'

Krystof had parked his staff car on the top road.

'Come on, Ruzena. I'll take you for a spin.' He tried to sound cheery, but she heard a new tone in his voice.

The main road was congested with army traffic so they motored down the twisting tunnel of back lanes to Polperro. Raucous squaddies packed the village pub. Krystof brought their shandies out to the sea wall where they had first met. They sat with their back to the sun-warmed granite and listened to the slap of the waves below them. She tasted her drink and it was bitter.

'We can have some ice cream soon,' he said.

'I don't want ice cream.' Rose bristled, feeling a torrid mix of despair and frustration grinding through her head. Each moment that passed took them closer to his departure.

Krystof sighed deeply, gazing around the busy little harbour. 'This is where it all began,' he said. 'But, Rose . . . No, look at me, I said look at me. This is not where it ends.'

She glared at him, then admitted, 'Krystof, I'm scared.'

'It is a shame that I cannot meet your parents tomorrow,' he said. 'I have to leave at dawn.'

'Well, I'm not going to go home now,' she snapped. 'Ted won't give me more time off.'

'Surely he will let you have one more day. They're expecting you.'

'I can't go. I don't want to. They'll say . . . *I told you so.* There—it's horrible, but they will. I'll have to tell them you've gone. I can't bear it.'

'Wire them, at least,' he said. 'Tell them you can't get the time off.'

'I'll tell them it's war work. Not that I swapped my day off to spend it with you. They wouldn't understand.'

They fell silent in mutual misery.

'This was not a good idea, coming here to Polperro,' muttered Krystof, looking around him. 'It's too crowded.'

'They've all got the same idea,' she said, her voice jaded and sad. 'They're all snatching their moments. Look, there's that girl. What's her name? Mabel. She's with a squaddie boyfriend, looks like.'

She pointed out Mabel Brown, the girl from the dance, sitting in the beer garden, her yellow hair glowing amongst a sea of khaki.

'Oh!' said Krystof, peering over. 'She's with Vaclav. He's in my company. He's from Moravia. Hey, Vaclav!'

The soldier looked over and waved and Mabel, on seeing Rose, gave a giggling salute, clutching his arm.

'Isn't it so sad,' she sighed. 'They're all going.'

Rose looked at Krystof. She whispered, 'I can't bear it here.'

'We both know where we want to be,' he said. 'The cove.'

She popped into the post office and quickly sent a telegram home. 'I'll go home soon,' she promised herself. 'I'll make it up to them.'

They lay on his jacket on the sand by their rock. His arms formed a shield around her but, even so, the dangerous outside world kept crashing into her thoughts. Her throat quivered with suppressed rage as she looked up at his face.

The wind was rising. Drops of blown rain and sea spray peppered the sand and yet the sun still cast a mellow light.

'Summer is over,' she said. 'Our glorious summer is over.'

'This should be a beautiful time,' said Krystof. 'September—our Zárí—is "the month that glows with colour". Did you notice the leaves in the hedgerows? How they are beginning to turn?'

'The way you speak, it's so beautiful,' she said. 'But I want it to be summer again. Not September, the autumn. Always our summer.'

He held her tightly and pressed his face to her neck. 'How can this be?' he asked, his voice muffled and broken. 'How can the war be like this when you are here with me. And I am here with you. I love you, Rose. I cannot leave you.'

She shuffled around so she could look at him, holding his lovely face in her hands, feeling her own strength rise as his faded. 'You won't leave me. You'll never leave my side. Not while you are loved by me.'

'How can I go out there and shoot a man dead?' he cried. 'I can't do that when I have held something as beautiful as you in my arms.'

In her head, her voice said, But you will have to.

She stopped him speaking with a kiss that took her own breath away.

'I love you, Krystof,' she said when at last he allowed her to pull away, 'and I will wait for you. I will wait for that day when you come strolling back to Pengared Farm, and climb over that silly locked gate, with Mutt and Jeff yapping around your ankles. I will be waiting.'

The sun was sinking into an inky sea as they made their way back up to the farm. The blackout was already down in Trelewin.

She sat on the top of the stile and gazed down at his face. A surge of courage pulsed through her veins. 'I want to be alone with you, tonight. We still have the night. You don't have to be back at base till dawn.'

'Oh, Ruzena . . . are you sure?'

They strolled back along the rutted track. 'I want to tell you something. Will once invited me up to London, and suggested we stay at the Ritz. I was horrified, worried what my parents would think. And, quite frankly, it made me feel sick. But now, with you, it is a whole new world, a whole new feeling. To be honest, I don't care any more what my parents think about you and me. And I wish we could have the Ritz.' They had reached the gate and began to climb over. 'But, Krystof, what I am trying to say is, we have the barn,' she said.

'Do you think we will get straw in our hair?' he asked.

They laughed gently, leaning forward to touch foreheads.

'Wait here a moment,' she said. 'I need to fetch something.'

Rose went upstairs and pulled the blanket from her bed.

Downstairs in the kitchen she wrapped bread and cheese in a tea towel and cut a large slice of apple pie. Betony, making her first batch of jam with plums from the orchard, watched her in silence. Mo gurgled from his high chair.

'Take this,' said Betony, handing Rose a bottle of her elderberry wine.

'Are you sure?'

'Are *you* sure?'

Rose told her, 'Never been more so in my whole life.'

She found Krystof waiting for her in the hayloft high up under the rafters where the last of the sun spun threads of gold through gaps in the roof tiles. She breathed the earthy fragrance of grain and wood, the freshness of new hay, and the scent of Krystof's skin. She left him to open the bundle of food while she began to arrange some straw bales and covered them with the blanket.

He watched her closely for a moment, then cleared his throat.

'Ruzena, we will not be lovers tonight,' he said.

She paused and glanced round. His face in the shadows was soft with love and an unusually deep contentment settled within her. She knew he was right, and it pleased her.

He went on. 'I don't want us to be like Hugh and Meg. I want it to be right. I think we should wait. I think we should be married. What do you say to that, Rose?'

Her hands shook as she pulled the cork from the wine. 'I am lost for words. It's like a dream.'

'But do you want to?' He sounded worried.

Rose sat close to him, cross-legged on the floor. 'More than you'll ever know,' she whispered, her heart pounding. 'Let's drink to us.'

He took a swig from the bottle and then handed it to her. '*Na zdraví.* Cheers, my Rose.'

'You need to ask my father's permission,' she said.

'Can we use Ted's telephone?'

'Oh, the line isn't working. It's been down for days,' she said in frustration. 'Nothing is ever straightforward, is it? But when I next go home—soon, I hope—I'll tell them the news. Can we get a special licence? What do people do in these circumstances? Can you get special leave?'

'I cannot answer your questions. But I will try my best to get something arranged,' he said.

She whispered, 'I can't believe you won't be here tomorrow.'

'I'll be *somewhere*,' he whispered back. 'Dartmoor or Salisbury Plain . . . but always with you.'

In silence, in the warm loft, they drank the sweet wine and ate the bread and cheese. When the bottle was finished, the laughter began. And when her tears began to flow, he stopped them with a look. Tears were replaced by more laughter, deeper and warmer than before.

As chilly midnight approached, she grew tired and sank into the hay bed next to his warm body. 'I can hear stars singing,' she whispered sleepily.

'We will watch the stars in Czechoslovakia. The night skies are clear and wide on my farm,' he told her. 'I will take you there. You will meet my family, my cows, my horses.' He pushed her hair behind her ears. 'How are you going to manage, leaving your parents behind?'

She thought of her home, her parlour, her parents sitting alone; she wrapped up that image and stowed it away. 'But *we* will be a family.'

Gradually the night shadows shifted and a grey dawn crept over them. She slept for just one hour inside his arms; a twitchy, nervous sleep. She felt his lips pressed to her forehead the whole time, his arms like a great cradle.

And then, as the sun inevitably rose, he pulled himself away from her. With no word, he put on his boots and jacket. He was being ripped from her. She tried her best to smile through her silent tears.

# Six

THE COLD WOKE HER. She did not hear the siren wailing over the headland from Trelewin; it only reached them at Pengared if the wind blew in their direction. Her dream had been of Krystof: a month had passed since he left, and she'd had one letter. He could tell her nothing of where he was, or what he was doing. The letter was short, but laced through with love. Whole sentences were blocked out by the censor's pen. She had cried when she read it, great fat tears of frustration. Now she stood in Meg's shoes; now she knew what it felt like to have someone 'out there' amid the excruciating uncertainty and looming danger. Her mother was right about not wanting to love. It hurt too much.

Rose shivered on the landing with Meg, staring out of the window into the night. The horizon towards Plymouth was red with flame. Meg put her arm round her shoulder. 'Come on, Ginge, it will be fine. Let's get to the cellar and make Ted heat us some warm milk.'

Huddled in the darkness, Rose imagined her parents sheltering in their Anderson and a twinge of guilt twisted her gut. She still had not been to visit them. With the end of the harvest, work was frantic.

In the morning, dazed and sleepy, she sat at the kitchen table to sip her cup of tea. She thought about the day ahead and felt weary: she had to see to the hens, turn the apples in storage, sweep the yard. Each raid became more difficult to bear and she felt her spirit washing away. When would it ever end? When would she see Krystof again?

'Oh, my goodness,' Betony exclaimed, stopping by the trap door to the cellar. She bent down to pick something up. 'Goodness gracious.'

Rose turned to catch sight of her engagement ring held delicately aloft between Betony's fingertips. 'You've found it?' She was amazed. 'Good God!'

'It was there, stuck between the floorboards all the time, Ginge.'

Betony handed her the ring, then turned towards the sound of rattling bicycle wheels along the track. Rose, fearfully following her gaze to the kitchen window, wrung her hands together. On reflex, she slipped the ring onto her finger.

In the yard Ted called out, 'Ho there!' and then Rose heard his long strides across the yard. There was a snatch of conversation between farmer and messenger. Betony kept herself pressed against the table and Meg was still upstairs, so Rose felt it was her duty to go to the back door and ask Ted who the telegram was for. She stood on the kitchen step, feeling the chill of the October morning on her hands and the tip of her nose. Ted was walking towards her, his face unreadable.

'What, Ted?' she asked. 'What is it?'

'You know a Mrs Brown?'

'Yes, the corner shop. Oh, dear. Poor Mr Brown. Has he succumbed?'

'I don't know about that, Rose.'

She flinched in shock and fixed her eyes on Ted. *Rose?* He'd called her Rose.

Betony was at her elbow. 'Get her inside.'

She let herself be led back into the kitchen, and she allowed them to seat her at the table. Suddenly irritated, Rose snatched the telegram from his hand and unfolded it. *House destroyed. Stop. Come home. Stop. Marion Brown. Stop.*

'Whatever does she mean?' she said to Ted and Betony. 'Why does she want me to go home? Has something happened to Mr Brown?' She looked up at Ted and Betony. 'Why would Mrs Brown want me to—' She felt her face stretching and tingling, as if a mask was being laid over it to shield her from the two faces that filled her view.

'Oh, Ginge,' whispered Betony, 'you need to go home.'

'But I want to stay here with you. I have to see to the hens, sweep the yard. I can't go home. Not now.'

She bent her head and stared at her lap. Her fingers twisted inside and out, tangling themselves. Her ring dug into her flesh. It took her back to a time when she was engaged to Will Bowman; back to a time when panic wasn't rising like cold vomit in her throat; when the ground wasn't rocking under her feet.

Meg's anguished face appeared suddenly close to hers. 'Come with me. We'll pack a few things.'

Rose let herself be guided like a child up the stairs. She sat on her bed, staring, her mouth agape, as Meg rummaged in her drawers.

'Do you want this jumper? These socks?'

'I can't do it.'

'These knickers? Where's your hairbrush?'

'I can't do it,' Rose said. 'I don't want to pack. I don't need anything. I don't care. Why would I need a hairbrush?'

Downstairs, Ted was pacing the kitchen, his face white. 'Petrol's run out. I am so sorry. I've used the last can.'

Meg took her hand. 'Come on, I'll come with you to the bus stop.'

Rose shook herself free and reached for a jar of Betony's plum jam from the dresser. 'I promised Mother I'd take some home.'

Ted ran his hand over his face and through his hair; Betony stared but said nothing, burying her face against Mo's soft cheek.

Fallen leaves were scattered in the bus's wake as it picked up speed along the top road. Jack Thimble eased himself down the gangway towards Rose, his face set and surly. She rummaged in her purse to find she had only a five-pound note. She proffered it with a shaking hand, knowing he got cross when passengers did not have the right change. He scrutinised her face, his eyes narrowing. When he did not respond, she pulled out the jar of jam from her bag and offered him that instead.

He shook his head, reeling off her ticket anyway, keeping his puzzled eyes fixed on hers. And then he seemed to understand. He reached into his breast pocket, pulled out a flask of brandy and offered her a nip.

Everything was normal. Stanley Crescent curved ahead of her, the houses neat and homely. Rose felt a blinding rush of relief as she stopped outside her house. Mrs Brown was losing her marbles, just like her poor husband. Her home wasn't destroyed. It looked fine.

The police rope round Rose's garden wall was fluttering in the wind. She walked straight through it. From the pavement behind her, she heard a voice shout, 'You can't go in there, love. It's too dangerous. Oi!'

There was something different, however, about the front door: it had sunk a little into the ground. And the window with the ship in full sail had a great crack through it. She felt an unsteadiness in her stomach. An instinct told her to use the side gate and go round the back. As she reached the end of the passage by the garage she sensed a strange smell: a smouldering. Her mother's enamel colander lay in the vegetable patch alongside a dented tin of milk, discarded among her father's charred cabbages. The chicken coop was a tangle of wire and singed straw; she spotted the brown corpse of a hen, feathers lifted by the breeze.

She stood still, pondering what was left of the garden, not able to take it in. Then she glanced at the house. The back of it was missing. Under the gutted roof, the bath was suspended and water spurted from broken pipes. Her parents' bed was shattered into sticks, lying on the parlour floor; every single object was coated in thick grey dust. Her eyes widened as she stared into the wreck of her home; the jar of Betony's jam slipped from her hands and smashed onto the ground.

'What a waste,' she whispered, staring at the sticky, oozing mess.

She looked up, expecting her parents to walk out of the rubble of the back parlour and tell her not to squander good food.

'Come on, Dad,' she said, her throat beginning to clamp tight in agony. 'Come on, Mother. I'm here now.'

A crater gaped open where the Anderson had once stood. The twisted corrugated-iron roof fanned out from it like the petals of a bizarre flower. 'Don't worry,' her father had said. 'We have our Anderson.'

In the pit lay one of her mother's best shoes. They must have been at a party for the evening, coming home for cocoa. They must have dashed out here when the siren blared.

Around her, leaves fell. She tilted her head to look at the sky and wished it would blow away. She wished that the sun had not risen, that this day had not happened. Her world was broken. Her childhood gone. Her body began to shake as if it was being sawn in two.

Then someone called out, 'Oi! You shouldn't be here, miss!'

She turned to glare. 'I don't care what you say,' she screamed. 'This is my home. This is my parents' house. Get off my property.'

There were two men, both in some sort of uniform.

One of them said, 'It's not safe, love. You have to leave.'

'Did you hear what I said,' she hissed. 'Get out!'

Another man stepped forward. 'Leave this to me, Reg.' This person came close to her and, through her half-blind, confused eyes, his frame seemed familiar.

'Dad?' she said.

'Oh, Rosebud.'

She let him come near her; she let him stand close. His arm went round her, ducking her face away from the worst of it. She looked up into Will's eyes. They were bright with shock.

He said, 'We took your parents away this morning. I am so sorry.'

'But where are they? I want to see them.'

'It's best you don't.'

How quiet it was in her garden. As Will held her, she watched each leaf as it fell, innocently, twirling to the ground. She began to cry, and pieces of herself started to break off. Parts of her life were scattered all over the ragged bombsite. Why was she still alive?

Clutching her mother's shoe, she kept her eyes on Will's sleeve, assimilating his presence as something from her past.

'We need to leave now, Rosebud,' he said. 'Let the authorities deal with it.'

She heard her own voice as if through fog. 'Will, wait.'

Picking her way back to the pit, she pulled out her mother's other shoe. Will took off his coat and put it round her. She let herself be led through the gate and back to the street.

A woman in glasses appeared, and it was many frozen moments before she realised it was Mrs Brown. She heard her say, 'Darling Rosie. What a dreadful shock. Will you come home with me? I have a spare bed now Mr Brown's in hospital. Come on, lovey.'

And she heard Will say, 'She's coming home with me.'

And 'Oh!' from Mrs Brown.

But she wasn't listening. She was shattered, empty of all thought or feeling. When Mrs Brown put her concerned face into her line of vision, she simply copied Will: 'I'm going home with him.'

His Ford was waiting, gleaming at the side of the road. He settled her into the passenger seat. She heard voices through the window.

'At least give me your address, Mr Bowman, so I can keep in touch.'

'Rose will be in contact with you, no doubt, when she feels able. Thanks for your concern. Good day.' He got into the car beside her. 'I'll take you back to mine, Rosebud,' he said.

She could not answer him; she could look neither left nor right.

As the Ford pulled away, a khaki car drew up behind it and a figure jumped out, waving frantically.

Will glanced in his rearview mirror. 'I see the army is here. Perhaps there's an unexploded bomb,' he muttered.

How could she possibly comment? Hot tears spilled from her eyes. Her head was churning, trying to stop the awful truth from reaching her consciousness. She could barely hear what Will was saying.

**W**ill's bachelor maisonette had one gas ring, tatty curtains and a smell of damp, but Rose had never seen anything as welcoming as the single bed in the narrow brown bedroom. She slumped onto it, and Will lifted her legs from the floor to the bed. She longed for sleep. He took off her shoes, pulled up a patched eiderdown and folded it over her shoulders.

When she opened her eyes it was dark. She began to shiver. She had no idea what the time was. The door to the room was ajar and she heard the striking of a match against its box. She thought that she was home and that Mother was lighting the ring under the kettle. And then, reality. She unfurled her legs and shuffled to the door.

Will was sitting in his armchair by the gas fire, smoking and reading; the radio babbled in the corner. He looked up and closed his book, turning the cover away from her. He switched off the radio. 'Ah, Rosebud. Just listening in on the Krauts,' he said. 'Tea? Toast?'

He told her to sit by the fire while he sliced bread in the kitchen. She tried to follow him but the kitchen was too small. He sent her back out, giving her the job of toasting bread in front of the gas flame.

Squatting in the half-light, she noticed the book cover was in German in a black gothic typeface. She held the toast as steadily as she could, feeling detached, as if she was watching herself in a film.

'Here we are, Rosebud.' Will gave her a cup of tea.

She took tentative sips as he stared at the ring on her finger.

'I knew it, Rosebud, I knew we couldn't be parted for long. I can't tell you how wonderful it is to see you wearing my ring. That silly argument we had, all that shouting. It's all in the past now.'

He sat on the floor by her feet and passed her a slice of toast, which she munched numbly. Reaching for her left hand, he turned the ring on her finger. 'And now *that's* back in its rightful place. And so are you.'

A memory made her pull her hand away from him.

He looked her over. 'Time you went to sleep again. Shock does that to a person. It's nearly midnight anyway. You need to sleep.'

In the bathroom, the reflection in Will's shaving mirror was not the girl she knew, but a woman Rose did not recognise. She had grey skin and eyes wide with an agony that she had yet to understand. She splashed water on her face and dressed in Will's pyjamas, rolling up the legs and sleeves so that they fitted.

He was arranging a pillow and blanket on the sofa. She asked, 'What are you doing?'

'I'm tired too, Rosebud. I'm turning in.'

'Will you sleep in there with me?'

He froze and looked at her, a brief shadow of triumph crossing his face. 'Whatever you want, Rosebud.'

She lay in the narrow bed, facing the wall. Will moved in behind her, his body like a dam that would prevent her spilling out of the bed, and out of herself. He made a warm prison for her.

'I am so sorry about your parents,' he said. There was a crack in his voice; an emotion she had not heard from him before.

'Please, don't talk,' she replied.

Suddenly, Krystof was holding her hand, laughing, surrounded by sunshine with hay in his hair. She felt a smile stretch her face. In the next breath, it fell away. The summer was over. Krystof had left her, walking away through falling leaves. Gone to war. Lost to the great, vast war. And this . . . this is the life she had expected, what her parents had always wanted. In Will's bed. Will taking care of her.

Will's asthmatic breathing was laboured and hot in her ear. She wanted to block it out and remove it all. But then what? There was simply nothing else. She turned her head to the sound of the breathing. She kissed him. She shuffled her body round to face him, hearing his grunt of surprise. He was soon finished with kissing. As he entered her, the pain blinded her to everything. It eliminated her life and all that had happened to her. And for that moment, and all the quick moments that followed, she felt no other pain. It was like mercy.

It was over, and he released her.

'I knew it, Rosebud,' he whispered. 'I knew you'd one day be mine.'

In the dull morning light, Will sat by the radio in his shirtsleeves. He ate toast with his mouth open, slurping his tea. Rose stood watching him from the bedroom door. She felt empty: no emotion, no spirit.

'Just off to work, dear,' he announced, glancing at his watch. 'Life goes on. You'll be all right here on your own, won't you? Perhaps you could do a bit of shopping. You can use my ration book for now, until you can get yours sent over from the farm. And don't buy anything frivolous like butter or sugar. I can get hold of all that, remember.'

She stared at him, barely listening, thinking how awful his table manners were. Her neck began to stiffen with shock and her ears filled with a rushing pressure. The squalid horror of what had happened to her parents began to replay itself in her mind's eye.

Will stood up, brushing crumbs from his trousers onto the floor, and walked over, wrapping his arms round her. 'How about I go to the town hall at lunchtime, Rosebud; see if I can set a date. After last night, well! Let's see if I can make an honest woman of you.'

She flinched with shock. 'But my parents?'

'It's what they would have wanted, you know that.'

'But where are they? I—I want to see them.'

'Oh, Rosebud, believe me. You wouldn't want to.' He drew away from her and said, lightly, 'So, what will you do today?'

'I—I could do a little housework,' she muttered, looking around her.

'Well, whatever you do, don't go round to Stanley Crescent. You're not fit to. It'll only set you back.'

'But I want something . . . something . . .'

'Believe me, before you arrived yesterday, I had a good look around. I found some papers, your birth certificate, but really . . . it's such a mess. The voluntary services are probably clearing it now.'

'I—I have my mother's shoes . . .'

'There you go! What's left there now is only fit for the scrap heap. We'll start afresh in our new house.'

'Our new . . .?'

'The Old Vicarage. It's high time I moved us out to Trelewin. The house is still mine. I just knew, *just knew*, it would only be a matter of time before you were.' He went on: 'The bank has agreed to a transfer. And I can register with Polperro ARP . . .'

But she wasn't listening to him. Her head filled with the sounds of the sea. The old, empty house would be her sanctuary. She'd be back near her friends; away from her destroyed life in Plymouth.

**M**rs Brown came knocking. 'I saw Mr Bowman in the town yesterday,' she trilled as she bustled in, 'and he told me your news, Rosie.'

'News?' Rose asked, distracted. 'Oh, the wedding.'

Rose put the kettle on the hob in Will's kitchen and sighed with weariness. It had been nearly two months since that dreadful day when she returned to Stanley Crescent. She felt lethargic and sick. Was this what grieving did to the body? she thought. She had no energy left.

'This is *exactly* what you need, my girl, after what has happened.' Mrs Brown settled herself in one of the chairs by the hearth. 'A fresh start. A new life. And I'm so glad that you have managed to'—she lowered her voice—'concede to an understanding with your fiancé. Forgiveness goes a long way, I say.'

'Forgiveness?' Rose asked from the kitchen, thinking, You've changed your tune. 'What do you mean?'

'Oh, your mother told me how much Mr Bowman adores you. She told me you threw him over—which I wasn't at all surprised at—but that he was distraught. Of course, I never told your mother that I saw him down at the Hoe with that woman. That would have made her see him in a different light, that's for sure . . .' Mrs Brown paused.

If only Mother and Father had known about the Wren, thought Rose. They would have been glad to see the back of Will. But what did it matter now? What did any of it matter?

'So, you forgave him, Rosie. Good for you. Now you can start afresh.'

Rose set down two cups of tea and turned on the gas fire. Overwhelmed with tiredness she rested back in the other armchair and took a sip of tea. Nausea swam up her gullet. 'Sorry, Mrs Brown,' she said, swallowing gingerly, 'but I think the milk in the tea must be off.'

'Nonsense.' Mrs Brown sipped her tea. 'It's fine. Now, something tells me you need some new clothes, seeing as your house. . .' The woman stopped herself and bent to her shopping bag. 'Look what I've got here.'

Rose barely glanced at what Mrs Brown was doing. She pushed her cup of tea away; the smell was revolting. Her stomach contracted.

Mrs Brown pulled out some brown woven material and a handful of silk. 'I've even got a scrap of parachute for the trimming. I could fashion a corsage from this.'

'A corsage?' Rose tried to sound interested.

'For your wedding suit. This is perfect.'

'Oh, the wedding . . .' Drowsiness washed over her.

'Now, now, we can't have you living like this, living in *sin* with Mr Bowman for much longer, can we?'

'Oh, I . . .?' Rose blushed. 'He sleeps on the sofa.' It had not occurred to her what others might be thinking. All she had wanted was somewhere to stay until it was time to go back to Cornwall.

'Bless you.' Mrs Brown smiled. 'You are such an innocent. Come on, let me measure your waist. Stand on this chair.' Rose obeyed. Mrs Brown wrapped the tape round her waist. 'Ah, twenty-five.' She wrote the measurement with a stub of pencil.

'Oh,' said Rose, 'I've put on weight. Must have been Betony's lovely cooking. Except I haven't had the pleasure for nearly two months now.'

Her mind slipped to Betony, Pengared and Meg.

'It will be nice for you to be back near the farm, away from here.' Mrs Brown chattered on, her eyes darting around the mean room. 'And a good steady man like Mr Bowman will soon set you straight. It's what you need right now, Rosie. In the circumstances.'

Mrs Brown tapped Rose on the bottom to indicate she should get down from the chair. And what were those circumstances? Rose wondered. Soon to be Mrs Bowman, living in a pretty hamlet by the sea; shielded from the war. But her parents were gone, and so was . . .

Suddenly, she clenched her hands into fists, desperate not to cry. Oh God, Krystof was gone. Their love and their summer were a lifetime ago. He had been sucked away into the war, just like her mother had said he would be. And here she was, allowing herself to be pulled away from him. Surely, if she had the strength to fight back . . .

'My dear, no tears, please,' Mrs Brown cried. The woman handed her a handkerchief and Rose began to mop her face, her wretchedness adding to the gripe of sickness in her stomach. She rested her hand over her waistband, hoping to soothe herself.

Mrs Brown glanced down, and then into Rose's face. 'Oh, my dear. I wonder . . . Do you think you might be . . .?'

'Goodness, Mrs Brown . . . what now?'

'Wrong side of the blanket, they say, but never mind, there's a war on. It must happen all the time these days. Just no one talks about it.'

'What on earth do you mean?'

'You're expecting, my dear! No wonder you're rushing to get married before Christmas. And I've got my work cut out to get this suit made. But don't worry. I'll have it run up in no time. Chop, chop.'

**R**ose pulled down the blackout to the darkening afternoon and sat at Will's desk to write three letters. The first was to Mrs Pike, district commissioner, South Cornwall Section, to explain that she was leaving the Women's Land Army now that she was to be married. Then she wrote to Betony and Ted that her parents' deaths had shattered her, and that she would not be returning to work now that she was to marry Will Bowman. She finished with a note for Meg, hearing, already, the exasperation and protestation ringing around the Pengared kitchen.

And then she heard the sound of Will's key turning in the lock.

'Hello, Rosebud, what are you up to?' asked Will, throwing down his coat and briefcase. He glanced at the letters on the desk. 'Ah, good, you're letting the country folk know. About time, too. I hope they don't think that it'll be open house at Trelewin. I'd rather those yokels weren't living in our back pockets to be honest with you.' He dipped to the gas fire and turned it up a notch. 'Christ, it's cold out there. Anyway, I've brought something home to warm us up: two tins of peaches. But perhaps we'll save them for Christmas Day in our new home. Only three days to go, and only two until our wedding,' he crowed. 'Am I the luckiest man alive, now I have you, Rosebud?'

She declined to answer him. 'Mrs Brown came back again today. She's going to make me my wedding suit.'

'Don't go getting any ideas about inviting that busybody,' he said. 'We'll pick witnesses off the street. We don't want any fuss, do we?'

'She's being very kind,' ventured Rose. 'She's gone to so much trouble.'

'Good, good. I'm sure you'll look a picture.' He walked over, wrapped his arms round her and caressed her bottom.

She struggled, pushing him away. 'None of that, please, Will.'

He pulled back but still held onto her, laughing. 'Ha, Rosebud, I always knew you were a traditional girl. Just you wait until our wedding night. Then you'll see how much I love you.' There was a sharp look in his eyes, just as there had been in the kitchen at Stanley Crescent.

'The thing is, Will'—Rose peeled his hands away—'I have some news for you. Mrs Brown suspected . . . I think I'm . . .' She began to cry.

'You're . . .? You're pregnant?' he exclaimed with a triumphant whoosh. 'I *am* the luckiest man alive.' His jubilant smile stretched wide. Then he stopped smiling. 'Hold on a moment, Rosebud. Is it mine?'

'Of *course* it is!' she bellowed, rushing from the room.

Sitting on the edge of the bed, Rose rested her head on her knees and covered her ears. She wanted to block out Will, block out the baby, block out her shivering terror.

Will knocked on the door.

'Hey, hey, I'm sorry,' he cooed, coming into the room. 'That was uncalled for. Look, I'm a rotter. I'm the cad who gets butter and peaches from under the counter. But I am here. I love you. And we're going to have a baby.'

His words made her jolt with disgust. How her father had hated the black market. It was criminal and an insult to the merchant sailors who risk their lives in the Atlantic. If only her father had known *that* about her fiancé. She looked at Will and felt her lip curl.

'Sometimes I think you hate me,' he said, his eyes searching her face. 'I admit I'm selfish, but I will look after you, like I promised your parents.' He wrung his hands, his face twisting pitifully. 'I'll never forgive myself for kissing that Wren. I'll never forgive myself for my behaviour on the night of the raid and what happened to your face . . . Will you ever forgive a pathetic man like me? There's a house in the country waiting for you, Rosebud. All you have to do is marry me, and we'll be happy.'

She looked up at him through her streaming tears. 'You insulted me,' she whispered. 'You think the child might not be yours.'

'I was thinking of your fancy man. Wondering if you . . .'

'What do you know? You know nothing about it!' She knew she had wanted to sleep with Krystof that night in the barn; wished she had.

'Look, Rosebud. You have to understand. Those men are gone. Who knows what Churchill has in mind for them? He will be a hero, your fellow. All we can do is sit and watch it all happen. And try to get on with our own lives.' Will's voice was plaintive, persuasive. 'It's the war, Rosebud. He would have had to have gone sooner or later.'

Abruptly, Rose stood up and dashed the tears from her eyes. She wanted to escape, leave this sordid place and contemptible man behind. But something caught her eye, made her stop. Her mother's shoes.

'I need to clean my mother's shoes in time for the wedding,' she said.

'I'll do that.' Will leapt up.

Rose held up her hand. 'No!' she cried. 'Let me do it myself.'

Sheepishly, he handed them to her and she slipped them on. Then she heard her mother's voice, ringing through her head, scolding her, pleading with her. *You're a fool to let him go for some fly-by-night squaddie who'll be gone in a few weeks. Will is your future, your life.*

How right she was, thought Rose. This is my life.

The first person Rose saw as she left Plymouth Town Hall as a married woman with Will was Mrs Brown, waiting in the drizzle. 'I just had to stop by on my way home to see you married,' Mrs Brown called. 'Congratulations! You look wonderful.'

Rose responded on reflex, as Will turned to shake the hand of the man he had collared to be a witness. 'Thank you, Mrs Brown. I'm glad to see you. You have been such a help to me.'

'Oh, hush. Anyone would do the same. And, Rosie, I have to mention . . . not sure how important it is . . .but you know on that day you came back, that dreadful day after the raid?'

Rose felt the woman's thin hand close tightly over her own. She said, 'Yes, that awful day . . .'

'Well, that army chap who pulled up in the car, you know, before you drove off—'

'I don't remember anything about an army chap.'

'Poor love. Of course. You've probably blotted it all out.' Mrs Brown pressed her hand on Rose's forearm. 'But this army chap . . . well, he wasn't English—'

Rose stiffened. 'He wasn't?'

'No. He was foreign,' Mrs Brown said with a trace of disdain. 'Not sure where from. Ah, look at your face, Rosie. More tears. You do make a lovely bride. So emotional, so beautiful . . .'

Rose tried to swallow. 'But wh—what did he say, this *chap*?'

'Oh, him! He said he was sorry. What for, I don't know. Sorry he was too late, or something. He'd heard about the raid the night before. He seemed to know who you were. He'd motored all the way from somewhere in the West Country that morning. I told him there and then that he needn't have bothered as you were being taken care of by your fiancé. That you would be safe with Mr Bowman. And he sort of . . .'

'Oh?' Rose pressed a hand to her throat.

'He sort of looked *crushed*. When I told him that you were going home with your Mr Bowman, he sort of *wilted*.'

'But what did he *say*?' She tried to focus on Mrs Brown's eyes and not her rain-splashed glasses.

'He said he had to be on duty that evening. Eighteen hundred hours, whatever that means. Colonel's orders. Threat of court martial.'

'But I don't understand!' Rose broke down, her head collapsing into her hands. 'He was there? At Stanley Crescent? He came to find me?'

'Was it important, Rosie? You'd gone with Mr Bowman. I thought—'

'But you didn't *think*! Why didn't you tell me before?'

Her sobbing brought Will to her side. 'I suggest you take your tittle-tattle elsewhere,' he barked. 'She's had enough to deal with already, don't you think? It's our wedding day, for God's sake.'

Mrs Brown backed off. 'I'm sorry, I was only trying to . . .'

Standing on the town hall steps, Rose's loneliness was complete. As Will handed her a handkerchief, she stared up at his face, and realised she didn't know him at all. She could barely remember who she was.

# Seven

THE RAIN FOLLOWED THEM all the way to Trelewin where the Old Vicarage stood in its dripping garden, its windows blank and unwelcoming. Rose shivered in the hallway while Will fetched their suitcases from the car. She didn't want to move any further. The stairs rose in front of her into the darkness. Her nose twitched at the smell of unlived-in spaces, undusted nooks, the aroma of mouse.

She braced herself and took some tentative steps across the hall, her mother's—*her*—shoes clipping on uneven Victorian mosaic tiles, and opened a door to the kitchen. A range sat in the hearth and beside it was a wooden dresser, not unlike Betony's. Reaching over the stained sink she pushed open a window and let in some damp air. She stuck her head in a cupboard and did not baulk at the stale smell inside. All she could think of was how she could clean it, clean all of it, with lemon juice and vinegar, just as her mother had shown her.

'There you are, *Mrs*,' Will called. 'What do you think of the place?'

'I—I quite like the kitchen,' she said.

'Well, could do with a lick of paint. And never mind these old loose tiles out here in the hall. I'll soon cover them up with lino.'

'No, let's leave the tiles. I'll get them restored once the war is over.'

'If you like,' he said. 'God, I didn't realise quite what a dump this place was. But never mind. Like I said, I bought it for a song.'

He came close to her and rested his hands on her shoulders. 'Have you recovered from earlier, Rosebud?'

'I—I feel a little better,' she lied.

'I want you to take care of yourself and'—he placed a hand flat on her stomach—'now there's to be a little one, you have to think of him as well. Come on, look in here.'

He ushered her through a doorway into a large room at the back of the house. In a former life, it would have been a grand sitting room; there was a fine mantelpiece and French windows that opened onto the terrace. Beyond the low garden wall, clothed in ivy, lay the church.

He said, 'I'd forgotten how close we are to the church. Once the war is over, they'll start ringing the bells again. I hope it doesn't bother us. If it does, I'll soon let the old vicar know.'

Will forced the latch on the French windows and they opened with a creak. The dank day entered the room in a blast of chilly air. And then, voices drifted over from the footpath beyond the garden wall.

'Oh, oh,' Will said, none too pleased. 'Looks like we have visitors.'

'Goodness, it's Betony and Meg. How wonderful!' Rose clapped her hands with joy. She rushed to the front door.

The two women were crunching over the gravel, carrying a cardboard box between them, red-faced and soaking but smiling happily.

'Ginge! We heard you'd arrived!' called Meg.

'How?'

'We have our spies. Didn't you see the bus earlier?'

'Mr Jack Thimble?'

Meg said, 'The very same. Told his wife. She told us. Hello again,

Will. How are you? I hope you carried your bride over the threshold?'

'Not in her condition, I wouldn't. Anyway, that's sentimental old rubbish. Carry her, indeed.'

The two women looked at Rose. 'Your condition? You mean . . .?'

'It's very early, I . . .'

Betony's eyes pierced Rose's for an uncomfortable moment, but then her voice brightened. 'Well, that's wonderful news, Ginge. We must help you get settled in. You must be worn out.'

Rose saw a glance of confusion between her two friends as she ushered them through. They set the box down on the kitchen table.

Betony said, 'Here's your first supper in your new house. Stew and dumplings, still piping hot and all packed in straw. Just return the casserole when you've finished.'

'Heaven.' She hugged them both in turn while Will leaned against the doorpost, tapping out a cigarette. 'We should have a drink to celebrate,' cried Rose. 'Don't we have a bottle of sherry somewhere, Will?'

He shook his head.

'We're so pleased you've come back,' said Meg to diffuse the silence. 'After all that happened, we weren't sure you would. We were so sorry, Ginge. And now here you are, married and expecting. It's all so sudden.' Meg's eyes were wide with the question, *Why?*

'I know from your letter that you've left the Land Army but would you like to continue to work at the farm? Light duties of course, until the baby comes?' asked Betony.

'No wife of mine will ever work,' piped up Will.

Betony ignored him. 'I'm going to start knitting,' she said. 'Little booties and jackets. Just you wait.'

'Oh, I've missed you, Ginge,' said Meg, hugging her. 'Come on, show us round this big old house, then.' She linked arms with Rose.

Rose said, 'I haven't even been upstairs yet, so we can discover it together.'

Will cleared his throat and they all looked round. Rose had forgotten he was standing there.

'I think it's best you ladies leave us to ourselves now. We've got a lot to do. We need to get settled.'

'Oh, but, Will . . .' Rose said.

Betony was flustered. 'Of course. We'll go, then. So sorry to interrupt.'

Meg piped up, 'Come over for Christmas dinner.'

'Oh, yes, do,' said Betony, her eyes shining. 'Not much as usual, but Ted dispatched a chicken yesterday. It will be lovely to have you.'

Will's hand rested on Rose's shoulder as he stood behind her. 'Thank you, but I want us to have our first Christmas dinner here alone.'

Rose said, 'But Mrs Brown gave us a hamper. We've got . . .' and stopped herself. 'Yes, thank you anyway, Betony. Will Hugh be home?'

Meg chipped in, 'No, but he's quite safe in Italy. He's guarding Italian towns as opposed to attacking them. He is very well.' She eyed Will Bowman with distaste. 'Come on, Betony,' she said, 'let's make tracks.'

'Ginge?' Will said, opening doors off the upstairs landing, tutting and then closing them again. 'Why do they have to call you Ginge? It sounds so awful. And, not least, rather unflattering.'

'I . . . I didn't like it at first,' she said, following him and peering into rooms behind him. 'But then it grew on me.' She opened a door onto a room at the front of the house to be confronted by a double bedstead in the middle of bare floorboards and a bay window offering an uninterrupted view of the sea.

'Ah ha.' Will came up behind her. 'This is my wedding present to you. Our marriage bed. Doesn't it look luxurious? And the view, how wonderful in the summer, hey, Rosebud? Think of us waking up to that.'

'My goodness . . .' She couldn't look at him, dreading having to share herself with him. At the maisonette she had managed to stall him, for the sake of appearances, but now the reality of sleeping with him left her cold. 'What a lovely surprise.'

'Come here, then.' He pulled her towards the bed. 'This is why I wanted the snooping locals gone. I want you all to myself.'

'Will . . . the baby?'

'Someone told me it was good for it. Now, come here, like a good wife. I'm going to make you smile like a bride should.'

The rain fell for the rest of December, and then in January the air grew still and the sodden earth froze hard. The countryside fell quiet in the grip of the chill, and not a soul walked by the Old Vicarage at Trelewin.

Shivering in pyjamas, jumper and socks, Rose scraped ice from the inside of the kitchen window. She stooped to the range and coaxed the banked-down coal into flame. Using both hands, she set the kettle to boil for tea, then was sick into the sink. She cried with every retch.

She picked up the bread knife and began to saw the loaf angrily, so that the knife scored the board again and again. If only he'd got there sooner. If only he hadn't had to go. If only she'd been stronger. But how could she have been? She'd had no idea what she was doing.

She watched through the window while the tea was brewing. Through the naked hedges she could see the postbox for Pengared—her only link with the outside world. He might write to her, yet, at the farm. *Stop it, you fool. You are married and pregnant. He has gone.*

Will came down the stairs in his suit and tie, whistling. 'Rosebud, I forgot to mention. I have to work late tonight. Don't wait up.' He crunched off over the gravel to catch the bus to the Polperro branch of the Western Bank where he had been transferred.

Another long day and evening alone in the house stretched before her. As the sound of the bus died away, Rose dressed in old trousers and a jumper. The kitchen was the warmest place in the house, but she forced herself to venture out into the other rooms and keep herself busy. In the sitting room, for some company, she switched on the radio and immediately turned the dial away from where Will always left it: hovering over Berlin. The friendly voices of the Light Programme drifted out as she swept the carpet.

She decided the place needed brightening up. Dragging Will's box of books in from the hallway, where it had been since the day they moved in, she took the books out and, one by one, dusted them off and lined the shelves: *British Songbirds, Jane Eyre, The Shell Book of the Countryside, Nicholas Nickleby*. At the bottom of the box were some novels in German; she remembered Will telling her it had been his favourite lesson at school. She flicked through a dogeared poetry book: *Des Müllers Blumen*. Will's schoolboy pen had translated it: *The miller's flowers. Tränenregen: showers of tears.* How pretty the language seemed on the page, she thought, compared to Mr Hitler's raging broadcasts. Thrusting her hand into the depths of the box, Rose pulled out a copy of *Mein Kampf*. She shrieked as if it had bitten her, dropped it back in the box and shoved the box back out into the hall. Suddenly, she was struck by a memory: Will reading it on the first night she stayed at the maisonette. She shook her head to banish the thought before the full awful scale of it fell like a cold axe through her skull.

Checking the time, she went to the kitchen window. Sure enough, Meg appeared by the postbox, thrust her hand in and pulled out a letter. Rose tapped energetically on the window and waved, but Meg neither heard nor saw her.

Dejected, she wandered back into the sitting room. She had already cleaned all the rooms they lived in. Tomorrow there would be nothing else to do. The baby fluttered inside her and she thought despairingly of the dark, empty weeks that lay ahead of her.

**A** week later, waking up more weary than when she had gone to bed, Rose pulled herself out from under the covers, leaving the snoring bulk of her husband behind. Last night, she had managed to dissuade him once again from what he half-jokingly called his 'conjugals'. Her swollen belly had become her shield, her excuse, and she patted it as she made her way downstairs in the cold darkness.

As soon as Will left for work, she dressed and waited in the kitchen, clutching a cup of tea to warm her fingers. Was it possible that the morning was infinitesimally lighter than the one before? She peered out into the gloom, desperate to spot the tiniest of green shoots poking through the leaf mould. What would this rambling garden reveal? Snowdrops and daffodils? *Father's favourite flowers.* Her hands shook and the cup thumped back down on the table.

It was Pengared postbox day, and soon enough, this time, Betony appeared. Rose stood at the window. Surely she'd see her? Surely she'd come and visit this time? Oh, why was Will so rude to them? She watched open-mouthed as Betony picked up her post, turned her slender back on her and disappeared down the footpath.

Rose could bear it no longer. Throwing on her coat and hat, she ran out of the house and plunged down the footpath.

'Betony!' she called, breathless, her feet like lead. 'Betony!' The full force of the icy air hit her as she reached the headland and began the climb, the cold scorching her throat, sweat drenching her back. 'Betony!'

At last she heard her. 'Ginge! You shouldn't be running!'

Rose doubled over with a cramp like a vice in her side. 'I-so-wanted-you-to-visit,' she spluttered. 'I-am-so-alone.'

'But we didn't know what to do,' Betony wailed, putting her arm round her. 'Ted said we shouldn't impose ourselves. I must say, your husband didn't make us feel very welcome.'

'I'm-so-sorry-he-was-so-rude-I've-been-going-out-of-my-mind.' Rose straightened, catching her breath. 'I had to escape. I saw you and ran!'

Betony peered at her, her face twisting with concern. 'You shouldn't be *escaping*. Come on. Come back with me to Pengared for the day.'

They linked arms and began to walk. 'Joel's gone,' said Betony. 'He's been called up. Something's going on, I know it. Have you noticed, even Polperro is empty of men now?'

'Really? I haven't been out at all.'

'Oh, Ginge, what have you been doing?'

'It's been too cold. Too awful.'

They fell into silent agreement until Rose said, 'What have you there?'

'Two letters,' Betony said, 'both from Hugh. One for Meg. One for us. But I wish . . . I wish I could stand here and read ours for myself.'

'Let me help you,' Rose said. 'Let me teach you to read.'

Betony flushed crimson. 'Would you? Ted has tried, but he's very impatient, bless him. I'm just too embarrassed to ask anyone else.'

Mutt and Jeff had not forgotten her; they bounded over as soon as Rose and Betony approached the farmyard gate, snuffling Rose's hands in search of those elusive biscuits.

'Where's Meg?' she asked.

'Over at the meadow,' said Betony. 'Here, take her letter. Careful as you go, it's still icy.'

As Rose picked her way across the yard, Ted strode towards her. Without a word he enfolded her in one of his huge hugs, his silent greeting speaking more to her than words could. She felt herself collapsing inside. 'Thank you, Ted,' she said and went to find Meg.

There she was, in the corner of Betony's meadow, cranking the starter handle of the Allis tractor. She looked up with a scream of delight. 'I knew it! I knew it wouldn't be long before you came back.' Meg ran to Rose, embracing her fiercely. 'Oh, Ginge, whatever *happened*?'

She swallowed hard, trying to be brave and searching for the right words. 'Krystof went to war,' she said, 'and Will was there for me.'

'But Ginge . . . surely Krystof . . .'

'Will is my husband.'

Meg's sharp eyes were unforgiving. 'Your husband made it very clear he did not want us to visit you.'

Rose distracted her with the letter. 'This is for you. Hugh.'

Meg snatched it gleefully, ripping open the envelope. 'Oh, he's fine. He's arranged his leave. At last! Oh, Ginge!' Meg skipped and hopped around her. 'We're getting married!'

'Meg!' Rose hugged her. 'When?'

'Beginning of June. I'd better go and see the vicar at Trelewin.'

'Ted and Betony have a letter from him, too. I expect he's broken the news to them. They'll be so happy. You are so happy! I wish . . .'

Meg stopped her jiggling around and looked at her. 'You *were* happy, Ginge. Remember the dance, the haymaking? I am so sorry for your parents. We've not been there for you, to help you through it. But you left us, Ginge.' Meg held her and Rose, resting her head on Meg's shoulder, felt her friend begin to sob. 'But we'll stand by you now.'

Meg extricated herself and wiped her face with the backs of her hands. 'Hey, look at me. So, are you going to help me today, or what?'

Rose smiled. 'I can try.'

Meg cranked the starter handle on the Allis and the spluttering engine broke the silence of the morning. She stepped up into the tractor seat. 'Come on, Ginge, you're not an invalid.'

Rose climbed up and slipped in beside Meg.

'Now, you haven't forgotten your promise to me, have you? I'm driving this contraption all the way to Polperro when this is over, and you are coming with me.'

'Just try to stop me.'

'That's my girl.'

'Where's Blossom?'

'Being a lazy arse in her stable.'

'And the herd?'

'At the knacker's.' Meg looked at her. 'But don't you dare go sentimental or we'll all go mad. Now, hop off and sort out the ploughshare.'

'Are we really going to do this?' asked Rose, climbing back down. 'Are we really going to break sod on Betony's meadow? First time in hundreds of years? It's the end of an era.'

'You bet. Orders from the Min of Ag. Bye bye, meadow.' The throbbing engine grumbled and the huge iron wheels began to roll forward.

How different it looked in the cold, pewter light of the February day. How far removed from last summer's golden days when they all made hay in the sunlight; when Krystof leaned in to pluck the seed heads from her hair, his fingertips leaving trails of ecstasy over her skin.

The tractor rumbled on and, strip by strip, the cold red earth was turned by the plough. Betony's meadow was no more.

Rose and Betony sat side by side in the lamplight of the warm Pengared kitchen, while Mo played quietly under the table.

'My third lesson,' said Betony. 'You're so patient.'

'It's the least I can do. You've been a great friend to me,' Rose replied.

Betony sighed. 'People think I'm stupid. They don't realise—I just can't see the words. They're like strange patterns.'

'You've done well so far. I'll be with you every step.' Rose picked up the old book that Betony had found in the cupboard. *The Return of the Soldier.* 'My goodness, I know this book. *My* mother had it.' *And where was that copy now? On a scrap heap somewhere?* 'It was written in 1918. This poor man, this soldier, loses his memory because of what happened in the trenches. When he comes home, he is so affected that he doesn't recognise his own wife.'

Betony was watching her closely, with her head cocked to one side. 'Go on,' she said.

'Right,' Rose said. 'Take a look at the first paragraph. Start here.'

'*I—no—If*,' read Betony, her cheeks flushed, her finger following the letters, her tongue protruding. '*If he—If he had . . .*'

'Good, Betony,' Rose said brightly. 'Stay calm. Remember to breathe. Hear the words in your head before you say them.'

Betony began to read, plucking at the words with her lips and setting them free from the page: '*If he had been anywhere interesting, anywhere where the fighting was really hot, he'd have found some way of telling me instead of just leaving it as "somewhere in France". He'll be all right.*'

Rose felt the smile freeze on her face. She grew cold with shock.

Betony sighed. 'How sad, and I haven't even got past the first page. And here we are, just twenty-odd years on and going through the same thing again. We know all about the waiting. The not knowing.'

Rose could barely speak. 'I don't think this book is appropriate to read at the moment.'

'Why, Ginge?'

Rose couldn't look at her.

Betony ventured, 'Is it because, possibly, you are thinking of *your* soldier? Are you afraid to talk about the return of *your* soldier?'

Rose lifted her face. 'There's nothing you or anyone can do to help me. This is all my doing. All my fault. He is gone for good. He won't be *returning*. Not after what happened.' She tugged angrily at her maternity blouse to emphasise her stomach. 'Not after *this!*'

Ignoring her fury, Betony said gently, 'Krystof came here, Ginge.'

Her body jolted. 'What?' Her voice croaked, '*When?*'

'On the morning after the raid, but you'd already gone. He'd heard about the air raid, had set out at dawn from Salisbury. He was already in deep trouble with his colonel, but he had to find you. He was due back on duty in two hours. He was never going to make it. He had already been threatened with court martial. They call it desertion.'

Rose's mouth hung open, a pressure building behind her eyes.

Betony said, 'He told me he had a special marriage licence. He wanted to find you and marry you that day. He said he was sorry he had not been in touch. Impossible, he said. He was taking a huge risk but hoped, eventually, his colonel would sympathise.'

'A licence,' Rose repeated. 'He came to my parents' house in Stanley Crescent. But I didn't see him. Mrs Brown told me on my wedding day. *After* I was married.'

They both fell silent, overwhelmed by the wretched irony.

'We thought that perhaps he had found you, and that you had got married,' said Betony. 'But then the weeks passed. Next thing we knew, we received your letter. Oh, if we could have done more, we would have, but we didn't know where you were.'

Rose's despair began to crush her. 'I was in shock. My parents . . . my home . . . I had no idea. This is worse, so much worse.' Her voice rang with bitterness. 'It's beyond repair. What did it look like to him? Seeing me go off like that, with Will? I betrayed him. He won't be returning to me now. I have ruined Krystof's happiness. I have ruined my own.'

Betony bit her lip, shaking her head. 'I don't know what to say.'

Rose dried her tears. 'I betrayed my parents, too. I was supposed to visit them that day in September, remember? But I chose Krystof. And now I am paying the price. I never saw my parents again.'

Betony swallowed. 'And what of Will?'

'As far as Will Bowman is concerned, us getting married, having a family; it's what my parents would have wanted.' A defeated calm returned and the clock on Betony's mantel ticked in the hollow silence.

When Rose spoke again, her voice cracked with anger: 'Is that the time? I must go. I have to get back to cook my husband's supper.'

She made a meat pie with scrag end from the Trelewin butcher, adding turnips to bulk it out. It was not as good as her mother's, but it would have to do.

The key turned in the front door and a blast of cold air reached her, across the hall and around the kitchen door.

'Something's cooking.' Will's banal voice rang out as he hung up his coat and stowed his briefcase. He poked his head round the door. 'What delight have I got to look forward to tonight?'

Rose cut into the pastry and slopped two portions onto plates, adding boiled cabbage stalks and a dab of mashed swede. They sat at opposite ends of the kitchen table. The congealing food swam before her as she tried to focus on her plate.

'We never did make it to the Ritz, did we, Rosebud,' said Will, loosening his tie and rolling up his shirtsleeves. 'Maybe we will, one day, to celebrate the birth of our first child.'

First child? Were there going to be more? Rose pushed her plate aside, the pressure behind her eyes escalating with every pulse.

Will forked chunks of meat into his mouth. 'Old Jones, the ledger clerk, got all patriotic in the staff room today, listening to Churchill on the radio. I soon shut him up when I told him that I had expected us all to be speaking German by now. He went all "Land of Hope and Glory" on me. Then got really shirty when I told him I already did speak German, thank you very much. He got so het up he started spitting on my newspaper. Disgusting man.'

She watched him prise some gristle out of his teeth.

'You're looking blank, Rosebud,' said Will. 'You must remember Jones. They brought him back from retirement because all the young clerks were called up. Our best boys go, and I'm stuck with Jones.'

She covered her eyes with her hand and let out a cry of despair. Tears rained onto the table.

She heard the scrape of his chair and felt the shadow of his large presence standing over her. 'Why are you crying?' he asked. 'Are you thinking of your parents? I'm sorry, Rosebud. So very, very sorry.'

The unusual softness in his voice made her glance at him. He was being kind. She had to tell him. If she didn't she'd choke.

'Krystof . . .' Her sobs asphyxiated her, her shoulders jerked. 'I'm thinking of Krystof. We missed each other by minutes.' Her words were strangled. 'I should have married him. Not you.'

'Well, I know that,' Will said, his voice tender and deep. He gazed at her through his lashes. 'I have known that all along.'

'You knew?' she blurted.

'I've noticed how unhappy you are. We need to put that right. We need to mend this . . . constant moping and crying.'

His words set off another torrent of tears.

'Now, now. Shush now.' He paused. 'I think you should go to him. I take it he's at Salisbury? I will drive you there myself. You can track him down. Have your fling, Rosebud. Get him out of your system.'

She gaped at him in disbelief. 'How can I? I'm married to you.'

'I am doing this to save our marriage. Go and have your pleasure with him. But remember, Rosebud. When it's all over, when it has run its course, which it will, I will be waiting for you.'

She looked down at her swollen belly. Shame engulfed her. 'An affair?' she asked, still incredulous. 'I can't. I can't go to him like *this*!'

'This is the hand you've been dealt. It's harsh, isn't it? So difficult, these days, for everyone.' He sat back and shrugged. 'It's your choice.'

Guardedly, she looked at his face and was surprised to see it remained placid, his eyes brimming with patience. He took her hands.

'Time to move on, Rosebud. Time to think of the little one.' He placed his hand on her stomach. 'He's gone,' Will whispered.

# Eight

WET SPRING UNFOLDED into tranquil summer. The sky over Trelewin grew wider, bluer, and leaves returned to the trees around the church-yard. With each passing week, Rose's stomach grew heavier and tighter.

She stood at the bedroom window at the front of the house and, shivering, watched the sea. The air felt cold for June. A blustery wind was fretting at the waves; a summer storm was coming. She thought of Meg and Hugh's wedding tomorrow and hoped the storm would pass. She moved away from the window and crossed the landing to the nurs-ery at the back. Betony had given her Mo's old cot and promised her the pram. Now, wiping the cot down, she wanted to feel hope and excite-ment, but these emotions eluded her. Poor little thing, she thought, tracing a finger over her stomach. I will try to love you.

She left the nursery and went into the small room that her husband called his office. I expect this needs a dust, she thought and looked at his typewriter on the paper-strewn desk. The window was open a chink, so she pushed at it in order to close it properly and a gust of wind whistled through, blowing the papers off the desk.

Sighing, she stopped to pick some of them up, feeling her baby shift in protest. 'What on earth?' she muttered out loud, realising that among the pages was a photograph of the Wren from the Anchor pub. It had been coloured at the studio: all blue eyes and red lipstick. Rose exhaled in shock. 'I don't believe it.' She bent to pick up the rest of the papers. The picture did not hurt her; she could not care less.

She sat down at the desk and began to leaf through the typewritten pages in her hand. They were all written in German.

'It's all very interesting, Rosebud,' Will had told her, when he tried to explain why he listened in on Radio Berlin. 'It's good to *know* your enemy, isn't it? And the book by the man himself? He has some fasci-nating ideas. Give him that. A great leader of men. Some would say Mr Hitler has charisma. You've seen the thousands, the millions who follow him. They can't all be fools. The fact that I have read his book is nothing for you to worry about. Nothing at all.'

A chill gripped the back of her neck as she turned over the cover of a pamphlet hidden among the papers. Even though she'd not studied German, she could read the words *Kristellnacht* and *Jüdisch*. The chill reached her bones. It was Nazi propaganda against the Jewish people. It was under her nose; in her house. She was as guilty as . . . with a shout of surprise, she dropped it and was on her feet, reaching up to the shelves, her fingers alighting on the spine of Oswald Mosley's *Tomorrow We Live*. Another man with charisma. The baby thumped inside her.

She tugged at a file next to the book and a sheaf of postcards fell into her lap. Some were tattered, some pristine; all showed naked women. She saw blonde hair, arms aloft, faces glancing over perky shoulders; flesh upon flesh, and swastikas. One of them was wearing an SS hat. 'Dear God,' she cried, pressing her hand to her forehead. 'How did he get hold of this stuff?'

Frantic now, she opened the drawers, plunging her hands through pens, paperclips, the trappings of an ordinary office. She found an envelope stuffed with banknotes; she counted, two hundred, three, *five*. And a letter from Sir Oswald Mosley's office, responding to Mr Will Bowman's congratulations on his recent release from prison.

What was she doing here with this man? Why had she not seen this? Why did she turn a blind eye when she unpacked the book all those months ago? But there had been clues all along. How on earth could a bank clerk afford a mortgage on a house like this? And the black marketing? Nylons, tins of peaches and bunches of flowers were all very well. But where did it end? On top of waves of disgust, lurched fear. He had hurt her before. He might hurt the baby.

Her hands trembled as she shuffled everything into place as best she could, making it look as it did when she first chanced upon it.

The picture of the smiling Wren was the least of her worries.

**R**ose could not sleep with the bulk of his body lying beside her. At half past five, she crept from the bed. She noted that the weather had changed for the better: the storm was over. She listened as the birds roused themselves, in treetop and on chimney pot, to pipe in the day. Was it really nearly a year ago that she had been up this early, ready to mow Betony's meadow?

Later on, struggling into the maternity dress that she had rummaged from Trelewin church jumble sale, she heard Will open the bedroom door behind her and walk in.

She picked up her hairbrush and sat at her dressing table to do her hair, her fingers shaking. 'What—what a lovely day for the wedding,' she managed. She felt his eyes boring into her spine.

'I came up here to tell you we're not going to the wedding.'

'But Meg's my best friend. How can I not go?'

He shifted his eyes to the side. 'You'll get overemotional and distraught. She'll have her parents there.'

'No,' she corrected him, 'only her mother. Meg lost her father many years ago. And I told you, she lost her brother Bertie at Dunkirk.' She swallowed and said bravely, 'What is the real reason?'

He looked peevish. 'I want to stay here and tune in. There are some interesting reports coming through on the radio.'

'All you think of is yourself and that blessed radio.' She faced him, trying not to reveal her rage. Her anger was edged with fear of him. 'Are you tuning in to Berlin again?' she asked, terror making her heart thump.

'Might do; there's a lot going on.'

'Well, you do that. In the meantime, I am going to my best friend's wedding. You, Will, can do what you like.'

He took a step back and sat on the bed. 'You seem different today, Rosebud.' His voice had a childish whine. 'Something's changed.'

She turned away again, defensively. 'Must be because of the baby.' Then she lightened her voice, lifting it into a half-laugh. 'But no need to worry. You never wanted to go to this wedding anyway. Don't forget, the day will be overrun with the locals.'

She gave him warm smiles until, satisfied, he shrugged and left the room. Alone again, she doubled over, clutching herself, her stomach churning with a stew of dread.

At midday, Meg walked into Trelewin church on the arm of her mother. She looked beautiful and grown-up in a white satin suit.

Hugh waited for her by the altar, leaning on a walking stick, a legacy of a booby-trapped mine in Italy. His eyes sparkled in his sunburnt face and his medals stood out against the khaki.

The vicar began to intone, his voice thin in the hushed church. After the signing of the register, Meg and Hugh sat side by side, holding hands as Betony stood up before everyone, looked the congregation in the eye, opened the Bible and began to read: '*When I was a child, I spoke as a child, I understood as a child, I thought as a child: but when I became a man, I put away childish things.*'

Rose, immensely proud of her friend, met Betony's smile.

The guests followed the beaming bride and groom out of the church into the quiet shimmering afternoon and trooped back across the headland to the farm. Betony had set up a table in the dappled shade of the orchard and spread out the wedding breakfast. Guests sat themselves on rugs and barefooted Mo pattered on a carpet of pink clover, taking sips from lemonade cups and eating other people's cake. Rose watched quietly from a comfy rocking chair, her stomach swollen before her.

'Ladies and gentlemen.' A ruddy-faced Ted stood up and cleared his throat. 'Boys and girls. As is so blatantly obvious, we are here to celebrate the wedding of my brother Hugh—brave soldier that he is, I heard him say he'd rather take on Rommel any day of the week—and his beauteous bride Meg.' There was a ripple of laughter and applause. 'What has not been so obvious is their love for each other, which has grown and matured like a good wine, since they first met nearly a year ago. Against all odds and in the face of adversity—not least Jerry's landmines—it seems my little brother and Pengared's stroppiest land-girl have found their way to true love. And I hope it is a lesson to us all.'

'Hear, hear,' someone called. Everyone cheered and clapped.

Ted said, 'Raise your glasses to the bride and groom.'

There followed a brief silence. Then Ted said, 'And here's to the King.'

Rose sipped her lemonade, Ted's words tearing into her. This is how it should have been, for her and Krystof: married at Trelewin church and then here at Pengared surrounded by their friends.

Everyone went back to eating and drinking and the chattering voices blurred into one. The afternoon stretched languidly on.

Meg's smiling face came into view. 'Come with me, Ginge.' She pulled her to her feet and led her away from the orchard and down the track. They stopped and leaned on the gate to Betony's meadow where, in place of the waving grasses of last year, rows of sugar beet stretched to the far hedges. 'We did good work here, didn't we, girl?' said Meg.

'It doesn't look as pretty now, does it?'

'Trust you to notice that. Times have to move on, Ginge.'

*The hairs on Krystof's arms shimmered in the afternoon light; the cutting machine whirred and clicked, punctuating their laughter.*

'I think I'm stuck in time,' Rose whispered.

'Oh, come on,' said Meg, 'you have your baby to look forward to.' She linked her arm and marched her further up the lane. 'That's what I want next. Mr and Mrs Cumberpatch are proud to announce . . . This way, Ginge; I wanted to show you our wedding present from Ted and Betony. It's just down here.'

They turned the corner. Ahead lay Cringle Cottage, thatched and squat.

'The old cottage?' Rose swallowed. How Krystof had loved it.

'You bet! They've given it to us. Do you like it?' Meg giggled. 'Look at it. It's beautiful. A great place to start married life.'

Turning away, Rose burst into violent sobs.

'Oh, Ginge,' cried Meg, mortified. 'I'm so sorry. I'm gloating.'

'You were right,' Rose said, choking on her tears. 'My turn *has* come.'

'What are you talking about?'

'Like you said, first day we met. You told me so. The war will touch me one way or another. Well, here we are, and look at me now.'

'But you have your baby. That's what's important. My mother told me that many women tolerate their husbands, just so they can have a family.'

'But my mother will never see it.' She could barely speak.

Meg pressed on. 'Just because Betony's meadow is no longer there, we are the richer for having had it. You have to remember your parents as they were. As the lovely people they were.'

Wretched crying made Rose's words difficult to understand. 'But I wanted Krystof. I love Krystof. I've never loved . . .'

'I don't mean to be hard on you, Ginge. You are married to Will.'

'I can't go home tonight. I don't want to. I can't do it.'

'Stay at Pengared then,' said Meg. 'Betony will love to have you, Rose. Give yourself time. You can't go on like this. I want you to be as happy as me. You've got to think about what you are going to do.'

Rose thought of what lay in the drawers in her husband's study. 'I know already what I'm going to do.'

The blissful sound of Blossom clopping across the yard and the noise of Mutt and Jeff barking woke Rose. Creeping downstairs, she left Betony a note of thanks and departed swiftly, unable to bear brushing shoulders with the old life she had left behind.

The headland was as green and fresh as ever, with gentle waves in the cove below. She ignored it all and set her sights on Trelewin. She walked through the front door and straight into the sitting room. Will was outside on the patio. The radio was blaring with a thunderous BBC voice. She reached for the dial and switched it off.

'Hey, what the—?' Will yelled. 'What are you doing? And where have you been?' He leapt up and walked to the radio to switch it back on.

She dodged round him and out into the sunlight, throwing her words back over her shoulder. 'I stayed at Pengared last night. I didn't feel like coming home.'

'Well, isn't that charming? My own wife doesn't want to come home to me.' He was grinning sarcastically.

'It was my best friend's wedding and I wanted to linger. It was too late to come home. What's a wife to do, when she has no husband to escort her?' She sat in a deckchair on the patio. 'And can't you keep the volume down? That thing is hurting my head.'

He leaned against the French windows, looking down on her. She sensed he was enjoying a feeling of power. 'You haven't heard, have you?' He cocked his head towards the radio in the room behind him.

She looked at him, puzzled. 'What do you mean?'

'Only the biggest-ever military operation in British history,' he crowed. 'They set sail before dawn yesterday.'

She was dazed. 'Ted's radio doesn't work. We didn't hear . . .'

Will was warming up. 'Bombers first. Then the fleet. Thousands and thousands of them. They landed in France yesterday. Canadians, Yanks, the British. From Southampton, Portsmouth, Dartmouth, Plymouth. The BBC are calling it the Second Front. This is only the second day. This is it. This is the big one, Rosebud.'

Wild questions flew out of her mouth. 'But what's happening?'

'Sounds like the British are doing all right. But you know how cagey the newsreaders are. They talk about "air operations" all the time. What the hell does that mean? They never tell the whole story. Could be the Yanks are taking a hammering.'

She blocked her ears with her hands. 'Shut up!'

Will said, 'Ah, yes. Of course. He's with the Yanks, isn't he?'

She could not answer him. She did not know where Krystof was.

'I've touched a nerve, Rosebud,' he jeered. 'Your little Slovak is out there somewhere, wading through waves up to his neck.'

'He is *Czech*!' she yelled.

'You say *is*, there, Rosebud. I'd use the past tense if I was you.'

She hauled herself out of the deckchair and walked away from her husband and the alarming voice on the radio. She reached the church-yard wall and sat on it, but she could still hear the radio. She was agitated, her body alive with shock. She said to herself, Yesterday, I sat here at first light, and at the same time, he was preparing, briefing his men. And all through the day, right through the night, while I slept, he was . . . he was . . . She rubbed her hands over her face and over her head. She pulled at her hair. 'How do I know? How will I ever know? Where will he sleep tonight?'

Easing herself down, she slipped off the wall and meandered quickly through the sleeping graves, telling the baby, 'He told me that he could not kill another man. But he will have to. He will *have* to.'

Pushing open the church door, she was enveloped by the dusty smell of hymn books. She walked unsteadily up the aisle. Sinking into a pew at the front, she raised her accusing face to the altar.

'So this is why all the men have disappeared.' Her voice cracked the silence. 'This is why all the men have gone from the pubs, the farms, the villages . . . Dear Mother and Father,' she prayed, whispering into palms wet with tears, 'you were right. Krystof has gone. I thought he was on Salisbury Plain, fighting mock battles.' She choked on despair. 'Now the battle is real. And how in heaven will my soldier ever return?'

She waited, wanting a response. Wanting an answer.

'I love him,' she whispered to God.

Anger consumed her then and, as she struggled to her feet, the baby objected with tapping little prods. 'Oh, it's not your fault,' she told it.

Outside the church, she glanced at the clock on the tower. Jack Thimble's bus was leaving in ten minutes. Once back at the house, she crept through the scullery door and slipped across the hall. A voice on the radio drifted from the sitting room and she caught sight of the back of Will's head, cocked to listen. She went upstairs and padded into the office for a moment, scarcely able to breathe.

'What are you doing up there?' Will called out. 'Where's my lunch?'

She came slowly back down the stairs. 'I need to go and buy some provisions.' Her false smile made her cheeks ache. 'I'm just going to catch the bus to Polperro. It will be here any minute.'

When she tried to pass him in the hall, he grabbed her arm. His gaze penetrated her. 'You'd better not be trying to leave me.'

She held her handbag—containing the envelope of money pilfered from his office—to her chest as sweat trickled down her back. 'I'm overwrought, that's all, Will,' she uttered in the sweetest voice she could muster. 'It's quite a shock, all of this. We can but hope for a good outcome for the troops.'

His face flicked from angry to jubilant. 'I think the German boys are going to give us a good kicking.'

She looked at him, at the sweat beading above his mouth, his eyes shifting back to the radio, his ears straining to hear. 'I won't be long.'

The cobbled streets were alive with anxiety. People leaned on gates, gathered in groups, listened on doorsteps. Radios hummed in the warm summer morning. Could this be the beginning of the end? Or only the start of something far worse? 'Shush-shush, everyone,' a woman cried. 'The King is on.'

Rose walked on down the hill and straight into the police station.

'I've come to report a crime,' she said to the constable at the desk.

**R**ose thought she had given it plenty of time. She waited in Polperro on a bench, knowing she had to go back sooner or later. At least to pack a case and head for Pengared and the warm embrace of her friends.

Suddenly she felt a lightness, an exquisite feeling; and then, deep inside, a belt tightened hard round her middle. 'I need to get you home,' she told the baby, and began to trudge back up the cobbles to the bus stop.

But even then, after she had bided her time, the police car was still parked on the gravel in front of the Old Vicarage.

An officer approached her. 'Mrs Bowman? We'll need to take a statement from you at some point.' He glanced down at her pregnant belly and back to her face. 'Perhaps when you are less indisposed.'

A young constable was loading boxes into the front seat of the car.

'Is that everything from the room upstairs?' his superior asked him.

'Yes, sir.'

The officer turned back to Rose. 'We'll need longer to search the rest of the house, madam.'

'I'd better go to my friends,' she said. She glanced towards the front door. Will appeared, flanked by two more policemen, his face white, his dark blue eyes fixed on her.

'Just let me say goodbye to my wife, damn you!' he cried, indignant.

They released him, keeping a watchful eye from a distance, as he bore down on her, his jaw set, his eyes never leaving her.

He leaned in close and held the top of her arm in a tight, spiteful grip. She flinched with pain as he bent to plant a kiss on her cheek. He whispered, his spit hitting her ear, 'I bought you this house. I pulled your parents' bodies from the rubble, and this is what you do to me.'

She looked at him, frozen. His eyes were brimming with tears.

'And when these monkeys set me free, which they will, eventually, Rosebud,' he hissed deep into her ear, 'I'm going to come and find you. And I'm going to kill you.'

**S**he heard the police car doors slam as she stumbled along the footpath, desperate to make it to the stile before another contraction split her body. Her legs buckled. Doubled over, she moaned in pain.

Climbing the stile, she felt an enormous warm deluge fall out of her and splash over the path like a torrent. And then, not knowing how, she found herself at the top of the headland. The pain came again. A hundred times worse. She fell to her knees and screamed into the long grass. Shaking violently, she pulled herself up and began to limp on.

She reached the farmyard gate and tried to call Betony's name but all that came out were stifled mews. Far away, Betany stood hoeing the sugar beet in the meadow. Rose lurched towards her across the yard. Only ten yards to go. Five. Four. Oh, the tearing agony. Was this the end of her life?

Rose fell, screaming, among the leafy tops of the sugar beet, her body sinking into a sea of searing pain. Betony was by her side. 'Don't try to fight it, Ginge. You've got to go with it. Ted is phoning for the doctor. But why didn't you telephone from home? Where's Will? Why did you come all the way here . . . oh, Ginge, go with it . . .'

Too many questions; too much commotion. All Rose managed was, 'He's . . . been . . . arrested. What is happening to me?' she whispered to Betony as her friend leaned over her. Rose's fingers reached up like claws and sank into her friend's hair.

'My gosh, Ginge, the baby's coming quickly!' cried Betony. 'Ouch! What are you doing to my hair?'

Black curtains closed in at the edges of Rose's eyes; all sound was muffled until a voice said deep in her ear, 'You've got a baby girl.'

Rose lay on her side among the sugar beet as Betony wrapped something in a towel and placed it next to her.

'There,' said Betony, kneeling down beside her. 'I was conceived in this meadow, and now your daughter has been born here. She's early, and she came quickly. The doctor will be here soon.'

Rose stared at the bundle. A hand emerged and unfurled like a flower.

Betony smoothed Rose's damp hair. 'Now, Ginge, what's all this about someone being arrested?'

Rose stirred herself and grabbed at her friend's hands. 'Have you heard? The troops? All the men? About what's happening in France?'

'Yes, yes,' said Betony. 'Ted fixed the radio at last. It's stupendous!'

Rose blurted, 'But Will Bowman's a disgusting Nazi!'

'Is he? Oh, dear,' said Betony. 'We always thought he was a complete rotter, an utter wrong 'un, but this really takes the biscuit.'

'I shopped him.' Rose began to laugh, then to cry. 'And Krystof . . .' she murmured. 'Krystof is somewhere in France. Like in your book, remember, Betony?'

'Don't you want to look at your baby?' Betony asked, soothingly.

Rose carefully parted the folds of cloth in Betony's arms. 'Why,' Rose said, 'she looks just like a little plucked chicken.'

# Nine

PERCHED ON THE FARMYARD GATE in the May sunshine, Rose said, 'All right, Mo, if you like you can walk her over to the hedge.' She watched the young boy hold Nancy's chubby hand and take small, patient steps while the little girl toddled beside him. She was born early, and was now walking early, Rose thought. Her straight, dark hair had been cut by Betony that morning and it framed her pale face, emphasising her long-lashed eyes.

Mo's care for and interest in her daughter were heartwarming, especially on the days when Rose could barely look at Nancy, the colour of her hair and the length of her lashes constantly bringing Will to mind. He can't hurt us now, Rose told herself. He is locked away in Bodmin jail.

She listened to the sounds of Pengared: birdsong, the cock crowing, Ted chopping wood, the dogs' friendly barking, through a mist of grinding regret. A year and a half had passed since she'd last seen Krystof and her heart was an aching void.

Then a new, unfamiliar sound. She cocked her head to listen. There came out of the blue a clear and joyful ringing. 'Mo!' she called in excitement. 'Mo! Quickly! Bring Nancy back here!' Could it be? Could it possibly be? The bells of Trelewin church, silenced for six years, were resounding across the headland.

Betony and Ted were running towards her across the yard. 'Can you hear the bells, Ginge?' Betony cried, in disbelief.

'This can only mean one thing,' cried Ted. 'By God! Is it the end?'

And then another sound made them all turn to look up the track. There was Meg, triumphant, sitting atop the spluttering Allis.

'Hey, everyone!' she screamed, standing up in the seat and waving like mad. 'Jack Thimble just told me. Hitler's dead! The war is over!'

Their cheers were dizzy with joy as they hugged and jumped

together; the children, squeezed in their arms, were tearful amid the melee. Mutt and Jeff yapped around their knees, tails lashing in rapture.

'Right, Ginge,' said Meg, 'the day has finally come.'

Rose laughed, remembering her promise. 'Goodness, yes, but we'd better telephone ahead and warn Polperro.'

Meg cried, 'All aboard then!'

'You're mad,' said Ted. 'You're both barmy.'

'Mad with joy!' cried Meg as Rose settled beside her, holding Nancy tightly. Meg started the tractor and it rumbled up the hill, driver and passengers all waving with gusto.

'Just look at this beautiful day! I'll never forget it!' Meg's voice sang out as the tractor chugged on, negotiating the lanes, trundling through tunnels of green. 'Oh, Ginge, you're crying?'

Rose wiped her face. 'It's a shock. It's been so hard. So long and hard and *bloody*. I was just wondering about . . .'

'I know, I'm thinking of everyone too. Ol' Kentucky from the dance. Did he make it? What about Joel? We haven't heard from him. Some lose the battle, some win.' Meg put her hand on Rose's knee and peered into her face. 'We're OK, aren't we?'

'We are,' she said, holding Nancy tighter than ever. 'We're alive. We made it.' She felt inexplicable guilt. 'We must be thankful.'

The tractor came to a spluttering stop at the top of Polperro's hill. Meg killed the engine and they sat and stared in amazement down the street. All the way to the harbour, everywhere they looked, people were moving in a mass, singing, cheering, dancing on the cobbles. Someone had wheeled the piano out of the pub and was bashing away on it. The landlord stood at the window passing pints of beer out. The happiness and noise surged closer and closer, drawing them in.

Meg cried, 'Joel! There's Joel! He's home!' and leapt off the tractor.

Rose held onto a fidgeting Nancy and watched Meg's curly head bobbing through the throng. Joel and Meg were suddenly hugging each other, whooping and jumping up and down in the crowd. Meg turned and waved, her face split in two by her smile.

Rose waved back, indicating that she would stay put. Someone handed her up a glass of lemonade, and someone else handed Nancy an orange. Rose felt the utter joy of the people envelop her, but inside her heart, sorrow sat like a lump of granite. 'Where's *my* soldier?' she whispered into Nancy's hair. 'Where can he be?'

The day that everyone had been longing for had arrived. But, now the war had ended, would they release Will Bowman? The memory of his last words to her still made her freeze in terror. She looked at Nancy. The little girl bit into the orange, the first she had ever seen, and chewed the peel, wrinkling her nose at its bitterness. The sudden desire to take care of her suddenly overwhelmed Rose. 'Oh, chicken. I am here for you.'

She held the child, trying to draw some strength from inside her, trying not to be envious of the laughing faces below her.

Suddenly, her eyes were drawn to someone. He was very still, not laughing or singing, his cap pulled low. No. It couldn't be. Not here.

The mass of people surged and she craned her neck, searching for the face again. She leaned over, straining, and saw him again: the curve of his face, the colour of his skin. He was standing there, by the lamp-post. He was not part of the celebrations; he was trying to pass through.

'No,' she breathed, suddenly feeling crushingly sick. 'No!'

She shuffled round on the tractor seat, trying to get down without dropping her child. She landed on the ground with Nancy clinging to her neck. The orange rolled away across the cobbles.

'You all right, love?' someone asked. 'Go steady now.'

'I just need to find him. Oh, God, I've lost him.'

On the ground, the crush of bodies shielded him from view. She forced her way forward, pushing people aside. Desperation made her fierce. 'Please, please, get out of the way! Krystof! Krystof!' She'd seen him, and now she would lose him. '*Kry-stof!*'

The crowd parted and he stepped into view. He looked older; his face was peaceful but lined; his eyes were weary but beautiful.

'Ruzena!' He plunged through the crowd to her. Rose felt a rush in her soul, an uncontrollable lifting of her heart.

But he stepped back from her. His jaw dropped. 'Who is this?'

'My daughter. Nancy, say hello. This is Krystof.'

He stared at Rose. 'You married him?'

'I did.' She lowered her eyes, suddenly feeling dreadful and ashamed.

'This proves it to me,' he said, his face blank, immovable. 'I should have known better and listened to the warnings in my head. You were stringing us both along.'

'Oh, no, Krystof, you don't understand!' Her words blurted in a frenzied stream. 'I was beside myself. I didn't know where you were!'

'So you went ahead and married him anyway. You didn't try any harder than that.' His voice was cold. He turned swiftly to go.

'Please don't go,' she cried. 'Please listen to me. Let me explain.'

'I can't listen to you any more. This is all I can give you. I have to go.'

She hurried after him, feeling the burden of Nancy, who now began to cry. 'The day my parents died I was deranged. I made a dreadful mistake, Krystof. I didn't get your message. You spoke to Mrs Brown, but she didn't tell me you'd come to Stanley Crescent until it was too late. I couldn't cope. You were gone. Don't leave me again,' she pleaded.

Krystof's voice broke. 'I thought about you all the way to Paris. I thought that maybe I had been mistaken. That he was just giving you a lift somewhere. But the things that woman told me . . . I wanted to marry you. I came for you.' He drew himself tall. 'I believed you loved me.'

'Stop, Krystof.' Rose set a squawking Nancy on the ground. 'You should believe, because it's true. I love you. I always have.' She embraced him, kissing him long, hard and deep. He wrapped his arms round her and she felt him press himself to her for a moment.

He pulled back. 'No.' He held her from him. 'You have his child.'

She blurted, 'My husband is in prison. We are separated.'

He uttered, 'But of course, *married*.'

Rose began to shake with dismay.

Sensing someone at her side, she turned to see Meg who was saying in wonder, 'Krystof, you made it!'

'Meg, please take Nancy for me.' Rose's voice was weak. 'I need to talk to Krystof.'

Meg gathered Nancy in her arms. She disappeared into the crowd.

Rose waited, head bowed. Krystof looked at her hard then took her hand. He pulled her up the street. 'Let's get away from here,' he said, opening the door of his army car.

He drove at speed down the lanes. Eventually he whispered, 'Why, Rose? I came for you. I had our *marriage* licence ready.' His teeth were gritted. She had never seen him angry. The war had changed him. The war had changed them both.

The night at the maisonette returned to her. The shock, and the horror of seeing her life destroyed . . . that had altered her. How she had allowed Will to claim her. How she had punished herself. 'But you weren't there!' she wailed. 'My parents were dead. I thought I had lost you too! Krystof, look at me!'

'I can't look at you,' he said. 'It hurts too much.'

Krystof pulled the car up outside the church in Trelewin and marched off along the path to the cove. Rose hurried to keep up.

'That's your home, isn't it? That's where you live with *him*.' He broke the silence, nodding at the Old Vicarage.

'I live at Pengared now,' she said awkwardly. 'The Old Vicarage still belongs to Will. I don't know what is going to happen to it now.'

Krystof shrugged. 'I'm sure you'll think of something.'

As they descended the ferny path to the cove in silence, she felt the cold and frightening space between them.

She sat on their rock, shivering despite the sunshine. Krystof walked to the wire. 'No need for this any more,' he said, giving the wire a half-hearted kick. When at last he turned to her, his face was shining with tears. He walked over and sat by her side, reluctantly allowing her to take his hand. Into the silence, he said, 'You know I love you, Ruzena. God knows I love you . . . but . . .'

Her voice trembled. 'Don't punish me, Krystof. Now that we have the chance to be together.'

'What chance?' His voice was a hoarse whisper, still edged with resentment. 'I was on my way to Pengared to ask where you were. I have to go away again. I've come all the way from liberated Europe, back here to England, only to be sent home.'

Rose lifted her hands to cover her mouth.

He said, 'There is a trainload of Czech servicemen leaving Plymouth for Prague tomorrow. And I have strict orders to be on it. Now the war is over your government doesn't need us any more.'

She felt as if he was choking her. 'Not again! No, Krystof!'

'I can't even begin to tell you what hell I have been through in the last year,' he muttered, unable to meet her eyes. He lowered his head and she watched his spirit breaking. 'I have not heard from my parents or brother in two years. I need to go back. My grandmother, my Babička, will need me. If she is still alive. I have to go home to Prague.'

'But I've only just found you again,' she wailed. 'At times I tried to forget you. But that was impossible. I soon realised my mistake, marrying the wrong man. My life was cold. It stopped. I have my daughter, and there are days when I resent her. But what has never changed, Krystof, through all of this, is my love for you.' She reached out with a trembling finger to touch his face. 'Please don't leave me again.'

He avoided her touch, got up abruptly and went to sit on another rock. His jaw was set, his fists clenched. She could not bear him being so close, yet punishing her, almost hating her. Through her tears she saw him gather his thoughts. He took a deep breath and walked back to her. He rested his forehead against hers, his embrace enfolding her. 'Oh, Ruzena, Ruzena,' he breathed. 'I never want to leave you.'

They kissed, as if kissing was the same as breathing, as if it would give them life. Give them time. Give them each other.

'You made it back to me. The least I can do is follow you home,' she declared. 'If you are going back to Prague then I'm coming too.'

As they climbed back up through the shady ferns, Krystof asked, 'Are you sure about it? There may be peace in Europe but there is also turmoil: battlefields, devastated cities. Your RAF did a good job in Germany, you know. Refugees, evacuees, starvation. Do you really think you can make the journey? What about your child?'

Rose swallowed hard on her fear. 'She will be safe with me.'

'My friend Vaclav is shipping out tomorrow with me,' Krystof said. 'Remember you met him in the pub in Polperro? He married Mabel yesterday. Remember her from the dance?' Rose nodded. 'Mabel is going to Prague. It might take a while to sort out but you must travel on the train with her. Two of you will be safer. Safer for Nancy.' Krystof fumbled in his pocket for a pen. He wrote on the back of an envelope. 'This is my house. This is where I live, in Prague. You must find me there.'

She took it as clouds of tears began to blind her.

'I haven't much time. I have to report back to Plymouth barracks.'

'Damn these bloody orders! The war is over!' she shrieked. 'I can't say goodbye now. I just can't.'

'Then we won't say goodbye. I will simply look at you.' He was holding her in his arms, leaning back to study her face. 'I see your green eyes, the little crinkles at the corner. I see the fire of your hair, your scar. Everything that makes you. Are you going to book your ticket?'

'Of course I am,' she sobbed, her tears hot and angry. 'I want to take a photograph of you, but I haven't a camera.'

'Your face is in here.' He touched his chest.

'I can't bear it,' she said, then a movement caught her eye and she looked up at the sky. 'Oh,' she cried. 'A swallow, the first of summer. He's early! He must have heard—the war is won!' She glanced back at Krystof but he was walking away from her. 'Krystof?'

Every few steps, he glanced back over his shoulder. 'We are not saying goodbye,' he called above the soaring sound of the waves.

Bereft, she watched as his presence peeled away from her side like a bandage unravelling until his waving figure faded into the horizon.

'I will never say goodbye,' she screamed to the sky.

The Plymouth travel office was busy with a long queue of people waiting. Rose sat beside Betony on an uncomfortable chair, crossing and recrossing her legs. On her lap sat her handbag containing the envelope of money she had filched from Will's study. The airless room was stifling; voices were pitched with anxiety; a typist tapped sporadically on her machine.

'Fill these forms in while you wait,' said a prim secretary, handing out sheets of paper. 'Seems like the whole of Europe is on the move.'

Betony tapped Rose on the sleeve and leaned in to whisper, 'Are you sure you're doing the right thing, Ginge?' Her voice cracked with concern. 'This has been bothering me for days. It could be so dangerous going all that way. And little Nancy . . . Goodness knows what a three-day journey across Europe will do to her. Have you seen the reports? What they're finding in Poland and Germany?'

'Nancy will be fine. I'll be with Mabel. She will help.'

'Huh—that flighty piece. What use would she be? This is such an enormous thing you're doing, Ginge. Have you really thought it through?'

'Krystof fought in the desert. Krystof helped liberate Paris. All I am doing is travelling across France and Germany to be with him.'

'But, Ginge, it would be safer to stay at home.'

Rose took a breath. 'Will Bowman threatened to kill me,' she said. 'And so to get me and Nancy as far away from him as I can will be the safest thing to do.'

'My God . . .' Betony breathed. 'You should tell the police.'

'No, that will make it far worse. Me calling the police in the first place was what set him off. And they let that Mosley out eventually—and his Mitford wife. It's only a matter of time before Will is set free too. And then what?'

Betony's eyes were spherical with shock. 'We won't breathe a word of where you are if he comes back to Trelewin.'

'Thank you, Betony. You and Ted, and Meg and Hugh, too, have been the best friends anyone could ever . . .'

'Next,' barked the bald-headed man behind the desk.

Rose sat down in front of him and Betony took a chair behind her.

'Have you your passport? Your identity card?'

Rose handed them over. She waited. He studied the form she had filled in, shaking his head, tutting.

'A passage to Prague, Czechoslovakia?' He sounded incredulous. 'Not in any hurry, I hope. You'll hardly get there before summer's out, the rate things are going. I thought most people would be coming the other way. Getting out of the likes of there. Are you a war bride, then?'

'Yes,' she lied. 'I'm taking my daughter with me.'

The man looked dubious. 'Not many girls go east. Most go west, following the GIs. He lifted an eyebrow and appraised her. He turned over the form. 'Mrs Bowman, is it?'

'Yes.' All her papers said her name was Bowman, Mrs.

He narrowed his eyes. 'That doesn't sound like a very Czechoslovakian surname to me.'

Betony, behind her, let out a sigh of resignation and began to put on her scarf. 'Come on, Ginge,' she whispered.

Rose spoke up. 'Er, there has been a mistake—my married name is—'

A loud voice resounded behind her, making her jump: 'Pepper? Pepper? Is that Pepper?'

Rose turned. 'Oh, Mrs Pike. How do you do?'

The South Cornwall district commissioner's robust, energetic frame filled the space beside Rose. 'My, my. You have grown into quite a young woman, haven't you? Early '43 when you passed out of our college, wasn't it, Pepper? You girls were exceptional.'

The man behind the desk leaned forward, his pate shining under the overhead light. 'Her name isn't Pepper any more, madam. It's Bowman.'

Mrs Pike smiled down on her appreciatively. 'Ah, so you married. How lovely for you,' she boomed. 'And where are you off to, then? Didn't go and marry a GI, did you, girl?'

'No, I—'

'She married a Mr Bowman, says here,' chipped in the official. 'Now can you move on, please, madam. I have to deal with this young woman.'

Mrs Pike scrutinised the man through her round spectacles. 'Excuse me, there's no need to be tetchy. We are only having a conversation.'

'And if you haven't noticed, there's a lot of people waiting. So—'

'I had noticed, but you can't use your usual excuse, that there's a war on. It won't wash any more. Try being civil instead.'

The man harrumphed and drew Rose's attention. 'That lady called you Pepper . . .?' he said.

'That's my maiden name,' Rose said quickly. 'My married name is—'

'Not very Czech sounding at all,' he bleated, shuffling the forms. 'I smell a rat. You say you are a war bride. But you're not married to a Czech man. You haven't the paperwork. None of it matches up. These papers could be forgeries. This isn't going any further. Next!'

Rose stared at the man, hating his sweating forehead and long superior nose. 'If you please, sir . . . I can explain . . .' she faltered.

Mrs Pike leaned in. 'Now, now, no need for all this fuss,' she clipped. 'Just issue her with a ticket to wherever she wants to go. That's a ticket to match her passport. And stop wasting everybody's time.'

# PART TWO

*Prague, September 1945*

# Ten

IT WAS LATE AT NIGHT when the train finally eased to a halt and let out a belching hiss of steam. Woken from her doze, Rose opened her eyes. Clouds of vapour obscured the windows, then evaporated to reveal a great gloomy vault of a station. The rusty, battered sign told her she had arrived: PRAHA.

The grinding and juddering of her journey had ceased, but the voices, sounds, fatigue and the gnawing hunger (Mabel's food had run out long before hers and Nancy's so they'd had to share) remained with her like a bad dream. The seasickness on the ferry; the busy Paris streets; the refugees of Stuttgart shuffling among the flattened ruins; starving faces; shattered lives. When the train had pulled across the Czech border and a brass band had struck up, they had laughed with hysterical relief.

Now, on Rose's lap, Nancy began to stir. She started to cry.

Rose tried to comfort her. She was ashen with exhaustion, but there was a blaze of purpose in her eyes.

Mabel, on the seat opposite, applied powder and lipstick, her wedding ring flashing on her finger. 'Thank God that's over with. Can't wait to see Vaclav. He'd better be there to meet me. And I hope he has learned some more English, for I don't know any Czech.'

They disembarked, Rose clutching Krystof's address written on the back of an envelope, holding Nancy tightly with one arm, her suitcase wrenching the other one. She was stooping with fatigue.

'Hey, Ginge, do you know the Czech for "porter"?' asked Mabel.

'No,' Rose said, then muttered under her breath, 'I don't even know the Czech for "please shut up".'

At the barrier, they gave up their tickets and were solemnly beckoned into an office by two uniformed officials. One sat behind the desk and flicked through their passports and visas, then wrote in a ledger. The other watched their faces. 'I hope this doesn't take too long,' whined Mabel. 'We're *British*. *English*.' She leaned over the desk. 'Do you understand? *We* helped *you* in the war. They should just let us through. There shouldn't be any need for all of this.'

Please be quiet, thought Rose. We *have* to stand it.

The officials spoke in their incomprehensible language, their straight faces giving nothing away. Rose strained to understand. She wrote down Krystof's address for them and they nodded indifferently. Mabel proudly showed them her marriage certificate. At last their passports were stamped and they were free to go.

'About time,' muttered Mabel.

Their train had been the last of the night. All the passengers had faded away and the empty echoing station concourse opened up before them. Rose felt utterly lost. 'What now, Nancy?' she said into her daughter's hair. She had been wondering all along if Krystof would be there to meet them. The station was deserted.

A man appeared by the entrance, his arms open wide. Suddenly, Mabel cried out 'Vaclav! Vaclav!' and sprinted off. Rose slowly approached the couple and waited politely for the kissing to stop.

'I haven't seen Krystof in weeks,' Vaclav told her. 'He is on leave. Had to travel to his country home for some reason or another. You need tram number eight.' He raised his voice over Mabel's giggling. 'That will take you to the Old Town Square. It's easy from there. Go straight on, turn left, right, left . . . left again. Here, take this.'

He fished in his pocket and poured some coins into Rose's hand.

She looked down at the unfamiliar money, unable to read the value. 'Oh! That's very kind of you, but . . . how do I . . .' she began.

'It's easy. You'll find it,' repeated Vaclav. 'We have just minutes to catch our last tram. I need to get this one home.' He saluted Rose and took his wife's arm. They set off together.

'Good luck, Ginge. Bye-eee,' called Mabel, barely looking back.

The station clock struck a quarter to midnight as Rose hoisted Nancy higher on her hip and walked out into the empty street. Night had fallen like an inky cloak. A solitary tram rumbled by, its lights feeble in the darkness. She hurried across the cobbles to where she thought it might pick up passengers; but it did not stop. She turned to the sound of a man calling. One of the officials, standing at the station exit, was gesticulating. Not understanding a word he said, but assuming he meant she should go towards the left, she raised her hand in thanks.

A wretched tiredness dragged her down. She contemplated the streets, greeting her with bottomless shadows. Buildings towered either side, shutting out the sky and the stars. Walls were pockmarked (bullet holes, she feared), bricks were crumbling, stucco peeling and ruined. Great studded doors were bolted against the night. Feeling Nancy's sleepy cheek against her shoulder, the suitcase tugging on her hand, she turned corner after corner. They were alone. From pitch-black lanes came the drip-drip of water, and a dog howled behind a wall. Footsteps approached and then receded without ever revealing their owner.

Shaking with nerves, she walked under the arch of a mighty stone gateway. She found herself, small and shivering, on the edge of an acre of cobbles. Putting her suitcase down, she told a protesting Nancy to sit on it. She wondered if this was the Old Town Square. A streetlamp shed a vague gleam on a medieval hall rising like a haunted storybook castle at the centre. Rubbing her aching arms, Rose gazed up at the wall of the ancient building, to see, by the glow of the gas lamp, a peculiar clock. It had not one but three faces, overlapping like arcs in a mathematical drawing. Shimmering with gold in the grim darkness, its long iron hands reached to point out indecipherable moments in time.

'Look at that clock, Nancy,' she whispered to her daughter.

In the empty stillness came the whirr of clockwork and the hands shifted to midnight. Chimes struck up and, suddenly, a figure of a grinning skeleton squatting beside the clock face lifted a bony hand to brandish an hourglass at them. Nancy screamed.

Rose turned her away. But over her daughter's shaking head she fixed her own eyes on the white, leering skull. Her parents would be broken skeletons now, buried in St Budeaux churchyard. 'Oh, Mother, Dad, help me!' she blurted. 'I'm so sorry I never said goodbye!'

Another noise singed her nerves as a tiny door above the clock creaked open to release a parade of mechanical doll figures shuffling out to mark the passing of the hour. Their wooden eyes in blank faces watched her, haunted her.

She gripped the suitcase handle, gathered Nancy close to her, turned and ran. What was she doing bringing her little girl here? Tears of panic burst from her eyes. She could scarcely breathe. *What if Krystof is not here? What if he decides not to remember me? What if he turns us away?*

She blundered down a dark lane, confronted with corner after corner: this way or that? What had Vaclav said? Oh, damn Vaclav!

A memory of Krystof's voice found its way into her head: *I live by the monastery of St Clement near the river. My house is called* At the Clementinum. But how would she ever find it? The street signs were indecipherable. There was no one to help her; no one to care.

Then in the darkness a match was struck. A figure emerged from inky shadows. The man spoke, his expression shielded by an enormous moustache. 'Please help us,' she said. With shaking hand, Rose drew out the envelope on which Krystof had written his address. The man's eyes widened and his moustache lifted in what Rose believed to be a smile. He spoke again, his finger pointing to a porch set in a stone wall.

'Thank you,' she said.

'Ah, *Anglický*,' he said, his voice and his footsteps drifting away.

Not daring to breathe, not daring to hope, Rose walked over to the arched entrance and pressed the bell. A great dripping silence returned to the street. Agitated, she lifted the huge knocker and rapped on the door. After excruciating, breathless moments, she heard the rattle of the latch, the drawing back of bolts. The door opened a chink and she saw the face of an old woman. Rose found a well of strength. She whispered, 'Krystof Novotny? Do you know him?'

It was no use. Her words were futile. Puzzled brown eyes glistened by the light of a candle. And then a crooked hand stretched past the door to touch her hair, then reach for Nancy's face.

'Ruzena?' came the deep voice, rolling the 'r' like a cat's purr.

Rose felt the woman grip her sleeve and pull her in. The door was shut behind her and she was inside a small vestibule. Mutely understanding the woman's gesture, she dropped her suitcase and began to climb the stairs. At the top, the woman extracted Nancy from her arms. Were there more stairs to climb? Or was their journey finally over?

The woman coaxed Rose into a room. Wooden panels glimmered in the light of a bank of candles. Thick ivy-green curtains shielded the windows and the polished parquet floor glimmered like a fish pond. In front of the window lay a cushioned, silken divan.

The woman led Rose to the bed and lay Nancy down. She made Rose sit, and in silence knelt to unlace Nancy's shoes. The little girl curled herself up on the bed and was, in one sigh, sound asleep. The woman turned her attention to Rose's laces. Sinking fast, Rose fixed her eyes on the top of the silver-grey head and the thick hair tied in a bun. 'Krystof?' Rose asked again, her voice a shadow.

She realised she was in her underthings and a nightgown was being pulled over her head. The woman gestured that she should lie down.

A glass of wine was held to her lips and she gratefully sipped its sweetness. She heard snatches of songs as the woman stroked her hair. Bohemian lullabies? Slovakian folk songs? Where was Krystof? Were these his songs? Who was this lady? She tried to keep her eyes open to ask these questions, but sleep began to draw her down.

Rose heard the drawing of heavy curtains and the chink of a china cup and saucer. The soft morning light was the colour of butter. She opened her eyes. Krystof was standing beside the bed, his tawny hair gilded by the sunshine through the window. His grey eyes gazed into hers with intensity. 'Welcome home, Ruzena.'

He had opened a leaded pane in the tall stone-mullioned window and the balmy breeze touched her face as gently as his fingertips smoothed her hair.

'The air is so soft, this time of year,' he said. 'I missed it when I was away. I missed it, but not half as much as I have missed you.'

'Where's Nancy?' she asked.

'Babička is giving her breakfast. My grandmother. She said she might well benefit from a bath.'

Rose sat up slowly, conscious of her head swimming.

Krystof smiled at her. 'You made it, Ruzena.' His eyes were shining with disbelief, shining with joy. 'Come and breathe the fresh air. It will make you feel better.' He drew her up from the bed and she padded barefoot with him to the window. 'Look, Ruzena. Drink in the first sight. It's always the best. It stays with you. Always.'

'Last night your beloved city frightened me. Frightened us both,' she said. 'There was a strange clock, a skeleton, footsteps, and a man with a huge moustache who showed me where you lived. But . . .' She stood on tiptoe, peering out the window. 'This is Prague.'

Red-tiled roofs and creamy yellow walls were laid out before her; layer on layer; an illogical jumble of streets. The sun bounced over eaves and chimney pots, tipping beams of gold onto ledges and gutters. A honeyed light, captured by a single pane of glass, winked at her. Above the roofs grew a forest of spires and turrets, dark and epic in antiquity. Some were topped with gold stars, some with crosses, some with gilded spheres. 'This is why I came.' She looked up at him and kissed him softly.

As they embraced, her terror, like last night, evaporated.

'Come and say hello to Babička,' he said. 'She is longing to meet you properly. She was worried you were outside for ages ringing the bell. It hasn't worked since the beginning of the war. If we're not too late, she may well have some breakfast for us, too.'

He wrapped a shawl round her shoulders and led her out of the room onto a landing. Stairs snaked downwards into the dark vestibule, where her suitcase still lay. 'How many floors have you here?' she asked as they walked up the stairs. Square patches on the gilded wallpaper indicated the ghosts of paintings long since removed. Above her head, carved plasterwork crumbled on the ceilings.

'Four floors. The narrow entrance downstairs, with my two shops either side. These I rent out: one is a café, one a tobacconist, but that's boarded up. Then the bedrooms. One is mine, where you slept, the other Babička's. On this floor are the kitchen and salon. Above us are the laundry and the bathroom.'

'I have never set foot inside a house like this before. It's beautiful.'

'But Babička could not look after it properly during the war. And then of course, my mother, my father . . .'

'Oh, Krystof, what?'

'So many stairs! This will keep you healthy!' he cried. 'But first, Babička.'

Stung by his refusal to talk, she followed him into a room at the back of the house. Squares of sunlight through the windows lay over the surface of a huge table and set the red-painted walls on fire. Nancy sat on a pile of cushions, drinking some milk from a tin cup. 'Mama,' she called.

'Oh, my darling chicken,' cried Rose and rushed to pick her up.

At one end by the stove, knitting furiously, sat the old woman.

Krystof said, 'Ruzena, this is Babička.'

The woman got up from the chair, exclaiming, 'Ruzena, Ruzena.'

'Her name is Lara,' said Krystof to Rose. 'My grandmother. Oh, she has some coffee. My goodness, we are to be treated.'

Lara's fingers brushed Rose's cheeks and then rested on Nancy's dark head, a glow of pride in her eyes. She bustled back to the range to set a coffee pot on the hob. Rose sat with Krystof at the long table, and set Nancy on her knee while Lara poured the steaming coffee into cups.

Questions tumbled through Rose's mind. Krystof must have had news about his family. What stopped him, just now, from speaking of them?

Lara brought black bread and a dab of butter to the table. She chattered away to Rose. Rose looked at Krystof for a translation.

Krystof told her, 'She says she is glad you have both arrived safely. She wants you to feel at home.'

Rose turned to Lara. 'Thank you so much for helping me last night,' she said. 'Krystof, how do I say "thank you"?'

'Dekuji ti,' he said.

She turned back to Lara. 'Dekuji ti, Babička.'

Rose sipped her coffee and wrinkled her nose: it was very strong but she knew she had to show her appreciation. The welcome from Lara and the closeness of Krystof made her throat tighten with pleasure. Lara picked Nancy up and walked with her round the room singing in her ear and blowing raspberries on her neck. The little girl laughed in delight. Rose watched her daughter. How far they had travelled to be here. And now they were safe.

'Come on, darling! I want to show you my beloved city.'

Outside *At the Clementinum* the streets were alive with mingling voices and faces, such a contrast to the deathly quiet of the night before. Krystof put his arm round her and she strolled with him, breathing smells and seeing sights she'd never dreamed of. Suddenly before her lay the river, and a cobbled bridge glimpsed through the arches of a majestic tower.

'This is the Old Town Bridge tower, the Vltava River, and over it, the ancient Charles Bridge,' said Krystof.

'These carvings, are they kingfishers?' she asked.

'Wenceslas's favourite bird,' he said.

'As in the Good King? I didn't know he really existed.' She laughed.

'Our patron saint. Murdered on his way to church.'

Together they walked onto the bridge and Rose contemplated the wide, green river flowing gently beneath. Upstream, white water tumbled over a weir and a flock of swans glided by. A hill rose before her, crowded again with a muddle of the red roofs of houses and churches, topped by the serene castle. She smiled at the sunlight on her face, the freedom she felt in her limbs, the warmth in her bones, walking by Krystof's side.

'Where's that music coming from?' she asked.

'Halfway along the bridge. There, see?' A trio of two violins and a cello were serenading the passers-by. 'They say that whoever is Czech is a musician. But I cannot play a note.' He laughed.

She glanced upwards. 'Oh, my goodness,' she cried. 'We're being watched.' Perched on the bridge's parapets on either side were statues of solemn men in flowing robes, brandishing bishops' crooks and crosses. Eyes in tortured, frozen faces glowered down on her, scrutinising her. She shuddered. 'Who *were* these men?'

'Saints and popes,' he said. 'Put to death, martyred. Like our good King. And so preserved in stone for ever to remind us.'

'It's as if they are being *paraded*, to teach us a lesson,' she said, seeing the faces twisted in agony. But, walking along the line, she saw, alongside the torment, some of the faces fixed in religious rapture.

She sighed. 'Such contrasts: day and night, ecstasy and agony. It's like a fairy tale.'

'We love it all,' said Krystof. 'We love the *drama*. Come on.'

She linked her arm through his, looking up at him in his trench coat, with his neat trilby cocked over one eye. 'How handsome you are,' she giggled. 'I tell you, Krystof . . .'

Suddenly, the beautiful music stopped. Rose glanced back to see a rowdy group of soldiers in dirty uniforms start to cross the bridge towards them. Some had slanting Slavic eyes, others were fair-haired. They were jostling, singing and laughing—but only with each other. Everyone else crept out of their way.

She held tightly onto Krystof's hand. 'What's going on?'

'Russian soldiers,' Krystof whispered. 'Don't catch their eye. They're always trouble.'

He led her quickly down some steps on the other side of the bridge to the water's edge. 'The Russians liberated us in May,' he said, 'which is all well and good. But they seem to have outstayed their welcome. There are hundreds of them. Undisciplined, making a nuisance.'

'But I thought the Americans liberated Prague?'

'Good old propaganda, it works for both sides, doesn't it? No, the Allies only got so far east into Germany, Czechoslovakia, Poland; they left the rest of Europe to the Soviets.'

'But even so, Krystof. Better them than the Germans?'

'Oh, yes.'

She watched him carefully. 'Vaclav mentioned that you'd been to the country. What about your family—'

He broke in. 'The Russians! I don't care much for their politics. We hoped for a new start for Czechoslovakia. A new republic. A return to the golden age we had fifty years ago when Babička was a girl.'

She asked, 'How do the Russians affect you? You're still an officer in the Czech army?'

'On leave at the moment. You're right. I had been out of town for a few weeks . . . got back late last night.' His voice drifted.

'But how does it work, with all these other troops here?'

'It doesn't *work*. Why do you think you saw not a soul on your walk through the city last night? The people of Prague are scared. They stay locked behind their doors at night.'

'Well, what does the government have to say?'

'So many questions! The Czech government and the army have an *understanding* with the Russians. You must remember our army is very weak. Our country is very weak, after years under the Nazis. Look at me. I've been given a desk job. I don't even wear a uniform.'

'Please tell me about your family?'

Pain shadowed his face like a series of clouds moving across the sun. He stood up. 'Come and see my favourite church.'

**K**rystof pushed open the great door and they stepped inside. Rose's eyes grew wide as she took in statues of the Virgin dripping with gold; cherubs dancing with angels. Krystof pointed out the jewelled altar at the far end as it captured the sun beaming down through monumental stained-glass windows. Then she recoiled when he showed her the rotting body of a saint inside a glass coffin.

'I have walked just one mile in this city,' she whispered to him, 'and everywhere I look I see images of pain and death.' They sat down on an ancient pew under a statue of a bleeding Christ. 'I feel I am being judged. All these statues, these saints . . . and God looking down on me. They know I am a married woman. They know . . .'

As if he wasn't listening, Krystof spoke up suddenly: 'We used to worship here every Sunday when we were up from the country. But now . . .' He rested the side of his head against hers. 'I cannot understand why people continue with their faith. The war . . . the dreadful atrocities. All my faith is gone. We are both orphans, Ruzena.'

'Oh, Krystof.' She watched as his face drained of colour; his eyes turned sharp with pain.

'My mother, my father, my younger brother Tomas. Murdered by German soldiers.' He was whispering and yet his voice was enormous.

A coldness crept into her bones as he told her how Tomas had, a year before, married his childhood sweetheart and they were living together in the farmhouse with his parents. When the soldiers stormed the village, he told her, the women and children were sent to the camps and all the men over sixteen were rounded up. Shot dead. Babička was in Prague at the time, visiting her friend in the Little Quarter—the only reason she survived.

'Why? But *why*?' Rose's voice caught in her throat.

He told her that the village had been made an example of—punished for the assassination of an important Nazi.

'The village was bulldozed,' he said. 'It no longer exists.'

Rose looked down at his hands; they were shaking. She tried to steady them with her own. She had lived with a man who supported these people. She had given birth to his child. Her stomach churned.

'I found out when I returned a few months ago. Babička had been alone for three years, her family dead. When I arrived she was nearly starving. She'd sold paintings, silver, our furniture on the black market to survive.' He looked up at the statues, the trappings of worship. 'I can't pray any more. I am finished. I am *angry*.' He touched her chin to turn her to face him. 'When I felt that you were on your way to me, I found a reason to live. And Babička has blossomed in just the few hours that you have been here. You are a good thing for us, Ruzena. You and Nancy.'

'And you are my good thing, Krystof,' she said into his hair.

**W**ho is that man?' she asked. 'And why is he staring?'

They had walked back across the bridge and were outside *At the Clementinum*. Krystof was fishing for his keys.

'Everyone stares at you, Ruzena. It's your red hair. Not many people in Czechoslovakia have such a red. Just like *Září* The month that glows with colour. How apt that you should arrive here in September.'

The man in question was standing outside the café next door to Krystof's house. He grinned widely at Krystof, showing teeth under a huge moustache and shouted a cheerful greeting.

Krystof glanced his way. 'Oh, that's Milan. He manages my café next door,' he said, calling back, '*Dobrý den*, Milan.'

'He's the man from last night,' whispered Rose.

Krystof walked over and shook Milan by the hand, as the man clapped him on the shoulder. 'Rose, this is Milan,' he said.

'Please tell him thank you,' she said.

Milan gazed at her hair, then his eyes began to travel down her body. Krystof told her, 'He wants us to step inside; he says he has some schnapps under the counter. I have told him, another time maybe.'

'I'm glad. Thank you,' she said to Krystof, avoiding Milan's eye.

Krystof opened his front door, waving away Milan's good-natured protests. As she shut the door behind her, Rose glanced back and saw the man's expression change. He was insulted.

They met Babička on the stairs. The old woman kissed them on the cheeks to say both hello and goodbye.

Krystof said, 'She has given Nancy her tea and put her to sleep; she is going for supper at her friend's house across in the Little Quarter.'

In the kitchen, Rose and Krystof sipped pheasant broth.

'How far is it to Babička's friend's house? Will she be getting a taxi back, or a tram?' asked Rose.

'Just over the Charles Bridge. I think she may well stay the night there.' Krystof looked at Rose and gently laughed. 'Didn't you see the little valise she was carrying? She is a wise old lady. She knows we would like to be alone tonight. Our first night.'

'Krystof,' she said, fully understanding his suggestion, 'we will be committing a sin. I am still married.'

'I'm sorry, Rose, I know. I am not being a gentleman. But you are estranged, separated. Your husband is in prison.'

Immediately, the awful memory of Will Bowman in the dark maisonette bedroom flashed through her mind. How utterly lost she had been. How mindlessly she had given herself away. And, now, how right being with Krystof felt. And yet, sex, in her mind, was connected only with her dreadful husband.

'I need some time,' she said, swallowing hard. 'I am a little . . . can I jus? . . . I am *surprised*. Remember in the barn at Pengared, how you wanted us to wait to be married. And I knew deep down you were right. Why have things changed?'

'I was a good Catholic back then. Now . . . so much has changed. All except me wanting you.' His eyes were serious. 'You are here now. We are together.' His lips found the back of her neck. '*Miluji ty.*'

'What did you say?'

'You know what I said. *I love you.*'

Krystof's face was transparent with desire and she felt a fierce warmth rise up in her body as it had done at Trelewin cove and again in the barn at Pengared. Suddenly she felt terrified. She walked away from him, opening the door to an empty room.

The room was bare, save for a grand chaise longue in the middle of naked floorboards. Lara had had to strip the room to pay for food. Rose sat down on the chaise. What was she *thinking*? Krystof was everything to her; she had crossed Europe for him. She loved him, so why could she not relax and let him make love to her?

After some minutes, she wiped away her tears. Patches on the salon walls revealed where paintings used to hang, and ragged, moth-eaten drapes at the windows were held together by remnants of gold thread. It must have been a wonderful room once, full of Babička's family and friends: glittering parties, conversation and music. She thought of her parents' back parlour and imagined the laughter there too.

Glancing up at the one remaining painting hanging over the fireplace, she turned cold. It was a wedding portrait. A man in a dark suit was seated, bursting with pride. Behind him stood a woman in a gown of eau de nil, a certain confidence in her eyes—the same grey eyes as Krystof. Her forehead was as strong as Lara's and her tiny hand was resting on the man's shoulder. The brushstroked date in the corner read 1923—the same year her parents had married. Rose sat transfixed by the painted faces, her tears drying in streaks. Krystof's parents looked so happy: they did not know how it would end.

Shivering with despair, she got up and walked to the window. As the beautiful evening glow began to fade, she contemplated the chances she'd had, and the chances she'd ruined by trying to be good and proper, trying to please others. The man she loved was waiting for her. He had escaped occupation, fought a long hard war, only to return to find his family murdered. And now he was sitting there, snubbed by her prissiness.

Leaving the room with the portrait to settle back into its closed tranquillity, she quietly shut the door.

She found Krystof by the kitchen stove, drinking a tot of schnapps in the twilight. She reached for the light switch. Nothing happened.

'Do the lights not work?' she asked.

'We haven't had electricity for six months.'

'Never mind, I like candlelight.' She took his hand. 'Krystof,' she said, 'shall we light some candles in the bedroom?'

**H**e closed the bedroom door. Her hands trembled as she lit the candles on the mantelpiece. She began to laugh softly, her nerves fizzing. He cradled her in his arms.

'Why do you laugh, Ruzena?'

'I am in shock. I still can't believe that I am here, with you.'

A sigh of warm air through the window brushed her skin and she began to shiver.

'Don't be nervous,' he said.

'Not nerves. I'm ecstatic.'

Even so, she drank from the small glass of schnapps that he handed her. Then he took the glass and knelt down. She touched his hair as he pressed his cheek to her stomach as if to listen to her body, the thumping of her heart. His hands moved to the buttons on the front of her dress, pausing first to ask the question with his eyes. She nodded in silence and watched as he undid the buttons with such patient composure that she was blinded with tears.

She whispered, 'You know I have had a baby . . . my body is not . . .'

'Do you think that matters to me?'

They kissed to say hello. They kissed to bridge the void of time and distance that had kept them apart. His fingers found the clips in her hair and he tossed them one by one onto the floor; he found the fastenings of her underwear.

'Oh, but Ruzena, you are beautiful!' he said and scooped her into his arms. They laughed together as he tottered towards the divan.

'You need to be naked too,' she giggled, and helped him undress.

She gasped at the breadth and beauty of his body. She nuzzled into him, unable to believe that she could be so happy. She let him guide her to a place where she could, at last, believe, and their laughter softened into sighs of wonder.

# Eleven

'I THINK I'VE FOUND just the thing,' Krystof called up the stairs. 'Ruzena, get up and come and look at this.'

The morning chill settled round her ankles as she descended the stairs to the vestibule. September had slid all too quickly into October and, although the days were still bright, mornings had a raw edge. Shivering, she opened the back door to see Krystof in the courtyard, dressed for the office in his smart suit, tie and trilby, beaming at her.

'Hurry up,' he cried. 'I've got to report at the barracks before eight this morning. First day back so I need to make a good impression.'

'What's that you've got there?' she asked.

'A pram for Nancy. Look. She'll love it. Isn't it perfect?'

'It's wonderful, Krystof.' Rose smiled. 'Where did you find it?'

'In the shed under a pile of old sacks,' he said, laughing. 'Don't look like that. Just be thankful! So what will you do today, while I'm working away pushing useless pieces of paper around on my desk?' he asked.

'I will help Babička, as usual, with the chores,' she said. 'Then I will take Nancy for a walk in her new pram and post my letter to Betony.' She cocked her head at him, puzzled. 'Do you think it's strange that I haven't heard from her yet? She hasn't replied to my first letter.'

'Not so strange,' said Krystof. 'Remember, the post will be in a very sorry state. Think how far that letter has to travel. Like you did.' He kissed the top of her head. 'Send another by all means. Do you think you will cope at the post office? Remember what to say?'

'Yes, yes. I've got to learn how to do it myself.'

'That's my good girl,' he said. 'Now I must be off.'

As she hugged him, she glanced at the top of the high garden wall to see a trail of cigarette smoke and Milan's dark head. He was standing in his own yard, as if he was waiting for something to happen.

**R**ose called goodbye to Babička, closed the front door behind her and pushed Nancy out into the chilly air. Grey clouds blew across the watery blue sky above the turrets and spires of the Old Town, and the weak sun winked at her occasionally from behind a rooftop. Market sellers in the Old Town Square were animated, dealing with long shuffling queues of people, all eager for the few loaves of bread on offer, the sparse, rotting vegetables. Lara had already been out at dawn to buy their provisions. There wasn't much left now.

Inside the post office Rose joined the end of another snaking queue. She reckoned she'd be there an hour. Shifting from one foot to the other and blowing on her fingers, boredom stretched her nerves. Speaking to the people of Prague was a trial. She did not want to be misunderstood. Mercifully Nancy slept, wrapped in her blanket.

A telegram, she thought. I will send a telegram instead. It will be quicker. She might hear from Betony sooner. In her head Rose repeated the words that Krystof had told her to say: '*Mohl byste to dat na postu?*'

At last she reached the service window. Queasy with nerves, she tried to speak but her tongue twisted the words. The stiff-faced clerk looked blankly at her, shaking his head. She tried again. Swallowing hard, she pushed forward ten crown notes. Frustrated tears stung her eyes. 'Please,' she said to the clerk, 'I'm *Anglický*. Please help me.'

To her astonishment, he shrugged and pulled down his blind with a snap. Furious and embarrassed, Rose spun the pram round and sped out of the building. She sat on a bench in the square, her shoulders sinking despondently. Nancy woke and began to cry. Rose picked her up and settled her on her lap, glancing around at the grand buildings. The leaden sky failed to bring life to the beauty of the city. Its spirit, like hers, was crushed by the gloom. Townspeople hurried by, glancing as was their wont, at her hair, which fell in a wave from under her hat. She noticed the holes in their shoes, the patched coats, and felt pity coiling in her belly.

She wondered about Mabel, who, Krystof told her, was living outside the city with Vaclav. Even a chat with that irritating girl would perk her up. She realised that without Krystof to talk to she was lonely. But his leave was now over and he had an important job to go to.

A large black Daimler rumbled across the square, a red flag with golden hammer and sickle fluttering on its bonnet. She watched it park outside one of the larger old guild houses which had a brand-new sign over its portal. The sign said *Ministerstuo Bezpečnost*. So that must be the Ministry of State Security, she thought with a shudder.

'*Ruský*,' someone next to her said.

She turned to behold the dark eyes of Milan glinting at her from under his woollen cap. 'Oh, *dobrý den*,' she greeted him.

He moved up the bench, shuffling closer. Her skin prickled with displeasure beneath her coat. Not wanting Milan to speak to or touch Nancy, she sat the child back in her pram and strapped her in.

The man said, '*Ruský všude*.'

She looked at him blankly, folding her hands demurely on her lap.

He sighed and appeared to try something different, patting his arms and pretending to shiver. '*Studený*,' he said.

'Ah.' Rose nodded, copying his actions. Was he saying he was cold? '*Studený nyni. Říjen*,' he insisted.

Relieved to have caught one word she knew, she said, 'Oh, yes. Krystof has taught me all the months of the year.' She spoke in English. '*Říjen* is October. The rutting season.'

Milan leaned in closer and she smelt the tobacco on his breath; his eyes were bright with pleasure. He gestured with his hips, as if he was, himself, rutting. '*Říjen! Říjen!*' he cried, laughing at his crudity.

Rose tried to avert her eyes. She shrank away.

He held out fat fingers and counted off the months of the year for her. He pointed to the trees and the leaves, and fluttered his hands.

'Ah, yes, *Listopad*,' she said, politely. 'Yes, next month is November, *Listopad*, the month of falling leaves.'

'*Listopad, studený*, cold,' he repeated, then when he got to January, '*Leden*,' he said, and began to shiver even more, as if he was in agony.

'Oh, yes,' she said, brightening a little, pleased to have understood. 'January, *Leden*—I know. It translates as *ice*. Very cold.'

Milan pointed a finger at her chest and said, '*Anglický*.' He gestured at his mouth and tapped the side of his temple. '*Anglický ucitelka!*'

She understood him. She looked at Milan and thought, You are quite odious but I am a stranger here and I ought to be open-minded. She took a breath. '*Ano,*' she said. 'Yes. I'll teach you English, if you teach me Czech.'

He nodded, his tongue poking out through his moustache.

**B**ack at *At the Clementinum* Rose left Nancy with Lara, telling her she had one more errand to do. Lara's angry stare was like a slap in the face. Was she cross about having to look after Nancy at short notice? Rose had no idea but resolved to make it up to her as soon as she returned.

At least the café was warm. Milan poured two cups of coffee at the counter and set them on a table, gesturing to her to be seated. The men, huddled at the tables, muffled in scarves and caps, stared at her before turning their backs and continuing to play dominoes, their murmuring punctuated by the clicking of ivory tiles.

Rose looked around her at the untidy crowd of tables and chairs. Gas lamps glowed, highlighting advertisement posters of beautiful girls holding burning cigarettes or mugs of frothing beer. She remembered Krystof telling her about the Czechoslovakian 'land-girls', and here they were in all their glory.

Milan tapped her on the arm impatiently. The first lesson began.

**M**uch later than she intended, and feeling guilty for leaving Nancy for so long with Lara, Rose returned to the house. She was climbing the stairs when voices reached her from the kitchen above. Lara's shrill, angry cry resounded through the house, stopping Rose in her tracks. Then, under this astonishing tirade, she caught snatches of Krystof's gentle voice: persuasive and apologetic.

As she reached the top of the stairs, Lara burst out of the kitchen door. She advanced on Rose in a frenzy, holding out her left hand and brandishing it in Rose's face. Rose stared wide-eyed in disbelief as the old woman began to tap furiously at the wedding ring on her own finger.

'What are you saying to me, Babička?' cried Rose, desperately.

'*Kurva!*' Lara hissed at her. The grandmother turned on her heel and stamped her way up the stairs.

Somewhere in the house, Nancy was crying.

'What's going on, Krystof?' asked Rose, her legs shaking as she walked into the kitchen. 'I am so sorry. I left Nancy with Babička this afternoon—obviously for far too long—but I won't be doing it again.'

'Sit down, Ruzena,' Krystof said, pouring a tot of schnapps for her.

'But first, I must go and see to Nancy. Is she all right?'

'Leave Nancy for a moment, please. Sit.' By the light of the lantern his face looked ashen, his forehead twisting with anxiety.

'Why is Babička so angry? I have never seen her so—'

'As you know,' he began, a hard edge to his voice, 'my family is—was—devoutly Catholic. And Babička remains so. Unfortunately, she has just found out that we are not married. And that Nancy is not my child.'

Rose gasped. 'But we did not pretend. We never told her . . .'

'Well, what's true is we didn't tell her *anything* and she assumed. She told me this morning that she was wondering about Nancy and how dark her hair was. No one in our family has that colouring.'

'That's why she glared at me earlier,' said Rose.

'And just now she asked me directly. I couldn't lie to her.'

'But you are like a father to Nancy,' said Rose. 'You always will be. And I want nothing more to do with Will, you know that . . .'

'Yes, but in the eyes of God—Babička's God—you are still married and we are living in sin. And she is angry.' Krystof looked incredibly tired. 'We have to try to make amends with her.'

'I will not allow my sham of a marriage to ruin our happiness! She will come round when she knows how much we love each other.'

'Yes.' He sounded dubious. 'She will calm down soon.'

'I hope so. I have never seen anyone so furious. Babička kept holding out her hand to me, tapping her wedding ring. Oh, what was the word she used . . . she literally hissed it at me. *Kurva*, was it?'

Krystof's eyes widened in shock. 'Good God,' he said, running his hand over his face. 'I don't believe it. *Kurva* means prostitute.'

**R**ose lay in the deep, delicious warmth of the bed beside Krystof. She squinted at the alarm clock. I wonder, she thought, *kolik je hodin*?

And then she gasped and laughed, waking Krystof with a start.

'What?' he asked, rolling over. 'What's the matter?'

'I just *thought* in Czech,' she said, with delight. 'I was wondering what the time was and there it was: *kolik je hodin?* What's the time?'

'If you're *thinking* it,' said Krystof, 'it must be sinking in.'

'At least now I won't have to spend so much time with Milan . . .' She shuddered. 'I'll tell him. I don't need his lessons any more.'

'What about his English?'

'I think Milan's up to scratch,' she said, feeling dismissive.

Before Krystof left for work, as was his habit, he lifted the sleeping Nancy from her cot and put her in the warm hollow that he left behind in the bed. Snuggled like this, Rose drifted off again to be woken by the flapping of the letter box below. She padded down the stairs.

'Oh, my goodness, it's for me!' she called out to herself in English, snatching the envelope up from the doormat. She thought carefully and then called out in Czech: 'A letter for me!'

Lara, crashing pots together in the kitchen above, ignored her. Rose was not in the least bit surprised: the old woman had hardly spoken to her since calling her a prostitute. Racing back up the stairs with the letter, Rose tried to put the ridiculous insult out of her mind.

'At long last, Nancy, my first letter must have got through,' Rose told her. 'Finally Auntie Betony has replied . . . Ahh, a telegram no less . . .'

She pulled out the chit of paper, and then her stomach dropped.

*Will Bowman released from prison STOP Back at Old Vicarage STOP To accuse you of kidnap in courts STOP We advise swift return STOP Cumberpatch*

She crushed the paper in her hands, her head sinking forwards. Would he ever let her go? She breathed steadily, waiting for her nerves to calm before getting up and dressing herself and her daughter.

'He can't do this to us,' she told Nancy brightly to convince herself. 'Kidnap. What a silly idea. I will divorce him, and I will marry Krystof. He is your father, Nancy. And we will be happy. A family.'

Nancy chuckled and pointed to a pair of Krystof's boots.

'That's right. Krystof.' Then, unable to control her sarcasm, Rose said, 'Come on, let's go to the warm kitchen and see if Babička will smile at us today.'

Lara, wielding a sharp knife, was in the midst of descaling a carp. '*Dobrý den*, Babička.' Rose spoke in Czech, hoping to appease the grandmother. 'I wondered, as the sun is shining, shall we both take Nancy for a walk? Perhaps over to the Little Quarter?'

Silence. Lara turned her back to reach for a bowl of eggs on the dresser, clumping it down on the table and resuming her work.

Rose sat Nancy on her pile of cushions and poured her some warm milk, trying to remember a word Milan had said, the word for cold.

'Er . . . Babička, perhaps it is too *stude* . . ..?' She hesitated.

Lara shrugged. She bent back to the fish.

'Can I help?' Rose tried again, walking to the table.

Lara gave a fierce shake of her head, then prepared to plunge the knife into the fish to slit it from neck to tail.

'I'd like us to be friends again, Babička. Please, for Krystof's sake.

I need your advice. Truth is, I've received some shocking news . . .'

Lara lifted her face and yelled, '*Skutečny?* Truth?'

'Oh, please, *prosím*, Babička.'

Lara threw an icy stare at Rose and in a flash, she took her eye off her task. The blade slipped. '*Jezis-Maria!*' The old woman screamed and clutched at her hand as blood oozed over the mess of fish scales.

Rose rushed over to her. 'Oh, Babička!'

The old woman flinched away, yelling angrily in a stream of incomprehensible words, and hurried into the scullery.

Rose hurried after her. She found her trying to turn on the tap with her elbow. There was no water.

'Babička, perhaps this will help,' she said, fetching a bottle of vinegar.

'*Ne, ne.*' Lara stared at her. Hatred and disgust boiled in her eyes. '*Kurva,*' she hissed.

Tears fell down Rose's cheeks. In her distress she cried out in English, 'Please don't say that to me. You don't understand.'

Lara went back into the kitchen. Rose followed. The old woman was standing by the table, staring hard at Nancy. The little girl sat cringing, her shoulders hunched with distress. Rose gently touched the old woman's arm. Lara yelled, flinging out her hand, sending the bowl of eggs crashing to the floor before marching out of the room.

Nancy began to cry as Rose sank to her knees to try to retrieve the mess. 'Oh, what a waste. What an utter waste.'

With Lara keeping to her room, not answering Rose's tapping on the door, Rose had no choice but to put Nancy to bed, press her finger to her lips and hope she stayed put. She went into the café. As she eschewed a table and walked straight to the counter she felt a murmuring among the patrons, their eyes flicking to look at her and then back down to their dominoes or beverage or schnapps.

Milan was leaning there, his large hairy arms folded in front of him. 'Find a table and I will serve you,' he grumbled.

'*Ne.* Not today. Or any day,' she said. 'I have come to tell you that there will be no more lessons. I think I am sufficiently fluent in Czech to get by, thank you very much. So I'm putting a stop to it.'

'Oh, no,' he said. 'That wasn't the deal. I am not *fully* fluent in English,' he said. 'So, you still have to teach me. The Party wants people like me. Translators.'

'The party?'

'The *Party*.'

'No, Milan. There was never any deal.'

She heard chuckling and turned to see that most of the men were laughing at Milan. Milan's face flushed red with fury.

'I'll give you double schnapps if you teach me now.'

'No, I don't want anything. I have to get back to my daughter.'

A customer called, 'Hey, Milan's been put in his place by the *Anglický*? Not even a double schnapps will tempt her. He's losing his touch.'

'Did he ever have a touch?' someone answered.

Rose watched as Milan's embarrassment seemed to swell his frame. 'Get out then,' he hissed, staring hard.

'With pleasure,' she said.

For the rest of the day, Rose busied herself in the kitchen. At last she heard Krystof's key in the lock below. Rushing to the kitchen door to greet him, she cried, 'Oh, Krystof, I've had an awful day—oh!'

She stopped talking when she saw him come into the lamplight. His face had the pallor of a corpse, his eyes were shining with shock.

'Nancy in bed?' he asked.

She nodded.

'And where's Babička?'

'Asleep in her room. I'm afraid she cut her finger badly. . .'

'Well, I'm glad she's in her room, as I don't want her to hear this.' He closed the door to the kitchen and pulled her to the table.

'What? What?' He was scaring her.

'I was walking back across the Charles Bridge, as usual, as I do every evening, when I saw two men walking towards me.' He was breathless. 'I thought they'd step aside—God, I've just had a thought. Wait!'

He jumped up. Rose followed him to the landing window. He stood in the darkness and carefully tilted his head from side to side, watching the street below. Finally he backed away and drew the curtain, gesturing that they should go back into the kitchen. He closed the door behind them and leaned on it.

'They're following me. The two men . . .' he said finally, his words disjointed by shock. 'The bridge was deserted. I was about halfway across. They were coming towards me. They stopped me with a hand to the chest. They asked me if I was Captain Novotny of the Tulka Regiment, Army of Czechoslovakia. I said, "Yes, of course I am." They introduced themselves. They said they were from the Communist Party. It was so dark that I could hardly see their faces. And then they asked, Would I like to join the Party. But it wasn't a question. It was a trap.'

Rose pressed her lips together, fighting her bubbling fear.

Krystof sat down next to her. 'I said, "No. No, thank you. I support the Social Democrats."'

'Of course you said no,' she said. 'Were they *Ruský*?'

'No, they were Czech. But they are under the influence of . . .'

She remembered the sleek Daimler with its fluttering red pennant in the square. She asked, 'What did they do?'

'One of them has followed me home. It's just intimidation. They know who I am.'

'Even so,' she said, her voice shaking. 'What does this *mean*?'

Krystof sighed. 'It means our Russian friends are here to stay. In a way, some people see it as a good thing. Our new government is desperate to get away from anything remotely right wing. I see their point, but I also see the whole of the East being eaten up by the Soviets.'

And here I am, Rose thought, in the centre of this mess, waiting for the debris to fall. The telegram from Pengared played on her mind, but she would not bother Krystof with that tonight.

To her astonishment, he suddenly laughed. 'One thing you can say,' he said, 'is that we've swapped one lot of occupying clowns for another. But at least the Germans had better manners.'

She joined in with his laughter, noting the edge of hysteria.

But then, as they held each other in the lamplight, she heard the telegram crinkle up in her pocket and a sick melancholy broke over her.

# Twelve

GOLDEN LEAVES WERE FALLING in streams from the trees. Brown smoke from coal fires floated in a layer above the chimney pots. From the kitchen window, Rose watched as Krystof spun Nancy round and round in her pram. The little girl shrieked with laughter.

Rose smiled and then her face dropped. On the other side of the wall, Milan was methodically sweeping up leaves in the café courtyard. She saw him step to the wall, carefully slide a loose brick to the side and press his eye to the hole.

Rose turned to see Lara walk into the kitchen with the post and she began to gesture towards the yard below. The old woman ignored Rose and placed the letters on the table. Then she went to the window and craned her neck to watch her grandson play. Glancing sideways at her, Rose noticed a thin smile twitch her lips.

After a while, the old lady turned to go, muttering to herself, 'She should learn to call him *Otec*.'

Rose felt hope rise like a bird. Lara had said that Nancy should call Krystof *Papa*. 'Babička will come round,' she told herself as she picked up the letter addressed to her.

Then she frowned. The envelope had already been torn open and resealed. She pulled out the letter. The folded sheet of thick, well-thumbed paper was headed with the name of a London solicitor. *Dear Mrs Bowman*, she read, *Re: Bowman vs Bowman*. Even across the miles, Will had the capacity to reach her.

> *. . . the very serious charge of kidnap will be brought to bear if you do not return to England with the child Nancy Sylvia Bowman . . . our client will petition for divorce on account of adultery, desertion and unreasonable behaviour . . . custody of the said child will be given to Mr Bowman . . . return immediately . . .*

She sat down at the kitchen table, let the letter fall into her lap and held her head in her hands. Betony had warned her in the telegram, but she had decided to ignore her. And now, just two weeks later, the full fury and cold patience of Will Bowman sat on her shoulders.

'But what of his conviction?' she cried out loud. She snatched up the letter again. In her shock, she'd missed out a paragraph.

> *. . . our client's contrition over his past misdemeanours stands him in good stead . . . has stood before an appeal judge . . . pardoned . . .*

Rose heard the back door to the yard open and Krystof and Nancy bundled in. She went to the top of the stairs. Her voice was hollow with shock. 'Krystof, please put Nancy down for a nap.'

'Oh, she's too excited for that. I thought she could have some milk and a *zákusek* from Milan next door.'

'I haven't got time for pastries! Take her to bed!'

Krystof looked at Rose aghast. 'What's the matter? What on earth?'

She handed him the letter and took Nancy from him. 'He has tracked me down,' Rose said. 'He says he wants me back in England or he will take Nancy away from me.' She turned to take Nancy up the stairs but the little girl began to wriggle and call for Krystof. Rose's hand flashed out and slapped her hard. 'Stop your crying!' she shouted. 'You do as you are told!'

Krystof cried, 'Ruzena, please!'

Rose stared at him over the top of her weeping child's face.

'Read it,' she said. 'Then you will know why I just did that.'

Feeling equal amounts of guilt, resentment and love for her child, she held Nancy close and walked up the stairs.

Unable to sleep they rose before dawn and, mindful of waking Lara and Nancy, crept quietly down the stairs. The night air in the street outside was so cold that Rose cried out. When they reached the Charles Bridge lined with its frozen statues, they turned left and walked along the embankment. The inky river slept in the darkness, its frigid depths unimaginable. They stopped at the next bridge along, the Legii, and leaned on the parapet. From here, the castle on the other bank was in deep shadow, but behind it, in the east, the veil of night was lifting and a pale greenness spread over the horizon.

'I can't believe it has come to this,' Rose said.

Krystof, ignoring her, spoke with conviction. 'I want to marry you, Rose Pepper.'

'Is that really the answer? How can we even start to think about that!' She took a deep, despairing breath. 'Why didn't we think of this before—why was I so hell-bent on getting away from England?'

She stopped. One glance at Krystof's face had told her why.

'I wanted my life with you to start as soon as possible,' she admitted. 'I should have divorced Will while he was still in prison, but I ran away. And, now, because of that, my chance of happiness with you is fading.'

Krystof's arms surrounded her. 'You have to return to England.' His voice cracked with reluctance. 'You need to set yourself free from this disgusting man. Show the courts you deserve custody of Nancy. Let them know of his appalling behaviour. Show them what a good mother you are.'

'But how can I leave when I have to be with you? I can't leave you.' She began to shiver, the cold reaching her stomach.

His whisper was edged with pain. 'But I cannot leave Babička.'

She heard the first stirrings of birds. Poor little creatures, how do they survive this bitterness? How did they not freeze when all around her was cold, so cold?

'No, no, don't cry.' Krystof stepped closer and wrapped his arms round her, tried to stop her shaking. 'Perhaps we will find a way. I will speak to people, people in high places . . . my superior at the barracks, perhaps.' Krystof's voice rose with hollow enthusiasm. 'Even Lucenka the old lamplighter woman has contacts. You'd be surprised.'

'But why should these people bother with us? It's useless.'

'Don't you dare say that, Rose Pepper.' Krystof was angry. 'I will not hear it.' But even as he spoke, she watched anger fade from his eyes as an awful realisation spread slowly over his face. 'If you leave Czechoslovakia,' Krystof said, 'the way things are . . . you may not be able to come back.'

'Then we do nothing,' Rose said.

As the sun pushed up into the stillness of the dawn, a sudden wind tore the last of the leaves from the trees, scattering them around their feet. She said, 'I remember leaves were falling in my parents' garden when I returned to find my home bombed . . . the life I knew . . . over.' The breeze sent icy fingers down the back of her neck. 'I feel exactly the same now, watching these leaves fall.'

The golden stone of the Charles Bridge began to emerge from the gloom and the silhouetted statues appeared like a line of chattering old men. Prague's beauty had never looked so transient nor so brittle.

'**On** days like today,' said Krystof, scraping the ice from the inside of the bedroom windowpanes, 'they say that birds fall dead from the sky. Frozen in mid-flight.'

'I thought the kitchen at the Old Vicarage was chilly.' Rose's teeth chattered. 'But this is monstrous.'

'You will get used to it. *Únor* is the month of floating ice. Of course it's going to be cold. But at least the ice is breaking on the river. Just think, in a month or two, the glorious spring will return.'

'Get back into bed, Krystof. Quickly. And in the spring?' she asked, responding to the edge of hope in his voice.

'I will resign from the army. We will sell this place. We can go and live in a *chalupa*—a little country house. Get away from Prague and its prying eyes. Perhaps have some chickens, a pig and a goat? What do you say, Ruzena?'

'I say *ano* to that. Yes,' she whispered.

'Nancy will love it. And Babička will agree, I am sure,' said Krystof. 'I take it she is giving Nancy her breakfast at the moment? Are things improving between you both?'

'She is being nice to Nancy,' said Rose. 'She can't ignore Nancy.'

Krystof asked, 'Have you seen our friend recently?'

'Our man who stands and watches?' she replied. 'No. I think even the *Ruský policie* are finding this weather too barbaric.'

'Well, I have a busy day. I want to fix that doorbell.' He laughed. 'It is driving me *blázniwý*.'

'Driving me crazy too,' said Rose, 'but it's too cold to even think about stepping outside.'

'It won't take long. Half an hour at the most,' he said. 'Talking of things driving us crazy . . . I saw Milan yesterday and said hello but he just stood and stared at me and stroked his moustache.'

'I find the man revolting. I avoid him at all costs.'

'Well, just think, when we move away, we can leave all of our troubles behind us. Including him.' Krystof's eyes sparkled at the thought. 'I'll even pass the café to him, if I have to, to keep him off our backs.'

'I don't think he deserves to be given the café,' said Rose, grumpily.

'Another thing I could do if it wasn't so bloody damn cold is to fill that hole in the wall. But the cement will freeze before I can do anything with it. I wonder where my tools are?'

**R**estless, Rose wandered the house, checking the fires in the bedrooms, making sure they were properly banked to preserve their warmth so that it lasted until the evening. She walked to the landing window and craned her neck to see if she could spot Krystof working below. The porch blocked her view, but she could hear the faint tapping of his hammer.

She watched the street like a hawk; as she predicted, the cold had driven even the hardiest of spies indoors. Shivering, her feet leaden, she knew she should go back to the kitchen and sit by the stove and watch Lara's stony face. It was too cold to stand there any longer.

Lara sat knitting, her mouth set in a pensive line. By her side, Nancy was having her nap in her cot brought close to the stove. As soon as Rose walked in, Lara stood up stiffly and poured some coffee from the enamel pot, punctuating the silence with a smattering of tutting and groans. She proffered the steaming cup and Rose deduced from the mute gesture that she should take the coffee to Krystof.

As she opened the front door a chink to call Krystof, the icy blast hit her like a blow. 'Krystof? Coffee for you. You must be nearly finished?' His chisel and screwdriver were laid neatly on the doorstep; his stepladder propped against the wall. 'Krystof?' He must have popped away for something from the ironmonger. Screws, perhaps? She pressed the bell. It still did not work.

At midday Rose, Lara and Nancy ate their soup in the quiet kitchen.

'Oh, isn't *Otec* a scoundrel?' she said to Nancy. 'I wonder where Krystof's gone?' Her mouth felt dry. He had been gone two hours.

Sitting close to the range, she held Nancy on her lap and read to her. The clock on the landing chimed three, and the sun began to sink. Glancing up, she saw that Lara was dozing.

Shutting the book and telling Nancy firmly to stay by the stove, Rose went back downstairs and opened the front door. But the doorway was empty. She folded up the stepladder and brought in Krystof's tools.

'How careless he is,' she muttered out loud as she closed the door. 'They might have been stolen.' But she was pretending.

'Krystof?' came Lara's despondent voice from the top of the stairs.

'*Ne*,' she told her.

In the shadows of the stairway, Rose saw lines of worry carve up the woman's face. 'Wait here, Babička,' Rose said, quickly bundling on her coat and hat. She went out into the cold.

Through the windows of the café she could see that all was dark and quiet. She took a deep breath and knocked on the door. There was utter silence. Eventually, a light showed at the back and Milan came out from behind the counter. She rattled the handle. 'Let me in!' she cried.

He shrugged and unlatched the door. 'I was asleep,' he moaned. 'It's my day off. The café is closed.'

'Krystof has gone,' she breathed urgently. 'Do you know where?'

He regarded her briefly and then told her, 'The *Ruský policie* came for Captain Novotny five hours ago.'

'*Why?* Why didn't you tell us?'

'His awful hammering stopped,' said Milan. 'It had given me a headache, so in the peace and quiet, I could sleep . . .'

'You stupid man!' she cried. 'Why have they taken him? He's done nothing wrong!'

Milan's hand gripped her arm. He put his face close to hers. 'Maybe he has.' His fingers tightened their grip; his other hand reached to touch her behind her ear. She flinched in disgust. 'I can tell you more,' he breathed. 'I know what's happened. If you teach me again, teach me more *Angliký* . . . If you stay here with me . . . tonight . . .'

With a murmur of fear, Rose whipped her arm away and fled from the café, feeling the roughness of his fingers still on her neck.

She stumbled through the front door to *At the Clementinum*, ran up the stairs and into the kitchen. 'Babička, Krystof has been arrested by the *Ruský policie*. Milan just told me. They took him away this morning.'

The dawn was sullen and unwelcome. In silence Rose and Lara ate breakfast and then Rose pushed a grizzling Nancy in the pram, along the empty, misty streets. Lara walked a few paces behind. As they crossed the Old Town Square, the mist swirled away and Rose spotted the shapeless figure of a woman shuffling from streetlamp to streetlamp. She hoisted up a long pole to pull on a ring, shutting off the gas. A large hairy dog trotted beside her like a horrific doppelganger.

'*Dobrý den,* Lucenka,' called Lara, her voice cracking in the cold.

The woman lifted a ragged gloved hand as a greeting. So this was Lucenka, thought Rose, the witch of the gas lamps. One by one, she snuffed the gas lamps out as Lara and Rose approached the Ministry of State Security, where Rose had seen the shining Daimler pull up all those weeks before. From each of its tall windows, floor on floor, hung two flags, flat in the frozen air. One, the Czech flag, the other, guarding it closely, was the blood-red Soviet banner.

Two guards stood to attention either side of the porch. Their rifles crossed automatically in front of the great studded door and one of them barked a question. Lara answered. In a smooth motion, the rifles were lowered and an arm reached out to open the door.

They stood in the entrance hall. Parquet stretched to right and left; a wide staircase swept upwards into endless gloom. Behind a small desk in the far corner sat a clerk in uniform writing in a protracted manner on a form. Rose parked the pram near the door and she and Lara approached the clerk. He ignored them.

Rose cleared her throat. 'Excuse me, sir.'

The man glared up at her, eyes like chips of steel. 'The ministry is not open yet.'

'May we wait, sir?' ventured Lara, her voice humble and hesitant.

He flicked his eyes to the old woman, pursed his lips and lifted his shoulders in a slow, insulting shrug. He was not going to say another word. They walked back to the wooden bench and sat.

The guard's pen continued to scribble and the clock on the desk ticked like a hollow torturous metronome. A phone rang behind a closed door along the corridor. Somewhere in the vaults of the building a door was shut with a sharp rap and footsteps clipped their approach along the corridor. Rose straightened her shoulders as a Russian officer appeared. He walked straight past, oblivious to them. The clerk got to his feet, his chair grating, and saluted. They spoke in staccato Russian, turning their broad backs on Lara and Rose. Then the officer retreated into an office and closed the door.

Rose heard Lara take a breath to speak out and swiftly placed a hand on her arm to stop her.

An hour dragged past and Rose felt her insides turn in agony. Suddenly, the man behind the desk looked up and addressed them.

Lara rose unsteadily to her feet, crying, '*Ano, ano*. Krystof Novotny. Captain Novotny, Tulka Regiment, Army of Czechoslovakia.'

Rose felt her heart pound. Surely, he must be here? There must be news. It was all a mistake and they must let him go. Mistaken identity, just a warning . . . She rushed to Lara's side, fixing her eyes on the guard's disdainful expression. Then it came to her, in waves of sickening comprehension. Of course he was here. All these people knew: the young guards outside knew, this clerk, the officer who had marched through an hour before, knew. But that meant nothing. She glanced in pity at Lara's open, eager and trusting face.

The guard used the very tips of his fingers to leaf through a pile of papers on the desk beside him. He drew out a buff file, its cover printed with Russian words. 'Hmm, Novotny,' he muttered.

Rose felt herself shaking. She tried to swallow her anger.

'Ah,' said the man, as if alighting on some new piece of information. He paused as if to relish the moment. 'Ah, yes.' He looked them in the eye for the first time and said, 'You will be informed.'

'What?' asked Lara, incredulous, her body sagging.

'We must leave,' Rose whispered to her, suddenly understanding.

The man's face was blank with inhumanity.

'*What?*' cried Lara, her thin voice cracking around the high ceiling.

Rose pulled Lara's trembling, frail figure away towards the door, and grasped the pram handles. Glancing back, she saw the guard had returned to his scribbling. His face had broken into a smile.

The following day, Rose again waited on the hard bench by the door. It was a weekday and there was a busier atmosphere. Officers strutted with paperwork and women in grey suits marched stiff-backed, holding bundles of buff files. After two hours, the desk clerk deigned to lift his head and call out, 'Novotny?'

She walked over with a trickle of hope. The clerk lifted a stamp and ground it into his inkpad, then stamped a file. 'You will be informed.'

Lara glanced up from her knitting with a hopeful smile. Rose shook her head and then watched as the old woman pressed her hands to the sides of her head and began to wail. Goose bumps prickled Rose's shivering arms. Lara balled up her fists and brought them down onto her thighs, hitting herself over and over until, breaking down, she hurried from the room.

Rose found Babička sitting bolt upright on the chaise longue in the freezing salon, her face sagging, staring at the portrait of her daughter on her wedding day. Tears fell down the old woman's face. Nancy toddled in, following her mother, and reached out for Lara.

The old woman broke her gaze to glance down at the child and an unexpected compassion transformed her face. She pulled Nancy onto her knee and Rose watched her tears fall into the little girl's hair.

**V**ery early on the sixth bitter morning without Krystof, as Rose left in the darkness for the ministry, she was stopped by an insistent rapping on the café window. She turned to see Milan opening the door.

'Come in here for a moment,' he hissed at her. 'I have some news.'

Cautiously, she did as he asked. He closed the door behind her.

'You teach me English properly, like we agreed before,' he said, his voice reverberating, 'and I will speak with the Party. I will help secure the release of Captain Novotny.' Milan reached for her. 'And perhaps we can be *friends*.' She felt his thumb massage her shoulder; his breathing on her cheek. 'Captain Novotny is a very brave man. A war hero.' He spoke deeply into her ear. 'He is my landlord, and I pay him good rent for this place. So he is rich. They don't like him at the Party. He is bourgeois. They know how influential he is . . . at the barracks . . . with his regiment. They want him to mend his ways. But I can convince them that he is not a threat to them. They will listen to me.'

She finally guessed his meaning. Krystof was in danger. But she said, 'No, Milan. I think you are causing more trouble for everyone.' She was surprised how steady her voice was. 'Please leave me alone.'

'Yes, you *are* alone. There is no one in Prague to help you. No one in this whole country who cares about you. I am your only hope.'

She went towards the door. 'I'm leaving. I am already late. I have to report to the ministry, and see if I can get some real news on Krystof.'

He gripped the top of her arm and leaned into her, his spittle hitting her lip. 'You are *kurva*. Everyone thinks it. Everyone knows it.' She watched in horror as he thrust his hips towards her. 'You remember,' he said, 'it's no longer the rutting season, but it can be if I want it to be. Come upstairs with me now to bed and you will see your captain home this evening.'

'I said . . . leave me alone.'

He gripped her shoulder. 'So he doesn't mean that much to you?'

'Please, you're hurting!' She fought her instinct to struggle, knowing it would make things worse. How could she deal with a man like this? His strength and belligerence were too much for her.

'You made a fool of me in front of my customers.'

'You made a fool of yourself, Milan.'

Inexplicably, he released her. He said, 'I tried to help you, silly girl. Just remember that. So it has come to this, then?' Turning to look over his shoulder, he shouted, 'Officers, if you please!'

Two men wearing black Homburgs and smart fur collars appeared from the back of the café. 'That will be all, Milan,' one of them said with a rumbling Russian accent. 'We don't need you any longer.'

The other approached Rose and held her elbow. 'Don't make a fuss and you won't be harmed, Mrs Bowman. You have to come with us.'

From the window, Rose could see the skeleton on the Town Hall clock. Twice now he had raised his bony arm and the chimes had struck. Two hours she had sat there, waiting, in dreadful silence.

The office at the ministry was frugal. Grey linoleum, an ordinary desk, a metal filing cabinet, a framed picture of Joseph Stalin. Beyond the closed door, she sensed, people, efficient people, were busy working. She heard typing. Incessant typing. But inside the room where she waited: utter quiet until the telephone rang, shrill and scolding. Sometimes Major Ivanov, ignoring her as he worked, would pick up the receiver and listen. Sometimes he'd just let it ring.

Rose shifted on the hard seat. Fear was fastening onto her spine. She fought it with all her strength, trying to clear her head.

Suddenly, the major spoke to her. 'Your file, Mrs Bowman, is very interesting to us.' He was Russian but spoke in Czech with sinister authority. He opened a buff folder and extracted a sheet of paper.

She glanced up, surprised, and saw that he was holding a copy of the letter she had been sent by Will Bowman's solicitors: the letter that had been opened and inexpertly resealed.

Major Ivanov shuffled the papers in his hand. 'What have we here? Ah, yes. Your husband is a Nazi convict. You have been accused by the British authorities of the kidnapping of a minor. You left England to be with your bourgeois lover, Comrade Novotny.'

Terror hit her in the stomach. 'Is Krystof . . .?'

He barked, 'No, you speak when I have finished. This is not a very good start, is it, Mrs Bowman? Not a good start at all, for someone wishing to come and live here in our Soviet state of Czechoslovakia.'

'Soviet state? Is it already? I thought . . .'

'Silence! Very soon to be part of the glorious Soviet Union. Now,' he said. 'We require your cooperation.'

'I just want to know that Captain Novotny is well. Is he . . .?'

'No questions.'

She bit her lip. Tears filled her eyes. She willed them to retreat.

'We only want the best for you, and your little'—he glanced back at the letter—'girl. We only want the best for Comrade Novotny. The Soviet Union cares for you. Joseph Stalin cares for you all.' He nodded up to the portrait. 'He liberated this country from Hitler. Liberated Europe.'

She looked up at the portrait: at the dark, slanted eyes of Stalin; at the surprisingly friendly moustache. 'But where is Krystof? Please tell me.' Her voice was small, frightened.

'He is downstairs, reconsidering his position.'

Frustration rose within her. 'I don't understand why Captain Novotny has been taken away from me. He is a good, loyal citizen. He fought for his country. He also helped in the fight against the Nazis. Is this how he is to be repaid?'

'Comrade Novotny is an enemy of the state. He knows that . . . after a few days in our care. He knows, now, that Soviet workers unite against the likes of him. He is bourgeois. He is also a commanding officer in the Czechoslovakian army, and we have to be careful. We have to rein him in. It is for his own good. For the good of the Party.'

'Krystof fought against the Nazis. He was on your side. And you do this to him.'

'It is for his own good. As I said before, Comrade Bowman. We care. The Party cares.' He stood up and walked round the desk. He stood close behind her. 'Now what are we going to do with you? You are rather unconventional. Not our usual idea of a sweet English rose.'

'Why don't you call me a *kurva* and be done with it,' she snapped. 'Milan thinks it. He thinks the whole of Prague knows it.'

'Milan is a stupid, self-important individual. We deal with Milan.'

'He is . . .?'

'As for *prostitute* . . . I do not believe it for one minute. But, Comrade Bowman,' he said, 'how do we know you are not a spy?'

'A spy? A spy! That is ridiculous!' Her mouth gaped with the horror.

'We have to watch you. We have to be careful the Nazi sympathy has not infiltrated here.' He reached out and tapped the side of her head. It felt like a violation.

'I hated it. I hated my husband. I had no idea.'

'What drove you to leave your home and drag your child across Europe to be with Comrade Novotny?'

Rose turned to face him, her eyes wide with fear. The answer was ludicrously simple. 'Because I love him.'

'Ha!' Major Ivanov strode back to his desk. He tidied more papers and put her file away. He walked over to the filing cabinet, extracted a new buff folder and sat back down. He began to leaf through the papers.

Rose swallowed hard. Was the waiting to start all over? Would they ever let her see Krystof? What was going to happen to her?

The skeleton raised his arm again, the cadaverous skull grinning.

'Oh.' Ivanov looked up. 'You are still here?'

'I don't know . . .'

'You are free to go. You have always been free to go.'

Rose sat at the kitchen table, while Lara dozed in her chair by the stove. The old woman had turned in on herself, shrinking down with worry. The dark corners of the room grew closer. Nancy was curled up in her cot by the open stove door. Rose thought that they would be safer in the kitchen; perhaps they should all sleep here. She knew she did not want to go back to her cold, empty bed.

She wanted to hear some news. English voices. Ear bent to the radio, she turned the dial. Radio waves crackled and, occasionally, the precise enunciation of a BBC man floated forward for a moment, just as hope did, to recede again into an unintelligible hiss. Sighing, she switched off the radio set.

Woken by the silence, Lara jerked, her eyes focusing on Rose. There was a grunt of realisation that the other chair was still empty. She took herself off to bed. Nancy slept on, blissfully unaware. Rose had never felt so alone.

She settled herself into Lara's still-warm chair and dozed. She did not hear the rattle of the latch below. She did not hear the shuffling footsteps as they mounted the stairs; the kitchen door opening.

Her eyes popped open. 'Who's there?' she hissed, thinking of Milan. She saw a haggard figure in the doorway, hanging onto the handle with both hands. She gasped in fright; then cried out in disbelief. And then flew from her chair towards him.

She took Krystof in her arms and pressed her face to his neck. She smelt the fusty rot of his clothes, his neglect and his terror. She drew herself away and looked him full in the face, plucking off his cap and unravelling his scarf, desperate to reveal him. She tried to mask her reaction. His face was puffy and unshaven, his eyes dull. Above his eyebrow, his skin had swollen angrily around a deep cut. Bruises, in varying shades of purple, grey and yellow, blossomed over his cheeks and chin. His hands were raw. She guided him to the stove. He recoiled with every laboured step.

'What have they done to you? Oh, Krystof, what has happened?'

'A Russian jackboot happened.' He exhaled in a groan of pain. 'My foot is broken. They stamped on it.'

'Oh God! I will get you into bed. You must sleep.'

'Sleep? I have not slept,' he said. 'They would not let me.'

She raked hot coals into a warming pan and went to put it in their bed. When she came back, she knelt in front of him. 'Oh, my love,' she whispered again, her eyes brimming with tears. She dashed them angrily away. 'We must fight them. They can't win.'

He shook his head, wincing. 'I haven't the strength.'

'But you are going to be all right?' Suddenly she was panicking. Her Krystof seemed remote, unrecognisable.

He drew a deep, raw breath. His eyes were two dark slits. 'Am I going to be all right? I don't think so, Ruzena. This changes everything.'

She lay awake all night, her hand on the back of his head as he dreamed; as he called out, twitched and shuffled. As he wept. He was delirious. She held his hand as he muttered, 'I shot a German boy.' Hours later, he spoke again: 'He was just a child in a Panzer uniform. He was combing his hair. I shot him. Him or me. East of Caen.'

In the morning Krystof turned to face her. He whispered, 'I am the enemy. I am bourgeois. Because of my property. Because I am an army officer. They will make our lives a misery, until I join the Party. They want to strip the army of its powers, of its men, of its weapons. In case we rise up against them. They will put us in prison.'

He shut his eyes and slept.

Rose got up and knocked on Lara's bedroom door. 'He's here,' she said. 'He's home.' Lara burst into tears and rushed to see for herself. She opened the door a crack and peered in at her grandson, shaking with disbelief, wiping at her wet face, unable to speak.

When Krystof woke, Rose gave him a bowl of porridge. '"You piece of filth" they called me, with every blow. "You stupid bourgeois traitor."' He took a mouthful of porridge, tried to swallow. 'They told me you and Babička wanted nothing more to do with me, because I am an enemy of the state. The cell was two metres by three. I paced it out before they broke my foot. It was deep underground, there was no air to breathe. I think it was an old wine cellar.'

Rose told him, 'We came to the ministry. We tried to find you . . .'

'They watched me through a spy hole. Every day, staring at four blank walls.' He chewed a little, tears in his eyes. 'Every night, lights went out at eight. Two hours later they would haul me to another cell. This one was a bit bigger. Questions, then. Interrogation.'

Rose saw that he could not look at her.

'I was returned to my cell at four in the morning. Two men holding me up. Lights went on at six. No sleep.' He dabbed at the porridge with the spoon. 'They made me stand in ice for hours. I dreamed of you. I dreamed you'd gone. I dreamed you loved me. I dreamed you didn't.'

Lara was standing in the doorway, listening. She came and sat on the bed and Rose jumped with surprise as Lara held her shaking hand, clutching Krystof's with her other.

'Sometimes,' said Krystof, 'I was taken to a normal office. The commander, Major somebody, sat under a picture of Uncle Joe Stalin. "Why don't you save yourself all this trouble?" he asked me, his pen poised over a confession they'd cooked up. A confession of bourgeois behaviour and an application to join the Party. All I had to do was sign.'

'Krystof, I know,' whispered Rose. 'Did you hear the typewriters? I never thought such everyday machines could sound so ominous.'

'He had a file on me, and I asked if I could read it. He laughed. Six days, Ruzena, I was alone, without sleep. I lived and died a hundred lifetimes. I dreamed you did not love me. But still I did not sign.'

Taking the spoon from him, Lara tried to feed her grandson.

Rose whispered, 'We came every day. They expected us. They ignored us. Every day. They just said, "You will be informed."'

Krystof said, 'They have taken my passport. They showed it to me and then put it in my file.'

So, Rose thought, her terror disabling her, we can never leave.

Krystof pushed the spoon away. Lara gathered up his porridge bowl and left the room.

He shuffled back under the covers. Rose lay down beside him. He drew her very close, as best he could with his shattered body.

'They are watching us, Ruzena.' He spoke deeply into her ear. 'They are listening. Every person is our enemy. From now on we pretend. We buy ourselves time. We buy ourselves a life. But I will never sign.'

# Thirteen

THE THAW WAS ALMOST COMPLETE; March had finally arrived.

Puffs of soft air from the west boosted Rose's mood as she crossed the steep cobbled lane in the Little Quarter. Krystof was fighting an infection in his foot and someone at his regiment had some penicillin on the black market. She was on her way to find his house under the shadow of the castle.

Something up the street caught her eye. The blonde hair was faded and hanging in rat's tails, but it was unmistakably Mabel.

'Hello, Mabel!' Rose called. Mabel hurried up the hill, keeping her head down, turning into an alleyway. But Rose was quick. She called again, as she dodged a man pushing a cart of scrap iron. 'Mabel!'

'There you are!' She put her hand on Mabel's shoulder from behind. Gone was Mabel's red lipstick, the powder. Fierce blotches covered her neck. 'We haven't seen each other—not since the night we got off that blessed train. I heard that you and Vaclav were living on the outskirts of the city. What brings you here to the Little Quarter?'

At first, Mabel stared at her as if she did not know her. 'Rose Pepper?'

'As was.'

Mabel's eyes brightened a little. 'I'm surprised you're still here. I'm on my way to see some bloke to buy my ticket home. Sold this.' She held up her wedding ring finger. It was naked. 'Vaclav left me.'

'Oh, gosh.'

'There's no need for sympathy, Pepper.' Mabel linked her arm. 'Come on, let's get into the warm. It's perishing out here. Have you any crowns? Good. This way.' Mabel led her through a small doorway into a dim, vaulted room under the rock of the castle. There were a few battered tables and a dusty counter.

'Two schnapps,' she told the proprietor.

In the half-light, Mabel's fair hair seemed to glow; she looked half pretty again. 'That's the only Czech I seem to have picked up,' she said.

Rose sat down and removed her gloves.

'As I said,' Mabel went on, 'Vaclav left me. He simply vanished. I'm renting now with an old biddy in the Jewish quarter. I have no money left. I keep selling what I can. I suppose this is the last straw.' She indicated her ring finger again. 'Now I can afford my ticket out of here. My parents warned me: don't trust Johnny Foreigner. How right they were.'

Rose slid her eyes to the floor, not able to think of her own parents, and what they said about Krystof. And what it made her do. She squared her shoulders. 'Did you actually see Vaclav leave, Mabel?'

'No. He just didn't come home one day. No one knows where he is.'

'Oh, Mabel, Krystof also vanished . . .'

'See! Just as I thought. These Czech men are all the same!'

'But Krystof returned. He had been interrogated, tortured. By the Russian state police at the ministry in the square. I wonder if Vaclav might be there?'

Mabel picked up her shot glass to sip her liqueur. Her fingers were trembling. 'Interrogated?' Mabel repeated. She wouldn't look at her.

Rose lowered her voice. 'Are you really going to leave?'

'What else can I do? The rent the old witch is charging is killing me. Awful woman. She's the lamplighter. She smells worse than her dog.'

'That's Lucenka. I know who she is.'

'One good thing about her is that she knows who I should go to to get a travel permit quickly. She has her contacts. Some man at a café near the monastery. Milan someone. Lucenka says I may have to give him more than these crowns I've got to secure the deal. If you know what I mean. I tell you, I'll do anything.'

Rose put her hand on Mabel's arm. 'But Mabel, I don't think—'

Mabel snatched her arm away. 'And I would do the same if I were you, too. Go home. Get back to Blighty.' Mabel took another sip.

'Mabel, you must go straight to the ministry. See if you can trace Vaclav. It might be that they are—'

'Ugh,' Mabel shuddered. 'Those awful Communists. I couldn't bear to. They're everywhere now, aren't they? I can't keep up.' She squinted at Rose. 'What are you still doing here?'

'I can't leave Krystof.'

Mabel looked at her as if she wanted to ask why not. 'So, Krystof came back to you?'

'Yes, I told you. He was released.'

Mabel wasn't listening. 'That's because he loves you. He fought his way out of there. You are very lucky. Vaclav the pig just wanted me in the bedroom. Well, he can get that now with his tart.'

'Mabel, perhaps Krystof knows about Vaclav. Perhaps he knows where Vaclav is. He might have heard. I mean, he is still rather ill at the moment and hasn't mentioned him . . . but he might know something. Would you like to come to my home and ask him?'

Mabel shrugged her shoulders. 'Haven't the time, Pepper. I have to get me to this damn Milan fellow. See if I can't score a ticket home.'

'Mabel, I know Milan. He is not to be trusted.'

'Look, dear, this girl can take care of herself, you know.' She stood up. 'Thanks for the drink, Pepper. It'll keep me warm.'

Out in the blustery street, Mabel said goodbye. Her hair seemed to match the grey of the stone walls, the pewter of the sky.

'Good luck, Rose Pepper, as was!' cried Mabel.

'You too,' Rose called, as the slight figure of the girl disappeared round a corner. 'You too.'

**A** rude hammering woke them. Now, from the street below, a hubbub of noise, hard Russian voices, filtered through the casement. 'Open up, Comrades,' came the cry. 'Open up in the name of the state.'

Krystof swore. *'Jezis-Maria.'* He hauled himself out of bed and limped to the window, pushed open the curtains and peered out.

Rose screwed her eyes up to the morning light, watching his face. How miraculous was the healing balm of time, she thought. Two months after his traumatic experience, she nearly had the same Krystof back with her. The bruises had faded; but what of his memories?

'What's going on, Krystof?' asked Rose.

'There are so many of them. Did they have to send so many?' muttered Krystof. 'Get dressed, Rose. We have visitors. Wake Babička up.' He shrugged his shirt on. 'Tell her to take Nancy and stay in the kitchen. Make her stay in there, for she is not afraid of them. That could prove a problem.'

But Rose's own fear made her annoyed with him. 'Who are they?'

'Red Army,' he said.

She made sure Lara and Nancy were safely locked in the kitchen, before Krystof went down to the vestibule and opened the front door.

Immediately Krystof was flung aside and a dozen men surged in brandishing old-fashioned rifles, and tramped up the stairs. Rose winced as they passed her. Then they set to: barging from room to room.

Following in protest into the salon she watched, aghast, as they scuffed the floor and tugged at the old curtains, discarding them as rags. A soldier poked at the painting of Krystof's parents with his penknife as Krystof limped up the stairs and stood close to Rose.

One of them tried the kitchen door, which Lara had locked from the inside. Rose could hear her shouting through the door. 'Touch anything of mine and I will stick your rifles up your arses!' she shrieked. 'Then I will kick you in the trousers!'

Major Ivanov brought up the rear of the rabble. 'Good morning, Comrade Bowman.' He bowed to Rose and then turned to Krystof. 'Comrade Novotny, we have been instructed to assess this house. We have come to confiscate your property in the name of the state.'

Krystof fixed his face with good humour. 'It's *Captain* Novotny.'

'Not any more,' said the major, taking out a clipboard. 'How many floors do you have here?'

A soldier interjected. 'Four, sir, plus a cellar.'

'What's up there?' Major Ivanov pointed up the stairs.

'Two attic rooms, sir,' said another dirty-faced boy-in-uniform, eager to please. 'And a *bathroom*.'

The major turned to Krystof. 'All property is theft. The state will not allow all this space for just two people, a child and'—he indicated the shut kitchen door—'the old woman who I believe is locked in that room.'

'My Babička,' Krystof corrected him. 'And by locking herself in there, she is protecting you all from the full force of her fury.'

The major ignored him. 'You will live with your mistress, her child and your grandmother up there in the attic. The rest of this house now belongs to the state.' He barked to his men, 'Clear these rooms!'

Krystof went to the kitchen door. Lara opened it and let him in. Immediately, eager-faced soldiers followed him and began to count the china on Lara's dresser, knocking the coffee pot off the stove, treading over the shards. She saw Krystof pick up Nancy and try to comfort her.

Rose held back on the landing, clinging to the banisters, watching, with increasing bewilderment, the plundering of Krystof's home.

Feeling her anger rising uncontrollably, she walked up to the next floor where the major had spread his papers on the windowsill.

'Perhaps you can enlighten me, Major,' she said. 'If we are to live upstairs in the attic, what will happen to the rest of the house?'

'It will be shared among the people,' he clipped, knowing his doctrine. 'Shared among the workers. The proletariat. Have you not read the manifesto? Now, to recap: who owns the café downstairs?'

'Captain Krystof Novotny.'

'The boarded-up *tabak*?'

'Captain Krystof Novotny.'

He began to laugh, a cold, hollow laugh, saying, 'I know you mean *Comrade* Novotny but I am tired of constantly correcting you. You will learn. Anyway, the café will be confiscated by the state, also.'

'His passport's been taken,' she blurted in panic. 'What do we do?'

Major Ivanov's eyes swept over her and the hardness in his bearing faded. 'As I told you before, at the ministry, you are free to go.'

She turned her face away. 'Please tell them to leave the painting. It's all he has. His parents, they . . .'

The major yelled in Russian to his men. One of them sheepishly walked back into the salon with the painting.

Major Ivanov turned back to her. He twitched his head and she saw, briefly, the man beneath the uniform. 'It does not have to be like this. All you people have to do is comply.'

As he shook his pen and began to write again, a loud thud and a crash drew Rose back to the banisters. She looked down the stairwell to see the pram in the vestibule buckling under the weight of a lead money chest that the soldiers had decided to steal.

Krystof rushed from the kitchen and looked down, aghast.

'You bastards,' he muttered. 'Nancy's pram. There is nothing in it, you fools!' he called. 'The reason it weighs a ton is because it's made of lead, not full of crowns. But we need that pram. It was my brother Tomas's. We've had it in the family for years.'

Lara appeared on the landing and, seeing the pram with its frame twisted and one wheel fallen off, she cried out, '*Ne, ne*. The pram!'

Rose tried to console her. 'I know, Babička. It's such a shame.'

'But it was for the little one! The *děť' átko*!'

'The baby?' asked Krystof.

'What are you saying, Babička?' asked Rose. 'For Nancy?'

Lara spluttered, '*Ne. Ne.* The *little* baby. Tomas was coming to collect the pram.' Lara wept. 'He never made it. The Nazis . . . came to the village . . . before he left . . . before he . . .'

'Collect it?' asked Krystof. 'What on earth for, Babička?'

Lara's sobs reached to the ceiling. 'For his own *děť' átko*. His own little boy.'

'Tomas had a son?' said Krystof. 'I had a baby nephew?'

Lara's voice was muffled with grief. 'They didn't even have time to christen him. I don't even know whether he had a name.'

Rose saw Major Ivanov gazing down at them, his face twitching from bewilderment to sorrow, his eyes drifting, not able to catch hers.

An enormous moon was suspended over Prague, like a fat white cheese against a velvet, navy night sky. It was a strangely tranquil night. The middle of May. The month of *Kveten*. The month of flowers. Their spring had come, thought Rose, watching from the attic window, and yet their future had not yet started. As she gazed along the roofscape, her strong love for the city was crushed with each alternate breath by her utter loathing of it. What was being whispered behind those shutters over there? What was being said behind closed doors? Were people listening for the sound of radio sets through their neighbours' walls? Were they keeping a record of times, dates, visitors, voices?

'Are you all right, Ruzena?' asked Krystof. He got up from the bed and came to stand beside her, his bad foot making him flinch.

'Where's Babička?' she asked, holding him.

'She is just at her toilet. She won't be long.'

Rose glanced around at their accommodation. The rescued portrait was leaning against the wall. They had been allowed to bring up two beds and two chairs. Their clothing was in the bathroom next door. They had to share the toilet, and the kitchen downstairs, with whoever was going to move into their old home. In the meantime, the soldiers were garrisoned below and a commotion of footsteps and a bevy of drunken, laughing voices came sporadically up the stairs.

She watched Krystof's face tighten with anger as he listened to the racket. 'I might not be able to give you much of a home, Ruzena, but remember that I love you. I always will.'

His tone made her question him. 'What do you mean? I know that you love me . . . What are you saying?'

'You have a home elsewhere, remember. Where you and your little girl can be safe.'

'Do you mean it's time for us to go to a *chalupa*?' She felt excitement fizz, her world opening up. 'Do you mean we can have our farm?'

'No. What I mean to say is, you have Pengared.'

'No!' she hissed. 'I will not go anywhere without you.'

He caught her and held her tight. 'Not so fierce, Ruzena. Not tonight. But we may have to have this conversation one day.' Slowly, he unbuttoned his shirt and took it off. He plucked at her nightgown and exposed her shoulders. His lips pressed enquiring kisses over her skin, up her throat.

She whispered, 'But Nancy?'

He glanced to the cot in the corner. 'Fast asleep.'

'And Babička? She is only next door.'

'She will knock.'

'What about them downstairs?'

'They can rot.'

She felt his heart thumping under her hands. She whispered, 'We will never be apart again, Krystof.' They made love briefly, tenderly, and with as much intensity as to last a lifetime.

As she lay curled in his arms, she watched the tension melt from his jaw, a light return to his face. He leaned over her, stroking her cheek. 'Remember the Polperro dance, Ruzena? Remember the haymaking?'

She smiled lovingly, thinking of the Cornish sunshine. 'One day,' she told him, 'we will sit on our rock again and watch the gentle waves of Trelewin cove. We have jumped the wire once and for all,' she said, trying to be brave for him, for herself.

But as she watched him drift off to sleep, she knew that the wire was still there, tightening around them, the rusted barbs cutting their flesh.

The moon was higher and the attic bedroom was soaked with pure white light when Rose suddenly came to. Lara was sitting bolt upright against her pillows. 'Ruzena,' she whispered.

'What is it, Babička? Are you all right?'

The old woman whispered back to her, but her words tumbled in Czech; a dialect Rose had not heard Lara speak before. She nudged Krystof awake. 'What is it?' he asked.

Lara began to speak.

Krystof sighed, rubbing his face sleepily. Half-awake, he said, 'Babička wants to tell you all about her days as a young lady . . . fêted in the gas-lit ballrooms of Wenceslas Square . . . Hosting her own parties here, downstairs in the salon. During the *fin de siècle* . . . Her belle époque . . . she dined . . . she played cards . . . she drank schnapps . . . everything glittered . . . it was Czechoslovakia's golden years.'

'Your golden republic?' asked Rose.

'Yes, and she says how you would have loved those days . . .'

Lara chuckled deep in her chest, wagging her finger at Krystof.

'I just told her,' said Krystof, 'that the winters were still bloody cold in those days, never mind the social whirl, but she says she never felt the cold. She was young and foolish.'

'She had a beautiful time?'

'She did. There was so much music, so much singing.'

Rose imagined the laughter tinkling down the hallway, the lamplight reflected in oil paintings, cards snapping over polished tables. She watched Lara's face in the semidarkness, trying to imagine the young girl whose long life had come to this. Lara's smile suddenly struck her with its unexpected warmth.

How Rose wanted to tell her about her own life, her friends, her parents, her own beautiful time as a young girl in the days before the war in her little Plymouth suburb.

'*Dobrou noc*,' whispered Lara.

'Good night, Babička,' Rose returned, understanding the settlement between them; the start of forgiveness. She snuggled down under the covers next to Krystof.

But the old woman stayed sitting upright and, as Rose drifted off to sleep, once or twice she opened her eyes to see Lara watching over her.

Rose woke to the sound of jackboots and riotous shouting from below. She rolled over in annoyance to see Krystof standing on the other side of the two beds, his face fixed. Lara was still sitting upright.

'Oh, Babička, couldn't you sleep?' she asked.

Krystof was shaking his head, unable to take his eyes off his grandmother's face.

Rose squinted, and cocked her head to the side.

Lara's face sagged down, her chin rested on her shoulder. Her hands were folded over the covers, her brown eyes wide open. She was dead.

The men carried Lara's coffin down the stairs as warm sunshine fell in long shafts through the high landing windows. Rose watched as Krystof, his face pale and haunted, cradled the head end, giving gentle instructions to the unusually decorous soldiers.

The hearse was waiting outside on the cobbles. Customers at Milan's café rose from the tables and removed their hats as the soldiers slid Lara's coffin into the open back of the car. Rose caught sight of Milan standing at the café window. Not wishing to linger under his gaze, she quickly encouraged Krystof into their waiting taxi.

In the back of the taxi, Krystof held Nancy on his lap and she clung to his neck, sensing, Rose decided, his distress. But what of her own? Her fingers began to shake as her shock at Lara's death suddenly became edged with other, more selfish, emotions.

Ahead of them, further along the river bank, the steep cliff of Vysehrad Hill loomed up. Up there, amid the tall trees, lay the cemetery where they were to bury Lara and where Krystof was to leave her. Feeling the bitter sting of relief that they *could* leave his Babička there,

Rose took Krystof's hand and leaned towards him, tears of shame in her eyes.

The tiny funeral cortège shuffling around the open grave included Lucenka and her dog. Rose took a step towards her, to welcome her as Lara's old friend, but Krystof whispered in her ear, 'Ignore her.'

'Why?' Rose whispered back. 'Might she not help us one day?'

'Exactly. But we don't know who is listening.'

The priest finished and Lara was lowered into the family plot next to her husband, Krystof's grandfather. Rose could not take her eyes off Krystof as he flinched at each clod of earth hitting the coffin. Something about that sound—hollow, final, dismal—thudded through her head and she was struck by the memory of her parents' funeral which, up until then, had been a merciful blur. She had been escorted by—held up by—Will and guided through it as if she were disabled. And now, as the tiny congregation turned away from the grave, her pain returned with such speed and intensity that she felt her knees give way.

She cried out, 'Krystof, I . . .' Then she felt her mouth snap shut. She couldn't tell him this and trample all over his grief.

He looked at her, understanding. 'Come, let's walk,' he said, hoisting Nancy high in his arms. They picked their way through the crowded city of graves and monuments, losing themselves among the ruins that populated Vyšehrad Hill. When they reached the edge of the cliff they gazed down at the river snaking through the golden stone houses.

Krystof made Rose look at him. 'I told you, the night Babička died,' he said, peering into her eyes. 'Your home is Pengared. I think now . . .' he said, wincing in disbelief at his own words, 'now we are free to go.'

'Free?'

'In the sense that Babička . . .'

'Oh.' Rose hadn't wanted to acknowledge what Lara's death meant to them both. And, she knew, neither had he.

'I know it's what you want,' Krystof said. 'I see it in your face every day.'

Rose felt a surge of hope. 'And when we get back to England, I can settle my divorce. Then we will be truly free.'

'I will talk to Lucenka,' said Krystof.

Rose felt anxiety tap her on the shoulder. 'Krystof . . . are you sure we can leave? They took your passport.'

'Lucenka is the only person who can deal with something that serious. She will get me the correct visas, documents, whatever. She knows the right people. She has the right contacts, not like Milan.'

'Oh, hang that man,' muttered Rose. 'I forgot to tell you. While you were ill, I bumped into Mabel. She told me she was renting a room at Lucenka's house, and that Milan was getting her some paperwork so she could leave. Mabel told me Vaclav was missing. That was in March. Two months ago now . . .'

Krystof shook his head, resting it in his hands. 'He was probably in the next cell to me. Do you know if he was ever released?'

'I have no idea. Mabel wouldn't believe me. She thought he had left *her* and was living with another woman. She was ready to leave Prague. Past caring. She's probably back in England now.'

'But with Milan's useless documents?' Krystof said. 'I doubt it very much. I would not trust him to get me a fake library card.'

The café manager's face loomed back into Rose's mind's eye. She shuddered. 'You were too weak for me to tell you before.'

'Tell me what?'

'What he tried to do. He called me . . . that word. He said that if I . . . slept with him, then he would ensure your release.'

Krystof slammed his hand hard onto the bench, his eyes ablaze with anger. 'How dare that man think he can even speak to you!'

'I told him to get lost. But of course . . . they still took me in.'

Krystof stood up, agitated, pacing the grass. 'It's my fault. I should have been firmer with Babička. I should not have let these people think that of you. Speak like that about you. To think I was going to leave the café to that weasel. Well now, he'll see what Communism really means. I no longer have a café to give him.'

Nancy, jolted by Krystof's rage, began to cry. Rose scooped her up to comfort her, speaking to Krystof quietly over her head. 'And I say we keep quiet. We say no more. Leave him to it. Walk away.'

**A**rriving back home, Krystof hesitated outside the front door.

'I see two very tired girls in front of me,' he said, lightly. 'You take Nancy in. Have a rest. Take a nap. I won't be long.'

Rose squinted at him, registering his false smile. 'Krystof, what are you going to do?'

'Just some unfinished business. I won't be long.'

Rose laid a sleepy Nancy on the bed.

'My goodness, chicken,' she said. 'It's nearly your birthday.' She tucked a lock of her daughter's dark hair behind her tiny ear. 'To think, nearly two years ago, Krystof was heading for Normandy, I was with . . . that man. And now here we are.'

She heard Krystof come up the stairs. He was right about not being long: she had barely had time to change out of her brown suit.

'The soldiers didn't heckle you today?' she asked.

'No, they're being very respectful. I think they liked Babička's spirit; the way she yelled at them. They remember her fondly,' Krystof said. 'But I'm surprised you didn't hear them cheer just now?'

She looked at him. 'Krystof, what have you done?'

'My business concerning the café is now finished. *Kaput*. Over with. Ouch!' He rubbed his fist, flexing his fingers, massaging the joints. 'I was just paying my respects to Milan.'

'Oh, Krystof. I said *walk away*,' she scolded, understanding.

He grinned. 'You knew I couldn't do that.'

'Did it hurt?'

'Yes.' He examined the knuckles. 'But I think it hurt him more. It's not good for Milan to be socked in the face by his ex-landlord and find himself sprawled on the cobbles in front of a group of jeering soldiers. Especially when they are supposed to be his comrades.'

Krystof took out the front door key to *At the Clementinum* from his trench-coat pocket. 'Won't be needing this any more,' he said. The bells of the monastery rang out clearly as he dropped the key down a drain.

Hearing the plop deep below the street, Rose looked at Krystof. 'That's the only spare?'

'Yes. That should annoy the commandant for a while.'

'We're really doing this, aren't we?' she said.

Krystof nodded. 'We are. We are mad fools, but . . . Are you all right?'

'No, but I will be once we are on the train.' She followed his gaze up to the attic window. 'Are you thinking of the portrait?' she asked.

'It's the only thing I regret leaving behind,' he said, shaking his head.

Rose distracted him. 'Now look,' she said brightly. 'I've packed as little as possible, as if we're going on holiday, in case we're searched.' Then, just as quickly, her spirits plummeted. 'But our tickets and visas are for Paris. That will draw attention, surely. Oh, Krystof . . .'

'Forgeries from Lucenka.' He sounded immensely confident. 'You can't have one without the other: a ticket without a visa. Permission has been granted from a higher authority. That's what it will look like to the "monkeys" at the station anyway. They'll just get out their rubber stamps and wave us through.' He paused, and looked at her. 'You and Nancy will be fine, but if there's a problem—'

'Krystof!'

'We have been through this,' he said, his words clipped, his nerves making him cranky. 'If for any reason they stop me getting on the Paris train, then there is the other plan. I take a local train that goes somewhere near to the Austrian border. I leave the train—throw myself off it if I have to—and sneak across the border. I will make my way to Vienna, and then on to Paris. I will find a way.'

'I can't even think of it,' she hissed. 'My nerves are in shreds.'

'I will find a way to follow you.' His voice was grave with promise. He picked up his suitcase. 'Goodbye, *At the Clementinum*.'

Glancing round, Rose saw Milan standing at his café window. His black eye was turning a nasty shade of yellow. She hissed under her breath, 'Milan's watching us again. Let's get going.'

'Don't worry,' said Krystof. 'Don't let him see we are concerned. That's it, Nancy. Smile and wave.'

As the little girl flapped her chubby hand in the direction of the café, a black shiny Daimler rumbled over the cobbles towards them, a Soviet pennant fluttering on its bonnet. Major Ivanov wound down the window. 'Good morning, Comrades. What a fine day.'

Krystof spoke reluctantly. 'Good morning to you.'

The major got out of his car and waved his driver away. 'I want to say how sorry I am for your recent loss,' he said. He stood tall, his authority tangible. 'Your beloved Babička. May I offer my condolences?'

'You may. Thank you,' said Krystof.

They know *everything*, thought Rose in wonder.

The major noticed the suitcases. 'Oh, so you are off somewhere? Visiting someone?' He knelt down so that his face was level with Nancy's. Rose watched a kindly smile stretch the Russian's face. 'And where are you off to in all this glorious sunshine, young lady?'

Nancy peeked out from the folds of Rose's hemline, and spoke her first—and only—Czech word: '*Chalupa*,' she burbled.

'Is that so? You're off to your *chalupa*? I wasn't aware you had one.'

'Nancy doesn't mean that—' said Krystof.

'It's—it's the property of friends,' stammered Rose, catching Krystof's eye. Even as her words left her lips, she cringed at her mistake.

'After the death of your beloved grandmother, I certainly understand,' said the major. 'Who might these friends be? Could it be Comrade Vaclav and his lovely wife Mabel?'

Rose opened her mouth to say no, but Krystof interjected, 'Yes, indeed. My old friend Vaclav.'

The major paused. 'Where might their *chalupa* be?'

'Moravia,' said Krystof.

Rose could not look at him. She knew that he regretted every word he had uttered.

'Well, now that it's summer,' said the major, breezily, 'I hear it is lovely in that part of the country. Have a good journey, Comrade. And you, too, Comrade.' He bowed towards Rose.

As Milan rushed outside and began to fuss with a chair and table for the major, Krystof gripped Rose's arm. They walked sedately away but as soon as they turned the first corner, they began to hurry.

Rose panted, 'Oh, Krystof, what have we said? Ivanov knows. I could see it in his face. Should we just give up, go back?'

'No, no. I think he is playing games. I think he pretends. To scare us. What an *utter* fool I was to mention Vaclav. If he *is* under arrest, then why on earth would we be going to stay at his country home?'

Over Krystof's shoulder, Nancy smiled at her mother and Will Bowman's blue eyes were laughing. Rose had to look away.

Oh, Nancy, she thought, as they lengthened their strides and headed for the station, one word from you . . . one word from you.

They skirted the edge of the Jewish Quarter and hurried past the end of a small winding lane. The lane was filled with Russian soldiers. They were banging on a door.

'That's Lucenka's house,' said Krystof, barely stopping.

'Oh, poor woman,' cried Rose. 'What do they want? And . . . what?'

Suddenly, with a crash, the door was forced open.

'This is serious,' said Krystof. 'But we're not going to wait around to find out why.' He turned to go, then stopped. They both heard, clearly, the strains of an English voice from behind the front door, asking with edgy indignation, 'What *do* you think you are doing?'

'Oh God, that's Mabel,' said Rose, turning back to the lane. 'She *hasn't* left yet. I wonder why? What's going on?'

Through the balmy morning air came a high-pitched scream. And then, muffled, one, two, three shots.

'Oh God!' cried Rose.

Krystof blazed at her. 'I said, come on! We have to keep going. We cannot waste our time here. We have a train to catch.'

Fear rose like a hand tight around her throat to choke her. This fear was real, so different from the make-believe horror of the first night when she ran from the wooden figures and the fake skeleton on the Town Hall clock. She believed this terror would kill her.

'If something goes wrong . . .' Krystof said, marching her on, 'I will make it, Ruzena. Listen to me. I will make it. I will follow you.'

She failed to believe him. Every ounce of her body was stretched, every weak breath she took she had to use to hold herself together. Somehow, her legs kept going across the treacherous cobbles.

Almost out of breath, she gasped, 'They've just killed Mabel.'

'We don't know that. Just keep going. Keep going.'

They hurried on and a stitch began to pull Rose's side apart. Not long now, not long, she told herself. The station was just round the corner.

'Ah,' said Krystof, slowing down suddenly. 'If it isn't Lucenka.'

The lamplighter woman was sitting at a table outside a café, smoking a pipe, her great woolly dog sprawled on the cobbles.

'*Tabak*, Novotny?' She offered him a pouch.

'*Ne, ne,* we are in a hurry. But,' Krystof ventured, 'did you know that there has been some trouble at your house?'

Lucenka shrugged and turned her mouth down. Her eyes were like those of a dead fish. 'Yes, yes,' she muttered. 'That girl will not listen to me. I told her Milan was no good.'

'I think you had better get back there,' said Rose, her lip curling, her voice quivering with disbelief at the woman's indifference.

'They told me, those *Ruskýs,* to give them half an hour,' said Lucenka. 'So I wait here, smoking my pipe, for half an hour.'

Rose and Krystof walked on in stunned silence.

**A**nnouncements reverberated from speakers, echoing round the high arched ceiling of the station. Rose felt tiny on the concourse. Krystof, holding Nancy, faced her. Idling engines hissed contentedly beyond the barriers while people crisscrossed the area, going about their daily business, catching their trains.

'We should be laughing,' Krystof said. 'We are going to our *chalupa.*'

She glanced at him. He looked back at her. Desperation on his face softened into adoration.

She said, 'I can hardly speak, let alone laugh.'

'Then let me tell you a story. I once saw Lucenka coming out of an alleyway with a face like a slapped arse, adjusting her clothing.'

'That old witch.' She longed to smile, but it felt painful to do so.

Krystof went on, 'And who should follow her out, buttoning himself up? Some young Red, who looked like *his* arse had been slapped.'

Her false smile made her face ache; her stomach twisted into knots.

'Now we know why,' he said. 'Now it is all falling into place. Although why anyone would want . . .'

'Krystof, I think I'm going to be sick.'

'Look, you hold onto the tickets, I want to take this off.' He handed the folded paperwork to her, then removed his trench coat and laid it over his arm. 'It is rather warm for the beginning of June, don't you think? Pity you will never see high summer in Prague. It gets very hot in the city then. Did you know the month of June translates as *Cerven*, the month of the colour red? Don't let the irony be lost on you.'

Her nerves fizzed to the surface. 'Krystof, be quiet, I can't stand it. Is the train in yet? Is it ready? Have they announced it?' she rattled. 'I just want to be on it. Once we're on it, we are halfway there.'

'Not quite, angel.' Krystof smiled indulgently.

'In my mind we will be,' she snapped.

'Ah,' he said, looking at the arrivals board. 'It's just come in.'

They both held one of Nancy's hands, each carrying a case in their other hand, Krystof with his trench coat over his arm as they walked towards the ticket barrier.

'We're going to make it,' she said and smiled up at Krystof.

'Almost there, Ruzena,' Krystof said. 'Almost halfway there.'

'Comrade Novotny.' The voice was behind them.

Two Red Army guards stood shoulder to shoulder, a wall of grey uniform, a smattering of red stars on lapels, caps and collars.

Turning good-naturedly, Krystof said, 'Yes, Comrade?'

'We'd like a brief word with you,' said one guard, his Czech not very good. 'Before you go to your *chalupa*. It is about your property.'

As Rose's eyes flicked between them, her stomach tightened. She wanted to shout with laughter at the horror of it all. How did *these* men know that they had told the major that they were going to a *chalupa*?

'Do you mean *At the Clementinum*?' said Krystof. 'Oh, I see. I do apologise. The key? It was a bit of a prank, you see. I threw it down the drain outside. I am sorry. I realise the major might want a spare while we are away. But my . . . my wife here has another one.' He turned to her. 'Your key, Ruzena. Your key.'

She plunged her hand into her pocket. Her fingers were trembling as she held it out.

'Thank you for the key, Comrade,' said the Russian. 'Please come to the stationmaster's office for a moment. We need you to sign it over.'

Krystof said, brightly, 'But I'm *giving* you the key, Comrade.'

'We need to complete some paperwork, Comrade.'

Rose saw Krystof tilt his head back for a split second to survey the guards' faces. Then she watched his face change. The look on his face made her heart freeze. Krystof was frightened. 'Ruzena.' He turned to her. 'Would you be so kind as to hold this for me while I talk to these gentlemen?' He handed her his folded trench coat.

'The train leaves in ten minutes,' she said, addressing the guards, more than Krystof. Her mouth tightened with panic.

The voice of one of the guards rumbled at her. 'You must get on the train with the child.'

She glared at Krystof. 'Did they say we could get on the train . . . and that you *cannot*?' she blurted in English.

'No, no,' Krystof cried, his agitation making him harsh, 'you're not quite grasping the translation . . . Get on the train. I am to follow, they say. I will follow.'

The guard cracked his rifle butt on the ground and bellowed, 'In Czech, please!'

Rose recoiled in shock, clutching Nancy to her. The guards moved forward and gripped Krystof by the elbows. They walked off across the concourse: a trio of men with Krystof limping in the middle. They went into the station office and the door was shut behind them.

Clutching the trench coat, her suitcase and Nancy's hand, Rose made her slow way to the ticket barrier. When she drew out her ticket and visa she realised that Krystof did not have his. She handed the collector all the paperwork and managed to make him understand that the gentleman delayed in the station office would follow shortly. And that this was *his* ticket. The collector waved her through. She walked to the train and stood on the platform outside the first carriage she came to. She stood, staring towards the office, the door of which she could just see, willing it to open.

She gazed up at the train. This could be their private compartment, theirs alone, all the way to Paris. This was where they would make their plans for the future. They were nearly halfway there.

The whistle blew long and urgent. She glanced nervously back to the concourse.

'All aboard! All aboard!' cried the train guard.

A railman walked the length of the train, slamming doors shut. The engine was building a head of steam. The noise assaulted her ears and a great belch of billowing smoke filled the great curved ceiling above.

On reflex, Rose climbed up the steps to the carriage, installed Nancy on a seat, folded the trench coat next to her and put her suitcase on the rack. She closed the door and pulled down the window, then leaned out, craning her neck.

'Come on, come on, Krystof,' she muttered.

Nancy knelt up on the seat, her blue eyes huge in her pale face and her finger pointing to the window, to beyond the train.

'Yes, darling. Your *Otec,* your Krystof will be here in a moment.'

She peered from the train window again. Suddenly she saw him. 'Krystof!' she screamed, waving as hard as she could. 'Quickly, Krystof!'

He had emerged from the office, flanked by the guards. He stood still and stared down the platform. She saw his eyes find her.

'Krystof, here!' she called. 'Your ticket is with the collector!'

The whistle sounded again. She felt the great wheels shudder beneath her and the platform seemed to move.

'Krystof!' she screamed. 'It's going! We're moving! Krystof!'

He remained motionless. He mouthed, *I will follow.*

Rose watched with horror as saw the ticket collector hand Krystof's papers to the guards. The soldiers were pressed either side of him, still holding his elbows. Then she saw that he was in handcuffs.

'Krystof!' The hiss of steam silenced her as the train pulled slowly away. She started to open the door. Krystof shook his head with such violence, his eyes piercing her with such passion, that he stopped her from leaping off the train. Again, he mouthed, *I will follow.*

His tawny head was still visible through the smoke and steam as she pulled the door shut, but he soon grew smaller and smaller as she was hauled away down the line.

'This isn't about a stupid key,' she breathed in pointless realisation.

She stared hard at the spot where Krystof stood until her eyes began to burn. The tracks merged behind the train to a point of infinity, and the platform, the station and Krystof disappeared.

She slumped back into the seat next to Nancy, bending double, Krystof's trench coat now bunched up on her lap. She pressed her face into it, smelling Krystof's scent. *He will be cold,* she thought. There was something heavy in the folds of the material. Puzzled, she lifted her tear-streamed face and began to unwrap it, burrowing until she came across the smooth, cool steel of his gun.

*Clever Kristof. You knew. You gave me the coat. At that moment. You were so brave.* Rose leaned forward to look out of the open window. The city had faded into green countryside dotted with the red roofs of farms.

If the guards had found the gun, they'd now both be dead; shot dead on the concourse. And what would have happened to Nancy?

No time to explain. No more life.

*I will follow,* he said.

**A** week later, Rose bought red roses from the flower seller at the Gare de l'Est. How appropriate they seemed and how frivolous they were. The room she was renting for herself and Nancy near the station was cheap but the crowns that she had found in one of Krystof's other pockets—now exchanged for francs—were not going very far.

She had left Nancy with the kindly *madame* at the hotel, and found a bench to sit on. The arrivals board indicated that the weekly train from Prague was due in half an hour.

She watched the people to pass the time: hurrying passengers, dawdling couples, the newspaper man. She bought *Le Figaro* and conjured up her schoolgirl French to read about the Nuremberg trials.

As the minute hand on the station clock eased itself towards the hour, every nerve in Rose's body burned and twitched.

The voice on the tannoy announced the train and she gathered herself together. Shaking hands straightened her brown wedding suit. Clutching her roses, she flashed a smile as she passed the ticket booth and the girl behind the window smiled back. She wanted to laugh out loud at the wondrous, warm excitement suddenly washing away the nerves.

At last, the great train eased to a halt. Doors slammed and the crowd of alighting passengers—people, like her, leaving the East—surged through in a mass of drab greys and browns, dressed, she thought wryly, just like her. Her eyes flicked from one face to the next, straining to catch a glimpse of his hair, his cheek, his eyes. She waited, jostled; the poor roses were crushed. The stream of humanity grew less and less until it petered out to nothing. And, still, she stayed on the platform.

**R**ose was hungry and cold. She put on Krystof's trench coat, tightened the belt and relished the warmth of it. Another week gone, and she couldn't stretch to flowers this time. Surely, by now, they would have finished with him? Surely, this time, he would have made the train?

Holding back, she watched the crowd alight from the Prague train and file through the ticket barrier. Twice, she thought she saw him: but both men melted away into the city; both those men were free.

A thought suddenly blinded her: he might not be coming on the Prague train. He might have done what he said he might do: escape by leaping from a train in Czechoslovakia and crossing the border. Her eyes frantically scanned the arrivals board: Zurich, Vienna, Amsterdam? How could she know? How could she possibly guess?

The girl tilted her head in sympathy. Rose walked on by.

A week later she was right on time. Unfailing hope made her buy roses again, but she felt her heart pounding with dread and futility. She heard a tapping sound and looked round to see the girl in the ticket office knocking on the window, waving her over. Rose's eyes widened. Perhaps the girl had news? Maybe there was a message left for her?

'*Mademoiselle*, would you like *du chocolat*?'

Rose stared, speechless. She bit her lip, feeling tears brighten her eyes and stop, suspended, at her lashes. She whispered, '*Oui, merci.*'

Handing her the steaming chocolate in a china cup and saucer, the girl said, her English as exquisite as her tiny face, 'The train is a little delayed. Due in ten minutes. Would you like to come in here and wait?'

Rose shook her head and watched the girl staring at the silent tears streaming down her face. She lifted the cup again and drank.

'*Merci beaucoup*,' Rose said as she heard the train coming to rest behind her. Hope drained the strength from Rose's limbs as she walked over and stood in her usual place. She tilted her chin up and waited. The shuffling, weary passengers filed by. Moment on moment, her head sank down and her heart crumbled. She tossed the roses into a bin.

# Fourteen

'ALL CHANGE. Last stop Trelewin. We go no further!' came the cry from Mr Thimble.

Wobbling with fatigue, Rose got to her feet. They could have waited in Paris for the next train, and the next, but something inside Rose had urged them to go home—or starve.

'Welcome back, miss,' said Jack Thimble. 'You all right with that suit-case? All right with the little one? All right to walk over the headland?'

'Yes, I am all right.'

'Telephone's working now,' he said, nodding towards the red box behind the hedge. 'You could call ahead to them Cumberpatches.'

'A good idea. Thank you, Mr Thimble,' she managed.

How peaceful it was, here in Trelewin among its quiet cottages, after the rattling of her journey. But there, behind its high hedge, loomed the Old Vicarage with its neglected garden and missing roof tiles. A plume of smoke from the chimney indicated its owner was home. She hurried to the call box and took out a penny.

Lifting the receiver, she spoke: 'Polperro two-five-four.'

'Connecting you.'

Betony's gentle voice suddenly filled her ear. 'Pengared Farm.'

Tears began to flow, to choke her. 'It's Rose. I'm home.'

Betony said, 'We'll come and get you. Stay where you are. Oh, Ginge.'

'I left him. I left him behind.'

Rose rested her suitcase down by a bench and sat, holding Nancy tightly. A village woman with her child walked towards her and, not recognising her, gave her a pitiful stare. Rose turned her face away, knowing she looked a fright; like a refugee.

Suddenly, as they passed her, the little boy pointed towards the Old Vicarage and said, 'Mummy, isn't that the Nazi's house?'

A burst of anger, like white lightning, flashed through Rose's head. She picked up Nancy and marched across the road, an incredible energy pumping through her blood. 'He'd better be home,' she muttered. She hammered on the front door. 'I want him to *know* how much this hurts.' She wanted to scream out her grief, spit in the face of the man at the root of it all. The front door opened.

'What?' Will Bowman asked, his bleary eyes not registering. He was barefoot, his shirt untucked. She smelt alcohol fumes. Suddenly, his eyes widened. 'Rosebud?'

She pushed past him. Immediately she was revolted. The air was damp and putrid. Piles of rubbish filled the corners. She saw mouse droppings by the wall. 'I see you've kept the place nice.' She saw plates of old food in the kitchen; overflowing ashtrays; and a pair of ladies' stockings bundled behind a cushion.

'Is this my daughter? Is this Nancy?' A crooked smile softened Will's face into a pathetic mask. He reached for the child.

'Don't you dare touch her!' Rose cried, flinching away.

'I have a right to hold her. She is my daughter, after all. So you tell me.' Before Rose could muster her answer, he demanded, 'What are you doing here, anyway? I thought you might be dead.'

'It's been touch and go,' she hissed.

'Then if you're not dead,' he said, 'aren't you supposed to be with your lover in Prague?'

'I had to leave,' she retorted. 'Haven't you heard what's been going on in Eastern Europe? Perhaps the BBC doesn't know half the truth.'

'And your lover? Has he come too?'

She slid her eyes to the floor.

'Your silence speaks volumes, Rosebud. So, your lover has left you.' His eyes narrowed as she stared at him. 'Well, well. You've got a nerve showing your face here. After what you did to me; and after you took my daughter away. Before I ever clapped eyes on her. Do you know, it was months before the screws at Bodmin jail even told me what you'd had—boy or girl.'

'How come they let you out, then?' she asked, thirsty for answers.

'They always release the likes of me eventually,' he said. 'Political prisoner. Has a romantic ring, doesn't it? I have to report to the police station every week for a year. A slap on the wrist, really. The threat's over. It's the bastard Communists now.'

Thinking suddenly of the major, she turned on Will. 'Don't you realise that your dreadful politics put your own daughter in danger? They opened your solicitor's letter to me. They knew you were a Nazi sympathiser. And they, rightly, abhor the Nazis. Your actions were more far reaching than you think. And to accuse me of kidnap!'

He took a step closer and reached for her hair, his voice unnaturally soft. 'Rosebud . . . I am sorry. But it's had the right effect. You've come back. Back to me. You've brought our daughter back to me . . .'

She batted his hand away. 'It stinks in here,' she retorted, shifting herself away. 'How on earth do you manage to entertain the ladies when it smells like this? It's revolting.'

'Let me hold her. Please. Just let me hold my little girl.'

Something coiled in Rose's heart. He was Nancy's father after all. But as she passed Nancy over, the little girl began to cry.

'Give her back to me,' Rose said, her voice shaking.

'Oh, no, she is here to stay, aren't you, Nancy?' he said, moving towards the stairs and placing Nancy on the bottom step. 'If you stay with me Rosebud, I will drop all charges of kidnap against you.'

Nancy shuffled around on the step and began to climb up the stairs.

'That's right, Nancy,' he called softly, 'you go up there.'

Rose leaned against the wall, exhausted. Will walked over to her.

'You just need a little comfort, too, don't you? A little lie-down?' he cooed. 'Perhaps we can be a family again. All forgiven. All forgotten. Just look at you.' His eyes roved up and down her figure. 'That coat is a bit big for you, but I know what lies beneath. And your eyes . . . I always told your parents how beautiful you were. They liked me.' He reached for the belt on her coat. 'They wanted us to be together.'

'Take your hand away,' she spat.

'Ah, that's my fighting girl. We're still married, you know.'

Fear crystallised her thoughts in a sudden rush. 'All I want is to live in peace with my daughter,' she hissed. 'She belongs to me.'

'Let's see, shall we,' he said, his fingers working their way over the buttons on her coat. He glanced up the stairs. Nancy had reached the landing. She sat there, hugging her knees, her eyes opaque with fear. 'Let's both call her and see who she goes to.'

'Don't be flippant. You know what I mean. Nancy, come here. Come to Mummy!' Rose broke away from him and raced to the stairs. Will caught up with her, grabbing her, his two hands on her shoulders. He wrenched her round, using his weight and strength, forcing her against the banisters. The rail pressed painfully into her spine.

'Listen, you,' he hissed, spit flying in her face. 'I gave you everything. I rescued you when your parents died. I identified their bodies at the morgue. What bits of them they found, anyway.'

She turned her head away, screwing up her eyes. The bomb that had obliterated her parents' lives had found her finally, detonating over her head in an almighty explosion.

'Look at me, Rosebud. Look at me!' he bellowed.

She opened her eyes.

'I put this roof over your head. Gave you a home. Gave you that child up there. And you repay me with nearly two years in prison, while you run off with your lover. Do you know what that does to a man? Remember what I told you, Rosebud, the day you grassed on me? Remember what I said I'd do?'

She felt the end of his finger trace the scar on her cheek. Her mouth curled up in revulsion. She could see the spittle on his mouth.

'You remember how I loved you?' He lowered his hand and slowly traced the curve of her body. 'Deep down, you love me,' he whispered, 'or you wouldn't have come back.'

'Get off me!' she screamed, struggling as he moved.

He pushed her down onto the stairs, her backbone crunching against the steps. His weight was on her. Rose thrashed and jerked, trying to escape. His force was crushing the breath out of her. She could no longer scream or plead with him. In a moment, he could take her. Her little girl was waiting upstairs on the landing. Rose wanted to live for her; she wanted her life back. She twisted her wrist, bending her elbow. She felt her way into the pocket of the coat and pulled out Krystof's gun. She pressed it to Will's chest.

He stopped. 'What on earth . . .? Good God.'

He stood up and backed away across the hall, holding up his hands. His eyes flicked from Krystof's gun to her face and back again.

He said, 'It's probably not loaded.'

'There's only one way to find out,' she said. She held firm, aiming it between his eyes. She took a step towards him.

'Now, Rose, come on.' He tried to make himself sound reasonable but his face registered blind fear. 'All right, what do you want?'

'I want you to leave this house and never come back. I want full custody of Nancy. I want a divorce. I want you to leave us in peace.' It was all she had ever wanted. As she spoke, she felt a tide of emotion rock her core. She had to hold herself together, to stop the tears.

'Well, Rosebud, what a tear-jerker.' His hateful face twisted into a sarcastic smile as he said, 'That's my daughter watching us, too, remember? You won't have peace, not from me, not for what you did to me.'

'What about what you did to me!' she screamed. 'You brainwashed me and my parents into thinking you were a decent man. You took me away from the man I should have been with. He was coming to find me. I wouldn't have married you . . . I wouldn't have had—oh!'

'Aha—so you wish you hadn't had Nancy, is that it? I bet she's a burden to your lover. I can't even be bothered to remember his name.'

'It's Krystof!' she yelled. 'And I love him. He loves us both.' She glared at him, fixing him with all her hatred. 'I hate you!'

'I never thought you had it in you,' he said. 'All this bravado. Just put the gun down and give me a kiss, like a good girl.'

'Enough!' she screamed. Both hands holding the gun began to shake. 'I've had enough!' She squeezed the trigger.

An inhuman force kicked her back. The bullet exploded into Will's shoulder and flung him back against the wall.

He started to scream as blood oozed out of the wound. His hands twitched over it, his mouth agape with horror. He sank down the wall, his knees buckling. His eyes began to glaze in pain but the snarl was still on his lips. 'You bitch,' he breathed, choking. 'You little whore bitch.'

'What did you call me?' she screamed. She lowered the gun two inches and fired again. And again. And again.

There came a hammering, an awful, insistent hammering. Ted was calling her name. He sounded urgent. He sounded angry. But how could he be angry? thought Rose. He doesn't know what I've done.

She pulled herself up from the hall floor, unfurled her quaking body and walked unsteadily to the front door. As she reached her hand to lift the latch she heard a whimpering sound. Looking back at Will's crumpled body, she saw that his open eyes were like glass, his legs in a peculiar position. She glanced up to the top of the stairs. Nancy was crouched there, clinging to the newel post, her eyes wide and dark, her mouth square with shock. There were no tears, just a horrified whine.

'Oh, Nancy,' she whispered. 'I'm so sorry.'

Her shaking fingers fumbled with the latch. Betony, Ted and Meg burst through the door. 'Good God, what's happened here?'

Rose stood in the centre of the hallway, beseeching her little girl at the top of the stairs. 'Come here, Nancy, come to Mummy. Mummy is so sorry. I am so sorry. Please come here for a hug.'

The little girl got to her feet and ran down the stairs, straight to Betony, who picked her up on reflex. Nancy curled her legs round her waist and buried her face in her shoulder.

'Nancy, I'm your Mummy!' cried Rose, horrified.

'Take them out of here!' came Ted's gruff bellow.

Rose felt Meg put her arm tightly round her shoulders and move her towards the front door. Rose looked back. Ted's quick, efficient hands were wrapping Krystof's gun in an old towel that had been lying in the corner. A tourniquet seemed to compress her brain, preventing her from feeling the horror of what she had just done.

'Keep walking,' said Betony, her face in Nancy's hair.

Meg was crying. 'You should never have come here on your own, Ginge, knowing that man as you do. What have you done?'

'It's pretty bloody obvious, isn't it?' snapped Betony. 'Now shut up, Meg, just keep her moving. It will be all right. Don't look back.'

Rose didn't know how she made it along the footpath, past the postbox, over the stile, following Betony and Meg onto the headland, becoming aware of the tug and crash of the waves below in the cove. A sigh from deep inside broke away from her.

'I won't be long, Betony,' Rose said. 'You go on.'

The wire had been removed. All traces of the crude wooden props and the cruel rusting spikes were gone. She found their rock and sat on it, looking out to sea. Gulls cried overhead and nested in the cliffside; the little rock pools shimmered in the afternoon sunshine. She wasn't alone: a family had been picnicking. Now the parents were rolling up their blanket, packing their basket, putting on their jumpers. There were two children: little girls who would not leave their rock pool, despite the mother and then the father getting cross. They were fascinated by the life below the still, bright surface of the water. Eventually, after a minute of tears, she watched the parents tenderly take hold of each child's hand and walk back along the beach, picking their way over shells, pebbles and seaweed. Their fading chattering and laughter reached her on the breeze.

'I wish you could see it like this,' she said to the sky.

She was left alone with the tumbling waves as they hissed, spent, across the smooth sand. The sound seemed to cradle her. It found the blackest, deepest part of her and forgave her. The waves set her free.

It was nearly dark when she made her way back up the ferny path. She wanted to get back to Pengared, to see Nancy, but something caught her eye. There was a light on at the back of the Old Vicarage. As she drew nearer she heard a clump-clump sound, a chink of metal against stone, a satisfying thump of spade penetrating earth.

Over the garden wall by the stile she saw Ted in the semidarkness, digging in the nettle-choked corner of the garden next to the churchyard. She hitched herself up onto the wall and sat very still. Ted would not look at her as he worked, sweat beading his ruddy face.

When the hole was deep enough he eased himself upright and glanced in her direction. She waited, her eyes huge in the twilight.

At last he spoke, his voice monotone as if he had been practising: 'I am very sorry to tell you this, Rose. Your husband has left you. He is going to divorce you for adultery, desertion, kidnap and cruelty, because of your flight to Czechoslovakia and back. But you have negotiated with his solicitors and you now have custody of your child. You are satisfied with the outcome. You are satisfied that he has absconded. You have no idea where he has gone. He left no forwarding address.' Ted stopped for a moment, breathless. 'You are relieved that it is all over, and that you can get on with your life.'

The hole was so deep that she could not see what was at the bottom of it. The dusk deepened. Many minutes passed before she could trust herself to say a word. 'And what are you doing, Ted?'

'I am planting you a nice flowering cherry, Rose, right by the wall.'

'You called me Rose,' she said. 'What's happened to Ginge?'

'I think the girl we knew as Ginge has gone.'

She turned away, tears blinding her. She pointed to the spindly sapling that leaned against the wall. 'Is that it?' she asked.

'I know. It looks small at the moment, but it will grow good and strong,' Ted said. 'The bark will be lovely, glossy and smooth. In springtime you will have blossom, in summer you will have cherries, and in the autumn you will have falling leaves.'

**N**ow that the empty Nazi's house was to have a new occupant, the villagers of Trelewin grew very generous. There was relief that they didn't have to put up with such a person in their midst any longer. They were pleased his young wife and daughter could be left in peace. They gave Rose a bed, new table and chairs, blankets and sheets; Jack Thimble's wife gave a stove that needed just one small repair. Betony made curtains and Ted splashed some paint about. Meg promised her the fireside chairs from Cringle Cottage, so that she could start nagging Hugh for some brand-new ones.

It took two weeks to clean the Old Vicarage from top to bottom.

Betony asked, 'Do you really want to move in here, Rose? Don't you want to live a long way away? Start again, somewhere else?'

'How can I?'

They were standing on the doorstep, watching Ted unload the suitcases from the back of his truck. Nancy was clinging onto Betony's hand. Her little face had closed in, her eyes were guarded. Only Betony was able to give her any comfort. Only Betony and Mo, who remembered his playmate tenderly from before and would not leave her side.

'No one else can live here,' Rose told Betony. 'Not with that thing in the . . .'

'You mean the cherry tree.'

The look between the two women was havy with a meaning which could never be voiced.

Rose rallied, trying to be practical. 'I need to be alone with Nancy, in our own home. I want to make amends for everything she has had to go through. Be a good mother.'

'Perhaps she won't remember what happened,' whispered Betony.

Rose suddenly felt incredibly brave. 'I also want to be where Krystof can find me. I need to keep an eye on the postbox just in case . . .'

'And, of course,' said Betony, her eyes shining with tears, 'you can make it into a nice home to bring up your new baby.'

Instinctively, Rose brushed her hand over her stomach. She felt a warm swaying inside herself. 'His baby.'

'Baby?' Nancy asked suddenly, looking up.

Rose squatted down and held her chubby hands. 'Yes, my darling.

We are going to have a little baby. A little brother or sister for you.'

But Nancy would not look at her. Instead, her eyes roamed around the gravel on the drive up to the front door of her new home. 'But where is my *Otec*?' she asked. 'Where is my Krystie?'

# PART THREE

### *Prague, September 1992*

## Fifteen

ROSE MANAGED to shake off her two daughters. She left them with a promise to meet later at a café near the Clementinum monastery.

'Try not to be late, Mum,' Lara said. 'We have a surprise—'

Nancy nudged her sister fiercely in the ribs. 'Hush, don't spoil it.'

But Rose was not listening. A café . . . There must be lots of cafés near the Clementinum. They can't possibly mean—

'Mum? Don't forget, will you?'

Suddenly noticing their thinly disguised concern, she smiled broadly at them. 'I'll be fine,' she said.

What sort of surprise had Lara meant? Rose wondered, as she walked along the river bank. The great pile of the castle rose up in front of her, surrounded by the familiar jumble of red-tiled roofs and spires. Smiling, she absorbed the city as if she was greeting an old friend.

She walked across the Legii Bridge, towards the Old Town side of the river. She found the spot where she and Krystof had stood that bitterly cold dawn to contemplate their fate. She remembered how the chestnut leaves had fallen around them, and how the cold had penetrated her bones, staying there for nearly fifty years.

There was a bench there now, and so she sat, resting her handbag on her knees, Krystof's three letters safe inside. In a moment, she thought.

People strolled past her, their chatter comforting. She was just one more elderly visitor, just a little old lady sitting on a bench. Who would guess at her story? Who could imagine what she had done?

She thought how she had come to be here in Prague again. How she had thought it might never be possible. The early years had been surprisingly easy. She'd received compensation from the government for the bombing of her parents' home; was able to sell the newly built property in Stanley Crescent. After seven years, Will Bowman was officially declared dead. Her daughters grew up, oblivious. Nancy, whose dark hair and often guarded eyes were a constant reminder; and Lara, whose bright innocence never left her, despite her own disastrous marriage and hasty divorce. The people of Trelewin closed ranks round Rose and her family; never questioning, never commenting. The estate was settled. The Old Vicarage was hers.

She did not want the house. The years grew longer, harder; the passing of time less bearable. Slowly, her friends died: Ted, then Hugh, then Meg. And now only Betony remained, loyal and silent to the truth. The truth of what made Ginge disappear, and of who Rose Pepper became.

Rose opened her handbag wide and stared into it. Pulling out the bundle wrapped in the silk scarf, she carefully loosened it. The first letter was postmarked *Praha, June 9, 1946*. She looked away, trying to recall. She and Nancy had been in Paris, waiting for the first train.

Her arthritic hands with their swollen knuckles shook, irritating her, as she pulled out a folded, almost transparent sheet, looped with the faded ink of the hand she had loved for so long.

Fumbling again, she fished out her magnifying glass, trying to be calm, and to keep breathing. His English was as perfect as ever:

*June 8, 1946, Mirov Prison, Czechoslovakia*
*Darling Ruzena,*

*How are you, my love? How I miss you. This is where the Soviets have put me. Those Red Guards who spoke Czech so ill at the station soon made it clear where they were taking me.*

*Imagine an old castle stronghold in the middle of the countryside. It is now a labour camp. There is a concrete exercise yard in the middle, barbed wire all round. We are all the same here: former Czech servicemen, all of us, and now enemies of the state. We are counted in and counted out: a roll call at every juncture of every tedious day.*

*They worry that we will rise up and fight them—but there is no need. There is not one man here, apart from me, fit enough to put on his army boots again. Vaclav is here. He has been here for months. He is very poorly. I cannot bring myself to tell him what happened to Mabel.*

*My Ruzena, when I think of the danger we were in, I am glad you got on that train. At least I know you and Nancy are safe. And please do not worry about me, for I am strong, very strong, knowing you love me.*

*This will reach you in Pengared where you will be safe. And you will know that I love you. You have always known that, haven't you?*
*Your Krystof*

Did he know? she asked herself, sitting on that breezy bench forty-six years later. Did he know that the Red Guards were coming for him? That he'd be arrested at the station? That, like the major said, she was free to go? That he had to get us on that train? So that we could be safe? So we could live a life? Without him?

*June 16, Mirov Prison, Czechoslovakia*
*My Ruzena,*

   *A week on and I know you must be safely home now, with Nancy and all your friends. I hope you have managed to negotiate with her father and somehow start to make arrangements. I think of you every moment. I think of the sea, the little cove, the sound and the smell of it. We will see it again together one day. Until then, hold on tight to our dream.*

   *We march, file in, are counted, fall out. Then we start work. Making string, sewing postbags. So, I think, I fought Rommel in the desert, and fought my way to Paris for this? It makes me laugh, Ruzena.*

   *They at least allow me one letter a week. I have begun to feel unwell, some irritating cough. I suppose I am out of shape.*

   *Please don't worry, my love. But don't write to me, for anything you say may be used against me. Speak to me in my dreams instead.*

   *God knows we love each other and that one day we shall be wife and husband, mother and father. God help me to make you happy, darling, and God help you to make me happy. You see, my faith is returning. I pray to God again these days. When we are old, my true love, we shall look at this piece of paper and see how our prayers have been answered. Good night, my sweetheart.*

   *Krystof*

Eyes misting, grief solidifying her blood, Rose grasped the third, and last, letter and tore at the fragile envelope. She was frantic to read more, desperate to hear again Krystof's voice in her head. She unfolded the single piece of paper. Shaking her head in confusion, she lifted her glasses to brush tears away from her eyes. Krystof hadn't written it. It was in someone else's handwriting. In Czech. Panic gripped her; she wanted to scream. And all the time people strolled by in the sunshine.

'I can't read it!' she cried out loud.

A man looked over, concerned.

Glad of her dark glasses to hide her pain, she smiled and waved her hand, hoping he would think her a silly old woman. She picked up the shreds of the third envelope, on which, she saw in confusion, Krystof had written her address.

She sat, stupefied and helpless. And then noticed the time.

I must go, Rose thought, I've got to find Nancy and Lara. Tell them the truth. They should know. We should all know.

Setting off through the labyrinth of streets, she was lost, frantic and late, hurrying down alleyways and turning blind corners, just as she had done on her first desperate encounter with the city.

'Three weeks!' she hissed to herself. 'I waited three stupid weeks. If I had just gone straight back to Pengared, I might have got the letters. And Will Bowman would never have got his hands on them, and stopped me knowing. He stole the truth. Three weeks led to forty-six years.'

Rose hurried past a crowd of people gathering under the Town Hall clock, waiting for the show. She glanced up quickly to see her old friend the skeleton begin his party piece. Heads turned as she hurried past muttering, 'But at least he didn't open them, read them. At least he didn't destroy them. Oh, imagine if he had. Imagine . . .'

Lara and Nancy were sitting outside the café, next door to *At the Clementinum*. The doorway to her old home was freshly painted and had a bronze plaque on it. It was now a hotel.

'Is this the surprise?' Rose asked, her imploding emotion making her bitter and vile. 'Dragging me back here?'

'You're late,' said Nancy.

'Sit down, Mum,' said Lara. 'Calm down. We thought you'd like to see the old place you've told us so much about. How convenient—it's still a café! We've ordered coffee.'

'I think, by the look on your face, Mum, you need something stronger,' said Nancy. She beckoned a waiter over and asked for some brandy.

Rose sat, stupefied, watching the aproned man scoot back into Milan's café door. 'I suppose the doorbell to the hotel works now,' she muttered, looking up to the lofty tiled roof in the attic under which she and Krystof spent their last night together. Where they'd left the portrait.

'Are you OK?' asked Lara, dipping her head in concern. 'Oh, you've read the letters, haven't you? Is everything all right?'

Rose looked at her daughters. Nancy was moulding her face into an expression of concern; Lara's eyes were wide and frightened. She had her fair hair in a ponytail and it took years off her. 'No, it is not all right,' Rose said. 'I can't read the last one. It's in Czech, and it is such a hard language. I could only ever speak it. *Think* it. I can't *read* it. Not now.'

'Mum.' Nancy leaned forward, her dark eyes scrutinising. 'There is someone here who can possibly help. He's just been to the gents'. This is our surprise for you, Mum. We hope you don't mind.'

'Who? Who can help?'

'Let me explain, Mum,' said Nancy. 'Myself, Mo and Lara had contacted the Red Cross to try to trace Krystof. They put us in touch with the Prague university students who were doing a study on the experience of ex-servicemen after the war. They were very kind to us, they . . . Ah, here he is. Karol. Karol, over here.'

Rose lifted her head and saw Krystof walk out of the café. His tawny hair was a little longer and his frame a little taller, but the way he moved, the way he slowly smiled over to her, told her it was him. His grey eyes were as soft as they had ever been, shining deeply with his love. *I will follow,* he had said.

Rose gripped the table and tried to stand. The deep-freeze of her heart burst at last and her face dissolved into a dreadful hot tide of tears. She began to choke as she called his name, 'Krystof! Krystof!' as if she was still screaming at him from the train window.

'No, no, Mum.' Nancy's voice was in her ear. 'Please sit down. Brandy, waiter, hurry, please!'

'Drink it. Oh, Mum, we're sorry.' Lara was on Rose's other side, supporting her as her knees buckled.

Rose felt the fire of alcohol on her lips and finally opened her eyes. He was still there, looking down on her.

'Mum, this is Karol. Karol, Krystof's nephew.'

The man sat down next to Rose. He took her hand. Even the sound—the quality—of his voice threatened to break her heart.

'I am Tomas's son,' he said. 'I never knew my uncle, but I did find out a little about him. How he fought in the war. I understand he used to live here. This was our family home.' He glanced over to the hotel.

'But—but . . . how did you . . .?'

Nancy said, 'We tracked him down by chance when we were making enquiries at the university before the trip.'

'No, no,' demanded Rose, turning on Karol. 'How come *you* are here? How come you *exist*? Are alive. You're *alive*.'

'I was plucked from the atrocity. I was a tiny baby, born just days before. I was—how the Nazis put it—*Germanised*. I was adopted by a family of the Third Reich; brought up in Moravia. When I was eighteen I left. I tried to track my family down. I tried to find survivors. I don't think there were any.'

Rose plunged her hand into her bag and pulled out the third letter.

'Please read it for me,' she said, her voice tiny and vanquished. 'Read it, please, and you may well find out.'

Karol moved his chair closer to her and unfolded the letter. Rose watched Karol's face, unable to take her eyes off him even though it was as if she was staring into the sun.

Karol said, 'The letter is written by Nurse Koste, at the Mirov Prison infirmary, dated June the 20th, 1946.' He paused. 'Would you like me to read it, Ruzena?'

*June 20th? I was still in Paris; it was the week before I murdered my husband.* Rose nodded, tears pooling over her lip. Karol cleared his throat.

*Dear Ruzena,*

*I am very sorry to inform you that Captain Krystof Novotny passed away today. He had been suffering from pneumonia. He was able to give me this envelope, for me to send a letter on to you. His last words to me were about a wire, to tell you about jumping a wire. I am sorry but I don't know if I have that correct. My condolences, madam. He was a very brave, very gentle man.*

# Epilogue

## *Cornwall, November 1992*

STANDING ON THE STEPS of the Old Vicarage at Trelewin, Rose watched the taxi come to a halt on the gravel. Karol got out and paid the driver. He folded his raincoat over his arm and stooped to pick up his suitcase.

Behind him the sky was a deep, astonishing blue; the late, slanting November sunshine was pure gold. Leaves—red, orange, burnt yellow—were spiralling through the air. *Listopad*, she thought. It was the season of falling leaves.

Rose breathed the damp air, smelling the salt of the sea. She closed her eyes for a moment to see a man, naked from the waist up, take a run and then a jump, clearing the wire with a cry of joy.

Karol smiled over at her and she tried to compose her face.

She heard urgent footsteps behind her, racing across the hall, and Lara sprinted past her, her arms outstretched, calling Karol's name.

Rose's daughter greeted her cousin with a hug and a cry of delight, her ponytail bouncing just as it had done when she was a child.

# Catherine Law

**Is *A Season of Leaves* your first novel?**

It is my first *published* novel. I have written others, all of which have since been shredded and recycled! My agent, who has believed in me through many manuscripts, and has the patience of a saint, has read them all. I feel that this novel is more focused and better planned, better researched.

**So when did you start to write?**

When I was a little girl I used to scribble stories and clip the pages together to make books. I've always had the desire to write. That's what drives me. Having a book deal has given me more confidence. It validates what I do.

**How did you research the various aspects of the Second World War and of the situation in Prague in the immediate aftermath of the war?**

I wanted to create authenticity in my writing and make the events of long ago ring true in the present, so I spent many hours soaking up the atmosphere of wartime and the hard, brutal facts at the Imperial War Museum in London. And I read a huge number of books about the war. I've been to Prague twice. The first time I went I was taken on a communist tour of the city; they pointed out where a big red star used to dominate an elegant square. I also